MW00755071

ENDER'S GAME

TOR BOOKS BY ORSON SCOTT CARD

Eye for Eye
The Folk of the Fringe
Future on Fire (editor)
Future on Ice (editor)*
Hart's Hope
Maps in a Mirror:
The Short Fiction of Orson Scott Card
Saints
Songmaster
The Worthing Saga
Wyrms

THE TALES OF ALVIN MAKER

Seventh Son
Red Prophet
Prentice Alvin

ENDER

Ender's Game
Speaker for the Dead
Xenocide

*forthcoming

ENDER'S GAME

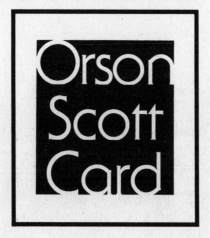

TOR

A TOM DOHERTY ASSOCIATES BOOK

NEW YORK

This is a work of fiction. All the characters and events portrayed in this book are fictitious, and any resemblance to real people or events is purely coincidental.

ENDER'S GAME

Copyright © 1977, 1985, 1991 by Orson Scott Card

All rights reserved, including the right to reproduce this book, or portions thereof, in any form.

Introduction copyright © 1991 by Orson Scott Card. First published in *Phoenix Rising*.

This book was printed on acid-free paper.

A Tor Book
Published by Tom Doherty Associates, LLC
49 West 24th Street
New York, NY 10010

Tor® is a registered trademark of Tom Doherty Associates, LLC
Cover art by John Harris.

Library of Congress Cataloging-in-Publication Data

Card, Orson Scott.
    Ender's Game / Orson Scott Card.
       p.   cm.
    "A Tom Doherty Associates book."
    ISBN 0-312-85323-8 (pbk.)
    ISBN 0-312-93208-1 (hc)
    I. Title.
  [PS3553.A655E5   1991]   91-9908
  813′ .54—dc20   CIP

Printed in the United States of America

20 19 18 17

For Geoffrey,
who makes me remember
how young and how old
children can be

CONTENTS

ACKNOWLEDGMENTS

Portions of this book were recounted in my first published science fiction story, "Ender's Game," in the August 1977 *Analog*, edited by Ben Bova; his faith in me and this story are the foundation of my career.

Harriet McDougal of Tor is that rarest of editors—one who understands a story and can help the author make it exactly what he meant it to be. They don't pay her enough. Harriet's task was made more than a little easier, however, because of the excellent work of my resident editor, Kristine Card. I don't pay her enough, either.

I am grateful also to Barbara Bova, who has been my friend and agent through thin and, sometimes, thick; and to Tom Doherty, my publisher, who let me talk him into doing this book at the ABA in Dallas, which shows either his superb judgment or how weary one can get at a convention.

INTRODUCTION

It makes me a little uncomfortable, writing an introduction to *Ender's Game*. After all, the book has been in print for six years now, and in all that time, nobody has ever written to me to say, "You know, *Ender's Game* was a pretty good book, but you know what it really needs? An introduction!" And yet when a novel goes back to print for a new hardcover edition, there ought to be *something* new in it to mark the occasion (something besides the minor changes as I fix the errors and internal contradictions and stylistic excesses that have bothered me ever since the novel first appeared). So be assured—the novel stands on its own, and if you skip this intro and go straight to the story, I not only won't stand in your way, I'll even *agree* with you!

The novelet "Ender's Game" was my first published science fiction. It was based on an idea—the Battle Room—that came to me when I was sixteen years old. I had just read Isaac Asimov's *Foundation* trilogy, which was (more or less) an extrapolation of the ideas in Gibbon's *Decline and Fall of the Roman Empire*, applied to a galaxy-wide empire in some far future time.

The novel set me, not to dreaming, but to *thinking*, which is Asimov's most extraordinary ability as a fiction writer. What *would* the future be like? How would things change? What would remain the same? The premise of *Foundation* seemed to be that even though you might change the props and the actors, the play of human history is always the same. And yet that fundamentally pessimistic premise (you mean we'll *never* change?) was tempered by Asimov's idea of a group of human beings who, not through genetic change, but through learned skills, are able to understand and heal the minds of other people.

It was an idea that rang true with me, perhaps in part because of my Mormon upbringing and beliefs: Human beings may be miserable specimens, in the main, but we *can* learn, and, through learning, become decent people.

Those were some of the ideas that played through my mind as I read *Foundation*, curled on my bed—a thin mattress on a slab of plywood, a bed my father had made for me—in my basement bedroom in our little rambler on 650 East in Orem, Utah. And then, as so many science fiction readers have done over the years, I felt a strong desire to write stories that would do for others what Asimov's story had done for me.

In other genres, that desire is usually expressed by producing thinly veiled rewrites of the great work: Tolkien's disciples far too often simply rewrite Tolkien, for example. In science fiction, however, the whole point is that the ideas are fresh and startling and intriguing; you imitate the great ones, not by rewriting *their* stories, but rather by creating stories that are just as startling and new.

But new in what way? Asimov was a scientist, and approached every field of human knowledge in a scientific manner—assimilating data, combining it in new and startling ways, thinking through the implications of each new idea. I was no scientist, and unlikely ever to be one, at least not a *real* scientist—not a physicist, not a chemist, not a biologist, not even an engineer. I had no gift for mathematics and no great love for it, either. Though I relished the study of logic and languages, and virtually inhaled histories and biographies, it never occurred to me at the time that these were just as valid sources of science fiction stories as astronomy or quantum mechanics.

How, then, could I possibly come up with a science fiction idea? What did *I* actually know about anything?

At that time my older brother Bill was in the army, stationed at Fort Douglas in Salt Lake City; he was nursing a hip-to-heel cast from a bike-riding accident, however, and came home on weekends. It was then that he had met his future wife, Laura Dene Low, while attending a church meeting on the BYU campus; and it was Laura who gave me *Foundation* to read. Perhaps, then, it was natural for my thoughts to turn to things military.

To me, though, the military didn't mean the Vietnam War, which was then nearing its peak of American involvement. I had no experience of that, except for Bill's stories of the miserable life in basic training, the humiliation of officer's candidate school, and his lonely but in many ways successful life as a noncom in Korea. Far more deeply rooted in my mind was my experience, five or six years earlier, of reading Bruce Catton's three-volume *Army of the Potomac*. I remembered so well the stories of the commanders in that war—the struggle to find a Union general capable of using McClellan's magnificent army to defeat Lee and Jackson and Stuart, and then, finally, Grant, who brought death to far too many of his soldiers, but also made their deaths mean something, by grinding away at Lee, keeping him from dancing and maneuvering out of reach. It was because of Catton's history that I had stopped enjoying chess, and had to revise the rules of *Risk* in order to play it—I had come to understand something of war, and not just because of the conclusions Catton himself had reached. I found meanings of my own in that history.

I learned that history is shaped by the use of power, and that different people, leading the same army, with, therefore, approximately the same power, applied it so differently that the army seemed to change from a pack of noble fools at Fredericksburg to panicked cowards melting away at Chancellorsville, then to the grimly determined, stubborn soldiers who held the ridges at Gettysburg, and then, finally, to the disciplined, professional army that ground Lee to dust in Grant's long campaign. It wasn't the soldiers who changed. It was the leader. And even though I could not then have articulated what I understood of military leadership, I knew that I *did* understand it. I understood, at levels deeper than speech, how a great military leader imposes his will on his enemy, and makes his own army a willing extension of himself.

So one morning, as my Dad drove me to Brigham Young High School along Carterville Road in the heavily wooded bottoms of the Provo River, I wondered: How would you train soldiers for combat in the future? I didn't bother thinking of new land-based weapons systems—what was on my mind, after *Foundation*, was space. Soldiers and commanders would have to think very differently in space, because the old ideas of up and down simply wouldn't apply anymore. I had read in Nordhoff's and Hall's history of World War I flying that it was very hard at first for new pilots to learn to look above and below them rather than merely to the right and left, to find the enemy approaching them in the air. How much worse, then, would it be to learn to think with no up and down at all?

The essence of training is to allow error without consequence. Three-dimensional warfare would need to be practiced in an enclosed space, so mistakes wouldn't send trainees flying off to Jupiter. It would need to offer a way to practice shooting without risk of injury; and yet trainees who were "hit" would need to be disabled, at least temporarily. The environment would need to be changeable, to simulate the different conditions of warfare—near a ship, in the midst of debris, near tiny asteroids. And it would need to have some of the confusion of real battle, so that the play-combat didn't evolve into something as rigid and formal as the meaningless marching and maneuvers that still waste an astonishing amount of a trainee's precious hours in basic training in our modern military.

The result of my speculations that morning was the Battle Room, exactly as you will see it (or have already seen in) in this book. It was a good idea, and something like it will certainly be used for training if ever there is a manned military in space. (Something very much like it has already been used in various amusement halls throughout America.)

But, having thought of the Battle Room, I hadn't the faintest idea of how to go about turning the idea into a story. It occurred to me then for the first time that the *idea* of the story is nothing compared to the importance of knowing how to find a character and a story to tell around that idea. Asimov, having had the idea of paralleling *The Decline and Fall,* still had no story; his genius—and the soul of the story—came when he personalized his history, making the psychohistorian Hari Seldon the god-figure, the plan-maker, the apocalyptic prophet of the story. I had no such character, and no idea of how to make one.

Years passed. I graduated from high school as a junior (just in time—Brigham Young High School was discontinued with the class of 1968) and went on to Brigham Young University. I started there as an archaeology major, but quickly discovered that doing archaeology is unspeakably boring compared to reading the books by Thor Heyerdahl (*Aku-Aku, Kon-Tiki*), Yigael Yadin (*Masada*), and James Michener (*The Source*) that had set me dreaming. Potsherds! Better to be a *dentist* than to spend your life trying to put together fragments of old pottery in endless desert landscapes in the Middle East.

By the time I realized that not even the semi-science of archaeology was for someone as impatient as me, I was already immersed in my real career. At the time, of course, I misunderstood myself: I thought I was in theatre because I loved performing. And I *do* love performing, don't get me wrong. Give me an audience and I'll hold onto them as long as I can, on any subject. But I'm not a good actor, and theatre was not to be my career. At the time, though, all I cared about was doing plays. Directing them. Building sets and making costumes and putting on makeup for them.

And, above all, *rewriting* those *lousy* scripts. I kept thinking, Why couldn't the playwright hear how dull that speech was? This scene could so easily be punched up and made far more effective.

Then I tried my hand at writing adaptations of novels for a reader's theatre class, and my fate was sealed. I was a playwright.

People came to my plays and clapped at the end. I learned—from actors and from audiences—how to shape a scene, how to build tension, and—above all—the necessity of being harsh with your own material, excising or rewriting anything that doesn't work. I learned to separate the *story* from the *writing*, probably the most important thing that any storyteller has to learn—that there are a thousand right ways to tell a story, and ten million wrong ones, and you're a lot more likely to find one of the latter than the former your first time through the tale.

My love of theatre lasted through my mission for the LDS Church. Even while I was in São Paulo, Brazil, as a missionary, I wrote a play called *Stone Tables* about the relationship between Moses and Aaron in the book of Exodus, which had standing-room-only audiences at its premiere (which I didn't attend, since I was still in Brazil!).

At the same time, though, that original impetus to write science fiction persisted.

I had taken fiction writing courses at college, for which I don't think I ever wrote science fiction. But on the side, I had started a series of stories about people with psionic powers (I had no idea this was a sci-fi cliché at the time) that eventually grew into *The Worthing Saga*. I had even sent one of the stories off to *Analog* magazine before my mission, and on my mission I wrote several long stories in the same series (as well as a couple of stabs at mainstream stories).

In all that time, the Battle Room remained an idea in the back of my mind. It wasn't until 1975, though, that I dusted it off and tried to write it. By then I had started a theatre company that managed to do reasonably well during the first summer and then collapsed under the weight of bad luck and bad management (myself) during the fall and winter. I was deeply in debt on the pathetic salary of an editor at BYU Press. Writing was the only thing I knew how to do *besides* proofreading and editing. It was time to get serious about writing something that might actually earn some money—and, plainly, playwriting wasn't going to be it.

I first rewrote and sent out "Tinker," the first Worthing story I wrote and the one that was still most effective. I got a rejection letter from Ben Bova at *Analog*, pointing out that "Tinker" simply didn't feel like science fiction—it felt like fantasy. So the Worthing stories were out for the time being.

What was left? That old Battle Room idea. It happened one spring day that a friend of mine, Tammy Mikkelson, was taking her boss's children to the circus in Salt Lake City; would I like to come along? I would. And since there was no ticket for me (and I've always detested the circus anyway—the clowns drive me up a wall), I spent the hours of the performance out on the lawn of the Salt Palace with a notebook on my lap, writing "Ender's Game" as I had written all my plays, in longhand on narrow-ruled paper. "Remember," said Ender. "The enemy's gate is *down*."

Maybe it was because of the children in the car on the way up that I decided that the trainees in the Battle Room were so young. Maybe it was because I, barely an adolescent myself, understood only childhood well enough to write about it. Or maybe it was because of something that impressed me in Catton's *Army of the Potomac*: that the soldiers were all so young and innocent. That they shot and bayoneted the enemy, and then slipped across the neutral ground between armies to trade tobacco, jokes, liquor, and food. Even though it was a deadly game, and the suffering and fear were terrible and real, it was still a game played by children, not all that different from the wargames my brothers and I had played, firing water-filled squirt bottles at each other.

"Ender's Game" was written and sold. I knew it was a strong story because *I* cared about it and believed in it. I had no idea that it would have the effect it had on the science fiction audience. While most people ignored it, of course, and continue to live full and happy lives without reading it or anything else by me, there was still a surprisingly large group who responded to the story with some fervency.

Ignored on the Nebula ballot, "Ender's Game" got onto the Hugo ballot and came in second. More to the point, I was awarded the John W. Campbell Award for best new writer. Without doubt, "Ender's Game" wasn't just my first sale—it was the launching pad of my career.

The same story did it again in 1985, when I rewrote it at novel length—the book, now slightly revised, that you are holding in your hands. At that point I thought of *Ender's Game*, the novel, existing only to set up the much more powerful (I thought) story of *Speaker for the Dead*. But when I finished the novel, I knew that the story had new strength. I had learned a great deal, both about life and about writing, in the decade since I wrote the novelet, and it came together for the first time in this book. Again the audience was kind to me: the Nebula and Hugo awards, foreign translations, and strong, steady sales that, for the first time in my career, actually earned out my advance and allowed me to receive royalties.

But it wasn't just a matter of having a quiet little cult novel that brought in a steady income. There was something more to the way that people responded to *Ender's Game*.

For one thing, the people that hated it *really* hated it. The attacks on the novel—and on me—were astonishing. Some of it I expected—I have a master's degree in literature, and in writing *Ender's Game* I deliberately avoided all the little literary games and gimmicks that make "fine" writing so impenetrable to the general audience. All the layers of meaning are there to be decoded, if you like to play the game of literary criticism—but if you don't care to play that game, that's fine with me. I designed *Ender's Game* to be as clear and accessible as any story of mine could possibly be. My goal was that the reader wouldn't have to be trained in literature or even in science fiction to receive the tale in its simplest, purest form. And, since a great many writers and critics have based their entire careers on the premise that anything that the general public can understand without mediation is worthless drivel, it is not surprising that they found my little novel to be despicable. If everybody came to agree that stories should be told this clearly, the professors of literature would be out of a job, and the writers of obscure, encoded fiction would be, not honored, but pitied for their impenetrability.

For some people, however, the loathing for *Ender's Game* transcended mere artistic argument. I recall a letter to the editor of *Isaac Asimov's Science Fiction Magazine*, in which a woman who worked as a guidance counselor for gifted children reported that she had only picked up *Ender's Game* to read it because her son had kept telling her it was a wonderful book. She read it and loathed it. Of course, I wondered what kind of guidance counselor would hold her son's tastes up to public ridicule, but the criticism that left me most flabbergasted was her assertion that my depiction of gifted children was hopelessly unrealistic. They just don't talk like that, she said. They don't *think* like that.

And it wasn't just her. There have been others with that criticism. Thus I began to realize that, as it is, *Ender's Game* disturbs some people because it challenges their assumptions about reality. In fact, the novel's very clarity may make it *more* challenging, simply because the story's vision of the world is so relentlessly plain. It was important to her, and to others, to believe that children don't actually think or speak the way the children in *Ender's Game* think and speak.

Yet I knew—I *knew*—that this was one of the truest things about *Ender's Game*. In fact, I realized in retrospect that this may indeed be part of the reason why it was so important to me, there on the lawn in front of the Salt Palace, to write a story in which gifted children are trained to fight in adult wars. Because never in my entire childhood did I feel like a child. I felt like a person all along—the same person that I am today. I never felt that I spoke childishly. I never felt that my emotions and desires were somehow less real than adult emotions and desires. And in writing *Ender's Game*, I forced the audience to experience the lives of these children from that perspective—the perspective in which their feelings and decisions are just as real and important as any adult's.

The nasty side of myself wanted to answer that guidance counselor by saying, The only reason you don't think gifted children talk this way is because they know better than to talk this way in front of *you*. But the truer answer is that *Ender's Game* asserts the personhood of children, and those who are used to thinking of children in another way—especially those whose whole career is based on that—are going to find *Ender's Game* a very unpleasant place to live. Children are a perpetual, self-renewing underclass, helpless to escape from the decisions of adults until they become adults themselves. And *Ender's Game*, seen in that context, might even be a sort of revolutionary tract.

Because the book *does* ring true with the children who read it. The highest praise I ever received for a book of mine was when the school librarian at Farrer Junior High in Provo, Utah, told me, "You know, *Ender's Game* is our most-lost book."

And then there are the letters. This one, for instance, which I received in March of 1991:

> Dear Mr. Card,
> I am writing to you on behalf of myself and my twelve friends and fellow students who joined me at a two-week residential program for gifted and talented students at Purdue

University this summer. We attended the class, "Philosophy and Science Fiction," instructed by Peter Robinson, and we range in age from thirteen through fifteen.

We are all in about the same position; we are very intellectually oriented and have found few people at home who share this trait. Hence, most of us are very lonely, and have been since kindergarten. When teachers continually compliment you, your chances of "fitting in" are about nil.

All our lives we've unconsciously been living by the philosophy, "The only way to gain respect is doing so well you can't be ignored." And, for me and Mike, at least, "beating the system" at school is how we've chosen to do this. Both Mike and I plan to be in calculus our second year of high school, schedules permitting. (Both of us are interested in science/math related careers.) Not to get me wrong; we're all bright and at the top of our class. However, in choosing these paths, most of us have wound up satisfied in ourselves, but very lonely.

This is why *Ender's Game* and *Speaker for the Dead* really hit home for us. These books were our "texts" for the class. We would read one hundred to two hundred pages per night and then discuss them (and other short stories and essays) during the day. At Purdue, it wasn't a "classroom" discussion, however. It was a group of friends talking about how their feelings and philosophies corresponded to or differed from the books'.

You couldn't *imagine* the impact your books had on us; *we* are the Enders of today. Almost everything written in *Ender's Game* and *Speaker* applied to each one of us on a very, very personal level. No, the situation isn't as drastic today, but all the feelings are there. Both your books, along with the excellent work of Peter Robinson, unified us into a tight web of people.

Ingrid's letter goes on, talking of the *Phoenix Rising*, the magazine that these students publish together in order to maintain their sense of community. (In response I have given them this introduction to publish in their magazine before its appearance in book form.)

Of course, I'm always glad when people like a story of mine; but something much more important is going on here. These readers found that *Ender's Game* was not merely a "mythic" story, dealing with general truths, but something much more personal: To them, *Ender's Game* was an epic tale, a story that expressed who they are as a community, a story that distinguished them from the other people around them. They didn't love Ender, or pity Ender (a frequent adult response); they *were* Ender, all of them. Ender's experience was not foreign or strange to them; in their minds, Ender's life echoed their own lives. The truth of the story was not truth in general, but *their* truth.

Stories can be read so differently—even clear stories, even stories that deliberately avoid surface ambiguities. For instance, here's another letter, likewise one that I received in mid-March of 1991. It was written on 16 February and postmarked the 18th. Those dates are important.

> Mr. Card,
> I'm an army aviator waiting out a sandstorm in Saudi Arabia. I've always wanted to write you and since my future is in doubt—I know when the ground war will begin—I decided today would be the day I'd write.
> I read *Ender's Game* during flight school four years ago. I'm a warrant officer, and our school, at least the first six weeks, is very different from the commissioned officers'. I was eighteen years old when I arrived at Ft. Rucker to start flight training, and the first six weeks almost beat me. Ender gave me courage then and many times after that. I've experienced the tiredness Ender felt, the kind that goes deep to your soul. It would be interesting to know what caused you to feel the same way. No one could describe it unless they experienced it, but I understand how personal that can be. There is one other novel that describes that frame of soul and mind that I cherish as much as *Ender's Game*. It's called *Armour* and its author is John Steakley. Ender and Felix [the protagonist of *Armour*] are always close by in my mind. Sadly, there is no sequel to *Armour* as there is to *Ender's Game*.
> We are the bastards of military aviation. Our helicopters may be the best in the world, but the equipment we wear and the systems in our helicopter, such as the navigation instruments, are at least twenty years behind the Navy and Air Force. I am very happy with the Air Force's ability to bomb with precision, but if they miss, the bombs still land on the enemy's territory. If we screw up, the guys we haul to the battle, the "grunts," die. We don't even have the armour plate for our chests—"chicken plate"—that the helicopter pilots did in Vietnam. Last year in El Salvador, army aviators flew a couple of civilian VIPs and twenty reporters over guerrilla-controlled territory and there were no flares in their launchers to counteract the heat-seeking missiles we knew the rebels had. One of our pilots and a crew member were killed last year on a training flight because they flew the sling load they were carrying into the trees at 70 miles an hour. It could have been prevented if our night vision goggles had a heads-up display like the Air Force has had for forty years. I'm sure you heard about Colonel Pickett being shot down in a Huey in El Salvador just a few months ago. That type of aircraft is at least thirty years old and there are no survivability measures installed. He was a good man, I knew him.

The reason I told you about these things is because I wanted to paint a picture for you. I love my job but we aren't like the "zoomies" that everyone makes movies about. We do our job with less technology, less political support, less recognition, and more risk than the rest, while the threat to us continues to modernize at an unbelievable rate. I'm not asking for sympathy but I was wondering if you and Mr. Steakley could write a novel about helicopters and the men that fly them for the Army twenty years in the future. There are many of us that read science fiction and after I read *Ender's Game* and *Armour* three times each I started letting my comrades read them. My wife cried when she read *Ender's Game*. There is a following here for a book like the one I requested. We have no speaker for us, the ones that will soon die, or the ones that survive. . .

As with those gifted young students who read this book as "their" story, this soldier—who, like most but not all of the Army aviators in the Gulf War, survived—did not read *Ender's Game* as a "work of literature." He read it as epic, as a story that helped define his community. It was not his only epic, of course—*Armour*, John Steakley's fine novel, was an equal candidate to be part of his self-story. What matters most, though, was his clear sense that, no matter how much these stories spoke to him, they were still not *exactly* his community's epic. He still felt the need for a "speaker for the dead" and for the living. He still felt a hunger, especially at a time when death might well be near, to have his own story, his friends' stories, told.

Why else do we read fiction, anyway? Not to be impressed by somebody's dazzling language—or at least I hope that's not our reason. I think that most of us, anyway, read these stories that we know are not "true" because we're hungry for another kind of truth: The mythic truth about human nature in general, the particular truth about those life-communities that define our own identity, and the most specific truth of all: our own self-story. Fiction, because it is not about somebody who actually lived in the real world, always has the possibility of being about ourself.

Ender's Game is a story about gifted children. It is also a story about soldiers. Captain John F. Schmitt, the author of the Marine Corps's *Warfighting*, the most brilliant and concise book of military strategy ever written by an American (and a proponent of the kind of thinking that was at the heart of the allied victory in the Gulf War), found *Ender's Game* to be a useful enough story about the nature of leadership to use it in courses he taught at the Marine University at Quantico. Watauga College, the interdisciplinary studies program at Appalachian State University—as *un*military a community as you could ever hope to find!—uses *Ender's Game* for completely different purposes—to talk about problem-solving and the self-creation of the individual. A graduate student in Toronto explored the political ideas in *Ender's Game*. A writer and critic at Pepperdine has seen *Ender's Game* as, in some ways, religious fiction.

All these uses are valid; all these readings of the book are "correct." For all these readers have placed themselves inside this story, not as spectators, but as participants, and so have looked at the world of *Ender's Game*, not with my eyes only, but also with their own.

This is the essence of the transaction between storyteller and audience. The "true" story is not the one that exists in my mind; it is *certainly* not the written words on the bound paper that you hold in your hands. The story in my mind is nothing but a hope; the text of the story is the tool I created in order to try to make that hope a reality. The story itself, the true story, is the one that the audience members create in their minds, guided and shaped by my text, but then transformed, elucidated, expanded, edited, and clarified by their own experience, their own desires, their own hopes and fears.

The story of *Ender's Game* is not this book, though it has that title emblazoned on it. The story is the one that you and I will construct together in your memory. If the story means anything to you at all, then when you remember it afterward, think of it, not as something I created, but rather as something that we made together.

Orson Scott Card
Greensboro, North Carolina
March 1991

ENDER'S GAME

1

THIRD

"I've watched through his eyes, I've listened through his ears, and I tell you he's the one. Or at least as close as we're going to get."

"That's what you said about the brother."

"The brother tested out impossible. For other reasons. Nothing to do with his ability."

"Same with the sister. And there are doubts about him. He's too malleable. Too willing to submerge himself in someone else's will."

"Not if the other person is his enemy."

"So what do we do? Surround him with enemies all the time?"

"If we have to."

"I thought you said you liked this kid."

"If the buggers get him, they'll make me look like his favorite uncle."

"All right. We're saving the world, after all. Take him."

The monitor lady smiled very nicely and tousled his hair and said, "Andrew, I suppose by now you're just absolutely sick of having that horrid monitor. Well, I have good news for you. That monitor is going to come out today. We're going to take it right out, and it won't hurt a bit."

Ender nodded. It was a lie, of course, that it wouldn't hurt a bit. But since adults always said it when it *was* going to hurt, he could count on that statement as an accurate prediction of the future. Sometimes lies were more dependable than the truth.

"So if you'll just come over here, Andrew, just sit right up here on the examining table. The doctor will be in to see you in a moment."

The monitor gone. Ender tried to imagine the little device missing from the back of his neck. I'll roll over on my back in bed and it won't be pressing there. I won't feel it tingling and taking up the heat when I shower.

And Peter won't hate me anymore. I'll come home and show him that the monitor's gone, and he'll see that I didn't make it, either. That I'll just be a normal kid now, like him. That won't be so bad then. He'll forgive me that I had my monitor a whole year longer than he had his. We'll be—

Not friends, probably. No, Peter was too dangerous. Peter got so angry. Brothers, though. Not enemies, not friends, but brothers—able to live in the same house. He won't hate me, he'll just leave me alone. And when he wants to play buggers and astronauts, maybe I won't have to play, maybe I can just go read a book.

But Ender knew, even as he thought it, that Peter wouldn't leave him alone. There was something in Peter's eyes, when he was in his mad mood, and whenever Ender saw that look, that glint, he knew that the one thing Peter would *not* do was leave him alone. I'm practicing piano, Ender. Come turn the pages for me. Oh, is the monitor boy too busy to help his brother? Is he too smart? Got to go kill some buggers, astronaut? No, no, I don't *want* your help. I can do it on my own, you little bastard, you little *Third*.

"This won't take long, Andrew," said the doctor.

Ender nodded.

"It's designed to be removed. Without infection, without damage. But there'll be some tickling, and some people say they have a feeling of something *missing*. You'll keep looking around for something, something you were looking for, but you can't find it, and you can't remember what it was. So I'll tell you. It's the monitor you're looking for, and it isn't there. In a few days that feeling will pass."

The doctor was twisting something at the back of Ender's head. Suddenly a pain stabbed through him like a needle from his neck to his groin. Ender felt his back spasm, and his body arched violently backward; his head struck the bed. He could feel his legs thrashing, and his hands were clenching each other, wringing each other so tightly that they arched.

"Deedee!" shouted the doctor. "I need you!" The nurse ran in, gasped. "Got to relax these muscles. Get it to me, now! What are you waiting for!"

Something changed hands; Ender could not see. He lurched to one side and fell off the examining table. "Catch him!" cried the nurse.

"Just hold him steady—"

"You hold him, doctor, he's too strong for me—"

"Not the whole thing! You'll stop his heart—"

Ender felt a needle enter his back just above the neck of his shirt. It burned, but wherever in him the fire spread, his muscles gradually unclenched. Now he could cry for the fear and pain of it.

"Are you all right, Andrew?" the nurse asked.

Andrew could not remember how to speak. They lifted him onto the table. They checked his pulse, did other things; he did not understand it all.

The doctor was trembling; his voice shook as he spoke. "They leave these things in the kids for three years, what do they expect? We could have switched him off, do you realize that? We could have unplugged his brain for all time."

"When does the drug wear off?" asked the nurse.

"Keep him here for at least an hour. Watch him. If he doesn't start talking in fifteen minutes, call me. Could have unplugged him forever. I don't have the brains of a bugger."

He got back to Miss Pumphrey's class only fifteen minutes before the closing bell. He was still a little unsteady on his feet.

"Are you all right, Andrew?" asked Miss Pumphrey.

He nodded.

"Were you ill?"

He shook his head.

"You don't look well."

"I'm OK."

"You'd better sit down, Andrew."

He started toward his seat, but stopped. Now what was I looking for? I can't think what I was looking for.

"Your seat is over there," said Miss Pumphrey.

He sat down, but it was something else he needed, something he had lost. I'll find it later.

"Your monitor," whispered the girl behind him.

Andrew shrugged.

"His monitor," she whispered to the others.

Andrew reached up and felt his neck. There was a bandaid. It was gone. He was just like everybody else now.

"Washed out, Andy?" asked a boy who sat across the aisle and behind him. Couldn't think of his name. Peter. No, that was someone else.

"Quiet, Mr. Stilson," said Miss Pumphrey. Stilson smirked.

Miss Pumphrey talked about multiplication. Ender doodled on his desk, drawing contour maps of mountainous islands and then telling his desk to display them in three dimensions from every angle. The teacher would know, of course, that he wasn't paying attention, but she wouldn't bother him. He always knew the answer, even when she thought he wasn't paying attention.

In the corner of his desk a word appeared and began marching around the perimeter of the desk. It was upside down and backward at first, but Ender knew what it said long before it reached the bottom of the desk and turned right side up.

THIRD

Ender smiled. He was the one who had figured out how to send messages and make them march—even as his secret enemy called him names, the method of delivery praised him. It was not *his* fault he was a Third. It was the government's idea, they were the ones who authorized it—how else could a Third like Ender have got into school? And now the monitor was gone. The experiment entitled Andrew Wiggin hadn't worked out after all. If they could, he was sure they would like to rescind the waivers that had allowed him to be born at all. Didn't work, so erase the experiment.

The bell rang. Everyone signed off their desks or hurriedly typed in reminders to themselves. Some were dumping lessons or data into their computers at home. A few gathered at the printers while something they wanted to show was printed out. Ender spread his hands over the child-size keyboard near the edge of the desk and wondered what it would feel like to have hands as large as a grown-up's. They must feel so big and awkward, thick stubby fingers and beefy palms. Of course, they had bigger keyboards—but how could their thick fingers draw a fine line, the way Ender could, a thin line so precise that he could make it spiral seventy-nine times from the center to the edge of the desk without the lines ever touching or overlapping. It gave him something to do while the teacher droned on about arithmetic. Arithmetic! Valentine had taught him arithmetic when he was three.

"Are you all right, Andrew?"

"Yes, ma'am."

"You'll miss the bus."

Ender nodded and got up. The other kids were gone. They would be waiting, though, the bad ones. His monitor wasn't perched on his neck, hearing what he heard and seeing what he saw. They could say what they liked. They might even hit him now—no one could see them anymore, and so no one would come to Ender's rescue. There were advantages to the monitor, and he would miss them.

It was Stilson, of course. He wasn't bigger than most other kids, but he was bigger than Ender. And he had some others with him. He always did.

"Hey Third."

Don't answer. Nothing to say.

"Hey, Third, we're talkin to you, Third, hey bugger-lover, we're talkin to you."

Can't think of anything to answer. Anything I say will make it worse. So will saying nothing.

"Hey, Third, hey, turd, you flunked out, huh? Thought you were better than us, but you lost your little birdie, Thirdie, got a bandaid on your neck."

"Are you going to let me through?" Ender asked.

"Are we going to let him through? Should we let him through?" They all laughed. "Sure we'll let you through. First we'll let your arm through, then your butt through, then maybe a piece of your knee."

The others chimed in now. "Lost your birdie, Thirdie. Lost your birdie, Thirdie."

Stilson began pushing him with one hand; someone behind him then pushed him toward Stilson.

"See-saw, marjorie daw," somebody said.

"Tennis!"

"Ping-pong!"

This would not have a happy ending. So Ender decided that he'd rather not be the unhappiest at the end. The next time Stilson's arm came out to push him, Ender grabbed at it. He missed.

"Oh, gonna fight me, huh? Gonna fight me, Thirdie?"

The people behind Ender grabbed at him, to hold him.

Ender did not feel like laughing, but he laughed. "You mean it takes this many of you to fight one Third?"

"We're *people*, not *Thirds*, turd face. You're about as strong as a fart!"

But they let go of him. And as soon as they did, Ender kicked out high and hard, catching Stilson square in the breastbone. He dropped. It took Ender by surprise—he hadn't thought to put Stilson on the ground with one kick. It didn't occur to him that Stilson didn't take a fight like this seriously, that he wasn't prepared for a truly desperate blow.

For a moment, the others backed away and Stilson lay motionless. They were all wondering if he was dead. Ender, however, was trying to figure out a way to forestall vengeance. To keep them from taking him in a pack tomorrow. I have to win this now, and for all time, or I'll fight it every day and it will get worse and worse.

Ender knew the unspoken rules of manly warfare, even though he was only six. It was forbidden to strike the opponent who lay helpless on the ground; only an animal would do that.

So Ender walked to Stilson's supine body and kicked him again, viciously, in the ribs. Stilson groaned and rolled away from him. Ender walked around him and kicked him again, in the crotch. Stilson could not make a sound; he only doubled up and tears streamed out of his eyes.

Then Ender looked at the others coldly. "You might be having some idea of ganging up on me. You could probably beat me up pretty bad. But just remember what I do to people who try to hurt me. From then on you'd be wondering when I'd get you, and how bad it would be." He kicked Stilson in the face. Blood from his nose spattered the ground nearby. "It wouldn't be this bad," Ender said. "It would be worse."

He turned and walked away. Nobody followed him. He turned a corner into the corridor leading to the bus stop. He could hear the boys behind him saying, "Geez. Look at him. He's wasted." Ender leaned his head against the wall of the corridor and cried until the bus came. I am just like Peter. Take my monitor away, and I am just like Peter.

2

PETER

"All right, it's off. How's he doing."

"You live inside somebody's body for a few years, you get used to it. I look at his face now, I can't tell what's going on. I'm not used to seeing his facial expressions. I'm used to feeling them."

"Come on, we're not talking about psychoanalysis here. We're soldiers, not witch doctors. You just saw him beat the guts out of the leader of a gang."

"He was thorough. He didn't just beat him, he beat him deep. Like Mazer Rackham at the—"

"Spare me. So in the judgment of the committee, he passes."

"Mostly. Let's see what he does with his brother, now that the monitor's off."

"His brother. Aren't you afraid of what his brother will do to *him*?"

"You were the one who told me that this wasn't a no-risk business."

"I went back through some of the tapes. I can't help it. I like the kid. I think we're going to screw him up."

"Of course we are. It's our job. We're the wicked witch. We promise gingerbread, but we eat the little bastards alive."

"I'm sorry, Ender," Valentine whispered. She was looking at the bandaid on his neck.

Ender touched the wall and the door closed behind him. "I don't care. I'm glad it's gone."

"What's gone?" Peter walked into the parlor, chewing on a mouthful of bread and peanut butter.

Ender did not see Peter as the beautiful ten-year-old boy that grown-ups saw, with dark, thick, tousled hair and a face that could have belonged to Alexander the Great. Ender looked at Peter only to detect anger or boredom, the dangerous moods that almost always led to pain. Now as Peter's eyes discovered the bandaid on his neck, the telltale flicker of anger appeared.

Valentine saw it too. "Now he's like us," she said, trying to soothe him before he had time to strike.

But Peter would not be soothed. "Like us? He keeps the little sucker till he's six years old. When did you lose yours? You were three. I lost mine before I was five. *He* almost made it, little bastard, little bugger."

This is all right, Ender thought. Talk and talk, Peter. Talk is fine.

"Well, now your guardian angels aren't watching over you," Peter said. "Now they aren't checking to see if you feel pain, listening to hear what I'm saying, seeing what I'm doing to you. How about that? How about it?"

Ender shrugged.

Suddenly Peter smiled and clapped his hands together in a mockery of good cheer. "Let's play buggers and astronauts," he said.

"Where's Mom?" asked Valentine.

"Out," said Peter. "I'm in charge."

"I think I'll call Daddy."

"Call away," said Peter. "You know he's never in."

"I'll play," Ender said.

"You be the bugger," said Peter.

"Let him be the astronaut for once," Valentine said.

"Keep your fat face out of it, fart mouth," said Peter. "Come on upstairs and choose your weapons."

It would not be a good game, Ender knew. It was not a question of winning. When kids played in the corridors, whole troops of them, the buggers never won, and sometimes the games got mean. But here in their flat, the game would start mean, and the bugger couldn't just go empty and quit the way buggers did in the real wars. The bugger was in it until the astronaut decided it was over.

Peter opened his bottom drawer and took out the bugger mask. Mother had got upset at him when Peter bought it, but Dad pointed out that the war wouldn't go away just because you hid bugger masks and wouldn't let your kids play with make-believe laser guns. Better to play the war games, and have a better chance of surviving when the buggers came again.

If I survive the games, thought Ender. He put on the mask. It closed him in like a hand pressed tight against his face. But this isn't how it feels to be a bugger, thought Ender. They don't wear this face like a mask, it *is* their face. On their home worlds, do the buggers put on human masks, and play?

And what do they call us? Slimies, because we're so soft and oily compared to them?

"Watch out, Slimy," Ender said.

He could barely see Peter through the eyeholes. Peter smiled at him. "Slimy, huh? Well, bugger-wugger, let's see how to break that face of yours."

Ender couldn't see it coming, except a slight shift of Peter's weight; the mask cut out his peripheral vision. Suddenly there was the pain and pressure of a blow to the side of his head; he lost balance, fell that way.

"Don't see too well, do you, bugger?" said Peter.

Ender began to take off the mask. Peter put his toe against Ender's groin. "Don't take off the mask," Peter said.

Ender pulled the mask down into place, took his hands away.

Peter pressed with his foot. Pain shot through Ender; he doubled up.

"Lie flat, bugger. We're gonna vivisect you, bugger. At long last we've got one of you alive, and we're going to see how you work."

"Peter, stop it," Ender said.

"Peter, stop it. Very good. So you buggers can guess our names. You can make yourselves sound like pathetic, cute little children so we'll love you and be nice to you. But it doesn't work. I can see you for what you really are. They meant you to be human, little Third, but you're really a bugger, and now it shows."

He lifted his foot, took a step, and then knelt on Ender, his knee pressing into Ender's belly just below the breastbone. He put more and more of his weight on Ender. It became hard to breathe.

"I could kill you like this," Peter whispered. "Just press and press until you're dead. And I could say that I didn't know it would hurt you, that we were just playing, and they'd believe me, and everything would be fine. And you'd be dead. Everything would be fine."

Ender could not speak; the breath was being forced from his lungs. Peter might mean it. Probably didn't mean it, but then he might.

"I do mean it," Peter said. "Whatever you think, I mean it. They only authorized you because I was so promising. But I didn't pan out. You did better. They think you're better. But I don't want a better little brother, Ender. I don't want a Third."

"I'll tell," Valentine said from the doorway.

"No one would believe you."

"They'd believe me."

"Then you're dead, too, sweet little sister."

"Oh, yes," said Valentine. "They'll believe that. 'I didn't know it would kill Andrew. And when he was dead, I didn't know it would kill Valentine *too*.'"

The pressure let up a little.

"So. Not today. But someday you two won't be together. And there'll be an accident."

"You're all talk," Valentine said. "You don't mean any of it."

"I don't?"

"And do you know why you don't mean it?" Valentine asked. "Because you want to be in government someday. You want to be elected. And they won't elect you if your opponents can dig up the fact that your brother and sister both died in suspicious accidents when they were little. Especially because of the letter I've put in my secret file in the city library, which will be opened in the event of my death."

"Don't give me that kind of crap," Peter said.

"It says, I didn't die a natural death. Peter killed me, and if he hasn't already killed Andrew, he will soon. Not enough to convict you, but enough to keep you from ever getting elected."

"You're his monitor now," said Peter. "You better watch him, day and night. You better be there."

"Ender and I aren't stupid. We scored as well as you did on everything. Better on some things. We're all such wonderfully bright children. You're not the smartest, Peter, just the biggest."

"Oh, I know. But there'll come a day when you aren't there with him, when you forget. And suddenly you'll remember, and you'll rush to him, and there he'll be, perfectly all right. And the next time you won't worry so much, and you won't come so fast. And every time, he'll be all right. And you'll think that I forgot. Even though you'll remember that I said this, you'll think that I forgot. And years will pass. And then there'll be a terrible accident, and I'll find his body, and I'll cry and cry over him, and you'll remember this conversation, Vally, but you'll be ashamed of yourself for remembering, because you'll know that I changed, that it really was an accident, that it's cruel of you even to remember what I said in a childhood quarrel. Except that it'll be true. I'm gonna save this up, and he's gonna die, and you won't do a thing, not a thing. But you go on believing that I'm just the biggest."

"The biggest asshole," Valentine said.

Peter leaped to his feet and started for her. She shied away. Ender pried off his mask. Peter flopped back on his bed and started to laugh. Loud, but with real mirth, tears coming to his eyes. "Oh, you guys are just super, just the biggest suckers on the planet earth."

"Now he's going to tell us it was all a joke," Valentine said.

"Not a joke, a game. I can make you guys believe anything. I can make you dance around like puppets." In a phony monster voice he said, "I'm going to kill you and chop you into little pieces and put you into the garbage hole." He laughed again. "Biggest suckers in the solar system."

Ender stood there watching him laugh and thought of Stilson, thought of how it felt to crunch into his body. This is who needed it. This is who should have got it.

As if she could read his mind, Valentine whispered, "No, Ender."

Peter suddenly rolled to the side, flipped off the bed, and got in position for a fight. "Oh, yes, Ender," he said. "Any time, Ender."

Ender lifted his right leg and took off his shoe. He held it up. "See there, on the toe? That's blood, Peter. It's not mine."

"Ooh. Ooh, I'm gonna die, I'm gonna die. Ender squished a capper-tiller and now he's gonna squish me."

There was no getting to him. Peter was a murderer at heart, and nobody knew it but Valentine and Ender.

Mother came home and commiserated with Ender about the monitor. Father came home and kept saying it was such a wonderful surprise, they had such fantastic children that the government told them to have three, and now the government didn't want to take any of them after all, so here they were with three, they still had a Third . . . until Ender wanted to scream at him, I know I'm a Third, I know it, if you want I'll go away so you don't have to be embarrassed in front of everybody, I'm sorry I lost the monitor and now you have three kids and no obvious explanation, so inconvenient for you, I'm sorry sorry sorry.

He lay in bed staring upward into the darkness. On the bunk above him, he could hear Peter turning and tossing restlessly. Then Peter slid off the bunk and walked out of the room. Ender heard the hushing sound of the toilet clearing; then Peter stood silhouetted in the doorway.

He thinks I'm asleep. He's going to kill me.

Peter walked to the bed, and sure enough, he did not lift himself up to his bed. Instead he came and stood by Ender's head.

But he did not reach for a pillow to smother Ender. He did not have a weapon.

He whispered, "Ender, I'm sorry, I'm sorry, I know how it feels, I'm sorry, I'm your brother, I love you."

A long time later, Peter's even breathing said that he was asleep. Ender peeled the bandaid from his neck. And for the second time that day he cried.

3

GRAFF

"The sister is our weak link. He really loves her."

"I know. She can undo it all, from the start. He won't want to leave her."

"So, what are you going to do?"

"Persuade him that he wants to come with us more than he wants to stay with her."

"How will you do that?"

"I'll lie to him."

"And if that doesn't work?"

"Then I'll tell the truth. We're allowed to do that in emergencies. We can't plan for everything, you know."

Ender wasn't very hungry during breakfast. He kept wondering what it would be like at school. Facing Stilson after yesterday's fight. What Stilson's friends would do. Probably nothing, but he couldn't be sure. He didn't want to go.

"You're not eating, Andrew," his mother said.

Peter came into the room. "Morning, Ender. Thanks for leaving your slimy washcloth in the middle of the shower."

"Just for you," Ender murmured.

"Andrew, you have to eat."

Ender held out his wrists, a gesture that said, So feed it to me through a needle.

"Very funny," Mother said. "I try to be concerned, but it makes no difference to my genius children."

"It was all your genes that made us geniuses, Mom," said Peter. "We sure didn't get any from Dad."

"I heard that," Father said, not looking up from the news that was being displayed on the table while he ate.

"It would've been wasted if you hadn't."

The table beeped. Someone was at the door.

"Who is it?" Mother asked.

Father thumbed a key and a man appeared on his video. He was wearing the only military uniform that meant anything anymore, the I.F., the International Fleet.

"I thought it was over," said Father.

Peter said nothing, just poured milk over his cereal.

And Ender thought, Maybe I won't have to go to school today after all.

Father coded the door open and got up from the table. "I'll see to it," he said. "Stay and eat."

They stayed, but they didn't eat. A few moments later, Father came back into the room and beckoned to Mother.

"You're in deep poo," said Peter. "They found out what you did to that kid at school, and now they're gonna make you do time out in the Belt."

"I'm only six, moron, I'm a juvenile."

"You're a Third, turd. You've got no rights."

Valentine came in, her hair in a sleepy halo around her face. "Where's Mom and Dad? I'm too sick to go to school."

"Another oral exam, huh?" Peter said.

"Shut up, Peter," said Valentine.

"You should relax and enjoy it," said Peter. "It could be worse."

"I don't know how."

"It could be an anal exam."

"Hyuk hyuk," Valentine said. "Where are Mother and Father?"

"Talking to a guy from IF."

Instinctively she looked at Ender. After all, for years they had expected someone to come and tell them that Ender had passed, that Ender was needed.

"That's right, look at him," Peter said. "But it might be me, you know. They might have realized I was the best of the lot after all." Peter's feelings were hurt, and so he was being a snot, as usual.

The door opened. "Ender," said Father, "you better come in here."

"Sorry, Peter," Valentine taunted.

Father glowered. "Children, this is no laughing matter."

Ender followed Father into the parlor. The I.F. officer rose to his feet when they entered, but he did not extend a hand to Ender.

Mother was twisting her wedding band on her finger. "Andrew," she said, "I never thought you were the kind to get in a fight."

"The Stilson boy is in the hospital," Father said. "You really did a number on him. With your shoe, Ender. That wasn't exactly fair."

Ender shook his head. He had expected someone from the school to come about Stilson, not an officer of the fleet. This was more serious than he had thought. And yet he couldn't think what else he could have done.

"Do you have any explanation for your behavior, young man?" asked the officer.

Ender shook his head again. He didn't know what to say, and he was afraid to reveal himself to be any more monstrous than his actions had made him out to be. I'll take it, whatever the punishment is, he thought. Let's get it over with.

"We're willing to consider extenuating circumstances," the officer said. "But I must tell you it doesn't look good. Kicking him in the groin, kicking him repeatedly in the face and body when he was down—it sounds like you really enjoyed it."

"I didn't," Ender whispered.

"Then why did you do it?"

"He had his gang there," Ender said.

"So? This excuses anything?"

"No."

"Tell me why you kept on kicking him. You had already won."

"Knocking him down won the first fight. I wanted to win all the next ones, too. So they'd leave me alone." Ender couldn't help it, he was too afraid, too ashamed of his own acts; though he tried not to, he cried again. Ender did not like to cry and rarely did; now, in less than a day, he had done it three times. And each time was worse. To cry in front of his mother and father and this military man, that was shameful. "You took away the monitor," Ender said. "I had to take care of myself, didn't I?"

"Ender, you should have asked a grown-up for help," Father began.

But the officer stood up and stepped across the room to Ender. He held out his hand. "My name is Graff, Ender. Colonel Hyrum Graff. I'm director of primary training at Battle School in the Belt. I've come to invite you to enter the school."

After all. "But the monitor—"

"The final step in your testing was to see what would happen when the monitor came off. We don't always do it that way, but in your case—"

"And he passed?" Mother was incredulous. "Putting the Stilson boy in the hospital? What would you have done if Andrew had killed him, given him a medal?"

"It isn't *what* he did, Mrs. Wiggin. It's *why*." Colonel Graff handed her a folder full of papers. "Here are the requisitions. Your son has been cleared by the I.F. Selective Service. Of course we already have your consent, granted in writing at the time conception was confirmed, or he could not have been born. He has been ours from then, if he qualified."

Father's voice was trembling as he spoke. "It's not very kind of you, to let us think you didn't want him, and then to take him after all."

"And this charade about the Stilson boy," Mother said.

"It wasn't a charade, Mrs. Wiggin. Until we knew what Ender's motivation was, we couldn't be sure he wasn't another—we had to know what the action meant. Or at least what Ender believed that it meant."

"Must you call him that stupid nickname?" Mother began to cry.

"That's the name he calls himself."

"What are you going to do, Colonel Graff?" Father asked. "Walk out the door with him now?"

"That depends," said Graff.

"On what?"

"On whether Ender wants to come."

Mother's weeping turned to bitter laughter. "Oh, so it's voluntary after all, how sweet!"

"For the two of you, the choice was made when Ender was conceived. But for Ender, the choice has not been made at all. Conscripts make good cannon fodder, but for officers we need volunteers."

"Officers?" Ender asked. At the sound of his voice, the others fell silent.

"Yes," said Graff. "Battle School is for training future starship captains and commodores of flotillas and admirals of the fleet."

"Let's not have any deception here!" Father said angrily. "How many of the boys at the Battle School actually end up in command of ships!"

"Unfortunately, Mr. Wiggin, that is classified information. But I *can* say that none of our boys who makes it through the first year has ever failed to receive a commission as an officer. And none has retired from a position of lower rank than chief executive officer of an interplanetary vessel. Even in the domestic defense forces within our own solar system, there's honor to be had."

"How many make it through the first year?" asked Ender.

"All who want to," said Graff.

Ender almost said, I want to. But he held his tongue. This would keep him out of school, but that was stupid, that was just a problem for a few days. It would keep him away from Peter—that was more important, that might be a matter of life itself. But to leave Mother and Father, and above all, to leave Valentine. And become a soldier. Ender didn't like fighting. He didn't like Peter's kind, the strong against the weak, and he didn't like his own kind either, the smart against the stupid.

"I think," Graff said, "that Ender and I should have a private conversation."

"No," Father said.

"I won't take him without letting you speak to him again," Graff said. "And you really can't stop me."

Father glared at Graff a moment longer, then got up and left the room. Mother paused to squeeze Ender's hand. She closed the door behind her when she left.

"Ender," Graff said, "if you come with me, you won't be back here for a long time. There aren't any vacations from Battle School. No visitors, either. A full course of training lasts until you're sixteen years old—you get your first leave, under certain circumstances, when you're twelve. Believe me, Ender, people change in six years, in ten years. Your sister Valentine will be a woman when you see her again, if you come with me. You'll be strangers. You'll still love her, Ender, but you won't know her. You see I'm not pretending it's easy."

"Mom and Daddy?"

"I know you, Ender. I've been watching the monitor disks for some time. You won't miss your mother and father, not much, not for long. And they won't miss you long, either."

Tears came to Ender's eyes, in spite of himself. He turned his face away, but would not reach up to wipe them.

"They *do* love you, Ender. But you have to understand what your life has cost them. They were born religious, you know. Your father was baptized with the name John Paul Wieczorek. Catholic. The seventh of nine children."

Nine children. That was unthinkable. Criminal.

"Yes, well, people do strange things for religion. You know the sanctions, Ender—they were not as harsh then, but still not easy. Only the first two children had a free education. Taxes steadily rose with each new child. Your father turned sixteen and invoked the Noncomplying Families Act to separate himself from his family. He changed his name, renounced his religion, and vowed never to have more than the allotted two children. He meant it. All the shame and persecution he went through as a child—he vowed no child of his would go through it. Do you understand?"

"He didn't want me."

"Well, no one *wants* a Third anymore. You can't expect them to be glad. But your father and mother are a special case. They both renounced their religions—your mother was a Mormon—but in fact their feelings are still ambiguous. Do you know what ambiguous means?"

"They feel both ways."

"They're ashamed of having come from noncompliant families. They conceal it. To the degree that your mother refuses to admit to anyone that she was born in Utah, lest they suspect. Your father denies his Polish ancestry, since Poland is still a noncompliant nation, and under international sanction because of it. So, you see, having a Third, even under the government's direct instructions, undoes everything they've been trying to do."

"I know that."

"But it's more complicated than that. Your father still named you with legitimate saints' names. In fact, he baptized all three of you himself as soon as he got you home after you were born. And your mother objected. They quarreled over it each time, not because she didn't want you baptized, but because she didn't want you baptized Catholic. They haven't really given up their religion. They look at you and see you as a badge of pride, because they were able to circumvent the law and have a Third. But you're also a badge of cowardice, because they dare not go further and practice the noncompliance they still feel is right. And you're a badge of public shame, because at every step you interfere with their efforts at assimilation into normal complying society."

"How can you know all this?"

"We monitored your brother and sister, Ender. You'd be amazed at how sensitive the instruments are. We were connected directly to your brain. We heard all that you heard, whether you were listening carefully or not. Whether you understood or not. *We* understand."

"So my parents love me and don't love me?"

"They love you. The question is whether they want you here. Your presence in this house is a constant disruption. A source of tension. Do you understand?"

"*I'm* not the one who causes tension."

"Not anything you *do,* Ender. Your life itself. Your brother hates you because you are living proof that he wasn't good enough. Your parents resent you because of all the past they are trying to evade."

"Valentine loves me."

"With all her heart. Completely, unstintingly, she's devoted to you, and you adore her. I told you it wouldn't be easy."

"What is it like, there?"

"Hard work. Studies, just like school here, except we put you into mathematics and computers much more heavily. Military history. Strategy and tactics. And above all, the Battle Room."

"What's that?"

"War games. All the boys are organized into armies. Day after day, in zero gravity, there are mock battles. Nobody gets hurt, but winning and losing matter. Everybody starts as a common soldier, taking orders. Older boys are your officers, and it's their duty to train you and command you in battle. More than that I can't tell you. It's like playing buggers and astronauts—except that you have weapons that work, and fellow soldiers fighting beside you, and your whole future and the future of the human race depends on how well you learn, how well you fight. It's a hard life, and you won't have a normal childhood. Of course, with your mind, and as a Third to boot, you wouldn't have a particularly normal childhood anyway."

"All boys?"

"A few girls. They don't often pass the tests to get in. Too many centuries of evolution are working against them. None of them will be like Valentine, anyway. But there'll be brothers there, Ender."

"Like Peter?"

"Peter wasn't accepted, Ender, for the very reasons that you hate him."

"I don't hate him. I'm just—"

"Afraid of him. Well, Peter isn't all bad, you know. He was the best we'd seen in a long time. We asked your parents to choose a daughter next—they would have anyway—hoping that Valentine would be Peter, but milder. She was too mild. And so we requisitioned you."

"To be half Peter and half Valentine."

"If things worked out right."

"Am I?"

"As far as we can tell. Our tests are very good, Ender. But they don't tell us everything. In fact, when it comes down to it, they hardly tell us anything. But they're better than nothing." Graff leaned over and took Ender's hands in his. "Ender Wiggin, if it were just a matter of choosing the best and happiest future for you, I'd tell you to stay home. Stay here, grow up, be happy. There are worse things than being a Third, worse things than a big brother who can't make up his mind whether to be a human being or a jackal. Battle School is one of those worse things. But we need you. The buggers may seem like a game to you now, Ender, but they damn near wiped us out last time. They had us cold, outnumbered and outweaponed. The only thing that saved us was that we had the most brilliant military commander we ever found. Call it fate, call it God, call it damnfool luck, we had Mazer Rackham.

"But we don't have him now, Ender. We've scraped together everything mankind could produce, a fleet that makes the one they sent against us last time seem like a bunch of kids playing in a swimming pool. We have some new weapons, too. But it might not be enough, even so. Because in the eighty years since the last war, they've had as much time to prepare as we have. We need the best we can get, and we need them fast. Maybe you're not going to work out for us, and maybe you are. Maybe you'll break down under the pressure, maybe it'll ruin your life, maybe you'll hate me for coming here to your house today. But if there's a chance that because you're with the fleet, mankind might survive and the buggers might leave us alone forever—then I'm going to ask you to do it. To come with me."

Ender had trouble focusing on Colonel Graff. The man looked far away and very small, as if Ender could pick him up with tweezers and drop him in a pocket. To leave everything here, and go to a place that was very hard, with no Valentine, no Mom and Dad.

And then he thought of the films of the buggers that everyone had to see at least once a year. The Scathing of China. The Battle of the Belt. Death and suffering and terror. And Mazer Rackham and his brilliant maneuvers, destroying an enemy fleet twice his size and twice his firepower, using the little human ships that seemed so frail and weak. Like children fighting with grown-ups. And we won.

"I'm afraid," said Ender quietly. "But I'll go with you."

"Tell me again," said Graff.

"It's what I was born for, isn't it? If I don't go, why am I alive?"

"Not good enough," said Graff.

"I don't want to go," said Ender, "but I will."

Graff nodded. "You can change your mind. Up until the time you get in my car with me, you can change your mind. After that, you stay at the pleasure of the International Fleet. Do you understand that?"

Ender nodded.

"All right. Let's tell them."

Mother cried. Father held Ender tight. Peter shook his hand and said, "You lucky little pinheaded fart-eater." Valentine kissed him and left her tears on his cheek.

There was nothing to pack. No belongings to take. "The school provides everything you need, from uniforms to school supplies. And as for toys— there's only one game."

"Good-bye," Ender said to his family. He reached up and took Colonel Graff's hand and walked out the door with him.

"Kill some buggers for me!" Peter shouted.

"I love you, Andrew!" Mother called.

"We'll write to you!" Father said.

And as he got into the car that waited silently in the corridor, he heard Valentine's anguished cry. "Come back to me! I love you forever!"

4

LAUNCH

"With Ender, we have to strike a delicate balance. Isolate him enough that he remains creative—otherwise he'll adopt the system here and we'll lose him. At the same time, we need to make sure he keeps a strong ability to lead."

"If he earns rank, he'll lead."

"It isn't that simple. Mazer Rackham could handle his little fleet and win. By the time this war happens, there'll be too much, even for a genius. Too many little boats. He has to work smoothly with his subordinates."

"Oh, good. He has to be a genius and nice, too."

"Not *nice*. Nice will let the buggers have us all."

"So you're going to isolate him."

"I'll have him completely separated from the rest of the boys by the time we get to the School."

"I have no doubt of it. I'll be waiting for you to get here. I watched the vids of what he did to the Stilson boy. This is not a sweet little kid you're bringing up here."

"That's where you're mistaken. He's even sweeter than he looks. But don't worry. We'll purge *that* in a hurry."

"Sometimes I think you enjoy breaking these little geniuses."

"There *is* an art to it, and I'm very, very good at it. But enjoy? Well, maybe. When they put back the pieces afterward, and it makes them better."

"You're a monster."

"Thanks. Does this mean I get a raise?"

"Just a medal. The budget isn't inexhaustible."

They say that weightlessness can cause disorientation, especially in children, whose sense of direction isn't yet secure. But Ender was disoriented before he left Earth's gravity. Before the shuttle launch even began.

There were nineteen other boys in his launch. They filed out of the bus and into the elevator. They talked and joked and bragged and laughed. Ender kept his silence. He noticed how Graff and the other officers were watching them. Analyzing. Everything we do means something, Ender realized. Them laughing. Me not laughing.

He toyed with the idea of trying to be like the other boys. But he couldn't think of any jokes, and none of theirs seemed funny. Wherever their laughter came from, Ender couldn't find such a place in himself. He was afraid, and fear made him serious.

They had dressed him in a uniform, all in a single piece; it felt funny not to have a belt cinched around his waist. He felt baggy and naked, dressed like that. There were TV cameras going, perched like animals on the shoulders of crouching, prowling men. The men moved slowly, catlike, so the camera motion would be smooth. Ender caught himself moving smoothly, too.

He imagined himself being on TV, in an interview. The announcer asking him, How do you feel, Mr. Wiggin? Actually quite well, except hungry. Hungry? Oh, yes, they don't let you eat for twenty hours before the launch. How interesting, I never knew that. All of us are quite hungry, actually. And all the while, during the interview, Ender and the TV guy would slink along smoothly in front of the cameraman, taking long, lithe strides. The TV guy was letting him be the spokesman for all the boys, though Ender was barely competent to speak for himself. For the first time, Ender felt like laughing. He smiled. The other boys near him were laughing at the moment, too, for another reason. They think I'm smiling at their joke, thought Ender. But I'm smiling at something much funnier.

"Go up the ladder one at a time," said an officer. "When you come to an aisle with empty seats, take one. There aren't any window seats."

It was a joke. The other boys laughed.

Ender was near the last, but not the very last. The TV cameras did not give up, though. Will Valentine see me disappear into the shuttle? He thought of waving at her, of running to the cameraman and saying, "Can I tell Valentine good-bye?" He didn't know that it would be censored out of the tape if he did, for the boys soaring out to Battle School were all supposed to be heroes. They weren't supposed to miss anybody. Ender didn't know about the censorship, but he did know that running to the cameras would be wrong.

He walked the short bridge to the door in the shuttle. He noticed that the wall to his right was carpeted like a floor. That was where the disorientation began. The moment he thought of the wall as a floor, he began to feel like he was walking on a wall. He got to the ladder, and noticed that the vertical surface behind it was also carpeted. I am climbing up the floor. Hand over hand, step by step.

And then, for fun, he pretended that he was climbing *down* the wall. He did it almost instantly in his mind, convinced himself against the best evidence of gravity until he reached an empty seat. He found himself gripping the seat tightly, even though gravity pulled him firmly against it.

The other boys were bouncing on their seats a little, poking and pushing, shouting. Ender carefully found the straps, figured out how they fit together to hold him at crotch, waist, and shoulders. He imagined the ship dangling upside down on the undersurface of the Earth, the giant fingers of gravity holding them firmly in place. But we will slip away, he thought. We are going to fall off this planet.

He did not know its significance at the time. Later, though, he would remember that it was even before he left Earth that he first thought of it as a planet, like any other, not particularly his own.

"Oh, already figured it out," said Graff. He was standing on the ladder.

"Coming with us?" Ender asked.

"I don't usually come down for recruiting," Graff said. "I'm kind of in charge there. Administrator of the School. Like a principal. They told me I had to come back or I'd lose my job." He smiled.

Ender smiled back. He felt comfortable with Graff. Graff was good. And he was principal of the Battle School. Ender relaxed a little. He would have a friend there.

Adults helped the other boys belt themselves in place, those who hadn't done as Ender did. Then they waited for an hour while a TV at the front of the shuttle introduced them to shuttle flight, the history of space flight, and their possible future with the great starships of the I.F. Very boring stuff. Ender had seen such films before.

Except that he had not been belted into a seat inside the shuttle. Hanging upside down from the belly of Earth.

The launch wasn't bad. A little scary. Some jolting, a few moments of panic that this might be the first failed launch since the early days of the shuttle. The movies hadn't made it plain how much violence you could experience, lying on your back in a soft chair.

Then it was over, and he really was hanging by the straps, no gravity anywhere.

But because he had already reoriented himself, he was not surprised when Graff came up the ladder backward, as if he were climbing down to the front of the shuttle. Nor did it bother him when Graff hooked his feet under a rung and pushed off with his hands, so that suddenly he swung upright, as if this were an ordinary airplane.

The reorientations were too much for some. One boy gagged; Ender understood then why they had been forbidden to eat anything for twenty hours before the launch. Vomiting in null gravity wouldn't be fun.

But for Ender, Graff's gravity game was fun. And he carried it further, imagining that Graff was actually hanging upside down from the center aisle, and then picturing him sticking straight out from a side wall. Gravity could go any which way. However I want it to go. I can make Graff stand on his head and he doesn't even know it.

"What do you think is so funny, Wiggin?"

Graff's voice was sharp and angry. What did I do wrong, thought Ender. Did I laugh out loud?

"I asked you a question, soldier!" barked Graff.

Oh yes. This is the beginning of the training routine. Ender had seen some military shows on TV, and they always shouted a lot at the beginning of training before the soldiers and the officer became good friends.

"Yes sir," Ender said.

"Well answer it, then!"

"I thought of you hanging upside down by your feet. I thought it was funny."

It sounded stupid, now, with Graff looking at him coldly. "To you I suppose it *is* funny. Is it funny to anybody else here?"

Murmurs of no.

"Well why isn't it?" Graff looked at them all with contempt. "Scumbrains, that's what we've got in this launch. Pinheaded little morons. Only one of you had the brains to realize that in null gravity directions are whatever you conceive them to be. Do you understand that, Shafts?"

The boy nodded.

"No you didn't. Of course you didn't. Not only stupid, but a liar too. There's only one boy on this launch with any brains *at all,* and that's Ender Wiggin. Take a good look at him, little boys. He's going to be a commander when you're still in diapers up there. Because he knows how to think in null gravity, and you just want to throw up."

This wasn't the way the show was supposed to go. Graff was supposed to pick on him, not set him up as the best. They were supposed to be against each other at first, so they could become friends later.

"Most of you are going to ice out. Get used to that, little boys. Most of you are going to end up in Combat School, because you don't have the brains to handle deep-space piloting. Most of you aren't worth the price of bringing you up here to Battle School because you don't have what it takes. Some of you might make it. *Some* of you might be worth something to humanity. But don't bet on it. I'm betting on only one."

Suddenly Graff did a backflip and caught the ladder with his hands, then swung his feet away from the ladder. Doing a handstand, if the floor was down. Dangling by his hands, if the floor was up. Hand over hand he swung himself back along the aisle to his seat.

"Looks like *you've* got it made here," whispered the boy next to him.

Ender shook his head.

"Oh, won't even talk to me?" the boy said.

"I didn't ask him to say that stuff," Ender whispered.

He felt a sharp pain on the top of his head. Then again. Some giggles from behind him. The boy in the next seat back must have unfastened his straps. Again a blow to the head. Go away, Ender thought. I didn't do anything to you.

Again a blow to the head. Laughter from the boys. Didn't Graff see this? Wasn't he going to stop it? Another blow. Harder. It really hurt. Where was Graff?

Then it became clear. Graff had deliberately caused it. It was worse than the abuse in the shows. When the sergeant picked on you, the others liked you better. But when the officer prefers you, the others hate you.

"Hey, fart-eater," came the whisper from behind him. He was hit on the head again. "Do you like this? Hey, super-brain, is this fun?" Another blow, this one so hard that Ender cried out softly with the pain.

If Graff was setting him up, there'd be no help unless he helped himself. He waited until he thought another blow was about to come. Now, he thought. And yes, the blow was there. It hurt, but Ender was already trying to sense the coming of the next blow. Now. And yes, right on time. I've got you, Ender thought.

Just as the next blow was coming, Ender reached up with both hands, snatched the boy by the wrist, and then pulled down on the arm, hard.

In gravity, the boy would have been jammed against Ender's seat back, hurting his chest. In null gravity, however, he flipped over the seat completely, up toward the ceiling. Ender wasn't expecting it. He hadn't realized how null gravity magnified the effects of even a child's movements. The boy sailed through the air, bouncing against the ceiling, then down against another boy in his seat, then out into the aisle, his arms flailing until he screamed as his body slammed into the bulkhead at the front of the compartment, his left arm twisted under him.

It took only seconds. Graff was already there, snatching the boy out of the air. Deftly he propelled him down the aisle toward the other man. "Left arm. Broken, I think," he said. In moments the boy had been given a drug and lay quietly in the air as the officer ballooned a splint around his arm.

Ender felt sick. He had only meant to catch the boy's arm. No. No, he had meant to hurt him, and had pulled with all his strength. He hadn't meant it to be so public, but the boy was feeling exactly the pain Ender had meant him to feel. Null gravity had betrayed him, that was all. I am Peter. I'm just like him. And Ender hated himself.

Graff stayed at the front of the cabin. "What are you, slow learners? In your feeble little minds, haven't you picked up one little fact? You were brought here to be *soldiers*. In your old schools, in your old families, maybe you were the big shot, maybe you were tough, maybe you were smart. But we chose the best of the best, and that's the only kind of kid you're going to meet now. And when I tell you Ender Wiggin is the best in this launch, take the hint, my little dorklings. Don't mess with him. Little boys have died in Battle School before. Do I make myself clear?"

There was silence the rest of the launch. The boy sitting next to Ender was scrupulously careful not to touch him.

I am not a killer, Ender said to himself over and over. I am not Peter. No matter what Graff says, I'm not. I was defending myself. I bore it a long time. I was patient. I'm not what he said.

A voice over the speaker told them they were approaching the school; it took twenty minutes to decelerate and dock. Ender lagged behind the others. They were not unwilling to let him be the last to leave the shuttle, climbing upward in the direction that had been down when they embarked. Graff was waiting at the end of the narrow tube that led from the shuttle into the heart of the Battle School.

"Was it a good flight, Ender?" Graff asked cheerfully.

"I thought you were my friend." Despite himself, Ender's voice trembled.

Graff looked puzzled. "Whatever gave you that idea, Ender?"

"Because you—" Because you spoke nicely to me, and honestly. "You didn't lie."

"I won't lie now, either," said Graff. "My job isn't to be friends. My job is to produce the best soldiers in the world. In the whole history of the world. We need a Napoleon. An Alexander. Except that Napoleon lost in the end, and Alexander flamed out and died young. We need a Julius Caesar, except that he made himself dictator, and died for it. My job is to produce such a creature, and all the men and women he'll need to help him. Nowhere in that does it say I have to make friends with children."

"You made them hate me."

"So? What will you do about it? Crawl into a corner? Start kissing their little backsides so they'll love you again? There's only one thing that will make them stop hating you. And that's being so good at what you do that they can't ignore you. I told them you were the best. Now you damn well better be."

"What if I can't?"

"Then too bad. Look, Ender, I'm sorry if you're lonely and afraid. But the buggers are out there. Ten billion, a hundred billion, a million billion of them, for all we know. With as many ships, for all we know. With weapons we can't understand. And a willingness to use those weapons to wipe us out. It isn't the world at stake, Ender. Just us. Just humankind. As far as the rest of the biosphere is concerned, we could be wiped out and it would adjust, it would get on with the next step in evolution. But humanity doesn't want to die. As a species, we have evolved to survive. And the way we do it is by straining and straining and, at last, every few generations, giving birth to genius. The one who invents the wheel. And light. And flight. The one who builds a city, a nation, an empire. Do you understand any of this?"

Ender thought he did, but wasn't sure, and so said nothing.

"No. Of course not. So I'll put it bluntly. Human beings are free except when humanity needs them. Maybe humanity needs you. To do something. Maybe humanity needs *me*—to find out what you're good for. We might both do despicable things, Ender, but if humankind survives, then we were good tools."

"Is that all? Just tools?"

"Individual human beings are all tools, that the others use to help us all survive."

"That's a lie."

"No. It's just a half truth. You can worry about the other half after we win this war."

"It'll be over before I grow up," Ender said.

"I hope you're wrong," said Graff. "By the way, you aren't helping yourself at all, talking to me. The other boys are no doubt telling each other that old Ender Wiggin is back there licking up to Graff. If word once gets around that you're a teachers' boy, you're iced for sure."

In other words, go away and leave me alone. "Goodbye," Ender said. He pulled himself hand over hand along the tube where the other boys had gone.

Graff watched him go.

One of the teachers near him said, "Is that the one?"

"God knows," said Graff. "If Ender isn't him, then he'd better show up soon."

"Maybe it's nobody," said the teacher.

"Maybe. But if that's the case, Anderson, then in my opinion God is a bugger. You can quote me on that."

"I will."

They stood in silence a while longer.

"Anderson."

"Mmm."

"The kid's wrong. I *am* his friend."

"I know."

"He's clean. Right to the heart, he's good."

"I've read the reports."

"Anderson, think what we're going to do to him."

Anderson was defiant. "We're going to make him the best military commander in history."

"And then put the fate of the world on his shoulders. For his sake, I hope it isn't him. I do."

"Cheer up. The buggers may kill us all before he graduates."

Graff smiled. "You're right. I feel better already."

5

GAMES

"You have my admiration. Breaking an arm—that was a master stroke."

"That was an accident."

"Really? And I've already commended you in your official report."

"It's too strong. It makes that other little bastard into a hero. It could screw up training for a lot of kids. I thought Ender might call for help."

"Call for help? I thought that was what you valued most in him—that he settles his own problems. When he's out there surrounded by an enemy fleet, there ain't gonna be nobody to help him if he calls."

"Who would have guessed the little sucker'd be out of his seat? And that he'd land just wrong against the bulkhead?"

"Just one more example of the stupidity of the military. If you had any brains, you'd be in a real career, like selling life insurance."

"You, too, mastermind."

"We've just got to face the fact that we're second rate. With the fate of humanity in our hands. Gives you a delicious feeling of power, doesn't it? Especially because this time if we lose there won't be any criticism of us at all."

"I never thought of it that way. But let's not lose."

"See how Ender handles it. If we've already lost him, if he can't handle this, who next? Who else?"

"I'll make up a list."

"In the meantime, figure out how to unlose Ender."

"I told you. His isolation can't be broken. He can never come to believe that anybody will ever help him out, *ever*. If he once thinks there's an easy way out, he's wrecked."

"You're right. That would be terrible, if he believed he had a friend."

"He can have friends. It's parents he can't have."

The other boys had already chosen their bunks when Ender arrived. Ender stopped in the doorway of the dormitory, looking for the sole remaining bed. The ceiling was low—Ender could reach up and touch it. A child-sized room, with the bottom bunk resting on the floor. The other boys were watching him, cornerwise. Sure enough, the bottom bunk right by the door was the only empty bed. For a moment it occurred to Ender that by letting the others put him in the worst place, he was inviting later bullying. Yet he couldn't very well oust someone else.

So he smiled broadly. "Hey, thanks," he said. Not sarcastically at all. He said it as sincerely as if they had reserved for him the best position. "I thought I was going to have to *ask* for low bunk by the door."

He sat down and looked in the locker that stood open at the foot of the bunk. There was a paper taped to the inside of the door.

PLACE YOUR HAND ON THE SCANNER
AT THE HEAD OF YOUR BUNK
AND SPEAK YOUR NAME TWICE.

Ender found the scanner, a sheet of opaque plastic. He put his left hand on it and said, "Ender Wiggin. Ender Wiggin."

The scanner glowed green for a moment. Ender closed his locker and tried to reopen it. He couldn't. Then he put his hand on the scanner and said, "Ender Wiggin." The locker popped open. So did three other compartments.

One of them contained four jumpsuits like the one he was wearing, and one white one. Another compartment contained a small desk, just like the ones at school. So they weren't through with studies yet.

It was the largest compartment that contained the prize. It looked like a spacesuit at first glance, complete with helmet and gloves. But it wasn't. There was no airtight seal. Still, it would effectively cover the whole body. It was thickly padded. It was also a little stiff.

And there was a pistol within. A lasergun, it looked like, since the end was solid, clear glass. But surely they wouldn't let children have lethal weapons—

"Not laser," said a man. Ender looked up. It was one he hadn't seen before. A young and kind-looking man. "But it has a tight enough beam. Well-focused. You can aim it and make a three-inch circle of light on a wall a hundred meters off."

"What's it for?" Ender asked.

"One of the games we play during recreation. Does anyone else have his locker open?" The man looked around. "I mean, have you followed directions and coded in your voices and hands? You can't get into the lockers until you do. This room is your home for the first year or so here at the Battle School, so get the bunk you want and stay with it. Ordinarily, we let you elect your chief officer and install him in the lower bunk by the door, but apparently that position has been taken. Can't recode the lockers now. So think about whom you want to choose. Dinner in seven minutes. Follow the lighted dots on the floor. Your color code is red yellow yellow—whenever you're assigned a path to follow, it will be red yellow yellow, three dots side by side—go where those lights indicate. What's your color code, boys?"

"Red, yellow, yellow."

"Very good. My name is Dap. I'm your mom for the next few months."

The boys laughed.

"Laugh all you like, but keep it in mind. If you get lost in the school, which is quite possible, don't go opening doors. Some of them lead outside." More laughter. "Instead just tell someone that your mom is Dap, and they'll call me. Or tell them your color, and they'll light up a path for you to get home. If you have a problem, come talk to me. Remember, I'm the only person here who's paid to be nice to you. But not too nice. Give me any lip and I'll break your face. OK?"

They laughed again. Dap had a room full of friends. Frightened children are so easy to win.

"Which way is down, anybody tell me?"

They told him.

"OK, that's true. But that direction is toward the *outside*. The ship is spinning, and that's what makes it feel like that is down. The floor actually curves around in *that* direction. Keep going long enough that way, and you come back to where you started. Except don't try it. Because up that way is teachers' quarters, and up that way is the bigger kids. And the bigger kids don't like Launchies butting in. You might get pushed around. In fact, you *will* get pushed around. And when you do, don't come crying to me. Got it? This is Battle School, not nursery school."

"What are we supposed to do, then?" asked a boy, a really small black kid who had a top bunk near Ender's.

"If you don't like getting pushed around, figure out for yourself what to do about it. But I warn you—murder is strictly against the rules. So is any deliberate injury. I understand there was one attempted murder on the way up here. A broken arm. That kind of thing happens again, somebody ices out. You got it?"

"What's icing out?" asked the boy with his arm puffed up in a splint.

"Ice. Put out in the cold. Sent Earthside. Finished at Battle School."

Nobody looked at Ender.

"So, boys, if any of you are thinking of being troublemakers, at least be clever about it, OK?"

Dap left. They still didn't look at Ender.

Ender felt the fear growing in his belly. The kid whose arm he broke—Ender didn't feel sorry for him. He was a Stilson. And like Stilson, he was already gathering a gang. A little knot of kids, several of the bigger ones. They were laughing at the far end of the room, and every now and then one of them would turn to look at Ender.

With all his heart, Ender wanted to go home. What did any of this have to do with saving the world? There was no monitor now. It was Ender against the gang again, only they were right in his room. Peter again, but without Valentine.

The fear stayed, all through dinner as no one sat by him in the mess hall. The other boys were talking about things—the big scoreboard on one wall, the food, the bigger kids. Ender could only watch in isolation.

The scoreboards were team standings. Win-loss records, with the most recent scores. Some of the bigger boys apparently had bets on the most recent games. Two teams, Manticore and Asp, had no recent score—these boxes were flashing. Ender decided they must be playing right now.

He noticed that the older boys were divided into groups, according to the uniforms they wore. Some with different uniforms were talking together, but generally the groups each had their own area. Launchies—their own group, and the two or three next older groups—all had plain blue uniforms. But the big kids, the ones that were on teams, they were wearing much more flamboyant clothing. Ender tried to guess which ones went with which name. Scorpion and Spider were easy. So were Flame and Tide.

A bigger boy came to sit by him. Not just a little bigger—he looked to be twelve or thirteen. Getting his man's growth started.

"Hi," he said.

"Hi," Ender said.

"I'm Mick."

"Ender."

"That's a name?"

"Since I was little. It's what my sister called me."

"Not a bad name here. Ender. Finisher. Hey."

"Hope so."

"Ender, you the bugger in your launch?"

Ender shrugged.

"I noticed you eating all alone. Every launch has one like that. Kid that nobody takes to right away. Sometimes I think the teachers do it on purpose. The teachers aren't very nice. You'll notice that."

"Yeah."

"So you the bugger?"

"I guess so."

"Hey. Nothing to cry about, you know?" He gave Ender his roll, and took Ender's pudding. "Eat nutritious stuff. It'll keep you strong." Mick dug into the pudding.

"What about you?" asked Ender.

"Me? I'm nothing. I'm a fart in the air conditioning. I'm always there, but most of the time nobody knows it."

Ender smiled tentatively.

"Yeah, funny, but no joke. I got nowhere here. I'm getting big now. They're going to send me to my next school pretty soon. No way it'll be Tactical School for me. I've never been a leader, you see. Only the guys who get to be leaders have a shot at it."

"How do you get to be a leader?"

"Hey, if I knew, you think I'd be like this? How many guys my size you see in here?"

Not many. Ender didn't say it.

"A few. I'm not the only half-iced bugger-fodder. A few of us. The other guys—they're all commanders. All the guys from my launch have their own teams now. Not me."

Ender nodded.

"Listen, little guy. I'm doing you a favor. Make friends. Be a leader. Kiss butts if you've got to, but if the other guys despise you—you know what I mean?"

Ender nodded again.

"Naw, you don't know nothing. You Launchies are all alike. You don't know nothing. Minds like space. Nothing there. And if anything hits you, you fall apart. Look, when you end up like me, don't forget that somebody warned you. It's the last nice thing anybody's going to do for you."

"So why did you tell me?" asked Ender.

"What are you, a smartmouth? Shut up and eat."

Ender shut up and ate. He didn't like Mick. And he knew there was no chance he would end up like that. Maybe that was what the teachers were planning, but Ender didn't intend to fit in with their plans.

I will not be the bugger of my group, Ender thought. I didn't leave Valentine and Mother and Father to come here just to be iced.

As he lifted the fork to his mouth, he could feel his family around him, as they always had been. He knew just which way to turn his head to look up and see Mother, trying to get Valentine not to slurp. He knew just where Father would be, scanning the news on the table while pretending to be part of the dinner conversation. Peter, pretending to take a crushed pea out of his nose—even Peter could be funny.

It was a mistake to think of them. He felt a sob rise in his throat and swallowed it down; he could not see his plate.

He could not cry. There was no chance that he would be treated with compassion. Dap was not Mother. Any sign of weakness would tell the Stilsons and Peters that this boy could be broken. Ender did what he always did when Peter tormented him. He began to count doubles. One, two, four, eight, sixteen, thirty-two, sixty-four. And on, as high as he could hold the numbers in his head: 128, 256, 512, 1024, 2048, 4096, 8192, 16384, 32768, 65536, 131072, 262144. At 67108864 he began to be unsure—had he slipped out a digit? Should he be in the ten millions or the hundred millions or just the millions? He tried doubling again and lost it. 1342 something. 16? Or 17738? It was gone. Start over again. All the doubling he could hold. The pain was gone. The tears were gone. He would not cry.

Until that night, when the lights went dim, and in the distance he could hear several boys whimpering for their mothers or fathers or dogs. Then he could not help himself. His lips formed Valentine's name. He could hear her voice laughing in the distance, just down the hall. He could see Mother passing his door, looking in to be sure he was all right. He could hear Father laughing at the video. It was all so clear, and it would *never* be that way again. I'll be old when I ever see them again, twelve at the earliest. Why did I say yes? What was I such a fool for? Going to school would have been nothing. Facing Stilson every day. And Peter. He was a pissant, Ender wasn't afraid of him.

I want to go home, he whispered.

But his whisper was the whisper he used when he cried out in pain when Peter tormented him. The sound didn't travel farther than his own ears, and sometimes not that far.

And his tears could fall unwanted on his sheet, but his sobs were so gentle that they did not shake the bed, so quiet they could not be heard. But the ache was there, thick in his throat and the front of his face, hot in his chest and in his eyes. I want to go home.

Dap came to the door that night and moved quietly among the beds, touching a hand here, a forehead there. Where he went there was more crying, not less. The touch of kindness in this frightening place was enough to push some over the edge into tears. Not Ender, though. When Dap came, his crying was over, and his face was dry. It was the lying face he presented to Mother and Father, when Peter had been cruel to him and he dared not let it show. Thank you for this, Peter. For dry eyes and silent weeping. You taught me how to hide anything I felt. More than ever, I need that now.

This was school. Every day, hours of classes. Reading. Numbers. History. Videos of the bloody battles in space, the Marines spraying their guts all over the walls of the bugger ships. Holos of the clean wars of the fleet, ships turning into puffs of light as the spacecraft killed each other deftly in the deep night. Many things to learn. Ender worked as hard as anyone; all of them struggled for the first time in their lives, as for the first time in their lives they competed with classmates who were at least as bright as they.

But the games—that was what they lived for. That was what filled the hours between waking and sleeping.

Dap introduced them to the game room on their second day. It was up, way above the decks where the boys lived and worked. They climbed ladders to where the gravity weakened, and there in the cavern they saw the dazzling lights of the games.

Some of the games they knew; some they had even played at home. Simple ones and hard ones. Ender walked past the two-dimensional games on video and began to study the games the bigger boys played, the holographic games with objects hovering in the air. He was the only Launchy in that part of the room, and every now and then one of the bigger boys would shove him out of the way. What're you doing here? Get lost. Fly off. And of course he would fly, in the lower gravity here, leave his feet and soar until he ran into something or someone.

Every time, though, he extricated himself and went back, perhaps to a different spot, to get a different angle on the game. He was too small to see the controls, how the game was actually done. That didn't matter. He got the movement of it in the air. The way the player dug tunnels in the darkness, tunnels of light, which the enemy ships would search for and then follow mercilessly until they caught the player's ship. The player could make traps: mines, drifting bombs, loops in the air that forced the enemy ships to repeat endlessly. Some of the players were clever. Others lost quickly.

Ender liked it better, though, when two boys played against each other. Then they had to use each other's tunnels, and it quickly became clear which of them was worth anything at the strategy of it.

Within an hour or so, it began to pall. Ender understood the regularities by then. Understood the rules the computer was following, so that he knew he could always, once he mastered the controls, outmaneuver the enemy. Spirals when the enemy was like this; loops when the enemy was like that. Lie in wait at one trap. Lay seven traps and then lure them like this. There was no challenge to it, then, just a matter of playing until the computer got so fast that no human reflexes could overcome it. That wasn't fun. It was the other boys he wanted to play. The boys who had been so trained by the computer that even when they played against each other they each tried to emulate the computer. Think like a machine instead of a boy.

I could beat them this way. I could beat them that way.

"I'd like a turn against you," he said to the boy who had just won.

"Lawsy me, what is this?" asked the boy. "Is it a bug or a bugger?"

"A new flock of dwarfs just came aboard," said another boy.

"But it *talks*. Did you know they could talk?"

"I see," said Ender. "You're afraid to play me two out of three."

"Beating you," said the boy, "would be as easy as pissing in the shower."

"And not half as fun," said another.

"I'm Ender Wiggin."

"Listen up, scrunchface. You nobody. Got that? You *nobody*, got that? You not anybody till you gots you first kill. Got that?"

The slang of the older boys had its own rhythm. Ender picked it up quick enough. "If I'm nobody, then how come you scared to play me two out of three?"

Now the other guys were impatient. "Kill the squirt quick and let's get on with it."

So Ender took his place at the unfamiliar controls. His hands were small, but the controls were simple enough. It took only a little experimentation to find out which buttons used certain weapons. Movement control was a standard wireball. His reflexes were slow at first. The other boy, whose name he still didn't know, got ahead quickly. But Ender learned a lot and was doing much better by the time the game ended.

"Satisfied, Launchy?"

"Two out of three."

"We don't allow two out of three games."

"So you beat me the first time I ever touched the game," Ender said. "If you can't do it twice, you can't do it at all."

They played again, and this time Ender was deft enough to pull off a few maneuvers that the boy had obviously never seen before. His patterns couldn't cope with them. Ender didn't win easily, but he won.

The bigger boys stopped laughing and joking then. The third game went in total silence. Ender won it quickly and efficiently.

When the game ended, one of the older boys said, "Bout time they replaced this machine. Getting so any pinbrain can beat it now."

Not a word of congratulation. Just total silence as Ender walked away.

He didn't go far. Just stood off in the near distance and watched as the next players tried to use the things he had shown them. Any pinbrain? Ender smiled inwardly. They won't forget me.

He felt good. He had won something, and against older boys. Probably not the best of the older boys, but he no longer had the panicked feeling that he might be out of his depth, that Battle School might be too much for him. All he had to do was watch the game and understand how things worked, and then he could use the system, and even excel.

It was the waiting and watching that cost the most. For during that time he had to endure. The boy whose arm he had broken was out for vengeance. His name, Ender quickly learned, was Bernard. He spoke his own name with a French accent, since the French, with their arrogant Separatism, insisted that the teaching of Standard not begin until the age of four, when the French language patterns were already set. His accent made him exotic and interesting; his broken arm made him a martyr; his sadism made him a natural focus for all those who loved pain in others.

Ender became their enemy.

Little things. Kicking his bed every time they went in and out of the door. Jostling him with his meal tray. Tripping him on the ladders. Ender learned quickly not to leave anything of his outside his lockers; he also learned to be quick on his feet, to catch himself. "Maladroit," Bernard called him once, and the name stuck.

There were times when Ender was very angry. With Bernard, of course, anger was inadequate. It was the kind of person he was—a tormentor. What enraged Ender was how willingly the others went along with him. Surely they knew there was no justice in Bernard's revenge. Surely they knew that he had struck first at Ender in the shuttle, that Ender had only been responding to violence. If they knew, they acted as if they didn't; even if they did not know, they should be able to tell from Bernard himself that he was a snake.

After all, Ender wasn't his only target. Bernard was setting up a kingdom, wasn't he?

Ender watched from the fringes of the group as Bernard established the hierarchy. Some of the boys were useful to him, and he flattered them outrageously. Some of the boys were willing servants, doing whatever he wanted even though he treated them with contempt.

But a few chafed under Bernard's rule.

Ender, watching, knew who resented Bernard. Shen was small, ambitious, and easily needled. Bernard had discovered that quickly, and started calling him Worm. "Because he's so *small*," Bernard said, "and because he *wriggles*. Look how he shimmies his butt when he walks."

Shen stormed off, but they only laughed louder. "Look at his *butt*. See ya, Worm!"

Ender said nothing to Shen—it would be too obvious, then, that he was starting his own competing gang. He just sat with his desk on his lap, looking as studious as possible.

He was not studying. He was telling his desk to keep sending a message into the interrupt queue every thirty seconds. The message was to everyone, and it was short and to the point. What made it hard was figuring out how to disguise who it was from, the way the teachers could. Messages from one of the boys always had their name automatically inserted. Ender hadn't cracked the teachers' security system yet, so he couldn't pretend to be a teacher. But he *was* able to set up a file for a nonexistent student, whom he whimsically named *God*.

Only when the message was ready to go did he try to catch Shen's eye. Like all the other boys, he was watching Bernard and his cronies laugh and joke, making fun of the math teacher, who often stopped in midsentence and looked around as if he had been let off the bus at the wrong stop and didn't know where he was.

Eventually, though, Shen glanced around. Ender nodded to him, pointed to his desk, and smiled. Shen looked puzzled. Ender held up his desk a little and then pointed at it. Shen reached for his own desk. Ender sent the message then. Shen saw it almost at once. Shen read it, then laughed aloud. He looked at Ender as if to say, Did you do this? Ender shrugged, to say, I don't know who did it but it sure wasn't me.

Shen laughed again, and several of the other boys who were not close to Bernard's group got out their desks and looked. Every thirty seconds the message appeared on every desk, marched around the screen quickly, then disappeared. The boys laughed together.

"What's so funny?" Bernard asked. Ender made sure he was not smiling when Bernard looked around the room, imitating the fear that so many others felt. Shen, of course, smiled all the more defiantly. It took a moment; then Bernard told one of his boys to bring out a desk. Together they read the message.

> COVER YOUR BUTT. BERNARD IS WATCHING.
> —GOD

Bernard went red with anger. "Who did this!" he shouted.

"God," said Shen.

"It sure as hell wasn't *you*," Bernard said. "This takes too much *brains* for a *worm*."

Ender's message expired after five minutes. After a while, a message from Bernard appeared on his desk.

> I KNOW IT WAS YOU.
> —BERNARD.

Ender didn't look up. He acted, in fact, as if he hadn't seen the message. Bernard just wants to catch me looking guilty. He doesn't know.

Of course, it didn't matter if he knew. Bernard would punish him all the more, because he had to rebuild his position. The one thing he couldn't stand was having the other boys laughing at him. He had to make clear who was boss. So Ender got knocked down in the shower that morning. One of Bernard's boys pretended to trip over him, and managed to plant a knee in his belly. Ender took it in silence. He was still watching, as far as the open war was concerned. He would do nothing.

But in the other war, the war of desks, he already had his next attack in place. When he got back from the shower, Bernard was raging, kicking beds and yelling at boys. "I didn't write it! Shut up!"

Marching constantly around every boy's desk was this message:

> I LOVE YOUR BUTT. LET ME KISS IT.
> —BERNARD

"I didn't write that message!" Bernard shouted. After the shouting had been going on for some time, Dap appeared at the door.

"What's the fuss?" he asked.

"Somebody's been writing messages using my name." Bernard was sullen.

"What message?"

"It doesn't matter what message!"

"It does to me." Dap picked up the nearest desk, which happened to belong to the boy who bunked above Ender. Dap read it, smiled very slightly, gave back the desk.

"Interesting," he said.

"Aren't you going to find out who did it?" demanded Bernard.

"Oh, I know who did it," Dap said.

Yes, Ender thought. The system was too easily broken. They mean us to break it, or sections of it. They know it was me.

"Well, who, then?" Bernard shouted.

"Are you shouting at me, soldier?" asked Dap, very softly.

At once the mood in the room changed. From rage on the part of Bernard's closest friends and barely contained mirth among the rest, all became somber. Authority was about to speak.

"No, sir," said Bernard.

"Everybody knows that the system automatically puts on the name of the sender."

"I didn't write that!" Bernard said.

"Shouting?" asked Dap.

"Yesterday someone sent a message that was signed GOD," Bernard said.

"Really?" said Dap. "I didn't know he was signed onto the system." Dap turned and left, and the room filled with laughter.

Bernard's attempt to be ruler of the room was broken—only a few stayed with him now. But they were the most vicious. And Ender knew that until he was through watching, it would go hard on him. Still, the tampering with the system had done its work. Bernard was contained, and all the boys who had some quality were free of him. Best of all, Ender had done it without sending him to the hospital. Much better this way.

Then he settled down to the serious business of designing a security system for his own desk, since the safeguards built into the system were obviously inadequate. If a six-year-old could break them down, they were obviously put there as a plaything, not serious security. Just another game that the teachers set up for us. And this is one I'm good at.

"How did you do that?" Shen asked him at breakfast.

Ender noted quietly that this was the first time another Launchy from his own class had sat with him at a meal. "Do what?" he asked.

"Send a message with a fake name. And Bernard's name! That was great. They're calling him Buttwatcher now. Just Watcher in front of the teachers, but everybody knows what he's watching."

"Poor Bernard," Ender murmured. "And he's so sensitive."

"Come on, Ender. You broke into the system. How'd you do it?"

Ender shook his head and smiled. "Thanks for thinking I'm bright enough to do that. I just happened to see it first, that's all."

"OK, you don't have to tell me," said Shen. "Still, it was great." They ate in silence for a moment. "*Do* I wiggle my butt when I walk?"

"Naw," Ender said. "Just a little. Just don't take such big long steps, that's all."

Shen nodded.

"The only person who'd ever notice was Bernard."

"He's a pig," said Shen.

Ender shrugged. "On the whole, pigs aren't so bad."

Shen laughed. "You're right. I wasn't being fair to the pigs."

They laughed together, and two other Launchies joined them. Ender's isolation was over. The war was just beginning.

6

THE GIANT'S DRINK

"We've had our disappointments in the past, hanging on for years, hoping they'll pull through, and then they don't. Nice thing about Ender, he's determined to ice within the first six months."

"Oh?"

"Don't you see what's going on here? He's stuck at the Giant's Drink in the mind game. Is the boy suicidal? You never mentioned it."

"Everybody gets the Giant sometime."

"But Ender won't leave it alone. Like Pinual."

"Everybody looks like Pinual at one time or another. But he's the only one who killed himself. I don't think it had anything to do with the Giant's Drink."

"You're betting my life on that. And look what he's done with his launch group."

"Wasn't his fault, you know."

"I don't care. His fault or not, he's poisoning that group. They're supposed to bond, and right where he stands there's a chasm a mile wide."

"I don't plan to leave him there very long, anyway."

"Then you'd better plan again. That launch is sick, and he's the source of the disease. He stays till it's cured."

"*I* was the source of the disease. I was isolating him, and it worked."

"Give him time with the group. To see what he does with it."

"We don't have time."

"We don't have time to rush too fast with a kid who has as much chance of being a monster as a military genius."

"Is this an order?"

"The recorder's on, it's always on, your ass is covered, go to hell."

"If it's an order, then I'll—"

"It's an order. Hold him where he is until we see how he handles things in his launch group. Graff, you give me ulcers."

"You wouldn't have ulcers if you'd leave the school to me and take care of the fleet yourself."

"The fleet is looking for a battle commander. There's nothing to take care of until you get me *that*."

They filed clumsily into the battleroom, like children in a swimming pool for the first time, clinging to the handholds along the side. Null gravity was frightening, disorienting; they soon found that things went better if they didn't use their feet at all.

Worse, the suits were confining. It was harder to make precise movements, since the suits bent just a bit slower, resisted a bit more than any clothing they had ever worn before.

Ender gripped the handhold and flexed his knees. He noticed that along with the sluggishness, the suit had an amplifying effect on movement. It was hard to get them started, but the suit's legs kept moving, and strongly, after his muscles had stopped. Give them a push *this* strong, and the suit pushes with twice the force. I'll be clumsy for a while. Better get started.

So, still grasping the handhold, he pushed off strongly with his feet.

Instantly he flipped around, his feet flying over his head, and landed flat on his back against the wall. The rebound was stronger, it seemed, and his hands tore loose from the handhold. He flew across the battleroom, tumbling over and over.

For a sickening moment he tried to retain his old up-and-down orientation, his body attempting to right itself, searching for the gravity that wasn't there. Then he forced himself to change his view. He was hurtling toward a wall. That was down. And at once he had control of himself. He wasn't flying, he was falling. This was a dive. He could choose how he would hit the surface.

I'm going too fast to catch ahold and stay, but I can soften the impact, I can fly off at an angle if I roll when I hit and use my feet—

It didn't work at all the way he had planned. He went off at an angle, but it was not the one he had predicted. Nor did he have time to consider. He hit another wall, this time too soon to have prepared for it. But quite accidently he discovered a way to use his feet to control the rebound angle. Now he was soaring across the room again, toward the other boys who still clung to the wall. This time he had slowed enough to be able to grip a rung. He was at a crazy angle in relation to the other boys, but once again his orientation had changed, and as far as he could tell, they were all lying on the floor, not hanging on a wall, and he was no more upside down than they were.

"What are you trying to do, kill yourself?" asked Shen.

"Try it," Ender said. "The suit keeps you from hurting yourself, and you can control your bouncing with your legs, like this." He approximated the movement he had made.

Shen shook his head—he wasn't trying any fool stunt like that. But one boy did take off, not as fast as Ender had, because he didn't begin with a flip, but fast enough. Ender didn't even have to see his face to know that it was Bernard. And right after him, Bernard's best friend, Alai.

Ender watched them cross the huge room, Bernard struggling to orient himself to the direction he thought of as the floor, Alai surrendering to the movement and preparing to rebound from the wall. No wonder Bernard broke his arm in the shuttle, Ender thought. He tightens up when he's flying. He panics. Ender stored the information away for future reference.

And another bit of information, too. Alai did not push off in the same direction as Bernard. He aimed for a corner of the room. Their paths diverged more and more as they flew, and where Bernard made a clumsy, crunching landing and bounce on his wall, Alai did a glancing triple bounce on three surfaces near the corner that left him most of his speed and sent him flying off at a surprising angle. Alai shouted and whooped, and so did the boys watching him. Some of them forgot they were weightless and let go of the wall to clap their hands. Now they drifted lazily in many directions, waving their arms, trying to swim.

Now, that's a problem, thought Ender. What if you catch yourself drifting? There's no way to push off.

He was tempted to set himself adrift and try to solve the problem by trial and error. But he could see the others, their useless efforts at control, and he couldn't think of what he would do that they weren't already doing.

Holding onto the floor with one hand, he fiddled idly with the toy gun that was attached to his suit in front, just below the shoulder. Then he remembered the hand rockets sometimes used by marines when they did a boarding assault on an enemy station. He pulled the gun from his suit and examined it. He had pushed all the buttons back in the room, but the gun did nothing there. Maybe here in the battleroom it would work. There were no instructions on it. No labels on the controls. The trigger was obvious—he had had toy guns, as all children had, almost since infancy. There were two buttons that his thumb could easily reach, and several others along the bottom of the shaft that were almost inaccessible without using two hands. Obviously, the two buttons near his thumb were meant to be instantly usable.

He aimed the gun at the floor and pulled back on the trigger. He felt the gun grow instantly warm; when he let go of the trigger, it cooled at once. Also, a tiny circle of light appeared on the floor where he was aiming.

He thumbed the red button at the top of the gun, and pulled the trigger again. Same thing.

Then he pushed the white button. It gave a bright flash of light that illuminated a wide area, but not as intensely. The gun was quite cold when the button was pressed.

The red button makes it like a laser—but it is not a laser, Dap had said—while the white button makes it a lamp. Neither will be much help when it comes to maneuvering.

So everything depends on how you push off, the course you set when you start. It means we're going to have to get very good at controlling our launches and rebounds or we're all going to end up floating around in the middle of nowhere. Ender looked around the room. A few of the boys were drifting close to walls now, flailing their arms to catch a handhold. Most were bumping into each other and laughing; some were holding hands and going around in circles. Only a few, like Ender, were calmly holding onto the walls and watching.

One of them, he saw, was Alai. He had ended up on another wall not too far from Ender. On impulse, Ender pushed off and moved quickly toward Alai. Once in the air, he wondered what he would say. Alai was Bernard's friend. What did Ender have to say to him?

Still, there was no changing course now. So he watched straight ahead, and practiced making tiny leg and hand movements to control which way he was facing as he drifted. Too late, he realized that he had aimed too well. He was not going to land *near* Alai—he was going to hit him.

"Here, snag my hand!" Alai called.

Ender held out his hand. Alai took the shock of impact and helped Ender make a fairly gentle landing against the wall.

"That's good," Ender said. "We ought to practice that kind of thing."

"That's what I thought, only everybody's turning to butter out there," Alai said. "What happens if we get out there together? We should be able to shove each other in opposite directions."

"Yeah."

"OK?"

It was an admission that all might not be right between them. Is it OK for us to do something together? Ender's answer was to take Alai by the wrist and get ready to push off.

"Ready?" said Alai. "Go."

Since they pushed off with different amounts of force, they began to circle each other. Ender made some small hand movements, then shifted a leg. They slowed. He did it again. They stopped orbiting. Now they were drifting evenly.

"Packed head, Ender," Alai said. It was high praise. "Let's push off before we run into that bunch."

"And then let's meet over in that corner." Ender did not want this bridge into the enemy camp to fail.

"Last one there saves farts in a milk bottle," Alai said.

Then, slowly, steadily, they maneuvered until they faced each other, spread-eagled, hand to hand, knee to knee.

"And then we just scrunch?" asked Alai.

"I've never done this before either," said Ender.

They pushed off. It propelled them faster than they expected. Ender ran into a couple of boys and ended up on a wall that he hadn't expected. It took him a moment to reorient and find the corner where he and Alai were to meet. Alai was already headed toward it. Ender plotted a course that would include two rebounds, to avoid the largest clusters of boys.

When Ender reached the corner, Alai had hooked his arms through two adjacent handholds and was pretending to doze.

"You win."

"I want to see your fart collection," Alai said.

"I stored it in your locker. Didn't you notice?"

"I thought it was my socks."

"We don't wear socks anymore."

"Oh yeah." A reminder that they were both far from home. It took some of the fun out of having mastered a bit of navigation.

Ender took his pistol and demonstrated what he had learned about the two thumb buttons.

"What does it do when you aim at a person?" asked Alai.

"I don't know."

"Why don't we find out?"

Ender shook his head. "We might hurt somebody."

"I meant why don't we shoot each other in the foot or something. I'm not Bernard, I never tortured cats for fun."

"Oh."

"It can't be too dangerous, or they wouldn't give these guns to kids."

"We're soldiers now."

"Shoot me in the foot."

"No, you shoot me."

"Let's shoot each other."

They did. Immediately Ender felt the leg of the suit grow stiff, immobile at the knee and ankle joints.

"You frozen?" asked Alai.

"Stiff as a board."

"Let's freeze a few," Alai said. "Let's have our first war. Us against them."

They grinned. Then Ender said, "Better invite Bernard."

Alai cocked an eyebrow. "Oh?"

"And Shen."

"That little slanty-eyed butt-wiggler?"

Ender decided that Alai was joking. "Hey, we can't all be niggers."

Alai grinned. "My grandpa would've killed you for that."

"My great great grandpa would have sold him first."

"Let's go get Bernard and Shen and freeze these bugger-lovers."

In twenty minutes, everyone in the room was frozen except Ender, Bernard, Shen, and Alai. The four of them sat there whooping and laughing until Dap came in.

"I see you've learned how to use your equipment," he said. Then he did something to a control he held in his hand. Everybody drifted slowly toward the wall he was standing on. He went among the frozen boys, touching them and thawing their suits. There was a tumult of complaint that it wasn't fair how Bernard and Alai had shot them all when they weren't ready.

"Why weren't you ready?" asked Dap. "You had your suits just as long as they did. You had just as many minutes flapping around like drunken ducks. Stop moaning and we'll begin."

Ender noticed that it was assumed that Bernard and Alai were the leaders of the battle. Well, that was fine. Bernard knew that Ender and Alai had learned to use the guns together. And Ender and Alai were friends. Now others might believe that Ender had joined his group, but it wasn't so. Ender had joined a new group. Alai's group. Bernard had joined it too.

It wasn't obvious to everyone; Bernard still blustered and sent his cronies on errands. But Alai now moved freely through the whole room, and when Bernard was crazy, Alai could joke a little and calm him down. When it came time to choose their launch leader, Alai was the almost unanimous choice. Bernard sulked for a few days and then he was fine, and everyone settled into the new pattern. The launch was no longer divided into Bernard's in-group and Ender's outcasts. Alai was the bridge.

———

Ender sat on his bed with his desk on his knees. It was private study time, and Ender was doing Free Play. It was a shifting, crazy kind of game in which the school computer kept bringing up new things, building a maze that you could explore. You could go back to events that you liked, for a while; if you left one alone too long, it disappeared and something else took its place.

Sometimes they were funny things. Sometimes exciting ones, and he had to be quick to stay alive. He had lots of deaths, but that was OK, games were like that, you died a lot until you got the hang of it.

His figure on the screen had started out as a little boy. For a while it had changed into a bear. Now it was a large mouse, with long and delicate hands. He ran his figure under a lot of large items of furniture depicted on the screen. He had played with the cat a lot, but now it was boring—too easy to dodge, he knew all the furniture.

Not through the mousehole this time, he told himself. I'm sick of the Giant. It's a dumb game and I can't ever win. Whatever I choose is wrong.

But he went through the mousehole anyway, and over the small bridge in the garden. He avoided the ducks and the divebombing mosquitoes—he had tried playing with them but they were too easy, and if he played with the ducks too long he turned into a fish, which he didn't like. Being a fish reminded him too much of being frozen in the battleroom, his whole body rigid, waiting for the practice to end so Dap would thaw him. So, as usual, he found himself going up the rolling hills.

The landslides began. At first he had got caught again and again, crushed in an exaggerated blot of gore oozing out from under a rockpile. Now, though, he had mastered the skill of running up the slopes at an angle to avoid the crush, always seeking higher ground.

And, as always, the landslides finally stopped being jumbles of rock. The face of the hill broke open and instead of shale it was white bread, puffy, rising like dough as the crust broke away and fell. It was soft and spongy; his figure moved more slowly. And when he jumped down off the bread, he was standing on a table. Giant loaf of bread behind him; giant stick of butter beside him. And the Giant himself leaning his chin in his hands, looking at him. Ender's figure was about as tall as the Giant's head from chin to brow.

"I think I'll bite your head off," said the Giant, as he always did.

This time, instead of running away or standing there, Ender walked his figure up to the Giant's face and kicked him in the chin.

The Giant stuck out his tongue and Ender fell to the ground.

"How about a guessing game?" asked the Giant. So it didn't make any difference—the Giant only played the guessing game. Stupid computer. Millions of possible scenarios in its memory, and the Giant could only play one stupid game.

The Giant, as always, set two huge shot glasses, as tall as Ender's knees, on the table in front of him. As always, the two were filled with different liquids. The computer was good enough that the liquids had never repeated, not that he could remember. This time the one had a thick, creamy looking liquid. The other hissed and foamed.

"One is poison and one is not," said the Giant. "Guess right and I'll take you into Fairyland."

Guessing meant sticking his head into one of the glasses to drink. He never guessed right. Sometimes his head was dissolved. Sometimes he caught on fire. Sometimes he fell in and drowned. Sometimes he fell out, turned green, and rotted away. It was always ghastly, and the Giant always laughed.

Ender knew that whatever he chose he would die. The game was rigged. On the first death, his figure would reappear on the Giant's table, to play again. On the second death, he'd come back to the landslides. Then to the garden bridge. Then to the mousehole. And then, if he still went back to the Giant and played again, and died again, his desk would go dark, "Free Play Over" would march around the desk, and Ender would lie back on his bed and tremble until he could finally go to sleep. The game was rigged but still the Giant talked about Fairyland, some stupid childish three-year-old's Fairyland that probably had some stupid Mother Goose or Pac-Man or Peter Pan, it wasn't even worth getting to, but he had to find some way of beating the Giant to get there.

He drank the creamy liquid. Immediately he began to inflate and rise like a balloon. The Giant laughed. He was dead again.

He played again, and this time the liquid set, like concrete, and held his head down while the Giant cut him open along the spine, deboned him like a fish, and began to eat while his arms and legs quivered.

He reappeared at the landslides and decided not to go on. He even let the landslides cover him once. But even though he was sweating and he felt cold, with his next life he went back up the hills till they turned into bread, and stood on the Giant's table as the shot glasses were set before him.

He stared at the two liquids. The one foaming, the other with waves in it like the sea. He tried to guess what kind of death each one held. Probably a fish will come out of the ocean one and eat me. The foamy one will probably asphyxiate me. I hate this game. It isn't fair. It's stupid. It's rotten.

And instead of pushing his face into one of the liquids, he kicked one over, then the other, and dodged the Giant's huge hands as the Giant shouted, "Cheater, cheater!" He jumped at the Giant's face, clambered up his lip and nose, and began to dig in the Giant's eye. The stuff came away like cottage cheese, and as the Giant screamed, Ender's figure burrowed into the eye, climbed right in, burrowed in and in.

The Giant fell over backward. The view shifted as he fell, and when the Giant came to rest on the ground, there were intricate, lacy trees all around. A bat flew up and landed on the dead Giant's nose. Ender brought his figure up out of the Giant's eye.

"How did you get here?" the bat asked. "Nobody ever comes here."

Ender could not answer, of course. So he reached down, took a handful of the Giant's eyestuff, and offered it to the bat.

The bat took it and flew off, shouting as it went, "Welcome to Fairyland."

He had made it. He ought to explore. He ought to climb down from the Giant's face and see what he had finally achieved.

Instead he signed off, put his desk in his locker, stripped off his clothes and pulled his blanket over him. He hadn't meant to kill the Giant. This was supposed to be a game. Not a choice between his own grisly death and an even worse murder. I'm a murderer, even when I play. Peter would be proud of me.

7

SALAMANDER

"Isn't it nice to know that Ender can do the impossible?"

"The player's deaths have always been sickening, I've always thought the Giant's Drink was the most perverted part of the whole mind game, but going for the eye like that—this is the one we want to put in command of our fleet?"

"What matters is that he won the game that couldn't be won."

"I suppose you'll move him now."

"We were waiting to see how he handled the thing with Bernard. He handled it perfectly."

"So as soon as he can cope with a situation, you move him to one he can't cope with. Doesn't he get any rest?"

"He'll have a month or two, maybe three, with his launch group. That's really quite a long time in a child's life."

"Does it ever seem to you that these boys aren't children? I look at what they do, the way they talk, and they don't seem like little kids."

"They're the most brilliant children in the world, each in his own way."

"But shouldn't they still act like children? They aren't *normal*. They act like—history. Napoleon and Wellington. Caesar and Brutus."

"We're trying to save the world, not heal the wounded heart. You're too compassionate."

"General Levy has no pity for anyone. All the videos say so. But don't hurt this boy."

"Are you joking?"

"I mean, don't hurt him more than you have to."

Alai sat across from Ender at dinner. "I finally figured out how you sent that message. Using Bernard's name."

"Me?" asked Ender.

"Come on, who else? It sure wasn't Bernard. And Shen isn't too hot on the computer. And I know it wasn't me. Who else? Doesn't matter. I figured out how to fake a new student entry. You just created a student named Bernard-blank, B-E-R-N-A-R-D-space, so the computer didn't kick it out as a repeat of another student."

"Sounds like that might work," said Ender.

"OK, OK. It *does* work. But you did that practically on the first day."

"Or somebody. Maybe Dap did it, to keep Bernard from getting too much control."

"I found something else. I can't do it with your name."

"Oh?"

"Anything with *Ender* in it gets kicked out. I can't get inside your files at all, either. You made your own security system."

"Maybe."

Alai grinned. "I just got in and trashed somebody's files. He's right behind me on cracking the system. I need protection, Ender. I need your system."

"If I give you my system, you'll know how I do it and you'll get in and trash *me*."

"You say *me?*" Alai asked. "I the sweetest friend you got!"

Ender laughed. "I'll set up a system for you."

"Now?"

"Can I finish eating?"

"You never finish eating."

It was true. Ender's tray always had food on it after a meal. Ender looked at the plate and decided he was through. "Let's go then."

When they got to the barracks, Ender squatted down by his bed and said, "Get your desk and bring it over here, I'll show you how." But when Alai brought his desk to Ender's bed, Ender was just sitting there, his lockers still closed.

"What up?" asked Alai.

In answer, Ender palmed his locker. "Unauthorized Access Attempt," it said. It didn't open.

"Somebody done a dance on your head, mama," Alai said. "Somebody eated your face."

"You sure you want my security system now?" Ender got up and walked away from his bed.

"Ender," said Alai.

Ender turned around. Alai was holding a little piece of paper. "What is it?"

Alai looked up at him. "Don't you know? This was on your bed. You must have sat on it."

Ender took it from him.

ENDER WIGGIN
ASSIGNED SALAMANDER ARMY
COMMANDER BONZO MADRID
EFFECTIVE IMMEDIATELY
CODE GREEN GREEN BROWN
NO POSSESSIONS TRANSFERRED

"You're smart, Ender, but you don't do the battleroom any better than me."

Ender shook his head. It was the stupidest thing he could think of, to promote him now. Nobody got promoted before they were eight years old. Ender wasn't even seven yet. And launches usually moved into the armies together, with most armies getting a new kid at the same time. There were no transfer slips on any of the other beds.

Just when things were finally coming together. Just when Bernard was getting along with everybody, even Ender. Just when Ender was beginning to make a real friend out of Alai. Just when his life was finally getting livable.

Ender reached down to pull Alai up from the bed.

"Salamander Army's in contention, anyway," Alai said.

Ender was so angry at the unfairness of the transfer that tears were coming to his eyes. Mustn't cry, he told himself.

Alai saw the tears but had the grace not to say so. "They're fartheads, Ender, they won't even let you take anything you *own*."

Ender grinned and didn't cry after all. "Think I should strip and go naked?"

Alai laughed, too.

On impulse Ender hugged him, tight, almost as if he were Valentine. He even thought of Valentine then and wanted to go home. "I don't want to go," he said.

Alai hugged him back. "I understand them, Ender. You *are* the best of us. Maybe they in a hurry to teach you everything."

"They don't want to teach me *everything*," Ender said. "I wanted to learn what it was like to have a friend."

Alai nodded soberly. "Always my friend, always the best of my friends," he said. Then he grinned. "Go slice up the buggers."

"Yeah." Ender smiled back.

Alai suddenly kissed Ender on the cheek and whispered in his ear, "Sa-

laam." Then, red-faced, he turned away and walked to his own bed at the
back of the barracks. Ender guessed that the kiss and the word were somehow forbidden. A suppressed religion, perhaps. Or maybe the word had
some private and powerful meaning for Alai alone. Whatever it meant to
Alai, Ender knew that it was sacred; that he had uncovered himself for
Ender, as once Ender's mother had done, when he was very young, before
they put the monitor in his neck, and she had put her hands on his head
when she thought he was asleep, and prayed over him. Ender had never
spoken of that to anyone, not even to Mother, but had kept it as a memory
of holiness, of how his mother loved him when she thought that no one,
not even he, could see or hear. That was what Alai had given him; a gift so
sacred that even Ender could not be allowed to understand what it meant.

After such a thing nothing could be said. Alai reached his bed and turned
around to see Ender. Their eyes held for only a moment, locked in understanding. Then Ender left.

There would be no green green brown in this part of the school; he would
have to pick up the colors in one of the public areas. The others would be
finished with dinner very soon; he didn't want to go near the mess hall. The
game room would be nearly empty.

None of the games appealed to him, the way he felt now. So he went to
the bank of public desks at the back of the room and signed on to his own
private game. He went quickly to Fairyland. The Giant was dead when he
arrived now; he had to climb carefully down the table, jump to the leg of
the Giant's overturned chair, and then make the drop to the ground. For a
while there had been rats gnawing at the Giant's body, but Ender had killed
one with a pin from the Giant's ragged shirt, and they had left him alone
after that.

The Giant's corpse had essentially finished its decay. What could be torn
by the small scavengers was torn; the maggots had done their work on the
organs; now it was a desiccated mummy, hollowed-out, teeth in a rigid grin,
eyes empty, fingers curled. Ender remembered burrowing through the eye
when it had been alive and malicious and intelligent. Angry and frustrated
as he was, Ender wished to do such violence again. But the Giant had become part of the landscape now, and so there could be no rage against him.

Ender had always gone over the bridge to the castle of the Queen of
Hearts, where there were games enough for him; but none of those appealed to him now. He went around the giant's corpse and followed the
brook upstream, to where it emerged from the forest. There was a playground there, slides and monkeybars, teeter-totters and merry-go-rounds,
with a dozen children laughing as they played. Ender came and found that
in the game he had become a child, though usually his figure in the games
was adult. In fact, he was smaller than the other children.

He got in line for the slide. The other children ignored him. He climbed up to the top, watched the boy before him whirl down the long spiral to the ground. Then he sat and began to slide.

He had not slid for a moment when he fell right through the slide and landed on the ground under the ladder. The slide would not hold him.

Neither would the monkey bars. He could climb a ways, but then at random a bar seemed to be insubstantial and he fell. He could sit on the seesaw until he rose to the apex; then he fell. When the merry-go-round went fast, he could not hold onto any of the bars, and centrifugal force hurled him off.

And the other children: their laughter was raucous, offensive. They circled around him and pointed and laughed for many seconds before they went back to their play.

Ender wanted to hit them, to throw them in the brook. Instead he walked into the forest. He found a path, which soon became an ancient brick road, much overgrown with weeds but still usable. There were hints of possible games off to either side, but Ender followed none of them. He wanted to see where the path led.

It led to a clearing, with a well in the middle, and a sign that said, "Drink, Traveler." Ender went forward and looked at the well. Almost at once, he heard a snarl. Out of the woods emerged a dozen slavering wolves with human faces. Ender recognized them—they were the children from the playground. Only now their teeth could tear; Ender, weaponless, was quickly devoured.

His next figure appeared, as usual, in the same spot, and was eaten again, though Ender tried to climb down into the well.

The next appearance, though, was at the playground. Again the children laughed at him. Laugh all you like, Ender thought. I know what you are. He pushed one of them. She followed him, angry. Ender led her up the slide. Of course he fell through; but this time, following so closely behind him, she also fell through. When she hit the ground, she turned into a wolf and lay there, dead or stunned.

One by one Ender led each of the others into a trap. But before he had finished off the last of them, the wolves began reviving, and were no longer children. Ender was torn apart again.

This time, shaking and sweating, Ender found his figure revived on the Giant's table. I should quit, he told himself. I should go to my new army.

But instead he made his figure drop down from the table and walk around the Giant's body to the playground.

This time, as soon as the child hit the ground and turned into a wolf, Ender dragged the body to the brook and pulled it in. Each time, the body sizzled as though the water were acid; the wolf was consumed, and a dark cloud of smoke arose and drifted away. The children were easily dispatched, though they began following him in twos and threes at the end. Ender found no wolves waiting for him in the clearing, and he lowered himself into the well on the bucket rope.

The light in the cavern was dim, but he could see piles of jewels. He passed them by, noting that, behind him, eyes glinted among the gems. A table covered with food did not interest him. He passed through a group of cages hanging from the ceiling of the cave, each containing some exotic, friendly-looking creature. I'll play with you later, Ender thought. At last he came to a door, with these words in glowing emeralds:

THE END OF THE WORLD

He did not hesitate. He opened the door and stepped through.

He stood on a small ledge, high on a cliff overlooking a terrain of bright and deep green forest with dashes of autumn color and patches here and there of cleared land, with oxdrawn plows and small villages, a castle on a rise in the distance, and clouds riding currents of air below him. Above him, the sky was the ceiling of a vast cavern, with crystals dangling in bright stalactites.

The door closed behind him; Ender studied the scene intently. With the beauty of it, he cared less for survival than usual. He cared little, at the moment, what the game of this place might be. He had found it, and seeing it was its own reward. And so, with no thought of consequences, he jumped from the ledge.

Now he plummeted downward toward a roiling river and savage rocks; but a cloud came between him and the ground as he fell, and caught him, and carried him away. It took him to the tower of the castle, and through the open window, bearing him in. There it left him, in a room with no apparent door in floor or ceiling, and windows looking out over a certainly fatal fall.

A moment ago he had thrown himself from a ledge carelessly; this time he hesitated.

The small rug before the fire unraveled itself into a long, slender serpent with wicked teeth.

"I am your only escape," it said. "Death is your only escape."

Ender looked around the room for a weapon, when suddenly the screen went dark. Words flashed around the rim of the desk.

REPORT TO COMMANDER IMMEDIATELY.
YOU ARE LATE.
GREEN GREEN BROWN.

Furious, Ender snapped off the desk and went to the color wall, where he found the ribbon of green green brown, touched it, and followed it as it lit up before him. The dark green, light green, and brown of the ribbon reminded him of the early autumn kingdom he had found in the game. I must go back there, he told himself. The serpent is a long thread; I can let myself down from the tower and find my way through that place. Perhaps it's called the end of the world because it's the end of the games, because I can go to one of the villages and become one of the little boys working and playing there, with nothing to kill and nothing to kill me, just living there.

As he thought of it, though, he could not imagine what "just living" might actually be. He had never done it in his life. But he wanted to do it anyway.

Armies were larger than launch groups, and the army barracks room was larger, too. It was long and narrow, with bunks on both sides; so long, in fact, that you could see the curvature of the floor as the far end bent upward, part of the wheel of the Battle School.

Ender stood at the door. A few boys near the door glanced at him, but they were older, and it seemed as though they hadn't even seen him. They went on with their conversations, lying and leaning on bunks. They were discussing battles, of course—the older boys always did. They were all much larger than Ender. The ten- and eleven-year-olds towered over him; even the youngest were eight, and Ender was not large for his age.

He tried to see which of the boys was the commander, but most were somewhere between battle dress and what the soldiers always called their sleep uniform—skin from head to toe. Many of them had desks out, but few were studying.

Ender stepped into the room. The moment he did, he was noticed.

"What do you want?" demanded the boy who had the upper bunk by the door. He was the largest of them. Ender had noticed him before, a young giant who had whiskers growing raggedly on his chin. "You're not a Salamander."

"I'm supposed to be, I think," Ender said. "Green green brown, right? I was transferred." He showed the boy, obviously the doorguard, his paper.

The doorguard reached for it. Ender withdrew it, just out of reach. "I'm supposed to give it to Bonzo Madrid."

Now another boy joined the conversation, a smaller boy, but still larger than Ender. "Not bahn-zoe, pisshead. Bone-So. The name's Spanish. Bonzo Madrid. Aqui nosotros hablamos español, Señor Gran Fedor."

"You must be Bonzo, then?" Ender asked, pronouncing the name correctly.

"No, just a brilliant and talented polyglot. Petra Arkanian. The only girl in Salamander Army. With more balls than anybody else in the room."

"Mother Petra she talking," said one of the boys, "she talking, she talking."

Another one chimed in. "Shit talking, shit talking, shit talking!"

Quite a few laughed.

"Just between you and me," Petra said, "if they gave the Battle School an enema, they'd stick it in at green green brown."

Ender despaired. He already had nothing going for him—grossly under-trained, small, inexperienced, doomed to be resented for early advance-ment. And now, by chance, he had made exactly the wrong friend. An outcast in Salamander Army, and she had just linked him with her in the minds of the rest of the army. A good day's work. For a moment, as Ender looked around at the laughing, jeering faces, he imagined their bodies cov-ered with hair, their teeth pointed for tearing. Am I the only human being in this place? Are all the others animals, waiting only to devour?

Then he remembered Alai. In every army, surely, there was at least one worth knowing.

Suddenly, though no one said to be quiet, the laughter stopped and the group fell silent. Ender turned to the door. A boy stood there, tall and slender, with beautiful black eyes and slender lips that hinted at refinement. I would follow such beauty, said something inside Ender. I would see as those eyes see.

"Who are you?" asked the boy quietly.

"Ender Wiggin, sir," Ender said. "Reassigned from launch to Salamander Army." He held out the orders.

The boy took the paper in a swift, sure movement, without touching En-der's hand. "How old are you, Wiggin?" he asked.

"Almost seven."

Still quietly, he said, "I asked how old you are, not how old you almost are."

"I am six years, nine months, and twelve days old."

"How long have you been working in the battleroom?"

"A few months, now. My aim is better."

"Any training in battle maneuvers? Have you ever been part of a toon? Have you ever carried out a joint exercise?"

Ender had never heard of such things. He shook his head.

Madrid looked at him steadily. "I see. As you will quickly learn, the offi-cers in command of this school, most notably Major Anderson, who runs the game, are fond of playing tricks. Salamander Army is just beginning to emerge from indecent obscurity. We have won twelve of our last twenty games. We have surprised Rat and Scorpion and Hound, and we are ready to play for leadership in the game. So of course, of course I am given such a useless, untrained, hopeless specimen of underdevelopment as yourself."

Petra said, quietly, "He isn't glad to meet you."

"Shut up, Arkanian," Madrid said. "To one trial, we now add another. But whatever obstacles our officers choose to fling in our path, we are still—"

"Salamander!" cried the soldiers, in one voice.

Instinctively, Ender's perception of these events changed. It was a pattern, a ritual. Madrid was not trying to hurt him, merely taking control of a surprising event and using it to strengthen his control of his army.

"We are the fire that will consume them, belly and bowel, head and heart, many flames of us, but one fire."

"Salamander!" they cried again.

"Even this one will not weaken us."

For a moment, Ender allowed himself to hope. "I'll work hard and learn quickly," he said.

"I didn't give you permission to speak," Madrid answered. "I intend to trade you away as quickly as I can. I'll probably have to give up someone valuable along with you, but as small as you are you are worse than useless. One more frozen, inevitably, in every battle, that's all you are, and we're now at a point where every frozen soldier makes a difference in the standings. Nothing personal, Wiggin, but I'm sure you can get your training at someone else's expense."

"He's all heart," Petra said.

Madrid stepped closer to the girl and slapped her across the face with the back of his hand. It made little sound, for only his fingernails had hit her. But there were bright red marks, four of them, on her cheek, and little pricks of blood marked where the tips of his fingernails had struck.

"Here are your instructions, Wiggin. I expect that it is the last time I'll need to speak to you. You will stay out of the way when we're training in the battleroom. You have to be there, of course, but you will not belong to any toon and you will not take part in any maneuvers. When we're called to battle, you will dress quickly and present yourself at the gate with everyone else. But you will not pass through the gate until four full minutes after the beginning of the game, and then you will remain at the gate, with your weapons undrawn and unfired, until such time as the game ends."

Ender nodded. So he was to be a nothing. He hoped the trade happened soon.

He also noticed that Petra did not so much as cry out in pain, or touch her cheek, though one spot of blood had beaded and run, making a streak down to her jaw. Outcast she may be, but since Bonzo Madrid was not going to be Ender's friend, no matter what, he might as well make friends with Petra.

He was assigned a bunk at the far end of the room. The upper bunk, so that when he lay on his bed he couldn't even see the door: The curve of the ceiling blocked it. There were other boys near him, tired-looking boys, sullen, the ones least valued. They had nothing of welcome to say to Ender.

Ender tried to palm his locker open, but nothing happened. Then he realized the lockers were not secured. All four of them had rings on them, to pull them open. Nothing would be private, then, now that he was in an army.

There was a uniform in the locker. Not the pale green of the Launchies, but the orange-trimmed dark green of Salamander Army. It did not fit well. But then, they had probably never had to provide such a uniform for a boy so young.

He was starting to take it off when he noticed Petra walking down the aisle toward his bed. He slid off the bunk and stood on the floor to greet her.

"Relax," she said. "I'm not an officer."

"You're a toon leader, aren't you?"

Someone nearby snickered.

"Whatever gave you that idea, Wiggin?"

"You have a bunk in the front."

"I bunk in the front because I'm the best sharpshooter in Salamander Army, and because Bonzo is afraid I'll start a revolution if the toon leaders don't keep an eye on me. As if I could start anything with boys like *these*." She indicated the sullen-faced boys on the nearby bunks.

What was she trying to do, make it worse than it already was? "Everybody's better than I am," Ender said, trying to dissociate himself from her contempt for the boys who would, after all, be his near bunkmates.

"I'm a girl," she said, "and you're a pissant of a six-year-old. We have so much in common, why don't we be friends?"

"I won't do your deskwork for you," he said.

In a moment she realized it was a joke. "Ha," she said. "It's all so military, when you're in the game. School for us isn't like it is for Launchies. History and strategy and tactics and buggers and math and stars, things you'll need as a pilot or a commander. You'll see."

"So you're my friend. Do I get a prize?" Ender asked. He was imitating her swaggering way of speaking, as if she cared about nothing.

"Bonzo isn't going to let you practice. He's going to make you take your desk to the battleroom and study. He's right, in a way—he don't want a totally untrained little kid to screw up his precision maneuvers." She lapsed into giria, the slangy talk that imitated the pidgin English of uneducated people. "Bonzo, he pre-*cise*. He so *careful*, he piss on a plate and never splash."

Ender grinned.

"The battleroom is open all the time. If you want, I'll take you in the off hours and show you some of the things I know. I'm not a great soldier, but I'm pretty good, and I sure know more than you."

"If you want," Ender said.

"Starting tomorrow morning after breakfast."

"What if somebody's using the room? We always went right after breakfast, in my launch."

"No problem. There are really nine battlerooms."

"I never heard of any others."

"They all have the same entrance. The whole center of the battle school, the hub of the wheel, is battlerooms. They don't rotate with the rest of the station. That's how they do the nullo, the no-gravity—it just holds still. No spin, no down. But they can set it up so that any one of the rooms is at the battleroom entrance corridor that we all use. Once you're inside, they move it along and another battleroom's in position."

"Oh."

"Like I said. Right after breakfast."

"Right," Ender said.

She started to walk away.

"Petra," he said.

She turned back.

"Thanks."

She said nothing, just turned around again and walked down the aisle.

Ender climbed back up on his bunk and finished taking off his uniform. He lay naked on the bed, doodling with his new desk, trying to decide if they had done anything to his access codes. Sure enough, they had wiped out his security system. He couldn't own anything here, not even his desk.

The lights dimmed a little. Getting toward bedtime. Ender didn't know which bathroom to use.

"Go left out of the door," said the boy on the next bunk. "We share it with Rat, Condor, and Squirrel."

Ender thanked him and started to walk on past.

"Hey," said the boy. "You can't go like that. Uniforms at all times out of this room."

"Even going to the toilet?"

"Especially. And you're forbidden to speak to anyone from any other army. At meals or in the toilet. You can get away with it sometimes in the game room, and of course whenever a teacher tells you to. But if Bonzo catch you, you dead, eh?"

"Thanks."

"And, uh, Bonzo get mad if you skin by Petra."

"She was naked when I came in, wasn't she?"

"She do what she like, but you keep you clothes on. Bonzo's orders."

That was stupid. Petra still looked like a boy, it was a stupid rule. It set her apart, made her different, split the army. Stupid stupid. How did Bonzo get to be a commander, if he didn't know better than that? Alai would be a better commander than Bonzo. He knew how to bring a group together.

I know to bring a group together, too, thought Ender. Maybe I'll be commander someday.

In the bathroom, he was washing his hands when somebody spoke to him. "Hey, they putting babies in Salamander uniforms now?"

Ender didn't answer. Just dried off his hands.

"Hey, look! Salamander's getting babies now! Look at this! He could walk between my legs without touching my balls!"

"Cause you got none, Dink, that's why," somebody answered.

As Ender left the room, he heard somebody else say, "It's Wiggin. You know, the smartass Launchie from the game room."

He walked down the corridor smiling. He may be short, but they knew his name. From the game room, of course, so it meant nothing. But they'd see. He'd be a good soldier, too. They'd all know his name soon enough. Not in Salamander Army, maybe, but soon enough.

Petra was waiting in the corridor that led to the battleroom. "Wait a minute," she said to Ender. "Rabbit Army just went in, and it takes a few minutes to change to the next battleroom."

Ender sat down beside her. "There's more to the battleroom than just switching from one to the next," he said. "For instance, why is there gravity in the corridor outside the room, just before we go in?"

Petra closed her eyes. "And if the battlerooms are really free-floating, what happens when one is connected? Why doesn't it start to move with the rotation of the school?"

Ender nodded.

"These are the mysteries," Petra said in a deep whisper. "Do not pry into them. Terrible things happened to the last soldier who tried. He was discovered hanging by his feet from the ceiling of the bathroom, with his head stuffed in the toilet."

Of course she was joking, but the message was clear. "So I'm not the first person to ask the question."

"You remember this, little boy." When she said *little boy* it sounded friendly, not contemptuous. "They never tell you any more truth than they have to. But any kid with brains knows that there've been some changes in science since the days of old Mazer Rackham and the Victorious Fleet. Obviously we can now control gravity. Turn it on and off, change the direction, maybe reflect it—I've thought of lots of neat things you could do with gravity weapons and gravity drives on starships. And think how starships could move near planets. Maybe tear big chunks out of them by reflecting the planet's own gravity back on itself, only from another direction, and focused down to a smaller point. But they say nothing."

Ender understood more than she said. Manipulation of gravity was one thing; deception by the officers was another; but the most important message was this: the adults are the enemy, not the other armies. They do not tell us the truth.

"Come, little boy," she said. "The battleroom is ready. Petra's hands are steady. The enemy is deadly." She giggled. "Petra the poet, they call me."

"They also say you're crazy as a loon."

"Better believe it, baby butt." She had ten target balls in a bag. Ender held onto her suit with one hand and the wall with the other, to steady her as she threw them, hard, in different directions. In the null gravity, they bounced every which way. "Let go of me," she said. She shoved off, spinning deliberately; with a few deft hand moves she steadied herself, and began aiming carefully at ball after ball. When she shot one, its glow changed from white to red. Ender knew that the color change lasted less than two minutes. Only one ball had changed back to white when she got the last one.

She rebounded accurately from a wall and came at high speed back to Ender. He caught her and held her against her own rebound—one of the first techniques they had taught him as a Launchy.

"You're good," he said.

"None better. And you're going to learn how to do it."

Petra taught him to hold his arm straight, to aim with the whole arm. "Something most soldiers don't realize is that the farther away your target is, the longer you have to hold the beam within about a two-centimeter circle. It's the difference between a tenth of a second and a half a second, but in battle that's a long time. A lot of soldiers think they missed when they were right on target, but they moved away too fast. So you can't use your gun like a sword, swish swish slice-em-in-half. You got to aim."

She used the ballcaller to bring the targets back, then launched them slowly, one by one. Ender fired at them. He missed every one.

"Good," she said. "You don't have any bad habits."

"I don't have any good ones, either," he pointed out.

"I give you those."

They didn't accomplish much that first morning. Mostly talk. How to think while you were aiming. You've got to hold your own motion and your enemy's motion in your mind at the same time. You've got to hold your arm straight out and aim with your body, so in case your arm is frozen you can still shoot. Learn where your trigger actually fires and ride the edge, so you don't have to pull so far each time you fire. Relax your body, don't tense up, it makes you tremble.

It was the only practice Ender got that day. During the army's drills in the afternoon, Ender was ordered to bring his desk and do his schoolwork, sitting in a corner of the room. Bonzo had to bring all his soldiers to the battleroom, but he didn't have to use them.

Ender did not do his schoolwork, however. If he couldn't drill as a soldier, he could study Bonzo as a tactician. Salamander Army was divided into the standard four toons of ten soldiers each. Some commanders set up their toons so that A toon consisted of the best soldiers, and D toon had the worst. Bonzo had mixed them, so that each consisted of good soldiers and weaker ones.

Except that B toon had only nine boys. Ender wondered who had been transferred to make room for him. It soon became plain that the leader of toon B was new. No wonder Bonzo was so disgusted—he had lost a toon leader to get Ender.

And Bonzo was right about another thing. Ender was not ready. All the practice time was spent working on maneuvers. Toons that couldn't see each other practiced performing precision operations together with exact timing; toons practiced using each other to make sudden changes of direction without losing formation. All these soldiers took for granted skills that Ender didn't have. The ability to make a soft landing and absorb most of the shock. Accurate flight. Course adjustment using the frozen soldiers floating randomly through the room. Rolls, spins, dodges. Sliding along the walls—a very difficult maneuver and yet one of the most valuable, since the enemy couldn't get behind you.

Even as Ender learned how much he did not know, he also saw things that he could improve on. The well-rehearsed formations were a mistake. It allowed the soldiers to obey shouted orders instantly, but it also meant they were predictable. Also, the individual soldiers were given little initiative. Once a pattern was set, they were to follow it through. There was no room for adjustment to what the enemy did against the formation. Ender studied Bonzo's formations like an enemy commander would, noting ways to disrupt the formation.

During free play that night, Ender asked Petra to practice with him.

"No," she said. "I want to be a commander someday, so I've got to play the game room." It was a common belief that the teachers monitored the games and spotted potential commanders there. Ender doubted it, though. Toon leaders had a better chance to show what they might do as commanders than any video player.

But he didn't argue with Petra. The after-breakfast practice was generous enough. Still, he had to practice. And he couldn't practice alone, except a few of the basic skills. Most of the hard things required partners or teams. If only he still had Alai or Shen to practice with.

Well, why *shouldn't* he practice with them? He had never heard of a soldier practicing with Launchies, but there was no rule against it. It just wasn't done; Launchies were held in too much contempt. Well, Ender was still being treated like a Launchy anyway. He needed someone to practice with, and in return he could help them learn some of the things he saw the older boys doing.

"Hey, the great soldier returns!" said Bernard. Ender stood in the doorway of his old barracks. He'd only been away for a day, but already it seemed like an alien place, and the others of his launch group were strangers. Almost he turned around and left. But there was Alai, who had made their friendship sacred. Alai was not a stranger.

Ender made no effort to conceal how he was treated in Salamander

Army. "And they're right. I'm about as useful as a sneeze in a spacesuit."
Alai laughed, and other Launchies started to gather around. Ender proposed his bargain. Free play, every day, working hard in the battleroom, under Ender's direction. They would learn things from the armies, from the battles Ender would see; he would get the practice he needed in developing soldier skills. "We'll get ready together."

A lot of boys wanted to come, too. "Sure," Ender said. "If you're coming to work. If you're just farting around, you're out. I don't have any time to waste."

They didn't waste any time. Ender was clumsy, trying to describe what he had seen, working out ways to do it. But by the time free play ended, they had learned some things. They were tired, but they were getting the knack of a few techniques.

"Where were you?" asked Bonzo.

Ender stood stiffly by his commander's bunk. "Practicing in a battleroom."

"I hear you had some of your old Launchy group with you."

"I couldn't practice alone."

"I won't have any soldiers in Salamander Army hanging around with Launchies. You're a soldier now."

Ender regarded him in silence.

"Did you hear me, Wiggin?"

"Yes, sir."

"No more practicing with those little farts."

"May I speak to you privately?" asked Ender.

It was a request that commanders were required to allow. Bonzo's face went angry, and he led Ender out into the corridor. "Listen, Wiggin, I don't want you, I'm trying to get rid of you, but don't give me any problems or I'll paste you to the wall."

A good commander, thought Ender, doesn't have to make stupid threats.

Bonzo grew annoyed at Ender's silence. "Look, you asked me to come out here, now talk."

"Sir, you were correct not to place me in a toon. I don't know how to do anything."

"I don't need you to tell me when I'm correct."

"But I'm going to become a good soldier. I won't screw up your regular drill, but I'm going to practice, and I'm going to practice with the only people who will practice with me, and that's my Launchies."

"You'll do what I tell you, you little bastard."

"That's right, sir. I'll follow all the orders that you're authorized to give. But free play is free. No assignments can be given. None. By anyone."

He could see Bonzo's anger growing hot. Hot anger was bad. Ender's anger was cold, and he could use it. Bonzo's was hot, and so it used him.

"Sir, I've got my own career to think of. I won't interfere in your training and your battles, but I've got to learn sometime. I didn't ask to be put into your army, you're trying to trade me as soon as you can. But nobody will take me if I don't know anything, will they? Let me learn something, and then you can get rid of me all the sooner and get a soldier you can really use."

Bonzo was not such a fool that anger kept him from recognizing good sense when he heard it. Still, he couldn't let go of his anger immediately.

"While you're in Salamander Army, you'll obey me."

"If you try to control my free play, I can get you iced."

It probably wasn't true. But it was possible. Certainly if Ender made a fuss about it, interfering with free play could conceivably get Bonzo removed from command. Also, there was the fact that the officers obviously saw something in Ender, since they had promoted him. Maybe Ender *did* have influence enough with the teachers to ice somebody. "Bastard," said Bonzo.

"It isn't my fault you gave me that order in front of everybody," Ender said. "But if you want, I'll pretend you won this argument. Then tomorrow you can tell me you changed your mind."

"I don't need you to tell me what to do."

"I don't want the other guys to think you backed down. You wouldn't be able to command as well."

Bonzo hated him for it, for the kindness. Ender tried to understand why. Maybe it seemed to Bonzo as if Ender were granting him his command as a favor. Galling, and yet he had no choice. No choice about anything. Well it was Bonzo's own fault, for giving Ender an unreasonable order. Still, he would only know that Ender had beaten him, and then rubbed his nose in it by being magnanimous.

"I'll have your ass someday," Bonzo said.

"Probably," said Ender. The lights out buzzer sounded. Ender walked back into the room, looking dejected. Beaten. Angry. The other boys drew the obvious conclusion.

And in the morning, as Ender was leaving for breakfast, Bonzo stopped him and spoke loudly. "I changed my mind, pinprick. Maybe by practicing with your Launchies you'll learn something, and I can trade you easier. Anything to get rid of you faster."

"Thank you, sir," Ender said.

"Anything," whispered Bonzo. "I hope you're iced."

Ender smiled gratefully and left the room. After breakfast he practiced again with Petra. All afternoon he watched Bonzo drill and figured out ways to destroy his army. During free play he and Alai and the others worked themselves to exhaustion. I can do this, thought Ender as he lay in his bed, his muscles throbbing, unknotting themselves. I can handle it.

Salamander Army had a battle four days later. Ender followed behind the real soldiers as they jogged along the corridors to the battleroom. There were two ribbons along the walls, the green green brown of Salamander and the black white black of Condor. When they came to the place where the battleroom had always been, the corridor split instead, with green green brown leading to the left and black white black to the right. Around another turn to the right, and the army stopped in front of a blank wall.

The toons formed up in silence. Ender stayed behind them all. Bonzo was giving his instructions. "A take the handles and go up. B left, C right, D down." He saw that the toons were oriented to follow instructions, then added, "And you, pinprick, wait four minutes, then come just inside the door. Don't even take your gun off your suit."

Ender nodded. Suddenly the wall behind Bonzo became transparent. Not a wall at all, then, but a forcefield. The battleroom was different, too. Huge brown boxes were suspended in midair, partially obstructing the view. So these were the obstacles that the soldiers called *stars*. They were distributed seemingly at random. Bonzo seemed not to care where they were. Apparently the soldiers already knew how to handle the stars.

But it soon became clear to Ender, as he sat and watched the battle from the corridor, that they did not know how to handle the stars. They did know how to softland on one and use it for cover, the tactics of assaulting the enemy's position on a star. They showed no sense at all of *which* stars mattered. They persisted in assaulting stars that could have been bypassed by wallsliding to a more advanced position.

The other commander was taking advantage of Bonzo's neglect of strategy. Condor Army forced the Salamanders into costly assaults. Fewer and fewer Salamanders were unfrozen for the attack on the next star. It was clear, after only four minutes, that Salamander Army could not defeat the enemy by attacking.

Ender stepped through the gate. He drifted slightly downward. The battlerooms he had practiced in always had their doors at floor level. For real battles, however, the door was set in the middle of the wall, as far from the floor as from the ceiling.

Abruptly he felt himself reorient, as he had in the shuttle. What had been down was now up, and now sideways. In nullo, there was no reason to stay oriented the way he had been in the corridor. It was impossible to tell, looking at the perfectly square doors, which way had been up. And it didn't matter. For now Ender had found the orientation that made sense. The enemy's gate was down. The object of the game was to fall toward the enemy's home.

Ender made the motions that oriented himself in his new direction. Instead of being spread out, his whole body presented to the enemy, now Ender's legs pointed toward them. He was a much smaller target.

Someone saw him. He was, after all, drifting aimlessly in the open. Instinctively he pulled his legs up under him. At that moment he was flashed, and the legs of his suit froze in position. His arms remained unfrozen, for without a direct body hit, only the limbs that were shot froze up. It occurred to Ender that if he had not been presenting his legs to the enemy, it would have been his body they hit. He would have been immobilized.

Since Bonzo had ordered him not to draw his weapon, Ender continued to drift, not moving his head or arms, as if they had been frozen, too. The enemy ignored him and concentrated their fire on the soldiers who were firing at them. It was a bitter battle. Outnumbered now, Salamander Army gave ground stubbornly. The battle disintegrated into a dozen individual shootouts. Bonzo's discipline paid off now, for each Salamander that froze took at least one enemy with him. No one ran or panicked, everyone remained calm and aimed carefully.

Petra was especially deadly. Condor Army noticed it and took great effort to freeze her. They froze her shooting arm first, and her stream of curses was only interrupted when they froze her completely and the helmet clamped down on her jaw. In a few minutes it was over. Salamander Army offered no more resistance.

Ender noted with pleasure that Condor could only muster the minimal five soldiers necessary to open the gate to victory. Four of them touched their helmets to the lighted spots at the four corners of Salamander's door, while the fifth passed through the forcefield. That ended the game. The lights came back on to their full brightness, and Anderson came out of the teacher door.

I could have drawn my gun, thought Ender, as the enemy approached the door. I could have drawn my gun and shot just one of them, and they would have been too few. The game would have been a draw. Without four men to touch the four corners and a fifth man to pass through the gate, Condor would have had no victory. Bonzo, you ass, I could have saved you from this defeat. Maybe even turned it to victory, since they were sitting there, easy targets, and they wouldn't have known at first where the shots were coming from. I'm a good enough shot for that.

But orders were orders, and Ender had promised to obey. He did get some satisfaction out of the fact that on the official tally Salamander Army recorded, not the expected forty-one disabled or eliminated, but rather forty eliminated and one damaged. Bonzo couldn't understand it, until he consulted Anderson's book and realized who it was. I was only damaged, Bonzo, thought Ender. I could still shoot.

He expected Bonzo to come to him and say, "Next time, when it's like that, you can shoot." But Bonzo didn't say anything to him at all until the next morning after breakfast. Of course, Bonzo ate in the commanders' mess, but Ender was pretty sure the odd score would cause as much stir there as it did in the soldiers' dining hall. In every other game that wasn't a draw, every member of the losing team was either eliminated—totally frozen—or disabled, which meant they had some body parts still unfrozen, but were unable to shoot or inflict damage on the enemy. Salamander was the only losing army with one man in the Damaged but Active category.

Ender volunteered no explanation, but the other members of Salamander Army let it be known why it had happened. And when other boys asked him why he hadn't disobeyed orders and fired, he calmly answered, "I obey orders."

After breakfast, Bonzo looked for him. "The order still stands," he said, "and don't you forget it."

It will cost you, you fool. I may not be a good soldier, but I can still help and there's no reason you shouldn't let me.

Ender said nothing.

An interesting side effect of the battle was that Ender emerged at the top of the soldier efficiency list. Since he hadn't fired a shot, he had a perfect record on shooting—no misses at all. And since he had never been eliminated or disabled, his percentage there was excellent. No one else came close. It made a lot of boys laugh, and others were angry, but on the prized efficiency list, Ender was now the leader.

He kept sitting out the army practice sessions, and kept working hard on his own, with Petra in the mornings and his friends at night. More Launchies were joining them now, not on a lark but because they could see results—they were getting better and better. Ender and Alai stayed ahead of them, though. In part, it was because Alai kept trying new things, which forced Ender to think of new tactics to cope with them. In part it was because they kept making stupid mistakes, which suggested things to do that no self-respecting, well-trained soldier would even have tried. Many of the things they attempted turned out to be useless. But it was always fun, always exciting, and enough things worked that they knew it was helping them. Evening was the best time of the day.

The next two battles were easy Salamander victories; Ender came in after four minutes and remained untouched by the defeated enemy. Ender began to realize that Condor Army, which had beaten them, was unusually good; Salamander, weak as Bonzo's grasp of strategy might be, was one of the better teams, climbing steadily in the ratings, clawing for fourth place with Rat Army.

Ender turned seven. They weren't much for dates and calendars at the Battle School, but Ender had found out how to bring up the date on his desk, and he noticed his birthday. The school noticed it, too; they took his measurements and issued him a new Salamander uniform and a new flash suit for the battleroom. He went back to the barracks with the new clothing on. It felt strange and loose, like his skin no longer fit properly.

He wanted to stop at Petra's bunk and tell her about his home, about what his birthdays were usually like, just tell her it was his birthday so she'd say something about it being a happy one. But nobody told birthdays. It was childish. It was what landsiders did. Cakes and silly customs. Valentine baked him his cake on his sixth birthday. It fell and it was terrible. Nobody knew how to cook anymore, it was the kind of crazy thing Valentine would do. Everybody teased Valentine about it, but Ender saved a little bit of it in his cupboard. Then they took out his monitor and he left and for all he knew, it was still there, a little piece of greasy yellow dust. Nobody talked about home, not among the soldiers; there had been no life before Battle School. Nobody got letters, and nobody wrote any. Everybody pretended that they didn't care.

But I do care, thought Ender. The only reason I'm here is so that a bug-ger won't shoot out Valentine's eye, won't blast her head open like the soldiers in the videos of the first battles with the buggers. Won't split her head with a beam so hot that her brains burst the skull and spill out like rising bread dough, the way it happens in my worst nightmares, in my worst nights, when I wake up trembling but silent, must keep silent or they'll hear that I miss my family, I want to go home.

It was better in the morning. Home was merely a dull ache in the back of his memory. A tiredness in his eyes. That morning Bonzo came in as they were dressing. "Flash suits!" he called. It was a battle. Ender's fourth game.

The enemy was Leopard Army. It would be easy. Leopard was new, and it was always in the bottom quarter in the standings. It had been organized only six months ago, with Pol Slattery as its commander. Ender put on his new battle suit and got into line; Bonzo pulled him roughly out of line and made him march at the end. You didn't need to do that, Ender said silently. You could have let me stay in line.

Ender watched from the corridor. Pol Slattery was young, but he was sharp, he had some new ideas. He kept his soldiers moving, darting from star to star, wallsliding to get behind and above the stolid Salamanders. Ender smiled. Bonzo was hopelessly confused, and so were his men. Leop-ard seemed to have men in every direction. However, the battle was not as lopsided as it seemed. Ender noticed that Leopard was losing a lot of men, too—their reckless tactics exposed them too much. What mattered, how-ever, was that Salamander *felt* defeated. They had surrendered the initiative completely. Though they were still fairly evenly matched with the enemy, they huddled together like the last survivors of a massacre, as if they hoped the enemy would overlook them in the carnage.

Ender slipped slowly through the gate, oriented himself so the enemy's gate was down, and drifted slowly eastward to a corner where he wouldn't be noticed. He even fired at his own legs, to hold them in the kneeling position that offered him the best protection. He looked to any casual glance like another frozen soldier who had drifted helplessly out of the battle.

With Salamander Army waiting abjectly for destruction, Leopard oblig-ingly destroyed them. When Salamander finally stopped firing, Leopard had nine boys left. They formed up and started to open the Salamander gate.

Ender aimed carefully with a straight arm, as Petra had taught him. Before anyone knew what was happening, he froze three of the soldiers who were about to press their helmets against the lighted corners of the door. Then some of the others spotted him and fired—but at first they hit only his already-frozen legs. It gave him time to get the last two men at the gate. Leopard had only four men left unfrozen when Ender was finally hit in the arm and disabled. The game was a draw, and they never had hit him in the body.

Pol Slattery was furious, but there had been nothing unfair about it. Everyone in Leopard Army assumed that it had been a strategy of Bonzo's, to leave a man till the last minute. It didn't occur to them that little Ender had fired against orders. But Salamander Army knew. Bonzo knew, and Ender could see from the way his commander looked at him that Bonzo hated him for rescuing him from total defeat. I don't care, Ender told himself. It will just make me easier to trade away, and in the meantime you won't drop so far in the standings. Just trade me. I've learned all I'm ever going to learn from *you*. How to fail with style, that's all you know, Bonzo.

What *have* I learned so far? Ender listed things in his mind as he undressed by his bunk. The enemy's gate is down. Use my legs as a shield in battle. A small reserve, held back until the end of the game, can be decisive. And soldiers can sometimes make decisions that are smarter than the orders they've been given.

Naked, he was about to climb into bed when Bonzo came toward him, his face hard and set. I have seen Peter like this, thought Ender, silent with murder in his eye. But Bonzo is not Peter. Bonzo has more fear.

"Wiggin, I finally traded you. I was able to persuade Rat Army that your incredible place on the efficiency list is more than an accident. You go over there tomorrow."

"Thank you, sir," Ender said.

Perhaps he sounded too grateful. Suddenly Bonzo swung at him, caught his jaw with a vicious open-handed slap. It knocked Ender sideways, into his bunk, and he almost fell. Then Bonzo slugged him, hard, in the stomach. Ender dropped to his knees.

"You disobeyed me," Bonzo said. Loudly, for all to hear. "No good soldier ever disobeys."

Even as he cried from the pain, Ender could not help but take vengeful pleasure in the murmurs he heard rising through the barracks. You fool, Bonzo. You aren't enforcing discipline, you're destroying it. They know I turned defeat into a draw. And now they see how you repay me. You made yourself look stupid in front of everyone. What is your discipline worth now?

The next day, Ender told Petra that for her sake the shooting practice in the morning would have to end. Bonzo didn't need anything that looked like a challenge now, and so she'd better stay clear of Ender for a while. She understood perfectly. "Besides," she said, "you're as close to being a good shot as you'll ever be."

He left his desk and flash suit in the locker. He would wear his Salamander uniform until he could get to the commissary and change it for the brown and black of Rat. He had brought no possessions with him; he would take none away. There were none to have—everything of value was in the school computer or his own head and hands.

He used one of the public desks in the game room to register for an earth-gravity personal combat course during the hour immediately after breakfast. He didn't plan to get vengeance on Bonzo for hitting him. But he did intend that no one would be able to do that to him again.

8
RAT

"Colonel Graff, the games have always been run fairly before. Either random distribution of stars, or symmetrical."

"Fairness is a wonderful attribute, Major Anderson. It has nothing to do with war."

"The game will be compromised. The comparative standings will become meaningless."

"Alas."

"It will take months. Years, to develop the new battlerooms and run the simulations."

"That's why I'm asking you now. To begin. Be creative. Think of every stacked, impossible, unfair star arrangement you can. Think of other ways to bend the rules. Late notification. Unequal forces. Then run the simulations and see which ones are hardest, which easiest. We want an intelligent progression here. We want to bring him along."

"When do you plan to make him a commander? When he's eight?"

"Of course not. I haven't assembled his army yet."

"Oh, so you're stacking it that way, too?"

"You're getting too close to the game, Anderson. You're forgetting that it is merely a training exercise."

"It's also status, identity, purpose, name; all that makes these children who they are comes out of this game. When it becomes known that the game can be manipulated, weighted, *cheated*, it will undo this whole school. I'm not exaggerating."

"I know."

"So I hope Ender Wiggin truly is the one, because you'll have degraded the effectiveness of our training method for a long time to come."

"If Ender isn't the one, if his peak of military brilliance does not coincide with the arrival of our fleet at the bugger homeworlds, then it doesn't really matter what our training method is or isn't."

"I hope you will forgive me, Colonel Graff, but I feel that I must report your orders and my opinion of their consequences to the Strategos and the Hegemon."

"Why not our dear Polemarch?"

"Everybody knows you have him in your pocket."

"Such hostility, Major Anderson. And I thought we were friends."

"We are. And I think you may be right about Ender. I just don't believe you, and you alone, should decide the fate of the world."

"I don't even think it's right for me to decide the fate of Ender Wiggin."

"So you won't mind if I notify them?"

"Of course I mind, you meddlesome ass. This is something to be decided by people who know what they're doing, not these frightened politicians who got their office because they happen to be politically potent in the country they come from."

"But you understand why I'm doing it."

"Because you're such a short-sighted little bureaucratic bastard that you think you need to cover yourself in case things go wrong. Well, if things go wrong we'll all be bugger meat. So trust me now, Anderson, and don't bring the whole damn Hegemony down on my neck. What I'm doing is hard enough without them."

"Oh, is it unfair? Are things stacked against you? You can do it to Ender, but you can't take it, is that it?"

"Ender Wiggin is ten times smarter and stronger than I am. What I'm doing to him will bring out his genius. If I had to go through it myself, it would crush me. Major Anderson, I know I'm wrecking the game, and I know you love it better than any of the boys who play. Hate me if you like, but don't stop me."

"I reserve the right to communicate with the Hegemony and the Strategoi at any time. But for now—do what you want."

"Thank you so very kindly."

"Ender Wiggin, the little farthead who leads the standings, what a pleasure to have you with us." The commander of Rat Army lay sprawled on a lower bunk wearing only his desk. "With you around, how can any army lose?" Several of the boys nearby laughed.

There could not have been two more opposite armies than Salamander and Rat. The room was rumpled, cluttered, noisy. After Bonzo, Ender had thought that undiscipline would be a welcome relief. Instead, he found that he had come to expect quiet and order, and the disorder here made him uncomfortable.

"We doing OK, Ender Bender. I Rose de Nose, Jewboy extraordinaire, and you ain't nothin but a pinheaded pinprick of a goy. Don't you forget it."

Since the I.F. was formed, the Strategos of the military forces had always been a Jew. There was a myth that Jewish generals didn't lose wars. And so far it was still true. It made any Jew in the Battle School dream of being Strategos, and conferred prestige on him from the start. It also caused resentment. Rat Army was often called the Kike Force, half in praise, half in parody of Mazer Rackham's Strike Force. There were many who liked to remember that during the Second Invasion, even though an American Jew, as President, was Hegemon of the alliance, an Israeli Jew was Strategos in overall command of I.F. defense, and a Russian Jew was Polemarch of the fleet, it was Mazer Rackham, a little-known, twice-court-martialled, half-Maori New Zealander whose Strike Force broke up and finally destroyed the bugger fleet in the action around Saturn.

If Mazer Rackham could save the world, then it didn't matter a bit whether you were a Jew or not, people said.

But it did matter, and Rose the Nose knew it. He mocked himself to forestall the mocking comments of anti-semites—almost everyone he defeated in battle became, at least for a time, a Jew-hater—but he also made sure everyone knew what he was. His army was in second place, bucking for first.

"I took you on, goy, because I didn't want people to think I only win because I got great soldiers. I want them to know that even with a little puke of a soldier like you I can still win. We only got three rules here. Do what I tell you and don't piss in the bed."

Ender nodded. He knew that Rose wanted him to ask what the third rule was. So he did.

"That *was* three rules. We don't do too good in math, here."

The message was clear. Winning is more important than anything.

"Your practice sessions with half-assed little Launchies are over, Wiggin. Done. You're in a big boys' army now. I'm putting you in Dink Meeker's toon. From now on, as far as you're concerned, Dink Meeker is God."

"Then who are you?"

"The personnel officer who hired God." Rose grinned. "And you are forbidden to use your desk again until you've frozen two enemy soldiers in the same battle. This order is out of self-defense. I hear you're a genius programmer. I don't want you screwing around with my desk."

Everybody erupted in laughter. It took Ender a moment to understand why. Rose had programmed his desk to display and animate a bigger-than-lifesize picture of male genitals, which waggled back and forth as Rose held the desk on his naked lap. This is just the sort of commander Bonzo would trade me to, thought Ender. How does a boy who spends his time like this win battles?

Ender found Dink Meeker in the game room, not playing, just sitting and watching. "A guy pointed you out," Ender said. "I'm Ender Wiggin."

"I know," said Meeker.

"I'm in your toon."

"I know," he said again.

"I'm pretty inexperienced."

Dink looked up at him. "Look, Wiggin, I know all this. Why do you think I asked Rose to get you for me?"

He had not been dumped, he had been picked up, he had been asked for. Meeker wanted him. "Why?" asked Ender.

"I've watched your practice sessions with the Launchies. I think you show some promise. Bonzo is stupid and I wanted you to get better training than Petra could give you. All she can do is shoot."

"I needed to learn that."

"You still move like you were afraid to wet your pants."

"So teach me."

"So learn."

"I'm not going to quit my freetime practice sessions."

"I don't want you to quit them."

"Rose the Nose does."

"Rose the Nose can't stop you. Likewise, he can't stop you from using your desk."

"So why did he order it?"

"Listen, Ender, commanders have just as much authority as you let them have. The more you obey them, the more power they have over you."

"What's to stop them from hurting me?" Ender remembered Bonzo's blow.

"I thought that was why you were taking personal attack classes."

"You've really been watching me, haven't you?"

Dink didn't answer.

"I don't want to get Rose mad at me. I want to be part of the battles now, I'm tired of sitting out till the end."

"Your standings will go down."

This time Ender didn't answer.

"Listen, Ender, as long as you're part of my toon, you're part of the battle."

Ender soon learned why. Dink trained his toon independently from the rest of Rat Army, with discipline and vigor; he never consulted with Rose, and only rarely did the whole army maneuver together. It was as if Rose commanded one army, and Dink commanded a much smaller one that happened to practice in the battleroom at the same time.

Dink started out the first practice by asking Ender to demonstrate his feet-first attack position. The other boys didn't like it. "How can we attack lying on our backs?" they asked.

To Ender's surprise, Dink didn't correct them, didn't say, "You aren't attacking on your back, you're dropping downward toward them." He had seen what Ender was doing, but he had not understood the orientation that it implied. It soon became clear to Ender that even though Dink was very, very good, his persistence in holding onto the corridor gravity orientation instead of thinking of the enemy gate as downward was limiting his thinking.

They practiced attacking an enemy-held star. Before trying Ender's feet-first method, they had always gone in standing up, their whole bodies available as a target. Even now, though, they reached the star and then assaulted the enemy from one direction only; "Over the top," cried Dink, and over they went. To his credit, he then repeated the exercise, calling, "Again, upside down," but because of their insistence on a gravity that didn't exist, the boys became awkward when the maneuver was under, as if vertigo seized them.

They hated the feet-first attack. Dink insisted that they use it. As a result, they hated Ender. "Do we have to learn how to fight from a Launchy?" one of them muttered, making sure Ender could hear. "Yes," answered Dink. They kept working.

And they learned it. In practice skirmishes, they began to realize how much harder it was to shoot an enemy who is attacking feet first. As soon as they were convinced of that, they practiced the maneuver more willingly.

That night was the first time Ender had come to one of his laundry practice sessions after a whole afternoon of work. He was tired.

"Now you're really in an army," said Alai, "you don't have to keep practicing with us."

"From you I can learn things that nobody knows," said Ender.

"Dink Meeker is the best. I hear he's your toon leader."

"Then let's get busy. I'll teach you what I learned from him today."

He put Alai and two dozen others through the same exercises that had worn him out all afternoon. But he put new touches on the patterns, made the boys try the maneuvers with one leg frozen, with both legs frozen, or using frozen boys for leverage to change directions.

Halfway through the practice, Ender noticed Petra and Dink together, standing in the doorway, watching. Later, when he looked again, they were gone.

So they're watching me, and what we're doing is known. He did not know whether Dink was his friend; he believed that Petra was, but nothing could be sure. They might be angry that he was doing what only commanders and toon leaders were supposed to do—drilling and training soldiers. They might be offended that a soldier would associate so closely with Launchies. It made him uneasy, to have older children watching.

"I thought I told you not to use your desk." Rose the Nose stood by Ender's bunk.

Ender did not look up. "I'm completing the trigonometry assignment for tomorrow."

Rose bumped his knee into Ender's desk. "I said not to use it."

Ender set the desk on his bunk and stood up. "I need trigonometry more than I need you."

Rose was taller than Ender by at least forty centimeters. But Ender was not particularly worried. It would not come to physical violence, and if it did, Ender thought he could hold his own. Rose was lazy and didn't know personal combat.

"You're going down in the standings, boy," said Rose.

"I expect to. I was only leading the list because of the stupid way Salamander Army was using me."

"Stupid? Bonzo's strategy won a couple of key games."

"Bonzo's strategy wouldn't win a salad fight. I was violating orders every time I fired my gun."

Rose hadn't known that. It made him angry. "So everything Bonzo said about you was a lie. You're not only short and incompetent, you're insubordinate, too."

"But I turned defeat into stalemate, all by myself."

"We'll see how you do all by yourself next time." Rose went away.

One of Ender's toonmates shook his head. "You dumb as a thumb."

Ender looked at Dink, who was doodling on his desk. Dink looked up, noticed Ender watching him, and gazed steadily back at him. No expression. Nothing. OK, thought Ender, I can take care of myself.

Battle came two days later. It was Ender's first time fighting as part of a toon; he was nervous. Dink's toon lined up against the right-hand wall of the corridor and Ender was very careful not to lean, not to let his weight slip to either side. Stay balanced.

"Wiggin!" called Rose the Nose.

Ender felt dread come over him from throat to groin, a tingle of fear that made him shudder. Rose saw it.

"Shivering? Trembling? Don't wet your pants, little Launchy." Rose hooked a finger over the butt of Ender's gun and pulled him to the forcefield that hid the battleroom from view. "We'll see how well you do *now,* Ender. As soon as that door opens, you jump through, go straight ahead toward the enemy's door."

Suicide. Pointless, meaningless self-destruction. But he had to follow orders now, this was battle, not school. For a moment Ender raged silently; then he calmed himself. "Excellent, sir," he said. "The direction I fire my gun is the direction of their main contingent."

Rose laughed. "You won't have time to fire anything, pinprick."

The wall vanished. Ender jumped up, took hold of the ceiling handholds, and threw himself out and down, speeding toward the enemy door.

It was Centipede Army, and they only began to emerge from their door when Ender was halfway across the battleroom. Many of them were able to get under cover of stars quickly, but Ender had doubled up his legs under him and, holding his pistol at his crotch, he was firing between his legs and freezing many of them as they emerged.

They flashed his legs, but he had three precious seconds before they could hit his body and put him out of action. He froze several more, then flung out his arms in equal and opposite directions. The hand that held his gun ended up pointing toward the main body of Centipede Army. He fired into the mass of the enemy, and then they froze him.

A second later he smashed into the forcefield of the enemy's door and rebounded with a crazy spin. He landed in a group of enemy soldiers behind a star; they shoved him off and spun him even more rapidly. He rebounded out of control through the rest of the battle, though gradually friction with the air slowed him down. He had no way of knowing how many men he had frozen before getting iced himself, but he did get the general idea that Rat Army won again, as usual.

After the battle Rose didn't speak to him. Ender was still first in the standings, since he had frozen three, disabled two, and damaged seven. There was no more talk about insubordination and whether Ender could use his desk. Rose stayed in his part of the barracks, and left Ender alone.

Dink Meeker began to practice instant emergence from the corridor—Ender's attack on the enemy while they were still coming out of the door had been devastating. "If one man can do that much damage, think what a toon can do." Dink got Major Anderson to open a door in the middle of a wall, even during practice sessions, instead of just the floor-level door, so they could practice launching under battle conditions. Word got around. From now on no one could take five or ten or fifteen seconds in the corridor to size things up. The game had changed.

More battles. This time Ender played a proper role within a toon. He made mistakes. Skirmishes were lost. He dropped from first to second in the standings, then to fourth. Then he made fewer mistakes, and began to feel comfortable within the framework of the toon, and he went back up to third, then second, then first.

After practice one afternoon, Ender stayed in the battleroom. He had noticed that Dink Meeker usually came late to dinner, and he assumed it was for extra practice. Ender wasn't very hungry, and he wanted to see what it was Dink practiced when no one else could see.

But Dink didn't practice. He stood near the door, watching Ender.

Ender stood across the room, watching Dink.

Neither spoke. It was plain Dink expected Ender to leave. It was just as plain that Ender was saying no.

Dink turned his back on Ender, methodically took off his flash suit, and gently pushed off from the floor. He drifted slowly toward the center of the room, very slowly, his body relaxing almost completely, so that his hands and arms seemed to be caught by almost nonexistent air currents in the room.

After the speed and tension of practice, the exhaustion, the alertness, it was restful just to watch him drift. He did it for ten minutes or so before he reached another wall. Then he pushed off rather sharply, returned to his flash suit, and pulled it on.

"Come on," he said to Ender.

They went to the barracks. The room was empty, since all the boys were at dinner. Each went to his own bunk and changed into regular uniforms. Ender walked to Dink's bunk and waited for a moment till Dink was ready to go.

"Why did you wait?" asked Dink.

"Wasn't hungry."

"Well, now you know why I'm not a commander."

Ender had wondered.

"Actually, they promoted me twice, and I refused."

Refused?

"The second time they took away my old locker and bunk and desk, assigned me to a commander's cabin, and gave me an army. But I just stayed in the cabin until they gave in and put me back into somebody else's army."

"Why?"

"Because I won't let them do it to me. I can't believe you haven't seen through all this crap yet, Ender. But I guess you're young. These other armies, they aren't the enemy. It's the teachers, they're the enemy. They get us to fight each other, to hate each other. The game is everything. Win win win. It amounts to nothing. We kill ourselves, go crazy trying to beat each other, and all the time the old bastards are watching us, studying us, discovering our weak points, deciding whether we're *good enough* or not. Well, good enough for what? I was six years old when they brought me here. What the hell did I know? *They* decided I was right for the program, but nobody ever asked me if the program was right for me."

"So why don't you go home?"

Dink smiled crookedly. "Because I can't give up the game." He tugged at the fabric of his flash suit, which lay on the bunk beside him. "Because I love this."

"So why not be a commander?"

Dink shook his head. "Never. Look what it does to Rosen. The boy's crazy. Rose de Nose. Sleeps in here with us instead of in his cabin. Why? Because he's scared to be alone, Ender. Scared of the dark."

"Rose?"

"But they made him a commander and so he has to act like one. He doesn't know what he's doing. He's winning, but that scares him worst of all, because he doesn't know *why* he's winning, except that I have something to do with it. Any minute somebody could find out that Rosen isn't some magic Israeli general who can win no matter what. He doesn't know why anybody wins or loses. Nobody does."

"It doesn't mean he's crazy, Dink."

"I know, you've been here a year, you think these people are normal. Well, they're not. *We're* not. I look in the library, I call up books on my desk. Old ones, because they won't let us have anything new, but I've got a pretty good idea what children are, and we're not children. Children can lose sometimes, and nobody cares. Children aren't in armies, they aren't *commanders,* they don't rule over forty other kids, it's more than anybody can take and not get crazy."

Ender tried to remember what other children were like, in his class at school, back in the city. But all he could think of was Stilson.

"I had a brother. Just a normal guy. All he cared about was girls. And flying. He wanted to fly. He used to play ball with the guys. A pickup game, shooting balls at a hoop, dribbling down the corridors until the peace officers confiscated your ball. We had a great time. He was teaching me how to dribble when I was taken." ·

Ender remembered his own brother, and the memory was not fond.

Dink misunderstood the expression on Ender's face. "Hey, I know, nobody's supposed to talk about home. But we came from *somewhere.* The Battle School didn't create us, you know. The Battle School doesn't create *anything.* It just destroys. And we all remember things from home. Maybe not good things, but we remember and then we lie and pretend that—look, Ender, why is it that *nobody* talks about home, *ever*? Doesn't that tell you how important it is? That nobody even admits that—oh hell."

"No, it's all right," Ender said. "I was just thinking about Valentine. My sister."

"I wasn't trying to make you upset."

"It's OK. I don't think of her very much, because I always get—like this."

"That's right, we never cry. I never thought of that. Nobody ever cries. We really are trying to be adults. Just like our fathers. I bet your father was like you. I bet he was quiet and took it, and then busted out and—"

"I'm not like my father."

"So maybe I'm wrong. But look at Bonzo, your old commander. He's got an advanced case of Spanish honor. He can't allow himself to have weaknesses. To be better than him, that's an insult. To be stronger, that's like cutting off his balls. That's why he hates you, because you didn't suffer when he tried to punish you. He hates you for that, he honestly wants to kill you. He's crazy. They're all crazy."

"And you aren't?"

"I be crazy too, little buddy, but at least when I be craziest, I be floating all alone in space and the crazy, she float out of me, she soak into the walls, and she don't come out till there be battles and little boys bump into the walls and squish out de crazy."

Ender smiled.

"And you be crazy too," said Dink. "Come on, let's go eat."

"Maybe you can be a commander and not be crazy. Maybe knowing about craziness means you don't have to fall for it."

"I'm not going to let the bastards run me, Ender. They've got you pegged, too, and they don't plan to treat you kindly. Look what they've done to you so far."

"They haven't done anything except promote me."

"And she make you life so easy, neh?"

Ender laughed and shook his head. "So maybe you're right."

"They think they got you on ice. Don't let them."

"But that's what I came for," Ender said. "For them to make me into a tool. To save the world."

"I can't believe you still believe it."

"Believe what?"

"The bugger menace. Save the world. Listen, Ender, if the buggers were coming back to get us, they'd *be here*. They aren't invading again. We beat them and they're gone."

"But the videos—"

"All from the First and Second Invasions. Your grandparents weren't born yet when Mazer Rackham wiped them out. You watch. It's all a fake. There *is* no war, and they're just screwing around with us."

"But why?"

"Because as long as people are afraid of the buggers, the I.F. can stay in power, and as long as the I.F. is in power, certain countries can keep their hegemony. But keep watching the vids, Ender. People will catch onto this game pretty soon, and there'll be a civil war to end all wars. *That's* the menace, Ender, not the buggers. And in *that* war, when it comes, you and I won't be friends. Because you're American, just like our dear teachers. And *I* am not."

They went to the mess hall and ate, talking about other things. But Ender could not stop thinking about what Dink had said. The Battle School was so enclosed, the game so important in the minds of the children, that Ender had forgotten there was a world outside. Spanish honor. Civil war. Politics. The Battle School was really a very small place, wasn't it?

But Ender did not reach Dink's conclusions. The buggers were real. The threat was real. The I.F. controlled a lot of things, but it didn't control the videos and the nets. Not where Ender had grown up. In Dink's home in the Netherlands, with three generations under Russian hegemony, perhaps it was all controlled, but Ender knew that lies could not last long in America. So he believed.

Believed, but the seed of doubt was there, and it stayed, and every now and then sent out a little root. It changed everything, to have that seed growing. It made Ender listen more carefully to what people meant, instead of what they said. It made him wise.

There weren't as many boys at the evening practice, not by half.

"Where's Bernard?" asked Ender.

Alai grinned. Shen closed his eyes and assumed a look of blissful meditation.

"Haven't you heard?" said another boy, a Launchy from a younger group. "Word's out that any Launchy who comes to your practice sessions won't ever amount to anything in anybody's army. Word's out that the commanders don't want any soldiers who've been damaged by your training."

Ender nodded.

"But the way I brain it," said the Launchy, "I be the best soldier I can, and any commander worth a damn, he take me. Neh?"

"Eh," said Ender, with finality.

They went on with practice. About a half hour into it, when they were practicing throwing off collisions with frozen soldiers, several commanders in different uniforms came in. They ostentatiously took down names.

"Hey," shouted Alai. "Make sure you spell my name right!"

The next night there were even fewer boys. Now Ender was hearing the stories—little Launchies getting slapped around in the bathrooms, or having accidents in the mess hall and the game room, or getting their files trashed by older boys who had broken the primitive security system that guarded the Launchies' desks.

"No practice tonight," Ender said.

"The hell there's not," said Alai.

"Give it a few days. I don't want any of the little kids getting hurt."

"If you stop, even one night, they'll figure it works to do this kind of thing. Just like if you'd ever backed down to Bernard back when he was being a swine."

"Besides," said Shen, "we aren't scared and we don't care, so you owe it to us to go on. We need the practice and so do you."

Ender remembered what Dink had said. The game was trivial, compared to the whole world. Why should anybody give every night of his life to this stupid, stupid game?

"We don't accomplish that much anyway," Ender said. He started to leave.

Alai stopped him. "They scare you, too? They slap you up in the bathroom? Stick you head in the pissah? Somebody gots a gun up you bung?"

"No," Ender said.

"You still my friend?" asked Alai, more quietly.

"Yes."

"Then I still you friend, Ender, and I stay here and practice with you."

The older boys came again, but fewer of them were commanders. Most were members of a couple of armies. Ender recognized Salamander uniforms. Even a couple of Rats. They didn't take names this time. Instead, they mocked and shouted and ridiculed as the Launchies tried to master difficult skills with untrained muscles. It began to get to a few of the boys.

"Listen to them," Ender said to the other boys. "Remember the words. If you ever want to make your enemy crazy, shout that kind of stuff at them. It makes them do dumb things, to be mad. But *we* don't get mad."

Shen took the idea to heart, and after each jibe from the older boys, he had a group of four Launchies recite the words, loudly, five or six times. When they started singing the taunts like nursery rhymes, some of the older boys launched themselves from the wall and came out for a fight.

The flash suits were designed for wars fought with harmless light; they offered little protection and seriously hampered movement if it came to hand-to-hand fighting in nullo. Half the boys were flashed, anyway, and couldn't fight; but the stiffness of their suits made them potentially useful. Ender quickly ordered his Launchies to gather in one corner of the room. The older boys laughed at them even more, and some who had waited by the wall came forward to join in the attack, seeing Ender's group in retreat.

Ender and Alai decided to throw a frozen soldier in the face of an enemy. The frozen Launchy struck helmet first, and the two caromed off each other. The older boy clutched his chest where the helmet had hit him, and screamed in pain.

The mockery was over. The rest of the older boys launched themselves to enter the battle. Ender didn't really have much hope of any of the boys getting away without some injury. But the enemy was coming haphazardly, uncoordinatedly; they had never worked together before, while Ender's little practice army, though there were only a dozen of them now, knew each other well and knew how to work together.

"Go nova!" shouted Ender. The other boys laughed. They gathered into three groups, feet together, squatting, holding hands so they formed small stars against the back wall. "We'll go around them and make for the door. Now!"

At his signal, the three stars burst apart, each boy launching in a different direction, but angled so he could rebound off a wall and head for the door. Since all of the enemy were in the middle of the room, where course changes were far more difficult, it was an easy maneuver to carry out.

Ender had positioned himself so that when he launched, he would rendez-vous with the frozen soldier he had just used as a missile. The boy wasn't frozen now, and he let Ender catch him, whirl him around and send him toward the door. Unfortunately, the necessary result of the action was for Ender to head in the opposite direction, and at a reduced speed. Alone of all his soldiers, he was drifting fairly slowly, and at the end of the battleroom where the older boys were gathered. He shifted himself so he could see that all his soldiers were safely gathered at the far wall.

In the meantime, the furious and disorganized enemy had just spotted him. Ender calculated how soon he would reach the wall so he could launch again. Not soon enough. Several enemies had already rebounded toward him. Ender was startled to see Stilson's face among them. Then he shuddered and realized he had been wrong. Still, it was the same situation, and this time they wouldn't sit still for a single combat settlement. There was no leader, as far as Ender knew, and these boys were a lot bigger than him.

Still, he had learned some things about weight-shifting in personal combat class, and about the physics of moving objects. Game battles almost never got to hand-to-hand combat—you never bumped into an enemy that wasn't frozen unless *you* were frozen yourself. So in the few seconds he had, Ender tried to position himself to receive his guests.

Fortunately, they knew as little about nullo fighting as he did, and the few who tried to punch him found that throwing a punch was pretty ineffective when their bodies moved backward just as quickly as their fists moved forward. But there were some in the group who had bone-breaking on their minds, as Ender quickly saw. He didn't plan to be there for it, though.

He caught one of the punchers by the arm and threw him as hard as he could. It hurled Ender out of the way of the rest of the first onslaught, though he still wasn't getting any closer to the door. "Stay there!" he shouted at his friends, who obviously were forming up to come and rescue him. "Just stay there!"

Someone caught Ender by the foot. The tight grip gave Ender some leverage; he was able to stamp firmly on the other boy's ear and shoulder, making him cry out and let go. If the boy had let go just as Ender kicked downward, it would have hurt him much less and allowed Ender to use the maneuver as a launch. Instead, the boy had hung on too well; his ear was torn and scattering blood in the air, and Ender was drifting even more slowly.

I'm doing it again, thought Ender. I'm hurting people again, just to save myself. Why don't they leave me alone, so I don't have to hurt them?

Three more boys were converging on him now, and this time they were acting together. Still, they had to grab him before they could hurt him. Ender positioned himself quickly so that two of them would take his feet, leaving his hands free to deal with the third.

Sure enough, they took the bait. Ender grasped the shoulders of the third boy's shirt and pulled him up sharply, butting him in the face with his helmet. Again a scream and a shower of blood. The two boys who had his legs were wrenching at them, twisting him. Ender threw the boy with the bleeding nose at one of them; they entangled, and Ender's leg came free. It was a simple matter then to use the other boy's hold for leverage to kick him firmly in the groin, then shove off him in the direction of the door. He didn't get that good a launch, so that his speed was nothing special, but it didn't matter. No one was following him.

He got to his friends at the door. They caught him and handed him along to the door. They were laughing and slapping him playfully. "You bad!" they said. "You scary! You flame!"

"Practice is over for the day," Ender said.

"They'll be back tomorrow," said Shen.

"Won't do them any good," said Ender. "If they come without suits, we'll do this again. If they come *with* suits, we can flash them."

"Besides," said Alai, "the teachers won't let it happen."

Ender remembered what Dink had told him, and wondered if Alai was right.

"Hey Ender!" shouted one of the older boys, as Ender left the battleroom. "You nothing, man! You be nothing!"

"My old commander Bonzo," said Ender. "I think he doesn't like me."

Ender checked the rosters on his desk that night. Four boys turned up on medical report. One with bruised ribs, one with a bruised testicle, one with a torn ear, and one with a broken nose and a loose tooth. The cause of injury was the same in all cases:

ACCIDENTAL COLLISION IN NULL G

If the teachers were allowing that to turn up on the official report, it was obvious they didn't intend to punish anyone for the nasty little skirmish in the battleroom. Aren't they going to do anything? Don't they care what goes on in this school?

Since he was back to the barracks earlier than usual, Ender called up the fantasy game on his desk. It had been a while since he last used it. Long enough that it didn't start him where he had left off. Instead, he began by the Giant's corpse. Only now, it was hardly identifiable as a corpse at all, unless you stood off a ways and studied it. The body had eroded into a hill, entwined with grass and vines. Only the crest of the Giant's face was still visible, and it was white bone, like limestone protruding from a discouraged, withering mountain.

Ender did not look forward to fighting with the wolf-children again, but to his surprise they weren't there. Perhaps, killed once, they were gone forever. It made him a little sad.

He made his way down underground, through the tunnels, to the cliff ledge overlooking the beautiful forest. Again he threw himself down, and again a cloud caught him and carried him into the castle turret room.

The snake began to unweave itself from the rug again, only this time Ender did not hesitate. He stepped on the head of the snake and crushed it under his foot. It writhed and twisted under him, and in response he twisted and ground it deeper into the stone floor. Finally it was still. Ender picked it up and shook it, until it unwove itself and the pattern in the rug was gone. Then, still dragging the snake behind him, he began to look for a way out.

Instead, he found a mirror. And in the mirror he saw a face that he easily recognized. It was Peter, with blood dripping down his chin and a snake's tail protruding from a corner of his mouth.

Ender shouted and thrust his desk from him. The few boys in the barracks were alarmed at the noise, but he apologized and told them it was nothing. They went away. He looked again into his desk. His figure was still there, staring into the mirror. He tried to pick up some of the furniture, to break the mirror, but it could not be moved. The mirror would not come off the wall, either. Finally Ender threw the snake at it. The mirror shattered, leaving a hole in the wall behind it. Out of the hole came dozens of tiny snakes, which quickly bit Ender's figure again and again. Tearing the snakes frantically from itself, the figure collapsed and died in a writhing heap of small serpents.

The screen went blank, and words appeared.

PLAY AGAIN?

Ender signed off and put the desk away.

The next day, several commanders came to Ender or sent soldiers to tell him not to worry, most of them thought the extra practice sessions were a good idea, he should keep it up. And to make sure nobody bothered him, they were sending a few of their older soldiers who needed extra practice to come join him. "They're as big as most of the buggers who attacked you last night. They'll think twice."

Instead of a dozen boys, there were forty-five that night, more than an army, and whether it was because of the presence of older boys on Ender's side or because they had had enough the night before, none of their enemies came.

Ender didn't go back to the fantasy game. But it lived in his dreams. He kept remembering how it felt to kill the snake, grinding it in, the way he tore the ear off that boy, the way he destroyed Stilson, the way he broke Bernard's arm. And then to stand up, holding the corpse of his enemy, and find Peter's face looking out at him from the mirror. This game knows too much about me. This game tells filthy lies. I am not Peter. I don't have murder in my heart.

And then a worse fear, that he *was* a killer, only better at it than Peter ever was; that it was this very trait that pleased the teachers. It's killers they need for the bugger wars. It's people who can grind the enemy's face into the dust and spatter their blood all over space.

Well, I'm your man. I'm the bloody bastard you wanted when you had me spawned. I'm your tool, and what difference does it make if I hate the part of me that you most need? What difference does it make that when the little serpents killed me in the game, I agreed with them, and was glad.

9

LOCKE AND DEMOSTHENES

"I didn't call you in here to waste time. How in hell did the computer do that?"

"I don't know."

"How could it pick up a picture of Ender's brother and put it into the graphics in this Fairyland routine?"

"Colonel Graff, I wasn't there when it was programmed. All I know is that the computer's never taken anyone to this place before. Fairyland was strange enough, but this isn't Fairyland anymore. It's beyond the End of the World, and—"

"I know the names of the places, I just don't know what they mean."

"Fairyland was programmed in. It's mentioned in a few other places. But nothing talks about the End of the World. We don't have any experience with it."

"I don't like having the computer screw around with Ender's mind that way. Peter Wiggin is the most potent person in his life, except maybe his sister Valentine."

"And the mind game is designed to help shape them, help them find worlds they can be comfortable in."

"You don't get it, do you, Major Imbu? I don't want Ender being comfortable with the end of the world. Our business here is not to be comfortable with the end of the world!"

"The End of the World in the game isn't necessarily the end of humanity in the bugger wars. It has a private meaning to Ender."

"Good. What meaning?"

"I don't know, sir. I'm not the kid. Ask him."

"Major Imbu, I'm asking *you*."

"There could be a thousand meanings."

"Try one."

"You've been isolating the boy. Maybe he's wishing for the end of *this* world, the Battle School. Or maybe it's about the end of the world he grew up with as a little boy, his home, coming here. Or maybe it's his way of coping with having broken up so many other kids here. Ender's a sensitive kid, you know, and he's done some pretty bad things to people's bodies, he might be wishing for the end of *that* world."

"Or none of the above."

"The mind game is a relationship between the child and the computer. Together they create stories. The stories are true, in the sense that they reflect the reality of the child's life. That's all I *know*."

"And I'll tell you what *I* know, Major Imbu. That picture of Peter Wiggin was not one that could have been taken from our files here at the school. We have nothing on him, electronically or otherwise, since Ender came here. And that picture is more recent."

"It's only been a year and a half, sir, how much can the boy change?"

"He's wearing his hair completely differently now. His mouth was redone with orthodontia. I got a recent photograph from landside and compared. The only way the computer here in the Battle School could have got that picture was by requisitioning it from a landside computer. And not even one connected with the I.F. That takes requisitionary powers. We can't just go into Guilford County North Carolina and pluck a picture out of school files. Did anyone at this school authorize getting this?"

"You don't understand, sir. Our Battle School computer is only a part of the I.F. network. If *we* want a picture, *we* have to get a requisition, but if the mind game program determines that the picture is necessary—"

"It can just go take it."

"Not just every day. Only when it's for the child's own good."

"OK, it's for his good. But *why*. His brother is dangerous, his brother was rejected for this program because he's one of the most-ruthless and unreliable human beings we've laid hands on. Why is he so important to Ender? Why, after all this time?"

"Honestly, sir, I don't know. And the mind game program is designed so that it can't tell us. It may not know itself, actually. This is uncharted territory."

"You mean the computer's making this up as it goes along?"

"You might put it that way."

"Well, that does make me feel a little better. I thought I was the only one."

Valentine celebrated Ender's eighth birthday alone, in the wooded back yard of their new home in Greensboro. She scraped a patch of ground bare of pine needles and leaves, and there scratched his name in the dirt with a twig. Then she made a small teepee of twigs and needles and lit a small fire. It made smoke that interwove with the branches and needles of the pine overhead. All the way into space, she said silently. All the way to the Battle School.

No letters had ever come, and as far as they knew their own letters had never reached him. When he first was taken, Father and Mother sat at the table and keyed in long letters to him every few days. Soon, though, it was once a week, and when no answers came, once a month. Now it had been two years since he went, and there were no letters, none at all, and no remembrance on his birthday. He is dead, she thought bitterly, because we have forgotten him.

But Valentine had not forgotten him. She did not let her parents know, and above all never hinted to Peter how often she thought about Ender, how often she wrote him letters that she knew he would not answer. And when Mother and Father had announced to them that they were leaving the city to move to North Carolina, of all places, Valentine knew that they never expected to see Ender again. They were leaving the only place where he knew to find them. How would Ender find them here, among these trees, under this changeable and heavy sky? He had lived deep in corridors all his life, and if he was still in the Battle School, there was less of nature there. What would he make of this?

Valentine knew why they had moved here. It was for Peter, so that living among trees and small animals, so that nature, in as raw a form as Mother and Father could conceive of it, might have a softening influence on their strange and frightening son. And, in a way, it had. Peter took to it right away. Long walks out in the open, cutting through woods and out into the open country—going sometimes for a whole day, with only a sandwich or two sharing space with his desk in the pack on his back, with only a small pocket knife in his pocket.

But Valentine knew. She had seen a squirrel half-skinned, spiked by its little hands and feet with twigs pushed into the dirt. She pictured Peter trapping it, staking it, then carefully parting and peeling back the skin without breaking into the abdomen, watching the muscles twist and ripple. How long had it taken the squirrel to die? And all the while Peter had sat nearby, leaning against the tree where perhaps the squirrel had nested, playing with his desk while the squirrel's life seeped away.

At first she was horrified, and nearly threw up at dinner, watching how Peter ate so vigorously, talked so cheerfully. But later she thought about it and realized that perhaps, for Peter, it was a kind of magic, like her little fires; a sacrifice that somehow stilled the dark gods that hunted for his soul. Better to torture squirrels than other children. Peter has always been a husbandman of pain, planting it, nurturing it, devouring it greedily when it was ripe; better he should take it in these small, sharp doses than with dull cruelty to children in the school.

"A model student," said his teachers. "I wish we had a hundred others in the school just like him. Studies all the time, turns in all his work on time. He loves to learn."

But Valentine knew it was a fraud. Peter loved to learn, all right, but the teachers hadn't taught him anything, ever. He did his learning through his desk at home, tapping into libraries and databases, studying and thinking and, above all, talking to Valentine. Yet at school he acted as though he were excited about the puerile lesson of the day. Oh, wow, I never knew that frogs looked like *this* inside, he'd say, and then at home he studied the binding of cells into organisms through the philotic collation of DNA. Peter was a master of flattery, and all his teachers bought it.

Still, it was good. Peter never fought anymore. Never bullied. Got along well with everybody. It was a new Peter.

Everyone believed it. Father and Mother said it, so often it made Valentine want to scream at them. It isn't the new Peter! It's the old Peter, only smarter!

How smart? Smarter than *you*, Father. Smarter than *you*. Mother. Smarter than anybody you have ever met.

But not smarter than me.

"I've been deciding," said Peter, "whether to kill you or what."

Valentine leaned against the trunk of the pine tree, her little fire a few smoldering ashes. "I love you, too, Peter."

"It would be so easy. You always make these stupid little fires. It's just a matter of knocking you out and burning you up. You're such a firebug."

"I've been thinking of castrating you in your sleep."

"No you haven't. You only think of things like that when I'm with you. I bring out the best in you. No, Valentine, I've decided not to kill you. I've decided that you're going to help me."

"I am?" A few years ago, Valentine would have been terrified at Peter's threats. Now, though, she was not so afraid. Not that she doubted that he was capable of killing her. She couldn't think of anything so terrible that she didn't believe Peter might do it. She also knew, though, that Peter was not insane, not in the sense that he wasn't in control of himself. He was in better control of himself than anyone she knew. Except perhaps herself. Peter could delay any desire as long as he needed to; he could conceal any emotion. And so Valentine knew that he would never hurt her in a fit of rage. He would only do it if the advantages outweighed the risks. And they did not. In a way, she actually preferred Peter to other people because of this. He always, always acted out of intelligent self-interest. And so, to keep herself safe, all she had to do was make sure it was more in Peter's interest to keep her alive than to have her dead.

"Valentine, things are coming to a head. I've been tracking troop movements in Russia."

"What are we talking about?"

"The world, Val. You know Russia? Big Empire? The Second Warsaw Pact? Rulers of Eurasia from the Netherlands to Pakistan?"

"They don't publish their troop movements, Peter."

"Of course not. But they do publish their passenger and freight train schedules. I've had my desk analyzing those schedules and figuring out when the secret troop trains are moving over the same tracks. Done it backward over the past three years. In the last six months, they've stepped up, they're getting ready for war. Land war."

"But what about the League? What about the buggers?" Valentine didn't know what Peter was getting at, but he often launched discussions like this, practical discussions of world events. He used her to test his ideas, to refine them. In the process, she also refined her own thinking. She found that while she rarely agreed with Peter about what the world *ought* to be, they rarely disagreed about what the world actually *was*. They had become quite deft at sifting accurate information out of the stories of the hopelessly ignorant, gullible news writers. The news herd, as Peter called them.

"The Polemarch is Russian, isn't he? And he knows what's happening with the fleet. Either they've found out the buggers aren't a threat after all, or we're about to have a big battle. One way or another, the bugger war is about to be over. They're getting ready for after the war."

"If they're moving troops, it must be under the direction of the Strategos."

"It's all internal, within the Warsaw Pact."

This was troubling. The facade of peace and cooperation had been undisturbed almost since the bugger wars began. What Peter had detected was a fundamental shift in the world order. She had a mental picture, as clear as memory, of the way the world had been before the buggers forced peace upon them. "So it's back to the way it was before."

"A few changes. The shields make it so nobody bothers with nuclear weapons anymore. We have to kill each other thousands at a time instead of millions." Peter grinned. "Val, it was bound to happen. Right now there's a vast international fleet and army in existence, with North American hegemony. When the bugger wars are over, all that power will vanish, because it's all built on fear of the buggers. And suddenly we'll look around and discover that all the old alliances are gone, dead and gone, except one, the Warsaw Pact. And it'll be the dollar against five million lasers. We'll have the asteroid belt, but they'll have Earth, and you run out of raisins and celery kind of fast out there, without Earth."

What disturbed Valentine most of all was that Peter did not seem at all worried. "Peter, why do I get the idea that you are thinking of this as a golden opportunity for Peter Wiggin?"

"For both of us, Val."

"Peter, you're twelve years old. I'm ten. They have a word for people our age. They call us children and they treat us like mice."

"But we don't *think* like other children, do we, Val? We don't *talk* like other children. And above all, we don't *write* like other children."

"For a discussion that began with death threats, Peter, we've strayed from the topic, I think." Still, Valentine found herself getting excited. Writing was something Val did better than Peter. They both knew it. Peter had even named it once, when he said that he could always see what other people hated most about themselves, and bully them, while Val could always see what other people liked best about themselves, and flatter them. It was a cynical way of putting it, but it was true. Valentine could persuade other people to her point of view—she could convince them that they wanted what she wanted them to want. Peter, on the other hand, could only make them fear what he wanted them to fear. When he first pointed this out to Val, she resented it. She had wanted to believe she was good at persuading people because she was right, not because she was clever. But no matter how much she told herself that she didn't ever want to exploit people the way Peter did, she enjoyed knowing that she could, in her way, control other people. And not just control what they did. She could control, in a way, what they wanted to do. She was ashamed that she took pleasure in this power, and yet she found herself using it sometimes. To get teachers to do what she wanted, and other students. To get Mother and Father to see things her way. Sometimes, she was able to persuade even Peter. That was the most frightening thing of all—that she could understand Peter well enough, could empathize with him enough to get inside him that way. There was more Peter in her than she could bear to admit, though sometimes she dared to think about it anyway. This is what she thought as Peter spoke: You dream of power, Peter, but in my own way I am more powerful than you.

"I've been studying history," Peter said. "I've been learning things about patterns in human behavior. There are times when the world is rearranging itself, and at times like that, the right words can change the world. Think what Pericles did in Athens, and Demosthenes—"

"Yes, they managed to wreck Athens twice."

"Pericles, yes, but Demosthenes was right about Philip—"

"Or provoked him—"

"See? This is what historians usually do, quibble about cause and effect when the point is, there are times when the world is in flux and the right voice in the right place can move the world. Thomas Paine and Ben Franklin, for instance. Bismarck. Lenin."

"Not exactly parallel cases, Peter." Now she was disagreeing with him out of habit; she saw what he was getting at, and she thought it might just be possible.

"I didn't expect *you* to understand. *You* still believe that teachers know something worth learning."

I understand more than you think, Peter. "So you see yourself as Bismarck?"

"I see myself as knowing how to insert ideas into the public mind. Haven't you ever thought of a phrase, Val, a clever thing to say, and said it, and then two weeks or a month later you hear some adult saying it to another adult, both of them strangers? Or you see it on a video or pick it up on a net?"

"I always figured I heard it before and only thought I was making it up."

"You were wrong. There are maybe two or three thousand people in the world as smart as us, little sister. Most of them are making a living somewhere. Teaching, the poor bastards, or doing research. Precious few of them are actually in positions of power."

"I guess we're the lucky few."

"Funny as a one-legged rabbit, Val."

"Of which there are no doubt several in these woods."

"Hopping in neat little circles."

Valentine laughed at the gruesome image and hated herself for thinking it was funny.

"Val, *we* can say the words that everyone else will be saying two weeks later. We can do that. We don't have to wait until we're grown up and safely put away in some career."

"Peter, you're *twelve*."

"Not on the nets I'm not. On the nets I can name myself anything I want, and so can you."

"On the nets we are clearly identified as students, and we can't even get into the real discussions except in audience mode, which means we can't *say* anything anyway."

"I have a plan."

"You always do." She pretended nonchalance, but she listened eagerly.

"We can get on the nets as full-fledged adults, with whatever net names we want to adopt, *if* Father gets us onto his citizen's access."

"And why would he do that? We already have student access. What do you tell him, I need citizen's access so I can take over the world?"

"No, Val. *I* won't tell him anything. *You'll* tell him how you're worried about me. How I'm trying so very hard to do well at school, but you know it's driving me crazy because I can never talk to anybody intelligent, everybody always talks down to me because I'm young, I never get to converse with my *peers*. You can prove that the stress is getting to me. There's even evidence."

Valentine thought of the corpse of the squirrel in the woods and realized that even that discovery was part of Peter's plan. Or at least he had *made* it part of his plan, after it happened.

"So you get him to authorize us to share his citizen's access. To adopt our own identities there, to conceal who we are so people will give us the intellectual respect we deserve."

Valentine could challenge him on ideas, but never on things like this. She could not say, What makes you think you deserve respect? She had read about Adolf Hitler. She wondered what he was like at the age of twelve. Not this smart, not like Peter that way, but craving honor, probably that. And what would it have meant to the world if in childhood he had been caught in a thresher or trampled by a horse?

"Val," Peter said. "I know what you think of me. I'm not a nice person, you think."

Valentine threw a pine needle at him. "An arrow through your heart."

"I've been planning to come talk to you for a long time. But I kept being afraid."

She put a pine needle in her mouth and blew it at him. It dropped almost straight down. "Another failed launch." Why was he pretending to be weak?

"Val, I was afraid you wouldn't believe me. That you wouldn't believe I could do it."

"Peter, I believe you could do anything, and probably will."

"But I was even more afraid that you'd believe me and try to stop me."

"Come on, threaten to kill me again, Peter." Did he actually believe *she* could be fooled by his nice-and-humble-kid act?

"So I've got a sick sense of humor. I'm sorry. You know I was teasing. I need your help."

"You're just what the world needs. A twelve-year-old to solve all our problems."

"It's not my fault I'm twelve right now. And it's not my fault that right now is when the opportunity is open. Right now is the time when I can shape events. The world is always a democracy in times of flux, and the man with the best voice will win. Everybody thinks Hitler got to power because of his armies, because they were willing to kill, and that's partly true, because in the real world power is always built on the threat of death and dishonor. But mostly he got to power on words, on the right words at the right time."

"I was just thinking of comparing you to him."

"I don't hate Jews, Val. I don't want to destroy anybody. And I don't want war, either. I want the world to hold together. Is that so bad? I don't want us to go back to the old way. Have you read about the world wars?"

"Yes."

"We can go back to that again. Or worse. We could find ourselves locked into the Warsaw Pact. Now, there's a cheerful thought."

"Peter, we're children, don't you understand that? We're going to school, we're growing up—" But even as she resisted, she wanted him to persuade her. She had wanted him to persuade her from the beginning.

But Peter didn't know that he had already won. "If I believe that, if I accept that, then I've got to sit back and watch while all the opportunities vanish, and then when I'm old enough it's too late. Val, listen to me. I know how you feel about me, you always have. I was a vicious, nasty brother. I was cruel to you and crueler to Ender before they took him. But I didn't hate you. I loved you both, I just had to be—had to have *control*, do you understand that? It's the most important thing to me, it's my greatest gift, I can see where the weak points are, I can see how to get in and use them, I just *see* those things without even trying. I could become a businessman and run some big corporation, I'd scramble and maneuver until I was at the top of everything and what would I have? Nothing. I'm going to rule, Val, I'm going to have control of something. But I want it to be something worth ruling. I want to accomplish something worthwhile. A Pax Americana through the whole world. So that when somebody else comes, after we beat the buggers, when somebody else comes here to defeat us, they'll find we've already spread over a thousand worlds, we're at peace with ourselves and impossible to destroy. Do you understand? I want to save mankind from self-destruction."

She had never seen him speak with such sincerity. With no hint of mockery, no trace of a lie in his voice. He was getting better at this. Or maybe he was actually touching on the truth. "So a twelve-year-old boy and his kid sister are going to save the world?"

"How old was Alexander? I'm not going to do it overnight. I'm just going to start now. If you'll help me."

"I don't believe what you did to those squirrels was part of an act. I think you did it because you love to do it."

Suddenly Peter wept into his hands. Val assumed that he was pretending, but then she wondered. It was possible, wasn't it, that he loved her, and that in this time of terrifying opportunity he was willing to weaken himself before her in order to win her love. He's manipulating me, she thought, but that doesn't mean he isn't sincere. His cheeks were wet when he took his hands away, his eyes rimmed in red. "I know," he said. "It's what I'm most afraid of. That I really am a monster. I don't want to be a killer but I just can't help it."

She had never seen him show such weakness. You're so clever, Peter. You saved your weakness so you could use it to move me now.

And yet it did move her. Because if it were true, even partly true, then Peter was not a monster, and so she could satisfy her Peter-like love of power without fear of becoming monstrous herself. She knew that Peter was calculating even now, but she believed that under the calculations he was telling the truth. It had been hidden layers deep, but he had probed her until he found her trust.

"Val, if you don't help me, I don't know what I'll become. But if you're there, my partner in everything, you can keep me from becoming—like that. Like the bad ones."

She nodded. You are only pretending to share power with me, she thought, but in fact I have power over you, even though you don't know it. "I will. I'll help you."

—

As soon as Father got them both onto his citizen's access, they began testing the waters. They stayed away from the nets that required use of a real name. That wasn't hard because real names only had to do with money. They didn't need money. They needed respect, and that they could earn. With false names, on the right nets, they could be anybody. Old men, middle-aged women, anybody, as long as they were careful about the way they wrote. All that anyone would see were their words, their ideas. Every citizen started equal, on the nets.

They used throwaway names with their early efforts, not the identities that Peter planned to make famous and influential. Of course they were not invited to take part in the great national and international political forums—they could only be audiences there until they were invited or elected to take part. But they signed on and watched, reading some of the essays published by the great names, witnessing the debates that played across their desks.

And in the lesser conferences, where common people commented about the great debates, they began to insert their comments. At first Peter insisted that they be deliberately inflammatory. "We can't learn how our style of writing is working unless we get responses—and if we're bland, no one will answer."

They were not bland, and people answered. The responses that got posted on the public nets were vinegar; the responses that were sent as mail, for Peter and Valentine to read privately, were poisonous. But they did learn what attributes of their writing were seized upon as childish and immature. And they got better.

When Peter was satisfied that they knew how to sound adult, he killed the old identities and they began to prepare to attract real attention.

"We have to seem completely separate. We'll write about different things at different times. We'll never refer to each other. You'll mostly work on the west coast nets, and I'll mostly work in the south. Regional issues, too. So do your homework."

They did their homework. Mother and Father worried sometimes, with Peter and Valentine constantly together, their desks tucked under their arms. But they couldn't complain—their grades were good, and Valentine was such a good influence on Peter. She had changed his whole attitude toward everything. And Peter and Valentine sat together in the woods, in good weather, and in pocket restaurants and indoor parks when it rained, and they composed their political commentaries. Peter carefully designed both characters so neither one had all of his ideas; there were even some spare identities that they used to drop in third party opinions. "Let both of them find a following as they can," said Peter.

Once, tired of writing and rewriting until Peter was satisfied, Val despaired and said, "Write it yourself, then!"

"I can't," he answered. "They can't both sound alike. Ever. You forget that someday we'll be famous enough that somebody will start running analyses. We have to come up as different people every time."

So she wrote on. Her main identity on the nets was Demosthenes—Peter chose the name. He called himself Locke. They were obvious pseudonyms, but that was part of the plan. "With any luck, they'll start trying to guess who we are."

"If we get famous enough, the government can always get access and find out who we really are."

"When that happens, we'll be too entrenched to suffer much loss. People might be shocked that Demosthenes and Locke are two kids, but they'll already be used to listening to us."

They began composing debates for their characters. Valentine would prepare an opening statement, and Peter would invent a throwaway name to answer her. His answer would be intelligent, and the debate would be lively, lots of clever invective and good political rhetoric. Valentine had a knack for alliteration that made her phrases memorable. Then they would enter the debate into the network, separated by a reasonable amount of time, as if they were actually making them up on the spot. Sometimes a few other netters would interpose comments, but Peter and Val would usually ignore them or change their own comments only slightly to accommodate what had been said.

Peter took careful note of all their most memorable phrases and then did searches from time to time to find those phrases cropping up in other places. Not all of them did, but most of them were repeated here and there, and some of them even showed up in the major debates on the prestige nets. "We're being read," Peter said. "The ideas are seeping out."

"The phrases, anyway."

"That's just the measure. Look, we're having some influence. Nobody quotes us by name, yet, but they're discussing the points we raise. We're helping set the agenda. We're getting there."

"Should we try to get into the main debates?"

"No. We'll wait until they ask us."

They had been doing it only seven months when one of the west coast nets sent Demosthenes a message. An offer for a weekly column in a pretty good newsnet.

"I can't do a weekly column," Valentine said. "I don't even have a monthly period yet."

"The two aren't related," Peter said.

"They are to me. I'm still a kid."

"Tell them yes, but since you prefer not to have your true identity revealed, you want them to pay you in network time. A new access code through their corporate identity."

"So when the government traces me—"

"You'll just be a person who can sign on through CalNet. Father's citizen's access doesn't get involved. What I can't figure out is why they wanted Demosthenes before Locke."

"Talent rises to the top."

As a game, it was fun. But Valentine didn't like some of the positions Peter made Demosthenes take. Demosthenes began to develop as a fairly paranoid anti-Russian writer. It bothered her because Peter was the one who knew how to exploit fear in his writing—she had to keep coming to him for ideas on how to do it. Meanwhile, his Locke followed her moderate, empathic strategies. It made sense, in a way. By having her write Demosthenes, it meant he also had some empathy, just as Locke also could play on others' fears. But the main effect was to keep her inextricably tied to Peter. She couldn't go off and use Demosthenes for her own purposes. She wouldn't know how to use him. Still, it worked both ways. He couldn't write Locke without her. Or could he?

"I thought the idea was to unify the world. If I write this like you say I should, Peter, I'm pretty much calling for war to break up the Warsaw Pact."

"Not war, just open nets and prohibition of interception. Free flow of information. Compliance with the League rules, for heaven's sake."

Without meaning to, Valentine started talking in Demosthenes' voice, even though she certainly wasn't speaking Demosthenes' opinions. "Everyone knows that from the beginning of the League the Second Warsaw Pact was to be regarded as a single entity where those rules were concerned. International free flow is still open. But between the Warsaw Pact nations these things are internal matters. That was why they were willing to allow American hegemony in the League."

"You're arguing Locke's part, Val. Trust me. You have to call for the Warsaw Pact to lose official status. You have to get a lot of people really angry. Then, later, when you begin to recognize the need for compromise—"

"Then they stop listening to me and go off and fight a war."

"Val, trust me. I know what I'm doing."

"How do you know? You're not any smarter than me, and you've never done this before either."

"I'm thirteen and you're ten."

"Almost eleven."

"And I know how these things work."

"All right, I'll do it your way. But I won't do any of these liberty or death things."

"You will too."

"And someday when they catch us and they wonder why your sister was such a warmonger, I can just bet you'll tell them that you told me to do it."

"Are you *sure* you're not having a period, little woman?"

"I hate you, Peter Wiggin."

What bothered Valentine most was when her column got syndicated into several other regional newsnets, and Father started reading it and quoting from it at table. "Finally, a man with some sense," he said. Then he quoted some of the passages Valentine hated worst in her own work. "It's fine to work with these hegemonist Russians with the buggers out there, but after we win, I can't see leaving half the civilized world as virtual serfs in the Russian Empire, can you, dear?"

"I think you're taking this all too seriously," said Mother.

"I like this Demosthenes. I like the way he thinks. I'm surprised he isn't in the major nets—I looked for him in the international relations debates and you know, he's never taken part in any of them."

Valentine lost her appetite and left the table. Peter followed her after a respectable interval.

"So you don't like lying to Father," he said. "So what? You're *not* lying to him. He doesn't think that you're really Demosthenes, and Demosthenes isn't saying things you really believe. They cancel each other out, they amount to nothing."

"That's the kind of reasoning that makes Locke such an ass." But what really bothered her was not that she was lying to Father— it was the fact that Father actually agreed with Demosthenes. She had thought that only fools would follow him.

A few days later Locke got picked up for a column in a New England newsnet, specifically to provide a contrasting view for their popular column from Demosthenes. "Not bad for two kids who've only got about eight pubic hairs between them," Peter said.

"It's a long way between writing a newsnet column and ruling the world," Valentine reminded him. "It's such a long way that no one has ever done it."

"They have, though. Or the moral equivalent. I'm going to say snide things about Demosthenes in my first column."

"Well, Demosthenes isn't even going to notice that Locke exists. Ever."

"For now."

With their identities now fully supported by their income from writing columns, they used Father's access now only for the throwaway identities. Mother commented that they were spending too much time on the nets. "All work and no play makes Jack a dull boy," she reminded Peter.

Peter let his hand tremble a little, and he said, "If you think I should stop, I think I might be able to keep things under control this time, I really do."

"No, no," Mother said. "I don't want you to *stop*. Just—be careful, that's all."

"I'm careful, Mom."

Nothing was different, nothing had changed in a year. Ender was sure of it, and yet it all seemed to have gone sour. He was still the leading soldier in the standings, and no one doubted that he deserved it now. At the age of nine he was a toon leader in Phoenix Army, with Petra Arkanian as his commander. He still led his evening practice sessions, and now they were attended by an elite group of soldiers nominated by their commanders, though any Launchy who wanted to could still come. Alai was also a toon leader, in another army, and they were still good friends; Shen was not a leader, but that was no barrier. Dink Meeker had finally accepted command and succeeded Rose the Nose in Rat Army's command. All is going well, *very* well, I couldn't ask for anything better—

So why do I hate my life?

He went through the paces of the practices and games. He liked teaching the boys in his toon, and they followed him loyally. He had the respect of everyone, and he was treated with deference in his evening practices. Commanders came to study what he did. Other soldiers approached his table at mess and asked permission to sit down. Even the teachers were respectful.

He had so much damn respect he wanted to scream.

He watched the young kids in Petra's army, fresh out of their launch groups, watched how they played, how they made fun of their leaders when they thought no one was looking. He watched the camaraderie of old friends who had known each other in the Battle School for years, who talked and laughed about old battles and long-graduated soldiers and commanders.

But with *his* old friends there was no laughter, no remembering. Just work. Just intelligence and excitement about the game, but nothing beyond that. Tonight it had come to a head in the evening practice. Ender and Alai were discussing the nuances of open-space maneuvers when Shen came up and listened for a few moments, then suddenly took Alai by the shoulders and shouted, "Nova! Nova! Nova!" Alai burst out laughing, and for a moment or two Ender watched them remember together the battle where open-room maneuvering had been for real, and they had dodged past the older boys and—

Suddenly they remembered that Ender was there. "Sorry, Ender," Shen said.

Sorry. For what? For being friends? "I was there, too, you know," Ender said.

And they apologized again. Back to business. Back to *respect*. And Ender realized that in their laughter, in their friendship, it had not occurred to them that he could have been included.

How could they think I was part of it? Did I laugh? Did I join in? Just stood there, watching, like a teacher.

That's how they think of me, too. Teacher. Legendary soldier. Not one of *them*. Not someone that you embrace and whisper Salaam in his ear. That only lasted while Ender still seemed a victim. Still seemed vulnerable. Now he was the master soldier, and he was completely, utterly alone.

Feel sorry for yourself, Ender. He typed the words on his desk as he lay on his bunk. POOR ENDER. Then he laughed at himself and cleared away the words. Not a boy or girl in this school who wouldn't be glad to trade places with me.

He called up the fantasy game. He walked as he often did through the village that the dwarves had built in the hill made by the Giant's corpse. It was easy to build sturdy walls, with the ribs already curved just right, just enough space between them to leave windows. The whole corpse was cut into apartments, opening onto the path down the Giant's spine. The public amphitheatre was carved into the pelvic bowl, and the common herd of ponies was pastured between the Giant's legs. Ender was never sure what the dwarves were doing as they went about their business, but they left him alone as he picked his way through the village, and in return he did them no harm either.

He vaulted the pelvic bone at the base of the public square, and walked through the pasture. The ponies shied away from him. He did not pursue them. Ender did not understand how the game functioned anymore. In the old days, before he had first gone to the End of the World, everything was combat and puzzles to solve—defeat the enemy before he kills you, or figure out how to get past the obstacle. Now, though, no one attacked, there was no war, and wherever he went, there was no obstacle at all.

Except, of course, in the room in the castle at the End of the World. It was the one dangerous place left. And Ender, however often he vowed that he would not, always went back there, always killed the snake, always looked his brother in the face, and always, no matter what he did next, died.

It was no different this time. He tried to use the knife on the table to pry through the mortar and pull out a stone from the wall. As soon as he breached the seal of the mortar, water began to gush in through the crack, and Ender watched his desk as his figure, now out of his control, struggled madly to stay alive, to keep from drowning. The windows of his room were gone, the water rose, and his figure drowned. All the while, the face of Peter Wiggin in the mirror stayed and looked at him.

I'm trapped here, Ender thought, trapped at the End of the World with no way out. And he knew at last the sour taste that had come to him, despite all his successes in the Battle School. It was despair.

—

There were uniformed men at the entrances to the school when Valentine arrived. They weren't standing like guards, but rather slouched around as if they were waiting for someone inside to finish his business. They wore the uniforms of I.F. Marines, the same uniforms that everyone saw in bloody combat on the videos. It lent an air of romance to this day at school; all the other kids were excited about it.

Valentine was not. It made her think of Ender, for one thing. And for another, it made her afraid. Someone had recently published a savage commentary on Demosthenes' collected writings. The commentary, and therefore her work, had been discussed in the open conference of the international relations net, with some of the most important people of the day attacking and defending Demosthenes. What worried her most was the comment of an Englishman: "Whether he likes it or not, Demosthenes cannot remain incognito forever. He has outraged too many wise men and pleased too many fools to hide behind his too-appropriate pseudonym much longer. Either he will unmask himself in order to assume leadership of the forces of stupidity he has marshalled, or his enemies will unmask him in order to better understand the disease that has produced such a warped and twisted mind."

Peter had been delighted, but then he would be. Valentine was afraid that enough powerful people had been annoyed by the vicious persona of Demosthenes that she would indeed be tracked down. The I.F. could do it, even if the American government was constitutionally bound not to. And here were I.F. troops gathered at Western Guilford Middle School, of all places. Not exactly the regular recruiting grounds for the I.F. Marines.

So she was not surprised to find a message marching around her desk as soon as she logged in.

> PLEASE LOG OFF AND GO TO DR.
> LINEBERRY'S OFFICE AT ONCE.

Valentine waited nervously outside the principal's office until Dr. Lineberry opened the door and beckoned her inside. Her last doubt was removed when she saw the soft-bellied man in the uniform of an I.F. colonel sitting in the one comfortable chair in the room.

"You're Valentine Wiggin," he said.

"Yes," she whispered.

"I'm Colonel Graff. We've met before."

Before? When had she had any dealings with the I.F.?

"I've come to talk to you in confidence, about your brother."

It's not just me, then, she thought. They have Peter. Or is this something new? Has he done something crazy? I thought he stopped doing crazy things.

"Valentine, you seem frightened. There's no need to be. Please, sit down. I assure you that your brother is well. He has more than fulfilled our expectations."

And now, with a great inward gush of relief, she realized that it was Ender they had come about. This must be the officer who had taken him away. Ender. It wasn't punishment at all, it was little Ender, who had disappeared so long ago, who was no part of Peter's plots now. You were the lucky one, Ender. You got away before Peter could trap you into his conspiracy.

"How do you feel about your brother, Valentine?"

"Ender?"

"Of course."

"How can I feel about him? I haven't seen him or heard from him since I was eight."

"Dr. Lineberry, will you excuse us?"

Lineberry was annoyed.

"On second thought, Dr. Lineberry, I think Valentine and I will have a much more productive conversation if we walk. Outside. Away from the recording devices that your assistant principal has placed in this room."

It was the first time Valentine had seen Dr. Lineberry speechless. Colonel Graff lifted a picture out from the wall and peeled a sound-sensitive membrane from the wall, along with its small broadcast unit. "Cheap," said Graff, "but effective. I thought you knew."

Lineberry took the device and sat down heavily at her desk. Graff led Valentine outside.

They walked out into the football field. The soldiers followed at a discreet distance; they split up and formed a large circle, to guard them from the widest possible perimeter.

"Valentine, we need your help for Ender."

"What kind of help?"

"We aren't even sure of that. We need you to help us figure out how you can help us."

"Well, what's wrong?"

"That's part of the problem. We don't know."

Valentine couldn't help but laugh. "I haven't seen him in three years! You've got him up there with you all the time!"

"Valentine, it costs more money than your father will make in his lifetime for me to fly to Earth and back to the Battle School again. I don't commute casually."

"The king had a dream," said Valentine, "but he forgot what it was, so he told his wise men to interpret the dream or they'd die. Only Daniel could interpret it, because he was a prophet."

"You read the Bible?"

"We're doing classics this year in advanced English. I'm not a prophet."

"I wish I could tell you everything about Ender's situation. But it would take hours, maybe days, and afterward I'd have to put you in protective confinement because so much of it is strictly confidential. So let's see what we can do with limited information. There's a game that our students play with the computer." And he told her about the End of the World and the closed room and the picture of Peter in the mirror.

"It's the computer that puts the picture there, not Ender. Why not ask the computer?"

"The computer doesn't know."

"*I'm* supposed to know?"

"This is the second time since Ender's been with us that he's taken this game to a dead end. To a game that seems to have no solution."

"Did he solve the first one?"

"Eventually."

"Then give him time, he'll probably solve this one."

"I'm not sure. Valentine, your brother is a very unhappy little boy."

"Why?"

"I don't know."

"You don't know much, do you?"

Valentine thought for a moment that the man might get angry. Instead, though, he decided to laugh. "No, not much. Valentine, why would Ender keep seeing your brother Peter in the mirror?"

"He shouldn't. It's stupid."

"Why is it stupid?"

"Because if there's ever anybody who was the opposite of Ender, it's Peter."

"How?"

Valentine could not think of a way to answer him that wasn't dangerous. Too much questioning about Peter could lead to real trouble. Valentine knew enough about the world to know that no one would take Peter's plans for world domination seriously, as a danger to existing governments. But they might well decide he was insane and needed treatment for his megalo-mania.

"You're preparing to lie to me," Graff said.

"I'm preparing not to talk to you anymore," Valentine answered.

"And you're afraid. Why are you afraid?"

"I don't like questions about my family. Just leave my family out of this."

"Valentine, I'm *trying* to leave your family out of this. I'm coming to you so I don't have to start a battery of tests on Peter and question your parents. I'm trying to solve this problem now, with the person Ender loves and trusts most in the world, perhaps the only person he loves and trusts at all. If we can't solve it this way, then we'll sequester your family and do as we like from then on. This is not a trivial matter, and I won't just go away."

The only person Ender loves and trusts at all. She felt a deep stab of pain, of regret, of shame that now it was Peter she was close to, Peter who was the center of her life. For you, Ender, I light fires on your birthday. For Peter I help fulfil all his dreams. "I never thought you were a nice man. Not when you came to take Ender away, and not now."

"Don't pretend to be an ignorant little girl. I saw your tests when you were little, and at the present moment there aren't very many college professors who could keep up with you."

"Ender and Peter hate each other."

"I knew that. You said they were opposites. Why?"

"Peter—can be hateful sometimes."

"Hateful in what way?"

"Mean. Just mean, that's all."

"Valentine, for Ender's sake, tell me what he does when he's being mean."

"He threatens to kill people a lot. He doesn't mean it. But when we were little, Ender and I were both afraid of him. He told us he'd kill us. Actually, he told us he'd kill Ender."

"We monitored some of that."

"It was because of the monitor."

"Is that all? Tell me more about Peter."

So she told him about the children in every school that Peter attended. He never hit them, but he tortured them just the same. Found what they were most ashamed of and told it to the person whose respect they most wanted. Found what they most feared and made sure they faced it often.

"Did he do this with Ender?"

Valentine shook her head.

"Are you sure? Didn't Ender have a weak place? A thing he feared most, or that he was ashamed of?"

"Ender never did anything to be ashamed of." And suddenly, deep in her own shame for having forgotten and betrayed Ender, she started to cry.

"Why are you crying?"

She shook her head. She couldn't explain what it was like to think of her little brother, who was so good, whom she had protected for so long, and then remember that now she was Peter's ally, Peter's helper, Peter's slave in a scheme that was completely out of her control. Ender never surrendered to Peter, but I have turned, I've become part of him, as Ender never was. "Ender never gave in," she said.

"To what?"

"To Peter. To being like Peter."

They walked in silence along the goal line.

"How would Ender ever be like Peter?"

Valentine shuddered. "I already told you."

"But Ender never did that kind of thing. He was just a little boy."

"We both wanted to, though. We both wanted to—to kill Peter."

"Ah."

"No, that isn't true. We never said it. Ender never said that he wanted to do that. I just—*thought* it. It was me, not Ender. He never said that he wanted to kill him."

"What *did* he want?"

"He just didn't want to be—"

"To be what?"

"Peter tortures squirrels. He stakes them out on the ground and skins them alive and sits and watches them until they die. He did that for a while, after Ender left; he doesn't do it now. But he did it. If Ender knew that, if Ender saw him, I think that he'd—"

"He'd what? Rescue the squirrels? Try to heal them?"

"No, in those days you didn't—undo what Peter did. You didn't cross him. But Ender would be kind to squirrels. Do you understand? He'd feed them."

"But if he fed them, they'd become tame, and that much easier for Peter to catch."

Valentine began to cry again. "No matter what you do, it always helps Peter. Everything helps Peter, everything, you just can't get away, no matter what."

"Are you helping Peter?" asked Graff.

She didn't answer.

"Is Peter such a very bad person, Valentine?"

She nodded.

"Is Peter the worst person in the world?"

"How can he be? I don't know. He's the worst person I know."

"And yet you and Ender are his brother and sister. You have the same genes, the same parents, how can he be so bad if—"

Valentine turned and screamed at him, screamed as if he were killing her. "Ender is not like Peter! He is not like Peter in any way! Except that he's smart, that's all—in every other way a person could possibly be like Peter he is nothing nothing nothing like Peter! Nothing!"

"I see," said Graff.

"I know what you're thinking, you bastard, you're thinking that I'm wrong, that Ender's like Peter. Well maybe *I'm* like Peter, but Ender isn't, he isn't at all, I used to tell him that when he cried, I told him that lots of times, you're not like Peter, you never like to hurt people, you're kind and good and not like Peter at all!"

"And it's true."

His acquiescence calmed her. "Damn right it's true. It's true."

"Valentine, will you help Ender?"

"I can't do anything for him now."

"It's really the same thing you always did for him before. Just comfort him and tell him that he never likes to hurt people, that he's good and kind and not like Peter at all. That's the most important thing. That he's not like Peter at all."

"I can see him?"

"No. I want you to write a letter."

"What good does that do? Ender never answered a single letter I sent."

Graff sighed. "He answered every letter he got."

It took only a second for her to understand. "You really stink."

"Isolation is—the optimum environment for creativity. It was *his* ideas we wanted, not the—never mind, I don't have to defend myself to you."

Then why are you doing it, she did not ask.

"But he's slacking off. He's coasting. We want to push him forward, and he won't go."

"Maybe I'd be doing Ender a favor if I told you to go stuff yourself."

"You've already helped me. You can help me more. Write to him."

"Promise you won't cut out anything I write."

"I won't promise any such thing."

"Then forget it."

"No problem. I'll write your letter myself. We can use your other letters to reconcile the writing styles. Simple matter."

"I want to see him."

"He gets his first leave when he's eighteen."

"You told him it would be when he was twelve."

"We changed the rules."

"Why should I help you!"

"Don't help me. Help Ender. What does it matter if that helps us, too?"

"What kind of terrible things are you doing to him up there?"

Graff chuckled. "Valentine, my dear little girl, the terrible things are only about to begin."

———

Ender was four lines into the letter before he realized that it wasn't from one of the other soldiers in the Battle School. It had come in the regular way—a MAIL WAITING message when he signed into his desk. He read four lines into it, then skipped to the end and read the signature. Then he went back to the beginning, and curled up on his bed to read the words over and over again.

ENDER,
THE BASTARDS WOULDN'T PUT ANY OF
MY LETTERS THROUGH TILL NOW. I
MUST HAVE WRITTEN A HUNDRED TIMES
BUT YOU MUST HAVE THOUGHT I NEVER
DID. WELL I DID. I HAVEN'T
FORGOTTEN YOU. I REMEMBER YOUR

BIRTHDAY. I REMEMBER EVERYTHING.
SOME PEOPLE MIGHT THINK THAT
BECAUSE YOU'RE BEING A SOLDIER
YOU ARE NOW A CRUEL AND HARD
PERSON WHO LIKES TO HURT PEOPLE,
LIKE THE MARINES IN THE VIDEOS,
BUT I KNOW THAT ISN'T TRUE. YOU
ARE NOTHING LIKE YOU-KNOW-WHO.
HE'S NICER-SEEMING BUT HE'S
STILL A SLUMBITCH INSIDE.
MAYBE YOU SEEM MEAN, BUT IT
WON'T FOOL ME. STILL PADDLING
THE OLD KNEW,
ALL MY LOVE TURKEY LIPS,
VAL
DON'T WRITE BACK THEY'LL PROBLY
SIKOWANALIZE YOUR LETTER.

Obviously it was written with the full approval of the teachers. But there was no doubt it was written by Val. The spelling of *psychoanalyze*, the epithet *slumbitch* for Peter, the joke about pronouncing *knew* like *canoe* were all things that no one could know but Val.

And yet they came pretty thick, as though someone wanted to make very sure that Ender believed that the letter was genuine. Why should they be so eager if it's the real thing?

It isn't the real thing anyway. Even if she wrote it in her own blood, it isn't the real thing because they made her write it. She'd written before, and they didn't let any of those letters through. Those might have been real, but this was asked for, this was part of their manipulation.

And the despair filled him again. Now he knew why. Now he knew what he hated so much. He had no control over his own life. They ran everything. They made all the choices. Only the game was left to him, that was all, everything else was them and their rules and plans and lessons and programs, and all he could do was go this way or that way in battle. The one real thing, the one precious real thing was his memory of Valentine, the person who loved him before he ever played a game, who loved him whether there was a bugger war or not, and they had taken her and put her on their side. She was one of them now.

He hated them and all their games. Hated them so badly that he cried, reading Val's empty asked-for letter again. The other boys in Phoenix Army noticed and looked away. *Ender Wiggin* crying? That was disturbing. Something terrible was going on. The best soldier in any army, lying on his bunk *crying*. The silence in the room was deep.

Ender deleted the letter, wiped it out of memory and then punched up the fantasy game. He was not sure why he was so eager to play the game, to get to the End of the World, but he wasted no time getting there. Only when he coasted on the cloud, skimming over the autumnal colors of the pastoral world, only then did he realize what he hated most about Val's letter. All that it said was about Peter. About how he was not at all like Peter. The words she had said so often as she held him, comforted him as he trembled in fear and rage and loathing after Peter had tortured him, that was all that the letter had said.

And that was what they had asked for. The bastards knew about *that*, and they knew about Peter in the mirror in the castle room, they knew about everything and to them Val was just one more tool to use to control him, just one more trick to play. Dink was right, they were the enemy, they loved nothing and cared for nothing and he was not going to do what they wanted, he was damn well not going to do anything for them. He had had only one memory that was safe, one good thing, and those bastards had plowed it into him with the rest of the manure—and so he was finished, he wasn't going to play.

As always the serpent waited in the tower room, unraveling itself from the rug on the floor. But this time Ender didn't grind it underfoot. This time he caught it in his hands, knelt before it, and gently, so gently, brought the snake's gaping mouth to his lips.

And kissed.

He had not meant to do that. He had meant to let the snake bite him on the mouth. Or perhaps he had meant to eat the snake alive, as Peter in the mirror had done, with his bloody chin and the snake's tail dangling from his lips. But he kissed it instead.

And the snake in his hands thickened and bent into another shape. A human shape. It was Valentine, and she kissed him again.

The snake could not be Valentine. He had killed it too often for it to be his sister. Peter had devoured it too often for Ender to bear it that it might have been Valentine all along.

Was this what they planned when they let him read her letter? He didn't care.

She arose from the floor of the tower room and walked to the mirror. Ender made his figure also rise and go with her. They stood before the mirror, where instead of Peter's cruel reflection there stood a dragon and a unicorn. Ender reached out his hand and touched the mirror and so did Valentine; the wall fell open and revealed a great stairway downward, carpeted and lined with shouting, cheering multitudes. Together, arm in arm, he and Valentine walked down the stairs. Tears filled his eyes, tears of relief that at last he had broken free of the room at the End of the World. And because of the tears, he didn't notice that every member of the multitude wore Peter's face. He only knew that wherever he went in this world, Valentine was with him.

Valentine opened the letter that Dr. Lineberry had given her. "Dear Valentine," it said, "We thank you and commend you for your efforts on behalf of the war effort. You are hereby notified that you have been awarded the Star of the Order of the League of Humanity, First Class, which is the highest military award that can be give to a civilian. Unfortunately, I.F. security forbids us to make this award public until after the successful conclusion of current operations, but we want you to know that your efforts resulted in complete success. Sincerely, General Shimon Levy, Strategos."

When she had read it twice, Dr. Lineberry took it from her hands. "I was instructed to let you read it, and then destroy it." She took a cigarette lighter from a drawer and set the paper afire. It burned brightly in the ashtray. "Was it good or bad news?" she asked.

"I sold my brother," Valentine said, "and they paid me for it."

"That's a bit melodramatic, isn't it, Valentine?"

Valentine went back to class without answering. That night Demosthenes published a scathing denunciation of the population limitation laws. People should be allowed to have as many children as they like, and the surplus population should be sent to other worlds, to spread mankind so far across the galaxy that no disaster, no invasion could ever threaten the human race with annihilation. "The most noble title any child can have," Demosthenes wrote, "is Third."

For you, Ender, she said to herself as she wrote.

Peter laughed in delight when he read it. "That'll make them sit up and take notice. Third! A noble title! Oh, you have a wicked streak."

10

DRAGON

"Now?"

"I suppose so."

"It has to be an order, Colonel Graff. Armies don't move because a commander says 'I suppose it's time to attack.'"

"I'm not a commander. I'm a teacher of little children."

"Colonel, sir, I admit I was on you, I admit I was a pain in the ass, but it worked, everything worked just like you wanted it to. The last few weeks Ender's even been, been—"

"Happy."

"Content. He's doing well. His mind is keen, his play is excellent. Young as he is, we've never had a boy better prepared for command. Usually they go at eleven, but at nine and a half he's top flight."

"Well, yes. For a few minutes there, it actually occurred to me to wonder what kind of a man would heal a broken child of some of his hurt, just so he could throw him back into battle again. A little private moral dilemma. Please overlook it. I was tired."

"Saving the world, remember?"

"Call him in."

"We're doing what must be done, Colonel Graff."

"Come on, Anderson, you're just dying to see how he handles all those rigged games I had you work out."

"That's a pretty low thing to—"

"So I'm a low kind of guy. Come on, Major. We're both the scum of the earth. I'm dying to see how he handles them, too. After all, our lives depend on him doing real well. Neh?"

"You're not starting to use the boys' slang, are you?"

"Call him in, Major. I'll dump the rosters into his files and give him his security system. What we're doing to him isn't all bad, you know. He gets his privacy again."

"Isolation, you mean."

"The loneliness of power. Go call him in."

"Yes sir. I'll be back with him in fifteen minutes."

"Good-bye. Yes sir yessir yezzir. I hope you had fun, I hope you had a nice, nice time being happy, Ender. It might be the last time in your life. Welcome, little boy. Your dear Uncle Graff has plans for you."

Ender knew what was happening from the moment they brought him in. Everyone expected him to go commander early. Perhaps not *this* early, but he had topped the standings almost continuously for three years, no one else was remotely close to him, and his evening practices had become the most prestigious group in the school. There were some who wondered why the teachers had waited this long.

He wondered which army they'd give him. Three commanders were graduating soon, including Petra, but it was beyond hope for them to give him Phoenix Army—no one ever succeeded to command of the same army he was in when he was promoted.

Anderson took him first to his new quarters. That sealed it—only commanders had private rooms. Then he had him fitted for new uniforms and a new flash suit. He looked on the forms to discover the name of his army.

Dragon, said the form. There was no Dragon Army.

"I've never heard of Dragon Army," Ender said.

"That's because there hasn't been a Dragon Army in four years. We discontinued the name because there was a superstition about it. No Dragon Army in the history of the Battle School ever won even a third of its games. It got to be a joke."

"Well, why are you reviving it now?"

"We had a lot of extra uniforms to use up."

Graff sat at his desk, looking fatter and wearier than the last time Ender had seen him. He handed Ender his hook, the small box that allowed commanders to go where they wanted in the battleroom during practices. Some said they worked magnetically, some said it was gravity. Many times during his evening practice sessions Ender had wished that he had a hook, instead of having to rebound off walls to get where he wanted to go. Now that he'd got quite deft at maneuvering without one, here it was. "It only works," Anderson pointed out, "during your regularly scheduled practice sessions." Since Ender already planned to have extra practices, it meant the hook would only be useful some of the time. It also explained why so many commanders never held extra practices. They depended on the hook, and it wouldn't do anything for them during the extra times. If they felt that the hook was their authority, their power over the other boys, then they were even less likely to work without it. That's an advantage I'll have over some of my enemies, Ender thought.

Graff's official welcome speech sounded bored and over-rehearsed. Only at the end did he begin to sound interested in his own words. "We're doing something unusual with Dragon Army. I hope you don't mind. We've assembled a new army by advancing the equivalent of an entire launch course early and delaying the graduation of quite a few advanced students. I think you'll be pleased with the quality of your soldiers. I hope you are, because we're forbidding you to transfer any of them."

"No trades?" asked Ender. It was how commanders always shored up their weak points, by trading around.

"None. You see, you've been conducting your extra practice sessions for three years now. You have a following. Many good soldiers would put unfair pressure on their commanders to trade them into your army. We've given you an army that can, in time, be competitive. We have no intention of letting you dominate unfairly."

"What if I've got a soldier I just can't get along with?"

"Get along with him." Graff closed his eyes, Anderson stood up and the interview was over.

Dragon was assigned the colors grey, orange, grey; Ender changed into his flash suit, then followed the ribbons of light until he came to the barracks that contained his army. They were there already, milling around near the entrance. Ender took charge at once. "Bunking will be arranged by seniority. Veterans to the back of the room, newest soldiers to the front."

It was the reverse of the usual pattern, and Ender knew it. He also knew that he didn't intend to be like many commanders, who never even saw the younger boys because they were always in the back.

As they sorted themselves out according to their arrival dates, Ender walked up and down the aisle. Almost thirty of his soldiers were new, straight out of their launch group, completely inexperienced in battle. Some were even underage—the ones nearest the door were pathetically small. Ender reminded himself that that's how he must have looked to Bonzo Madrid when he first arrived. Still, Bonzo had had only one underage soldier to cope with.

Not one of the veterans belonged to Ender's elite practice group. None had ever been a toon leader. None, in fact, was older than Ender himself, which meant that even his veterans didn't have more than eighteen months' experience. Some he didn't even recognize, they had made so little impression.

They recognized Ender, of course, since he was the most celebrated soldier in the school. And some, Ender could see, resented him. At least they did me one favor—none of my soldiers is older than me.

As soon as each soldier had a bunk, Ender ordered them to put on their flash suits and come to practice. "We're on the morning schedule, straight to practice after breakfast. Officially you have a free hour between breakfast and practice. We'll see what happens after I find out how good you are." After three minutes, though many of them still weren't dressed, he ordered them out of the room.

"But I'm naked!" said one boy.

"Dress faster next time. Three minutes from first call to running out the door—that's the rule this week. Next week the rule is two minutes. Move!" It would soon be a joke in the rest of the school that Dragon Army was so dumb they had to practice getting dressed.

Five of the boys were completely naked, carrying their flash suits as they ran through the corridors; few were fully dressed. They attracted a lot of attention as they passed open classroom doors. No one would be late again if he could help it.

In the corridors leading to the battleroom, Ender made them run back and forth in the halls, fast, so they were sweating a little, while the naked ones got dressed. Then he led them to the upper door, the one that opened into the middle of the battleroom just like the doors in the actual games. Then he made them jump up and use the ceiling handholds to hurl themselves into the room. "Assemble on the far wall," he said. "As if you were going for the enemy's gate."

They revealed themselves as they jumped, four at a time, through the door. Almost none of them knew how to establish a direct line to the target, and when they reached the far wall few of the new ones had any idea how to catch on or even control their rebounds.

The last boy out was a small kid, obviously underage. There was no way he was going to reach the ceiling handhold.

"You can use a side handhold if you want," Ender said.

"Go suck on it," said the boy. He took a flying leap, touched the ceiling handhold with a finger tip, and hurtled through the door with no control at all, spinning in three directions at once. Ender tried to decide whether to like the little kid for refusing to take a concession or to be annoyed at his insubordinate attitude.

They finally got themselves together along the wall. Ender noticed that without exception they had lined up with their heads still in the direction that had been up in the corridor. So Ender deliberately took hold of what they were treating as a floor and dangled from it upside down. "Why are you upside down, soldier?" he demanded.

Some of them started to turn the other way.

"Attention!" They held still. "I said why are you upside down!"

No one answered. They didn't know what he expected.

"I said why does every one of you have his feet in the air and his head toward the ground!"

Finally one of them spoke. "Sir, this is the direction we were in coming out of the door."

"Well what difference is that supposed to make! What difference does it make what the gravity was back in the corridor! Are we going to fight in the corridor? Is there any gravity here?"

No sir. No *sir*.

"From now on, you forget about gravity before you go through that door. The old gravity is gone, erased. Understand me? Whatever your gravity is when you get to the door, remember—the enemy's gate is *down*. Your feet are toward the enemy gate. Up is toward your own gate. North is that way, south is that way, east is that way, west is—what way?"

They pointed.

"That's what I expected. The only process you've mastered is the process of elimination, and the only reason you've mastered that is because you can do it in the toilet. What was the circus I saw out here! Did you call that forming up? Did you call that flying? Now everybody, launch and form up on the ceiling! Right now! Move!"

As Ender expected, a good number of them instinctively launched, not toward the wall with the door in it, but toward the wall that Ender had called *north*, the direction that had been up when they were in the corridor. Of course they quickly realized their mistake, but too late—they had to wait to change things until they had rebounded off the north wall.

In the meantime, Ender was mentally grouping them into slow learners and fast learners. The littlest kid, the one who had been last out of the door, was the first to arrive at the correct wall, and he caught himself adroitly. They had been right to advance him. He'd do well. He was also cocky and rebellious, and probably resented the fact that he had been one of the ones Ender had sent naked through the corridors.

"You!" Ender said, pointing at the small one. "Which way is down?"

"Toward the enemy door." The answer was quick. It was also surly, as if to say, OK, OK, now get on with the important stuff.

"Name, kid?"

"This soldier's name is Bean, sir."

"Get that for size or for brains?" The other boys laughed a little. "Well, Bean, you're right onto things. Now listen to me, because this matters. Nobody's going to get through that door without a good chance of getting hit. In the old days, you had ten, twenty seconds before you even had to move. Now if you aren't already streaming out of the door when the enemy comes out, you're frozen. Now, what happens when you're frozen?"

"Can't move," one of the boys said.

"That's what frozen *means*," Ender said. "But what *happens* to you?"

It was Bean, not intimidated at all, who answered intelligently. "You keep going in the direction you started in. At the speed you were going when you were flashed."

"That's true. You five, there on the end, move!" Startled, the boys looked at each other. Ender flashed them all. "The next five, move!"

They moved. Ender flashed them, too, but they kept moving, heading toward the walls. The first five, though, were drifting uselessly near the main group.

"Look at these so-called soldiers," Ender said. "Their commander ordered them to move, and now look at them. Not only are they frozen, they're frozen right here, where they can get in the way. While the others, because they moved when they were ordered, are frozen down there, plugging up the enemy's lanes, blocking the enemy's vision. I imagine that about five of you have understood the point of this. And no doubt Bean is one of them. Right, Bean?"

He didn't answer at first. Ender looked at him until he said, "Right, sir."

"Then what is the point?"

"When you are ordered to move, move fast, so if you get iced you'll bounce around instead of getting in the way of your own army's operations."

"Excellent. At least I have one soldier who can figure things out. " Ender could see resentment growing in the way the other soldiers shifted their weight and glanced at each other, the way they avoided looking at Bean. Why am I doing this? What does this have to do with being a good commander, making one boy the target of all the others? Just because they did it to me, why should I do it to him? Ender wanted to undo his taunting of the boy, wanted to tell the others that the little one needed their help and friendship more than anyone else. But of course Ender couldn't do that. Not on the first day. On the first day even his mistakes had to look like part of a brilliant plan.

Ender hooked himself nearer the wall and pulled one of the boys away from the others. "Keep your body straight," said Ender. He rotated the boy in midair so his feet pointed toward the others. When the boy kept moving his body, Ender flashed him. The others laughed. "How much of his body could you shoot?" Ender asked a boy directly under the frozen soldier's feet.

"Mostly all I can hit is his feet."

Ender turned to the boy next to him. "What about you?"

"I can see his body."

"And you?"

A boy a little farther down the wall answered. "All of him."

"Feet aren't very big. Not much protection." Ender pushed the frozen soldier out of the way. Then he doubled his legs under him, as if he were kneeling in midair, and flashed his own legs. Immediately the legs of his suit went rigid, holding them in that position.

Ender twisted himself in the air, so that he knelt above the other boys.
"What do you see?" he asked.

A lot less, they said.

Ender thrust his gun between his legs. "I can see fine," he said, and pro-
ceeded to flash the boys directly under him. "Stop me!" he shouted. "Try
and flash me!"

They finally did, but not until he had flashed more than a third of them.
He thumbed his hook and thawed himself and every other frozen soldier.
"Now," he said, "which way is the enemy's gate?"

"Down!"

"And what is our attack position?"

Some started to answer with words, but Bean answered by flipping himself
away from the wall with his legs doubled under him, straight toward the
opposite wall, flashing between his legs all the way.

For a moment Ender wanted to shout at him, to punish him; then he
caught himself, rejected the ungenerous impulse. Why should I be so angry
at this little boy? "Is Bean the only one who knows how?" Ender shouted.

Immediately the entire army pushed off toward the opposite wall, kneeling in the air, firing between their legs, shouting at the top of their lungs.
There may be a time, thought Ender, when this is exactly the strategy I'll
need—forty screaming boys in an unbalancing attack.

When they were all at the other side, Ender called for them to attack
him, all at once. Yes, thought Ender. Not bad. They gave me an untrained
army, with no excellent veterans, but at least it isn't a crop of fools. I can
work with this.

When they were assembled again, laughing and exhilarated, Ender began
the real work. He had them freeze their legs in the kneeling position. "Now,
what are your legs good for, in combat?"

Nothing, said some boys.

"Bean doesn't think so," said Ender.

"They're the best way to push off walls."

"Right," Ender said.

The other boys started to complain that pushing off walls was movement,
not combat.

"There is no combat without movement," Ender said. They fell silent and
hated Bean a little more. "Now, with your legs frozen like this, can you
push off walls?"

No one dared answer, for fear they'd be wrong.

"Bean?" asked Ender.

"I've never tried it, but maybe if you faced the wall and doubled over at
the waist—"

"Right but wrong. Watch me. My back's to the wall, legs are frozen.
Since I'm kneeling, my feet are against the wall. Usually, when you push

off you have to push downward, so you string out your body behind you like a string *bean*, right?"

Laughter.

"But with my legs frozen, I use pretty much the same force, pushing downward from the hips and thighs, only now it pushes my shoulders and my feet backward, shoots out my hips, and when I come loose my body's tight, nothing stringing out behind me. Watch this."

Ender forced his hips forward, which shot him away from the wall; in a moment he readjusted his position and was kneeling, legs downward, rushing toward the opposite wall. He landed on his knees, flipped over on his back, and jackknifed off the wall in another direction. "Shoot me!" he shouted. Then he set himself spinning in the air as he took a course roughly parallel to the boys along the far wall. Because he was spinning, they couldn't get a continuous beam on him.

He thawed his suit and hooked himself back to them. "That's what we're working on for the first half hour today. Build up some muscles you didn't know you had. Learn to use your legs as a shield and control your movements so you can get that spin. Spinning doesn't do any good up close, but far away, they can't hurt you if you're spinning—at that distance the beam has to hit the same spot for a couple of moments, and if you're spinning it can't happen. Now freeze yourself and get started."

"Aren't you going to assign lanes?" asked a boy.

"No I'm not going to assign lanes. I want you bumping into each other and learning how to deal with it all the time, except when we're practicing formations, and then I'll usually have you bump into each other on purpose. Now move!"

When he said *move*, they moved.

Ender was the last one out after practice, since he stayed to help some of the slower ones improve on technique. They'd had good teachers, but the inexperienced soldiers fresh out of their launch groups were completely helpless when it came to doing two or three things at the same time. It was fine to practice jackknifing with frozen legs, they had no trouble maneuvering in midair, but to launch in one direction, fire in another, spin twice, rebound with a jackknife off a wall, and come out firing, facing the right direction—that was way beyond them. Drill drill drill, that was all Ender would be able to do with them for a while. Strategies and formations were nice, but they were nothing if the soldiers didn't know how to handle themselves in battle.

He had to get this army ready *now*. He was early at being a commander, and the teachers were changing the rules now, not letting him trade, giving him no top-notch veterans. There was no guarantee that they'd give him the usual three months to get his army together before sending them into battle.

At least in the evenings he'd have Alai and Shen to help him train his new boys.

He was still in the corridor leading out of the battleroom when he found himself face to face with little Bean. Bean looked angry. Ender didn't want problems right now.

"Ho, Bean."

"Ho, Ender."

Pause.

"*Sir*," Ender said softly.

"I know what you're doing, Ender, sir, and I'm warning you."

"Warning me?"

"I can be the best man you've got, but don't play games with me."

"Or what?"

"Or I'll be the worst man you've got. One or the other."

"And what do you want, love and kisses?" Ender was getting angry now. Bean looked unworried. "I want a toon."

Ender walked back to him and stood looking down into his eyes. "Why should you get a toon?"

"Because I'd know what to do with it."

"Knowing what to do with a toon is easy," Ender said. "It's getting them to do it that's hard. Why would any soldier want to follow a little pinprick like you?"

"They used to call *you* that, I hear. I hear Bonzo Madrid still does."

"I asked you a question, soldier."

"I'll earn their respect, sir, if you don't stop me."

Ender grinned. "I'm helping you."

"Like hell," said Bean.

"Nobody would notice you, except to feel sorry for the little kid. But I made sure they *all* noticed you today. They'll be watching every move you make. All you have to do to earn their respect now is be perfect."

"So I don't even get a chance to learn before I'm being judged."

"Poor kid. Nobody's treatin' him fair." Ender gently pushed Bean back against the wall. "I'll tell you how to get a toon. Prove to me you know what you're doing as a soldier. Prove to me you know how to use other soldiers. And then prove to me that somebody's willing to follow you into battle. Then you'll get your toon. But not bloody well until."

Bean smiled. "That's fair. *If* you actually work that way, I'll be a toon leader in a month."

Ender reached down and grabbed the front of his uniform and shoved him into the wall. "When I say I work a certain way, Bean, then that's the way I work."

Bean just smiled. Ender let go of him and walked away. When he got to his room he lay down on his bed and trembled. What am I doing? My first practice session, and I'm already bullying people the way Bonzo did. And Peter. Shoving people around. Picking on some poor little kid so the others'll have somebody they all hate. Sickening. Everything I hated in a commander, and I'm doing it.

Is it some law of human nature that you inevitably become whatever your first commander was? I can quit right now, if that's so.

Over and over he thought of the things he did and said in his first practice with his new army. Why couldn't he talk like he always did in his evening practice group? No authority except excellence. Never had to give orders, just made suggestions. But that wouldn't work, not with an army. His informal practice group didn't have to learn to do things together. They didn't have to develop a group feeling; they never had to learn how to hold together and trust each other in battle. They didn't have to respond instantly to commands.

And he could go to the other extreme, too. He could be as lax and incompetent as Rose the Nose, if he wanted. He could make stupid mistakes no matter what he did. He had to have discipline, and that meant demanding—and getting—quick, decisive obedience. He had to have a well-trained army, and that meant drilling the soldiers over and over again, long after they thought they had mastered a technique, until it was so natural to them that they didn't have to think about it anymore.

But what was this thing with Bean? Why had he gone for the smallest, weakest, and possibly the brightest of the boys? Why had he done to Bean what had been done to Ender by commanders that he despised?

Then he remembered that it hadn't begun with his commanders. Before Rose and Bonzo treated him with contempt, he had been isolated in his launch group. And it wasn't Bernard who began that, either. It was Graff.

It was the teachers who had done it. And it wasn't an accident. Ender realized that now. It was a strategy. Graff had deliberately set him up to be separate from the other boys, made it impossible for him to be close to them. And he began now to suspect the reasons behind it. It wasn't to unify the rest of the group—in fact, it was divisive. Graff had isolated Ender to make him struggle. To make him prove, not that he was competent, but that he was far better than everyone else. That was the only way he could win respect and friendship. It made him a better soldier than he would ever have been otherwise. It also made him lonely, afraid, angry, untrusting. And maybe those traits, too, made him a better soldier.

That's what I'm doing to you, Bean. I'm hurting you to make you a better soldier in every way. To sharpen your wit. To intensify your effort. To keep you off balance, never sure what's going to happen next, so you always have to be ready for anything, ready to improvise, determined to win no matter what. I'm also making you miserable. That's why they brought you to me, Bean. So you could be just like me. So you could grow up to be just like the old man.

And me—am I supposed to grow up like Graff? Fat and sour and unfeeling, manipulating the lives of little boys so they turn out factory perfect, generals and admirals ready to lead the fleet in defense of the homeland? You get all the pleasures of the puppeteer. Until you get a soldier who can do more than anyone else. You can't have that. It spoils the symmetry. You must get him in line, break him down, isolate him, beat him until he gets in line with everyone else.

Well, what I've done to you this day, Bean, I've done. But I'll be watching you, more compassionately than you know, and when the time is right you'll find that I'm your friend, and you are the soldier you want to be.

Ender did not go to classes that afternoon. He lay on his bunk and wrote down his impressions of each of the boys in his army, the things he noticed right about them, the things that needed more work. In practice tonight, he would talk with Alai and they'd figure out ways to teach small groups the things they needed to know. At least he wouldn't be in this thing alone.

But when Ender got to the battleroom that night, while most others were still eating, he found Major Anderson waiting for him. "There has been a rule change, Ender. From now on, only members of the same army may work together in a battleroom during freetime. And, therefore, battlerooms are available only on a scheduled basis. After tonight, your next turn is in four days."

"Nobody else is holding extra practices."

"They are now, Ender. Now that you command another army, they don't want their boys practicing with you. Surely you can understand that. So they'll conduct their own practices."

"I've always been in another army from them. They still sent their soldiers to me for training."

"You weren't commander then."

"You gave me a completely green army, Major Anderson, sir— "

"You have quite a few veterans."

"They aren't any good."

"Nobody gets here without being brilliant, Ender. Make them good."

"I needed Alai and Shen to—"

"It's about time you grew up and did some things on your own, Ender. You don't need these other boys to hold your hand. You're a commander now. So kindly act like it, Ender."

Ender walked past Anderson toward the battleroom. Then he stopped, turned, asked a question. "Since these evening practices are now regularly scheduled, does it mean I can use the hook?"

Did Anderson almost smile? No. Not a chance of that. "We'll see," he said.

Ender turned his back and went on into the battleroom. Soon his army arrived, and no one else; either Anderson waited around to intercept anyone coming to Ender's practice group, or word had already passed through the whole school that Ender's informal evenings were through.

It was a good practice, they accomplished a lot, but at the end of it Ender was tired and lonely. There was a half hour before bedtime. He couldn't go into his army's barracks—he had long since learned that the best commanders stay away unless they have some reason to visit. The boys have to have a chance to be at peace, at rest, without someone listening, to favor or despise them depending on the way they talk and act and think.

So he wandered to the game room, where a few other boys were using the last half hour before final bell to settle bets or beat their previous scores on the games. None of the games looked interesting, but he played one anyway, an easy animated game designed for Launchies. Bored, he ignored the objectives of the game and used the little player-figure, a bear, to explore the animated scenery around him.

"You'll never win that way."

Ender smiled, "Missed you at practice, Alai."

"*I* was there. But they had your army in a separate place. Looks like you're big time now, can't play with the little boys anymore."

"You're a full cubit taller than I am."

"Cubit! Has God been telling you to build a boat or something? Or are you in an archaic mood?"

"Not archaic, just arcane. Secret, subtle, roundabout. I miss you already, you circumcised dog."

"Don't you know? We're enemies now. Next time I meet you in battle, I'll whip your ass."

It was banter, as always, but now there was too much truth behind it. Now when Ender heard Alai talk as if it were all a joke, he felt the pain of losing his friend, and the worse pain of wondering if Alai really felt as little pain as he showed.

"You can try," said Ender. "I taught you everything you know. But I didn't teach you everything *I* know."

"I knew all along that you were holding something back, Ender."

A pause. Ender's bear was in trouble on the screen. He climbed a tree. "I wasn't, Alai. Holding anything back."

"I know," said Alai. "Neither was I."

"Salaam, Alai."

"Alas, it is not to be."

"What isn't?"

"Peace. It's what *salaam* means. Peace be unto you."

The words brought forth an echo from Ender's memory. His mother's voice reading to him softly, when he was very young. Think not that I am come to bring peace on earth. I came not to bring peace, but a sword. Ender had pictured his mother piercing Peter the Terrible with a bloody rapier, and the words had stayed in his mind along with the image.

In the silence, the bear died. It was a cute death, with funny music. Ender turned around. Alai was already gone. Ender felt as if part of himself had been taken away, an inward prop that was holding up his courage and confidence. With Alai, to a degree impossible even with Shen, Ender had come to feel a unity so strong that the word *we* came to his lips much more easily than *I*.

But Alai had left something behind. Ender lay in bed, dozing into the night, and felt Alai's lips on his cheek as he muttered the word *peace*. The kiss, the word, the peace were with him still. I am only what I remember, and Alai is my friend in a memory so intense that they can't tear him out. Like Valentine, the strongest memory of all.

The next day he passed Alai in the corridor, and they greeted each other, touched hands, talked, but they both knew that there was a wall now. It might be breached, that wall, sometime in the future, but for now the only real conversation between them was the roots that had already grown low and deep, under the wall, where they could not be broken.

The most terrible thing, though, was the fear that the wall could never be breached, that in his heart Alai was glad of the separation, and was ready to be Ender's enemy. For now that they could not be together, they must be infinitely apart, and what had been sure and unshakable was now fragile and insubstantial; from the moment we are not together, Alai is a stranger, for he has a life now that will be no part of mine, and that means that when I see him we will not know each other.

It made him sorrowful, but Ender did not weep. He was done with that. When they had turned Valentine into a stranger, when they had used her as a tool to work on Ender, from that day forward they could never hurt him deep enough to make him cry again. Ender was certain of that.

And with that anger, he decided he was strong enough to defeat them—the teachers, his enemies.

11

VENI VIDI VICI

"You can't be serious about this schedule of battles."

"Yes I can."

"He's only had his army three and a half weeks."

"I told you. We did computer simulations on probable results. And here is what the computer estimated Ender would do."

"We want to teach him, not give him a nervous breakdown."

"The computer knows him better than we do."

"The computer is also not famous for having mercy."

"If you wanted to be merciful, you should have gone to a monastery."

"You mean this *isn't* a monastery?"

"This is best for Ender, too. We're bringing him to his full potential."

"I thought we'd give him two years as commander. We usually give them a battle every two weeks, starting after three months. This is a little extreme."

"Do we *have* two years to spare?"

"I know. I just have this picture of Ender a year from now. Completely useless, worn out, because he was pushed farther than he or any living person could go."

"We told the computer that our highest priority was having the subject remain useful after the training program."

"Well, as long as he's useful—"

"Look, Colonel Graff, you're the one who made me prepare this, over my protests, if you'll remember."

"I know, you're right, I shouldn't burden you with my conscience. But my eagerness to sacrifice little children in order to save mankind is wearing thin. The Polemarch has been to see the Hegemon. It seems Russian intelligence is concerned that some of the active citizens on the nets are already figuring how America ought to use the I.F. to destroy the Warsaw Pact as soon as the buggers are destroyed."

"Seems premature."

"It seems insane. Free speech is one thing, but to jeopardize the League over nationalistic rivalries—and it's for people like that, short-sighted, suicidal people, that we're pushing Ender to the edge of human endurance."

"I think you underestimate Ender."

"But I fear that I also underestimate the stupidity of the rest of mankind. Are we absolutely sure that we ought to win this war?"

"Sir, those words sound like treason."

"It was black humor."

"It wasn't funny. When it comes to the buggers, nothing—"

"Nothing is funny, I know."

Ender Wiggin lay on his bed staring at the ceiling. Since becoming commander, he never slept more than five hours a night. But the lights went off at 2200 and didn't come on again until 0600. Sometimes he worked at his desk, anyway, straining his eyes to use the dim display. Usually, though, he stared at the invisible ceiling and thought.

Either the teachers had been kind to him after all, or he was a better commander than he thought. His ragged little group of veterans, utterly without honor in their previous armies, were blossoming into capable leaders. So much so that instead of the usual four toons, he had created five, each with a toon leader and a second; every veteran had a position. He had the army drill in eight-man toon maneuvers and four-man half-toons, so that at a single command, his army could be assigned as many as ten separate maneuvers and carry them out at once. No army had ever fragmented itself like that before, but Ender was not planning to do anything that had been done before, either. Most armies practiced mass maneuvers, preformed strategies. Ender had none. Instead he trained his toon leaders to use their small units effectively in achieving limited goals. Unsupported, alone, on their own initiative. He staged mock wars after the first week, savage affairs in the practice room that left everybody exhausted. But he knew, with less than a month of training, that his army had the potential of being the best fighting group ever to play the game.

How much of this did the teachers plan? Did they know they were giving him obscure but excellent boys? Did they give him thirty Launchies, many of them underage, because they knew the little boys were quick learners, quick thinkers? Or was this what any similar group could become under a commander who knew what he wanted his army to do, and knew how to teach them to do it?

The question bothered him, because he wasn't sure whether he was con-founding or fulfilling their expectations.

All he was sure of was that he was eager for battle. Most armies needed three months because they had to memorize dozens of elaboration forma-tions. We're ready now. Get us into battle.

The door opened in darkness. Ender listened. A shuffling step. The door closed.

He rolled off his bunk and crawled in the darkness the two meters to the door. There was a slip of paper there. He couldn't read it, of course, but he knew what it was. Battle. How kind of them. I wish, and they deliver.

Ender was already dressed in his Dragon Army flash suit when the lights came on. He ran down the corridor at once, and by 0601 he was at the door of his army's barracks.

"We have a battle with Rabbit Army at 0700. I want us warmed up in gravity and ready to go. Strip down and get to the gym. Bring your flash suits and we'll go to the battleroom from there."

What about breakfast?

"I don't want anybody throwing up in the battleroom."

Can we at least take a leak first?

"No more than a decaliter."

They laughed. The ones who didn't sleep naked stripped down; everyone bundled up their flash suits and followed Ender at a jog through the corri-dors to the gym. He put them through the obstacle course twice, then split them into rotations on the tramp, the mat, and the bench. "Don't wear yourselves out, just wake yourselves up." He didn't need to worry about exhaustion. They were in good shape, light and agile, and above all excited about the battle to come. A few of them spontaneously began to wres-tle—the gym, instead of being tedious, was suddenly fun, because of the battle to come. Their confidence was the supreme confidence of those who have never been in the contest, and think they are ready. Well, why shouldn't they think so? They are. And so am I.

At 0640 he had them dress out. He talked to the toon leaders and their seconds while they dressed. "Rabbit Army is mostly veterans, but Carn Carby was made their commander only five months ago, and I never fought them under him. He was a pretty good soldier, and Rabbit has done fairly well in the standings over the years. But I expect to see formations, and so I'm not worried."

At 0650 he made them all lie down on the mats and relax. Then, at 0656, he ordered them up and they jogged along the corridor to the battleroom. Ender occasionally leaped up to touch the ceiling. The boys all jumped to touch the same spot on the ceiling. Their ribbon of color led to the left; Rabbit Army had already passed through to the right. And at 0658 they reached their gate to the battleroom.

The toons lined up in five columns. A and E were ready to grab the side handholds and flip themselves out toward the sides. B and D lined up to catch the two parallel ceiling holds and flip upward into null gravity. C toon were ready to slap the sill of the doorway and flip downward.

Up, down, left, right; Ender stood at the front, between columns so he'd be out of the way, and reoriented them. "Which way is the enemy's gate?"

Down, they all said, laughing. And in that moment *up* became north, *down* became south, and *left* and *right* became east and west.

The grey wall in front of them disappeared, and the battleroom was visible. It wasn't a dark game, but it wasn't a bright one either—the lights were about half, like dusk. In the distance, in the dim light, he could see the enemy door, their lighted flash suits already pouring out. Ender knew a moment's pleasure. Everyone had learned the wrong lesson from Bonzo's misuse of Ender Wiggin. They all dumped through the door immediately, so that there was no chance to do anything other than name the formation they would use. Commanders didn't have time to think. Well, Ender would take the time, and trust his soldiers' ability to fight with flashed legs to keep them intact as they came late through the door.

Ender sized up the shape of the battleroom. The familiar open grid of most early games, like the monkey bars at the park, with seven or eight stars scattered through the grid. There were enough of them, and in forward enough positions, that they were worth going for. "Spread to the near stars," Ender said. "C try to slide the wall. If it works, A and E will follow. If it doesn't, I'll decide from there. I'll be with D. Move."

All the soldiers knew what was happening, but tactical decisions were entirely up to the toon leaders. Even with Ender's instructions, they were only ten seconds late getting through the gate. Rabbit Army was already doing some elaborate dance down at the end of the room. In all the other armies Ender had fought in, he would have been worrying right now about making sure he and his toon were in their proper place in their own formation. Instead, he and all his men were only thinking of ways to slip around past the formation, control the stars and the corners of the room, and then break the enemy formation into meaningless chunks that didn't know what they were doing. Even with less than four weeks together, the way they fought already seemed like the only intelligent way, the only *possible* way. Ender was almost surprised that Rabbit Army didn't know already that they were hopelessly out of date.

C toon slipped along the wall, coasting with their bent knees facing the enemy. Crazy Tom, the leader of C toon, had apparently ordered his men to flash their own legs already. It was a pretty good idea in this dim light, since the lighted flash suits went dark wherever they were frozen. It made them less easily visible. Ender would commend him for that.

Rabbit Army was able to drive back C toon's attack, but not until Crazy Tom and his boys had carved them up, freezing a dozen Rabbits before retreating to the safety of a star. But it was a star behind the Rabbit formation, which meant they were going to be easy pickings now.

Han Tzu, commonly called Hot Soup, was the leader of D toon. He slid quickly along the lip of the star to where Ender knelt. "How about flipping off the north wall and kneeling on their faces?"

"Do it," Ender said. "I'll take B south to get behind them." Then he shouted, "A and E slow on the walls!" He slid footward along the star, hooked his feet on the lip, and flipped himself up to the top wall, then rebounded down to E toon's star. In a moment he was leading them down against the south wall. They rebounded in near perfect unison and came up behind the two stars that Carn Carby's soldiers were defending. It was like cutting butter with a hot knife. Rabbit Army was gone, just a little cleanup left to do. Ender broke his toons up into half-toons to scour the corners for any enemy soldiers who were whole or merely damaged. In three minutes his toon leaders reported the room clean. Only one of Ender's boys was completely frozen—one of C toon, which had borne the brunt of the assault—and only five were disabled. Most were damaged, but those were leg shots and many of them were self-inflicted. All in all, it had gone even better than Ender expected.

Ender had his toon leaders do the honors at the gate—four helmets at the corners, and Crazy Tom to pass through the gate. Most commanders took whoever was left alive to pass the gate; Ender could have picked practically anyone. A good battle.

The lights went full, and Major Anderson himself came through the teachergate at the south end of the battleroom. He looked very solemn as he offered Ender the teacher hook that was ritually given to the victor in the game. Ender used it to thaw his own army's flash suits, of course, and he assembled them in toons before thawing the enemy. Crisp, military appearance, that's what he wanted when Carby and Rabbit Army got their bodies under control again. They may curse us and lie about us, but they'll remember that we destroyed them, and no matter what they say other soldiers and other commanders will see that in their eyes; in those Rabbit eyes, they'll see us in neat formation, victorious and almost undamaged in our first battle. Dragon Army isn't going to be an obscure name for long.

Carn Carby came to Ender as soon as he was unfrozen. He was a twelve-year-old, who had apparently made commander only in his last year at the school. So he wasn't cocky, like the ones who made it at eleven. I will remember this, thought Ender, when I am defeated. To keep dignity, and give honor where it's due, so that defeat is not disgrace. And I hope I don't have to do it often.

Anderson dismissed Dragon Army last, after Rabbit Army had straggled through the door that Ender's boys had come through. Then Ender led his army through the enemy's door. The light along the bottom of the door reminded them of which way was down once they got back to gravity. They all landed lightly on their feet, running. They assembled in the corridor. "It's 0715," Ender said, "and that means you have fifteen minutes for breakfast before I see you all in the battleroom for the morning practice." He could hear them silently saying, Come on, we won, let us celebrate. All right, Ender answered, you may. "And you have your commander's permission to throw food at each other during breakfast."

They laughed, they cheered, and then he dismissed them and sent them jogging on to the barracks. He caught his toon leaders on the way out and told them that he wouldn't expect anyone to come to practice till 0745, and that practice would be over early so the boys could shower. Half an hour for breakfast, and no shower right after a battle—it was still stingy, but it would look lenient compared to fifteen minutes. And Ender liked having the announcement of the extra fifteen minutes come from the toon leaders. Let the boys learn that leniency comes from their toon leaders, and harshness from their commander—it will bind them better in the small, tight knots of this fabric.

Ender ate no breakfast. He wasn't hungry. Instead he went to the bathroom and showered, putting his flash suit in the cleaner so it would be ready when he was dried off. He washed himself twice and let the water run and run on him. It would all be recycled. Let everybody drink some of my sweat today. They had given him an untrained army, and he had won, and not just nip and tuck, either. He had won with only six frozen or disabled. Let's see how long other commanders keep using their formations now that they've seen what a flexible strategy can do.

He was floating in the middle of the battleroom when his soldiers began to arrive. No one spoke to him, of course. He would speak, they knew, when he was ready, and not before.

When all were there, Ender hooked himself near them and looked at them, one by one. "Good first battle," he said, which was excuse enough for a cheer, and an attempt to start a chant of Dragon, Dragon, which he quickly stopped. "Dragon Army did all right against Rabbits. But the enemy isn't always going to be that bad. If that had been a good army, C toon, your approach was so slow they would have had you from the flanks before you got into good position. You should have split and angled in from two directions, so they couldn't flank you. A and E, your aim was wretched. The tallies show that you averaged only one hit for every two soldiers. That means most of the hits were made by attacking soldiers close in. That can't go on—a competent enemy would cut up the assault force unless they have much better cover from the soldiers at a distance. I want every toon to work on distance marksmanship at moving and unmoving targets. Half-toons take turns being targets. I'll thaw the flash suits every three minutes. Now move."

"Will we have any stars to work with?" asked Hot Soup. "To steady our aim?"

"I don't want you to get used to having something to steady your arms. If your arm isn't steady, freeze your elbows! Now move!"

The toon leaders quickly got things going, and Ender moved from group to group to make suggestions and help soldiers who were having particular trouble. The soldiers knew by now that Ender could be brutal in the way he talked to groups, but when he worked with an individual he was always patient, explaining as often as necessary, making suggestions quietly, listening to questions and problems and explanations. But he never laughed when they tried to banter with him, and they soon stopped trying. He was commander every moment they were together. He never had to remind them of it; he simply *was*.

They worked all day with the taste of victory in their mouths, and cheered again when they broke half an hour early for lunch. Ender held the toon leaders until the regular lunch hour, to talk about the tactics they had used and evaluate the work of their individual soldiers. Then he went to his own room and methodically changed into his uniform for lunch. He would enter the commanders' mess about ten minutes late. Exactly the timing that he wanted. Since this was his first victory, he had never seen the inside of the commanders' mess hall and had no idea what new commanders were expected to do, but he did know that he wanted to enter last today, when the scores of the morning's battles were already posted. Dragon Army will not be an obscure name now.

There was no great stir when he came in. But when some of them noticed how small he was, and saw the dragons on the sleeves of the uniform, they stared at him openly, and by the time he got his food and sat at a table, the room was silent. Ender began to eat, slowly and carefully, pretending not to notice that he was the center of attention. Gradually conversation and noise started up again, and Ender could relax enough to look around.

One entire wall of the room was a scoreboard. Soldiers were kept aware of an army's overall record for the past two years; in here, however, records were kept for each commander. A new commander couldn't inherit a good standing from his predecessor—he was ranked according to what he had done.

Ender had the best ranking. A perfect won-lost record, of course, but in the other categories he was far ahead. Average soldiers-disabled, average enemy-disabled, average time-elapsed-before-victory—in every category he was ranked first.

When he was nearly through eating, someone came up behind him and touched his shoulder.

"Mind if I sit?" Ender didn't have to turn around to know it was Dink Meeker.

"Ho Dink," said Ender. "Sit."

"You gold-plated fart," said Dink cheerfully. "We're all trying to decide whether your scores up there are a miracle or a mistake."

"A habit," said Ender.

"One victory is not a habit," Dink said. "Don't get cocky. When you're new they seed you against weak commanders."

"Carn Carby isn't exactly on the bottom of the rankings." It was true. Carby was just about in the middle.

"He's OK," Dink said, "considering that he only just started. Shows some promise. You don't show promise. You show threat."

"Threat to what? Do they feed you less if I win? I thought you told me this was all a stupid game and none of it mattered."

Dink didn't like having his words thrown back at him, not under these circumstances. "You were the one who got me playing along with them. But I'm not playing games with you, Ender. You won't beat *me*."

"Probably not," Ender said.

"I taught you," Dink said.

"Everything I know," said Ender. "I'm just playing it by ear right now."

"Congratulations," said Dink.

"It's good to know I have a friend here." But Ender wasn't sure Dink was his friend anymore. Neither was Dink. After a few empty sentences, Dink went back to his table.

Ender looked around when he was through with his meal. There were quite a few small conversations going on. Ender spotted Bonzo, who was now one of the oldest commanders. Rose the Nose had graduated. Petra was with a group in a far corner, and she didn't look at him once. Since most of the others stole glances at him from time to time, including the ones Petra was talking with, Ender was pretty sure she was deliberately avoiding his glance. That's the problem with winning right from the start, thought Ender. You lose friends.

Give them a few weeks to get used to it. By the time I have my next battle, things will have calmed down in here.

Carn Carby made a point of coming to greet Ender before the lunch period ended. It was, again, a gracious gesture, and, unlike Dink, Carby did not seem wary. "Right now I'm in disgrace," he said frankly. "They won't believe me when I tell them you did things that nobody's ever seen before. So I hope you beat the snot out of the next army you fight. As a favor to me."

"As a favor to you," Ender said. "And thanks for talking to me."

"I think they're treating you pretty badly. Usually new commanders are cheered when they first join the mess. But then, usually a new commander has had a few defeats under his belt before he first makes it in here. I only got in here a month ago. If anybody deserves a cheer, it's you. But that's life. Make them eat dust."

"I'll try." Carn Carby left, and Ender mentally added him to his private list of people who also qualified as human beings.

That night, Ender slept better than he had in a long time. Slept so well, in fact, that he didn't wake up until the lights came on. He woke up feeling good, jogged on out to take his shower, and did not notice the piece of paper on his floor until he came back and started dressing in his uniform. He only saw the paper because it moved in the wind as he snapped out the uniform to put it on. He picked up the paper and read it.

PETRA ARKANIAN, PHOENIX ARMY, 0700

It was his old army, the one he had left less than four weeks before, and he knew their formations backward and forward. Partly because of Ender's influence, they were the most flexible of armies, responding relatively quickly to new situations. Phoenix Army would be the best able to cope with Ender's fluid, unpatterned attack. The teachers were determined to make life interesting for him.

0700, said the paper, and it was already 0630. Some of his boys might already be heading for breakfast. Ender tossed his uniform aside, grabbed his flash suit, and in a moment stood in the doorway of his army's barracks.

"Gentlemen, I hope you learned something yesterday, because today we're doing it again."

It took a moment for them to realize that he meant a battle, not a practice. It had to be a mistake, they said. Nobody ever had battles two days in a row.

He handed the paper to Fly Molo, the leader of A toon, who immediately shouted "Flash suits" and started changing clothes.

"Why didn't you tell us earlier?" demanded Hot Soup. Hot had a way of asking Ender questions that nobody else dared ask.

"I thought you needed the shower," Ender said. "Yesterday Rabbit Army claimed we only won because the stink knocked them out."

The soldiers who heard him laughed.

"Didn't find the paper till you got back from the showers, right?"

Ender looked for the source of the voice. It was Bean, already in his flash suit, looking insolent. Time to repay old humiliations, is that it, Bean?

"Of course," Ender said, contemptuously. "I'm not as close to the floor as you are."

More laughter. Bean flushed with anger.

"It's plain we can't count on old ways of doing things," Ender said. "So you'd better plan on battles anytime. And often. I can't pretend I like the way they're screwing around with us, but I do like one thing—that I've got an army that can handle it."

After that, if he had asked them to follow him to the moon without space suits, they would have done it.

Petra was not Carn Carby; she had more flexible patterns and responded much more quickly to Ender's darting, improvised, unpredictable attack. As a result, Ender had three boys flashed and nine disabled at the end of the battle. Petra was not gracious about bowing over his hand at the end, either. The anger in her eyes seemed to say, I was your friend, and you humiliate me like this?

Ender pretended not to notice her fury. He figured that after a few more battles, she'd realize that in fact she had scored more hits against him than he expected anyone ever would again. And he was still learning from her. In practice today he would teach his toon leaders how to counter the tricks Petra had played on them. Soon they would be friends again.

He hoped.

At the end of the week Dragon Army had fought seven battles in seven days. The score stood 7 wins and 0 losses. Ender had never had more losses than in the battle with Phoenix Army, and in two battles he had suffered not one soldier frozen or disabled. No one believed anymore that it was a fluke that put him first in the standings. He had beaten top armies by un-heard-of margins. It was no longer possible for the other commanders to ignore him. A few of them sat with him at every meal, carefully trying to learn from him how he had defeated his most recent opponents. He told them freely, confident that few of them would know how to train their sol-diers and their toon leaders to duplicate what his could do. And while Ender talked with a few commanders, much larger groups gathered around the opponents Ender had defeated, trying to find out how Ender might be beaten.

There were many, too, who hated him. Hated him for being young, for being excellent, for having made their victories look paltry and weak. Ender saw it first in their faces when he passed them in the corridors; then he began to notice that some boys would get up in a group and move to another table if he sat near them in the commanders' mess; and there began to be elbows that accidently jostled him in the game room, feet that got entangled with his when he walked into and out of the gym, spittle and wads of wet paper that struck him from behind as he jogged through the corridors. They couldn't beat him in the battleroom, and knew it—so instead they would attack him where it was safe, where he was not a giant but just a little boy. Ender despised them—but secretly, so secretly that he didn't even know it himself, he feared them. It was just such little torments that Peter had al-ways used, and Ender was beginning to feel far too much at home.

These annoyances were petty, though, and Ender persuaded himself to accept them as another form of praise. Already the other armies were begin-ning to imitate Ender. Now most soldiers attacked with knees tucked under them; formations were breaking up now, and more commanders were send-ing out toons to slip along the walls. None had caught on yet to Ender's five-toon organization—it gave him the slight advantage that when they had accounted for the movements of four units, they wouldn't be looking for a fifth.

Ender was teaching them all about null gravity tactics. But where could Ender go to learn new things?

He began to use the video room, filled with propaganda vids about Mazer Rackham and other great commanders of the forces of humanity in the First and Second Invasion. Ender stopped the general practice an hour early, and allowed his toon leaders to conduct their own practice in his absence. Usually they staged skirmishes, toon against toon. Ender stayed long enough to see that things were going well, then left to watch the old battles.

Most of the vids were a waste of time. Heroic music, closeups of commanders and medal-winning soldiers, confused shots of marines invading bugger installations. But here and there he found useful sequences: ships, like points of light, maneuvering in the dark of space, or, better still, the lights on shipboard plotting screens, showing the whole of a battle. It was hard, from the videos, to see all three dimensions, and the scenes were often short and unexplained. But Ender began to see how well the buggers used seemingly random flight paths to create confusion, how they used decoys and false retreats to draw the I.F. ships into traps. Some battles had been cut into many scenes, which were scattered through the various videos; by watching them in sequence, Ender was able to reconstruct whole battles. He began to see things that the official commentators never mentioned. They were always trying to arouse pride in human accomplishments and loathing of the buggers, but Ender began to wonder how humanity had won at all. Human ships were sluggish; fleets responded to new circumstances unbearably slowly, while the bugger fleet seemed to act in perfect unity, responding to each challenge instantly. Of course, in the First Invasion the human ships were completely unsuited to fast combat, but then so were the bugger ships; it was only in the Second Invasion that the ships and weapons were swift and deadly.

So it was from the buggers, not the humans, that Ender learned strategy. He felt ashamed and afraid of learning from them, since they were the most terrible enemy, ugly and murderous and loathsome. But they were also very good at what they did. To a point. They always seemed to follow one basic strategy only—gather the greatest number of ships at the key point of conflict. They never did anything surprising, anything that seemed to show either brilliance or stupidity in a subordinate officer. Discipline was apparently very tight.

And there was one oddity. There was plenty of talk about Mazer Rackham but precious little video of his actual battle. Some scenes from early in the battle, Rackham's tiny force looking pathetic against the vast power of the main bugger fleet. The buggers had already beaten the main human fleet out in the comet shield, wiping out the earliest starships and making a mockery of human attempts at high strategy—that film was often shown, to arouse again and again the agony and terror of bugger victory. Then the fleet coming to Mazer Rackham's little force near Saturn, the hopeless odds, and then—

Then one shot from Mazer Rackham's little cruiser, one enemy ship blowing up. That's all that was ever shown. Lots of film showing marines carving their way into bugger ships. Lots of bugger corpses lying around inside. But no film of buggers killing in personal combat, unless it was spliced in from the First Invasion. It frustrated Ender that Mazer Rackham's victory was so obviously censored. Students in the Battle School had much to learn from Mazer Rackham, and everything about his victory was concealed from view. The passion for secrecy was not very helpful to the children who had to learn to accomplish again what Mazer Rackham had done.

Of course, as soon as word got around that Ender Wiggin was watching the war vids over and over again, the video room began to draw a crowd. Almost all were commanders, watching the same vids Ender watched, pretending they understood why he was watching and what he was getting out of it. Ender never explained anything. Even when he showed seven scenes from the same battle, but from different vids, only one boy asked, tentatively, "Are some of those from the same battle?"

Ender only shrugged, as if it didn't matter.

It was during the last hour of practice on the seventh day, only a few hours after Ender's army had won its seventh battle, that Major Anderson himself came into the video room. He handed a slip of paper to one of the commanders sitting there, and then spoke to Ender. "Colonel Graff wishes to see you in his office immediately."

Ender got up and followed Anderson through the corridors. Anderson palmed the locks that kept students out of the officers' quarters; finally they came to where Graff had taken root on a swivel chair bolted to the steel floor. His belly spilled over both armrests now, even when he sat upright. Ender tried to remember. Graff hadn't seemed particularly fat at all when Ender first met him, only four years ago. Time and tension were not being kind to the administrator of the Battle School.

"Seven days since your first battle, Ender," said Graff.

Ender did not reply.

"And you've won seven battles, once a day."

Ender nodded.

"Your scores are unusually high, too."

Ender blinked.

"To what, commander, do you attribute your remarkable success?"

"You gave me an army that does whatever I can think for it to do."

"And what have you thought for it to do?"

"We orient downward toward the enemy gate and use our lower legs as a shield. We avoid formations and keep our mobility. It helps that I've got five toons of eight instead of four of ten. Also, our enemies haven't the time to respond effectively to our new techniques, so we keep beating them with the same tricks. That won't hold up for long."

"So you don't expect to keep winning."

"Not with the same tricks."

Graff nodded. "Sit down, Ender."

Ender and Anderson both sat. Graff looked at Anderson, and Anderson spoke next. "What condition is your army in, fighting so often?"

"They're all veterans now."

"But how are they doing? Are they tired?"

"If they are, they won't admit it."

"Are they still alert?"

"You're the ones with the computer games that play with people's minds. You tell *me*."

"We know what *we* know. We want to know what *you* know."

"These are very good soldiers, Major Anderson. I'm sure they have limits, but we haven't reached them yet. Some of the newer ones are having trouble because they never really mastered some basic techniques, but they're working hard and improving. What do you want me to say, that they need to rest? Of course they need to rest. They need a couple of weeks off. Their studies are shot to hell, none of us are doing any good in our classes. But you know that, and apparently you don't care, so why should I?"

Graff and Anderson exchanged glances. "Ender, why are you studying the videos of the bugger wars?"

"To learn strategy, of course."

"Those videos were created for propaganda purposes. All our strategies have been edited out."

"I know."

Graff and Anderson exchanged glances again. Graff drummed on his table. "You don't play the fantasy game anymore," he said.

Ender didn't answer.

"Tell me why you don't play it."

"Because I won."

"You never win *everything* in that game. There's always more."

"I won."

"Ender, we want to help you be as happy as possible, but if you—"

"You want to make me the best soldier possible. Go down and look at the standings. Look at the all-time standings. So far you're doing an excellent job with me. Congratulations. Now when are you going to put me up against a good army?"

Graff's set lips turned to a smile, and he shook a little with silent laughter.

Anderson handed Ender a slip of paper. "Now," he said.

BONZO MADRID, SALAMANDER ARMY, 1200

"That's ten minutes from now," said Ender. "My army will be in the middle of showering up after practice."

Graff smiled, "Better hurry, then, boy."

He got to his army's barracks five minutes later. Most were dressing after their showers; some had already gone to the game room or the video room to wait for lunch. He sent three younger boys to call everyone in, and made everyone else dress for battle as quickly as they could.

"This one's hot and there's no time," Ender said. "They gave Bonzo notice about twenty minutes ago, and by the time we get to the door they'll have been inside for a good five minutes at least."

The boys were outraged, complaining loudly in the slang that they usually avoided around the commander. What they doing to us? They be crazy, neh?

"Forget why, we'll worry about that tonight. Are you tired?"

Fly Molo answered. "We worked our butts off in practice today. Not to mention beating the crap out of Ferret Army this morning."

"Same day nobody ever do two battles!" said Crazy Tom.

Ender answered in the same tone. "Nobody ever beat Dragon Army, either. This be your big chance to lose?" Ender's taunting question was the answer to their complaints. Win first, ask questions later.

All of them were back in the room, and most of them were dressed. "Move!" shouted Ender, and they ran along behind him, some of them still dressing when they reached the corridor outside the battleroom. Many of them were panting, a bad sign; they were too tired for this battle. The door was already open. There were no stars at all. Just empty, empty space in a dazzlingly bright room. Nowhere to hide, not even in darkness.

"My heart," said Crazy Tom, "they haven't come out yet, either."

Ender put his hand across his own mouth, to tell them to be silent. With the door open, of course the enemy could hear every word they said. Ender pointed all around the door, to tell them that Salamander Army was undoubtedly deployed against the wall all around the door, where they couldn't be seen but could easily flash anyone who came out.

Ender motioned for them all to back away from the door. Then he pulled forward a few of the taller boys, including Crazy Tom, and made them kneel, not squatting back to sit on their heels, but fully upright, so they formed an L with their bodies. He flashed them. In silence the army watched him. He selected the smallest boy, Bean, handed him Tom's gun, and made Bean kneel on Tom's frozen legs. Then he pulled Bean's hands, each holding a gun, through Tom's armpits.

Now the boys understood. Tom was a shield, an armored spacecraft, and Bean was hiding inside. He was certainly not invulnerable, but he would have time.

Ender assigned two more boys to throw Tom and Bean through the door, but signalled them to wait. He went on through the army, quickly assigning groups of four—a shield, a shooter, and two throwers. Then, when all were frozen or armed or ready to throw, he signalled the throwers to pick up their burdens, throw them through the door, and then jump through themselves.

"Move!" shouted Ender.

They moved. Two at a time the shield-pairs went through the door, backward so that the shield would be between the shooter and the enemy. The enemy opened fire at once, but they mostly hit the frozen boy in front. In the meantime, with two guns to work with and their targets neatly lined up and spread flat along the wall, the Dragons had an easy time of it. It was almost impossible to miss. And as the throwers also jumped through the door, they got handholds on the same wall with the enemy, shooting at a deadly angle so that the Salamanders couldn't figure out whether to shoot at the shield-pairs slaughtering them from above or the throwers shooting at them from their own level. By the time Ender himself came through the door, the battle was over. It hadn't taken a full minute from the time the first Dragon passed through the door until the shooting stopped. Dragon had lost twenty frozen or disabled, and only twelve boys were undamaged. It was their worst score yet, but they had won.

When Major Anderson came out and gave Ender the hook, Ender could not contain his anger. "I thought you were going to put us against an army that could match us in a fair fight."

"Congratulations on the victory, commander."

"Bean!" shouted Ender. "If you had commanded Salamander Army, what would you have done?"

Bean, disabled but not completely frozen, called out from where he drifted near the enemy door. "Keep a shifting pattern of movement going in front of the door. You never hold still when the enemy knows exactly where you are."

"As long as you're cheating," Ender said to Anderson, "why don't you train the other army to cheat intelligently!"

"I suggest that you remobilize your army," said Anderson.

Ender pressed the buttons to thaw both armies at once. "Dragon Army dismissed!" he shouted immediately. There would be no elaborate formation to accept the surrender of the other army. This had not been a fair fight, even though they had won—the teachers had meant them to lose, and it was only Bonzo's ineptitude that had saved them. There was no glory in *that*.

Only as Ender himself was leaving the battleroom did he realize that Bonzo would not realize that Ender was angry at the teachers. Spanish honor. Bonzo would only know that he had been defeated even when the odds were stacked in his favor; that Ender had had the youngest child in his army publicly state what Bonzo should have done to win; and that Ender had not even stayed to receive Bonzo's dignified surrender. If Bonzo had not already hated Ender, he would surely have begun; and hating him as he did, this would surely turn his rage murderous. Bonzo was the last person to strike me, thought Ender. I'm sure he has not forgotten that.

Nor had he forgotten the bloody affair in the battleroom when the older boys tried to break up Ender's practice session. Nor had many others. They were hungry for blood then; Bonzo will be thirsting for it now. Ender toyed with the idea of taking advanced personal defense; but with battles now possible not only every day, but twice in the same day, Ender knew he could not spare the time. I'll have to take my chances. The teachers got me into this—they can keep me safe.

Bean flopped down on his bunk in utter exhaustion—half the boys in the barracks were already asleep, and it was still fifteen minutes before lights out. Wearily he pulled his desk from its locker and signed on. There was a test tomorrow in geometry and Bean was woefully unprepared. He could always reason things out if he had enough time, and he had read Euclid when he was five, but the test had a time limit so there wouldn't be a chance to think. He had to know. And he didn't know. And he would probably do badly on the test. But they had won twice today, and so he felt good.

As soon as he signed on, however, all thoughts of geometry were banished. A message paraded around the desk:

SEE ME AT ONCE—ENDER

The time was 2150, only ten minutes before lights out. How long ago had Ender sent it? Still, he'd better not ignore it. There might be another battle in the morning—the thought made him weary—and whatever Ender wanted to talk to him about, there wouldn't be time then. So Bean rolled off the bunk and walked emptily through the corridor to Ender's room. He knocked.

"Come in," said Ender.

"Just saw your message."

"Fine," said Ender.

"It's near lights out."

"I'll help you find your way in the dark."

"I just didn't know if you knew what time it was—"

"I always know what time it is."

Bean sighed inwardly. It never failed. Whenever he had any conversation with Ender, it turned into an argument. Bean hated it. He recognized Ender's genius and honored him for it. Why couldn't Ender ever see anything good in him?

"Remember four weeks ago, Bean? When you told me to make you a toon leader?"

"Eh."

"I've made five toon leaders and five assistants since then. And none of them was you." Ender raised his eyebrows. "Was I right?"

"Yes, sir."

"So tell me how you've done in these eight battles."

"Today was the first time they disabled me, but the computer listed me as getting eleven hits before I had to stop. I've never had less than five hits in a battle. I've also completed every assignment I've been given."

"Why did they make you a soldier so young, Bean?"

"No younger than you were."

"But why?"

"I don't know."

"Yes you do, and so do I."

"I've tried to guess, but they're just guesses. You're—very good. They knew that, they pushed you ahead—"

"Tell me *why*, Bean."

"Because they need us, that's why." Bean sat down on the floor and stared at Ender's feet. "Because they need somebody to beat the buggers. That's the only thing they care about."

"It's important that you know that, Bean. Because most boys in this school think the game is important *for itself*, but it isn't. It's only important because it helps them find kids who might grow up to be real commanders, in the real war. But as for the game, screw that. That's what they're doing. Screwing up the game."

"Funny. I thought they were just doing it to us."

"A game nine weeks earlier than it should have come. A game every day. And now two games in the same day. Bean, I don't know what the teachers are doing, but my army is getting tired, and I'm getting tired, and they don't care at all about the rules of the game. I've pulled the old charts up from the computer. No one has ever destroyed so many enemies and kept so many of his own soldiers whole in the history of the game."

"You're the best, Ender."

Ender shook his head. "Maybe. But it was no accident that I got the soldiers I got. Launchies, rejects from other armies, but put them together and my worst soldier could be a toon leader in another army. They've loaded things my way, but now they're loading it all against me. Bean, they want to break us down."

"They can't break you."

"You'd be surprised." Ender breathed sharply, suddenly, as if there were a stab of pain, or he had to catch a sudden breath in a wind; Bean looked at him and realized that the impossible was happening. Far from baiting him, Ender Wiggin was actually confiding in him. Not much. But a little. Ender was human and Bean had been allowed to see.

"Maybe you'll be surprised," said Bean.

ORSON SCOTT CARD   140

"There's a limit to how many clever new ideas I can come up with every day. Somebody's going to come up with something to throw at me that I haven't thought of before, and I won't be ready."

"What's the worst that could happen? You lose one game."

"Yes. That's the worst that could happen. I can't lose *any* games. Because if I lose *any*—"

He didn't explain himself, and Bean didn't ask.

"I need you to be clever, Bean. I need you to think of solutions to problems we haven't seen yet. I want you to try things that no one has ever tried because they're absolutely stupid."

"Why me?"

"Because even though there are some better soldiers than you in Dragon Army—not many, but some—there's nobody who can think better and faster than you." Bean said nothing. They both knew it was true.

Ender showed him his desk. On it were twelve names. Two or three from each toon. "Choose five of these," said Ender. "One from each toon. They're a special squad, and you'll train them. Only during the extra practice sessions. Talk to me about what you're training them to do. Don't spend too long on any one thing. Most of the time you and your squad will be part of the whole army, part of your regular toons. But when I need you. When there's something to be done that only you can do."

"These are all new," said Bean. "No veterans."

"After last week, Bean, all our soldiers are veterans. Don't you realize that on the individual soldier standings, all forty of our soldiers are in the top fifty? That you have to go down seventeen places to find a soldier who *isn't* a Dragon?"

"What if I can't think of anything?"

"Then I was wrong about you."

Bean grinned. "You weren't wrong."

The lights went out.

"Can you find your way back, Bean?"

"Probably not."

"Then stay here. If you listen very carefully, you can hear the good fairy come in the night and leave our assignment for tomorrow."

"They won't give us another battle tomorrow, will they?"

Ender didn't answer. Bean heard him climb into bed. He got up from the floor and did likewise. He thought of a half dozen ideas before he went to sleep. Ender would be pleased—every one of them was stupid.

12

BONZO

"General Pace, please sit down. I understand you have come to me about a matter of some urgency."

"Ordinarily, Colonel Graff, I would not presume to interfere in the internal workings of the Battle School. Your autonomy is guaranteed, and despite our difference in ranks I am quite aware that it is my authority only to advise, not to order you to take action."

"Action?"

"Do not be disingenuous with me, Colonel Graff. Americans are quite apt at playing stupid when they choose to, but I am not to be deceived. You know why I am here."

"Ah. I guess this means Dap filed a report."

"He feels—paternal toward the students here. He feels your neglect of a potentially lethal situation is more than negligence—that it borders on conspiracy to cause the death or serious injury of one of the students here."

"This is a school for children, General Pace. Hardly a matter to bring the chief of I.F. military police here for."

"Colonel Graff, the name of Ender Wiggin has percolated through the high command. It has even reached my ears. I have heard him described modestly as our only hope of victory in the upcoming invasion. When it is his life or health that is in danger, I do not think it untoward that the military police take some interest in preserving and protecting the boy. Do you?"

"Damn Dap and damn you too, sir, I know what I'm doing."

"Do you?"

"Better than anyone else."

"Oh, that is obvious, since nobody else has the faintest idea what you're doing. You have known for eight days that there is a conspiracy among some of the more vicious of these 'children' to cause the beating of Ender Wiggin, if they can. And that some members of this conspiracy, notably the boy named Bonito de Madrid, commonly called Bonzo, are quite likely to exhibit no self-restraint when this punishment takes place, so that Ender Wiggin, an inestimably important international resource, will be placed in serious danger of having his brains pasted on the walls of your orbiting schoolhouse. And you, fully warned of this danger, propose to do exactly—"

"Nothing."

"You can see how this excites our puzzlement."

"Ender Wiggin has been in this situation before. Back on Earth, the day he lost his monitor, and again when a large group of older boys—"

"I did not come here ignorant of the past. Ender Wiggin has provoked Bonzo Madrid beyond human endurance. And you have no military police standing by to break up disturbances. It is unconscionable."

"When Ender Wiggin holds our fleets in his control, when he must make the decisions that bring us victory or destruction, will there be military police to come save him if things get out of hand?"

"I fail to see the connection."

"Obviously. But the connection is there. Ender Wiggin must believe that no matter what happens, no adult will ever, ever step in to help him in any way. He must believe, to the core of his soul, that he can only do what he and the other children work out for themselves. If he does not believe that, then he will never reach the peak of his abilities."

"He will also not reach the peak of his abilities if he is dead or permanently crippled."

"He won't be."

"Why don't you simply graduate Bonzo? He's old enough."

"Because Ender knows that Bonzo plans to kill him. If we transfer Bonzo ahead of schedule, he'll know that we saved him. Heaven knows Bonzo isn't a good enough commander to be promoted on merit."

"What about the other children? Getting them to help him?"

"We'll see what happens. That is my first, final, and only decision."

"God help you if you're wrong."

"God help us all if I'm wrong."

"I'll have you before a capital court martial. I'll have your name disgraced throughout the world if you're wrong."

"Fair enough. But do remember, if I happen to be right, to make sure I get a few dozen medals."

"For what!"
"For keeping you from meddling."

Ender sat in a corner of the battleroom, his arm hooked through a hand-hold, watching Bean practice with his squad. Yesterday they had worked on attacks without guns, disarming enemies with their feet. Ender had helped them with some techniques from gravity personal combat—many things had to be changed, but inertia in flight was a tool that could be used against the enemy as easily in nullo as in Earth gravity.

Today, though, Bean had a new toy. It was a deadline, one of the thin, almost invisible twines used during construction in space to hold two objects together. Deadlines were sometimes kilometers long. This one was just a bit longer than a wall of the battleroom, and yet it looped easily, almost invisibly, around Bean's waist. He pulled it off like an article of clothing and handed one end to one of his soldiers. "Hook it to a handhold and wind it around a few times." Bean carried the other end across the battleroom.

As a tripwire it wasn't too useful, Bean decided. It was invisible enough, but one strand of twine wouldn't have much chance of stopping an enemy that could easily go above or below it. Then he got the idea of using it to change his direction of movement in midair. He fastened it around his waist, the other end still fastened to a handhold, slipped a few meters away, and launched himself straight out. The twine caught him, changed his direction abruptly, and swung him in an arc that crashed him brutally against the wall.

He screamed and screamed. It took Ender a moment to realize that he wasn't screaming in pain. "Did you see how fast I went! Did you see how I changed direction!"

Soon all of Dragon Army stopped work to watch Bean practice with the twine. The changes in direction were stunning, especially when you didn't know where to look for the twine. When he used the twine to wrap himself around a star, he attained speeds no one had ever seen before.

It was 2140 when Ender dismissed the evening practice. Weary but delighted at having seen something new, his army walked through the corridors back to the barracks. Ender walked among them, not talking, but listening to their talk. They were tired, yes—a battle every day for more than four weeks, often in situations that tested their abilities to the utmost. But they were proud, happy, close—they had never lost, and they had learned to trust each other. They trusted their fellow soldiers to fight hard and well; trusted their leaders to use them rather than waste their efforts; above all trusted Ender to prepare them for anything and everything that might happen.

As they walked the corridor, Ender noticed several older boys seemingly engaged in conversations in branching corridors and ladderways; some were in their corridor, walking slowly in the other direction. It became too much of a coincidence, however, that so many of them were wearing Salamander uniforms, and that those who weren't were often older boys belonging to armies whose commanders most hated Ender Wiggin. A few of them looked at him, and looked away too quickly; others were too tense, too nervous as they pretended to be relaxed. What will I do if they attack my army here in the corridor? My boys are all young, all small, and completely untrained in gravity combat. When would they learn?

"Ho, Ender!" someone called. Ender stopped and looked back. It was Petra. "Ender, can I talk to you."

Ender saw in a moment that if he stopped and talked, his army would quickly pass him by and he would be alone with Petra in the hallway. "Walk with me," Ender said.

"It's just for a moment."

Ender turned around and walked on with his army. He heard Petra running to catch up. "All right, I'll walk with you," Ender tensed when she came near. Was she one of them, one of the ones who hated him enough to hurt him?

"A friend of yours wanted me to warn you. There are some boys who want to kill you."

"Surprise," said Ender. Some of his soldiers seemed to perk up at this. Plots against their commander were interesting news, it seemed.

"Ender, they can do it. He said they've been planning it ever since you went commander—"

"Ever since I beat Salamander, you mean."

"I hated you after you beat Phoenix Army, too, Ender."

"I didn't say I blamed anybody."

"It's true. He told me to take you aside today and warn you, on the way back from the battleroom, to be careful tomorrow because—"

"Petra, if you had actually taken me aside just now, there are about a dozen boys following along who would have taken me in the corridor. Can you tell me you didn't notice them?"

Suddenly her face flushed. "No, I didn't. How can you think I did? Don't you know who your friends are?" She pushed her way through Dragon Army, got ahead of him, and scrambled up a ladderway to a higher deck.

"Is it true?" asked Crazy Tom.

"Is what true?" Ender scanned the room and shouted for two roughhousing boys to get to bed.

"That some of the older boys want to kill you?"

"All talk," said Ender. But he knew that it wasn't. Petra had known something, and what he saw on the way here tonight wasn't imagination.

"It may be all talk, but I hope you'll understand when I say you've got five toon leaders who are going to escort you to your room tonight."

"Completely unnecessary."

"Humor us. You owe us a favor."

"I owe you nothing." He'd be a fool to turn them down. "Do as you want." He turned and left. The toon leaders trotted along with him. One ran ahead and opened his door. They checked the room, made Ender promise to lock it, and left him just before lights out.

There was a message on his desk.

DON'T BE ALONE. EVER. —DINK

Ender grinned. So Dink was still his friend. Don't worry. They won't do anything to me. I have my army.

But in the darkness he did not have his army. He dreamed that night of Stilson, only he saw now how small Stilson was, only six years old, how ridiculous his tough-guy posturing was; and yet in the dream Stilson and his friends tied Ender so he couldn't fight back, and then everything that Ender had done to Stilson in life, they did to Ender in the dream. And afterward Ender saw himself babbling like an idiot, trying hard to give orders to his army, but all his words came out as nonsense.

He awoke in darkness, and he was afraid. Then he calmed himself by remembering that the teachers obviously valued him, or they wouldn't be putting so much pressure on him; they wouldn't let anything happen to him, nothing bad, anyway. Probably when the older kids attacked him in the battleroom years ago, there were teachers just outside the room, waiting to see what would happen; if things had got out of hand, they would have stepped in and stopped it. I probably could have sat there and done nothing, and they would have seen to it I came through all right. They'll push me as hard as they can in the game, but outside the game they'll keep me safe.

With that assurance, he slept again, until the door opened softly and the morning's war was left on the floor for him to find.

They won, of course, but it was a grueling affair, with the battleroom so filled with a labyrinth of stars that hunting down the enemy during mop-up took forty-five minutes. It was Pol Slattery's Badger Army, and they refused to give up. There was a new wrinkle in the game, too—when they disabled or damaged an enemy, he thawed in about five minutes, the way it worked in practice. Only when the enemy was completely frozen did he stay out of action the whole time. But the gradual thawing did not work for Dragon Army. Crazy Tom was the one who realized what was happening, when they started getting hit from behind by people they thought were safely out of the way. And at the end of the battle, Slattery shook Ender's hand and said, "I'm glad you won. If I ever beat you, Ender, I want to do it fair."

"Use what they give you," Ender said. "If you've ever got an advantage over the enemy, use it."

"Oh, I did," said Slattery. He grinned. "I'm only fair-minded before and after battles."

The battle took so long that breakfast was over. Ender looked at his hot, sweating, tired soldiers waiting in the corridor and said, "Today you know everything. No practice. Get some rest. Have some fun. Pass a test." It was a measure of their weariness that they didn't even cheer or laugh or smile, just walked into the barracks and stripped off their clothes. They would have practiced if he had asked them to, but they were reaching the end of their strength, and going without breakfast was one unfairness too many.

Ender meant to shower right away, but he was also tired. He lay down on his bed in his flash suit, just for a moment, and woke up at the beginning of lunchtime. So much for his idea of studying more about the buggers this morning. Just time to clean up, go eat, and head for class.

He peeled off his flash suit, which stank from his sweat. His body felt cold, his joints oddly weak. Shouldn't have slept in the middle of the day. I'm beginning to slack off. I'm beginning to wear down. Can't let it get to me.

So he jogged to the gym and forced himself to climb the rope three times before going to the bathroom to shower. It didn't occur to him that his absence in the commanders' mess would be noticed, that showering during the noon hour, when his own army would be wolfing down their first meal of the day, he would be completely, helplessly alone.

Even when he heard them come into the bathroom he paid no attention. He was letting the water pour over his head, over his body; the muffled sound of footsteps was hardly noticeable. Maybe lunch was over, he thought. He started to soap himself again. Maybe somebody finished practice late.

And maybe not. He turned around. There were seven of them, leaning back against the metal sinks or standing closer to the showers, watching him. Bonzo stood in front of them. Many were smiling, the condescending leer of the hunter for his cornered victim. Bonzo was not smiling, however.

"Ho," Ender said.

Nobody answered.

So Ender turned off the shower, even though there was still soap on him, and reached for his towel. It wasn't there. One of the boys was holding it. It was Bernard. All it would take for the picture to be complete was for Stilson and Peter to be there, too. They needed Peter's smile; they needed Stilson's obvious stupidity.

Ender recognized the towel as their opening point. Nothing would make him look weaker than to chase naked after the towel. That was what they wanted, to humiliate him, to break him down. He wasn't going to play. He refused to feel weak because he was wet and cold and unclothed. He stood strongly, facing them, his arms at his sides. He fastened his gaze on Bonzo.

"Your move," Ender said.

"This is no game," said Bernard. "We're tired of you, Ender. You graduate today. On ice."

Ender did not look at Bernard. It was Bonzo who hungered for his death, even though he was silent. The others were along for the ride, daring themselves to see how far they might go. Bonzo knew how far he would go.

"Bonzo," Ender said softly. "Your father would be proud of you."

Bonzo stiffened.

"He would love to see you now, come to fight a naked boy in a shower, smaller than you, and you brought six friends. He would say, Oh, what honor."

"Nobody came to fight you," said Bernard. "We just came to talk you into playing fair with the games. Maybe lose a couple now and then."

The others laughed, but Bonzo didn't laugh, and neither did Ender.

"Be proud, Bonito, pretty boy. You can go home and tell your father, Yes, I beat up Ender Wiggin, who was barely ten years old, and I was thirteen. And I had only six of my friends to help me, and somehow we managed to defeat him, even though he was naked and wet and alone—Ender Wiggin is so *dangerous* and *terrifying* it was all we could do not to bring two hundred."

"Shut your mouth, Wiggin," said one of the boys.

"We didn't come to hear the little bastard talk," said another.

"You shut up," said Bonzo. "Shut up and stand out of the way." He began to take off his uniform. "Naked and wet and alone, Ender, so we're even. I can't help that I'm bigger than you. You're such a genius, you figure out how to handle me." He turned to the others. "Watch the door. Don't let anyone else in."

The bathroom wasn't large, and plumbing fixtures protruded everywhere. It had been launched in one piece, as a low-orbit satellite, packed full of the water reclamation equipment; it was designed to have no wasted space. It was obvious what their tactics would have to be. Throw the other boy against fixtures until one of them does enough damage that he stops.

When Ender saw Bonzo's stance, his heart sank. Bonzo had also taken classes. And probably more recently than Ender. His reach was better, he was stronger, and he was full of hate. He would not be gentle. He will go for my head, thought Ender. He will try above all to damage my brain. And if this fight is long, he's bound to win. His strength can control me. If I'm to walk away from here, I have to win quickly, and permanently. He could still feel again the sickening way that Stilson's bones had given way. But this time it will be my body that breaks, unless I can break him first.

Ender stepped back, flipped the showerhead so it turned outward, and turned on pure hot water. Almost at once the steam began to rise. He turned on the next, and the next.

"I'm not afraid of hot water," said Bonzo. His voice was soft.

But it wasn't the hot water that Ender wanted. It was the heat. His body still had soap on it, and his sweat moistened it, made his skin more slippery than Bonzo would expect.

Suddenly there was a voice from the door. "Stop it!" For a moment Ender thought it was a teacher, come to stop the fight, but it was only Dink Meeker. Bonzo's friends caught him at the door, held him. "Stop it, Bonzo!" Dink cried. "Don't hurt him!"

"Why not?" asked Bonzo, and for the first time he smiled. Ah, thought Ender, he loves to have someone recognize that he is the one in control, that he has power.

"Because he's the best, that's why! Who else can fight the buggers! That's what matters, you fool, the buggers!"

Bonzo stopped smiling. It was the thing he hated most about Ender, that Ender really mattered to other people, and, in the end, Bonzo did not. You've killed me with those words, Dink. Bonzo doesn't want to hear that I might save the world.

Where are the teachers? thought Ender. Don't they realize that the first contact between us in this fight might be the end of it? This isn't like the fight in the battleroom, where no one had the leverage to do any terrible damage. There's gravity in here, and the floor and walls are hard and jutted with metal. Stop this now or not at all.

"If you touch him you're a buggerlover!" cried Dink. "You're a traitor, if you touch him you deserve to die!" They jammed Dink's face backward into the door and he was silent.

The mist from the showers dimmed the room, and the sweat was streaming down Ender's body. Now, before the soap is carried off me. Now, while I'm still too slippery to hold.

Ender stepped back, letting the fear he felt show in his face. "Bonzo, don't hurt me," he said. "Please."

It was what Bonzo was waiting for, the confession that he was in power. For other boys it might have been enough that Ender had submitted; for Bonzo, it was only a sign that his victory was sure. He swung his leg as if to kick, but changed it to a leap at the last moment. Ender noticed the shifting weight and stooped lower, so that Bonzo would be more off-balance when he tried to grab Ender and throw him.

Bonzo's tight, hard ribs came against Ender's face, and his hands slapped against his back, trying to grip him. But Ender twisted, and Bonzo's hands slipped. In an instant Ender was completely turned, yet still inside Bonzo's grasp. The classic move at this moment would be to bring up his heel into Bonzo's crotch. But for that move to be effective required too much accuracy, and Bonzo expected it. He was already rising onto his toes, thrusting his hips backward to keep Ender from reaching his groin. Without seeing him, Ender knew it would bring his face closer, almost in Ender's hair; so instead of kicking, he lunged upward off the floor, with the powerful lunge of the soldier bounding from the wall, and jammed his head into Bonzo's face.

Ender whirled in time to see Bonzo stagger backward, his nose bleeding, gasping from surprise and pain. Ender knew that at this moment he might be able to walk out of the room and end the battle.The way he had escaped from the battleroom after drawing blood. But the battle would only be fought again. Again and again until the will to fight was finished. The only way to end things completely was to hurt Bonzo enough that his fear was stronger than his hate.

So Ender leaned back against the wall behind him, then jumped up and pushed off with his arms. His feet landed in Bonzo's belly and chest. Ender spun in the air and landed on his toes and hands; he flipped over, scooted under Bonzo, and this time when he kicked upward into Bonzo's crotch, he connected, hard and sure.

Bonzo did not cry out in pain. He did not react at all, except that his body rose a little in the air. It was as if Ender had kicked a piece of furniture. Bonzo collapsed, fell to the side, and sprawled directly under the spray of steaming water from a shower. He made no movement whatever to escape the murderous heat.

"My God!" someone shouted. Bonzo's friends leaped to turn off the water. Ender slowly rose to his feet. Someone thrust his towel at him. It was Dink. "Come on out of here," Dink said. He led Ender away. Behind them they heard the heavy clatter of adults running down a ladderway. Now the teachers would come. The medical staff. To dress the wounds of Ender's enemy. Where were they before the fight, when there might have been no wounds at all?

There was no doubt now in Ender's mind. There was no help for him. Whatever he faced, now and forever, no one would save him from it. Peter might be scum, but Peter had been right, always right; the power to cause pain is the only power that matters, the power to kill and destroy, because if you can't kill then you are always subject to those who can, and nothing and no one will ever save you.

Dink led him to his room, made him lie on the bed. "Are you hurt anywhere?" he asked.

Ender shook his head.

"You took him apart. I thought you were dead meat, the way he grabbed you. But you took him apart. If he'd stood up longer, you would've killed him."

"He meant to kill me."

"I know it. I know him. Nobody hates like Bonzo. But not anymore. If they don't ice him for this and send him home, he'll never look you in the eye again. You or anybody. He had twenty centimeters on you, and you made him look like a crippled cow standing there chewing her cud."

All Ender could see, though, was the way Bonzo looked as Ender kicked upward into his groin. The empty, dead look in his eyes. He was already finished then. Already unconscious. His eyes were open, but he wasn't thinking or moving anymore, just that dead, stupid look on his face, that terrible look, the way Stilson looked when I finished with him.

"They'll ice him, though," Dink said. "Everybody knows he started it. I saw them get up and leave the commanders' mess. Took me a couple of seconds to realize you weren't there, either, and then a minute more to find out where you had gone. I told you not to be alone."

"Sorry."

"They're bound to ice him. Troublemaker. Him and his stinking honor."

Then, to Dink's surprise, Ender began to cry. Lying on his back, still soaking wet with sweat and water, he gasped his sobs, tears seeping out of his closed eyelids and disappearing in the water on his face.

"Are you all right?"

"I didn't want to hurt him!" Ender cried. "Why didn't he just leave me alone!"

He heard his door open softly, then close. He knew at once that it was his battle instructions. He opened his eyes, expecting to find the darkness of early morning, before 0600. Instead, the lights were on. He was naked, and when he moved the bed was soaking wet. His eyes were puffy and painful from crying. He looked at the clock on his desk. 1820, it said. It's the same day. I already had a battle today, I had two battles today—the bastards know what I've been through, and they're doing this to me.

WILLIAM BEE, GRIFFIN ARMY, TALO MOMOE,
TIGER ARMY, 1900

He sat on the edge of the bed. The note trembled in his hand. I can't do this, he said silently. And then not silently. "I can't do this."

He got up, bleary, and looked for his flash suit. Then he remembered—he had put it in the cleaner while he showered. It was still there.

Holding the paper, he walked out of his room. Dinner was nearly over, and there were a few people in the corridor, but no one spoke to him, just watched him, perhaps in awe of what had happened at noon in the bathroom, perhaps because of the forbidding, terrible look on his face. Most of his boys were in the barracks.

Ho, Ender. There gonna be a practice tonight?

Ender handed the paper to Hot Soup. "Those sons of bitches," he said. "Two at once?"

"Two armies!" shouted Crazy Tom.

"They'll just trip over each other," said Bean.

"I've got to clean up," Ender said. "Get them ready, get everybody together, I'll meet you there, at the gate."

He walked out of the barracks, A tumult of conversation rose behind them. He heard Crazy Tom scream, "Two fart-eating armies! We'll whip their butts!"

The bathroom was empty. All cleaned up. None of the blood that poured from Bonzo's nose into the shower water. All gone. Nothing bad ever happened here.

Ender stepped under the water and rinsed himself, took the sweat of combat and let it run down the drain. All gone, except they recycled it and we'll be drinking Bonzo's bloodwater in the morning. All the life gone out of it, but his blood just the same, his blood and my sweat, washed down in their stupidity or cruelty or whatever it was that made them let it happen.

He dried himself, dressed in his flash suit, and walked to the battleroom. His army was waiting in the corridor, the door still not opened. They watched him in silence as he walked to the front to stand by the blank grey forcefield. Of course they all knew about his fight in the bathroom today; that and their own weariness from the battle that morning kept them quiet, while the knowledge that they would be facing two armies filled them with dread.

Everything they can do to beat me, thought Ender. Everything they can think of, change all the rules, they don't care, just so they beat me. Well, I'm sick of the game. No game is worth Bonzo's blood pinking the water on the bathroom floor. Ice me, send me home, I don't want to play anymore.

The door disappeared. Only three meters out there were four stars together, completely blocking the view from the door.

Two armies weren't enough. They had to make Ender deploy his forces blind.

"Bean," said Ender. "Take your boys and tell me what's on the other side of this star."

Bean pulled the coil of twine from his waist, tied one end around him, handed the other end to a boy in his squad, and stepped gently through the door. His squad quickly followed. They had practiced this several times, and it took only a moment before they were braced on the star, holding the end of the twine. Bean pushed off at great speed, in a line almost parallel to the door; when he reached the corner of the room, he pushed off again and rocketed straight out toward the enemy. The spots of light on the wall showed that the enemy was shooting at him. As the rope was stopped by each edge of the star in turn, his arc became tighter, his direction changed, and he became an impossible target to hit. His squad caught him neatly as he came around the star from the other side. He moved all his arms and legs so those waiting inside the door would know that the enemy hadn't flashed him anywhere.

Ender dropped through the gate.

"It's really dim," said Bean, "but light enough you can't follow people easily by the lights on their suits. Worst possible for seeing. It's all open space from this star to the enemy side of the room. They've got eight stars making a square around their door. I didn't see anybody except the ones peeking around the boxes. They're just sitting there waiting for us."

As if to corroborate Bean's statement, the enemy began to call out to them. "Hey! We be hungry, come and feed us! Your ass is draggin'! Your ass is Dragon!"

Ender's mind felt dead. This was stupid. He didn't have a chance, outnumbered two to one and forced to attack a protected enemy. "In a real war, any commander with brains at all would retreat and save this army."

"What the hell," said Bean. "It's only a game."

"It stopped being a game when they threw away the rules."

"So, you throw 'em away, too."

Ender grinned. "OK. Why not. Let's see how they react to a formation."

Bean was appalled. "A formation! We've never done a formation in the whole time we've been an army!"

"We've still got a month to go before our training period is normally supposed to end. About time we started doing formations. Always have to know formations." He formed an A with his fingers, showed it to the blank door, and beckoned. A toon quickly emerged and Ender began arranging them behind the star. Three meters wasn't enough room to work in, the boys were frightened and confused, and it took nearly five minutes just to get them to understand what they were doing.

Tiger and Griffin soldiers were reduced to chanting catcalls, while their commanders argued about whether to try to use their overwhelming force to attack Dragon Army while they were still behind the star. Momoe was all for attacking—"We outnumber him two to one"— while Bee said, "Sit tight and we can't lose, move out and he can figure out a way to beat us."

So they sat tight, until finally in the dusky light they saw a large mass slip out from behind Ender's star. It held its shape, even when it abruptly stopped moving sideways and launched itself toward the dead center of the eight stars where eighty-two soldiers waited.

"Doobie doo," said a Griffin. "They're doing a formation."

"They must have been putting that together for all five minutes," said Momoe. "If we'd attacked while they were doing it, we could've destroyed them."

"Eat it, Momoe," whispered Bee. "You saw the way that little kid flew. He went all the way around the star and back behind without ever touching a wall. Maybe they've all got hooks, did you think of that? They've got something new there."

The formation was a strange one. A square formation of tightly-packed bodies in front, making a wall. Behind it, a cylinder, six boys in circumference and two boys deep, their limbs outstretched and frozen so they couldn't possibly be holding on to each other. Yet they held together as tightly as if they had been tied—which, in fact, they were.

From inside the formation, Dragon Army was firing with deadly accuracy, forcing Griffins and Tigers to stay tightly packed on their stars.

"The back of that sucker is open," said Bee. "As soon as they get between the stars, we can get around behind—"

"Don't talk about it, do it!" said Momoe. Then he took his own advice
and ordered his boys to launch against the wall and rebound out behind the
Dragon formation.

In the chaos of their takeoff, while Griffin Army held tight to their stars,
the Dragon formation abruptly changed. Both the cylinder and the front
wall split in two, as boys inside it pushed off; almost at once, the formations
also reversed direction, heading back toward the Dragon gate. Most of the
Griffins fired at the formations and the boys moving backward with them;
and the Tigers took the survivors of Dragon Army from behind.

But there was something wrong. William Bee thought for a moment and
realized what it was. Those formations couldn't have reversed direction in
midflight unless someone pushed off in the opposite direction, and if they
took off with enough force to make that twenty-man formation move backward, they must be going *fast*.

There they were, six small Dragon soldiers down near William Bee's own
door. From the number of lights showing on their flash suits, Bee could see
that three of them were disabled and two of them damaged; only one was
whole. Nothing to be frightened of. Bee casually aimed at them, pressed
the button, and—

Nothing happened.

The lights went on.

The game was over.

Even though he was looking right at them, it took Bee a moment to realize what had just happened. Four of the Dragon soldiers had their helmets
pressed on the corners of the door. And one of them had just passed
through. They had just carried out the victory ritual. They were getting
destroyed, they had hardly inflicted any casualties, and they had the gall to
perform the victory and end the game right under their noses.

Only then did it occur to William Bee that not only had Dragon Army
ended the game, it was possible that, under the rules, they had won it. After
all, no matter what happened, you were not certified as the winner unless
you had enough unfrozen soldiers to touch the corners of the gate and pass
someone through into the enemy's corridor. Therefore, by one way of thinking, you could argue that the ending ritual *was* victory. The battleroom certainly recognized it as the end of the game.

The teachergate opened and Major Anderson came into the room. "Ender," he called, looking around.

One of the frozen Dragon soldiers tried to answer him through jaws that
were clamped shut by the flash suit. Anderson hooked over to him and
thawed him.

Ender was smiling. "I beat you again, sir," he said.

"Nonsense, Ender," Anderson said softly. "Your battle was with Griffin and Tiger."

"How stupid do you think I am?" said Ender.

Loudly, Anderson said, "After that little maneuver, the rules are being revised to require that all of the enemy's soldiers must be frozen or disabled before the gate can be reversed."

"It could only work once anyway," Ender said.

Anderson handed him the hook. Ender unfroze everyone at once. To hell with protocol. To hell with everything. "Hey!" he shouted as Anderson moved away. "What is it next time? My army in a cage without guns, with the rest of the Battle School against them? How about a little equality?"

There was a loud murmur of agreement from the other boys, and not all of it came from Dragon Army. Anderson did not so much as turn around to acknowledge Ender's challenge. Finally, it was William Bee who answered. "Ender, if you're on one side of the battle, it won't be equal no matter what the conditions are."

Right! called the boys. Many of them laughed. Talo Momoe began clapping his hands. "Ender Wiggin!" he shouted. The other boys also clapped and shouted Ender's name.

Ender passed through the enemy gate. His soldiers followed him. The sound of them shouting his name followed him through the corridors.

"Practice tonight?" asked Crazy Tom.

Ender shook his head.

"Tomorrow morning then?"

"No."

"Well, when?"

"Never again, as far as I'm concerned."

He could hear the murmurs behind him.

"Hey, that's not fair," said one of the boys. "It's not our fault the teachers are screwing up the game. You can't just stop teaching us stuff because—"

Ender slammed his open hand against the wall and shouted at the boy. "I don't care about the game anymore!" His voice echoed through the corridor. Boys from other armies came to their doors. He spoke quietly into the silence. "Do you understand that?" And he whispered. "The game is over."

He walked back to his room alone. He wanted to lie down, but he couldn't because the bed was wet. It reminded him of all that had happened today, and in fury he tore the mattress and blankets from the bedframe and shoved them out into the corridor. Then he wadded up a uniform to serve as a pillow and lay on the fabric of wires strung across the frame. It was uncomfortable, but Ender didn't care enough to get up.

He had only been there a few minutes when someone knocked on the door.

"Go away," he said softly. Whoever was knocking didn't hear him or didn't care. Finally Ender said to come in.

It was Bean.

"Go away, Bean."

Bean nodded but didn't leave. Instead he looked at his shoes. Ender almost yelled at him, cursed at him, screamed at him to leave. Instead he noticed how very tired Bean looked, his whole body bent with weariness, his eyes dark from lack of sleep; and yet his skin was still soft and translucent, the skin of a child, the soft curved cheek, the slender limbs of a little boy. He wasn't eight years old yet. It didn't matter he was brilliant and dedicated and good. He was a child. He was *young*.

No he isn't, thought Ender. Small, yes. But Bean has been through a battle with a whole army depending on him and on the soldiers that he led, and he performed splendidly, and they won. There's no youth in that. No childhood.

Taking Ender's silence and softening expression as permission to stay, Bean took another step into the room. Only then did Ender see the small slip of paper in his hand.

"You're transferred?" asked Ender. He was incredulous, but his voice came out sounding uninterested, dead.

"To Rabbit Army."

Ender nodded. Of course. It was obvious. If I can't be defeated with my army, they'll take my army away. "Carn Carby's a good man," said Ender. "I hope he recognizes what you're worth."

"Carn Carby was graduated today. He got his notice while we were fighting our battle."

"Well, who's commanding Rabbit then?"

Bean held his hands out helplessly. "Me."

Ender looked at the ceiling and nodded. "Of course. After all, you're only four years younger than the regular age."

"It isn't funny. I don't know what's going on here. All the changes in the game. And now this. I wasn't the only one transferred, you know. They graduated half the commanders, and transferred a lot of our guys to command their armies."

"Which guys?"

"It looks like—every toon leader and every assistant."

"Of course. If they decide to wreck my army, they'll cut it to the ground. Whatever they're doing, they're thorough."

"You'll still win, Ender. We all know that. Crazy Tom, he said, 'You mean I'm supposed to figure out how to beat Dragon Army?' Everybody knows you're the best. They can't break you down, no matter what they—"

"They already have."

"No, Ender, they can't—"

"I don't care about their game anymore, Bean. I'm not going to play it anymore. No more practices. No more battles. They can put their little slips of paper on the floor all they want, but I won't go. I decided that before I went through the door today. That's why I had you go for the gate. I didn't think it would work, but I didn't care. I just wanted to go out in style."

"You should've seen William Bee's face. He just stood there trying to figure out how he had lost when you only had seven boys who could wiggle their toes and he only had three who couldn't."

"Why should I want to see William Bee's face? Why should I want to beat anybody?" Ender pressed his palms against his eyes. "I hurt Bonzo really bad today, Bean. I really hurt him bad."

"He had it coming."

"I knocked him out standing up. It was like he was dead, standing there. And I kept hurting him."

Bean said nothing.

"I just wanted to make sure he never hurt me again."

"He won't," said Bean. "They sent him home."

"Already?"

"The teachers didn't say much, they never do. The official notice says he was graduated, but where they put the assignment—you know, tactical school, support, precommand, navigation, that kind of thing—it just said Cartagena, Spain. That's his home."

"I'm glad they graduated him."

"Hell, Ender, we're just glad he's gone. If we'd known what he was doing to you, we would've killed him on the spot. Was it true he had a whole bunch of guys gang up on you?"

"No. It was just him and me. He fought with honor." If it weren't for his honor, he and the others would have beaten me together. They might have killed me, then. His sense of honor saved my life. "I didn't fight with honor," Ender added. "I fought to win."

Bean laughed. "And you did. Kicked him right out of orbit."

A knock on the door. Before Ender could answer, the door opened. Ender had been expecting more of his soldiers. Instead it was Major Anderson. And behind him came Colonel Graff.

"Ender Wiggin," said Graff.

Ender got to his feet. "Yes sir."

"Your display of temper in the battleroom today was insubordinate and is not to be repeated."

"Yes sir," said Ender.

Bean was still feeling insubordinate, and he didn't think Ender deserved the rebuke. "I think it was about time somebody told a teacher how we felt about what you've been doing."

The adults ignored him. Anderson handed Ender a sheet of paper. A full-sized sheet. Not one of the little slips of paper that served for internal orders within the Battle School; it was a full-fledged set of orders. Bean knew what it meant. Ender was being transferred out of the school.

"Graduated?" asked Bean. Ender nodded. "What took them so long? You're only two or three years early. You've already learned how to walk and talk and dress yourself. What will they have left to teach you?"

Ender shook his head. "All I know is, the game's over." He folded up the paper. "None too soon. Can I tell my army?"

"There isn't time," said Graff. "Your shuttle leaves in twenty minutes. Besides, it's better not to talk to them after you get your orders. It makes it easier."

"For them or for you?" Ender asked. He didn't wait for an answer. He turned quickly to Bean, took his hand for a moment, and then headed for the door.

"Wait," said Bean. "Where are you going? Tactical? Navigational? Support?"

"Command School," Ender answered.

"*Pre*-command?"

"Command," said Ender, and then he was out the door. Anderson followed him closely. Bean grabbed Colonel Graff by the sleeve. "Nobody goes to Command School until they're sixteen!"

Graff shook off Bean's hand and left, closing the door behind him.

Bean stood alone in the room, trying to grasp what this might mean. Nobody went to Command School without three years of Pre-command in either Tactical or Support. But then, nobody left Battle School without at least six years, and Ender had had only four.

The system is breaking up. No doubt about it. Either somebody at the top is going crazy, or something's gone wrong with the war, the real war, the bugger war. Why else would they break down the training system like this, wreck the game the way they did? Why else would they put a little kid like me in command of an army?

Bean wondered about it as he walked back down the corridor to his own bed. The lights went out just as he reached his bunk. He undressed in darkness, fumbling to put his clothing in a locker he couldn't see. He felt terrible. At first he thought he felt bad because he was afraid of leading an army, but it wasn't true. He knew he'd make a good commander. He felt himself wanting to cry. He hadn't cried since the first few days of homesickness after he got here. He tried to put a name on the feeling that put a lump in his throat and made him sob silently, however much he tried to hold it down. He bit down on his hand to stop the feeling, to replace it with pain. It didn't help. He would never see Ender again.

Once he named the feeling, he could control it. He lay back and forced himself to go through the relaxing routine until he didn't feel like crying anymore. Then he drifted off to sleep. His hand was near his mouth. It lay on his pillow hesitantly, as if Bean couldn't decide whether to bite his nails or suck on his fingertips. His forehead was creased and furrowed. His breathing was quick and light. He was a soldier, and if anyone had asked him what he wanted to be when he grew up, he wouldn't have known what they meant.

—

When he was crossing into the shuttle, Ender noticed for the first time that the insignia on Major Anderson's uniform had changed. "Yes, he's a colonel now," said Graff. "In fact, Major Anderson has been placed in command of the Battle School, as of this afternoon. I have been reassigned to other duties."

Ender did not ask him what they were.

Graff strapped himself into a seat across the aisle from him. There was only one other passenger, a quiet man in civilian clothes who was introduced as General Pace. Pace was carrying a briefcase, but Graff carried no more luggage than Ender did. Somehow that was comforting to Ender, that Graff also came away empty.

Ender spoke only once on the voyage home. "Why are we going home?" he asked. "I thought Command School was in the asteroids somewhere."

"It is," said Graff. "But the Battle School has no facilities for docking long-range ships. So you get a short landside leave."

Ender wanted to ask if that meant he could see his family. But suddenly, at the thought that it might be possible, he was afraid, and so he didn't ask. Just closed his eyes and tried to sleep. Behind him, General Pace was studying him; for what purpose, Ender could not guess.

It was a hot summer afternoon in Florida when they landed. Ender had been so long without sunlight that the light nearly blinded him. He squinted and sneezed and wanted to get back indoors. Everything was far away and flat; the ground, lacking the upward curve of Battle School floors, seemed instead to fall away, so that on level ground Ender felt as though he were on a pinnacle. The pull of real gravity felt different and he scuffed his feet when he walked. He hated it. He wanted to go back home, back to the Battle School, the only place in the universe where he belonged.

"Arrested?"

"Well, it's a natural thought. General Pace *is* the head of the military police. There *was* a death in the Battle School."

"They didn't tell me whether Colonel Graff was being promoted or court-martialed. Just transferred, with orders to report to the Polemarch."

"Is that a good sign or bad?"

"Who knows? On the one hand, Ender Wiggin not only survived, he passed a threshold, he graduated in dazzlingly good shape, you have to give old Graff credit for that. On the other hand, there's the fourth passenger on the shuttle. The one traveling in a bag."

"Only the second death in the history of the school. At least it wasn't a suicide this time."

"How is murder better, Major Imbu?"

"It wasn't murder, Colonel. We have it on video from two angles. No one can blame Ender."

"But they might blame Graff. After all this is over, the civilians can rake over our files and decide what was right and what was not. Give us medals where they think we were right, take away our pensions and put us in jail where they decide we were wrong. At least they had the good sense not to tell Ender that the boy died."

"It's the second time, too."

"They didn't tell him about Stilson, either."

"The kid is scary."

"Ender Wiggin isn't a killer. He just wins—thoroughly. If anybody's going to be scared, let it be the buggers."

"Makes you almost feel sorry for them, knowing Ender's going to be coming after them."

"The only one I feel sorry for is Ender. But not sorry enough to suggest they ought to let up on him. I just got access to the material that Graff's been getting all this time. About fleet movements, that sort of thing. I used to sleep easy at night."

"Time's getting short?"

"I shouldn't have mentioned it. I can't tell you secured information."

"I know."

"Let's leave it at this: they didn't get him to Command School a day too soon. And maybe a couple of years too late."

13

VALENTINE

"Children?"

"Brother and sister. They'd layered themselves five times through the nets—writing for companies that paid for their memberships, that sort of thing. Devil of a time tracking them down."

"What are they hiding?"

"Could be anything. The most obvious thing to hide, though, is their ages. The boy is fourteen, the girl is twelve."

"Which one is Demosthenes?"

"The girl. The twelve-year-old."

"Pardon me. I don't really think it's funny, but I can't help but laugh. All this time we've been worried, all the time we've been trying to persuade the Russians not to take Demosthenes too seriously, we held up Locke as proof that Americans weren't all crazy warmongers. Brother and sister, pubescent—"

"And their last name is Wiggin."

"Ah. Coincidence?"

"*The* Wiggin is a third. They are one and two."

"Oh, excellent. The Russians will never believe—"

"That Demosthenes and Locke aren't as much under our control as *the* Wiggin."

"*Is* there a conspiracy? Is someone controlling them?"

"We have been able to detect *no* contact between these two children and any adult who might be directing them."

"That is not to say that someone might not have invented some method you can't detect. It's hard to believe that two children— "

"I interviewed Colonel Graff when he arrived from the Battle School. It is his best judgment that nothing these children have done is out of their reach. Their abilities are virtually identical with—*the* Wiggin. Only their temperaments are different. What surprised him, however, was the orientation of the two personas. Demosthenes is definitely the girl, but Graff says the girl was rejected for Battle School because she was too pacific, too conciliatory, and above all, too empathic."

"Definitely not Demosthenes."

"And the boy has the soul of a jackal."

"Wasn't it Locke that was recently praised as 'The only truly open mind in America'?"

"It's hard to know what's really happening. But Graff recommended, and I agree, that we should leave them alone. Not expose them. Make no report at this time except that we have determined that Locke and Demosthenes have no foreign connections and have no connections with any domestic group, either, except those publicly declared on the nets."

"In other words, give them a clean bill of health."

"I know Demosthenes seems dangerous, in part because he—or she—has such a wide following. But I think it's significant that the one of the two of them who is most ambitious has chosen the moderate, wise persona. And they're still just talking. They have influence, but no power."

"In my experience, influence *is* power."

"If we ever find them getting out of line, we can easily expose them."

"Only in the next few years. The longer we wait, the older they get, and the less shocking it is to discover who they are."

"You know what the Russian troop movements have been. There's always the chance that Demosthenes is *right*. In which case—"

"We'd better have Demosthenes around. All right. We'll show them clean, for now. But watch them. And I, of course, have to find ways of keeping the Russians calm."

In spite of all her misgivings, Valentine was having fun being Demosthenes. Her column was now being carried on practically every newsnet in the country, and it was fun to watch the money pile up in her attorney's accounts. Every now and then she and Peter would, in Demosthenes' name, donate a carefully calculated sum to a particular candidate or cause: enough money that the donation would be noticed, but not so much that the candidate would feel she was trying to buy a vote. She was getting so many letters now that her newsnet had hired a secretary to answer certain classes of routine correspondence for her. The fun letters, from national and international leaders, sometimes hostile, sometimes friendly, always diplomatically trying to pry into Demosthenes' mind—those she and Peter read together, laughing in delight sometimes that people like *this* were writing to children, and didn't know it.

Sometimes, though, she was ashamed. Father was reading Demosthenes regularly; he never read Locke, or if he did, he said nothing about it. At dinner, though, he would often regale them with some telling point Demosthenes had made in that day's column. Peter loved it when Father did that—"See, it shows that the common man is paying attention"—but it made Valentine feel humiliated for Father. If he ever found out that all this time *I* was writing the columns he told us about, and that I didn't even believe half the things I wrote, he would be angry and ashamed.

At school, she once nearly got them in trouble, when her history teacher assigned the class to write a paper contrasting the views of Demosthenes and Locke as expressed in two of their early columns. Valentine was careless, and did a brilliant job of analysis. As a result, she had to work hard to talk the principal out of having her essay published on the very newsnet that carried Demosthenes' column. Peter was savage about it. "You write too much like Demosthenes, you can't get published, I should kill Demosthenes now, you're getting out of control."

If he raged about that blunder, Peter frightened her still more when he went silent. It happened when Demosthenes was invited to take part in the President's Council on Education for the Future, a blue-ribbon panel that was designed to do nothing, but do it splendidly. Valentine thought Peter would take it as a triumph, but he did not. "Turn it down," he said.

"Why should I?" she asked. "It's no work at all, and they even said that because of Demosthenes' well-known desire for privacy, they would net all the meetings. It makes Demosthenes into a respectable person, and—"

"And you love it that you got that before I did."

"Peter, it isn't you and me, it's Demosthenes and Locke. We made them up. They aren't real. Besides, this appointment doesn't mean they like Demosthenes better than Locke, it just means that Demosthenes has a much stronger base of support. You knew he would. Appointing him pleases a large number of Russian-haters and chauvinists."

"It wasn't supposed to work this way. Locke was supposed to be the respected one."

"He is! Real respect takes longer than official respect. Peter, don't be angry at me because I've done well with the things you told me to do."

But he was angry, for days, and ever since then he had left her to think through all her own columns, instead of telling her what to write. He probably assumed that this would make the quality of Demosthenes' columns deteriorate, but if it did no one noticed. Perhaps it made him even angrier that she never came to him weeping for help. She had been Demosthenes too long now to need anyone to tell her what Demosthenes would think about things.

And as her correspondence with other politically active citizens grew, she began to learn things, information that simply wasn't available to the general public. Certain military people who corresponded with her dropped hints about things without meaning to, and she and Peter put them together to build up a fascinating and frightening picture of Warsaw Pact activity. They were indeed preparing for war, a vicious and bloody earthbound war. Demosthenes wasn't wrong to suspect that the Second Warsaw Pact was not abiding by the terms of the League.

And the character of Demosthenes gradually took on a life of his own. At times she found herself thinking like Demosthenes at the end of a writing session, agreeing with ideas that were supposed to be calculated poses. And sometimes she read Peter's Locke essays and found herself annoyed at his obvious blindness to what was really going on.

Perhaps it's impossible to wear an identity without becoming what you pretend to be. She thought of that, worried about it for a few days, and then wrote a column using that as a premise, to show that politicians who toadied to the Russians in order to keep the peace would inevitably end up subservient to them in everything. It was a lovely bite at the party in power, and she got a lot of good mail about it. She also stopped being frightened of the idea of becoming, to a degree, Demosthenes. He's smarter than Peter and I ever gave him credit for, she thought.

Graff was waiting for her after school. He stood leaning on his car. He was in civilian clothes, and he had gained weight, so she didn't recognize him at first. But he beckoned to her, and before he could introduce himself she remembered his name.

"I won't write another letter," she said. "I never should have written that one."

"You don't like medals, then, I guess."

"Not much."

"Come for a ride with me, Valentine."

"I don't ride with strangers."

He handed her a paper. It was a release form, and her parents had signed it.

"I guess you're not a stranger. Where are we going?"

"To see a young soldier who is in Greensboro on leave."

She got in the car. "Ender's only ten years old," she said. "I thought you told me last time he'd be eligible for a leave when he was sixteen."

"He skipped a few grades."

"So he's doing well?"

"Ask him when you see him."

"Why me? Why not the whole family?"

Graff sighed. "Ender sees the world his own way. We had to persuade him to see you. As for Peter and your parents, he was not interested. Life at the Battle School was—intense."

"What do you mean, he's gone crazy?"

"On the contrary, he's the sanest person I know. He's sane enough to know that his parents are not particularly eager to reopen a book of affection that was closed quite tightly four years ago. As for Peter—we didn't even suggest a meeting, and so he didn't have a chance to tell us to go to hell."

They went out Lake Brandt Road and turned off just past the lake, following a road that wound down and up until they came to a white clapboard mansion that sprawled along the top of a hill. It looked over Lake Brandt on one side and a five-acre private lake on the other. "This is the house that Medly's Mist-E-Rub built," said Graff. "The I.F. picked it up in a tax sale about twenty years ago. Ender insisted that his conversation with you should not be bugged. I promised him it wouldn't be, and to help inspire confidence, the two of you are going out on a raft he built himself. I should warn you, though. I intend to ask you questions about your conversation when it is finished. You don't have to answer, but I hope you will."

"I didn't bring a swimming suit."

"We can provide one."

"One that isn't bugged?"

"At some point, there must be trust. For instance, I know who Demosthenes really is."

She felt a thrill of fear run through her, but said nothing.

"I've known since I landed from the Battle School. There are, perhaps, six of us in the world who know his identity. Not counting the Russians—God only knows what they know. But Demosthenes has nothing to fear from us. Demosthenes can trust our discretion. Just as I trust Demosthenes not to tell Locke what's going on here today. Mutual trust. We tell each other things."

Valentine couldn't decide whether it was Demosthenes they approved of, or Valentine Wiggin. If the former, she would not trust them; if the latter, then perhaps she could. The fact that they did not want her to discuss this with Peter suggested that perhaps they knew the difference between them. She did not stop to wonder whether she herself knew the difference anymore.

"You said he built the raft. How long has he been here?"

"Two months. We meant his leave to last only a few days. But you see, he doesn't seem interested in going on with his education."

"Oh. So I'm therapy again."

"This time we can't censor your letter. We're just taking our chances. We need your brother badly. Humanity is on the cusp."

This time Val had grown up enough to know just how much danger the world was in. And she had been Demosthenes long enough that she didn't hesitate to do her duty. "Where is he?"

"Down at the boat slip."

"Where's the swimming suit?"

Ender didn't wave when she walked down the hill toward him, didn't smile when she stepped onto the floating boat slip. But she knew that he was glad to see her, knew it because of the way his eyes never left her face.

"You're bigger than I remembered." she said stupidly.

"You too," he said. "I also remembered that you were beautiful."

"Memory does play tricks on us."

"No. Your face is the same, but I don't remember what beautiful means anymore. Come on. Let's go out into the lake."

She looked at the small raft with misgivings.

"Don't stand up on it, that's all," he said. He got on by crawling, spiderlike, on toes and fingers. "It's the first thing I built with my own hands since you and I used to build with blocks. Peter-proof buildings."

She laughed. They used to take pleasure in building things that would stand up even when a lot of the obvious supports had been removed. Peter, in turn, liked to remove a block here or there, so the structure would be fragile enough that the next person to touch it would knock it down. Peter was an ass, but he did provide some focus to their childhood.

"Peter's changed," she said.

"Let's not talk about him," said Ender.

"All right."

She crawled onto the boat, not as deftly as Ender. He used a paddle to maneuver them slowly toward the center of the private lake. She noticed aloud that he was sunbrowned and strong.

"The strong part comes from Battle School. The sunbrowning comes from this lake. I spend a lot of time on the water. When I'm swimming, it's like being weightless. I miss being weightless. Also, when I'm here on the lake, the land slopes up in every direction."

"Like living in a bowl."

"I've lived in a bowl for four years."

"So we're strangers now?"

"Aren't we, Valentine?"

"No," she said. She reached out and touched his leg. Then, suddenly, she squeezed his knee, right where he had always been most ticklish.

But almost at the same moment, he caught her wrist in his hand. His grip was very strong, even though his hands were smaller than hers and his own arms were slender and tight. For a moment he looked dangerous; then he relaxed. "Oh, yes," he said. "You used to tickle me."

"Not any more," she said, taking back her hand.

"Want to swim?"

In answer, she dropped herself over the side of the raft. The water was clear and clean, and there was no chlorine in it. She swam for a while, then returned to the raft and lay on it in the hazy sunlight. A wasp circled her, then landed on the raft beside her head. She knew it was there, and ordinarily would have been afraid of it. But not today. Let it walk on this raft, let it bake in the sun as I'm doing.

Then the raft rocked, and she turned to see Ender calmly crushing the life out of the wasp with one finger. "These are a nasty breed," Ender said. "They sting you without waiting to be insulted first." He smiled. "I've been learning about preemptive strategies. I'm very good. No one ever beat me. I'm the best soldier they ever had."

"Who would expect less?" she said. "You're a Wiggin."

"Whatever that means," he said.

"It means that you are going to make a difference in the world." And she told him what she and Peter were doing.

"How old is Peter, fourteen? Already planning to take over the world?"

"He thinks he's Alexander the Great. And why shouldn't he be? Why shouldn't *you* be, too?"

"We can't *both* be Alexander."

"Two faces of the same coin. And I am the metal in between." Even as she said it, she wondered if it was true. She had shared so much with Peter these last few years that even when she thought she despised him, she understood him. While Ender had been only a memory till now. A very small, fragile boy who needed her protection. Not this cold-eyed, dark-skinned manling who kills wasps with his fingers. Maybe he and Peter and I are all the same, and have been all along. Maybe we only thought we were different from each other out of jealousy.

"The trouble with coins is, when one face is up, the other face is down."

And right now you think you're down. "They want me to encourage you to go on with your studies."

"They aren't studies, they're games. All games, from beginning to end, only they change the rules whenever they feel like it." He held up a limp hand. "See the strings?"

"But you can use them, too."

"Only if they want to be used. Only if they think they're using you. No, it's too hard, I don't want to play anymore. Just when I start to be happy, just when I think I can handle things, they stick in another knife. I keep having nightmares, now that I'm here. I dream I'm in the battleroom, only instead of being weightless, they're playing games with gravity. They keep changing its direction. So I never end up on the wall I launched for. I never end up where I meant to go. And I keep pleading with them just to let me get to the door, and they won't let me out, they keep sucking me back in."

She heard the anger in his voice and assumed it was directed at her. "I suppose that's what I'm here for. To suck you back in."

"I didn't want to see you."

"They told me."

"I was afraid that I'd still love you."

"I hoped that you would."

"My fear, your wish—both granted."

"Ender, it really is true. We may be young, but we're not powerless. We play by their rules long enough, and it becomes our game." She giggled. "I'm on a presidential commission. Peter is so angry."

"They don't let me use the nets. There isn't a computer in the place, except the household machines that run the security system and the lighting. Ancient things. Installed back a century ago, when they made computers that didn't hook up with anything. They took away my army, they took away my desk, and you know something? I don't really mind."

"You must be good company for yourself."

"Not me. My memories."

"Maybe that's who you are, what you remember."

"No. My memories of strangers. My memories of the buggers."

Valentine shivered, as if a cold breeze had suddenly passed. "I refuse to watch the bugger vids anymore. They're always the same."

"I used to study them for hours. The way their ships move through space. And something funny, that only occurred to me lying out here on the lake. I realized that all the battles in which buggers and humans fought hand to hand, all those are from the First Invasion. All the scenes from the Second Invasion, when our soldiers are in I.F. uniforms, in those scenes the buggers are always already dead. Lying there, slumped over their controls. Not a sign of struggle or anything. And Mazer Rackham's battle—they never show us any footage from that battle."

"Maybe it's a secret weapon."

"No, no, I don't care about how we killed them. It's the buggers themselves. I don't know anything about them, and yet someday I'm supposed to fight them. I've been through a lot of fights in my life, sometimes games, sometimes—not games. Every time, I've won because I could understand the way my enemy thought. From what they *did*. I could tell what they thought I was doing, how they wanted the battle to take shape. And I played off of that. I'm very good at that. Understanding how other people think."

"The curse of the Wiggin children." She joked, but it frightened her, that Ender might understand her as completely as he did his enemies. Peter always understood her, or at least thought he did, but he was such a moral sinkhole that she never had to feel embarrassed when he guessed even her worst thoughts. But Ender—she did not want him to understand her. It would make her naked before him. She would be ashamed. "You don't think you can beat the buggers unless you know them."

"It goes deeper than that. Being here alone with nothing to do, I've been thinking about myself, too. Trying to understand why I hate myself so badly."

"No, Ender."

"Don't tell me 'No, Ender.' It took me a long time to realize that I did, but believe me, I did. Do. And it came down to this: In the moment when I truly understand my enemy, understand him well enough to defeat him, then in that very moment I also love him. I think it's impossible to really understand somebody, what they want, what they believe, and not love them the way they love themselves. And then, in that very moment when I *love* them—"

"You beat them." For a moment she was not afraid of his understanding.

"No, you don't understand. I *destroy* them. I make it impossible for them to ever hurt me again. I grind them and grind them until they don't *exist*."

"Of course you don't." And now the fear came again, worse than before. Peter has mellowed, but you, they've made you into a killer. Two sides of the same coin, but which side is which?

"I've really hurt some people, Val. I'm not making this up."

"I know, Ender." How will you hurt me?

"See what I'm becoming, Val?" he said softly. "Even you are afraid of me." And he touched her cheek so gently that she wanted to cry. Like the touch of his soft baby hand when he was still an infant. She remembered that, the touch of his soft and innocent hand on her cheek.

"I'm not," she said, and in that moment it was true.

"You should be."

No. I shouldn't. "You're going to shrivel up if you stay in the water. Also, the sharks might get you."

He smiled. "The sharks learned to leave me alone a long time ago." But he pulled himself onto the raft, bringing a wash of water across it as it tipped. It was cold on Valentine's back.

"Ender, Peter's going to do it. He's smart enough to take the time it takes, but he's going to win his way into power—if not right now, then later. I'm not sure yet whether that'll be a good thing or a bad thing. Peter can be cruel, but he knows the getting and keeping of power, and there are signs that once the bugger war is over, and maybe even before it ends, the world will collapse into chaos again. The Russian Empire was on its way to hegemony before the First Invasion. If they try for it afterward—"

"So even Peter might be a better alternative."

"You've been discovering some of the destroyer in yourself, Ender. Well, so have I. Peter didn't have a monopoly on that, whatever the testers thought. And Peter has some of the builder in him. He isn't kind, but he doesn't break every good thing he sees anymore. Once you realize that power will always end up with the sort of people who crave it, I think that there are worse people who could have it than Peter."

"With that strong a recommendation, I could vote for him myself."

"Sometimes it seems absolutely silly. A fourteen-year-old boy and his kid sister plotting to take over the world." She tried to laugh. It wasn't funny. "We aren't just ordinary children, are we. None of us."

"Don't you sometimes wish we were?"

She tried to imagine herself being like the other girls at school. Tried to imagine life if she didn't feel responsible for the future of the world. "It would be so dull."

"I don't think so." And he stretched out on the raft, as if he could lie on the water forever.

It was true. Whatever they did to Ender in the Battle School, they had spent his ambition. He really did not want to leave the sun-warmed waters of this bowl.

No, she realized. No, he *believes* that he doesn't want to leave here, but there is still too much of Peter in him. Or too much of me. None of us could be happy for long, doing nothing. Or perhaps it's just that none of us could be happy living with no other company than ourself.

So she began to prod again. "What is the one name that everyone in the world knows?"

"Mazer Rackham."

"And what if you win the next war, the way Mazer did?"

"Mazer Rackham was a fluke. A reserve. Nobody believed in him. He just happened to be in the right place at the right time."

"But suppose you do it. Suppose you beat the buggers and your name is known the way Mazer Rackham's name is known."

"Let somebody else be famous. Peter wants to be famous. Let him save the world."

"I'm not talking about fame, Ender. I'm not talking about power, either. I'm talking about accidents, just like the accident that Mazer Rackham happened to be the one who was there when somebody had to stop the buggers."

"If I'm here," said Ender, "then I won't be there. Somebody else will. Let them have the accident."

His tone of weary unconcern infuriated her. "I'm talking about *my* life, you self-centered little bastard." If her words bothered him, he didn't show it. Just lay there, eyes closed. "When you were little and Peter tortured you, it's a good thing I didn't lie back and wait for Mom and Dad to save you. They never understood how dangerous Peter was. I knew you had the monitor, but I didn't wait for *them,* either. Do you know what Peter used to do to me because I stopped him from hurting you?"

"Shut up," Ender whispered.

Because she saw that his chest was trembling, because she knew that she had indeed hurt him, because she knew that just like Peter, she had found his weakest place and stabbed him there, she fell silent.

"I can't beat them," Ender said softly. "I'll be out there like Mazer Rackham one day, and everybody will be depending on me, and I won't be able to do it."

"If you can't, Ender, then nobody could. If you can't beat them, then they deserve to win because they're stronger and better than us. It won't be your fault."

"Tell it to the dead."

"If not you, then who?"

"Anybody."

"Nobody, Ender. I'll tell you something. If you try and lose then it isn't your fault. But if you don't try and we lose, then it's all your fault. You killed us all."

"I'm a killer no matter what."

"What else should you be? Human beings didn't evolve brains in order to lie around on lakes. Killing's the first thing we learned. And a good thing we did, or we'd be dead, and the tigers would own the earth."

"I could never beat Peter. No matter what I said or did. I never could."

So it came back to Peter. "He was years older than you. And stronger."

"So are the buggers."

She could see his reasoning. Or rather, his unreasoning. He could win all he wanted, but he knew in his heart that there was always someone who could destroy him. He always knew that he had not really won, because there was Peter, undefeated champion.

"You want to beat Peter?" she asked.

"No," he answered.

"Beat the buggers. Then come home and see who notices Peter Wiggin anymore. Look him in the eye when all the world loves and reveres you. That'll be defeat in his eyes, Ender. That's how you win."

"You don't understand," he said.

"Yes I do."

"No you don't. I don't want to beat Peter."

"Then what do you want?"

"I want him to love me."

She had no answer. As far as she knew, Peter didn't love anybody.

Ender said nothing more. Just lay there. And lay there.

Finally Valentine, the sweat dripping off her, the mosquitos beginning to hover as the dusk came on, took one final dip in the water and then began to push the raft in to shore. Ender showed no sign that he knew what she was doing, but his irregular breathing told her that he was not asleep. When they got to the shore, she climbed onto the dock and said, "*I* love you, Ender. More than ever. No matter what you decide."

He didn't answer. She doubted that he believed her. She walked back up the hill, savagely angry at them for making her come to Ender like this. For she had, after all, done just what they wanted. She had talked Ender into going back into his training, and he wouldn't soon forgive her for that.

—

Ender came in the door, still wet from his last dip in the lake. It was dark outside, and dark in the room where Graff waited for him.

"Are we going now?" asked Ender.

"If you want to," Graff said.

"When?"

"When you're ready."

Ender showered and dressed. He was finally used to the way civilian clothes fit together, but he still didn't feel right without a uniform or a flash suit. I'll never wear a flash suit again, he thought. That was the Battle School game, and I'm through with that. He heard the crickets chirping madly in the woods; in the near distance he heard the crackling sound of a car driving slowly on gravel.

What else should he take with him? He had read several of the books in the library, but they belonged to the house and he couldn't take them. The only thing he owned was the raft he had made with his own hands. That would stay here, too.

The lights were on now in the room where Graff waited. He, too, had changed clothing. He was back in uniform.

They sat in the back seat of the car together, driving along country roads to come at the airport from the back. "Back when the population was growing," said Graff, "they kept this area in woods and farms. Watershed land. The rainfall here starts a lot of rivers flowing, a lot of underground water moving around. The Earth is deep, and right to the heart it's alive, Ender. We people only live on the top, like the bugs that live on the scum of the still water near the shore."

Ender said nothing.

"We train our commanders the way we do because that's what it takes—they have to think in certain ways, they can't be distracted by a lot of things, so we isolate them. You. Keep you separate. And it works. But it's so easy, when you never meet people, when you never know the Earth itself, when you live with metal walls keeping out the cold of space, it's easy to forget why Earth is worth saving. Why the world of people might be worth the price you pay."

So that's why you brought me here, thought Ender. With all your hurry, that's why you took three months, to make me love Earth. Well, it worked. All your tricks worked. Valentine, too; she was another one of your tricks, to make me remember that I'm not going to school for myself. Well, I remember.

"I may have used Valentine," said Graff, "and you may hate me for it, Ender, but keep this in mind—it only works because what's between you, that's real, that's what matters. Billions of those connections between human beings. That's what you're fighting to keep alive."

Ender turned his face to the window and watched the helicopters and dirigibles rise and fall.

They took a helicopter to the I.F. spaceport at Stumpy Point. It was officially named for a dead Hegemon, but everybody called it Stumpy Point, after the pitiful little town that had been paved over when they made the approaches to the vast islands of steel and concrete that dotted Pamlico Sound. There were still waterbirds taking their fastidious little steps in the saltwater, where mossy trees dipped down as if to drink. It began to rain lightly, and the concrete was black and slick; it was hard to tell where it left off and the Sound began.

Graff led him through a maze of clearances. Authority was a little plastic ball that Graff carried. He dropped it into chutes, and doors opened and people stood up and saluted and the chutes spat out the ball and Graff went on. Ender noticed that at first everyone watched Graff, but as they penetrated deeper into the spaceport, people began watching Ender. At first it was the man of real authority they noticed, but later, where everyone had authority, it was his cargo they cared to see.

Only when Graff strapped himself into the shuttle seat beside him did Ender realize Graff was going to launch with him.

"How far?" asked Ender. "How far are you going with me?"

Graff smiled thinly. "All the way, Ender."

"Are they making you administrator of Command School?"

"No."

So they had removed Graff from his post at Battle School solely to accompany Ender to his next assignment. How important am I, he wondered. And like a whisper of Peter's voice inside his mind, he heard the question, How can I use this?

He shuddered and tried to think of something else. Peter could have fantasies about ruling the world, but Ender didn't have them. Still, thinking back on his life in Battle School, it occurred to him that although he had never sought power, he had always had it. But he decided that it was a power born of excellence, not manipulation. He had no reason to be ashamed of it. He had never, except perhaps with Bean, used his power to hurt someone. And with Bean, things had worked well after all. Bean had become a friend, finally, to take the place of the lost Alai, who in turn took the place of Valentine. Valentine, who was helping Peter in his plotting. Valentine, who still loved Ender no matter what happened. And following that train of thought led him back to Earth, back to the quiet hours in the center of the clear water ringed by a bowl of tree-covered hills. That is the Earth, he thought. Not a globe thousands of kilometers around, but a forest with a shining lake, a house hidden at the crest of the hill, high in the trees, a grassy slope leading upward from the water, fish leaping and birds strafing to take the bugs that lived at the border between water and sky. Earth was the constant noise of crickets and winds and birds. And the voice of one girl, who spoke to him out of his far-off childhood. The same voice that had once protected him from terror. The same voice that he would do anything to keep alive, even return to school, even leave Earth behind again for another four or forty or four thousand years. Even if she loved Peter more.

His eyes were closed, and he had not made any sound but breathing; still, Graff reached out and touched his hand across the aisle. Ender stiffened in surprise, and Graff soon withdrew, but for a moment Ender was struck with the startling thought that perhaps Graff felt some affection for him. But no, it was just another calculated gesture. Graff was creating a commander out of a little boy. No doubt Unit 17 in the course of studies included an affectionate gesture from the teacher.

The shuttle reached the IPL satellite in only a few hours. Inter-Planetary Launch was a city of three thousand inhabitants, breathing oxygen from the plants that also fed them, drinking water that had already passed through their bodies ten thousand times, living only to service the tugs that did all the oxwork in the solar system and the shuttles that took their cargoes and passengers back to the Earth or the Moon. It was a world where, briefly, Ender felt at home, since its floors sloped upward as they did in the Battle School.

Their tug was fairly new; the I.F. was constantly casting off its old vehicles and purchasing the latest models. It had just brought a vast load of drawn steel processed by a factory ship that was taking apart minor planets in the asteroid belt. The steel would be dropped to the Moon, and now the tug was linked to fourteen barges. Graff dropped his ball into the reader again, however, and the barges were uncoupled from the tug. It would be making a fast run this time, to a destination of Graff's specification, not to be stated until the tug had cut loose from IPL.

"It's no great secret," said the tug's captain. "Whenever the destination is unknown, it's for ISL." By analogy with IPL, Ender decided the letters meant Inter-Stellar Launch.

"This time it isn't," said Graff.

"Where then?"

"I.F. Command."

"I don't have security clearance even to know where that is, sir."

"Your ship knows," said Graff. "Just let the computer have a look at this, and follow the course it plots." He handed the captain the plastic ball.

"And I'm supposed to close my eyes during the whole voyage, so I don't figure out where we are?"

"Oh, no, of course not. I.F. Command is on the minor planet Eros, which should be about three months away from here at the highest possible speed. Which is the speed you'll use, of course."

"Eros? But I thought that the buggers burned that to a radioactive—ah. When did I receive security clearance to know this?"

"You didn't. So when we arrive at Eros, you will undoubtedly be assigned to permanent duty there."

The captain understood immediately, and didn't like it. "I'm a pilot, you son of a bitch, and you got no right to lock me up on a rock!"

"I will overlook your derisive language to a superior officer. I do apologize, but my orders were to take the fastest available military tug. At the moment I arrived, that was you. It isn't as though anyone were out to get you. Cheer up. The war may be over in another fifteen years, and then the location of I.F. Command won't have to be a secret anymore. By the way, you should be aware, in case you're one of those who relies on visuals for docking, that Eros has been blacked out. Its albedo is only slightly brighter than a black hole. You won't see it."

"Thanks," said the captain.

It was nearly a month into the voyage before he managed to speak civilly to Colonel Graff.

The shipboard computer had a limited library—it was geared primarily to entertainment rather than education. So during the voyage, after breakfast and morning exercises, Ender and Graff would usually talk. About Command School. About Earth. About astronomy and physics and whatever Ender wanted to know.

And above all, he wanted to know about the buggers.

"We don't *know* much," said Graff. "We've never had a live one in custody. Even when we caught one unarmed and alive, he died the moment it became obvious he was captured. Even the *he* is uncertain—the most likely thing, in fact, is that most bugger soldiers are females, but with atrophied or vestigial sexual organs. We can't tell. It's their psychology that would be most useful to you, and we haven't exactly had a chance to interview them."

"Tell me what you know, and maybe I'll learn something that I need."

So Graff told him. The buggers were organisms that could conceivably have evolved on Earth, if things had gone a different way a billion years ago. At the molecular level, there were no surprises. Even the genetic material was the same. It was no accident that they looked insectlike to human beings. Though their internal organs were now much more complex and specialized than any insects, and they had evolved an internal skeleton and shed most of the exoskeleton, their physical structure still echoed their ancestors, who could easily have been very much like Earth's ants. "But don't be fooled by that," said Graff. "It's just as meaningful to say that our ancestors could easily have been very much like squirrels."

"If that's all we have to go on, that's *something*," said Ender.

"Squirrels never built starships," said Graff. "There are usually a few changes on the way from gathering nuts and seeds to harvesting asteroids and putting permanent research stations on the moons of Saturn."

The buggers could probably see about the same spectrum of light as human beings, and there was artificial lighting in their ships and ground installations. However, their antennae seemed almost vestigial. There was no evidence from their bodies that smelling, tasting, or hearing were particularly important to them. "Of course, we can't be sure. But we can't see any way that they could have used sound for communication. The oddest thing of all was that they also don't have any communication devices on their ships. No radios, nothing that could transmit or receive any kind of signal."

"They communicate ship to ship. I've seen the videos, they talk to each other."

"True. But body to body, mind to mind. It's the most important thing we learned from them. Their communication, however they do it, is instantaneous. Lightspeed is no barrier. When Mazer Rackham defeated their invasion fleet, they all closed up shop. At once. There was no time for a signal. Everything just stopped."

Ender remembered the videos of uninjured buggers lying dead at their posts.

"We knew then that it was possible. To communicate faster than light. That was seventy years ago, and once we knew what could be done, we did it. Not *me*, mind you, I wasn't born then."

"How is it possible?"

"I can't explain philotic physics to you. Half of it nobody understands anyway. What matters is we built the ansible. The official name is Philotic Parallax Instantaneous Communicator, but somebody dredged the name *ansible* out of an old book somewhere and it caught on. Not that most people even know the machine exists."

"That means that ships could talk to each other even when they're across the solar system," said Ender.

"It means," said Graff, "that ships could talk to each other even when they're across the galaxy. And the buggers can do it without machines."

"So they knew about their defeat the moment it happened," said Ender. "I always figured—everybody always said that they probably only found out they lost the battle twenty-five years ago."

"It keeps people from panicking," said Graff. "I'm telling you things that you can't know, by the way, if you're ever going to leave I.F. Command. Before the war's over."

Ender was angry. "If you know me at all, you know I can keep a secret."

"It's a regulation. People under twenty-five are assumed to be a security risk. It's very unjust to a good many responsible children, but it helps narrow the number of people who might let something slip."

"What's all the secrecy for, anyway?"

"Because we've taken some terrible risks, Ender, and we don't want to have every net on earth second-guessing those decisions. You see, as soon as we had a working ansible, we tucked it into our best starships and launched them to attack the buggers home systems."

"Do we know where they are?"

"Yes."

"So we're not waiting for the Third Invasion."

"We *are* the Third Invasion."

"We're attacking them. Nobody says that. Everybody thinks we have a huge fleet of warships waiting in the comet shield—"

"Not one. We're quite defenseless here."

"What if they've sent a fleet to attack us?"

"Then we're dead. But our ships haven't seen such a fleet, not a sign of one."

"Maybe they gave up and they're planning to leave us alone."

"Maybe. You've seen the videos. Would you bet the human race on the chance of them giving up and leaving us alone?"

Ender tried to grasp the amounts of time that had gone by. "And the ships have been traveling for seventy years—"

"Some of them. And some for thirty years, and some for twenty. We make better ships now. We're learning how to play with space a little better. But every starship that is not still under construction is on its way to a bugger world or outpost. Every starship, with cruisers and fighters tucked into its belly, is out there approaching the buggers. Decelerating. Because they're almost there. The first ships we sent to the most distant objectives, the more recent ships to the closer ones. Our timing was pretty good. They'll all be arriving in combat range within a few months of each other. Unfortunately, our most primitive, outdated equipment will be attacking their homeworld. Still, they're armed well enough—we have some weapons the buggers never saw before."

"When will they arrive?"

"Within the next five years, Ender. Everything is ready at I.F. Command. The master ansible is there, in contact with all our invasion fleet; the ships are all working, ready to fight. All we lack, Ender, is the battle commander. Someone who knows what the hell to do with those ships when they get there."

"And what if no one knows what to do with them?"

"We'll just do our best, with the best commander we can get."

Me, thought Ender. They want me to be ready in five years. "Colonel Graff, there isn't a chance I'll be ready to command a fleet in time."

Graff shrugged. "So. Do your best. If you aren't ready, we'll make do with what we've got."

That eased Ender's mind.

But only for a moment. "Of course, Ender, what we've got right now is nobody."

Ender knew that this was another of Graff's games. Make me believe that it all depends on me, so I can't slack off, so I push myself as hard as possible.

Game or not, though, it might also be true. And so he would work as hard as possible. It was what Val had wanted of him. Five years. Only five years until the fleet arrives, and I don't know anything yet. "I'll only be fifteen in five years," Ender said.

"Going on sixteen," said Graff. "It all depends on what you know."

"Colonel Graff," he said. "I just want to go back and swim in the lake."

"After we win the war," said Graff. "Or lose it. We'll have a few decades before they get back here to finish us off. The house will be there, and I promise you can swim to your heart's content."

"But I'll still be too young for security clearance."

"We'll keep you under armed guard at all times. The military knows how to handle these things."

They both laughed, and Ender had to remind himself that Graff was only acting like a friend, that everything he did was a lie or a cheat calculated to turn Ender into an efficient fighting machine. I'll become exactly the tool you want me to be, said Ender silently, but at least I won't be *fooled* into it. I'll do it because I choose to, not because you tricked me, you sly bastard.

The tug reached Eros before they could see it. The captain showed them the visual scan, then superimposed the heat scan on the same screen. They were practically on top of it—only four thousand kilometers out—but Eros, only twenty-four kilometers long, was invisible if it didn't shine with reflected sunlight.

The captain docked the ship on one of the three landing platforms that circled Eros. It could not land directly because Eros had enhanced gravity, and the tug, designed for towing cargoes, could never escape the gravity well. He bade them an irritable good-bye, but Ender and Graff remained cheerful. The captain was bitter at having to leave his tug; Ender and Graff felt like prisoners finally paroled from jail. When they boarded the shuttle that would take them to the surface of Eros, they repeated perverse misquotations of lines from the videos that the captain had endlessly watched, and laughed like madmen. The captain grew surly and withdrew by pretending to go to sleep. Then, almost as an afterthought, Ender asked Graff one last question.

"Why are we fighting the buggers?"

"I've heard all kinds of reasons," said Graff. "Because they have an overcrowded system and they've got to colonize. Because they can't stand the thought of other intelligent life in the universe. Because they don't think we *are* intelligent life. Because they have some weird religion. Because they watched our old video broadcasts and decided we were hopelessly violent. All kinds of reasons."

"What do you believe?"

"It doesn't matter what I believe."

"I want to know anyway."

"They must talk to each other directly, Ender, mind to mind. What one thinks, another can also think; what one remembers, another can also remember. Why would they ever develop language? Why would they ever learn to read and write? How would they know what reading and writing were if they saw them? Or signals? Or numbers? Or anything that we use to communicate? This isn't just a matter of translating from one language to another. They don't have a language at all. We used every means we could think of to communicate with them, but they don't even have the machinery to know we're signaling. And maybe they've been trying to think to us, and they can't understand why we don't respond."

"So the whole war is because we can't talk to each other."

"If the other fellow can't tell you his story, you can never be sure he isn't trying to kill you."

"What if we just left them alone?"

"Ender, we didn't go to them first, they came to us. If they were going to leave us alone, they could have done it a hundred years ago, before the First Invasion."

"Maybe they didn't know we were intelligent life. Maybe—"

"Ender, believe me, there's a century of discussion on this very subject. Nobody knows the answer. When it comes down to it, though, the real decision is inevitable: If one of us has to be destroyed, let's make damn sure we're the ones alive at the end. Our genes won't let us decide any other way. Nature can't evolve a species that hasn't a will to survive. Individuals might be bred to sacrifice themselves, but the race as a whole can never decide to cease to exist. So if we can we'll kill every last one of the buggers, and if they can they'll kill every last one of us."

"As for me," said Ender, "I'm in favor of surviving."

"I know," said Graff. "That's why you're here."

14

ENDER'S TEACHER

"Took your time, didn't you, Graff? The voyage isn't short, but the three-month vacation seems excessive."

"I prefer not to deliver damaged merchandise."

"Some men simply have no sense of hurry. Oh well, it's only the fate of the world. . . . Never mind me. You must understand our anxiety. We're here with the ansible, receiving constant reports of the progress of our starships. We have to face the coming war every day. If you can call them days. He's such a very *little* boy."

"There's greatness in him. A magnitude of spirit."

"A killer instinct, too, I hope."

"Yes."

"We've planned out an impromptu course of study for him. All subject to your approval, of course."

"I'll look at it. I don't pretend to know the subject matter, Admiral Chamrajnagar. I'm only here because I know Ender. So don't be afraid that I'll try to second-guess the order of your presentation. Only the pace."

"How much can we tell him?"

"Don't waste his time on the physics of interstellar travel."

"What about the ansible?"

"I already told him about that, and the fleets. I said they would arrive at their destination within five years."

"It seems there's very little left for us to tell him."

"You can tell him about the weapons systems. He has to know enough to make intelligent decisions."

"Ah. We can be useful after all, how very kind. We've devoted one of the five simulators to his exclusive use."

"What about the others?"

"The other simulators?"

"The other children."

"You were brought here to take care of Ender Wiggin."

"Just curious. Remember, they were all my students at one time or another."

"And now they are all mine. They are entering into the mysteries of the fleet, Colonel Graff, to which you, as a soldier, have never been introduced."

"You make it sound like a priesthood."

"And a god. And a religion. Even those of us who command by ansible know the majesty of flight among the stars. I can see you find my mysticism distasteful. I assure you that your distaste only reveals your ignorance. Soon enough Ender Wiggin will also know what I know; he will dance the graceful ghost dance through the stars, and whatever greatness there is within him will be unlocked, revealed, set forth before the universe for all to see. You have the soul of a stone, Colonel Graff, but I sing to a stone as easily as to another singer. You may go to your quarters and establish yourself."

"I have nothing to establish except the clothing I'm wearing."

"You own nothing?"

"They keep my salary in an account somewhere on Earth. I've never needed it. Except to buy civilian clothes on my—vacation."

"A non-materialist. And yet you are unpleasantly fat. A gluttonous ascetic? Such a contradiction."

"When I'm tense, I eat. Whereas when you're tense, you spout solid waste."

"I like you, Colonel Graff. I think we shall get along."

"I don't much care, Admiral Chamrajnagar. I came here for Ender. And neither of us came here for you."

Ender hated Eros from the moment he shuttled down from the tug. He had been uncomfortable enough on Earth, where floors were flat; Eros was hopeless. It was a roughly spindle-shaped rock only six and a half kilometers thick at its narrowest point. Since the surface of the planetoid was entirely devoted to absorbing sunlight and converting it to energy, everyone lived in the smooth-walled rooms linked by tunnels that laced the interior of the asteroid. The closed-in space was no problem for Ender—what bothered him was that all the tunnel floors noticeably sloped downward. From the start, Ender was plagued by vertigo as he walked through the tunnels, especially the ones that girdled Eros's narrow circumference. It did not help that gravity was only half of Earth-normal—the illusion of being on the verge of falling was almost complete.

There was also something disturbing about the proportions of the rooms—the ceilings were too low for the width, the tunnels too narrow. It was not a comfortable place.

Worst of all, though, was the number of people. Ender had no important memories of the scale of the cities of Earth. His idea of a comfortable number of people was the Battle School, where he had known by sight every person who dwelt there. Here, though, ten thousand people lived within the rock. There was no crowding, despite the amount of space devoted to life support and other machinery. What bothered Ender was that he was constantly surrounded by strangers.

They never let him come to know anyone. He saw the other Command School students often, but since he never attended any class regularly, they remained only faces. He would attend a lecture here or there, but usually he was tutored by one teacher after another, or occasionally helped to learn a process by another student, whom he met once and never saw again. He ate alone or with Colonel Graff. His recreation was in a gym, but he rarely saw the same people in it twice.

He recognized that they were isolating him again, this time not by setting the other students to hating him, but rather by giving them no opportunity to become friends. He could hardly have been close to most of them anyway—except for Ender, the other students were all well into adolescence.

So Ender withdrew into his studies and learned quickly and well. Astrogation and military history he absorbed like water; abstract mathematics was more difficult, but whenever he was given a problem that involved patterns in space and time, he found that his intuition was more reliable than his calculation—he often saw at once a solution that he could only prove after minutes or hours of manipulating numbers.

And for pleasure, there was the simulator, the most perfect videogame he had ever played. Teachers and students trained him, step by step, in its use. At first, not knowing the awesome power of the game, he had played only at the tactical level, controlling a single fighter in continuous maneuvers to find and destroy an enemy. The computer-controlled enemy was devious and powerful, and whenever Ender tried a tactic he found the computer using it against him within minutes.

The game was a holographic display, and his fighter was represented only by a tiny light. The enemy was another light of a different color, and they danced and spun and maneuvered through a cube of space that must have been ten meters to a side. The controls were powerful. He could rotate the display in any direction, so he could watch from any angle, and he could move the center so that the duel took place nearer or farther from him.

Gradually, as he became more adept at controlling the fighter's speed, direction of movement, orientation, and weapons, the game was made more complex. He might have two enemy ships at once; there might be obstacles, the debris of space; he began to have to worry about fuel and limited weapons; the computer began to assign him particular things to destroy or accomplish, so that he had to avoid distractions and achieve an objective in order to win.

When he had mastered the one-fighter game, they allowed him to step back into the four-fighter squadron. He spoke commands to simulated pilots of four fighters, and instead of merely carrying out the computer's instructions, he was allowed to determine tactics himself, deciding which of several objectives was the most valuable and directing his squadron accordingly. At any time he could take personal command of one of the fighters for a short time, and at first he did this often; when he did, however, the other three fighters in his squadron were soon destroyed, and as the games became harder and harder he had to spend more and more of his time commanding the squadron. When he did, he won more and more often.

By the time he had been at Command School for a year, he was adept at running the simulator at any of fifteen levels, from controlling an individual fighter to commanding a fleet. He had long since realized that as the battleroom was to Battle School, so the simulator was to Command School. The classes were valuable, but the real education was the game. People dropped in from time to time to watch him play. They never spoke—hardly anyone ever did, unless they had something specific to teach him. The watchers would stay, silently watching him run through a difficult simulation, and then leave just as he finished. What are you doing, he wanted to ask. Judging me? Determining whether you want to trust the fleet to me? Just remember that I didn't ask for it.

He found that a great deal of what he had learned at Battle School transferred to the simulator. He would routinely reorient the simulator every few minutes, rotating it so that he didn't get trapped into an up-down orientation, constantly reviewing his position from the enemy point of view. It was exhilarating at last to have such control over the battle, to be able to see every point of it.

It was also frustrating to have so little control, too, for the computer-controlled fighters were only as good as the computer allowed. They took no initiative. They had no intelligence. He began to wish for his toon leaders, so that he could count on some of the squadrons doing well without having his constant supervision.

At the end of his first year he was winning every battle on the simulator, and played the game as if the machine were a natural part of his body. One day, eating a meal with Graff, he asked, "Is that all the simulator does?"

"Is what all?"

"The way it plays now. It's easy, and it hasn't got any harder for a while."

"Oh."

Graff seemed unconcerned. But then, Graff always seemed unconcerned. The next day everything changed. Graff went away, and in his place they gave Ender a companion.

He was in the room when Ender awoke in the morning. He was an old man, sitting cross-legged on the floor. Ender looked at him expectantly, waiting for the man to speak. He said nothing. Ender got up and showered and dressed, content to let the man keep his silence if he wanted. He had long since learned that when something unusual was going on, something that was part of someone else's plan and not his own, he would find out more information by waiting than by asking. Adults almost always lost their patience before Ender did.

The man still hadn't spoken when Ender was ready and went to the door to leave the room. The door didn't open. Ender turned to face the man sitting on the floor. He looked to be about sixty, by far the oldest man Ender had seen on Eros. He had a day's growth of white whiskers that grizzled his face only slightly less than his close-cut hair. His face sagged a little and his eyes were surrounded by creases and lines. He looked at Ender with an expression that bespoke only apathy.

Ender turned back to the door and tried again to open it.

"All right," he said, giving up. "Why's the door locked?"

The old man continued to look at him blankly.

So this is a game, thought Ender. Well, if they want me to go to class, they'll unlock the door. If they don't, they won't. I don't care.

Ender didn't like games where the rules could be anything and the objective was known to them alone. So he wouldn't play. He also refused to get angry. He went through a relaxing exercise as he leaned on the door, and soon he was calm again. The old man continued to watch him impassively.

It seemed to go on for hours, Ender refusing to speak, the old man seeming to be a mindless mute. Sometimes Ender wondered if he were mentally ill, escaped from some medical ward somewhere in Eros, living out some insane fantasy here in Ender's room. But the longer it went on, with no one coming to the door, no one looking for him, the more certain he became that this was something deliberate, meant to disconcert him. Ender did not want to give the old man the victory. To pass the time he began to do exercises. Some were impossible without the gym equipment, but others, especially from his personal defense class, he could do without any aids.

The exercises moved him around the room. He was practicing lunges and kicks. One move took him near the old man, as he had come near him before, but this time the old claw shot out and seized Ender's left leg in the middle of a kick. It pulled Ender off his feet and landed him heavily on the floor.

Ender leapt to his feet immediately, furious. He found the old man sitting calmly, cross-legged, not breathing heavily, as if he had never moved. Ender stood poised to fight, but the other's immobility made it impossible for Ender to attack. What, kick the old man's head off? And then explain it to Graff—oh, the old man kicked me, and I had to get even.

He went back to his exercises; the old man kept watching.

Finally, tired and angry at this wasted day, a prisoner in his room, Ender went back to his bed to get his desk. As he leaned over to pick up the desk, he felt a hand jab roughly between his thighs and another hand grab his hair. In a moment he had been turned upside down. His face and shoulders were being pressed into the floor by the old man's knee, while his back was excruciatingly bent and his legs were pinioned by the old man's arm. Ender was helpless to use his arms, he couldn't bend his back to gain slack so he could use his legs. In less than two seconds the old man had completely defeated Ender Wiggin.

"All right," Ender gasped. "You win."

The man's knee thrust painfully downward. "Since when," asked the man, his voice soft and rasping, "do you have to tell the enemy when he has won?"

Ender remained silent.

"I surprised you once, Ender Wiggin. Why didn't you destroy me immediately afterward? Just because I looked peaceful? You turned your back on me. Stupid. You have learned nothing. You have never had a teacher."

Ender was angry now, and made no attempt to control or conceal it. "I've had too many teachers, how was I supposed to know you'd turn out to be a—"

"An enemy, Ender Wiggin," whispered the old man. "I am your enemy, the first one you've ever had who was smarter than you. There is no teacher but the enemy. No one but the enemy will tell you what the enemy is going to do. No one but the enemy will ever teach you how to destroy and conquer. Only the enemy shows you where you are weak. Only the enemy tells you where he is strong. And the rules of the game are what you can do to him and what you can stop him from doing to you. I am your enemy from now on. From now on I am your teacher."

Then the old man let Ender's legs fall. Because he still held Ender's head to the floor, the boy couldn't use his arms to compensate, and his legs hit the surface with a loud crack and a sickening pain. Then the old man stood and let Ender rise.

Slowly Ender pulled his legs under him, with a faint groan of pain. He knelt on all fours for a moment, recovering. Then his right arm flashed out, reaching for his enemy. The old man quickly danced back and Ender's hand closed on air as his teacher's foot shot forward to catch Ender on the chin.

Ender's chin wasn't there. He was lying flat on his back, spinning on the floor, and during the moment that his teacher was off balance from his kick,

Ender's feet smashed into the old man's other leg. He fell in a heap—but close enough to strike out and hit Ender in the face. Ender couldn't find an arm or a leg that held still long enough to be grabbed, and in the meantime blows were landing on his back and arms. Ender was smaller—he couldn't reach past the old man's flailing limbs. Finally he managed to pull away and scramble back near the door.

The old man was sitting cross-legged again, but now the apathy was gone. He was smiling. "Better, this time, boy. But slow. You will have to be better with a fleet than you are with your body or no one will be safe with you in command. Lesson learned?"

Ender nodded slowly. He ached in a hundred places.

"Good," said the old man. "Then we'll never have to have such a battle again. All the rest with the simulator. *I* will program your battles now, not the computer; I will devised the strategy of your enemy, and you will learn to be quick and discover what tricks the enemy has for you. Remember, boy. From now on the enemy is more clever than you. From now on the enemy is stronger than you. From now on you are always about to lose."

The old man's face grew serious again. "You will be about to lose, Ender, but you will win. You will learn to defeat the enemy. He will teach you how."

The teacher got up. "In this school, it has always been the practice for a young student to be chosen by an older student. The two become companions, and the older boy teaches the younger one everything he knows. Always they fight, always they compete, always they are together. I have chosen you."

Ender spoke as the old man walked to the door. "You're too old to be a student."

"One is never too old to be a student of the enemy. I have learned from the buggers. You will learn from me."

As the old man palmed the door open, Ender leaped into the air and kicked him in the small of the back with both feet. He hit hard enough that he rebounded onto his feet, as the old man cried out and collapsed on the floor.

The old man got up slowly, holding onto the door handle, his face contorted with pain. He seemed disabled, but Ender didn't trust him. Yet in spite of his suspicion he was caught off guard by the old man's speed. In a moment he found himself on the floor near the opposite wall, his nose and lip bleeding where his face had hit the bed. He was able to turn enough to see the old man standing in the doorway, wincing and holding his back. The old man grinned.

Ender grinned back. "Teacher," he said. "Do you have a name?"

"Mazer Rackham," said the old man. Then he was gone.

From then on, Ender was either with Mazer Rackham or alone. The old man rarely spoke, but he was there; at meals, at tutorials, at the simulator, in his room at night. Sometimes Mazer would leave, but always, when Mazer wasn't there, the door was locked, and no one came until Mazer returned. Ender went through a week in which he called him Jailor Rackman. Mazer answered to the name as readily as to his own, and showed no sign that it bothered him at all. Ender soon gave it up.

There were compensations. Mazer took Ender through the videos of the old battles from the First Invasion and the disastrous defeats of the I.F. in the Second Invasion. These were not pieced together from the censored public videos, but whole and continuous. Since many videos were working in the major battles, they studied bugger tactics and strategies from many angles. For the first time in his life, a teacher was pointing out things that Ender had not already seen for himself. For the first time, Ender had found a living mind he could admire.

"Why aren't you dead?" Ender asked him. "You fought your battle seventy years ago. I don't think you're even sixty years old."

"The miracle of relativity," said Mazer. "They kept me here for twenty years after the battle, even though I begged them to let me command one of the starships they launched against the bugger home planet and the bugger colonies. Then they—came to understand some things about the way soldiers behave in the stress of battle."

"What things?"

"You've never been taught enough psychology to understand. Enough to say that they realized that even though I would never be able to command the fleet—I'd be dead before the fleet even arrived—I was still the only person able to understand the things I understood about the buggers. I was, they realized, the only person who had ever defeated the buggers by intelligence rather than luck. They needed me here to—teach the person who *would* command the fleet."

"So they sent you out in a starship, got you up to a relativistic speed—"

"And then I turned around and came home. A very dull voyage, Ender. Fifty years in space. Officially, only eight years passed for me, but it felt like five hundred. All so I could teach the next commander everything I knew."

"Am I to be the commander, then?"

"Let's say that you're our best bet at present."

"There are others being prepared, too?"

"No."

"That makes me the only choice, then, doesn't it?"

Mazer shrugged.

"Except you. You're still alive, aren't you? Why not you?"

Mazer shook his head.

"Why not? You won before."

"I cannot be the commander for good and sufficient reasons."

"Show me how you beat the buggers, Mazer."

Mazer's face went inscrutable.

"You've shown me every other battle seven times at least. I think I've seen ways to beat what the buggers did before, but you've never shown me how you actually *did* beat them."

"The video is a very tightly kept secret, Ender."

"I know. I've pieced it together, partly. You, with your tiny reserve force, and their armada, those great big heavy-bellied starships launching their swarms of fighters. You dart in at one ship, fire at it, an explosion. That's where they always stop the clips. After that, it's just soldiers going into bugger ships and already finding them dead inside."

Mazer grinned. "So much for tightly kept secrets. Come on, let's watch the video."

They were alone in the video room, and Ender palmed the door locked. "All right, let's watch."

The video showed exactly what Ender had pieced together. Mazer's suicidal plunge into the heart of the enemy formation, the single explosion, and then—

Nothing. Mazer's ship went on, dodged the shock wave, and wove his way among the other bugger ships. They did not fire on him. They did not change course. Two of them crashed into each other and exploded—a needless collision that either pilot could have avoided. Neither made the slightest movement.

Mazer sped up the action. Skipped ahead. "We waited for three hours," he said. "Nobody could be believe it." Then the I.F. ships began approaching the bugger starships. Marines began their cutting and boarding operations. The videos showed the buggers already dead at their posts.

"So you see," said Mazer, "you already knew all there was to see."

"Why did it happen?"

"Nobody knows. I have my personal opinions. But there are plenty of scientists who tell me I'm less than qualified to have opinions."

"You're the one who won the battle."

"I thought that qualified me to comment, too, but you know how it is. Xenobiologists and xenopsychologists can't accept the idea that a starpilot scooped them by sheer guesswork. I think they all hate me because, after they saw these videos, they had to live out the rest of their natural lives here on Eros. Security, you know. They weren't happy."

"Tell me."

"The buggers don't talk. They think to each other, and it's instantaneous, like the philotic effect. Like the ansible. But most people always thought that meant a controlled communication, like language—I think you a thought and then you answer me. I never believed that. It's too *immediate*, the way they respond together to things. You've seen the videos. They aren't conversing and deciding among possible courses of action. Every ship acts like part of a single organism. It responds the way your body responds during combat, different parts automatically, thoughtlessly doing everything they're supposed to do. They aren't having a mental conversation between people with different thought processes. *All* their thoughts are present, together, at once."

"A single person, and each bugger is like a hand or a foot?"

"Yes. I wasn't the first person to suggest it, but I was the first person to believe it. And something else. Something so childish and stupid that the xenobiologists laughed me to silence when I said it after the battle. The buggers are *bugs*. They're like ants and bees. A queen, the workers. That was maybe a hundred million years ago, but that's how they started, that kind of pattern. It's a sure thing none of the buggers *we* saw had any way of making more little buggers. So when they evolved this ability to think together, wouldn't they still keep the queen? Wouldn't the queen still be the center of the group? Why would that ever change?"

"So it's the queen who controls the whole group."

"I had evidence, too. Not evidence that any of them could see. It wasn't there in the First Invasion, because that was exploratory. But the Second Invasion was a colony. To set up a new hive, or whatever."

"And so they brought a queen."

"The videos of the Second Invasion, when they were destroying our fleets out in the comet shell." He began to call them up and display the buggers' patterns. "Show me the queen's ship."

It was subtle. Ender couldn't see it for a long time. The bugger ships kept moving, all of them. There was no obvious flagship, no apparent nerve center. But gradually, as Mazer played the videos over and over again, Ender began to see the way that all the movements focused on, radiated from a center point. The center point shifted, but it was obvious, after he looked long enough, that the eyes of the fleet, the *I* of the fleet, the perspective from which all decisions were being made, was one particular ship. He pointed it out.

"You see it. I see it. That makes two people out of all of those who have seen this video. But it's true, isn't it."

"They make that ship move just like any other ship."

"They know it's their weak point."

"But you're right. That's the queen. But then you'd think that when you went for it, they would have immediately focused all their power on you. They could have blown you out of the sky."

"I know. That part I don't understand. Not that they didn't try to stop me—they were firing at me. But it's as if they really couldn't believe, until it was too late, that I would actually *kill* the queen. Maybe in their world, queens are never killed, only captured, only checkmated. I did something they didn't think an enemy would ever do."

"And when she died, the others all died."

"No, they just went stupid. The first ships we boarded, the buggers were still alive. Organically. But they didn't move, didn't respond to anything, even when our scientists vivisected some of them to see if we could learn a few more things about buggers. After a while they all died. No will. There's nothing in those little bodies when the queen is gone."

"Why don't they believe you?"

"Because we didn't find a queen."

"She got blown to pieces."

"Fortunes of war. Biology takes second place to survival. But some of them *are* coming around to my way of thinking. You can't live in this place without the evidence staring you in the face."

"What evidence is there in Eros?"

"Ender, look around you. Human beings didn't carve this place. We like taller ceilings, for one thing. This was the buggers' advance post in the First Invasion. They carved this place out before we even knew they were here. We've living in a bugger hive. But we already paid our rent. It cost the marines a thousand lives to clear them out of these honeycombs, room by room. The buggers fought for every meter of it."

Now Ender understood why the rooms had always felt wrong to him. "I knew this place wasn't a human place."

"This was the treasure trove. If they had known we would win that first war, they probably would never have built this place. We learned gravity manipulation because they enhanced the gravity here. We learned efficient use of stellar energy because they blacked out this planet. In fact, that's how we discovered *them*. In a period of three days, Eros gradually disappeared from telescopes. We sent a tug to find out why. It found out. The tug transmitted its videos, including the buggers boarding and slaughtering the crew. It kept right on transmitting through the entire bugger examination of the boat. Not until they finally dismantled the entire tug did the transmissions stop. It was their blindness—they never had to transmit anything by machine, and so with the crew dead, it didn't occur to them that anybody could be watching."

"Why did they kill the crew?"

"Why not? To them, losing a few crew members would be like clipping your nails. Nothing to get upset about. They probably thought they were routinely shutting down our communications by turning off the workers running the tug. Not murdering living, sentient beings with an independent genetic future. Murder's no big deal to them. Only queen-killing, really, is murder, because only queen-killing closes off a genetic path."

"So they didn't know what they were doing."

"Don't start apologizing for them, Ender. Just because they didn't know they were killing human beings doesn't mean they weren't killing human beings. We do have a right to defend ourselves as best we can, and the only way we found that works is killing the buggers before they kill us. Think of it this way. In all the bugger wars so far, they've killed thousands and thousands of living, thinking beings. And in all those wars, we've killed only one."

"If you hadn't killed the queen, Mazer, would we have lost the war?"

"I'd say the odds would have been three to two against us. I still think I could have trashed their fleet pretty badly before they burned us out. They have great response time and a lot of firepower, but we have a few advantages, too. Every single one of our ships contains an intelligent human being who's thinking on his own. Every one of us is capable of coming up with a brilliant solution to a problem. They can only come up with one brilliant solution at a time. The buggers think fast, but they aren't smart all over. But on *our* side, even when some incredibly timid and stupid commanders lost the major battles of the Second Invasion, some of their subordinates were able to do real damage to the bugger fleet."

"What about when our invasion reaches them? Will we just get the queen again?"

"The buggers didn't learn interstellar travel by being dumb. That was a strategy that could work only once. I suspect that we'll never get near a queen unless we actually make it to their home planet. After all, the queen doesn't have to be *with* them to direct a battle. The queen only has to be present to have little baby buggers. The Second Invasion was a colony—the queen was coming to populate the Earth. But this time—no, that won't work. We'll have to beat them fleet by fleet. And because they have the resources of dozens of star systems to draw on, my guess is they'll outnumber us by a lot, in every battle."

Ender remembered his battle against two armies at once. And I thought they were cheating. When the real war begins, it'll be like that every time. And there won't be any gate I can go for.

"We've only got two things going for us, Ender. We don't have to aim particularly well. Our weapons have great spread."

"Then we aren't using the nuclear missiles from the First and Second Invasions?"

"Dr. Device is much more powerful. Nuclear weapons, after all, were weak enough to be used on Earth at one time. The Little Doctor could never be used on a planet. Still, I wish I'd had one during the Second Invasion."

"How does it work?"

"I don't know, not well enough to build one. At the focal point of two beams, it sets up a field in which molecules can't hold together anymore. Electrons can't be shared. How much physics do you know, at that level?"

"We spend most of our time on astrophysics, but I know enough to get the idea."

"The field spreads out in a sphere, but it gets weaker the farther it spreads. Except that where it actually runs into a lot of molecules, it gets stronger and starts over. The bigger the ship, the stronger the new field."

"So each time the field hits a ship, it sends out a new sphere—"

"And if their ships are too close together, it can set up a chain that wipes them all out. Then the field dies down, the molecules come back together, and where you had a ship, you now have a lump of dirt with a lot of iron molecules in it. No radioactivity, no mess. Just dirt. We may be able to trap them close together on the first battle, but they learn fast. They'll keep their distance from each other."

"So Dr. Device isn't a missile—I can't shoot around corners."

"That's right. Missiles wouldn't do any good now. We learned a lot from them in the First Invasion, but they also learned from us—how to set up the Ecstatic Shield, for instance."

"The Little Doctor penetrates the shield?"

"As if it weren't there. You can't *see* through the shield to aim and focus the beams, but since the generator of the Ecstatic Shield is always in the exact center, it isn't hard to figure it out."

"Why haven't I ever been trained with this?"

"You always have. We just let the computer tend to it for you. Your job is to get into a superior strategic position and choose a target. The shipboard computers are much better at aiming the Doctor than you are."

"Why is it called Dr. Device?"

"When it was developed, it was called a Molecular Detachment Device. M.D. Device."

Ender still didn't understand.

"M.D. The initials stand for Medical Doctor, too. M.D. Device, therefore Dr. Device. It was a joke." Ender didn't see what was funny about it.

They had changed the simulator. He could still control the perspective and the degree of detail, but there were no ship's controls anymore. Instead, it was a new panel of levers, and a small headset with earphones and a small microphone.

The technician who was waiting there quickly explained how to wear the headset.

"But how do I control the ships?" asked Ender.

Mazer explained. He wasn't going to control ships anymore. "You've reached the next phase of your training. You have experience in every level of strategy, but now it's time for you to concentrate on commanding an entire fleet. As you worked with toon leaders in Battle School, so now you will work with squadron leaders. You have been assigned three dozen such leaders to train. You must teach them intelligent tactics; you must learn their strengths and limitations; you must make them into a whole."

"When will they come here?"

"They're already in place in their own simulators. You will speak to them through the headset. The new levers on your control panel enable you to see from the perspective of any of your squadron leaders. This more closely duplicates the conditions you might encounter in a real battle, where you will know only what your ships can see."

"How can I work with squadron leaders I never see?"

"And why would you need to see them?"

"To know who they are, how they think—"

"You'll learn who they are and how they think from the way they work with the simulator. But even so, I think you won't be concerned. They're listening to you right now. Put on the headset so you can hear them."

Ender put on the headset.

"Salaam," said a whisper in his ears.

"Alai," said Ender.

"And me, the dwarf."

"Bean."

And Petra, and Dink; Crazy Tom, Shen, Hot Soup, Fly Molo, Carn Carby, all the best students Ender had fought with or fought against, everyone that Ender had trusted in Battle School. "I didn't know you were here," he said. "I didn't know you were coming."

"They've been flogging us through the simulator for three months now," said Dink.

"You'll find that I'm by far the best tactician," said Petra. "Dink tries, but he has the mind of a child."

So they began working together, each squadron leader commanding individual pilots, and Ender commanding the squadron leaders. They learned many ways of working together, as the simulator forced them to try different situations. Sometimes the simulator gave them a larger fleet to work with; Ender set them up then in three or four toons that consisted of three or four squadrons each. Sometimes the simulator gave them a single starship with its twelve fighters, and he chose three squadron leaders with four fighters each.

It was pleasure; it was play. The computer-controlled enemy was none too bright, and they always won despite their mistakes, their miscommunications. But in the three weeks they practiced together, Ender came to know them very well. Dink, who deftly carried out instructions but was slow to improvise; Bean, who couldn't control large groups of ships effectively but could use a few like a scalpel, reacting beautifully to anything the computer threw at him; Alai, who was almost as good a strategist as Ender and could be entrusted to do well with half a fleet and only vague instructions.

The better Ender knew them, the faster he could deploy them, the better he could use them. The simulator would display the situation on the screen. In that moment Ender learned for the first time what his own fleet would consist of and how the enemy fleet was deployed. It took him only a few minutes now to call the squadron leaders that he needed, assign them to certain ships or groups of ships, and give them their assignments. Then, as the battle progressed, he would skip from one leader's point of view to another's, making suggestions and, occasionally, giving orders as the need arose. Since the others could see only their own battle perspective, he would sometimes give them orders that made no sense to them; but they, too, learned to trust Ender. If he told them to withdraw, they withdrew, knowing that either they were in an exposed position, or their withdrawal might entice the enemy into a weakened posture. They also knew that Ender trusted them to do as they judged best when he gave them no orders. If their style of fighting were not right for the situation they were placed in, Ender would not have chosen them for that assignment.

The trust was complete, the working of the fleet quick and responsive. And at the end of three weeks, Mazer showed him a replay of their most recent battle, only this time from the enemy's point of view.

"This is what he saw as you attacked. What does it remind you of? The quickness of response, for instance?"

"We look like a bugger fleet."

"You match them, Ender. You're as fast as they are. And here—look at this."

Ender watched as all his squadrons moved at once, each responding to its own situation, all guided by Ender's overall command, but daring, improvising, feinting, attacking with an independence no bugger fleet had ever shown.

"The bugger hive-mind is very good, but it can only concentrate on a few things at once. All your squadrons can concentrate a keen intelligence on what they're doing, and what they've been assigned to do is also guided by a clever mind. So you see that you do have some advantages. Superior, though not irresistible, weaponry; comparable speed and greater available intelligence. These are your advantages. Your disadvantage is that you will always, always be outnumbered, and after each battle your enemy will learn more about you, how to fight you, and those changes will be put into effect instantly."

Ender waited for his conclusion.

"So Ender, we will now begin your education. We have programmed the computer to simulate the kinds of situations we might expect in encounters with the enemy. We are using the movement patterns we saw in the Second Invasion. But instead of mindlessly following these same patterns, I will be controlling the enemy simulation. At first you will see easy situations that you are expected to win handily. Learn from them, because I will always be there, one step ahead of you, programming more difficult and advanced patterns into the computer so that your next battle is more difficult, so that you are pushed to the limit of your abilities."

"And beyond?"

"The time is short. You must learn as quickly as you can. When I gave myself to starship travel, just so I would still be alive when you appeared, my wife and children all died, and my grandchildren were my own age when I came back. I had nothing to say to them. I was cut off from all the people that I loved, everything I knew, living in this alien catacomb and forced to do nothing of importance but teach student after student, each one so hopeful, each one, ultimately, a weakling, a failure. I teach, I teach, but no one learns. You, too, have great promise, like so many students before you, but the seeds of failure may be in you, too. It's my job to find them, to destroy you if I can, and believe me, Ender, if you can be destroyed I can do it."

"So I'm not the first."

"No, of course you're not. But you're the last. If you don't learn, there'll be no time to find anyone else. So I have hope for you, if only because you are the only one left to hope for."

"What about the others? My squadron leaders?"

"Which of them is fit to take your place?"

"Alai."

"Be honest."

Ender had no answer, then.

"I am not a happy man, Ender. Humanity does not ask us to be happy. It merely asks us to be brilliant on its behalf. Survival first, then happiness as we can manage it. So, Ender, I hope you do not bore me during your training with complaints that you are not having fun. Take what pleasure you can in the interstices of your work, but your work is first, learning is first, winning is everything because without it there is nothing. When you can give me back my dead wife, Ender, then you can complain to me about what this education costs you."

"I wasn't trying to get out of anything."

"But you will, Ender. Because I am going to grind you down to dust, if I can. I'm going to hit you with everything I can imagine, and I will have no mercy, because when you face the buggers they will think of things I *can't* imagine, and compassion for human beings is impossible for them."

"You can't grind me down, Mazer."

"Oh, can't I?"

"Because I'm stronger than you."

Mazer smiled. "We'll see about that, Ender."

———

Mazer wakened him before morning; the clock said 0340, and Ender felt groggy as he padded along the corridor behind Mazer. "Early to bed and early to rise," Mazer intoned, "makes a man stupid and blind in the eyes."

He had been dreaming that buggers were vivisecting him. Only instead of cutting open his body, they were cutting up his memories and displaying them like holographs and trying to make sense of them. It was a very odd dream, and Ender couldn't easily shake loose of it, even as he walked through the tunnels to the simulator room. The buggers tormented him in his sleep, and Mazer wouldn't leave him alone when he was awake. Between the two of them he had no rest. Ender forced himself awake. Apparently Mazer meant it when he said he meant to break Ender down—and forcing him to play when tired and sleepy was just the sort of cheap and easy trick Ender should have expected. Well, today, it wouldn't work.

He got to the simulator and found his squadron leaders already on the wire, waiting for him. There was no enemy yet, so he divided them into two armies and began a mock battle, commanding both sides so he could control the test that each of his leaders was going through. They began slowly, but soon were vigorous and alert.

Then the simulator field went blank, the ships disappeared, and everything changed at once. At the near edge of the simulator field they could see the shapes, drawn in holographic light, of three starships from the human fleet. Each would have twelve fighters. The enemy, obviously aware of the human presence, had formed a globe with a single ship at the center. Ender was not fooled—it would not be a queen ship. The buggers outnumbered Ender's fighter force by two to one, but they were also grouped much closer together than they should have been—Dr. Device would be able to do much more damage than the enemy expected.

Ender selected one starship, made it blink in the simulator field, and spoke into the microphone. "Alai, this is yours; assign Petra and Vlad to the fighters as you wish." He assigned the other two starships with their fighter forces, except for one fighter from each starship that he reserved for Bean. "Slip the wall and get below them, Bean, unless they start chasing you—then run back to the reserves for safety. Otherwise, get in a place where I can call on you for quick results. Alai, form your force into a compact assault at one point in their globe. Don't fire until I tell you. This is maneuver only."

"This one's easy, Ender," Alai said.

"It's easy, so why not be careful? I'd like to do this without the loss of a single ship."

Ender grouped his reserves in two forces that shadowed Alai at a distance; Bean was already off the simulator, though Ender occasionally flipped to Bean's point of view to keep track of where he was.

It was Alai, however, who played the delicate game with the enemy. He was in a bullet-shaped formation, and probed the enemy globe. Wherever he came near, the bugger ships pulled back, as if to draw him in toward the ship in the center. Alai skimmed to the side; the bugger ships kept up with him, withdrawing wherever he was close, returning to the sphere pattern when he had passed.

Feint, withdraw, skim the globe to another point, withdraw again, feint again; and then Ender said, "Go on in, Alai."

His bullet started in, while he said to Ender, "You know they'll just let me through and surround me and eat me alive."

"Just ignore that ship in the middle."

"Whatever you say, boss."

Sure enough, the globe began to contract. Ender brought the reserves forward; the enemy ships concentrated on the side of the globe nearer the reserves. "Attack them there, where they're most concentrated," Ender said.

"This defies four thousand years of military history," said Alai, moving his fighters forward. "We're supposed to attack where we outnumber them."

"In this simulation they obviously don't know what our weapons can do. It'll only work once, but let's make it spectacular. Fire at will."

Alai did. The simulation responded beautifully: first one or two, then a dozen, then most of the enemy ships exploded in dazzling light as the field leapt from ship to ship in the tight formation. "Stay out of the way," Ender said.

The ships on the far side of the globe formation were not affected by the chain reaction, but it was a simple matter to hunt them down and destroy them. Bean took care of stragglers that tried to escape toward his end of space. The battle was over. It had been easier than most of their recent exercises.

Mazer shrugged when Ender told him so. "This is a simulation of a real invasion. There had to be one battle in which they didn't know what we could do. Now your work begins. Try not to be too arrogant about the victory. I'll give you the real challenges soon enough."

Ender practiced ten hours a day with his squadron leaders, but not all at once; he gave them a few hours in the afternoon to rest. Simulated battles under Mazer's supervision came every two or three days, and as Mazer had promised, they were never so easy again. The enemy quickly abandoned its attempt to surround Ender, and never again grouped its forces closely enough to allow a chain reaction. There was something new every time, something harder. Sometimes Ender had only a single starship and eight fighters; once the enemy dodged through an asteroid belt; sometimes the enemy left stationary traps, large installations that blew up if Ender brought one of his squadrons too close, often crippling or destroying some of Ender's ships. "You cannot absorb losses!" Mazer shouted at him after one battle. "When you get into a *real* battle you won't have the luxury of an infinite supply of computer-generated fighters. You'll have what you brought with you and *nothing more*. Now get used to fighting without unnecessary waste."

"It wasn't unnecessary waste," Ender said. "I can't win battles if I'm so terrified of losing a ship that I never take any risks."

Mazer smiled. "Excellent, Ender. You're beginning to learn. But in a real battle, you would have superior officers and, worst of all, civilians shouting those things at you. Now, if the enemy had been at all bright, they would have caught you *here,* and taken Tom's squadron." Together they went over the battle; in the next practice, Ender would show his leaders what Mazer had shown him, and they'd learn to cope with it the next time they saw it.

They thought they had been ready before, that they had worked smoothly together as a team. Now, though, having fought through real challenges together, they all began to trust each other more than ever, and battles became exhilarating. They told Ender that the ones who weren't actually playing would come into the simulator rooms and watch. Ender imagined what it would be like to have his friends there with him, cheering or laughing or gasping with apprehension; sometimes he thought it would be a great distraction, but other times he wished for it with all his heart. Even when he had spent his days lying out in the sunlight on a raft in a lake, he had not been so lonely. Mazer Rackham was his companion, was his teacher, but was not his friend.

He made no complaint, though. Mazer had told him there would be no pity, and his private unhappiness meant nothing to anyone. Most of the time it meant nothing even to Ender. He kept his mind on the game, trying to learn from the battles. And not just the particular lessons of that battle, but what the buggers might have done if they had been more clever, and how Ender would react if they did it in the future. He lived with past battles and future battles both, waking and sleeping, and he drove his squadron leaders with an intensity that occasionally provoked rebelliousness.

"You're too kind to us," said Alai one day. "Why don't you get annoyed with us for not being brilliant *every* moment of *every* practice. If you keep coddling us like this we'll think you like us."

Some of the others laughed into their microphones. Ender recognized the irony, of course, and answered with a long silence. When he finally spoke, he ignored Alai's complaint. "Again," he said, "and this time without self-pity." They did it again, and did it right.

But as their trust in Ender as a commander grew, their friendship, remembered from the Battle School days, gradually disappeared. It was to each other that they became close; it was with each other that they exchanged confidences. Ender was their teacher and commander, as distant from them as Mazer was from him, and as demanding.

They fought all the better for it. And Ender was not distracted from his work.

At least, not while he was awake. As he drifted off to sleep each night, it was with thoughts of the simulator playing through his mind. But in the night he thought of other things. Often he remembered the corpse of the Giant, decaying steadily; he did not remember it, though, in the pixels of the picture on his desk. Instead it was real, the faint odor of death still lingering near it. Things were changed in his dreams. The little village that had grown up between the Giant's ribs was composed of buggers now, and they saluted him gravely, like gladiators greeting Caesar before they died for his entertainment. He did not hate the buggers in his dream; and even though he knew that they had hidden their queen from him, he did not try

to search for her. He always left the Giant's body quickly, and when he got
to the playground, the children were always there, wolven and mocking;
they wore faces that he knew. Sometimes Peter and sometimes Bonzo,
sometimes Stilson and Bernard; just as often, though, the savage creatures
were Alai and Shen, Dink and Petra; sometimes one of them would be
Valentine, and in his dream he also shoved her under the water and waited
for her to drown. She writhed in his hands, fought to come up, but at last
was still. He dragged her out of the lake and onto the raft, where she lay
with her face in the rictus of death. He screamed and wept over her, crying
again and again that it was a game, a game, he was only playing!—

Then Mazer Rackham shook him awake. "You were calling out in your
sleep," he said.

"Sorry," Ender said.

"Never mind. It's time for another battle."

Steadily the pace increased. There were usually two battles a day now,
and Ender held practices to a minimum. He would use the time while the
others rested to pore over the replays of past games, trying to spot his own
weaknesses, trying to guess what would happen next. Sometimes he was
fully prepared for the enemy's innovations; sometimes he was not.

"I think you're cheating," Ender told Mazer one day.

"Oh?"

"You can observe my practice sessions. You can see what I'm working
on. You seem to be ready for everything I do."

"Most of what you see is computer simulations," Mazer said. "The computer is programmed to respond to your innovations only after you use them
once in battle."

"Then the computer is cheating."

"You need to get more sleep, Ender."

But he could not sleep. He lay awake longer and longer each night, and his
sleep was less restful. He woke too often in the night. Whether he was waking
up to think more about the game or to escape from his dreams, he wasn't sure.
It was as if someone rode him in his sleep, forcing him to wander through his
worst memories, to live in them again as if they were real. Nights were so real
that days began to seem dreamlike to him. He began to worry that he would
not think clearly enough, that he would be too tired when he played. Always
when the game began, the intensity of it awoke him, but if his mental abilities
began to slip, he wondered, would he notice it?

And he seemed to be slipping. He never had a battle anymore in which
he did not lose at least a few fighters. Several times the enemy was able to
trick him into exposing more weakness than he meant to; other times the
enemy was able to wear him down by attrition until his victory was as much
a matter of luck as strategy. Mazer would go over the game with a look of
contempt on his face. "Look at this," he would say. "You didn't have to
do this." And Ender would return to practice with his leaders, trying to

keep up their morale, but sometimes letting slip his disappointment with their weaknesses, the fact that they made mistakes.

"Sometimes we make mistakes," Petra whispered to him once. It was a plea for help.

"And sometimes we don't," Ender answered her. If she got help, it would not be from him. He would teach; let her find her friends among the others.

Then came a battle that nearly ended in disaster. Petra led her force too far; they were exposed, and she discovered it in a moment when Ender wasn't with her. In only a few moments she had lost all but two of her ships. Ender found her then, ordered her to move them in a certain direction; she didn't answer. There was no movement. And in a moment those two fighters, too, would be lost.

Ender knew at once that he had pushed her too hard—because of her brilliance he had called on her to play far more often and under much more demanding circumstances than all but a few of the others. But he had no time now to worry about Petra, or to feel guilty about what he had done to her. He called on Crazy Tom to command the two remaining fighters, then went on, trying to salvage the battle; Petra had occupied a key position, and now all of Ender's strategy came apart. If the enemy had not been too eager and clumsy in exploiting their advantage, Ender would have lost. But Shen was able to catch a group of the enemy in too tight a formation and took them out with a single chain reaction. Crazy Tom brought his two surviving fighters in through the gap and caused havoc with the enemy, and though his ships and Shen's as well were finally destroyed, Fly Molo was able to mop up and complete the victory.

At the end of the battle, he could hear Petra crying out, trying to get a microphone, "Tell him I'm sorry, I was just so tired, I couldn't think, that was all, tell Ender I'm sorry."

She was not there for the next few practices, and when she did come back she was not as quick as she had been, not as daring. Much of what had made her a good commander was lost. Ender couldn't use her anymore, except in routine, closely supervised assignments. She was no fool. She knew what had happened. But she also knew that Ender had no other choice, and told him so.

The fact remained that she had broken, and she was far from being the weakest of his squad leaders. It was a warning—he could not press his commanders more than they could bear. Now, instead of using his leaders whenever he needed their skills, he had to keep in mind how often they had fought. He had to spell them off, which meant that sometimes he went into battle with commanders he trusted a little less. As he eased the pressure on them, he increased the pressure on himself.

Late one night he woke up in pain. There was blood on his pillow, the taste of blood in his mouth. His fingers were throbbing. He saw that in his sleep he had been gnawing on his own fist. The blood was still flowing smoothly. "Mazer!" he called. Rackham woke up and called at once for a doctor.

As the doctor treated the wound, Mazer said, "I don't care how much you eat, Ender, self-cannibalism won't get you out of this school."

"I was asleep," Ender said. "I don't want to get out of Command School."

"Good."

"The others. The ones who didn't make it."

"What are you talking about?"

"Before me. Your other students, who didn't make it through the training. What happened to them?"

"They didn't make it. That's all. We don't punish the ones who fail. They just—don't go on."

"Like Bonzo."

"Bonzo?"

"He went home."

"Not like Bonzo."

"*What*, then? What happened to them? When they failed?"

"Why does it matter, Ender?"

Ender didn't answer.

"None of them failed at *this* point in their course, Ender. You made a mistake with Petra. She'll recover. But Petra is Petra, and you are you."

"Part of what I am is her. Is what she made me."

"You won't fail, Ender. Not this early in the course. You've had some tight ones, but you've always won. You don't know what your limits are yet, but if you've reached them already you're a good deal feebler than I thought."

"Do they die?"

"Who?"

"The ones who fail."

"No, they don't die. Good heavens, boy, you're playing games."

"I think that Bonzo died. I dreamed about it last night. I remembered the way he looked after I jammed his face with my head. I think I must have pushed his nose back into his brain. The blood was coming out of his eyes. I think he was dead right then."

"It was just a dream."

"Mazer, I don't want to keep dreaming these things. I'm afraid to sleep. I keep thinking of things that I don't want to remember. My whole life keeps playing out as if I were a recorder and someone else wanted to watch the most terrible parts of my life."

"We can't drug you if that's what you're hoping for. I'm sorry if you have bad dreams. Should we leave the light on at night?"

"Don't make fun of me!" Ender said. "I'm afraid I'm going crazy."

The doctor was finished with the bandage. Mazer told him he could go. He went.

"Are you really afraid of that?" Mazer asked.

Ender thought about it and wasn't sure.

"In my dreams," said Ender, "I'm never sure whether I'm really me."

"Strange dreams are a safety valve, Ender. I'm putting you under a little pressure for the first time in your life. Your body is finding ways to compensate, that's all. You're a big boy now. It's time to stop being afraid of the night."

"All right," Ender said. He decided then that he would never tell Mazer about his dreams again.

The days wore on, with battles every day, until at last Ender settled into the routine of the destruction of himself. He began to have pains in his stomach. They put him on a bland diet, but soon he didn't have an appetite for anything at all. "Eat," Mazer said, and Ender would mechanically put food in his mouth. But if nobody told him to eat, he didn't eat.

Two more of his squadron leaders collapsed the way that Petra had; the pressure on the rest became all the greater. The enemy outnumbered them by three or four to one in every battle now; the enemy also retreated more readily when things went badly, regrouping to keep the battle going longer and longer. Sometimes battles lasted for hours before they finally destroyed the last enemy ship. Ender began rotating his squadron leaders within the same battle, bringing in fresh and rested ones to take the place of those who were beginning to get sluggish.

"You know," said Bean one time, as he took over command of Hot Soup's four remaining fighters, "this game isn't quite as fun as it used to be."

Then one day in practice, as Ender was drilling his squadron leaders, the room went black and he woke up on the floor with his face bloody where he had hit the controls.

They put him to bed then, and for three days he was very ill. He remembered seeing faces in his dreams, but they weren't real faces, and he knew it even while he thought he saw them. He thought he saw Valentine sometimes, and sometimes Peter; sometimes his friends from the Battle School, and sometimes the buggers vivisecting him. Once it seemed very real when he saw Colonel Graff bending over him, speaking softly to him, like a kind father. But then he woke up and found only his enemy, Mazer Rackham.

"I'm awake," said Ender.

"So I see," Mazer answered. "Took you long enough. You have a battle today."

So Ender got up and fought the battle and won it. But there was no second battle that day, and they let him go to bed earlier. His hands were shaking as he undressed.

During the night he thought he felt hands touching him gently. Hands with affection in them, and gentleness. He dreamed he heard voices.

"You haven't been kind to him."

"That wasn't the assignment."

"How long can he go on? He's breaking down."

"Long enough. It's nearly finished."

"So soon?"

"A few days, and then he's through."

"How will he do, when he's already like this?"

"Fine. Even today, he fought better than ever."

In his dream, the voices sounded like Colonel Graff and Mazer Rackham. But that was the way dreams were, the craziest things could happen, because he dreamed he heard one of the voices saying, "I can't bear to see what this is doing to him." And the other voice answered, "I know. I love him too." And then they changed into Valentine and Alai, and in his dream they were burying him, only a hill grew up where they laid his body down, and he dried out and became a home for buggers, like the Giant was.

All dreams. If there was love or pity for him, it was only in his dreams.

He woke up and fought another battle and won. Then he went to bed and slept again and dreamed again and then he woke up and won again and slept again and he hardly noticed when waking became sleeping. Nor did he care.

The next day was his last day in Command School, though he didn't know it. Mazer Rackham was not in the room with him when he woke up. He showered and dressed and waited for Mazer to come unlock the door. He didn't come. Ender tried the door. It was open.

Was it an accident that Mazer had let him be free this morning? No one with him to tell him he must eat, he must go to practice, he must sleep. Freedom. The trouble was, he didn't know what to do. He thought for a moment that he might find his squadron leaders, talk to them face to face, but he didn't know where they were. They could be twenty kilometers away, for all he knew. So, after wandering through the tunnels for a little while, he went to the mess hall and ate breakfast near a few marines who were telling dirty jokes that Ender could not begin to understand. Then he went to the simulator room for practice. Even though he was free, he could not think of anything else to do.

Mazer was waiting for him. Ender walked slowly into the room. His step was slightly shuffling, and he felt tired and dull.

Mazer frowned. "Are you awake, Ender?"

There were other people in the simulator room. Ender wondered why they were there, but didn't bother to ask. It wasn't worth asking; no one would tell him anyway. He walked to the simulator controls and sat down, ready to start.

"Ender Wiggin," said Mazer. "Please turn around. Today's game needs a little explanation."

Ender turned around. He glanced at the men gathered at the back of the room. Most of them he had never seen before. Some were even dressed in civilian clothes. He saw Anderson and wondered what he was doing there, who was taking care of the Battle School if he was gone. He saw Graff and remembered the lake in the woods outside Greensboro, and wanted to go home. Take me home, he said silently to Graff. In my dream you said you loved me. Take me home.

But Graff only nodded to him, a greeting, not a promise, and Anderson acted as though he didn't know him at all.

"Pay attention, please, Ender. Today is your final examination in Command School. These observers are here to evaluate what you have learned. If you prefer not to have them in the room, we'll have them watch on another simulator."

"They can stay." Final examination. After today, perhaps he could rest.

"For this to be a fair test of your ability, not just to do what you have practiced many times, but also to meet challenges you have never seen before, today's battle introduces a new element. It is staged around a planet. This will affect the enemy's strategy, and will force you to improvise. Please concentrate on the game today."

Ender beckoned Mazer closer, and asked him quietly, "Am I the first student to make it this far?"

"If you win today, Ender, you will be the first student to do so. More than that I'm not at liberty to say."

"Well, I'm at liberty to hear it."

"You can be as petulant as you want, tomorrow. Today, though, I'd appreciate it if you would keep your mind on the examination. Let's not waste all that you've already done. Now, how will you deal with the planet?"

"I have to get someone behind it, or it's a blind spot."

"True."

"And the gravity is going to affect fuel levels—cheaper to go down than up."

"Yes."

"Does the Little Doctor work against a planet?"

Mazer's face went rigid. "Ender, the buggers never deliberately attacked a civilian population in either invasion. You decide whether it would be wise to adopt a strategy that would invite reprisals."

"Is the planet the only new thing?"

"Can you remember the last time I've given you a battle with only one new thing? Let me assure you, Ender, that I will not be kind to you today. I have a responsibility to the fleet not to let a second-rate student graduate. I will do my best against you, Ender, and I have no desire to coddle you. Just keep in mind everything you know about yourself and everything you know about the buggers, and you have a fair chance of amounting to something."

Mazer left the room.

Ender spoke into the microphone. "Are you there?"

"All of us," said Bean. "Kind of late for practice this morning, aren't you?"

So they hadn't told the squadron leaders. Ender toyed with the idea of telling them how important this battle was to him, but decided it would not help them to have an extraneous concern on their minds. "Sorry," he said. "I overslept."

They laughed. They didn't believe him.

He led them through maneuvers, warming up for the battle ahead. It took him longer than usual to clear his mind, to concentrate on command, but soon enough he was up to speed, responding quickly, thinking well. Or at least, he told himself, I think that I'm thinking well.

The simulator field cleared. Ender waited for the game to appear. What will happen if I pass the test today? Is there another school? Another year or two of grueling training, another year of isolation, another year of people pushing me this way and that way, another year without any control over my own life? He tried to remember how old he was. Eleven. How many years ago did he turn eleven? How many days? It must have happened here at the Command School, but he couldn't remember the day. Maybe he didn't even notice it at the time. Nobody noticed it, except perhaps Valentine.

And as he waited for the game to appear, he wished he could simply lose it, lose the battle badly and completely so that they would remove him from training, like Bonzo, and let him go home. Bonzo had been assigned to Cartagena. He wanted to see travel orders that said Greensboro. Success meant it would go on. Failure meant he could go home.

No, that isn't true, he told himself. They need me, and if I fail, there might not be any home to return to.

But he did not believe it. In his conscious mind he knew it was true, but in other places, deeper places, he doubted that they needed him. Mazer's urgency was just another trick. Just another way to make me do what they want me to do. Another way to keep me from resting. From doing nothing, for a long, long time.

Then the enemy formation appeared, and Ender's weariness turned to despair.

The enemy outnumbered him a thousand to one; the simulator glowed green with them. They were grouped in a dozen different formations, shifting positions, changing shapes, moving in seemingly random patterns through the simulator field. He could not find a path through them—a space that seemed open would close suddenly, and another appear, and a formation that seemed penetrable would suddenly change and be forbidding. The planet was at the far edge of the field, and for all Ender knew there were just as many enemy ships beyond it, out of the simulator's range.

As for his own fleet, it consisted of twenty starships, each with only four fighters. He knew the four-fighter starships—they were old-fashioned, slug-gish, and the range of their Little Doctors was half that of the newer ones. Eighty fighters, against at least five thousand, perhaps ten thousand enemy ships.

He heard his squadron leaders breathing heavily; he could also hear, from the observers behind him, a quiet curse. It was nice to know that one of the adults noticed that it wasn't a fair test. Not that it made any difference. Fairness wasn't part of the game, that was plain. There was no attempt to give him even a remote chance at success. All that I've been through, and they never meant to let me pass at all.

He saw in his mind Bonzo and his vicious little knot of friends, confront-ing him, threatening him; he had been able to shame Bonzo into fighting him alone. That would hardly work here. And he could not surprise the enemy with his ability as he had done with the older boys in the battleroom. Mazer knew Ender's abilities inside and out.

The observers behind him began to cough, to move nervously. They were beginning to realize that Ender didn't know what to do.

I don't care anymore, thought Ender. You can keep your game. If you won't even give me a chance, why should I play?

Like his last game in Battle School, when they put two armies against him.

And just as he remembered that game, apparently Bean remembered it, too, for his voice came over the headset, saying, "Remember, the enemy's gate is *down*."

Molo, Soup, Vlad, Dumper, and Crazy Tom all laughed. They remem-bered, too.

And Ender also laughed. It *was* funny. The adults taking all this so seri-ously, and the children playing along, playing along, believing it too until suddenly the adults went too far, tried too hard, and the children could see through their game. Forget it, Mazer. I don't care if I pass your test, I don't care if I follow your rules. If you can cheat, so can I. I won't let you beat me unfairly—I'll beat you unfairly first.

In that final battle in Battle School, he had won by ignoring the enemy, ignoring his own losses; he had moved against the enemy's gate.

And the enemy's gate was down.

If I break this rule, they'll never let me be a commander. It would be too dangerous. I'll never have to play a game again. And that is victory.

He whispered quickly into the microphone. His commanders took their parts of the fleet and grouped themselves into a thick projectile, a cylinder aimed at the nearest of the enemy formations. The enemy, far from trying to repel him, welcomed him in, so he could be thoroughly entrapped before they destroyed him. Mazer is at least taking into account the fact that by now they would have learned to respect me, thought Ender. And that does buy me time.

Ender dodged downward, north, east, and down again, not seeming to follow any plan, but always ending up a little closer to the enemy planet. Finally the enemy began to close in on him too tightly. Then, suddenly, Ender's formation burst. His fleet seemed to melt into chaos. The eighty fighters seemed to follow no plan at all, firing at enemy ships at random, working their way into hopeless individual paths among the bugger craft.

After a few minutes of battle, however, Ender whispered to his squadron leaders once more, and suddenly a dozen of the remaining fighters formed again into a formation. But now they were on the far side of one of the enemy's most formidable groups; they had, with terrible losses, passed through—and now they had covered more than half the distance to the enemy's planet.

The enemy sees now, thought Ender. Surely Mazer sees what I'm doing.

Or perhaps Mazer cannot believe that I would do it. Well, so much the better for me.

Ender's tiny fleet darted this way and that, sending two or three fighters out as if to attack, then bringing them back. The enemy closed in, drawing in ships and formations that had been widely scattered, bringing them in for the kill. The enemy was most concentrated beyond Ender, so he could not escape back into open space, closing him in. Excellent, thought Ender. Closer. Come closer.

Then he whispered a command and the ships dropped like rocks toward the planet's surface. They were starships and fighters, completely unequipped to handle the heat of passage through an atmosphere. But Ender never intended them to reach the atmosphere. Almost from the moment they began to drop, they were focusing their Little Doctors on one thing only. The planet itself.

One, two, four, seven of his fighters were blown away. It was all a gamble now, whether any of his ships would survive long enough to get in range. It would not take long, once they could focus on the planet's surface. Just a moment with Dr. Device, that's all I want. It occurred to Ender that perhaps the computer wasn't even equipped to show what would happen to a planet if the Little Doctor attacked it. What will I do then, shout Bang, you're dead?

Ender took his hands off the controls and leaned in to watch what happened. The perspective was close to the enemy planet now, as the ship hurtled into its well of gravity. Surely it's in range now, thought Ender. It must be in range and the computer can't handle it.

Then the surface of the planet, which filled half the simulator field now, began to bubble; there was a gout of explosion, hurling debris out toward Ender's fighters. Ender tried to imagine what was happening inside the planet. The field growing and growing, the molecules bursting apart but finding nowhere for the separate atoms to go.

Within three seconds the entire planet burst apart, becoming a sphere of bright dust, hurtling outward. Ender's fighters were among the first to go; their perspective suddenly vanished, and now the simulator could only display the perspective of the starships waiting beyond the edges of the battle. It was as close as Ender wanted to be. The sphere of the exploding planet grew outward faster than the enemy ships could avoid it. And it carried with it the Little Doctor, not so little anymore, the field taking apart every ship in its path, erupting each one into a dot of light before it went on.

Only at the very periphery of the simulator did the M.D. field weaken. Two or three enemy ships were drifting away. Ender's own starships did not explode. But where the vast enemy fleet had been, and the planet they protected, there was nothing meaningful. A lump of dirt was growing as gravity drew much of the debris downward again. It was glowing hot and spinning visibly; it was also much smaller than the world had been before. Much of its mass was now a cloud still flowing outward.

Ender took off his headphones, filled with the cheers of his squadron leaders, and only then realized that there was just as much noise in the room with him. Men in uniform were hugging each other, laughing, shouting; others were weeping; some knelt or lay prostrate, and Ender knew they were caught up in prayer. Ender didn't understand. It seemed all wrong. They were supposed to be angry.

Colonel Graff detached himself from the others and came to Ender. Tears streamed down his face, but he was smiling. He bent over, reached out his arms, and to Ender's surprise he embraced him, held him tightly, and whispered, "Thank you, thank you, Ender. Thank God for you, Ender."

The others soon came, too, shaking his hand, congratulating him. He tried to make sense of this. Had he passed the test after all? It was *his* victory, not theirs, and a hollow one at that, a cheat; why did they act as if he had won with honor?

The crowd parted and Mazer Rackham walked through. He came straight to Ender and held out his hand.

"You made the hard choice, boy. All or nothing. End them or end us. But heaven knows there was no other way you could have done it. Congratulations. You beat them, and it's all over."

All over. Beat them. Ender didn't understand. "I beat *you*."

Mazer laughed, a loud laugh that filled the room. "Ender, you never played *me*. You never played a *game* since I became your enemy."

Ender didn't get the joke. He had played a great many games, at a terrible cost to himself. He began to get angry.

Mazer reached out and touched his shoulder. Ender shrugged him off. Mazer then grew serious and said, "Ender, for the past few months you have been the battle commander of our fleets. This was the Third Invasion. There were no games, the battles were real, and the only enemy you fought was the buggers. You won every battle, and today you finally fought them at their home world, where the queen was, all the queens from all their colonies, they all were there and you destroyed them completely. They'll never attack us again. You did it. You."

Real. Not a game. Ender's mind was too tired to cope with it all. They weren't just points of light in the air, they were real ships that he had fought with and real ships he had destroyed. And a real world that he had blasted into oblivion. He walked through the crowd, dodging their congratulations, ignoring their hands, their words, their rejoicing. When he got to his own room he stripped off his clothes, climbed into bed, and slept.

———

Ender awoke when they shook him. It took a moment to recognize them. Graff and Rackham. He turned his back on them. Let me sleep.

"Ender, we need to talk to you," said Graff.

Ender rolled back to face them.

"They've been playing out the videos on Earth all day, all night since the battle yesterday."

"Yesterday?" He had slept through until the next day.

"You're a hero, Ender. They've seen what you did, you and the others. I don't think there's a government on Earth that hasn't voted you their highest medal."

"I killed them all, didn't I?" Ender asked.

"All who?" asked Graff. "The buggers? That was the idea."

Mazer leaned in close. "That's what the war was for."

"All their queens. So I killed all their children, all of everything."

"*They* decided that when they attacked us. It wasn't your fault. It's what had to happen."

Ender grabbed Mazer's uniform and hung onto it, pulling him down so they were face to face. "I didn't want to kill them all. I didn't want to kill anybody! I'm not a killer! You didn't want me, you bastards, you wanted Peter, but you made me do it, you tricked me into it!" He was crying. He was out of control.

"Of course we tricked you into it. That's the whole point," said Graff. "It had to be a trick or you couldn't have done it. It's the bind we were in. We had to have a commander with so much empathy that he would think like the buggers, understand them and anticipate them. So much compassion that he could win the love of his underlings and work with them like a perfect machine, as perfect as the buggers. But somebody with that much compassion could never be the killer we needed. Could never go into battle willing to win at all costs. If you knew, you couldn't do it. If you were the kind of person who would do it even if you knew, you could never have understood the buggers well enough."

"And it had to be a child, Ender," said Mazer. "You were faster than me. Better than me. I was too old and cautious. Any decent person who knows what warfare is can never go into battle with a whole heart. But you didn't know. We made sure you didn't know. You were reckless and brilliant and young. It's what you were born for."

"We had pilots with our ships, didn't we."

"Yes."

"I was ordering pilots to go in and die and I didn't even know it."

"*They* knew it, Ender, and they went anyway. They knew what it was for."

"You never asked me! You never told me the truth about anything!"

"You had to be a weapon, Ender. Like a gun, like the Little Doctor, functioning perfectly but not knowing what you were aimed at. *We* aimed you. We're responsible. If there was something wrong, we did it."

"Tell me later," Ender said. His eyes closed.

Mazer Rackham shook him. "Don't go to sleep, Ender," he said. "It's very important."

"You're finished with me," Ender said. "Now leave me alone."

"That's why we're here," Mazer said. "We're trying to tell you. They're not through with you, not at all. It's crazy down there. They're going to start a war. Americans claiming the Warsaw Pact is about to attack, and the Russians are saying the same thing about the Hegemon. The bugger war isn't twenty-four hours dead and the world down there is back to fighting again, as bad as ever. And all of them are worried about you. All of them want you. The greatest military leader in history, they want you to lead their armies. The Americans. The Hegemon. Everybody but the Warsaw Pact, and they want you dead."

"Fine with me," said Ender.

"We have to take you away from here. There are Russian marines all over Eros, and the Polemarch is Russian. It could turn to bloodshed at any time."

Ender turned his back on them again. This time they let him. He did not sleep, though. He listened to them.

"I was afraid of this, Rackham. You pushed him too hard. Some of those lesser outposts could have waited until after. You could have given him some days to rest."

"Are you doing it, too, Graff? Trying to decide how I could have done it better? You don't know what would have happened if I hadn't pushed. Nobody knows. I did it the way I did it, and it worked. Above all, it worked. Memorize that defense, Graff. You may have to use it, too."

"Sorry."

"I can see what it's done to him. Colonel Liki says there's a good chance he'll be permanently damaged, but I don't believe it. He's too strong. Winning meant a lot to him, and he won."

"Don't tell me about strong. The kid's eleven. Give him some rest, Rackham. Things haven't exploded yet. We can post a guard outside his door."

"Or post a guard outside another door and pretend that it's his."

"Whatever."

They went away. Ender slept again.

Time passed without touching Ender, except with glancing blows. Once he awoke for a few minutes with something pressing his hand, pushing downward on it, with a dull, insistent pain. He reached over and touched it; it was a needle passing into a vein. He tried to pull it out, but it was taped on and he was too weak. Another time he awoke in darkness to hear people near him murmuring and cursing. His ears were ringing with the loud noise that had awakened him; he did not remember the noise. "Get the lights on," someone said. And another time he thought he heard someone crying softly near him.

It might have been a single day; it might have been a week; from his dreams, it could have been months. He seemed to pass through lifetimes in his dreams. Through the Giant's Drink again, past the wolf-children, reliving the terrible deaths, the constant murders; he heard a voice whispering in the forest, You had to kill the children to get to the End of the World. And he tried to answer, I never wanted to kill anybody. Nobody ever asked me if I wanted to kill anybody. But the forest laughed at him. And when he leapt from the cliff at the End of the World, sometimes it was not clouds that caught him, but a fighter that carried him to a vantage point near the surface of the buggers' world, so he could watch, over and over, the eruption of death when Dr. Device set off a reaction on the planet's face; then closer and closer, until he could watch individual buggers explode, turn to light, then collapse into a pile of dirt before his eyes. And the queen, surrounded by infants; only the queen was Mother, and the infants were Valentine and all the children he had known in Battle School. One of them had Bonzo's face, and he lay there bleeding through the eyes and nose, saying, You have no honor. And always the dream ended with a mirror or a pool of water or the metal surface of a ship, something that would reflect his face back to him. At first it was always Peter's face, with blood and a snake's tail coming from the mouth. After a while, though, it began to be his own face, old and sad, with eyes that grieved for a billion, billion murders—but they were his own eyes, and he was content to wear them.

That was the world Ender lived in for many lifetimes during the five days of the League War.

When he awoke again he was lying in darkness. In the distance he could hear the thump, thump of explosions. He listened for a while. Then he heard a soft footstep.

He turned over and flung out a hand, to grasp whoever was sneaking up on him. Sure enough, he caught someone's clothing and pulled him down toward his knees, ready to kill him if need be.

"Ender, it's me, it's me!"

He knew the voice. It came out of his memory as if it were a million years ago.

"Alai."

"Salaam, pinprick. What were you trying to do, kill me?"

"Yes. I thought you were trying to kill *me*."

"I was trying not to wake you up. Well, at least you have some survival instinct left. The way Mazer talks about it, you were becoming a vegetable."

"I was trying to. What's the thumping?"

"There's a war going on here. Our section is blacked out to keep us safe."

Ender swung his legs out to sit up. He couldn't do it, though. His head hurt too bad. He winced in pain.

"Don't sit up, Ender. It's all right. It looks like we might win it. Not all the Warsaw Pact people went with the Polemarch. A lot of them came over when the Strategos told them you were loyal to the I.F."

"I was asleep."

"So he lied. You weren't plotting treason in your dreams, were you? Some of the Russians who came in told us that when the Polemarch ordered them to find you and kill you, they almost killed *him*. Whatever they may feel about other people, Ender, they love you. The whole world watched our battles. Videos, day and night. I've seen some. Complete with your voice giving the orders. It's all there, nothing censored. Good stuff. You've got a career in the vids."

"I don't think so," said Ender.

"I was joking. Hey, can you believe it? We won the war. We were so eager to grow up so we could fight in it, and it was us all the time. I mean, we're kids, Ender. And it was us." Alai laughed. "It was you, anyway. You were good, bosh. I didn't know how you'd get us out of that last one. But you did. You were good."

Ender noticed the way he spoke in the past. I *was* good. "What am I *now*, Alai?"

"Still good."

"At what?"

"At—anything. There's a million soldiers who'd follow you to the end of the universe."

"I don't want to go to the end of the universe."

"So where do you want to go? They'll follow you."

I want to go home, thought Ender, but I don't know where it is.

The thumping went silent.

"Listen to that," said Alai.

They listened. The door opened. Someone stood there. Someone small. "It's over," he said. It was Bean. As if to prove it, the lights went on.

"Ho, Bean," Ender said.

"Ho, Ender."

Petra followed him in, with Dink holding her hand. They came to Ender's bed. "Hey, the hero's awake," said Dink.

"Who won?" asked Ender.

"We did, Ender," said Bean. "You were there."

"He's not *that* crazy, Bean. He meant who won just now." Petra took Ender's hand. "There was a truce on Earth. They've been negotiating for days. They finally agreed to accept the Locke Proposal."

"He doesn't know about the Locke Proposal—"

"It's very complicated, but what it means here is that the I.F. will stay in existence, but without the Warsaw Pact in it. So the Warsaw Pact marines are going home. I think Russia agreed to it because they're facing a revolt of the Islamic States. Everybody's got troubles. About five hundred died here, but it was worse on Earth."

"The Hegemon resigned," said Dink. "It's crazy down there. Who cares."

"You OK?" Petra asked him, touching his head. "You scared us. They said you were crazy, and we said *they* were crazy."

"I'm crazy," said Ender. "But I think I'm OK."

"When did you decide that?" asked Alai.

"When I thought you were about to kill me, and I decided to kill you first. I guess I'm just a killer to the core. But I'd rather be alive than dead."

They laughed and agreed with him. Then Ender began to cry and embraced Bean and Petra, who were closest. "I missed you," he said. "I wanted to see you so bad."

"You saw us pretty bad," Petra answered. She kissed his cheek.

"I saw you magnificent," said Ender. "The ones I needed most, I used up soonest. Bad planning on my part."

"Everybody's OK now," said Dink. "Nothing was wrong with any of us that five days of cowering in blacked-out rooms in the middle of a war couldn't cure."

"I don't have to be your commander anymore, do I?" asked Ender. "I don't want to command anybody again."

"You don't have to command anybody," said Dink, "but you're always our commander."

Then they were silent for a while.

"So what do we do now?" asked Alai. "The bugger war's over, and so's the war down there on Earth, and even the war here. What do we do now?"

"We're kids," said Petra. "They'll probably make us go to school. It's a law. You have to go to school till you're seventeen."

They all laughed at that. Laughed until tears streamed down their faces.

15

SPEAKER FOR THE DEAD

The lake was still; there was no breeze. The two men sat together in chairs on the floating dock. A small wooden raft was tied up at the dock; Graff hooked his foot in the rope and pulled the raft in, then let it drift out, then pulled it in again.

"You've lost weight."

"One kind of stress puts it on, another takes it off. I am a creature of chemicals."

"It must have been hard."

Graff shrugged. "Not really. I knew I'd be acquitted."

"Some of us weren't so sure. People were crazy for a while there. Mistreatment of children, negligent homicide—those videos of Bonzo's and Stilson's deaths were pretty gruesome. To watch one child do that to another."

"As much as anything, I think the videos saved me. The prosecution edited them, but we showed the whole thing. It was plain that Ender was not the provocateur. After that, it was just a second-guessing game. I said I did what I believed was necessary for the preservation of the human race, and it worked; we got the judges to agree that the prosecution had to prove beyond doubt that Ender would have won the war *without* the training we gave him. After that, it was simple. The exigencies of war."

"Anyway, Graff, it was a great relief to us. I know we quarreled, and I know the prosecution used tapes of our conversations against you. But by then I knew that you were right, and I offered to testify for you."

"I know, Anderson. My lawyers told me."

"So what will you do now?"

"I don't know. I'm still relaxing. I have a few years of leave accrued. Enough to take me to retirement, and I have plenty of salary that I never used, sitting around in banks. I could live on the interest. Maybe I'll do nothing."

"It sounds nice. But I couldn't stand it. I've been offered the presidency of three different universities, on the theory that I'm an educator. They don't believe me when I say that all I ever cared about at the Battle School was the game. I think I'll go with the other offer."

"Commissioner?"

"Now that the wars are over, it's time to play games again. It'll be almost like vacation, anyway. Only twenty-eight teams in the league. Though after years of watching those children flying, football is like watching slugs bash into each other."

They laughed. Graff sighed and pushed the raft with his foot.

"That raft. Surely you can't float on it."

Graff shook his head. "Ender built it."

"That's right. This is where you took him."

"It's even been deeded over to him. I saw to it that he was amply rewarded. He'll have all the money he ever needs."

"If they ever let him come back to use it."

"They never will."

"With Demosthenes agitating for him to come home?"

"Demosthenes isn't on the nets anymore."

Anderson raised an eyebrow. "What does *that* mean?"

"Demosthenes has retired. Permanently."

"You know something, you old farteater. You know who Demosthenes is."

"Was."

"Well, tell me!"

"No."

"You're no fun anymore, Graff."

"I never was."

"At least you can tell me *why*. There were a lot of us who thought Demosthenes would be Hegemon someday."

"There was never a chance of that. No, even Demosthenes' mob of political cretins couldn't persuade the Hegemon to bring Ender back to Earth. Ender is far too dangerous."

"He's only eleven. Twelve, now."

"All the more dangerous because he could so easily be controlled. In all the world, the name of Ender is one to conjure with. The child-god, the miracle worker, with life and death in his hands. Every petty tyrant-to-be would like to have the boy, to set him in front of an army and watch the world either flock to join or cower in fear. If Ender came to Earth, he'd want to come here, to rest, to salvage what he can of his childhood. But they'd never let him rest."

"I see. Someone explained that to Demosthenes?"

Graff smiled. "Demosthenes explained it to someone else. Someone who could have used Ender as no one else could have, to rule the world and make the world like it."

"Who?"

"Locke."

"Locke is the one who argued for Ender to stay on Eros."

"All is not always as it seems."

"It's too deep for me, Graff. Give me the game. Nice, neat rules. Referees. Beginnings and endings. Winners and losers and then everybody goes home to their families."

"Get me tickets to some games now and then, all right?"

"You won't really stay here and retire, will you?"

"No."

"You're going into the Hegemony, aren't you?"

"I'm the new Minister of Colonization."

"So they're doing it."

"As soon as we get the reports back on the bugger colony worlds. I mean, there they are, already fertile, with housing and industry in place, and all the buggers dead. Very convenient. We'll repeal the population limitation laws—"

"Which everybody hates—"

"And all those thirds and fourths and fifths will get on starships and head out for worlds known and unknown."

"Will people really go?"

"People always go. Always. They always believe they can make a better life than in the old world."

"What the hell, maybe they can."

—

At first Ender believed that they would bring him back to Earth as soon as things quieted down. But things were quiet now, had been quiet for a year, and it was plain to him now that they would not bring him back at all, that he was much more useful as a name and a story than he would ever be as an inconvenient flesh-and-blood person.

And there was the matter of the court martial on the crimes of Colonel Graff. Admiral Chamrajnagar tried to keep Ender from watching it, but failed; Ender had been awarded the rank of admiral, too, and this was one of the few times he asserted the privileges the rank implied. So he watched the videos of the fights with Stilson and Bonzo, watched as the photographs of the corpses were displayed, listened as the psychologists and lawyers argued whether murder had been committed or the killing was in self-defense. Ender had his own opinion, but no one asked him. Throughout the trial, it was really Ender himself under attack. The prosecution was too clever to charge him directly, but there were attempts to make him look sick, perverted, criminally insane.

"Never mind," said Mazer Rackham. "The politicians are afraid of you, but they can't destroy your reputation yet. That won't be done until the historians get at you in thirty years."

Ender didn't care about his reputation. He watched the videos impassively, but in fact he was amused. In battle I killed ten billion buggers, whose queens, at least, were as alive and wise as any man, who had not even launched a third attack against us, and no one thinks to call it a crime.

All his crimes weighed heavy on him, the deaths of Stilson and Bonzo no heavier and no lighter than the rest.

And so, with that burden, he waited through the empty months until the world that he had saved decided he could come home.

One by one, his friends reluctantly left him, called home to their families, to be received with heroes' welcomes in hometowns they barely remembered. Ender watched the videos of their homecomings, and was touched when they spent much of their time praising Ender Wiggin, who taught them everything, they said, who taught them and led them into victory. But if they called for him to be brought home, the words were censored from the videos and no one heard the plea.

For a time, the only work in Eros was cleaning up after the bloody League War and receiving the reports of the starships, once warships, that were now exploring the bugger colony worlds.

But now Eros was busier than ever, more crowded than it had ever been during the war, as colonists were brought here to prepare for their voyages to the empty bugger worlds. Ender took part in the work, as much as they would let him; it did not occur to them that this twelve-year-old boy might be as gifted at peace as he was at war. But he was patient with their tendency to ignore him, and learned to make his proposals and suggest his plans through the few adults who listened to him, and let them present them as their own. He was concerned, not about getting credit, but about getting the job done.

The one thing he could not bear was the worship of the colonists. He learned to avoid the tunnels where they lived, because they would always recognize him—the world had memorized his face—and then they would scream and shout and embrace him and congratulate him and show him the children they had named after him and tell him how he was so young it broke their hearts and *they* didn't blame him for any of his murders because it wasn't his fault he was just a *child*—

He hid from them as best he could.

There was one colonist, though, he couldn't hide from.

He wasn't inside Eros that day. He had gone up with the shuttle to the new ISL, where he had been learning to do surface work on the starships; it was unbecoming to an officer to do mechanical labor, Chamrajnagar told him, but Ender answered that since the trade he had mastered wasn't much called for now, it was about time he learned another skill.

They spoke to him through his helmet radio and told him that someone was waiting to see him as soon as he could come in. Ender couldn't think of anyone he wanted to see, and so he didn't hurry. He finished installing the shield for the ship's ansible and then hooked his way across the face of the ship and pulled himself up into the airlock.

She was waiting for him outside the changing room. For a moment he was annoyed that they would let a colonist come to bother him here, where he came to be alone; then he looked again, and realized that if the young woman were a little girl, he would know her.

"Valentine," he said.

"Hi, Ender."

"What are you doing here?"

"Demosthenes retired. Now I'm going with the first colony."

"It's fifty years to get there—"

"Only two years if you're aboard the ship."

"But if you ever came back, everybody you knew on Earth would be dead—"

"That was what I had in mind. I was hoping, though, that someone I knew on Eros might come with me."

"I don't want to go to a world we stole from the buggers. I just want to go home."

"Ender, you're never going back to Earth. I saw to that before I left."

He looked at her in silence.

"I tell you that now, so that if you want to hate me, you can hate me from the beginning."

They went to Ender's tiny compartment in the ISL and she explained. Peter wanted Ender back on Earth, under the protection of the Hegemon's Council. "The way things are right now, Ender, that would put you effectively under Peter's control, since half the council now does just what Peter wants. The ones that aren't Locke's lapdogs are under his thumb in other ways."

"Do they know who he really is?"

"Yes. He isn't publicly known, but people in high places know him. It doesn't matter any more. He has too much power for them to worry about his age. He's done incredible things, Ender."

"I noticed the treaty a year ago was named for Locke."

"That was his breakthrough. He proposed it through his friends from the public policy nets, and then Demosthenes got behind it, too. It was the moment he had been waiting for, to use Demosthenes' influence with the mob and Locke's influence with the intelligentsia to accomplish something noteworthy. It forestalled a really vicious war that could have lasted for decades."

"He decided to be a statesman?"

"I think so. But in his cynical moments, of which there are many, he pointed out to me that if he had allowed the League to fall apart completely, he'd have had to conquer the world piece by piece. As long as the Hegemony existed, he could do it in one lump."

Ender nodded. "That's the Peter that I knew."

"Funny, isn't it? That Peter would save millions of lives."

"While I killed billions."

"I wasn't going to say that."

"So he wanted to use me?"

"He had plans for you, Ender. He would publicly reveal himself when you arrived, going to meet you in front of all the videos. Ender Wiggin's older brother, who also happened to be the great Locke, the architect of peace. Standing next to you, he would look quite mature. And the physical resemblance between you is stronger than ever. It would be quite simple for him, then, to take over."

"Why did you stop him?"

"Ender, you wouldn't be happy spending the rest of your life as Peter's pawn."

"Why not? I've spent my life as someone's pawn."

"Me too. I showed Peter all the evidence that I had assembled, enough to prove in the eyes of the public that he was a psychotic killer. It included full-color pictures of tortured squirrels and some of the monitor videos of the way he treated you. It took some work to get it all together, but by the time he saw it, he was willing to give me what I wanted. What I wanted was your freedom and mine."

"It's not my idea of freedom to go live in the house of the people that I killed."

"Ender, what's done is done. Their worlds are empty now, and ours is full. And we can take with us what their worlds have never known—cities full of people who live private, individual lives, who love and hate each other for their own reasons. In all the bugger worlds, there was never more than a single story to be told; when we're there, the world will be full of stories, and we'll improvise their endings day by day. Ender, Earth belongs to Peter. And if you don't go with me now, he'll have you there, and use you up until you wish you'd never been born. Now is the only chance you'll get to get away."

Ender said nothing.

"I know what you're thinking, Ender. You're thinking that I'm trying to control you just as much as Peter or Graff or any of the others."

"It crossed my mind."

"Welcome to the human race. Nobody controls his own life, Ender. The best you can do is choose to fill the roles given you by good people, by people who love you. I didn't come here because I wanted to be a colonist. I came because I've spent my whole life in the company of the brother that I hated. Now I want a chance to know the brother that I love, before it's too late, before we're not children anymore."

"It's already too late for that."

"You're wrong, Ender. You think you're grown up and tired and jaded with everything, but in your heart you're just as much a kid as I am. We can keep it secret from everybody else. While you're governing the colony and I'm writing political philosophy, they'll never guess that in the darkness of night we sneak into each other's room and play checkers and have pillowfights."

Ender laughed, but he had noticed some things she dropped too casually for them to be accidental. "Governing?"

"I'm Demosthenes, Ender. I went out with a bang. A public announcement that I believed so much in the colonization movement that I was going in the first ship myself. At the same time, the Minister of Colonization, a former colonel named Graff, announced that the pilot of the colony ship would be the great Mazer Rackham, and the governor of the first colony it established would be Ender Wiggin."

"They might have asked *me*."

"I wanted to ask you myself."

"But it's already announced."

"No. They'll be announcing it tomorrow, if you accept. Mazer accepted a few hours ago, back in Eros."

"You're telling everyone that you're Demosthenes? A fourteen-year-old girl?"

"We're only telling them that Demosthenes is going with the colony. Let them spend the next fifty years poring over the passenger list, trying to figure out which one of them is the great demagogue of the Age of Locke."

Ender laughed and shook his head. "You're actually having fun, Val."

"I can't think why I shouldn't."

"All right," said Ender. "I'll go. Maybe even as governor, as long as you and Mazer are there to help me. My abilities are a little underused at present."

She squealed and hugged him, for all the world like a typical teenage girl who just got the present that she wanted from her little brother.

"Val," he said. "I just want one thing clear. I'm not going for you. I'm not going in order to be governor, or because I'm bored here. I'm going because I know the buggers better than any other living soul, and maybe if I go there I can understand them better. I stole their future from them; I can only begin to repay by seeing what I can learn from their past."

The voyage was long. By the end of it, Val had finished the first volume of her history of the bugger wars and transmitted it by ansible, under Demosthenes' name, back to Earth, and Ender had won something better than the adulation of the passengers. They knew him now, and he had won their love and their respect.

He worked hard on the new world. He quickly understood the differences between military and civilian leadership, and governed by persuasion rather than fiat, and by working as hard as anyone at the tasks involved in setting up a self-sustaining economy. But his most important work, as everyone agreed, was exploring what the buggers had left behind, trying to find among structures, machinery, and fields long untended some things that human beings could use, could learn from. There were no books to read—the buggers never needed them. With all things present in their memories, all things spoken as they were thought, when the buggers died their knowledge died with them.

And yet. From the sturdiness of the roofs that covered their animal sheds and their food supplies, Ender learned that winter would be hard, with heavy snows. From fences with sharpened stakes that pointed outward he learned that there were marauding animals that were a danger to the crops or the herds. From the mill he learned that the long, foul-tasting fruits that grew in the overgrown orchards were dried and ground into meal. And from the slings that once were used to carry infants along with adults into the fields, he learned that even though the buggers were not much for individuality, they did care for their young.

Life settled down, and years passed. The colony lived in wooden houses and used the tunnels of the bugger city for storage and manufactories. They were governed by a council now, and administrators were elected, so that Ender, though they still called him governor, was in fact only a judge. There were crimes and quarrels, alongside kindness and cooperation; there were people who loved each other and people who did not; it was a human world. They did not wait so eagerly for each new transmission from the ansible; the names that were famous on Earth meant little to them now. The only name they knew was that of Peter Wiggin, the Hegemon of Earth; the only news that came was news of peace, of prosperity, of great ships leaving the littoral of Earth's solar system, passing the comet shield and filling up the bugger worlds. Soon there would be other colonies on this world, Ender's World; soon there would be neighbors; already they were halfway here; but no one cared. They would help the newcomers when they came, teach them what they had learned, but what mattered in life now was who would marry whom, and who was sick, and when was planting time, and why should I pay him when the calf died three weeks after I got it.

"They've become people of the land," said Valentine. "No one cares now that Demosthenes is sending the seventh volume of his history today. No one here will read it."

Ender pressed a button and his desk showed him the next page. "Very insightful, Valentine. How many more volumes until you're through?"

"Just one. The story of Ender Wiggin."

"What will you do, wait to write it until I'm dead?"

"No. Just write it, and when I've brought it up to the present day, I'll stop."

"I have a better idea. Take it up to the day we won the final battle. Stop it there. Nothing that I've done since then is worth writing down."

"Maybe," said Valentine. "And maybe not."

The ansible had brought them word that the new colony ship was only a year away. They asked Ender to find a place for them to settle in, near enough to Ender's colony that the two colonies could trade, but far enough apart that they could be governed separately. Ender used the helicopter and began to explore. He took one of the children along, an eleven-year-old boy named Abra; he had been only three when the colony was founded, and he remembered no other world than this. He and Ender flew as far away as Ender thought the new colony should be, then camped for the night and got a feel for the land on foot the next morning.

It was on the third morning that Ender suddenly began to feel an uneasy sense that he had been in this place before. He looked around; it was new land, he had never seen it. He called out to Abra.

"Ho, Ender!" Abra called. He was on top of a steep low hill. "Come up!"

Ender scrambled up, the turves coming away from his feet in the soft ground. Abra was pointing downward. "Can you believe this?" he asked.

The hill was hollow. A deep depression in the middle, partially filled with water, was ringed by concave slopes that cantilevered dangerously over the water. In one direction the hill gave way to two long ridges that made a V-shaped valley; in the other direction the hill rose to a piece of white rock, grinning like a skull with a tree growing out of its mouth.

"It's like a giant died here," said Abra, "and the Earth grew up to cover his carcass."

Now Ender knew why it had looked familiar. The Giant's corpse. He had played here too many times as a child not to know this place. But it was not possible. The computer in the Battle School could not possibly have seen this place. He looked through his binoculars in a direction he knew well, fearing and hoping that he would see what belonged in that place.

Swings and slides. Monkey bars. Now overgrown, but the shapes still unmistakable.

"Somebody had to have built this," Abra said. "Look, this skull place, it's not rock, look at it. This is concrete."

"I know," said Ender. "They built it for me."

"What?"

"I know this place, Abra. The buggers built it for me."

"The buggers were all dead fifty years before we got here."

"You're right, it's impossible, but I know what I know. Abra, I shouldn't take you with me. It might be dangerous. If they knew me well enough to build this place, they might be planning to—"

"To get even with you."

"For killing them."

"So don't go, Ender. Don't do what they want you to do."

"If they want to get revenge, Abra, I don't mind. But perhaps they don't. Perhaps this is the closest they could come to talking. To writing me a note."

"They didn't know how to read and write."

"Maybe they were learning when they died."

"Well, I'm sure as hell not sticking around here if you're taking off somewhere. I'm going with you."

"No. You're too young to take the risk of—"

"Come on! You're Ender *Wiggin*. Don't tell me what eleven-year-old kids can do!"

Together they flew in the copter, over the playground, over the woods, over the well in the forest clearing. Then out to where there was, indeed, a cliff, with a cave in the cliff wall and a ledge right where the End of the World should be. And there in the distance, just where it should be in the fantasy game, was the castle tower.

He left Abra with the copter. "Don't come after me, and go home in an hour if I don't come back."

"Eat it, Ender, I'm coming with you."

"Eat it yourself, Abra, or I'll stuff you with mud."

Abra could tell, despite Ender's joking tone, that he meant it, and so he stayed.

The walls of the tower were notched and ledged for easy climbing. They meant him to get in.

The room was as it had always been. Ender remembered well enough to look for a snake on the floor, but there was only a rug with a carved snake's head at one corner. Imitation, not duplication; for a people who made no art, they had done well. They must have dragged these images from Ender's own mind, finding him and learning his darkest dreams across the lightyears. But why? To bring him to this room, of course. To leave a message for him. But where was the message, and how would he understand it?

The mirror was waiting for him on the wall. It was a dull sheet of metal, in which the rough shape of a human face had been scratched. They tried to draw the image I should see in the picture.

And looking at the mirror he could remember breaking it, pulling it from the wall, and snakes leaping out of the hidden place, attacking him, biting him wherever their poisonous fangs could find purchase.

How well do they know me, wondered Ender. Well enough to know how often I have thought of death, to know that I am not afraid of it. Well enough to know that even if I feared death, it would not stop me from taking that mirror from the wall.

He walked to the mirror, lifted, pulled away. Nothing jumped from the space behind it. Instead, in a hollowed-out place, there was a white ball of silk with a few frayed strands sticking out here and there. An egg? No. The pupa of a queen bugger, already fertilized by the larval males, ready, out of her own body, to hatch a hundred thousand buggers, including a few queens and males. Ender could see in his mind the slug-like males clinging to the walls of a dark tunnel, and the large adults carrying the infant queen to the mating room; each male in turn penetrated the larval queen, shuddered in ecstasy, and died, dropping to the tunnel floor and shriveling. Then the new queen was laid before the old, a magnificent creature clad in soft and shimmering wings, which had long since lost the power of flight but still contained the power of majesty. The old queen kissed her to sleep with the gentle poison in her lips, then wrapped her in threads from her belly, and commanded her to become herself, to become a new city, a new world, to give birth to many queens and many worlds—

How do I know this, thought Ender. How can I see these things, like memories in my own mind.

As if in answer, he saw the first of all his battles with the bugger fleets. He had seen it before on the simulator; now he saw it as the hive-queen saw it, through many different eyes. The buggers formed their globe of ships, and then the terrible fighters came out of the darkness and the Little Doctor destroyed them in a blaze of light. He felt then what the hive-queen felt, watching through her workers' eyes as death came to them too quickly to avoid, but not too quickly to be anticipated. There was no memory of pain or fear, though. What the hive-queen felt was sadness, a sense of resignation. She had not thought these words as she saw the humans coming to kill, but it was in words that Ender understood her: The humans did not forgive us, she thought. We will surely die.

"How can you live again?" he asked.

The queen in her silken cocoon had no words to give back; but when he closed his eyes and tried to remember, instead of memory came new images. Putting the cocoon in a cool place, a dark place, but with water, so she wasn't dry, so that certain reactions could take place in the cocoon. Then time. Days and weeks, for the pupa inside to change. And then, when the cocoon had changed to a dusty brown color, Ender saw himself splitting open the cocoon, and helping the small and fragile queen emerge. He saw himself taking her by the forelimb and helping her walk from her birthwater to a nesting place, soft with dried leaves on sand. Then I am alive, came the thought in his mind. Then I am awake. Then I make my ten thousand children.

"No," said Ender. "I can't."

Anguish.

"Your children are the monsters of our nightmares now. If I awoke you, we would only kill you again."

There flashed through his mind a dozen images of human beings being killed by buggers, but with the image came a grief so powerful he could not bear it, and he wept their tears for them.

"If you could make them feel as you can make me feel, then perhaps they could forgive you."

Only me, he realized. They found me through the ansible, followed it and dwelt in my mind. In the agony of my tortured dreams they came to know me, even as I spent my days destroying them; they found my fear of them, and found also that I had no knowledge I was killing them. In the few weeks they had, they built this place for me, and the Giant's corpse and the playground and the ledge at the End of the World, so I would find this place by the evidence of my eyes. I am the only one they know, and so they can only talk to me, and through me. We are like you; the thought pressed into his mind. We did not mean to murder, and when we understood, we never came again. We thought we were the only thinking beings in the universe, until we met you, but never did we dream that thought could arise from the lonely animals who cannot dream each other's dreams. How were we to know? We could live with you in peace. Believe us, believe us, believe us.

He reached into the cavity and took out the cocoon. It was astonishingly light, to hold all the hope and future of a great race within it.

"I'll carry you," said Ender, "I'll go from world to world until I find a time and a place where you can come awake in safety. And I'll tell your story to my people, so that perhaps in time they can forgive you, too. The way that you've forgiven me."

He wrapped the queen's cocoon in his jacket and carried her from the tower.

"What was in there?" asked Abra.

"The answer," said Ender.

"To what?"

"My question." And that was all he said of the matter; they searched for five more days and chose a site for the colony far to the east and south of the tower.

Weeks later he came to Valentine and told her to read something he had written; she pulled the file he named from the ship's computer, and read it.

It was written as if the hive-queen spoke, telling all that they had meant to do, and all that they had done. Here are our failures, and here is our greatness; we did not mean to hurt you, and we forgive you for our death. From their earliest awareness to the great wars that swept across their home world, Ender told the story quickly, as if it were an ancient memory. When he came to the tale of the great mother, the queen of all, who first learned to keep and teach the new queen instead of killing her or driving her away, then he lingered, telling how many times she had finally to destroy the child of her body, the new self that was not herself, until she bore one who understood her quest for harmony. This was a new thing in the world, two queens that loved and helped each other instead of battling, and together they were stronger than any other hive. They prospered; they had more daughters who joined them in peace; it was the beginning of wisdom.

If only we could have talked to you, the hive-queen said in Ender's words. But since it could not be, we ask only this: that you remember us, not as enemies, but as tragic sisters, changed into a foul shape by fate or God or evolution. If we had kissed, it would have been the miracle to make us human in each other's eyes. Instead we killed each other. But still we welcome you now as guestfriends. Come into our home, daughters of Earth; dwell in our tunnels, harvest our fields; what we cannot do, you are now our hands to do for us. Blossom, trees; ripen, fields; be warm for them, suns; be fertile for them, planets: they are our adopted daughters, and they have come home.

The book that Ender wrote was not long, but in it was all the good and all the evil that the hive-queen knew. And he signed it, not with his name, but with a title:

SPEAKER FOR THE DEAD

On Earth, the book was published quietly, and quietly it was passed from hand to hand, until it was hard to believe that anyone on Earth might not have read it. Most who read it found it interesting; some who read it refused to set it aside. They began to live by it as best they could, and when their loved ones died, a believer would arise beside the grave to be the Speaker for the Dead, and say what the dead one would have said, but with full candor, hiding no faults and pretending no virtues. Those who came to such services sometimes found them painful and disturbing, but there were many who decided that their life was worthwhile enough, despite their errors, that when they died a Speaker should tell the truth for them.

On Earth it remained a religion among many religions. But for those who traveled the great cave of space and lived their lives in the hive-queen's tunnels and harvested the hive-queen's fields, it was the only religion. There was no colony without its Speaker for the Dead.

No one knew and no one really wanted to know who was the original Speaker. Ender was not inclined to tell them.

When Valentine was twenty-five years old, she finished the last volume of her history of the bugger wars. She included at the end the complete text of Ender's little book, but did not say that Ender wrote it.

By ansible she got an answer from the ancient Hegemon, Peter Wiggin, seventy-seven years old with a failing heart.

"I know who wrote it," he said. "If he can speak for the buggers, surely he can speak for me."

Back and forth across the ansible Ender and Peter spoke, with Peter pouring out the story of his days and years, his crimes and his kindnesses. And when he died, Ender wrote a second volume, again signed by the Speaker for the Dead. Together, his two books were called the Hive-Queen and the Hegemon, and they were holy writ.

"Come on," he said to Valentine one day. "Let's fly away and live forever."

"We can't," she said. "There are miracles even relativity can't pull off, Ender."

"We have to go. I'm almost happy here."

"So stay."

"I've lived too long with pain. I won't know who I am without it."

So they boarded a starship and went from world to world. Wherever they stopped, he was always Andrew Wiggin, itinerant speaker for the dead, and she was always Valentine, historian errant, writing down the stories of the living while Ender spoke the stories of the dead. And always Ender carried with him a dry white cocoon, looking for the world where the hive-queen could awaken and thrive in peace. He looked a long time.

MW00753691

NEMESIS

Also by Lindsey Davis

The Course of Honour
Rebels and Traitors

THE FALCO SERIES

The Silver Pigs
Shadows in Bronze
Venus in Copper
The Iron Hand of Mars
Poseidon's Gold
Last Act in Palmyra
Time to Depart
A Dying Light in Corduba
Three Hands in the Fountain
Two for the Lions
One Virgin Too Many
Ode to a Banker
A Body in the Bath House
The Jupiter Myth
The Accusers
Scandal Takes a Holiday
See Delphi and Die
Saturnalia
Alexandria

NEMESIS

LINDSEY DAVIS

MINOTAUR BOOKS ✿ NEW YORK

This is a work of fiction. All of the characters, organizations, and events portrayed in this novel are either products of the author's imagination or are used fictitiously.

NEMESIS. Copyright © 2010 by Lindsey Davis. All rights reserved. Printed in the United States of America. For information, address St. Martin's Press, 175 Fifth Avenue, New York, N.Y. 10010.

www.minotaurbooks.com

Library of Congress Cataloging-in-Publication Data

Davis, Lindsey.
    Nemesis / Lindsey Davis.—1st U.S. ed.
        p. cm.
    ISBN 978-0-312-59542-5
    1. Falco, Marcus Didius (Fictitious character)—Fiction.   2. Private investigators—Rome—Fiction.   3. Murder—Investigation—Fiction.   4. Rome—History—Vespasian, 69–79—Fiction.   I. Title.
    PR6054.A8925N46 2010
    823'.914—dc22

                                                                            2010021847

First published in Great Britain by Century, a division of Random House

First U.S. Edition: September 2010

10 9 8 7 6 5 4 3 2 1

PRINCIPAL CHARACTERS

Marcus Didius Falco	a man of mixed fortunes and seeker after truth
Helena Justina	his true love, sought and won
Falco's family	low grade, but not as bad as they seem:
Junilla Tacita	formidable wife to the deplorable Geminus
Maia Favonia	Falco's sister, the best of the bunch
Flavia Albia	heart-broken and ready to break heads
Katutis	Falco's secretary, a disappointed man
Helena's family	high class, but not as good as they look:
Aulus Camillus Aelianus	keeping a low profile
Quintus Camillus Justinus	keeping his career on target, thanks to:
Claudia Rufina	his wife and financial backer
Lentullus	an accident waiting to happen

Falco's associates in Rome

Lucius Petronius Longus	an upright vigiles enquirer (low pay)
Lucius Petronius Rectus	his brother, feeling off colour
Nero	their ox, another one gone missing
Tiberius Fusculus	Petro's second in command
Sergius	their whip man (always encouraging)
Clusius	a devious rival auctioneer (low motives)

Gaius	a dubious apprentice (high hopes)
Gornia	a tight-lipped porter (no comment)
Septimus Parvo	a family lawyer (*absolutely* no comment)
Thalia	a contortionist with a problem to wriggle out of
Philadelphion and Davos	her lovers, keeping well off the scene
Minas of Karystos	a lawyer, on the up
Hosidia Meline	a bride (on the make?)

Also in Rome

Tiberius Claudius Laeta	a smooth bureaucrat with high aspirations
Momus	a rough-edged auditor with low habits
Tiberius Claudius Anacrites	the Chief Spy, a high-flyer of low worth
The Melitans	his agents (dodgy connections)
Perella	an assassin who wants a new job (her boss's)
Heracleides	party-planner to the stars
Nymphidias	his thieving chef
Scorpus	a singer, spying on spies (an idiot)
Alis	a fortune-teller who blames Mum (a wise woman)
Arrius Persicus	a philanderer, oversexed and over-budget
A courier	newly wed and newly dead
Volusius	Mum's boy, a numerate victim

In Latium

Januaria	a waitress at Satricum, an all-rounder
Livia Primilla & Julius Modestus	complainants in high dudgeon
Sextus Silanus	their nephew in Lanuvium, in low spirits
Macer	their loyal overseer, gone missing
Syrus	their runaway slave, fatally roughed up
A butcher in Lanuvium	a very careless creditor
The horrible Claudii	neighbours from Hades:
Aristocles and Casta	cold-natured, hot-tempered parents (deceased)
Claudius Nobilis	so notorious, he has 'gone to see his granny'
Pius and Virtus	the twins, 'working away from home'
Probus	'upholding the family name'
Felix	'lost'
Plotia and Byrta	downtrodden wives
Demetria	runaway wife of Claudius Nobilis (low esteem)
Costus	her new boyfriend (asking for trouble)
Vexus	her father (anticipating the worst)
Thamyris	employer of Nobilis and Costus (over-confident)
Silvius	an officer of the Urban Cohorts, undercover

Plus full supporting cast
Jason the python, dogs, missing persons, slaves (non-persons),
personal beauticians, impersonal magistrates

And featuring
The Praetorian Guards   bastards!

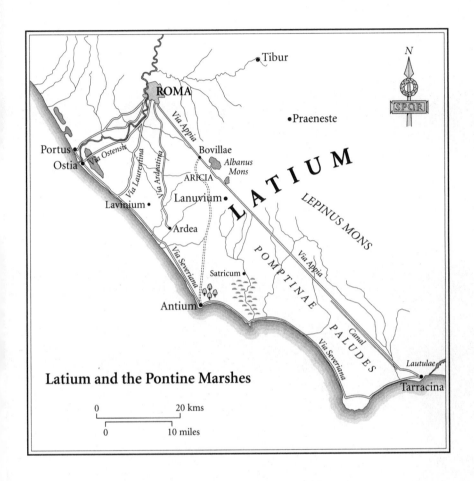

N

SPQR

Tibur

ROMA

Praeneste

Portus

Ostia

Via Ostensis

Via Appia

Bovillae

Via Laurentina

Via Ardeatina

Albanus
Mons

ARICIA

Lavinium

Lanuvium

LATIUM

Ardea

LEPINUS MONS

Via Severiana

Satricum

Via Appia

P O M P T I N A E

Antium

P A L U D E S

Canal

Via Severiana

Lautulae

Latium and the Pontine Marshes

Tarracina

0   20 kms

0   10 miles

ROME AND LATIUM: SUMMER, AD 77

I

I find it surprising more people are not killed over dinner at home. In my work we reckon that murder is most likely to happen among close acquaintances. Someone will finally snap after years of being wound up to blind rage by the very folk who best know how to drive them to distraction. For once it will be just too much to watch someone else eating the last sesame pancake—which, of course, was snatched with a triumphant laugh that was intended to rankle. So a victim expires with honey still dribbling down their chin—though it happens less often than you might expect.

Why are more kitchen cleavers not sunk between the fat shoulders of appalling uncles who get the slaves pregnant? Or that sneaky sister who shamelessly grabs the most desirable bedroom, with its glimpse of a corner of the Temple of Divine Claudius and almost no cracks in the walls? Or the crude son who farts uncontrollably, however many times he is told . . .

Even if people do not stab or strangle their own, you would expect more to rush out into the streets and vent their frustration upon the first person they meet. Perhaps they do. Perhaps even the random killing of strangers, which the vigiles call 'a motiveless crime', sometimes has an understandable domestic cause.

It could so easily have happened to us.

I grew up in a large family, crammed into a couple of small, sour rooms. All around our apartment were other teeming groups, too noisy, too obstreperous and all packed together far too close. Perhaps the thing that saved us from tragedy was that my father left home—his only escape from a situation he had come to find hideous, and an event which at least saved us from the burden of more children. Later my brother took himself off to the army; eventually I saw the sense of it and did the same. My sisters moved out to harass the feckless men they bullied into marriage. My mother, having brought up seven, was left alone but continued to have a strong influence on all of us. Even my father, once he returned to Rome, viewed Ma with wary respect.

As she continually reminded us, mothers can never retire. So, when my wife went into labour with our third child, in came Ma to boss everyone about, even though she was becoming frail and had eyesight problems. Helena's own mama rushed to our house too, the noble Julia Justa rolling up her sleeves to interfere in her genteel way. We had employed a perfectly decent midwife.

At first the mothers battled for dominance. In the end, when they were both badly needed, all that stopped.

My new son died on the day he was born. At once, we felt we were living in a tragedy that was unique to us. I suppose that is how it always seems.

The birth had been easy, a short labour like our second daughter's. Favonia had taken a week to seize upon existence but then she thrived. I thought the same would happen. But when this baby emerged, he was already fading. He never responded to us; he slipped away within hours.

The midwife said a mother should hold a dead baby; afterwards she and Julia Justa had to wrestle to make Helena give up the body again. Helena went into deep shock. Women cleaned up, as they do. Helena Justina stayed in the bedroom, refusing comfort, ignoring food, declining to see her daughters, even distant with me. My sister Maia said this day would be black in Helena's calendar for the rest of her life; Maia knew what it was to lose a child. At first I could not believe Helena would ever come out of it. It seemed to me, we might never even reach that point where grief only overtook her on anniversaries. She stayed frozen at the moment when she was told her boy was dead.

All action fell to me. It was not a legal necessity, but I named him: Marcus Didius Justinianus. In my place many fathers would not have bothered. His birth would not be registered; he had no civic identity. Perhaps I was wrong. I just had to decide what to do. His mother had survived, but for the moment I was alone trying to hold the family together, trying to choose what formalities were appropriate. It all became even more difficult after I learned what else had happened on that day.

The tiny swaddled bundle had been placed in a room we rarely used. What was I to do next? A newborn should receive no funeral rites; he was too small for full cremation. Adult burials must be held outside the city; families who can afford it build a mausoleum beside a highroad for their embalmed bodies or cremation urns. That had never been for us; ashes of the plebeian Didii are kept in a cupboard for a time, and then mysteriously lost.

My mother revealed that she had always taken her stillborns to the Campagna farm where she grew up, but I could not leave my distraught family. Helena's father, the senator, offered me a niche in the tumbledown columbarium of the Camilli on the Via Appia, saying sadly, 'It will be a very small urn!' I thought about it, but was too proud. We live in a patriarchal society; he was my son. I don't give two figs for formal rules, but disposal was my responsibility.

Some people inter newborn babies under a slab in a new building; none was available and I jibbed at making our child into a votive offering. I don't annoy the gods; I don't encourage them either. We lived in an old town house at the foot of the Aventine, with a back exit, but almost no ground. If I dug a tiny grave among the sage and rosemary, there was a horrendous possibility children at play or cooks digging holes to bury fish bones might one day turn up little Marcus' ribs accidentally.

I climbed up to our roof terrace and sat alone with the problem.

The answer came to me just before stiffness set in. I would take my sad bundle out to my father's house. We ourselves had once lived there, up on the Janiculan Hill across the Tiber; in fact, I was the idiot who first bought the inconvenient place. I had since worked a swap with my father but it still seemed like home. Although Pa was a reprobate, his villa offered the baby a resting place where, when Helena was ready for it, we could put up a memorial stone.

I wondered briefly why my father had not yet come with condolences. Normally when people wanted time alone, he was a first-footer. He could smell tragedy like newly cooked bread. He was bound to let himself in with that house key he would never give back to me, then irritate us with his insensitivity. The thought of Pa issuing platitudes to shake Helena out of her sadness was dire. He would probably try to get me drunk. Wine was bound to feature in my recovery one day, but I wanted to choose how, when and where the medicine was applied. The dose would be poured by my best friend Petronius Longus. The only reason I had not sought him out so far, was delicacy because he too had lost young children. Besides, I had things to do first.

My mother was staying at our house. She would continue to do so, as long as she believed she was needed. Perhaps that would be longer than we really wanted, but Ma would do what she thought best.

Helena wanted no part in the funeral. She turned away, weeping, when I told her what I planned to do. I hoped she approved. I hoped she knew that dealing with this was the only way I could try to help her. Albia, our teenaged foster daughter, intended to accompany me but in the end even she was too upset. Ma might have made the pilgrimage but I gratefully left her to look after little Julia and Favonia. I would not ask her to see Pa, from whom she had been bitterly estranged for thirty years. If I *had* asked, she might have forced herself to come and support me, but I had enough to endure without that worry.

So I went alone. And I was alone, therefore, when the subdued slaves at my father's house told me the next piece of bad news. On the same day that I lost my son, I lost my father too.

2

As I turned off the informal roadway into Pa's rough carriage drive, nothing appeared amiss. No smoke came from the new bath house. There was no one in sight; the gardeners had clearly decided that late afternoon was their time to down tools. The gardens, designed by Helena when we lived here, were looking in good fettle. Since Pa was an auctioneer, the statuary was exquisite. I thought Pa must be down in Rome, at his warehouse or his office in the Saepta Julia; otherwise on a warm summer evening I would expect to hear a low buzz and chinking wine paraphernalia as he entertained associates or neighbours, sprawling on the benches that permanently stood out beneath the old pine trees.

I had come in a closed litter. The dead baby lay in a basket on the opposite seat. I left it there temporarily. The bearers dropped me by the short flight of steps in the porch. I banged my fist on the big double doors to announce my presence and went straight indoors.

A peculiar scene met me. All the household slaves and freedmen stood assembled in the atrium as if they had been waiting for me.

I was startled. I was even more startled by the size of the sombre crowd filling the hallway. Tray-toters, pillow-plumpers, earwax-extractors, dust-dampers. I had never realised how many staff Pa kept. My father was missing from the scene. My heart started pounding unevenly.

I was wearing a black tunic instead of my usual hues. Still lost in the horror of the baby's death, I must have looked grim. The slaves seemed prepared for it, and oddly relieved to see me. 'Marcus Didius— you heard!'

'I heard nothing.'

Throats were cleared. 'Our dear master passed away.'

I was taken aback by that crazy phrase 'dear master'. Most people knew Pa as 'that bastard, Favonius' or even 'Geminus—may he rot in Hades with a bald crow perpetually eating his liver'. The bird would be pecking sooner than expected, apparently.

The whole bunch were deferring to me with new-found humility. If they felt awkward doing it, that was nothing to how I felt. They stood trying to hide the anxieties that characterise slaves of a newly dead citizen while they wait to know what will be done with them.

It could hardly be my problem, so I gave them no help. My father and I had been on bad terms after he left Ma; our reconciliation in recent years was patchy. He had no rights over me and I took no responsibility for him. Somebody else must be designated to deal with his effects. Somebody else would keep or sell the slaves.

I would have to tell the family he was gone. That would cause all sorts of bad feelings.

This was turning into a bad year.

Officially, it was the year of the consuls Vespasianus Augustus and Titus Caesar (Vespasian, our elderly, curmudgeonly, much-admired Emperor, in his eighth consulship, and his lively elder son and heir, notching up his sixth). Later, 'suffect' consuls took over, which was a way of sharing the workload and the honours. The suffects that year were Domitian Caesar (the much-less-liked younger son) and an unknown senator called Gnaeus Julius Agricola—a non-notable; some years afterwards he became governor of Britannia. Say no more. He was too insignificant for a civilised province, so the Senate finessed him by pretending that Britain was a challenge where they wanted a man they could trust . . .

I ignore the civic calendar. Still, there are years you remember.

Duty began weighing on me. Death wreaks havoc on survivors' lifestyles. For years I had been forced to play at being the family head, since my father reneged and my only brother was dead. Pa ran away with his redhead when I was about seven—an even thirty years ago. My mother never spoke to him again and most of us were loyal to Ma. Even after he returned sheepishly to Rome, calling himself Geminus as a half-hearted disguise, Pa kept apart from the family for years. More recently he did impose himself when it suited him. He was a snob about my connections to a senatorial family, so I had to see most of him. Recently my sister Maia took over his accounts at the auction house, one of my nephews was learning the business, and another sister ran a bar he owned.

Once the twittering slaves made their announcement, I foresaw big changes.

'Who is going to tell me what happened?'

First spokesman was a wine-pourer, not quite as handsome as he thought, who wanted to get himself noticed: 'Marcus Didius, your beloved father was found dead early this morning.'

He had been dead all day and I did not know. I had been struggling with the baby's birth and death and all the while this had been happening too.

'Was it natural?'

'What else could it be, sir?' I could think of a few answers.

Nema, Pa's personal bodyslave, who was known to me, stepped up to give me details. Yesterday, my father came home from work at the Saepta Julia at a normal time, had dinner and retired to bed, early for him. Nema had heard him moving about this morning, apparently at his ablutions, then came a sudden loud thump. Nema ran in and Pa was dead on the floor.

Since I was known to spend my working life questioning such statements, Nema and the others looked worried. I suspected they had discussed how to convince me the story was accurate. They said a slave with some medical knowledge had diagnosed a heart attack.

'We did not send for a doctor. You know Geminus. He would loathe the cost, when it was obvious that nothing could be done . . .'

I knew. Pa could be stupidly generous, but like most men who accrued a lot of money he was more often stingy. Anyway, the diagnosis was reasonable. His lifestyle was tough; he had been looking tired; we were all not long returned from a physically demanding trip to Egypt.

Even so, any doubts would bring the slaves under suspicion. Legally, their position was dangerous. If their master's passing was seen as unnatural, they could all be put to death. They were scared—particularly scared of me. I am an informer. I fix credit checks and character references. I deliver subpoenas, act for disappointed beneficiaries, defend accused parties in civil actions. In the course of this work I frequently run across corpses, not all of them persons who have died quietly of old age at home. So I tend to look for problems. Jealousy, greed and lust have a bad habit of causing people to end up on a bier prematurely. Clients may hire me to investigate the suspicious death of a lover or a business partner.

Sometimes it turns out that my client actually killed the deceased and hired me as a cover, which at least is neat.

'Shall I fetch the will?' asked Quirinius, whose main job had been to detain creditors with sweet drinks and pastries on a patio, while Pa scarpered by a back exit.

'Save it for the heir.'

'Back in an instant!'

Dear gods.

Me? My father's heir? On the other hand, who else was there? What friend or close relation, other than me, could Pa have lumbered? He knew half of Rome, but who counted with him enough for this? Had he died intestate, it would have become my role in any case. I had always imagined he *would* die intestate, come to that.

Misgiving gave way to dread. It seemed Pa was going to make me responsible for unravelling the complex rats' nest of his business affairs. I would have to become familiar with his dubious private life. A named heir does not automatically inherit the estate (though he is entitled to at least a quarter); his duty is to become an extension of the dead man, honouring his gods, coughing up for his charities, preserving property, paying debts (a frequent reason to back out of being an executor, believe me). He makes arrangements for specified bequests and tactfully fends off people who have been disinherited. He shares out the booty as instructed.

I would have to do it all. This was typical of my father. I don't know why I felt so unprepared.

The will was apparently hard to find. That wasn't suspicious; Pa hated documentation. He liked to keep everything vague. If he had to have written evidence, he tried to lose the scroll among a lot of mess.

The slaves kept staring. I cleared my throat and gazed at the mosaic floor. When I was bored with counting tesserae, I had to look at them.

They were a mixed bunch. Various nationalities and jobs. Some had worked for Pa for decades, others I failed to recognise. It was unlikely he came by any of them in the usual way. Not for my father a trip to the slave market when he needed a specific worker, with genteel haggling then a routine purchase. In his world, many business debts were settled by payment in kind. Some executors find antique vases of great value, which have been payments in lieu of fees. But since my father dealt in antique vases anyway, he accepted other commodities. He had acquired a curiously colourful *familia* in this way. Sometimes it worked out well; he had a wonderful panpipe-player, though he himself had a tin ear. But most of the staff looked unimpressive. Bankrupts' cast-offs. Two kitchen staff were blind; that could be entertaining. A gardener had only one arm. I spotted a few vacant expressions, not to mention the usual rheumy eyes, raw wounds and sinister rashes.

While we went on waiting, they plucked up courage to petition me. Very few of these frightened household members were already freedmen; Pa had made lavish promises, but never got around to issuing formal deeds of manumission. That was typical; he managed to screw decent service out of his staff, but preferred to keep them reliant on him. I quickly learned that many of these anxious souls had families, even though slaves are not allowed to marry. They pressed me to grant their freedom, plus the same for various wives and children. Pa did own some of these, so their fates could be untangled and regularised, if I was willing. But others belonged to neighbours, so that was a mess. Other owners would not appreciate me trying to fix up fairytale solutions for *their* handmaids and bootboys.

Another worry for the slaves was where they would all end up. They realised that the villa might have to be sold shortly. They might be heading for the slave-market and a very uncertain future.

While we hung around in embarrassment, surprisingly one of the women asked, 'Would you like to see him now?'

I nearly said *must I?* but that would have been an impiety.

Don't be like that, my boy! Is it too much to show respect to your poor old father? . . .

A freedman was guarding the room. A curtain of scent wafted at me from the doorway, cassia and myrrh, traditional funeral incenses, the costly ones. Who authorised that? I hesitated on the threshold then went in.

I had viewed plenty of corpses. That was work. This was duty. I preferred the other kind.

No need to wonder about identity. On a rather fine couch in this dim room off a peaceful corridor, lay my deceased parent: Marcus Didius Favonius, also known as Geminus, descendant of a long line of dubious Aventine plebeians and honoured among the dealers, tricksters and shysters of the Saepta Julia. He had been washed and anointed, dressed in an embroidered tunic and a toga; given a wreath; his eyes had been closed by respectful hands and a ridiculous flower garland positioned round his neck. His haematite seal ring, his other gold ring with the head of an emperor, and the key to his bankbox at the Saepta lay in a small bronze dish, emphasising that the trappings of his life were no longer needed. Lying on his back, laid out so neatly on two mattresses, that garrulous sociable soul, now permanently silent, seemed thinner but essentially the same as when I saw him last week at our house. Unkempt grey curls warned how my own would be in a decade's time. A lifetime of enjoying meals and doing business over cups of wine showed in his solid belly. Still, he had been a short, wide-bodied man who was used to moving heavy furniture and marble artefacts. His hairy arms and legs were strongly muscled. Down in Rome he often walked, even though he could afford a litter.

This motionless corpse was not my father. Gone were the characteristics that made him: the bright, devious eyes; the raucous, complicated jokes; the endless lust for barmaids; the aptitude for making money out of nothing; those flares of generosity that always led to pleading for reciprocal favours and affection. Gone for ever was what my mother called his cracking grin. No one could more surely clinch a deal. No one enjoyed making a sale so deeply. I had hated having him in my life—but now suddenly could not envisage life without him.

I backed out of the room, feeling queasy.

In the entrance hall Quirinius, flustered, told me, 'I thought I knew where his will was kept, but I've searched high and low and I can't find it.'

'Gone missing?' As a professional habit, I made it sound ominous; not that I cared.

He was reprieved. To my surprise, we were being joined by new arrivals; people had come from the city for the funeral. Bemused, I learned that messengers had been sent earlier today to the family and my father's business colleagues. My litter must have crossed with them.

Word must have flown around Rome. Father had belonged to an auctioneers' burial club; mainly he went for the wine. Although he had not paid his subscription for the last six months, the other members seemed to bear no grudges (well, that was Pa). Undertakers had been marshalled. A calm dignitary was in charge.

Gornia, the elderly assistant from the antiques warehouse, was one of the first comers. 'I brought up an altar we had kicking about, young Marcus. Rather nice Etruscan piece, with a winged figure . . .' A benefit of the profession. They could always lay hands on an altar. They had access to most things, and I was just thinking Gornia might help me pick out an urn for the ashes, when one of the funeral club people produced an alabaster item which apparently matched my father's instructions. (What instructions?) The man handed it to me discreetly, brushing aside my murmur about payment. I had the feeling I had blundered into a closed world where everything would be made easy for me today. The debts would come later. Probably not small. I, of course, would be expected to pay them, but I was too sensible to upset myself thinking of that before I had to.

A remarkable crowd gathered. Men I had never seen before claimed to be decades-old colleagues. Squeezing out tears that could almost be genuine, strangers gripped my hand like familiar old uncles and told me what an unexpected tragedy this was. They promised me assistance with unspecified needs. One or two actually winked heavily. I had no idea what they meant.

Family arrived too. With sombre gowns and veiled heads, my sisters—Allia, Galla, Junia—pushed through to the front, dragging with them my nightmare brothers-in-law and Mico, Victorina's widower. I viewed this as deep hypocrisy. Even Petronius Longus appeared, bringing my youngest sister Maia, who at least had some right to be here because she had worked with Pa. It was Maia who thrust a set of tablets at me.

'You'll need the will.'

'So I am shocked to hear. He kept it at the office?' I was just making conversation. I shoved the thing through my belt.

'This was his latest version!' Maia scoffed. 'Some urgent change

– 14 –

had to be made last week so he brought it down to the Saepta. He did love fiddling with it.'

'Know what it says?'

'The misery wouldn't say.'

'Haven't you looked?'

'Don't be shocking—it's sealed with seven seals!'

No time to be amazed by Maia's restraint (if that was true), another marvel happened. A small figure, veiled in blackest black, jumped nimbly off a hired donkey (cheaper than a carrying chair), with the manner of one who expected reverence. She received it. At once the crowd gave way for her, and apparently without surprise at her presence. If the day had seemed unreal before, it became madness now. I didn't need to peek beneath the veil. My mother was taking back her rights.

Luckily no one could see her expression. I knew she would not throw herself inconsolably on the bier, or rend her hair. She would send Pa to the Underworld with a cackle, delighted that he had gone first. She was here to make certain the renegade actually left for the Styx. The smug words I heard through that veil all day were, 'I never like to gloat!'

I saluted Ma gravely and made sure a couple of my sisters led her by the hands, with instructions to ensure that she always had a good view of proceedings and that she didn't pinch any silver trays or old Greek vases from the house. I knew how a son ought to handle his widowed mother. I had advised enough clients on this point.

A procession lined up, like some reptile slowly awakening in the sun. In a daze, I found myself propelled to the front of a long funeral train. We made our way a short distance to an area of the garden that Pa must have already chosen as his resting place. He had planned everything, I gathered. I was fascinated to find he had this morbid streak. His corpse was carried on a bier, on its double mattress, with an ivory headrest. I was one of the eight bearers, with Petronius and the other brothers-in-law—Verontius, the crooked road contractor; Mico the worst plasterer in Rome; Lollius, the constantly unfaithful boatman; Gaius Baebius, the most boring customs clerk in that far from rollicking profession. Numbers were made up by Gornia and a fellow called Clusius, some leading light in auctioneering, probably the one who hoped to scoop up most of my father's business in the next few weeks. There were torches, as is traditional even in daytime. There were horn-players and flautists. Curiously, they all could play. To my relief, there were no hired mourners wailing and, thank Pluto, no mime artists pretending to be Pa.

The undertakers must have brought equipment and, unnoticed, had already constructed a pyre. It was three levels high. Funereal odours soon covered the hillside: not just more myrrh and cassia, but frankincense and cinnamon. No one in Rome would be able to buy banquet garlands today; we had all the flowers. High on the Janiculan, a breeze helped the flames get going after I plunged in the first torch. We stood around, as you have to for hours, waiting for the corpse to be consumed, while people with no sense reminisced about Pa. The kinder ones simply watched in silence. Much later I was to drown the ashes with wine—just a mediocre vintage; in respect for Pa, I reserved his best for drinking. Though I was still not certain how much of the organisation was my responsibility, I invited everyone to a feast in nine days' time, after the set period of formal mourning. That encouraged them to leave. It was a good step back down to Rome and they had gathered I was not offering overnight accommodation.

They knew I had special troubles. They had all seen how, just before the undertakers opened my father's eyes on the bier so he could see his way on to Charon's ferry, I had clambered up and laid upon his breast the body of my one-day-old son.

So on the sun-drenched slopes of the Janiculan Hill, one long, strange July evening, we paid our respects to Marcus Didius Favonius. Neither he nor tiny Marcus Didius Justinianus would have to face the dark alone. Wherever they were going, they set off there together, with my tiny son clasped for eternity in the strong arms of his grandfather.

3

I shed some tears. People expect it. Sometimes at the funeral of a reprobate it seems easier than when you are honouring a man who really deserved grief.

Before they left, the jostling started. Relatives, business associates, friends, so-called friends and even strangers all made subtle or blatant attempts to find out whether they would receive a legacy. My mother stayed aloof from this. She and Pa had never declared themselves divorced, so she was convinced she had rights. She was waiting for my sisters to take her back to Rome, but they were queuing to come up and speak to me, showing affection that unsettled me. I could not remember the last time Allia, Galla or Junia had felt the need to kiss my cheek. One by one their feckless husbands each clasped my hand in strong, silent communion. Only Gaius Baebius came right out with a concern: 'What's going to happen about Flora's, Marcus?' He meant the Aventine bar that my sister Junia managed for our father.

'Just give me a few days, Gaius—'

'Well, I suppose Junia can go on running the place as usual.'

'That would be helpful.' I ground my teeth. 'I hope it's not a chore. Apollonius is a perfectly good waiter. Or if Junia really can't face it, why doesn't she just close up the shutters, until we know what's what?'

'Oh, Junia won't give way to her grief !'

Junia stood in uncharacteristic silence, forced by the situation to have her husband speak for her: he like a true Roman patriarch and she like an inconsolable bereaved daughter. Yes, the lies and deceit had started.

I caught Maia's eye and wondered again whether she had sneaked a look at the will. I could have unsealed the tablets. It is traditional to read a will in public straight after the funeral.

Stuff that for a game of soldiers. I wanted to inspect and evaluate this dodgy document when I was safely by myself. It remained in my belt. Every time I bent a few inches, the chunky tablets stuck in my ribs, reminding me. Every time someone fished for information, I played at being too overcome with sorrow to think about it.

'Cut that out!' muttered Petronius Longus, while *he* acted out supporting me. 'Some of us know you would have gone to live as a pork-chop trader in Halicarnassus if you could have escaped being your father's son.'

'No point. He'd only have turned up,' I answered gloomily. 'Offering me a cheap price for bones—and expecting me to leave the marrow in as a favour.'

Petro and Maia stayed until last, helping to shepherd out the rest, then giving orders to the slaves. 'Keep the house running as normal. Keep it clean and secure.'

'You will have instructions later this week about the funeral feast, then you will be told where you will each be working afterwards . . .'

I watched them, moving now like a long-established couple, although they had only lived together formally for one or two years. They had met after Maia was married and a mother, a status she respected with more diligence than her late husband deserved. Each now had children from first marriages, all of whom were currently outside in the portico, quietly occupying themselves. Throughout the day Petronilla, Cloelia, Marius, Rhea and Ancus had behaved in magical contrast to the brats my other sisters dragged along. They would have shown up my own pair, had I brought them. My daughters were cute but unmanageable. Helena said they got it from me.

Petronius, tall and hefty, was not in formal funeral clothes, but had simply thrown an extra-dark cloak over the battered brown gear he usually wore. I guessed that back in Rome he was due at the vigiles' patrol house for a night shift. I thanked him for coming all the more; he just shrugged. 'We've got a really puzzling case, Falco. I'd welcome your advice—'

My sister laid a hand on his arm. 'Lucius, not now.' Maia, with her dark curls and characteristic quick movements, looked odd and unfamiliar in black; she usually flitted about in very bright colours. Her face was pale, but she was businesslike.

I would have hugged her, but now the house had emptied, Maia broke away and threw herself onto a couch. 'Did you see this coming, sis?'

'Not really, though Pa had complained of feeling off-colour. Your Egypt trip knocked it out of him.'

'Not my idea. I had banned him. I knew he'd be a menace, and he was.'

'Oh I realise. Look,' Maia said, 'I won't annoy you with details, but I went quickly through the diary with Gornia. We will carry on with all the booked auctions but won't take any new orders. You'll have a lot of sorting out, whatever happens to the business.'

'Oh Jupiter! Sorting out—what a nightmare . . . Why me?' I finally managed to voice it out loud.

Petronius looked surprised. 'You are the son. He thought a lot of you.'

'No, he thought Marcus was a self-righteous prig,' my sister disagreed in a casual tone. She threw insults as if she had hardly noticed doing it, though her barbs were generally apt and always intentional. 'Still, Marcus always does a good job. And apart from behaving like a bastard at every opportunity, Father was a traditionalist.'

'Maybe all fathers are bastards,' I commented. I like to be fair. 'He knew what I thought of him. I told him often enough.'

'Well, he knew you were honest!' said Maia, laughing a little. She had faith in me. I had never felt certain just how she regarded Pa. We were the two youngest in our family, long-time allies against the others; she was my favourite and held me in great affection. She had worked with my father because he had paid her, at a time when she had been desperate financially. Newly widowed then—it was about three years ago—she appreciated being in a family business during that hard period. She needed the security. Pa, to do him justice, offered it. He railed against having a woman interfering yet he let her do much as she wanted as his office manager. He recognised how good she was at organisation. He also liked having one of his own privy to his secrets, rather than a hired hand or a slave. That was why he let Junia run Flora's Caupona too, even though her attitude upset half the customers. And that, I suppose, was why he landed me with his will.

I pulled it out. I held the tied and sealed tablets nervously between both hands, making no attempt to pull the strings undone. 'So tell me about this, Maia.' Maia just sniffed. 'He rewrote it last week? Why was that?'

'One of his whims. He sent for the lawyer straight after that drama-dealer, Thalia, came to see him at the Saepta.'

'*Thalia?*' That was unexpected.

'You know the creature, I believe? She wears the shortest skirts in the Empire.'

'And frolics suggestively with wild beasts.'

'Who is this? Should I know her?' Sitting on the end of Maia's couch, his long legs crossed and his hands behind his head, Petronius showed himself keen for gossip. Maia kicked him, and he massaged the bare soles of her tired feet for her; neither really seemed aware they were doing it.

I shrugged. 'Have Helena and I not mentioned her? She's a circus and theatre manager. Runs actors and musicians—does rather well. Her speciality is exotic animal acts. I do mean exotic! Her indecent dance with a python would make your eyes water.'

A gleam came into Petro's eyes. 'I'd like to see that! But Marcus, my boy, I thought you gave up your fancy girlfriends!'

'Oh I have; honest, legate! No, no; she's a family friend. Thalia's a good sort, though I hate her pesky snake, Jason. I could have done without her travelling to Alexandria with my damned father. She came to buy lions. Pa cadged a free ride on her ship. I believe that was the first time they met, and I can't imagine they would have any business together back in Rome.'

'Oh, they were close!' Maia snorted. 'They rushed into a closet with the door closed and there was some ghastly giggling. I did *not* take in a galley tray of almond fancies.' She looked prudish. 'When they emerged, Thalia seemed extremely happy with the outcome and our father positively glowed—the revolting way he did when some busty fifteen-year-old barmaid gave him a free drink.'

Petronius winced. I just looked rueful. 'Thalia's a woman of the world, Maia, with her own money; she can't have been scrounging. What she likes from men, insofar as she likes them for anything, is purely physical . . . What did Geminus say?'

'Nothing. I could see he was bursting to make *some* grand pronouncement,' Maia replied, 'but the Thalia woman glared at him and for once he held his tongue. Immediately she left, the lawyer was booked, however. Next day Geminus went into a huddle with *him*. He couldn't resist letting on he was playing with his will. Since he was dying to tell me the details, I refused to show any curiosity.'

Like Maia, I hated to be manipulated into feeling any interest. I was exhausted. I decided I would have dinner here, sleep at the villa, then rise early to go home to Helena. I tossed the will on to a low table. 'It will keep.'

'My bet is, that will be a whole year's work and twice as much trouble,' Petronius warned.

'Well, I'll give it proper attention tomorrow. The timing must be a coincidence, Maia. I can't imagine Thalia's visit was connected.'

Then Maia exclaimed, 'Oh, Marcus. You can be such an innocent!'

After Maia and Petronius left, the slaves found me something to eat and somewhere to sleep. I had to stop them putting me in my father's room. Assuming his legal identity was bad enough. I drew the line at his bed.

Food revived me. Pa always ate well. The excellent panpipe-player whootled gently for me too. I was ready to be irritated, but it was quite relaxing. He seemed surprised when I congratulated him on his arpeggios. It looked as if he was hanging around in case I required other services—not that my father would have stood for that. I dismissed the musician without rancour. Who knows what kind of debauched household he originally came from?

Then, of course, I did what you or anyone else would have done: I opened up the tablets.

4

My life changed for ever at that moment.

My father's will was quite short and surprisingly simple. There were no outrageous clauses. It was a routine family testament.

'I, Marcus Didius Favonius, have made a will and command my sons to be my heirs.'

So it was legally proper, but well out of date. Despite all the talk of revisions, this had been written long before he died—twenty years ago, to be precise. It was soon after my father returned to Rome from Capua, where he had originally fled with his girlfriend when he left home, and when he set up again as an auctioneer here, trading under the new name of Geminus. Flora, the girlfriend, never had children. At that time 'my sons' meant my brother and me. Festus later died in Judaea. Clearly Pa, who had been close to him, had never been able to face writing him out.

The customary seven witnesses had signed. They ought to be present again when the will was opened, but to Hades with that. Some names were vaguely familiar, business contacts, men of my father's age. I knew that at least two had died in the intervening period. A couple came to the funeral.

As was customary, the tablet named some people who might have had a claim but specifically disinherited them as main heirs: Pa chose to dispense with the equal treatment that the law would have given his four surviving daughters if, say, he had died intestate. I could see why he had never made my sisters aware this would happen. Their reaction would be vicious. The bastard must have imagined with enjoyment my discomfiture when I had to pass on the news.

He left no instructions about making any slaves free. They too would be disappointed, though executors can be flexible. They were bound to know that, so they would continue canvassing me. I would take my time over making decisions.

Next came a list of specific annuities to be paid out: quite a high figure to Mother, which surprised and pleased me. There were smaller sums for my sisters, so they had not been ignored completely. It was usually assumed married daughters had received their share of the family loot in their dowries. (*What dowries?* I could hear them all shriek.) Nothing had been done for Marina who, well after the will was made, became my brother's lover and mother of a child who was presumed to be fathered by Festus. An enormous sum was earmarked for Flora, Pa's mistress of two decades, though since she had died that no longer counted. I would keep quiet about it; there was no point upsetting Ma. After that, the rest went to the specified heirs: 'my sons'. So with Festus dead, everything else my father had owned would come to me.

I was seriously shocked. It was completely unexpected. Unless I uncovered enormous debts—and I reckoned Pa was too canny for that—then he had bequeathed me a substantial amount.

I tried to stay calm, but I was human. I began to reckon up mentally. My father had never owned much land—not land in the traditional Roman sense of rolling fields that could be ploughed and grazed and tended by battalions of rural workers, not land that counted formally towards social status. But this was a grand house in a splendid location, and he had owned another, even bigger villa on the coast below Ostia. I only discovered his place at Ostia last year, so there might be further properties he kept secret. The two I knew about were well staffed—and house-trained slaves were valuable in themselves. Above all, these houses were furnished expensively—crammed to the rafters with wonderful goods. I knew Pa kept instant-access funds in a chest bolted into the wall at the Saepta Julia and he had more money with a Forum banker; his cash flow rose and fell with the ups and downs of self-employment, much as my own did. However, throughout his life, his real investments followed his real interest: art and antiques.

I looked around. This was merely a bedroom for casual visitors. It was lightly furnished, compared with the areas Pa used himself. Even so, the bed I was lolling on had intricate bronze fittings, a well-upholstered mattress supported on decent webbing, a striking wool coverlet and tasselled pillows. There was a heavy folding stool in the room, like a magistrate's. An old Eastern carpet hung on one wall on a runner that had gilded finials. On a shelf—which was grey-veined marble, with polished onyx ends—stood a row of ancient south Italian vases that would sell for a figure big enough to feed a family for a year.

This was one unimportant room. Multiply it by all the other rooms in at least two large houses, plus whatever stock was crammed into various warehouses and the treasures currently on display at Pa's office in the Saepta . . . I began to feel light-headed.

Complete upheaval faced me. Nothing in my life could ever be as I had expected: neither my life, nor the lives of my wife and my children. If this will was genuine, and it was the latest version, and if my brother Festus really had died in the desert (which was undeniable, because I had spoken to people who saw it happen), then I would be able to live without anxiety for the rest of my days. I could give my daughters dowries lavish enough to secure them consuls, if they wanted idiots as husbands. I could stop being an informer. I need never work again. I could waste my life being a benefactor of out-of-the-way temples and playing at patron to dim-witted poets.

My father had not just made me his legal representative. He had left me a great fortune.

5

The morning after the funeral I returned home at first light.
     After only a few hours' sleep I felt drained. My house still lay
quiet. I crawled on to a couch in a spare room, unwilling to disturb
Helena. It was still barely a day since her labour and loss. But by then
she had been told about my father, so was on the alert. Just as she
always heard my return from late-night surveillances, Helena roused
herself and found me. I felt her drop a coverlet over me, then she slid
under it too. She was still distraught over the baby, but now the greater
need was to comfort me. Our love held strong. Extra trouble brought
us back close. For a time we lay side by side, holding hands. Too soon,
the dog snuffled in and found us, then we began the slow slide back to
normality.

     When I told Helena she had married better than she thought and
might be about to acquire a stupendous dress allowance, she sighed.
'He never mentioned his intentions, but I always suspected it. When
you raged at him, I think Geminus enjoyed secretly knowing that one
day he would give you all this. Because you are a realist you would
accept his generosity . . . He loved you, Marcus. He was very proud
of you.'

     'It's too much.'

'Nonsense.'

'I can say no to it.'

'Legally.'

'I might.'

'You won't. Just say yes, then give it away if you feel that way later.'

'It will ruin my life.'

'Your life is in your own hands, just as it always was. You won't change,' Helena said. 'You need to work. It is what you enjoy: grappling with puzzles that no one else will undertake and righting society's wrongs. Don't become a man of leisure; you'll go mad—and you'll drive the rest of us crazy.'

I pretended to think she just wanted reasons to pack me out of the house every morning as before. But she knew that I accepted she was right.

During the nine days of mourning, Helena and I told everyone that 'in the style of the divine Emperor Augustus and his unparalleled wife Livia', we would not be seen in public. Platitudes always work. Nobody considered that we regarded Augustus and Livia as two-faced, double-dealing, power-mad manipulators.

After the nine days, we could both just about face people again. Helena Justina was beside me at the feast, when I returned to the Janiculan.

I knew what the funeral feast would be like. I thought the day would hold no surprises. Even more hangers-on managed to bring themselves up the hill than had struggled there for the cremation. Free food, free drink, and the chance to hear or pass on gossip, brought fools out in flocks. Relatives we had forgotten were ours somehow turned up. Mother's brothers, Fabius and Junius, who were rarely seen together because they feuded so tenaciously, both came all the way from the Campagna; at least they brought root vegetables as presents, unlike the other shiftless guests. If they had ulterior motives they were too dumb to say. I thought Fabius and Junius were simply acknowledging the end of an era that only they and Ma now remembered.

I had primed my more reliable nephews—restless Gaius, over-weight Cornelius, sensible Marius—to pass among the throng, muttering that there were far more debts than anticipated and that I might refuse to be the heir . . . It held off some of the graspers from overt begging.

Together Helena and I went through the motions of hosting the banquet. Stuffing merrily, people were no trouble. As the long meal drew to a close, I watched the tall and stately Helena Justina pass among the guests with my secretary, Katutis, at her shoulder. He was new. I had acquired a trained Egyptian scribe at just the right moment. He was thrilled to have deaths in the family; it provided more work than I found for him normally. While Helena prised out people's names, Katutis busily wrote them all down in level Greek script in case I needed to know later. I was nervous that some of Pa's dubious business arrangements might jump up and bite. Helena had also pointed out several women who looked like off-duty barmaids, flaunting their best outfits and seemingly unaware that mourning women should leave off their jewellery. These blowsy, bulging dames might just be good-hearted old friends of my social papa; perhaps they adored him as a lovable rogue who left good tips by his empty wine-cup. Or they could have deeper motives. Helena was collecting their data along with details of all those old men who felt no need to explain who they were, as they called me Young Marcus and tapped their bulbous red noses as if we shared enormous secrets.

As we went about our duties, Helena murmured, 'I have said we are hoping for a mention in the *Daily Gazette* society column: *Seen at a banquet in his elegant Janiculan villa to celebrate the life of much-admired man-about-the-Forum, Marcus Didius Favonius, were the following persons of note* . . . Now watch the would-be persons of note rush up to help Katutis spell their names right.'

'I don't want Pa in the news.'

'No, darling. Why alert the tax authorities?' Helena's voice was thin, but she was regaining her sense of humour. Inheritance tax is five percent, paid into the Treasury's military fund. The army was going to like me a lot.

I had used my mourning period for the traditional purpose of starting to inventory the legacy. For most people nine days is enough to cover this formality; I had barely tickled the edge.

Supposedly incommunicado, I had worked like a bath-house stoker among Pa's many possessions. I set aside the least desirable items to sell to pay the tax. I also established with Gornia that we would auction some stuff that would either fail to sell, or sell for a disappointing amount; this would show picky officials that my inventory valuations were blamelessly modest. A citizen is obliged to pay his taxes, but may adopt any legal measures to minimise the damage. I knew all about that. I had been Vespasian's Census fixer. I investigated every variation of fiscal fraud and tax-dodging—and I now planned to use my experience. Pa would expect it.

I had had an interesting chat with a treasury official about whether, if I sold goods at auction, I must pay the one per cent auction tax on top of the five per cent for inheritance; you can guess his answer.

'Thalia is here; have you seen her, Marcus?'

'I glimpsed her.' She was lurking at the far end of a table, looking more wrapped up and respectable than usual. 'Nice of her to hang back and not bother us.' In fact her demure behaviour had set up anxiety.

'I shall have a word!' Helena declared, making me oddly apprehensive.

As she paraded through the guests, Helena identified the surviving witnesses to Father's will: four of those shaky old fellows who had grasped my hand interminably. I made sure they each had a drink poured from the special amphora of Falernian, which probably shortened their lives by several months; it flowed like rich olive oil and was dangerously potent. Their presence allowed me to read out the will formally. I pretended the contents came as news to me; nobody was fooled. A restrained silence fell. My sisters heard their fates without making a public scene, but assumed foreboding expressions. Ma was too heavily veiled for anyone to see her reaction. She had seemed quiet all day, as if losing the old devil at last had knocked all the spirit out of her.

Soon afterwards, people began to leave. Helena told me it was because I was viewed as tight-fisted. 'Everybody is whispering that things would have been very different—they mean, more money for them—if Festus had survived.'

That suited me. But many just went because the food and drink were running out. There had been plenty. Some of it was going home in people's pockets. Anyone who brought their own napkin made sure they took it away laden.

'I swear there were some "grieving friends" who came with little baskets specially,' I complained to Maia. Then I noticed her basket.

'Marcus, darling, I'm family. Any leftover egg-and-anchovy tart is mine!' She backed down slightly. 'You don't want waste, do you?'

Helena had identified my father's lawyer. Once we were freed from saying farewells in the portico, she brought him to me indoors.

He was surprisingly young, twenty-five or so. He introduced himself as Septimus Parvo. His accent was decent, though not screamingly aristocratic; it sounded as if he had learned how to speak from an elocution teacher, after a plebeian upbringing. His dress was neat, his manner polite. He told me he avoided cut-throat court cases at the Basilica Julia, instead working as a backstreet family lawyer.

'I'll keep your name handy then. I'm an informer myself. We may be able to do business.' The veiled surprise in Parvo's expression reminded me that most people expected I would now retire. It was still too early for me to be certain, though I thought Helena was probably right; work would always claim me. 'You're far too young to have prepared my father's will, Parvo—assuming the date is right?'

'No, my own late father did that. We have worked for many years with Didius Geminus—we always called him that. Or do you prefer to say Favonius, Falco?'

'To be frank, I just called him an incorrigible swine.'

The young man kept his expression neutral. He managed to avoid glancing around the salon we were in: the walls were drab because Pa never paid out for fresco decorators, but the room was adorned with a fabulous collection of furniture. Given how much I had just inherited, Parvo may have been wondering at my attitude.

Helena rejoined us. She led in Thalia. It was the first time I had ever seen the circus entertainer looking nervous. Normally she was as brazen as she was statuesque, even when not wrapped in her python.

'This is Thalia, Parvo. Have you met?'

She was a tall, striking woman, with muscled thighs like wharfside baulks, which were impossible to ignore through a fringed cloak that barely covered her toned body, minute skirt and tightly laced circus boots. Faced with this vision, Parvo inclined his head twitchily, as if he could tell Thalia ate men like him as pre-lunch snacks. 'No— but I heard a lot about you, Thalia.' Always a wily operator, Thalia made no reply to that thumping phrase. 'We are about to discuss the will,' Parvo murmured, acknowledging that Thalia should be part of the conversation, though not immediately saying why.

The women seated themselves in comfortable half-round chairs, filling in time by arranging cushions. Thalia folded the cloak so it just covered her legs, in a curiously modest gesture. I glanced at Helena, then waited. She had given me a 'don't say anything impetuous' look, the put-down that strong-minded wives inherit from their mothers. You know, the look you should always pay attention to, though the mischievous Fates somehow make you foolishly ignore it.

Parvo must be a piecework lawyer, not paid by the hour. He moved things along: 'Falco, when we spoke just now, did I detect a query?'

'Only that I was surprised by the will's date. I understand Pa made frequent revisions—and didn't that include one last week?'

'Yes, I brought that for you,' Parvo replied calmly. 'It is a codicil. Your father did indeed frequently make changes, but he always left the will itself alone.'

'Your fee for a codicil is much cheaper than your fee for a new will?' I guessed drily.

Parvo smiled his acknowledgement of what Pa called value for money and others might stigmatise as meanness. 'Apart from that, a codicil is often a more flexible way of giving instructions.'

I braced myself. 'So what usefully flexible orders has the old beggar left?'

Without comment, Parvo passed me a scroll, the ink so fresh and black it almost still smelt sooty. I read it. I raised my eyebrows and passed it to Helena, who read it too. We both looked at the lawyer.

'Marcus Didius Falco, your father hereby makes a solemn request of you called a *fideicommissum*. That is a good faith undertaking.' Filthy misnomer. Good faith did not come into this. 'It affects any child of Marcus Didius Geminus, otherwise Favonius, which is born to him after the date of this codicil—including a child born posthumously. You are charged with treating any child that you know your father intended to acknowledge as your sister or brother, according to the terms of the will.' Parvo knew what instruction he was handing me. A new female child must be given the same as my sisters' annuities. A *male* child would halve my inheritance. 'I shall leave you with that, Falco. Should you have any queries, anything at all, I gave your wife my address. Delighted to meet you, Helena Justina—and you too, Thalia.'

Being an experienced family lawyer, he fired the arrow then at once made off.

Helena and I turned to our old friend Thalia. Helena balanced her chin on her clasped hands, in silence. It was left to me: 'Do I gather, Thalia, that you are pregnant?'

She eyed me ruefully. 'Properly caught out, Falco.'

Thalia looked well-preserved. Across an arena she could pass for a lithe girl, but near to, I put her at approaching forty. Gracious Roman manners barred me from suggesting she was too old for this. Maybe she had thought so herself, while freely indulging in love play. That sexual promiscuity of an athletic kind had occurred was in no doubt. Thalia referred to her appetite for pleasure as consistently as she denounced as pitiful the brave men she bedded.

'Would this have been on your Egyptian trip?'

'I wondered why I was feeling so queasy all the time in Alexandria.'

'Geminus believed he was responsible?'

'Oh, he didn't need persuading. The sweet duck was ecstatic,' boasted Thalia. 'It must have happened on the boat when we were going out to Egypt. We had a few cuddles to keep out the sea breezes.'

'I'm rather surprised by the results!'

Thalia grinned. She was recovering her confidence. 'I can't say I'm happy to be a mother at my age—but when I told him the news, your dear father was just thrilled. He was so proud to find out his ballista was still firing missiles.'

I believed that. Pa—vain, foolish and ridiculous—would eagerly take the blame.

'You told my father you were expecting, he accepted it was his responsibility, and if he hadn't died, he would have acknowledged the baby?'

'That's right, Falco,' said Thalia meekly.

'What does Davos say?'

'Nothing to do with him.' Davos was Thalia's long-lost love, in theory. Helena and I had witnessed them being reunited out in Syria. It had seemed like a heart-warming development—for about three months. As far as I knew, he was now leading a summer theatre tour in southern Italy. No chance of pinning this baby on Davos. 'The Girl from Andros' and her pal 'The Girl from Perinthos' would give him foolproof alibis.

'And have you mentioned it to Philadelphion?'

'Why would I do that?'

Thalia gave me a hard defiant stare. She was sticking to her story, even though she realised I thought it much more likely her child had been procreated by a womanising zoo keeper we knew in Alexandria. He was firmly married—and what's more had a tenacious official mistress. None of that had stopped him unofficially discussing the price of lion cubs with his old crony Thalia in the humid privacy of her travel tent.

– 33 –

'You're right.' I managed not to appear angry. 'Philadelphion had enough baby animals to hand-rear.'

I rarely pray to the gods but on this occasion it did seem permissible to offer up a plea to Juno Lucina, light-bearer to pregnant women, that Thalia was not expecting male twins or triplets to reduce my heritage even further. Suddenly I knew how that old mythical king felt about the interlopers Romulus and Remus. I saw why he put those threatening twins straight into the Tiber in a basket; if I did it, I would make sure there were no nearby female wolves available for suckling.

'So Marcus, my dear,' Thalia wheedled. 'It's lucky we know each other so well—now that I'm going to be giving you a little sister or brother! And do I gather the precious babe is to receive a bit of money from your lovely father?'

'Get it born first!' I answered her, perhaps too cruelly.

6

'You hypocrite—I saw your face!' Helena accused me. She smoothed her skirts, rattling her bracelets in annoyance. 'Marcus Didius Falco—' That was a subtle clue. Helena used formality like a fisherman's trident. I was well speared. 'Can it be that you have become a miser, over a fortune you never expected—and it's only nine days since you heard about it?'

'Human nature. The dark side of greed.' I forced a grin cautiously. 'What I really hate is this pregnancy of Thalia's being passed off as our problem. Pa was riddled with vanity and befuddled by drink if he couldn't see she was conning him. Being fleeced by a friend is loathsome.'

Helena shook her head. 'What if she's right? No child can ever truly know its father, nor any father know his child. Unless there is some way of testing the blood in our veins, we are all left with the word of our mothers—and most of us are none the worse for it.'

'The world is full of wicked mothers who have no idea who their children belong to. Roll on the day some scientific investigator finds out how to prove paternity. Maybe that silver-haired fox Philadelphion will do it.'

'Given that Philadelphion may be the real parent, that would be a nice irony. But uncertainty has advantages,' Helena maintained. 'Besides, you can't blame Thalia asking Geminus for help—'

'She's a highly successful entrepreneur. What help can she need?'

'She can't dance with the python during a pregnancy!'

'I would not put it past her. Modesty isn't in her repertoire.' Even Thalia's normal acrobatics were gross. 'If she's out of action for a while, her troupe will go on working. She'll have funds.'

'But Marcus, she wanted to plan for the baby's future. She didn't know your father would die,' Helena insisted. 'No one expected it.'

'I agree, she can't have intended settling down with him—she's far too independent.' I shuddered at the thought of Thalia as a stepmother. 'Still, she got him to promise something. He obviously told her he would change his will. And she was happy for him to do so!'

'As you said—she is a very good businesswoman.'

Growling, I went off to the Saepta Julia, where I was burying my anger in the monumental task of exploring my father's affairs.

It was the day that crawler Cluvius turned up. He was nagging to know whether I intended carrying on Pa's business, or could Cluvius and his auctioneer cronies siphon off work that would have been ours? 'People approach the Guild for advice. We assume you don't want to be bothered, Marcus Didius . . .'

On the spot, I decided. 'Business as usual!' I snapped crushingly. 'I'll be lending a hand myself.' I had spare capacity. Informing was quiet in summer. People are too hot to worry about professional fortune-hunters marrying their daughters. Of course they *should* worry—because long steamy July and August nights are when those bold girls are most likely to let lovers in at the window . . .

'Feel free to ask any of us for advice then,' Cluvius offered peevishly.

That clinched it. From that moment I became a joint auctioneer-informer. I would manumit one or two of the better slaves from Pa's ménage then train them up as freedmen assistants, a few in the auction house, a couple on my client casework. There could be a handy crossover. The auction helpers could scout for people in the kind of difficulty I solved as an informer. And it was traditional for both trades to operate out of the Saepta Julia.

Strange how you can worry for years over your career, and do nothing about it—then alter it instantly without a qualm. This was like falling in love all over again. Certainty thumped down on me. There was no going back.

'Yes, Cluvius; I'm moving back into my old office. That will help me keep an eye on the competition!' I may have looked naïve but if Cluvius knew that the 'office' I referred to was where I had once worked with the Chief Spy picking off Census defaulters, he might see me as a more serious rival. Anacrites and I had done well. Even Vespasian, a byword for stinginess, had felt moved to reward us with social elevation. I had skills; I had contacts too. I rubbed my gold ring thoughtfully, but Cluvius still didn't get it.

He was leaving. Thank you, gods!

He dropped one more innocent-sounding question from the doorway to catch me off-guard. I hadn't seen that feeble trick since Nero appointed his racehorse a consul: 'I suppose nothing came of that amphitheatre contract? Tricky, pinning down the Treasury; I dare say it fell through . . .'

I knew nothing about this. I tapped my nose, implying some delicate and secret deal. As soon as Cluvius wandered off, I bounded into the back of the warehouse and briskly tackled Gornia.

The porter groaned. 'Oh, he must be on about the statues.'

Not news I wanted. The last time Pa and I were involved in statuary—our one and only operation together—we caught a bad cold. I could hardly bear to remember. Pa claimed he'd learned his lesson. Maybe I had too. Or maybe he at least could never resist a challenge . . . 'If that leech Cluvius is curious, do I sniff nice profits?'

'Oh just let Cluvius wet himself.' Gornia, a spindly old cove with about sixty years of working for Pa behind him, was as exciting as that porridge our forebears called a national dish. I mean, before they discovered the better joys of oysters and expensive turbot. 'You don't want to worry about him, Marcus Didius.'

I wondered if I could trust Gornia. His attitude was an aspect of the business I had not yet resolved. Even though he had stuck by Pa, he might not be so loyal to me.

'Statues? Amphitheatre? Gornia, would that be the great lump of unfinished masonry our beloved Emperor is dumping on the south side of the Forum? Where Nero's giant lake was? Where they need so much travertine cladding, they had to open a new marble quarry?'

'That's the beauty. Soon to be covered with statues,' said Gornia, looking nonchalant. 'They need thousands of the buggers, I believe.'

'Thousands?'

'Well, there will be three tiers of eighty arches, at least two tiers with some statuary in each arch.' He seemed well informed on the building plans.

'So "thousands" actually means a hundred and sixty? Two hundred and forty if they do the top tier?'

'Big fellows! Plus the odd hero driving a quadriga, with a full rack of fiery steeds, to shove up over entrances.'

I slumped on a stone seat. Foreboding dropped on me like a smelly old blanket, but I leaned back with a nonchalant air. 'Whisper to me what my cherished papa had to do with it?'

'Well . . . you know him!'

'Yes, I am afraid so.'

'He tried anything.'

'Tell me the worst.'

'The old fool lined up to supply a few old stone toffs for the exterior.'

I had already learned that Gornia avoided discussing problems. He had handled Pa by keeping out of awkward chats. When he did comment it was wry, dry and plastered as floridly as a banker's dining room with dangerous understatement. 'How many stone toffs,' I asked gently, 'is "a few"?'

'Not sure I know.'

'I bet. Does my sister have figures?'

'Oh, he didn't want to involve Maia.'

'Why not? Dodgy contract?' With Pa, no contract at all was more usual. I had another thought. 'Was this transaction off the books?'

'Our books?'

'No, the Treasury books. Don't say this is a corrupt deal?'

Gornia looked disapproving. 'He always said you were a prig, Marcus Didius!'

'I don't mess with the government; that's why I'm still alive. Was Pa behind with the order or something?' I remembered that his Rome warehouse had been significantly short of statues when I surveyed the stock.

'He sent samples. We'd scraped the moss off the second-hand ones. The officials were happy.'

'So what's the problem?'

Gornia looked shifty. 'Who mentioned a problem?'

'You did, Gornia, by not coming clean. What's up? Are we over-due on deliveries, or are we done?'

'It's our call. They pay by the piece, as and when. They're just happy to get enough suitable figures. Anyone who can meet the specifica-tions is in. The spec,' Gornia added quickly, 'is simple; there's a height rule, that's all.'

'That will be for visual uniformity.' I sounded like an interior de-signer. 'I bet it's surprisingly difficult to find ready-mades to fit the arches . . . We have stock?'

'The old man collected a marble or two at the place on the coast, I believe.'

'Be more specific?'

'Oh . . . maybe a hundred,' said Gornia.

'*A hundred?*' My voice was faint. 'That's bulk-buying by a maniac.'

'You did ask. Don't worry about it, I told you.'

'I am relaxed.' I was anxious. 'So, Gornia—excuse me, but why don't we just hand this huge batch over, and collect our fees? I don't want to be stuck with a glut of forgotten heroes and disgraced gener-als.' Everyone who might buy such junk had gone to their summer villas at Neapolis. There, many would be gazing at horrible statues my father had sold them on previous occasions, and thinking *never again.*

'It will work out,' Gornia assured me. 'Geminus said to hold off a bit ...' He looked embarrassed. 'We ought to pay for them.'

Now I saw it. This was neither unexpected nor insurmountable: 'Daylight! No ready funds?'

Odd, that. There were plenty of funds, as I knew well. In fact I was looking for outgoings, to set against the inheritance tax.

'We had the collateral. We just couldn't pass it to the vendors. I went. I went down there with the cash myself. Geminus always sent me, because I look so ordinary,' Gornia told me endearingly. 'Nobody ever robs me on the road. But I couldn't find them.'

'His suppliers?'

'They vanished.' Gornia looked relieved to squeeze it out. 'Bit of a novelty, isn't it?'

My father had been in many scrapes. Sometimes debt featured, but he covered it eventually. His cash flow only faltered temporarily. He was good at what he did.

It was rare for anyone in Rome, and never Geminus, to try to pay a creditor but to fail. I was used to the other system: those with claims came forward at a run. Their invoices were immaculate. They brought their own strongboxes to take away their cash. I coughed up. They were happy. End of story.

I decided I had better look at these statues myself. Then I would seek out the suppliers. I was an informer; I should be able to track them down.

I knew many good reasons why people who *owe* money vanish. But when people who are *owed* payment disappear, it tends to be because either they have grown old and confused—or they have quietly died. If Livia Primilla and Julius Modestus (those were their names) had passed away, fellow feeling made me want to help whatever poor heir needed to collect in this debt.

I just wanted to be a good citizen. But this was when the situation gently began tipping from straightforward into the kind of dark enquiry I was used to.

7

Modestus and Primilla lived at Antium, nearly thirty miles away. I dreaded announcing to Helena that I was going on a trip. The baby's death still gnawed. It was the wrong time to leave home. However, some god was on my side. Some deity with time on their hands in Olympus decided Falco needed help.

I entered my house with a cautious step. After working the key gently, I let the door swing to with care, glad no one was acting as door porter. I had the classic bearing of a guilty bastard slinking in and hoping to avoid notice. It was the ninth hour, evening, the period when busy men return, freshly bathed and ready for a good dinner. In houses all through Rome such men were about to have ructions with tired wives, layabout sons or indecent daughters.

Drawing upon six hundred years of a Roman's right to behave crassly, I flexed my shoulders. This house was where Pa had lived for twenty years but quite unlike the Janiculan spread. Crammed against the Aventine cliff on the Tiber's bank, our town house lacked the depth to allow a classic atrium with an open roof and vistas across peristyle gardens. Here, we lived vertically. I felt easy with that because I had grown up in the tall apartment blocks where the poor fester. We lived mainly upstairs because sometimes the river flooded in. Plain rooms off the corridors on the ground floor were non-domestic and silent at this hour. I walked across the empty entrance hall and went up.

Albia, my foster daughter, rushed down towards me. She was trying not to trip over the hem of a blue gown she thought particularly suited her. Her dark hair looked more fancifully arranged than usual, though with a lopsided tilt as if she had pinned it hastily herself. She burst out excitedly, 'Aulus has come home to Rome!'

Well, that could be good. Or not. He was a promising fellow. Still, she was too happy about his arrival. Something would have to be done. Helena was not up to it; this would be my problem.

Aulus Camillus Aelianus was Helena's brother, the elder of two. Though neither was a disaster, as pillars of the community this pair wobbled. Aulus once loathed me because I was an informer, but later saw sense. He was maturing; I liked to think he benefited from my patronage. Like his brother Quintus, he worked with me sometimes, when I felt strong enough for in-depth training of the hare-brained. Lately Aulus had been away studying law, first in Athens then Alexandria. This could either make him more useful to me, or give him a separate new career.

I was aware Albia and he had struck up a friendship. As a father who expected the worst, it made me glad Aulus was spending time abroad, since he was a senator's son and Albia was a foundling from Britain with a bleak history; they had no scope for romance, and anything else was unthinkable. On our recent family travels to Greece and to Egypt I had noticed Helena try to keep them apart, with limited success. Albia saw no problem. Aulus was something of a loner, and taking his time getting suitably married, so he liked having Albia to giggle with. He must know it could never go further. They were chums. It would pass. It had to.

'Aulus is *here*?'

'Come and see him!' Eyes bright, my innocent fosterling rushed ahead of me into the salon where we received visitors.

I detected a strained atmosphere at once.

Helena was sitting in a basket chair, her feet very neatly together on a footstool. She looked pale and weary. Our small daughters, Julia and Favonia, were lolling against her knees. Those scamps had been subdued since we lost the baby. Even at four and two, they had a good sense of trouble. Now Father was home but for once they did not hurl themselves upon me, shrieking. Their dark eyes came to me, with the open curiosity of children who recognised a crisis; my intelligent tots were watching closely what would happen now.

'*Aulus!*' Albia had cried out with joy too readily. He grinned, but it was sheepish. He was a poor actor. Albia's chum had come home looking indefinably hunted.

Albia tensed. She was very bright. I moved alongside and took her hand, like any fond father in company. But Albia was not like other people's daughters. She had come from the rowdy streets of Londinium, a harsh, remote city. Her Roman sophistication was a cloak she soon hurled off, immediately anyone upset her.

Seated on a couch, Aulus was a couple of years short of thirty, with a flop of dark hair, athletically built. Right beside him—when there were various other seats available, some more comfortable—perched a silent young woman. If there was trouble in the room, she was it. I kept tight hold of Albia.

Of foreign appearance, the young woman wore layers of expensive drapery in dark silk-shot linen. Her gold necklaces and ear-rings were rather formal for an unannounced visit to friends. Aulus must have brought her from Athens, but if she was Greek, she was not bearing gifts.

'Marcus!' Family gatherings were Helena Justina's strong point; she could direct bad-tempered relatives like a theatre producer getting an uncoordinated chorus into line. 'And Albia, my dear—here's a surprise.' Over our children's heads, her dark eyes sent me complicated messages. Without appearing to hurry, she began unhappily: 'Aulus has come back to Italy to settle down. He thinks he has learned enough; he wants to use his knowledge.' That, and his talent for upsetting everyone, I reckoned.

'So who's your new friend?' I asked him bluntly.

He cleared his throat. 'This is Hosidia.' He looked hopelessly at Albia.

'Hello, Hosidia.' I don't discriminate. I use the same brisk tone for tipsy barmaids showing their bosoms, hard-hearted females who have knifed their mothers, and Athenian dames who are looking down their nose as if they think I am the slave who cleans the silver. This Hosidia appeared to be costing up our metalware—the comport with the honey-glazed nutty titbits and the small but exquisite drinks tray. (Thanks to my father's perfect taste, our best service was small, but second to none.) If she had been under investigation, I would have put her on the suspects list. I really did not like the way she was assessing my pierce-patterned wine strainer.

'Marcus Didius Falco,' Aulus introduced me formally. He sounded unsure how Hosidia would react. I thought he could not know her well; nowhere near well enough, if I had judged this situation right.

Helena wanted Aulus to come clean, but as he held back she said politely, 'Hosidia is the daughter of my brother's tutor, Marcus. You remember the famous professor, Minas of Karystos, don't you?'

Jupiter help us! I raised an eyebrow, which Hosidia could take as admiration of her papa's intellect if she chose. In front of his daughter, I refrained from saying, 'That disgusting boozer, never in the classroom, trying to kill his students with his terrible all-night parties?'

Minas of Karystos was a decent court prosecutor when he could stand up straight, though that was rare. I knew Decimus Camillus, my father-in-law, was appalled by the shameless fees Minas charged. Perhaps this explained the son's recall. Camillus senior had decided to staunch the haemorrhage of cash. He can't have banked on the tutor's daughter.

Helena was looking overwrought. 'Marcus, would you believe my little brother has gone and got married?'

'No!' Call me a cynic, but I believed it all too sourly.

Aulus would have been an easy mark. He thought himself astute, but that just put him in more danger.

I saw it all. Albia, however, was taken aback. After one wild glance, she wrenched her hand free from mine and tore from the room.

Nobody commented on Albia running out. I thought Aulus jumped, but he stayed put.

Helena continued bleakly, 'The wedding happened in a rush, because of Aulus coming home. Minas is delighted—'

Minas must have set it up. However big a rissole Minas of godforsaken Karystos was in Athens, the glory of Greece had passed away. Rome was the only place for any ambitious professional. Marrying off his sombre daughter to a Roman senator's son must have been in the mind of the unscrupulous law teacher from the moment he grabbed his new pupil, fresh off the boat, and promised to make him a master of jurisprudence.

Demonstrating to the newlyweds how a good husband arrives home, whatever shocks await, I crossed the room sedately, then bent and kissed my dear wife's cheek. In the style of a good Roman marriage, she was the companion who shared my closest secrets, so to demonstrate our private affection to Aulus and his bride, I murmured a love greeting in Helena's neat ear. I managed not to nibble her lobe, though I considered it, which may have shown in my face.

'Seems Albia may want to leave town,' I then muttered. 'I could vanish to Pa's *villa maritima* for a few days. Call it executor business. Shall I take her away for some breathing space?'

Helena kissed me back formally like a matron who knows the father of the family is up to no good. 'Let's talk later, darling.'

In the style of a good Roman marriage, I took that as settled.

8

Toward nightfall, to escape the tantrums that were rattling shutters in my house, I went out to see Petronius Longus. He was on duty with the vigiles, at the Fourth Cohort's secondary patrol house. It was a calm, masculine environment where only the grunts of criminals being brutally thrashed ever disturbed the tranquillity. July and August were always quiet. Members of the public used fewer oil lamps and cooking fires, so they set fewer of their tenements on fire. For the vigiles, nights became tedious. Patrols could be stood down. While they waited for emergencies, the firefighters liked to sit in their exercise yard telling one another moral fables. Well, that was one way to describe it. They were ex-slaves, a rough lot.

Petronius sat apart in a small office, wrestling with his latest unsolved case. Drink was barred on these premises, but he gave me a slurp from the beaker he had under the table. He hid it again in case the tribune dropped in, then we swapped gossip.

'Helena is hopping mad at her brother, and our girlie is distraught.'

'Albia's how old? Seventeen?—Thundering Jove, was it that long ago you and I were in Britain during the Rebellion?' That was when she must have lost her parents. 'Did Aelianus touch her?' We were fathers. We were paranoid with good reason. We had been lads in the army together, then dirty bastards about town. We knew what happens.

'Albia is bound to deny it.' I had not asked her. Why invite tears? Indeed, why give your daughter a reason to hurl abuse at you? 'He's been away a lot, which is one good thing,' I went on gloomily. 'We ran into him a couple of times when we were travelling, but as far as I know, they just wrote to each other.'

'Oh *letters!*' scoffed Petro darkly. He did not have my literary leanings. 'Soulmates, eh? Falco my friend, you are in deep donkey shit.' He handed me his beaker again, though it was a joyless panacea. 'What's his new wife like? A looker?'

'A spender.'

'And a Greek prosecutor's daughter?'

'Guilty until proven innocent. We met her father in Athens. As a boozer he makes Bacchus look restrained.'

'Jupiter and Mars!' Petronius Longus viewed all lawyers as pests. Lawyers so easily demolished the criminal cases he put together; he ignored the fact that this feat was achievable because the vigiles' definition of 'proof' was simply a man whose face they did not like who walked down a street where they happened to be. 'How are the senator and his wife taking this?'

I laughed drily. 'Considering all three of their children have now, without permission, taken a spouse who is either foreign or plebeian, Helena says Decimus and Julia are calm. They have to be careful showing opinions, because not only is the Hellenic bride living in their house with the captured Aulus, but her go-getting, influence-seeking, hard-drinking Athenian father came to Rome too. Of course he would do. A niche among the ruling class, with access to a wine cellar? His sole purpose in fixing up the marriage.'

'The bastard!'

I shared Petro's curse, then put my troubles aside and let him tell me his. He was stumped on a peculiar case: a family who went to their mausoleum to hold a funeral discovered that someone had broken in and dumped an unknown body. Foul play among the tombs was commonplace. Some people would have just chucked out the corpse for the crows, but this family was sensible enough to notice disturbing elements. It was the body of a well-kept man of mature age, not the usual young rape or mugging victim, and he was laid out in an odd ritual position.

'Violence. Someone really enjoyed it.' Petronius was very experienced. He knew when death had been caused by an unexpected drunken fury and when it had a perverted smell.

'You think there will be other victims?'

'Dreading it, Falco.' He dealt with atrocity all the time, but never became inured to humans' absence of humanity.

I told him if anyone could solve this case it was him, and I meant it. Then I went home to be ready for an early start next morning on the trip to my father's villa.

'Is this the future?' Petronius joked. 'You swan off to your extravagant holiday home—while I get stuck here with a sordid serial killer?'

I grinned and told him to get used to it. He ought to know I wouldn't change.

Albia and I went down to the sea on the Via Laurentina. All the best people have villas north of where that road hits the coast, turning towards Ostia. My father had his place a little to the south. He said he liked the privacy. There were reasons. They were mostly commercial, relevant to his dedicated avoidance of paying import tax.

Pa had left me a litter and bearers but I had forgotten I owned it. Automatically, I hired a donkey cart, which gave me an excuse to concentrate on driving. Albia sat bolt upright beside me. Throughout her childhood she had been a scavenger for both food and affection; she still had stick-thin arms and, when she was unhappy, a gaunt look. No fancy ringlets today; she had let her hair dangle loose, though Helena had run with a bone comb and tidied her up for the trip. Even though there was bright sun beating on the highway, the girl hunched in a shawl, making herself suffer.

We rode twenty miles in silence then Albia could no longer keep it up. She was bursting to accuse me of cruelty. 'Why do I have to be dragged along with you? Am I forced to work in your business, like some horrible slave?'

'No, I have a posse of grateful slaves and freedmen for that now. They may be Paphlagonian poltroons but unlike you, Flavia Albia, they are meek.'

'I hope they all cheat you.'

I was the villain. Nothing new. 'Bound to. So cheer up, will you?'

We drove on for a while.

'I'd like to rip his head off.' Aelianus deserved all he got, but I owed it to the senator and Julia Justa to preserve his well-barbered bonce. So I merely said Helena and I hated to see Albia so unhappy; we had thought she might appreciate a chance to avoid Aulus. 'Yes,' agreed Albia thoughtfully. '*Then* I'll rip his head off—when he thinks he's got away with it.'

Helena Justina had taken in our British waif because she was so spirited, so torn with grief and loneliness, and had been so unjustly served by fate. Found as a baby in the ruins of Londinium, no one knew or would ever know whether Albia was a Briton or some half-and-half little bun, a dead trader's offspring born to a local woman, maybe. She could even be fully Roman, though it was unlikely. When we offered to adopt her, we had wormed a certificate of citizenship out of the British governor, who owed me favours. We now gave Albia education, sustenance, security and friendship, though not much more was feasible. In the snobbery of Rome, she would have a hard fight. I was middle-class now, with the Emperor's approval, but since I had plebeian origins, even my own daughters would need more than elocution lessons if they were to be accepted. I lived with a senator's daughter but that was Helena's choice. It was legal, but eccentric.

'I hope Aulus did not make you any promises.' I broached the subject tentatively, still not brave enough to say I hoped he had not slept with her.

'Of course he wouldn't; I'm a barbarian!' Albia snapped furiously. Her voice then dropped. 'I was just stupid.'

'Well, it must seem impossible at the moment, but one day you will get over him.'

'I *never* will!' Albia retorted. Her loves and hates were equally intense. I had a dark feeling she was right; she never would recover. After knocking about with street life in Londinium, Albia knew how to stay safe at that level, but she had trusted Aelianus. He was one of the family, *her* family now. She had dropped her guard.

'Maybe it's a good thing we are going to Antium, or I might rip his head off myself.'

'You never would,' sneered Albia bitterly.

'Since he is actually married, there is not much I can do about the situation, and you know that.'

'If he wasn't married would you do anything?'

I gave her no answer. Aulus was overdue for marriage. I thought his choice was a disaster, but I would have seriously opposed any offer for Albia—for both their sakes.

'You talk about righting injustice, but you never do it,' she grumbled.

'*Conciliation*—there's a fine Latin word . . . I hope you never have to see me stick a sword in someone's ribs.' It had been known. But I believed retribution should fit the degree of the crime. 'Aelianus has been thoughtless and disloyal. Young men are like that. Young women can be just as bad—or worse.'

'Oh I don't expect anyone to stand up for me!' Albia was back on the verge of tears now. My heart ached for her. 'You are both men. He is your friend, your relative, your assistant. You will stick by him—'

'He was your friend too.' I was nervous that Aulus might have the crazy idea they could carry on as friends. He was that kind of innocent. 'I'd say, value your past—but move on and forget him. Do it for yourself.'

Poor Albia was far from being ready to move on. She turned away but I heard her weeping all the rest of our journey to the villa.

9

Silence.

Pa's shoreline villa can never have rung with a summer social life, because he was rarely in residence; the one time I was here before, I had gathered activity was infrequent. Having an absentee owner was typical for a seaside villa. For security, he left more than a skeleton staff, though they lived in a separate wing from the main house. They stayed on the alert because he would turn up at any time—it depended what incoming ships from Spain or the East had agreed to quietly offload artworks at sea to save him paying duty. He and Gornia then took a boat out into the shipping lanes. It was not a process I intended to repeat. Mind you, I would keep the boat.

I reminded the slaves who I was and explained the situation. They made themselves look downcast over my father's death, though did not feel called upon to shed real tears. This was much as I felt myself, so I did not complain.

Naturally they assumed Albia was some fluffball I wanted to seduce behind my wife's back. That is what slaves always think. It's the male behaviour most see from their masters. Wearied by driving, my reaction was short-tempered.

I felt old. Once, finding myself with custody of a delightful young girl, I would have been tempted. I could still remember those happy days, but ambivalence was a vice I had lost. I was married. Albia was family. I viewed her as a grumpy teenager I had to keep safe despite her yen for rebellion, while she saw me as hideous, elderly and past it, just like any father.

Disappointed of scandal, the slaves—who seemed good-natured enough once they got used to a situation—made us a barbecue on the beach. Grilled fish, freshly caught from the sea and smoke-cooked in a drizzle of olive oil, can mend most griefs. Albia tried to continue the feud. But she smiled slightly when I pointed out that she was enjoying not enjoying anything. At least she ate. Being forlorn had not affected her appetite.

Next day I surveyed the property. It was even bigger and more luxurious than I remembered, and packed with treasures. Albia followed me around with her mouth agape, muttering, 'This is *yours?*'

'It's mine. Or only half of it, if Thalia's sprog pops out with male genitalia.'

'You could castrate him.' Albia's harsh new mood produced intriguing legal questions.

This villa, protected from sun and storms by pine trees, was where Pa had kept his favourite collection, items he really liked and enjoyed. I liked them too. I would have to come back soon for a long visit; there was so much stuff to catalogue. I needed to bring Helena, to show her the glorious location, the rampant antiques and furnishings. Maybe this would become our permanent summer retreat. If she hated the place, which I thought unlikely, there was so much to sell I would have to time our auctions carefully, so as not to flood the market.

'Are you planning to liberate any faithful slaves in your dear father's name, Marcus Didius?' The usual question.

As ever, I responded with a noncommittal sigh. I could free a percentage in Pa's name. I would do it if I could. I wanted to evaluate them first. What happened to them would have nothing to do with how well each had served my father during his life; it depended on how much manumission tax I would have to pay if I freed them or what price they would fetch in the slave market. Any with specialist training or pretty faces were in greater danger of being either kept as slaves or sold. Already I was thinking like a tycoon. If they had a high market value, I was less inclined to give them their release.

The monumental statues for the amphitheatre contract were lined up in rows in the woods. Close to, they were a ragbag: anonymous men of note in triumphal poses, batoned and breastplated; some were weathered about the face and drapery as if they had already adorned public places. I wondered if they had been stolen from their plinths; however, some had their plinths with them.

One batch appeared new. They had been carved to the same model, but with different arms or helmets. I was not surprised. Jobbing sculptors regularly provide a basic figure in an old-fashioned toga, then let you commission a true-life head of your grandaddy at a cut-price rate. So why not cloned dignitaries for an amphitheatre?

I counted them. One hundred and eleven. Jupiter! Pa had cornered the market. Trust him. The Flavian amphitheatre would be virtually: *statues courtesy of Geminus*. No wonder that creep Cluvius wanted me to step aside and let him muscle in.

I gave instructions that the statues were to be brought up to Rome using whatever haulage system Geminus had put in place. 'And I want to see a hundred and eleven arrive. A hundred and twelve will prove to me that you are really conscientious.' My humour was lost on the steward. Foolish; if he failed to notice my jokes, he could end up at the slave market.

'I could stay here to supervise,' volunteered Albia.

'No thanks.' I was not giving her a chance to bolt. 'Lass, if you want to run away, check logistics with me first. For a workable escape you need a plan, a budget, detailed road maps, a stout stick, proper footwear and a good hat.'

'You are no fun, Marcus Didius.' Albia openly acknowledged that I read her well. 'I want to go back to Britannia.'

'No.'

'Helena's Aunt Aelia would let me stay with them—'

'I said no, Albia.'

On to the next stage of our trip.

We could take the coast road down to Antium, a straight run but a poor track, all dreary dunes and sandflies, or we could go by sea. For that we would have to go up to Ostia, almost ten miles in the wrong direction, then the misery of a major trading port, followed by horrible seasickness for me. I opted to continue by cart, south down the Via Severiana, maybe fifteen miles. It only took a day, though it was a long hot one. We then stayed at a mediocre inn. It looked over a sea packed with delicious wildlife, yet the dish of the day was week-old eggs. Even my omelette was tough.

Next morning we tried to find the statue-sellers. Gornia was right. Their house was locked up, with nobody there. Not even a watchman answered our knocking. Albia tried to climb in from a balcony but the place was well shuttered.

I made standard enquiries. Primilla and Modestus had kept to themselves, as prosperous middle-rankers often do. They had a substantial home on the seashore, no obvious financial worries, no ugly rumours about why they did a flit. None of the neighbours had seen them for months or knew where they had gone. True, the neighbours shied away from my questions, though this was a town where imperial celebrities had long clustered; people were discreet.

Antium was once the capital of the Volsci, who tussled with Rome over a long period in the remote past. Once it became ours, the city lay far enough from Rome for men of means, wanting to avoid riots and creditors, to favour it as a retreat. Palatial villas lined the shore. Cicero owned a grand place. The disgustingly rich Maecenas had a house. The old imperial family, the Julio-Claudians, had a particular liking for this spot. It was at Antium that Augustus received formal acclaim as Father of his Country. Caligula and Nero were born here; Nero founded a veterans' colony and created a new harbour.

The new Flavians were bound to arrive on this part of the coast soon. Land agents must be keeping lists of suitable homes for up-and-coming Caesars whose pocket money came from the spoils of war.

This was a superb location for commercial dealers. The town had a slightly dusty, off-season look but it could easily perk up. By reputation the fine foreshore villas were beautified with exclusive original art and expensive modern reproductions. Most of the enormous houses were still lived in, and by people with funds for house and garden makeovers. It was astonishing that a pair of reputable art dealers would leave a place with such potential.

A Temple of Fortune was the big public monument. I applied there for information. Since Gornia's fruitless visit, a certain Sextus Silanus, a nephew of Primilla's, had left a message that enquirers should consult him. I had to pay the priests extortionately to be told; it would have been friendlier if the nephew had just chalked up a note on his uncle's locked front door.

The bad news was, Silanus lived at Lanuvium. To get there we had to take an unnamed road through famously unhealthy country on the northern edge of the Pontine plain. The Pontine Marshes have a fearsome reputation. Still, they should have dried out in summer and Lanuvium was on a spur of the Via Appia, which led straight back to Rome.

10

Lanuvium was an extremely ancient hilltop city in Latium, on the Alban Hills, lying just south of the Via Appia. The town was dominated by a clutch of temples, especially the richly endowed Temple of Juno Sospes, to which belonged much of the land between here and the coast. We knew, from passing through it, that the soil was unusually fertile, though the area was very thinly populated. For most of the route we saw no one but a few pasty-looking slaves. The state of the road suggested vehicles were unusual and the labourers stared at us as if they never saw travellers. Well, they stared until Albia glared at them. Then they turned away nervously.

'There are many rivers draining the hills; they carry down rich alluvium silt.' I was taking on Helena's role, had she been with us. Just because Albia had a broken heart, she need not be ignorant. 'So the Pontine plain has some of the best land in Italy for grazing animals and growing crops, but you won't see many people. The water table is very high and the sand dunes on the coast trap the floods, so for much of the year, especially south of here, it is a pestilential place. Clouds of biting insects make the marshes almost uninhabitable—keep yourself well covered up; they carry horrible diseases.' We were north of the real swamps, which suited me. Attempts had been made to drain them. The attempts all failed.

The high citadel at Lanuvium must be healthier. From its acropolis there were gracious views over the plain to the faraway ocean. Like most places with vistas, this had been heavily colonised by the villa-owning fraternity. To cater for their property maintenance needs, small artisan businesses thrived. Silanus was a terracotta specialist.

A row of freckled children sat on the kerb outside his premises. When our cart drew up, they all swarmed aboard. I tried to strike a bargain that they would look after the outfit, by which I meant they were not to kick the donkey or remove the wheels. I hoped they were too small to shift the money chest. Feigning acute shyness, none of them spoke. When I went into the workshop, Albia stationed herself at the doorway, observing the nippers sternly. In her present mood, she was scary; that would work.

The children must have inherited their freckles from their mother. She never appeared; I soon gathered she was dead—probably exhausted and deceased in childbirth, judging by the perilous number of offspring she had left behind.

Silanus was a stocky, pockmarked fellow with the faint tetchiness craftsmen have, caused by the anxieties of sole trading. As a gesture to personality, he wore a bracelet on his upper left arm that was pretending to be gold. His tunic was dull and ragged, but he was in work clothes so that told me nothing. The stock in his shop was good: well-made, fancy Greek-style acroteria for roof finials, a few gargoyles, routine racks of tiles and wall flues, plus the usual decorative wares for the home, plant tubs and balcony trays. It was all handsome. I would have bought from him.

He gave the impression he wanted to be friendly, but was biting it back. I softened him up, mainly by telling him how much cash I had brought for his uncle and aunt. He was stuck in an awkward situation. His relatives had mysteriously vanished. They had no children. As the only nephew, he felt obliged to take charge, though he did not even know if Primilla and Modestus were alive. Unlike me, he felt he had no legal position as an heir, so was not free to negotiate.

I sympathised. 'So what happened? I work in this line; maybe I can give you advice.' Silanus was not the type to trust informers, or even to know what we did. 'Silanus, whatever has gone on? I saw their house at Antium; it's quite deserted. Your uncle and aunt must have had staff, but they too have dematerialised. Have you brought the slaves here?'

Appreciating his practical difficulties must have won his trust. Silanus sighed. 'They ran away. I haven't started a fugitive-hunt. Let them go, if they can make a life.' This man was neither greedy nor vindictive. A decent sort. Not something I often came across. I tried not to find it suspicious.

He seemed upset about his missing aunt and uncle, troubled by the situation, completely dispirited. 'I was told that my uncle left first, then my aunt went to look for him. She had the sense to order one of their slaves to come and tell me, if she too vanished.'

'So where did Primilla and Modestus go?'

'You don't want to know, Falco.'

I was agog. 'Try me.'

'They went to see the Claudii.' Silanus spoke as if I ought to know what that meant. When I merely raised my eyebrows, he went back to the start of the story. 'Uncle and Auntie owned property, farmland. Made their money that way, originally, but you know how it is. Nobody stays on the plain, because they soon get sick. Anyone sick soon passes away. Only slaves can be persuaded to stay there for husbandry. People who can afford to move do so. They come up to the hills or go over to the coast. So about twenty years ago Modestus became an art dealer in Antium—though they always kept their land.'

'My father did business with them, as I told you; Geminus knew them for a long time . . . So whatever happened?'

'A boundary dispute flared up. I knew about it—squabbles have been grumbling on for years. Some of their neighbours are notoriously difficult to deal with. A few months ago cattle strayed on to Uncle's land and did a lot of damage. Modestus likes to assert his rights—he went to have it out. He never came back. Aunt Primilla is a spunky woman herself; she set off to find him. She too has never been seen since.'

'These neighbours are the Claudii you mentioned? . . . So have you reported it? Called in the authorities?'

'I did my best. It was a long time before I heard anything. Once I knew my folks had gone missing, I had to get someone to look after my business before I could go over to Antium. I managed to interest the local magistrate. A posse went to investigate. They found nothing. The Claudii all denied ever seeing my relatives. So nothing can be done.'

'That sounds feeble!'

'Ah well . . . it's the badlands, Falco. Strangers don't go there.'

'What—upset the web-footed marsh sprites and they drown you?' I was amazed. 'Troublemaking is a homely Pontine tradition and everyone has to put up with it?'

As I raved, Silanus looked boot-faced. 'The fact is, Falco, I know perfectly well what happened. My aunt and uncle upset the wrong people and have paid for it. Nobody can find any trace of them. No one locally saw anything. There is no evidence. So I'm not going to tackle the Claudii and be made to disappear myself, am I? So yes, that is how bullies get away with it—but no, I will not leave my children orphans.'

I asked if he wanted to hire me to investigate. He said no. Partly, that was a relief. I was reluctant to do country work. Especially in the Pontine Marshes. That's suicide.

This would not have done for me, yet I did understand why Sextus Silanus was letting the mystery rest. He was practical. How many times had I advised clients to take such a sensible route (and how many had ignored me)?

Regarding the money Pa owed, we agreed that I would hand it over and call the account closed. Silanus would bank the cash at the Temple of Juno Sospes, until enough time passed for him to feel he could have it himself. Realistically, that would be soon. One glance at all the children he was bringing up said it. And I did not blame him.

He came out to collect the money. Shooing his freckled infants off the cart, he confirmed he was a single-handed parent; he had six under fourteen.

I bought a load of his fine terracotta wares. It would pay a few food bills for him, and anyway I liked the stuff. Albia helped me choose.

As Silanus waved us off, he asked, with a desperation I could almost forgive, 'Your daughter seems a very nice young lady—Does she have a husband, Falco?'

'Get lost!' Albia and I roared in unison.

Bad timing, Silanus.

11

This strange disappearance of two respectable art dealers continued to haunt me. Driving allows you time to muse. Still, I had concerns of my own. If Silanus wanted to abandon hope, it was depressing, but his own affair. I went on my way, relieved of the cash and freed up to sell the statues. The curious episode was over.

Or was it? I should have known better.

The Via Appia is a legendary highway built four hundred years ago by Appius Claudius. It runs down across the Pontine Marshes, straight as a javelin for fifty miles between Rome and Tarracina. That entails causeways where it crosses swamps, but the northern part is wide, well-paved and, if your donkey can summon the energy, pleasantly fast. I had hired a decent working beast; she didn't bite or lie down in the gutter, though nor did she exert herself. We trickled sedately down a sliproad and hit the famous highway just before it climbed the Alban Hills, passing Lakes Nemi and Albanus.

Giving a friendly lecture to Albia (who barely responded) I had to admit that Appius, a great builder who also constructed the first

Roman aqueduct, was better than average, for a patrician. As a free-born city boy, I found some of his policies questionable—allowing the sons of manumitted slaves to enter the Senate and extending the vote to rural folk who owned no land. Still, Appius Claudius also published the law, stopping the priests from keeping it as their private mystery. That made him a patron of informers.

We went north for ten miles. With only another two or three to go, we reached the tombs among the stone pines that line the approach to Rome's Twelfth District. On a bright and baking afternoon this sometimes lonesome vicinity made for good travelling. We hit shade. I was cheerful; I could detect the smell of home and the donkey could sniff her stable. Albia just snuffled miserably but soon I could hand her over to Helena.

Then we ran into the vigiles. Since the Twelfth is looked after by the Fourth Cohort, these were a section of Petro's men.

Outside the city boundary, discipline evaporated. Some, inevitably, were lying under pine trees for a nap. However, others applied themselves fairly well. They told me they were on the case Petronius had told me about: the corpse dumped in a mausoleum. One ritual laying-out was not enough for Petro. Armed with crowbars and a love of violence, his troops were bashing open mausoleums and peering inside for other bodies that ought not to be there. In the crumbly roadside necropolis, many tombs were so ancient nobody knew who built them. They were easy to search, once the vigiles scraped the sleeping vagrants off their worn old entrance steps. Others, even the oldest, were still used by families; thanks to good diet and our nation's virility, some Roman clans had long pedigrees.

One cranky owner must have stipulated he had to be present; I saw Tiberius Fusculus, Petro's trusty, hiding his impatience while the blighted toff fumbled interminably with a padlock. I pulled up the cart and when Fusculus was free again, he strolled over. He was overweight, hot and red-faced. Albia gave him a drink of water. 'Take it all. Who cares?' She dispensed her generosity with airy fatalism, as if she herself did not care if she died of thirst.

Avoiding Albia's aggression like a wise man, Fusculus told me that no more corpses had been found. 'Well, plenty—' Fusculus joked, '—but none we link to the case.'

'Will Petronius pull you off it soon?'

'Not yet, Falco. Obstinate beggar is convinced we have turned up a ritual killer.'

'Then Petronius Longus must sit it out until the next new moon, or there's a "rho" in the month, or the red tunic comes home from the laundry—whatever weird trigger tells this killer it's time for him to shed more gore.'

'Normally,' Fusculus agreed, 'the boss would be happy to lie low. Especially in summer when he likes to get home early to your revered sister and have a nap on their nice sun terrace.'

I was amused. Petro had his eccentric side; he never liked anybody knowing his habits and he had not even told his men that he was living with Maia. They all knew of course. 'What's different?' I asked.

'Sealed lips. State secret.'

'Very grown-up! And are you going to share it?'

'Absolutely bloody not, Falco. This is so utterly *sub rosa*, one word to you and I'd be spit-roasted with a bunch of oregano pushed up my bum.'

Tired of boys' talk, Albia interrupted. 'I suppose, Tiberius Fusculus, that means Uncle Lucius has not told *you* his thinking on this?'

He gazed at her almost as speculatively as Silanus had before he asked if she was married. 'Bright girlie. No, *Uncle Lucius*—tight bastard—has not revealed his mighty thoughts.'

I grinned. 'I'll have to ask him myself then.'

'You do that, Falco.' Fusculus reapplied himself to searching tombs. I clucked up the donkey. As the cart jerked and moved off, Fusculus called after us without rancour, 'The big clue is—we found luggage!'

Interesting.

It was *so* interesting I was dying to ask Petronius about it. First, I returned the cart to the hire stables, took Albia home, and gave a good show of being safely back with my family. After about half an hour

I nipped out to see Petro. Helena spotted me going. I winked and promised to share any gossip as soon as I came back. She sighed, but did not intervene.

Petronius, amazingly, was trying on his toga. This rare sight made me chortle—until I found out why. It was dusk, so the sweltering streets had cooled a fraction; not enough for loading pounds of heavy white wool on your shoulders, though. No option, it seemed: Petro had to stand in for his tribune, Rubella. The Fourth Cohort's senior officer had been summoned to a high-status conference on the Palatine.

Petronius would normally have been taken along too, in order to whisper corrections whenever Rubella got information wrong—mishandling facts was any lazy tribune's prerogative. As it was July, Rubella was away. Since he had not bothered to inform the Prefect of Vigiles he had snatched a vacation, if Petro wanted, he could land Rubella in mule dung. However, he would be a fool to do so.

'Falco, you know what I think of Rubella—'

I assured him I thought the same. Marcus Rubella was an over-promoted, super-ambitious, unreliable, self-seeking squit. However, I thought he was the best the cohort would get. 'Fill me in, Petro.'

'On *Rubella*?'

'On the case, idiot.'

'We found a hidden pack that must have belonged to that murder victim. Maybe he noticed he was being followed, so he tucked away his stuff just before he was grabbed.'

'What's the palace connection?'

'He was carrying a draft petition to the Emperor.'

'About?'

Petronius winced. 'Ghastly moans. Complaining about local crime. *This public disgrace has been allowed to fester far too long; the authorities in our region simply will not address the issue . . . The Emperor should take the initiative and refuse to tolerate nuisances caused by criminals who boast they have special protection . . .* Nobody will ever listen, of course. Still, I shoved it onwards to the top—gave the poor bastard his last chance of an audience. Least I could do, I thought.'

'You know who he is?'

'I said it's a draft, you noodle! Nobody signs their name on a private rough.'

'Silly me! So it was no help?'

'I'd have kept it, if it had been useful. Obviously I had to mention to the scroll-beetles that the writer was discovered ripped open from crotch to gullet, with his hands removed.'

The details were new. I pulled a face. 'Pluto! That would have made your report attract notice.'

'Seems so. What came over me? Now some schnoozle wants a brief.'

'Minding his back,' I said. 'You'll handle it. You know your stuff. And you've been there before.' Petronius had attended at the Palace with me. We once had a policy discussion with the Emperor and a full phalanx of flunkies. Vespasian took our measure. Even so, we ticed a money-making commission out of him that time. 'Who sent the summons?'

'Some grunt called Laeta.'

I pulled up short. 'Claudius Laeta? I'll come with you.'

'Keep out of it. I don't need a nursemaid, Falco.'

'Laeta is trouble. Appearing amenable is his speciality. Then he'll extract your balls and twist them up in an old knitted sock, swing it round his head and knock you down with your own magic machinery.'

'For a spare-time poet, your imagery stinks,' opined my old friend dourly. But he must have been nervous about the meeting, because he let me tag along.

Unlike him, I did not go togate. Laeta was head of the main secretariat. The man had sent me on so many dubious missions, he would receive no respect from me. The only good thing about Laeta was his constantly trying to double-cross Anacrites, the Chief Spy. I watched from the sidelines and tried to play them off against each other.

Petronius and I ambled gently from the patrol house. I was enjoying my return. I threw back my head and breathed in the last heat of a warm city day. I heard the low buzz of voices from families and groups of friends, eating, chatting, gathering to enjoy those quiet hours of the day before they resumed their usual habits of fornicating with each other's wives and cheating each other at business or dice. Strings of shrieking garland-girls were going home; nobody would buy dinner flowers now. Sounds of flutes and a drummer vied with the clatter of crockery from an alley, obviously the back door to several bars. Wafts of frying food, swum in oil and enlivened with thyme and rosemary, floated just above street level.

I had missed Rome. Petronius pointed out with a grin that I had only been away three days, during which I should have been happy, since at Pa's villa I had all those expensive new possessions to count. Always generous, Petro bore no grudge for my good fortune. Like me, perhaps he did not yet take it seriously.

On descending the Aventine, to cross to the Palatine we had a choice of passing around the Circus Maximus at the starting-gate end or hoofing down past the apse. The racetrack was absolutely in our way. Even if Petro could have used influence to get inside and cut straight across, there was no point because then we would have had the Palatine's vertical face ahead of us. Since we both grew up on the Aventine, we were used to this inconvenience. Sometimes we detoured one way, sometimes the other. Either by-pass was long and frustrating. As it was his meeting tonight, I let him choose; he opted for the starting-gates, then wending gently through the Forum Boarium. It stank of raw blood and butchery but gave us a clear run at the Palatine via regular approaches. Petronius was not in a mood to slide through a back door and get lost in the pernicious maze of corridors.

He presented himself to the Praetorian Guard, managing not to be rude to those braggarts. If I stood on my rights with the Guards when they threatened to push us around, Petronius would shrug and dump me. I followed my friend's lead meekly.

Neither of us had any idea at that moment, but we were beginning an adventure that would be as difficult and dangerous as any we had ever attempted. And its connection with the Palatine overlords would be much more than simple bureaucracy.

12

The tall vaulted corridors of the old Palace had their usual evening hush. This was the time I liked to come here. The crowds of jabbering petitioners had given up and gone home, leaving residual odours of garlic sausage and sweat. People were about, but the daytime tension relaxed. The night shift was efficient, but unexcitable. They put anything important or awkward on hold for the day shift.

Slaves padded past us, setting out oil lamps. Under our frugal Emperor, there was never quite enough light. The slaves had mastered the art of implying they had too much work to break off and tell us whether the office we were looking for was down the right- or left-hand corridor, let alone to admit whether the imperial family was in residence or had all gone away to some summer villa . . .

Systems here had stayed the same since Tiberius organised this part of the Palatine. The imperial livery had changed and there was less open fornication; little else altered. Emperors came and went while bureaucracy continued, as rampant as mould. Vespasian and Titus lived in Nero's repulsively opulent Golden House on the other side of the Forum, while élite secretariats kept their old offices in this historic complex. The bigger the name, the grander the office. Laeta had a suite. Its doorknobs were gilded and a quiet slave constantly mopped the marble floor outside. She was probably there to eavesdrop on pre-admission visitors.

'This place always reeks of suspicion,' Petro mumbled, keeping an eye on the mopper. Once she looked up and automatically he smiled at her. Like any healthy Roman male, he kept in practice as a flirt.

I agreed. 'To say they all plot is like saying slugs eat lettuce.'

Laeta worked late. As a bureaucrat he genuinely believed his vital work required more than an ordinary business day, even from an expert like him. He kept us waiting. That was to make us impressed that he should find time for us. Petronius and I slouched on corridor benches below a high, elegant ceiling and remarked loudly that being so disorganised at his rank was pathetic. We made sure the usher heard. Enlivening the life of underlings is a ploy worth spending time on.

Maia and Helena said we had never grown up. We could be mature—though kicking our heels in boredom brought out the worst in us.

Finally Petronius was called in and I followed. When he saw me on his marble threshold, Laeta looked irritated. He was a middle-aged, middle ranker with an astute gaze. He was bursting to ask what I was doing there; he wondered whether somebody had failed to brief him on a policy issue—or, worse, had he been briefed but had forgotten it? He felt obliged to nod a greeting, but some unease showed.

We shimmied across the doormat—a pleasing integral mosaic— and began our next role-play. It involved extravagant respect from Petronius, while I stared as if flattering a senior official had never occurred to me. Petro declared he was honoured to meet such an important man of whom (he said) he had heard much, all of it impressive. Laeta fended off a blush. Everyone must suck up to him, but he was unsure how to take it from us. Well, I said he was astute.

Tiberius Claudius Laeta was a rising comet, experienced but still with a decade or two of conniving in him. His forenames indicated he had been a slave in the imperial house, freed under a previous emperor; from his age it would be Claudius. The imperial household had produced many senior bureaucrats, including my bugbear Anacrites, who had wormed his way up to be Chief Spy very quickly and, to me, quite unaccountably; he was the kind of light garbage that floats. Anacrites was younger than Laeta and had been freed by Nero—hardly a recommendation, to have that eye-rolling maniac think well of you.

'You submitted a man's petition, Watch Captain.' Prepared for the meeting, he waved it at us.

'Found in a murder victim's baggage,' Petro confirmed. 'I assessed it as the dead man's last words. Delivery seemed the decent thing.'

'Yes, you explained—' Laeta laid down the tablet abruptly, hoping to cut off bloody descriptions of the corpse. I made a grab to see what was written. Laeta was too refined to snatch the tablet back but watched jealously, like a man seeing his lover depart on an international journey.

The complaint was as Petro had described. The handwriting was decent, the language civil service Greek. If the author was not a professional scribe, he had certainly had general clerical training. One aspect surprised me: a tone of familiarity. 'Had this man written in before?'

'One of our regulars.' Laeta sounded weary.

'Classic aggrieved citizen?'

'Let's say, *detailed*!' Free Roman citizens have the right to petition the Emperor. That did not mean Vespasian personally read every scroll. He thought he did. So did those who made petition-writing their hobby. In truth, officials like Laeta censored out the batty ramblings of obsessives, at the same time as they were checking for unhinged threats against the Emperor's person and simple-minded do-gooders offering religious advice.

'Bit of a menace then?' Petronius asked, more mildly than me.

Laeta was too professional to insult a member of the public. His duty required him to be fair, to defend the high principle of equal access to the Emperor. 'On the one side—' elbows on the table, he turned back his left hand as if holding up a market weight, '—he has the right to campaign. And on the other—' he balanced the hypothetical weight with his other hand, '—resources are limited, so we just cannot investigate every perceived problem.'

Perceived said a lot. No wonder Laeta looked relaxed. He *perceived* he could ignore such stuff.

'Did this fellow always make the same complaint?' I asked.

'Usually. He worried over law-and-order issues. He was agitated about a large tribe of petty criminals who should, in his opinion, be exterminated. The fact is,' Laeta informed us smoothly, 'all over the Empire, groups exist who arouse their neighbours' prejudice, perhaps because they seem feckless or a little different. They live rough, they rebuff approaches from the community. People suspect them of stealing, of luring away women, insulting priests, depressing property values and having lewd habits. Drink and putting curses on cattle are a constant theme of complaints.'

'Living next door to deadbeats can be a real problem,' Petronius corrected him. He had no truck with social misfits. He didn't believe curse tablets could make cows barren, but he did reckon that when people bestirred themselves to complain formally, the thefts and assaults they protested about were probably real. To him, Laeta's bland remarks were official excuses for inaction.

To be angry about neighbours' bad behaviour would seem a crazy waste of time where we grew up. On the Aventine, there were too many persons of lewd habits to write petitions about it. Everyone drank, to take away the pain of existence. Nobody wore themselves out trying to have ethical standards. Even joining the army when we were eighteen was such a nod to the establishment it had made Petro and me objects of raucous derision.

'Of course we take all such reports seriously,' Laeta assured us. Tell that to the man who wrote in, I thought.

'You rush to rootle out the villains?' I teased him. 'Their horrid shacks are upended by military-style machines, their filthy possessions tossed away, and the pilfering layabouts are made to take regular jobs in nasty occupations?'

Laeta scowled. 'We ask the district magistrate to make enquiries.'

'And if your correspondent writes again—*when* he does, since he refuses to give up—you just send another soft request to the same magistrate who let everyone down the first time?'

'Dispersed responsibility, Falco.' Laeta let my jibes trickle off like river water from a cormorant.

'Well, it's hardly corrupt, but I'd define it as inept and complacent.'

'Always yourself!' smiled Laeta. 'I do admire that, Falco . . . Sometimes these complaints die down,' he said to Petronius, as if addressing the reasonable man in our pairing. 'So much better if a situation is dealt with peacefully, and at the local level. Nevertheless, should there be a flare-up that the local authorities cannot handle, it will be tackled—tackled aggressively.'

'This involves more than bad neighbours,' Petronius assessed. He was glum. 'Now a man has died. Tortured, killed, and his body deposited in a blasphemous way. He appears to have been coming to Rome to appeal to the Emperor personally. That, to me, places a moral duty on Rome to look into what happened—and to pursue the victim's complaints.'

'Quite.' Laeta, too, became more subdued. He clasped his hands on the surface of his shining marble table. Mention of moral duties always casts a blight on bureaucrats. He admitted, in a frank way that from him was an apology, 'It now appears the man's petitions were justified.'

We had reached the crux of the meeting. Claudius Laeta half rose from his throne-like chair, so he could wriggle out of his toga. In palace code, this told us whatever was said next must be in confidence. Petronius Longus eagerly shrugged off his own formal robe. He and I moved closer to Laeta. We three were alone in the enormous room, but all of us dropped our voices.

'What are we dealing with?' The expert now, Petronius was terse, calm and impressive.

'The misfit family are called the Claudii. Mean anything?'

I had heard the name only recently so I pricked up my ears, though Petronius shook his head, asking, 'Are they in Rome?'

'They may set their sights on moving to the city,' Laeta answered. 'So far we are spared.'

'Did your writer name names?'

'Often. He mainly railed against a brutish wastrel called Claudius Nobilis.'

'Anybody talked to him?'

'I believe he is frequently the subject of enquiries. However . . .' Petronius glanced my way as we waited. 'It is a little delicate.'

'Why?' I asked bluntly.

'These people are freedmen,' Laeta said. 'Not just anybody's freedmen—they originally came from the imperial family.'

Petronius chewed it over for a moment then clarified: 'The current Emperor's family name is Flavius. So not Vespasian's *familia*?'

'Yes and no.' Laeta's backside must be purpose-made for fence-sitting.

I saw the problem all right. 'All the imperial possessions passed over when Vespasian took the throne. Not just official buildings and mansions, but all the Julio-Claudians' vast portfolio of palaces, villas and farms—together with, presumably, their battalions of slaves. Claudian freedmen might transfer their respect to the Flavians—if they thought there was anything in it for them. As there generally is, with imperial connections.'

'The Flavians in turn must have been happy to accumulate powers of patronage—or not, in this case!' joked Petro.

Claudius Laeta had a chilly demeanour as we scoffed. 'Most freedmen of the old imperial house transferred their allegiance to the new.'

'And that's why you are here!' I told him, with a wicked smile.

He cut me off. 'We acknowledge an inherited problem. Someone tried to dump it in the past—unsuccessfully. Slaves *should* be freed as a reward for good service—' Just what my father's band all kept reminding me. 'It is clear this clan were disposed of because they were perennial pests.' Laeta sniffed. Slaves and ex-slaves are riddled with snobbery. 'None ever held a useful position or trained in a specialism. When they were freed, none took decent work or tried to set up businesses. Their imperial past makes them arrogant; it is thought— both by themselves and others—to give them protection from the law.'

'Wrong of course?' I asked.

'They exploit the belief, and people are afraid of them.'

Petronius and I shared another glance. 'So it will look bad,' he suggested, 'if moves are made against them on your orders, Laeta—but you find no evidence and can make no charges stick?'

'Indeed.'

'So what's the plan? I assume you asked me here because there is one?'

Laeta powered into a summary: 'Local initiatives have failed. Time and time again, in fact. I want to send expert examiners from Rome. Look at it with fresh eyes. We need a sophisticated approach, backed up by energetic action.'

The usual plan, apparently. The one that usually fails.

'You want them evicted?' A shift behind his eyes told me—and Laeta, if Laeta was observant—Petronius Longus thought this was asking for trouble.

'Only,' Laeta insisted, 'if the accusations are true. If these people are causing a very serious nuisance.'

'Murder would be defined as "very serious"?'

'Yes, murder would justify intervention from Rome. More than one murder certainly.'

'What action has been taken so far?'

'Your dead man was reported missing, by relatives I understand. Regional forces did visit the Claudii, since they were implicated . . .'

'And the regionals buggered it!' Petronius was frank, but Laeta looked unfazed. Well, he started life as a slave. He had heard crudity in many languages. As an official in Rome, he shared Petro's sneer at the regions too.

'Perhaps they were under-experienced . . . They found nothing. It means any new investigation has to be conducted with extra sensitivity. It would be a bad day if imperial freedmen—which the Claudii are, and that must never be forgotten—came to accuse the Emperor of harassment.'

I asked, 'Have they lawyered up?'

'Not yet.' Laeta clearly assumed they would. Social menaces are well versed in finding legal teams to defend them, and an imperial connection was attractive; it guaranteed the brief would attract notice.

'Can they afford it?'

'There are always lawyers, Petronius, who find it a challenge to take on the government.'

'*Pro bono?* That really would be a glory of democracy,' I scoffed.

'It would be a pile-bursting pain in the arse!' Laeta's turn to be crude.

'So you want the vigiles involved?' Petronius Longus was torn between his yearning to pursue an intriguing case and his distaste for taking orders.

Laeta flexed his fingers. He summed up the position in a careful intellectual way: 'The Praetorians would look heavy-handed. The army is never used against Roman citizens in Italy. Yes, it seems right to use the vigiles. And since you have prior knowledge, Petronius Longus, you should lead the mission.'

'Going out of Rome?'

'Going to Latium.'

'My tribune will need a docket.'

'Your tribune will be comforted with all the honeyed instructions he requires.'

'This is Marcus Rubella,' Petronius warned, on the verge of smiling.

'Ah, the wondrous Rubella!' Laeta had met him. 'Then I shall use my most impressive seal when I write to him.'

'Better bump up his budget,' I advised. 'To help him calm down.'

Laeta tinkled with laughter. 'Oh Falco, there are limits!'

Foreseeing a long summer away from his family, Petronius became grumpy. He could not refuse when the Palace commanded. If this had been his own idea, he would have been gagging for it; orders from a scroll-beetle were much less welcome. He tapped the dead man's tablet with a heavy index finger. 'So does the petition-writer have a name, Laeta?' Claudius Laeta made a show of ruffling through other documents to check.

I leaned towards him and offered helpfully, 'He is called Julius Modestus—am I right?' When Laeta confirmed it, I was not surprised.

13

Petronius shot me a dark look. He thought I had known all along. In fact, I had only just decided for sure the coincidences added up.

To Laeta I breezed, 'Lucius Petronius and I are already on this. We have been working together; I am just back from reconnaissance.' Now it was Laeta's turn to look annoyed with me; he thought I was angling for payment. He was right too. 'If you are sending in headquarters assessors it makes sense to include me. I'll do it for my usual rates.'

'You're too expensive, Falco.'

'You can't afford to peel manpower off the Fourth Cohort. Petronius and I have history as a team; he can't tackle this alone—and if Vespasian wants to distance himself from these freedmen, he knows I'm his man.'

To my surprise, Laeta reluctantly nodded. Probably he thought if this went wrong, he now had someone else to blame.

'It's more than neighbourhood annoyance,' said Petronius, impatient with our negotiations. 'The tomb death was not a singleton, an accident of tempers flaring; Modestus had been stalked, all the way to Rome. He was mutilated—the killer returned to the body for more of that after death.'

I saw Laeta moisten dry lips. 'I need to demonstrate we are dealing with more than one random murder.' He was still worrying over the bureaucracy.

'Modestus' wife is also missing, most certainly dead too. Not even a body,' said Petro. 'The killer may have kept her corpse for—'

'I see!' Laeta must be squeamish.

'Treats in the larder,' explained Petro relentlessly. Laeta closed his eyes. Petro scowled sombrely, mentally dwelling on the circumstances.

'Other murders are likely, going back over many years, Laeta,' I weighed in. 'Petronius reckons this killer will strike again, until he is captured and stopped.'

'Ah, one of those!' Laeta pretended to be a crime expert. 'No one has ever suggested the Claudii are *that* bad.'

'When such murderers are exposed, people are always surprised,' I pointed out. '*He kept to himself, but he never seemed violent. None of us had any idea*—that's how repeat killers get away with it. Only with hindsight does it all seem bloody obvious.'

I was supposed to have the reputation for mischief, but it was Petro who asked, 'You came up through the imperial household yourself, Laeta. Did you ever encounter these backwoodsmen? Were you slaves together?'

Claudius Laeta battled a shudder. 'No; absolutely not. Though it's a small world. I am sure you could find palace staff who have met them in the past . . . But during their time in the imperial *familia,* these were merely low-grade rural slaves. It is said they worked originally at a villa beloved of the Emperor Augustus at Antium. Nero tore it down—how typical of the man—and rebuilt on a scale that he fancied was more glamorous. Probably at that time the Claudii were deemed superfluous. You know, there is a difference between rough country slaves, labouring anonymously in the fields as shepherds, mowers, tillers or harvesters, and those of us who are fortunate enough to be trained for duties close to emperors.'

'Understood!' Petronius could be a bastard. 'So, they were batch field workers . . .' He kept pushing. 'Your paths never crossed?'

'No.' Laeta remained polite but cold. 'You could ask Momus,' he added offhandedly to me. He managed to imply I had no scruples in my choice of personal contacts.

Momus started life as a gruesome slave-overseer. Since he lacked both intellect and morals, he had been assigned to a palace audit section; according to him, his job description was to audit the spies. Interpreting that as an order to cut staff numbers, Momus strove to make Anacrites fall down a very deep well or float off a high parapet. I got on well with Momus. Laeta, who was more fastidious, regarded him as a major disease—but possibly useful.

'He is foul—though he knows the slave rostas. I intend to have a chat!' I assured Laeta happily. Now Laeta was wondering if Momus knew any secrets about *him* and would Momus tell *me*? 'Careful intelligence will be needed on this case, Laeta. I suppose it's a coup for you, grabbing the job from Anacrites?'

'So sad for him.' Claudius Laeta beamed, a disconcerting sight. 'I hear the Emperor has posted dear Anacrites on a mission to Istria—insultingly straightforward and boringly diplomatic. Here, he could have been gaining praise by saving the Emperor from association with the menace of the Claudii—Anacrites will be *livid*!'

Laeta was smiling. Petronius Longus and I were smiling too. The job stank. But we were all united in a bond of happiness that we had a chance to snatch credit away from the Chief Spy.

Before we left, Laeta found it in himself to say to me, a little awkwardly, 'I was so sorry to hear about your father and your child, Falco.'

He had left it too late in the conversation. It failed to come over as genuine. I brushed his condolences aside.

14

As we left, Petronius and I took a detour past the smelly hutch Momus normally occupied; there was no sign of him. I did not make enquiries. Momus was grisly; I preferred not to know about his leisure time. His room must have been shabby to start with, but he had let it grow squalid; in a palace full of slaves with buckets and sponges he had no need to endure this. Even Petronius, who saw the world's worst in his work for the vigiles, raised an eyebrow at the rancid accommodation.

On the opposite side of a long corridor lay Anacrites' office. Now we knew he was away, I opened the door and invited Petro inside. They had met a couple of times and Petro had a personal interest. Anacrites, who made a habit of hanging around my family, at one time took a shine to Maia. Maia saw through him; sensing he was dangerous, she backed out of whatever relationship they had. His response was to send men who trashed her home, terrifying Maia and her four young children. Even now, Anacrites could not see how that vicious action only proved she was right to drop him.

I would pay him back. He thought he had got away with it. He still hung around my mother as if she had adopted him, and he greeted me like an old, affectionate colleague. He would learn.

The good result had been Maia taking up with Petro soon afterwards. He knew her story. He, too, had not forgotten. Like me, he
was determined to deal with Anacrites one day, one day at the right
moment.

The spy's room was cramped but at least clean. It had an almost
medical smell; I had always noticed that, though never pinpointed the
source. One of his staff must have endemic veruccas, or enduring
the spy day in and day out had given someone migraines.

We strolled over and squinted sideways at the stuff on his table,
deliberately shifting pens and styluses in subtle ways, to worry him
when he came back. Everything had been laid out pedantically; he
was bound to notice changes.

There were no confidential tablets; Anacrites was tenaciously secretive. Petronius looked with longing at some secured cupboards, but
we were not in a mood to force locks. Usually, however late it was,
our bugbear had a dandruffy clerk or one of his dreadful agents moping in here with him. As soon as he was sent abroad, they must have
all rushed off. The room was strangely still and quiet. The strife and
duplicity that emanated from it had been placed on hold.

We stared around, then Petronius shook his head slightly, bemused. I wriggled my shoulders as if to slough off the very air the spy
had breathed. We left without a word.

By the time we emerged from the rambling old buildings, the night
had taken a shift onwards. Still simmering with remains of the day's
heat, Rome had become its darker self. Families and workers were
back in their homes. The streets now carried streams of delivery carts,
each alley ringing with the trundle of battered wooden wheels and
the bloody-minded curses of crude drivers. Stray dogs ran for their
lives from heavy-duty wagons that were so laden they could neither
swerve nor stop in a hurry. Even the burglars and muggers who
emerged at dusk kept their sandalled feet well back from the kerb.

We sensed their presence, as they skulked through streets where they had conveniently blown out any lamps. None of them bothered us. We looked too capable.

I saw Petronius savour the warm air, trying to tell whether various wafts of smoke from baths and cookshops meant fire duty for the vigiles. He was in full professional mode, alert for any kind of trouble.

He and I made a few quick plans as we strolled, via the winding lane at the foot of the Capitol, back to our own haunts. He then returned to the patrol house, up on the Aventine. I watched him go, with that familiar fast, loping stride. Quietly I continued along the Marble Embankment to my house.

15

'Marcus, darling, you should be ashamed! Why ever didn't you tell us about the funeral?'

Let's call Marina my sister-in-law, though it had always been a title of convenience. She and my legionary brother, Festus, had never lived together, though the ditsy dumpling claimed they would have done, but for his tactlessness in getting himself killed. She still made out our scamp would have settled down on his return—a concept he guffawed at, as I more accurately recollected. Suggestions of marriage always made Festus need a very large veal pie and so much drink to wash it down he would fall unconscious on the caupona counter.

Still, he had loved children. Once Marina had a baby we all agreed to accept as fathered by Festus, she needed somebody to sponge off. The Didius family pitied her plight. We understood want. We admired efficient begging too. Little Marcia was a dear child (possibly a factor that should make us think she was not ours), so we subsidised Marina for her daughter's sake. I say 'we'. The others always left the fine details to me. By details, I mean actually handing out cash.

Inevitably my father's death had brought Marina, dragging Marcia, to pay respects (her words). She had her large beautiful eyes on the legacy.

'Marcia will be no trouble. I brought her a lunch pack. I'll pick her up when I've run a few errands . . .'

Marina was a fabulous specimen, though common. She turned heads so frequently she had no idea it was possible for a woman to walk past a scaffold, a wine bar, a fish stall or a cohort of soldiers without whistles and loud invitations to share grimy fellows' flagons. It looked as if the food she had so unnecessarily brought for her daughter was part of a workman's sardine ration, in fact. Women loathed her. Helena, and even young Albia, greeted her arrival with embittered sighs. While they hoped she would leave quickly, I prayed she had not worked out how much money to ask me for. She had, of course.

'You never even invited Marcia to your party at Saturnalia. Everyone ignores us nowadays. Whoever thought Festus would be so quickly forgotten? Marcia hadn't seen her gramps for ages and now she'll never have the chance again—' (Wails from Marina's well-primed daughter.) 'Geminus was *so* fond of her; it's *such* a tragedy! And I blame you, Marcus.'

Since the child was listening, I refrained from spelling out that Geminus lost count of his grandchildren, and that my niece could have been brought to see Pa at the Saepta any day. Suitably prompted, he would have reminisced about Festus and handed out hot pancakes. Given his eye for a promising woman, Marina would probably have walked away with some piece of jewellery. The fact was, she had been too busy leading her life of play and pleasure—until she heard that Pa was gone and how much he had left behind.

Marina dumped Marcia on us 'to play with her little cousins'. Marcia was a fast-growing skinny-rib of ten, so she and my much younger girls had nothing in common, but Marcia spent hours diligently tying hair ribbons and my daughters were willing little dolls.

Primed by her mother, Marcia set about charming me in her own style. 'Uncle Marcus, just give us the money.'

'What money?'

'A big bag of cash to make us feel less sad that Grandpa died.'

'How does that work?'

'Mother is happy, so I'm happy—and you will be happy too. You don't want us littering up your smart hall every morning.'

'Is that going to happen?'

'Yes, *Marcus darling*—' Marcia did a priceless imitation of her effusive mama. 'Until you give in, I shall be dumped here to work on you.'

I said I was packing for a business trip to Latium.

My niece turned withering great brown eyes on me. What she lacked in her mother's extraordinary beauty—and she was on course to inherit most of that—she made up in character. If the character was dubious, it only proved a Didius really had spawned her. A handful at three, at ten she was now ferociously bright and spirited.

Marcia suggested that, if I was busy, I should simply give her the password for my Forum bankbox, then she would withdraw a sum she thought suitable. Nothokleptes, my banker, would probably be so surprised he would hand over everything.

I said Marcia must be joking, then we both collapsed in giggles.

Two days later it was Marcia, a dedicated gossip-winkler, who told me that Petro's brother was at Maia's house.

'Petronius must have sent for him. Auntie Maia is put out.'

'Nobody knew Lucius even had a brother!' Helena exclaimed. We were at lunch, tucking into our own goat's cheese, olives and flatbread, plus more sardines; Marina's scaffolder must be really keen on her, though he had a tedious diet.

'Lucius has a brother.' I wiped my oily chin on a napkin. 'Rectus. He lives in the country; Petro despises that.'

'His brother is always off-colour,' Marcia informed us. Information stuck to her like mud on a wall. 'He has marsh fever. First it nearly killed him, now it keeps coming back. But Lucius Petronius has turned down the official guide you were offered by the man at the Palace and asked his brother instead. He trusts him. Anyway, he's brought Nero.'

'*Spot!*' Helena and I corrected her briskly. Nero was an ox, of dubiously rakish character. Petronius, his poorly brother and some hick cousins jointly owned him. Calling the beast by the name of an emperor who had been damned-to-the-memory could be defined as an offence. I was once arrested for it in Herculaneum—though the real reason was that Spot tried to rape a donkey. A snooty Herculaneum citizen, its owner, failed to see the funny side.

'If this is the same ox, he's a sex maniac. I'm not driving him!'

'Why do you need a guide?' Helena interrupted, swift to pick up any detail I was trying to hide. She homed in on the fact that when I first discussed Laeta's mission, I implied Petro and I were just retracing my journey to Antium. She fixed me with accusing eyes. I acted casual. It never works.

'They need a guide,' Marcia piped up before I could stop her, 'to show them the way in the Pontine Marshes. That's where they have to find the murderers, if those men go into hiding and think nobody will ever dare to go after them there since it is so horribly unhealthy.'

'Thank you, Marcia,' I replied coolly. She gave me her clever-little-girlie smile. I would have biffed her, but refused to be dragged down to her level.

Helena Justina, my companion in work and my soulmate in life, was now inspecting me as if I was one of the more repulsive insects from the fetid swamps under discussion. 'O father of my children—' She adjusted an ear-ring, an expressive punctuation. 'Would that be the Pontine Marshes which have such a reputation for disease and death?'

I wiped my chin again as if I had missed a smear the first time. I placed the napkin on the serving table, neatly alongside my food-bowl; I straightened my spoon, rearranged my chewed olive stones in a more aesthetic pattern, then could no longer stall. 'We may not have to go there.'

'But if you do, Falco?' Helena generally called me 'Falco' when I had let her down unspeakably—and had been so careless that she found out.

I had done my research. I spent the past couple of days in libraries—not what people generally expect of informers, but unless there is a good reason to hang around barmaids and Forum lags, I like to use reputable sources. The scrolls depressed me. 'The good thing,' I chirruped, 'is that we are going in summer, when much of low-lying, scenic Old Latium dries out.'

Unfortunately, Helena was well read too. 'Marcus, the modern theory is that drying out the land seasonally has only provided better summer breeding-grounds for flies!'

'Olympus, is that what they say?' I was genuinely glum.

A row of silver bangles jingled together on Helena's left arm. 'The flies are hideous. Even in the forests, clouds of them rise up at every step. The Pontine Marshes are so dangerous nobody will live there. What's that proverb—*You grow rich in a year, but you die in six months?*'

Sometimes I liked having a partner who supplied me with background. At other moments I understood the men who married girls who had no time for arguments as they devoted themselves to athletes and actors. 'I won't be staying a year—not even six months.'

'Six hours will be too long if the wrong fly bites you.'

'Either we can pin the killings on our man, or we come straight home. In any case,' I countered feebly, 'as Marcia said, Petronius Longus is in charge of the logistics. He is bringing the best possible guardian—his own brother.'

My niece Marcia gave us a sniff that reminded me of my mother at her most disparaging. 'Everyone thinks Petronius Rectus has gone off like a pint of bad prawns.'

Much later, that evening when the house was quiet, Helena Justina and I discussed my journey properly in my small private study. I sat in an old basket chair I kept there purposely, so she could lean her elbows on the arms while she told me what a swine I was. At other times, the dog jumped up on it. Tonight, Helena pinched my reading couch, so I was reduced to the chair and the dog jumped on my lap.

Helena had thrown off her shoes and her jewellery, pulled out the ornamental pins from her fine hair and was massaging her head with those long fingers as if the pull of a chignon had made her scalp hurt. But I was the real headache.

'Listen, fruit. The old rules apply. If you ask me not to, I won't go.'

Helena thought about that, for about two heartbeats, which was longer than usual in fact. 'The rule is we travel together, Marcus.'

Now I was stuck, as she intended. If I said it would be irresponsible and unfair to our children for both parents to risk death in the marshes, it just emphasised how stupid it was even for one of us to go.

Helena did not wait for me to bluster. 'I can't come. Julia and Favonia need me here for reassurance.' They had played up a lot after we lost the baby. They probably needed me here too. Typically, Helena did not waste breath pointing that out.

'I am sorry a big case has come up so soon. Well, maybe I'm sorry it has come up at all.'

'Marcus, I know you will always need to work.'

'I could become a full-time antique dealer, a permanent auctioneer. Do you want me to do that?'

Helena made an impatient gesture, left-handed; lamplight hit silver in a ring I once gave her. We had not addressed the issue of my future, but now we dealt with it. 'I think you will be good at it,' Helena told me, 'but you would hate to do it permanently. You enjoy being an informer—it was one of the first things that struck me about you. And you're very good. So be honest. You and Lucius Petronius have been offered a mystery and as usual you can't resist.'

'My connection with Modestus caused it. Apparently a new career won't save me from mysteries!'

'So your argument is, you owe something to Modestus? Not profits. I know what the statues brought in.'

'You checked!'

'I check a lot of things,' Helena said, to worry me. I grinned happily. I kept few secrets from her. She was too likely to expose me.

When the statues went forward to the amphitheatre project, their modest price was the best Geminus could negotiate. Vespasian never wasted cash. 'Pa always decried sudden swish rewards,' I said. 'He reckoned it's the regular accumulation of small sums that matters, not a hiccup that may thrill you for a moment yet never come again.'

Helena smiled. She had been oddly fond of my father, as he always was of her. 'He was right—though I believe he had his thrills too. What pleased your father could be a beautiful artefact—' Often in the form of a willing woman, though I refrained from interrupting with that comment. 'But to him, any business finesse was delectable. You inherited it, Marcus. You get the same boost from your work. So you want the satisfaction of explaining what happened to this man and his wife, especially when nobody else can solve it. Then, since no one else will take them on, you and Lucius see these Claudii as your challenge.'

Helena understood—but explaining was not the point. 'You don't want me to go.'

'That's not it, Marcus. *I want you to come back!*'

Helena took in a breath, not despair, more exasperation. It was no more than if I had gone out in my newest tunic when the streets were muddy. She would let me go to the marshes once I promised to take care. Promises were not worth making in this situation, though for her I stretched the point.

Next morning, Helena and Maia visited apothecaries. A large basket of herbal ointments to keep away flies would be going on the mission with us. If we were sensible men we would use them.

If Petro and I were not sensible, our women would find out. So we thanked them politely for caring and agreed to take precautions against dying. 'You are taking swords, aren't you? What's the difference?'

I loved Helena Justina. I wanted to survive with her for many years. But did she think Hercules slathered himself with brimstone and pennyroyal when he departed for his twelve labours?

Actually it was worse. Petronius and I had been supplied with bunches of nettles to hang all around the ox cart, then numerous soapstone boxes of a concoction in which not only pennyroyal but wormwood, rue, sage, tansy, myrtle and spearmint were mingled in an olive oil base. Some individual ingredients were attractively aromatic, but the combination smelt foul.

'I'll use this stuff, if you will,' I told Petro.

He said, anything would be worth it to save us being bitten. For bites, he showed me, our determined women had sent another box. Their sandalwood and lavender bite-salve would scent us like a pair of Pamphyllian dancing masters. We were hard men, but that really terrified us.

16

We detoured to call on Sextus Silanus. We had to pass on the tragic news of his uncle's death. Petronius would explain the circumstances. My role would be to watch this conversation unobserved, judging the nephew's reaction. He had benefited financially from the death. Some investigators would pin the murder straight on him. When motive gives you a quick way to clear up a case, who needs facts?

Silanus came to the shop door, saw our cavalcade, recognised me, and expected the worst. Petronius Longus always looked as if he had a grim purpose. His bearing and sombre face gave away the reason for our visit. The numbers in our group also indicated that Modestus and his fate were at last of official concern.

We had the ox cart, containing some of us and our baggage. On dilapidated mules were a couple of Petro's men, all he could safely scrounge from duty: Auctus looked too fragile to fight fires but he had been in the cohort for years and everyone accepted him; he was riding Basiliscus, a skeletal beast with a bent ear and bad breath. Ampliatus had an eye missing and rode a brindled, knock-kneed mule called Corex who kept running away. Although the vigiles are ex-slaves, most were not quite so off-putting; these were the only two men who would volunteer for our destination.

Petronius had left Fusculus behind in charge, though we wished we could have had that steady fellow with us. Somebody had to do Marcus Rubella's vital job; at least, that would be Rubella's view.

In charge of the cart, Petro's brother had a similar relaxed driving style, holding the reins in one hand loosely and letting the ox make his own pace. Otherwise there was little resemblance between them. Maybe there had been a frisky lupin-seller in the neighbourhood just before Rectus was born, though I did not risk the joke. Rectus was older, shorter, of squashy shape and slumped posture, an unsociable fellow who seemed hard to like. They had had very little to do with one another for years. I was sure Petro once told me his brother was a bit of a fixer and mixer, though he gave no sign of it. Perhaps age or the marsh fever had slowed him down. When anyone asked Rectus about the fever (which we did frequently, because we were all petri-fied), he just grunted; if pushed further, he let out a sardonic laugh and turned away. I decided not to discuss him with Petronius. Let him volunteer a comment if he wanted to.

Completing our party was a brother of Helena's, Justinus. I worked with him in Rome and had also taken him on missions in rough country. I knew he would be reliable. Helena had begged me not to expose him to danger, but he was no longer a lad; it was his choice. He was keen to escape the bad atmosphere at home, caused by his brother's new wife and pushy father-in-law. On this trip Justinus had brought his barmy batman, Lentullus. The dopiest, clumsiest ex-legionary in the Empire, Lentullus was devoted to Quintus in a wide-eyed way. He limped badly on one leg and would probably try to tame the Pontine flies as pets.

I planned that if we ran into hostility from local dignitaries, re-sentful of imperial interference, then Camillus Justinus, as a senator's son with the smart travel clothes and uppercrust accent, could be shoved forward to charm them.

We first tackled officialdom at Lanuvium. I was right; we were given the brush-off. If there's one thing I hate about travel outside Rome it is small-town magistrates who think they count for something. The petty toffs who ran Lanuvium had so little sense of proportion they called their town council the Senate and their magistrate a Dictator. That was the title used in ancient times for a leader with unrestricted powers who was called upon to rescue the nation in an emergency. On mention of the Claudii, the Lanuvium Dictator rapidly assumed other emergency powers: declaring that this problem was outside his jurisdiction. He kindly suggested we try Antium instead.

He had cow dung on his boots and I wasn't certain he could read— yet he managed to dismiss Laeta's request for civic aid as briskly as if he was swatting wasps on a saucer of relish.

'I'm getting a feel for this,' Petronius remarked in annoyance as we left.

'You mean,' suggested Justinus, 'it feels like stepping in a slurry pit?'

'And helplessly falling over!'

We spent the next half-hour despondently embroidering this with such details as falling in the manure while wearing your best cloak and with a girl you fancied watching . . .

Our detour to Lanuvium was partly a waste of time, but we did see Silanus. Petronius had asked him a few questions that confirmed the body found in the tomb was his uncle: a man in his sixties, nearly bald, thin build; usually wearing a lapis signet ring, which had not been found. I saw Petro thinking that the killer might have kept it as a trophy and that if we ever caught up with him, the ring might be good evidence. Her nephew said Livia Primilla was about fifteen years younger; in good health, blue eyes, greying hair, kept herself nicely, wore good clothes and jewellery. Unfortunately, even though they dealt in statues and must know the artistic community, the couple had never commissioned portraits of themselves.

Silanus gave us directions to his uncle and aunt's farm. It was near Satricum, adjacent to land farmed by the Claudius freedmen: 'If you can call what the Claudii do *farming*.'

They did own cattle: Silanus said his uncle had a long history of bad relations with them but the most recent ugly incidents began when the Claudii let a rampaging bunch of young bullocks break down a fence. Modestus had an overseer who went to demand compensation for the damage, but was badly beaten up.

Silanus confirmed that Modestus had a hobby of writing angry letters. He had complained directly to the obnoxious Claudii. He also badgered the town council in Antium; those wits'-end worthies may have lost patience with his demands. After he and Primilla disappeared and Silanus appealed for help, the magistrate had to investigate, but his men may not have put much effort into it.

'Some of the Claudii are just loafers; they go into town and act up—minor thefts from homes and businesses, insults, writing their names on walls, guzzling wine then causing a disturbance after dark . . . You know.'

'Everyday life, where we come from,' Petronius said, though he made it clear he was sympathetic.

We were indoors at the time; Silanus went to look outside to check what his children were doing. Lentullus, a big child himself, was talking to them; he had them feeding grass to the ox. 'One or two Claudii have more violent reputations. People don't like anything to do with them.'

'Particular names?' asked Petro.

Silanus shook his head. 'When Modestus was railing, I had my own troubles. It always sounded like exaggeration. Anyway, there never seemed much I could do . . .'

'A man called Nobilis has been mentioned.'

'Means nothing to me.' Silanus fell silent. Now he blamed himself for not taking more interest previously.

I said quietly, 'You were right the other day. Why make yourself another victim? Your conscience is clear. Leave it to the professionals.'

I had watched Petronius silently weighing up the nephew as a harassed family man of basic honesty. Turning a piece of terracotta in his big hands, Petro asked, 'A slave brought you the news of your aunt's disappearance—can I speak to him?'

'Syrus. I don't have him,' said Silanus. 'There was a man I owed money to. I handed over the slave to pay off the debt.'

He had paid the butcher. That's how it is. Syrus may have loyally carried out instructions from Primilla that had brought him on a day's journey, and the result of his information would make Silanus and his children financially secure. But unlucky Syrus was a slave. His reward for diligence was to be exchanged for half a year's supply of skillet offal.

Our conversation seemed to have finished. But as Silanus saw us off outside, he brought out awkwardly, 'I have to ask—are you expecting to find Aunt Primilla?'

I let Petronius answer. 'We shall do all we can. You understand that we already suspect what happened. Whether any trace of her remains is a question I can't answer yet. I'm sorry.'

Silanus accepted it. But he had one more worry. We had told him how Modestus died. 'Will she have suffered . . . the same kind of injuries?'

Petronius Longus grasped his shoulders. 'Don't think about it. She won't be suffering now. My advice is, try to live as normally as possible until we report back. Whatever happened to Livia Primilla is long over.'

He would not give fake reassurance, nor could he offer comfort.

We had brought what remained of the late Julius Modestus with us from Rome. In such circumstances, the vigiles used a tame undertaker to cremate the body before it was returned to the family. All Silanus received was a plain urn with the ashes.

Petronius implied the cremation had been carried out when they thought the dead man might never be identified. But I saw the nephew's face. He recognised concern for him: preventing any chance that he or his children might see the decayed, beaten, mutilated and tortured corpse.

17

The butcher in Lanuvium was typical. He was built like an unhealthy boxer, with a cleaver through his belt. A row of meat joints hung along the front of his shop, just where his horrible nitty head would bang into them all day. He had blood on his tunic. It looked and smelt as if it was weeks old so if you ate his meat you would keel over. But if we all avoided the produce of off-putting butchers, we would be stuck with a diet of lettuce leaves and the Empire would be overrun by beefy barbarians.

He no longer possessed the slave Syrus. We groaned, thinking this was the start of an interminable chain of petty debt pay-offs. In Rome it would have been. The butcher would have sweetened a brothel-keeper who then passed on the goods to buy a sack of hay . . .

Sophisticated barter had yet to arrive in Lanuvium. They were simply careless. 'Syrus? I only had him two days. He ran away.'

'Not much of a debt cancellation!' Petronius grinned. 'If I were you, I'd take the old "sleep-with-my-sister" settlement next time.' City wit really goes down well in country districts. The butcher gave him a glare that made me squeamish. Still lost in his joke, Petro appeared to ignore the frosty looks but went on in formal vigiles mode: 'Have you reported your slave as a fugitive, sir?' The 'sir' was satirical, if you knew Petro.

'What's the point?'

'He may turn up.'

'That good-for-nothing is long gone.'

'Well, we do like to have runaways listed properly; apart from being useful if we catch them involved in a felony, it helps deter the next one from trying it if he knows he'll be on a list for the bounty-hunters . . . Where do you think this Syrus is headed? Would he go back home to Antium?'

The butcher was full of bluster and certainty. 'Oh he's chased off where they all go—straight up to the Via Appia, hop on the back of a winecart, and disappear in Rome. They think the streets are paved with gold. Maybe they are. I think I'll go myself one day!'

Petronius Longus remained undaunted. 'Better give me his description and I'll have a docket sent on your behalf in case he's rounded up. You may get him back, sir. The Rome vigiles are adept at spotting country runaways . . .' He implied that agricultural incomers stood out in our sophisticated city. It wasn't true. A loser in flight from a farm looked little different from one on the loose from a town house—well, once the townee had rolled up his smart uniform and shoved it under a bush. 'Let me take down a few details. Height?'

'Middling.'

'Weight?'

'Middling.'

'Distinguishing marks?'

'None visible.' The butcher leered. 'I hadn't got around to inspecting his rude bits!'

'Trained for any fancy duties?'

'General runabout.'

'I suppose,' Petronius deduced, 'he was wearing a rough-sewn, homespun tunic and worn country shoes? Well, thank you for your keen observation, sir. That gives us some very useful points to go on.'

Petro was a po-faced, placid humorist. The butcher could not decide whether he was being mocked or praised.

18

We could have stayed the night in Lanuvium but we all agreed that somewhere else—anywhere else—might suit us better. I remembered there was a hamlet about halfway down to Antium; it would put us well on our way tomorrow, so we headed off there. It was a very ancient settlement, a place that made us feel we had strayed into Old Latium back when it was New. They claimed to have ninety inhabitants; they must have been counting in their goats. I kept expecting to run into the old hero Aeneas, tramping across this low-lying bog that the gods had sent him to colonise, still wearing the loincloth in which he escaped from Troy.

There was a cluster of poor houses, gathered together for company because it was near a crossroads; about a mile further on, a bridge crossed a river. There, a rutted track led off the narrow road. Rectus said the track wandered south, passing close to Satricum, so we could have nipped down there immediately, but we still planned to try in Antium to learn about the official efforts to find Modestus and Primilla. We only expected disdain from another magistrate. But why abandon a well-tried system just because it doesn't work?

A man and his wife conjured up basic meals for travellers. If there were places to stay, we preferred not to investigate. We ate, drank, told stories, then camped out. Next day, the man had gone to check his fig tree, but his wife made us a simple breakfast. Then we pressed on.

At Antium our qualms proved groundless. The magistrate was not going to be the least bit unhelpful; we were not even able to meet the man. His house was locked up and he was away.

'So . . .' Petronius Longus mused thoughtfully. 'If you live in a scenic old town on the coast, when summer comes you still have to go off on holiday?'

'That lummock with the fig tree nipped down here and warned him you were coming,' gloated his brother. This was pretty well the first opinion he had volunteered on anything. The rest of us gazed at Petronius Rectus and carefully kept quiet, as we belatedly assessed him as a crackpot fantasist.

We asked around. That was a lark. Half the people refused to speak to us, the rest said they knew nothing.

After these fruitless forays, we did move on to Satricum. It was another very ancient township, on low-lying ground, right at the edge of the Pontine Marshes. Around this remote crossroads, cultures had clashed for aeons. The warlike Volscians had fought over the archaic place; they probably still lived here. Not only did it feel as if we might bump into a bunch of slant-eyed, smiling Etruscan ancestors, there was an end-of-civilisation atmosphere, brought about by the little town's proximity to the dreaded wetlands.

A tightly built settlement was going about its business. Up on a hill stood a temple to Mater Matuta: the mother of the morning, Eos, Aurora—the rosy-fingered harbinger who unlocks the gates of heaven so the sun can roll out each day. We climbed the acropolis like good tourists and saw the ancient goddess, chiselled in pitted stone, enthroned and mourning her son Memnon, killed at Troy by Achilles, whose corpse lay across her lap.

She was a goddess of provender as well, and a game girl who had been cursed by the jealous Venus into a habit of taking many lovers (the kind of curse most young girls fervently pray for). The Mater Matuta at Satricum looked a bit weathered for lovers, but had done her job with opening the gates for Helios today. The sky was clear blue and the sun shone brilliantly.

'That's the Pontine deception,' Petronius Rectus informed us gloomily. 'Gorgeous weather, vegetation blooming—death behind every bush.' As a travel companion, the man was a laugh a minute.

We went back to our lodging house, in need of a drink.

It had taken us a while to find an inn that could accommodate seven of us. Satricum might be a crossroads, but most people who came this way must be heading somewhere else. It had little to attract visitors. The main feature was the old temple; that was hardly a unique shrine. Mater Matuta once flourished all across mainland Italy. She had a temple in Rome, right beside the Cattle Market Forum and so close to my house the memory made me homesick.

Perhaps a mother mourning her dead son was a sight I was not yet ready for. Heaviness fell upon me. I lost myself in my own thoughts.

Most of us were spinning out the evening in the inn courtyard. Auctus and Ampliatus, the two vigiles, were outside on a bench at the roadside. Although they were ex-slaves, we were equals on this trip and the rest of us genuinely wanted to include them; they stubbornly remained aloof. Meanwhile, as Justinus was a senator's son it was his birthright to chat up the girl who had served us. He was, however, unsure whether Lentullus, who had only recently joined his household, would report to his wife Claudia anything he got up to. Petro and I had our wives under control, or so we convinced ourselves; even though flirting with bar staff went against our noble natures, we did the necessary with the waitress, just as we had done for the past twenty years.

We were picking her brains. What did you think I meant, legate?

Because it was the largest roadhouse in the area—the only acceptable inn, it seemed—this had to be where the posse that came to look for Modestus and Primilla also took a breather. At first the waitress was reluctant to say much. The riders from Antium counted as local to her; we were foreign. Under the curious eye of his older brother, Petronius set about persuading her how much he hated gossip and admired a discreet waitress, but how much more he liked a civic-minded young woman who poured wine so nicely while she revealed all. (All she *knew*, legate; don't go off pop.) It took him about ten minutes before she had sat down with us and was gabbling information just as fast as he could ask the questions. Rectus, Justinus and Lentullus were impressed. I had seen Petro reach this point in half the time, but in those days he was young and in army uniform.

Her name was Januaria. She looked fifteen, was probably twenty, and would be killed by hard work before another decade passed. She had stabled our ox, cooked our dinner, explained the wine list (that took no effort), pulled heavy benches closer to the table, filled jugs from a cask and served us, including several detours to the two vigiles outside. None of us had asked, but it was understood that if we wanted, she would go to bed with us as well; all seven, if necessary, on whatever rotation basis we suggested. It would probably cost no more than a soft-boiled egg.

Januaria obligingly told us a posse turned up here about two months ago. A town magistrate who was hoping to go home as soon as possible arrived on horseback, in charge of volunteers who were hoping at least for a fight. After a hearty lunch, they toddled off into the marshes to tackle the Claudii. Following ingrained tradition, those scurrilous runts all swore blind they never saw Modestus or Primilla after the broken fence incident. They provided alibis for one another, in the usual way of large families.

'Then there wasn't much more to be done. Suspicion fell mainly on Probus and Nobilis.'

'Nobilis and Probus? *Noble* and *Honourable*?' I could hardly believe the irony of these names.

The simple girl didn't see my point. 'Those two are the best known—and most feared. They hang around together a lot. But Probus now has his own business—he buys and sells harness; second-hand mostly.' That probably meant stolen, though she did not suggest it. 'Nobilis has been working for Thamyris, a grain supplier in Antium, though Probus swore blind to the militia that his brother had gone away. So he couldn't have done anything, could he?'

'Away where?' asked Petronius. 'Campania? Rome? Overseas?'

'No, somewhere real foreign.' The girl knew nothing of other regions of Italy, let alone the overseas provinces. Our glorious Empire meant little to her. She had never even been to Antium, which was only seven miles away.

'When did he leave?'

'We haven't seen him in Satricum for months, but that's not unusual. The Claudii come and go.'

'Do you think he fled because he knew people would be looking for him?'

'He's never been scared before.'

I shoved Petronius along his bench and muscled in. It took effort. He was bigger than me and resisting like a recalcitrant old hog. 'So, excellent young lady with the beautiful eyes—' Januaria giggled as if no man had ever chatted her up before. Clearly few from Rome stayed here. 'What do you know about these rascals, the Claudii? Are there many of them?'

'Plenty. They live a bit rough, except some of the girls, who got away and married and have families.'

'I'm Falco, by the way.' I gave her my best smile, the version with dimples, which has been called seductive.

Sadly Januaria lost her chance with me. There was a landlord keeping an eye on her in case she snatched five minutes to herself. We never found out whether he was her husband or father, or even her owner if she was a slave. Around here, arrangements were freestyle. All three situations might apply simultaneously. In Rome we have a wide range of social entertainments on offer; in country dumps they tend to be stuck with witchcraft and incest.

The man was a waddling, inquisitive slob in a meal-sack apron. When he put in an appearance, the girl slid to her feet and made off indoors. She knew he had come out to stop her gossiping. Maybe he beat her if she slacked. In the country, people who may be kindness itself to their valuable animals treat staff management as harshly as an arena blood sport.

We never found out his name. We never wanted to be that friendly.

He just liked to do all the talking himself. They had a system. This wastrel chatted to customers; Januaria did everything else.

'Oh yes, fine sirs! I can tell you all about the Claudii!'

He said he remembered them arriving here. He was a child then. They had been manumitted in the time of the Emperor Gaius, which would be forty years ago. Freed from the rural farms of Antonia, the Emperor Claudius' mother, they arrived near Satricum and took possession of some soggy fields they claimed had been given to them. No imperial land agent had ever come to question it, though that could be because the sodden fields in question were rubbish. The Claudii hit the district like a plague of rats. Since then, anything portable had to be locked up, which the landlord said included all women younger than great-grandmothers.

The father was called Aristocles. He was a cold, odd man who certainly beat his children; people reckoned he knocked his wife about too, though some said that in fact he was frightened of her. Others maintained both parents acted together as a terrible team; the mother once hit a three-year-old so hard he lost an ear. This matriarch, a woman known as Casta, had borne about twenty offspring, in whom she showed little interest, although they all strangely revered her. The children were feral and generally disliked. The boys became renowned for wild tempers. They had bad relations with their girlfriends, when they were able to find any. Their sisters, who knew no other kind of man, tended to ruin any hope of a new life by choosing work-shy, thieving wife-beaters who resembled their own kin. The whole family were regularly suspected of burglary and arson, though it took a brave person to accuse them. Criticism of one was viewed as an attack on them all. It would bring the whole tribe into town, out for retaliation.

'Isn't it rumoured they have imperial protection?' I asked.

'Oh they do. Everybody knows about it.'

'How does that work?'

'We just all know. The Claudii have powers in Rome looking after them. That's why nobody official tries to clear them out. That's why most of us steer clear of them.'

'Did they give the posse from Antium any trouble?' Petronius asked.

'Oh no, laddie. Resistance would have proved they were up to no good, wouldn't it? That's their trickery. When troops go down there to their camp, they act meek as lambs. They make out that all complaints against them are dreamed up out of local spite. They pretend to be helpful. They throw open their doors to let their places be searched.'

'But no evidence is found?'

'They are very clever.'

Petronius leaned his chin on his hands. He was thinking about bullies who fester in society, accepted as a hazard of life, while they terrorise communities for years. He had to deal with situations like this in Rome. There were foul alleyways that nobody went down. Even the vigiles would only venture there in groups and they whistled loudly first, to let it be known they were coming. They would not want to surprise anyone. They gave the specially violent ones good time to get away.

The landlord decided he had said enough, though he gave us directions for tomorrow. Rectus, our intended guide, looked down his nose; the information was of the 'take the first turn out of town then just keep going straight' variety. This always leads you to sharp bends and forks in the road with no signboard. 'You can't miss it,' said the innkeeper, complaisantly. Our hearts sank.

We turned in early. My dinner lay heavy in my guts and even after it deigned to go down I had an ache in the pit of my stomach. I cannot have been the only one. We all knew we were about to visit one of the most dangerous areas on earth.

19

First thing next morning, Petronius and I handed round the insecticide ointments Helena and Maia had made us bring. Amidst a lot of joshing about the reek, and how scared of our women Petro and I must be, surprising amounts were applied to exposed skin. Petronius Rectus called us a bunch of fragile florets, but even the two vigiles dipped into the pots and daubed their foreheads.

None of us bothered much with breakfast, except Rectus. Since he had already had a dose of marsh fever, nothing worried him. We were tense, but he was placid. Immediately he had stuffed himself, he harnessed up Nero the ox, then without a word, threw his pack on the cart and set off. Luckily the rest of us were ready to go. You couldn't call the man surly; he just never bothered to communicate. His distaste for talk was religious. Being in his brother's company seemed to make Petro equally gloomy. I didn't try to chivvy him out of it; I was gloomy myself.

There were towns on the coast, west of us; there were stopping points along the Via Appia, to the east. Between them, once we put Satricum behind us, the way ahead was a vast empty quarter. We had a sense that the sea was somewhere over on our right hand, less than ten miles away though we never caught a glimpse. When Appius

Claudius struck his great road south from Rome, he only added to the problems of this low-lying interior, his hefty causeways interfering with the water table. There were tracks, down which the ox could just haul his cart, though in narrow parts we had to dismount and manhandle the vehicle. These tracks all had the look of overgrown, deserted byways that would take you miles into nowhere then peter out without warning.

Everywhere had a wild beauty. The sun burned bright, its effects tempered by coastal breezes. Seabirds and marsh birds cried incessantly. Clouds of butterflies roamed fitfully, seeking out aromatic mints and oregano. Crickets jumped ahead of us. As we expected, there was a mass of insect life. Black bugs and tiny midge-like flies swarmed in clouds everywhere we stopped for a breather, along with worrying bright red things that looked as if they had already dined on blood. I reckoned there must be snakes too.

We were crossing great tracts of scrubland. We did see small fields, planted with grain or fast-growing crops to take advantage of the short summer period when the land at least partly dried out. Everything that grew, grew with astonishing vigour; the soil was both well watered and enriched with silt from all the rivers and tributaries that poured off the Lepini mountains. We never saw anyone tending the fields.

Where there had been grazing to keep down the foliage, the ground was covered with maquis—small, very tough bushes, some of which were broad-leaved, though more were of the vicious, prickly kind. If you stepped too far off the track, you were likely to find yourself sinking suddenly up to the ankle in swamp water. Its suck would be ominous. Once you managed to pull out your foot safely, your heart would be pattering.

Where there had been no attempt at agriculture, larger vegetation had grown. There were wild olives and figs, which could have been reassuring as domesticated trees, though left to nature they had become enormous rampaging monsters, forming impenetrable thickets. Rectus broke his silence to say happily that the forests would be even thicker, the further across the marsh we went.

Sometimes in the distance we glimpsed cattle, generally where the levels remained flooded. They probably belonged to someone, but were not visibly herded. We did not risk approaching them. Trampling the edges of dark saltponds and stagnant pools where fallen vegetation putrefied, these beasts in their lonely location gave me a grim shiver. Once in Germania, I had had an encounter with a wild aurochs; I glanced at Camillus Justinus and knew he too was remembering our narrow escape from that huge bovine throwback.

Supposedly, the threat here was human. The Pontine Marshes had a sinister reputation as a place where brigands and highwaymen holed up. They must be brigands who could endure being bitten, stung, afflicted with foot-rot and driven crazy by isolation. We were gathering an idea of what to expect if we ever found the people we had come to interview.

We knew that the Claudii deliberately lived far enough from habitation to make visits inconvenient. We were fit men, equipped for this, but by afternoon we felt exhausted. We were despondent too, thinking we might never track down our quarries. Rectus assured us we were not lost. That depended how much faith we put in him.

'I wish I was one of those herons and could just flap up and fly out of here. I bet this is a place where you could wander in endless circles!' chattered Lentullus when we paused for rest. He must be twenty-five now, but he wittered like a mindless child. Justinus and I had known him since he was an army recruit with a fervent imagination and a knack for getting into trouble. We reminded him that we got him safely back to civilisation last time; he looked unconvinced.

'Stay on the track,' Justinus warned his bright-eyed batman. 'If you get stuck in a deep sinkhole I'm not pulling you out, in case it brings a boggle-eyed sprite swirling to the surface.' Now who was using too much imagination?

We all had the creeps. Long periods of silence descended on us. The invigorating effect of fresh air turned into sun-glaze and skin-burn. Eyes were dry. We started to itch, but when we slapped at imagined insects, they were never there.

Something about wild places brings misery to the surface. I began to be afflicted by griefs and guilts I thought I had left behind in Rome. Now that I had mastered the endless tasks involved in Pa's estate, my brain found space to heal itself—which it did as spitefully as possible, by way of reliving moments of misery. Over and over, I went through again that long day of Helena's labour and how we lost our baby son; over and over, I daydreamed that I was back at my father's villa, while his gaggle of slaves informed me he had gone.

Avoiding the others, I lolled in the cart, thinking about life and death. Death, mostly.

When it was too late to get back to Satricum the same day and while we all tried to avoid raising the unwelcome subject of having to camp out for the night on this sodden ground, we came upon something.

We had been travelling an intermittently raised track through shoulder-high brushwood. Occasional clearings widened out in a ragged fashion. Somebody must use this route. In one part they had actually laid wicker hurdles where the track had sunk, though the hurdles had then been half submerged too. Quite suddenly we broached a bigger space. A tilting heap of trash grew out of the ground amongst a fungoid clutter that was definitely human in origin. It looked abandoned. It looked like the windblown rubbish that piles against bushes in forests. Not so, though. Someone had carefully collected this detritus, over a long period. There was a lopsided shack at the heart of the mess which appeared to be roofed and lived in.

'This is it, boys!' declared Rectus, as if he had knowingly led us to it.

'Ooh, I don't like it!' crooned Lentullus, like someone listening to a ghost story around a winter fire.

We stood and looked. Nero the ox lowered his head and nuzzled around in clumps of reedy grass. His tail flicked manically, as he was tormented by flies. We were too tired and dispirited to advance on the hovel immediately. If a will-o'-the-wisp had wafted out in a swirl of mist and cried *'Boo!'* we would have turned tail obediently.

One end of the building had a squashed look and slumped low, as if it was in the process of being swallowed by the swamp. This was a lean-to with nothing to lean against. At times over various decades, attempts had been made to patch up rotten parts. Items of hardware that may have been stolen from other people's porticoes or looted from stationary vehicles on market day were attached like trophies: a Medusa-faced tile end, a metal knocker solidified with its own verdigris, half of a baker's giant stone flour grinder. Around the shack were piles of old building materials, large-scale food containers that dribbled rancid waste, cartwheels, broken pieces of armour and incomplete fishing equipment. There was a table groaning under masses of machinery parts—rusty bits off pulleys, cranes and ploughs—ugly metalwork the purpose of which had been long forgotten and which would never be identified and reused. It all looked shabby. Most totters would have rejected it.

Parked between what must have been the door and a window that had been boarded-up was a row of heavy-duty spears and javelins. They were cruder than army issue, gross objects made for intimidation. No one in Rome could have such a vile armoury displayed against his house; decent folk just had a lantern they forgot to light most evenings and a tile saying *cave canem* to act as a cheap watchdog. Weapons were illegal in the city. In the country, anything was permissible. Out here in the wild, the hunting excuse let any small-time character who wanted to look big decorate his home with this all too obvious panoply. It didn't mean he was able to use it properly, though even an amateur who wielded one of those wicked beasts would be capable of inflicting harm.

Petronius Longus reached into the ox cart and quietly buckled on his sword.

I would have followed suit, but just then a man appeared in the tumbledown abode. Above three snaggled wooden entrance steps, with rotten treads, it had a two-part stable door. Without warning, he looked out through the top. Perhaps he had heard us coming. Obviously he had seen us now.

Petronius and I at once strode forward to speak to him. Wild barking announced that a vile-tempered dog was behind the lower section of the door, desperate to attack us. The man wore a filthy sleeveless tunic, a week-old beard and a scowl. No chance of a civilised traveller–host relationship here: he wasn't going to ask us in for pastries in a mock-marble peristyle. When Petro said we had come from Rome—a pedigree that must have been obvious—without a word, the rude householder swung back the lower door so that a powerful, ragged mastiff came bounding down the steps in a slather of rabid froth and sheer blind rage.

Justinus and Lentullus rushed forward. As always in a crisis, Lentullus knew no fear; he acted before he thought, then he fainted with terror afterwards. That was how he had nearly lost his leg. Now he grabbed the ferocious, snarling dog with both hands around its neck as it leapt at us. He hung on, intent on saving his beloved master. The man from the shack loped after the dog and lunged for it feebly; more by luck than judgement, he looped a chain around its heavy neck and clapped on a padlock. 'Good boy, Fangs! He's just being friendly,' he mumbled, in the manner of all lacklustre owners. He had no understanding of his dog's capabilities and strength, no hope of controlling it. He would be lucky if he wasn't found one day, savaged to death by his own animal.

We stepped away. The berserk Fangs was now straining to drag his chain free of the big tree to which its other end was fixed. He so much wanted to kill us, he seemed likely to strangle himself. We would have no qualms about letting him. Thwarted, he started hurling himself at the tree.

'Sorry, I forgot he was there. We don't see many people and he gets excitable. Quiet, boy!'

There was no way the dog could be silenced, until the owner lobbed half an old amphora at him. It missed. The weighty crock could well have cracked the canine skull. Fangs seemed to know about this wine-jar trick. Immediately he piped down and slunk to the base of the tree where he just sat, bored and whining.

We all stood in the clearing and went through introductory formalities.

'I am Probus, one of the Claudii,' said the man from the shack. 'I expect you have heard of us.' He folded his arms and stared, not openly hostile yet proud of their notoriety.

'One of the brothers?' asked Petronius, not denying we had been told about these people.

'That I am.'

'Are you the family spokesman?'

'Can be.'

'Do any of the rest live around here?'

'Several.'

'Give me some names?' Petro appeared quite patient, though I thought he wanted to kick this swamp slug in the throat. In Rome he would have had the bastard up against a wall; the problem here was lack of walls. Nobody wanted to go near the tree where Fangs was chained. Pushing a suspect hard up against the shack would most likely cause the whole wreck to keel over.

'Names?' Probus gave Petro a slow look, then wiped his nose on where his sleeve would be if he had sleeves. His arm was hairy enough, and muscular. He slouched like a wimp, but I bet he fought dirty. 'Names, eh?' He was medium height, well built in a slovenly way, with his belt drooping to groin level and a small paunch hanging over it. 'Everyone around here knows who we are.'

'I come from Rome,' Petronius told him again in a mild tone. 'SPQR. I'd like to hear some details.'

'I'm very busy,' Probus boasted. 'No time to draw a family tree.'

'And there are a lot of you, I gather.' Petronius still sounded friendly. I was waiting for him to explode. A cloud of midges began to swirl in front of my face and I biffed at them in irritation. 'Did I hear of twenty siblings?'

'Justus was the eldest—' Probus counted on his filthy fingers. He had on a silly face, playing clever bastards. I felt my attitude harden.

This could be the swine who had tortured a man for remonstrating about a trespass, beat him, cut off his extremities and left him to moulder. The gods only knew what had been done afterwards to the missing wife. That probably happened close to here.

'Go on,' Petro encouraged him, far too politely.

'Justus dropped dead last year—according to you lot, he probably died of a bad conscience. Then two girls, me, Felix—Felix, the happy and fortunate—and a clever little sod too; well we lost him early, naturally . . . another sister, the twins Virtus and Pius, and Era, then triplets who all died at birth, Providentia, Nobilis—he's the one you people usually blame, every time an apple falls from a tree and the owner squeals, *Those Claudii stole it!*—'

I had had enough. Probus continued his long list, but his sly, teasing attitude was more than I could take. Every name made me angrier. 'Let's stop messing about!' Petronius snatched at my arm but I shook him off. 'Probus, you know why we have come. A body was found; it was not pretty. Stop lying and admit that Modestus and his wife came here to complain.'

I strode forward. The thug stepped back in mock alarm. 'Oh they came!' he delighted in telling me. His black teeth showed in a gleeful grin. 'And they're not here now—however many of you cocky Romans barge about looking for them!'

That was all he said, because I socked him. I hit him low and hard, then as he doubled up, I struck again. If I had been alone with him, I would have carried on for half an hour. I felt so much aggression, I startled myself.

'Falco!'

Petro and one of the others dragged me off. 'Don't make me wish I hadn't let you come,' muttered Lucius Petronius, eye to eye with me and speaking low.

I wrenched free and stumbled away from him. Then I left him to deal with it. I walked off stiffly into the forest by myself.

20

I strode through the woods in a straight line. No point getting lost. When I came upon a path, I poked a stick in the ground, upright, to show me where to turn on my way back. I had no plan. I was not following the precept that sometimes on a bogged-down investigation, striking out blind can lead you to a clue. I was just overwrought.

I had calmed down by the time I came across more marsh-dwellers.

I walked into a similar campsite, just as poor as the last, just as untidy, just as unedifying. It had scenic advantages, however. It looked out on fields, for one thing. They were not bad fields either, my country background told me that, though their boundary fences were in a bad state.

Three horrible hutments, arranged in a rough triangle, formed a kind of shabby hamlet, not one to feature in a tourists' guidebook. What distinguished these from Probus' lair was that each had a couple of beaten-up chairs outside for admiring the view or making it easier to shout abuse at the sky. Each had a washing line. No man who cultivates a reputation as a dangerous long-term pest pegs out his smalls. So a couple of the Claudius women were in view, one slowly hanging up limp garments, another seated in a dispirited pose on the steps of what was probably her home. Her cowed demeanour suggested she was not allowed to use the chairs. On a nearby patch of ground, some tousled children were kicking a bucket about; I counted four though from the racket there could be others.

The girl with the laundry had the thin body of a child of fourteen and the face of someone two or three decades older. Pain lurked in her eyes. It would stay there. She had seen things she would never forget but she was never going to share them. Her drab dress was short, shapeless, frayed, a grey piece of rag that looked older than she was. Nonetheless, she wore a string of crude stone beads and even a bangle that could pass for gold for a pawnbroker who was ninety and short-sighted. Some man who wanted to signify she had a lot to be grateful for had given her those. She should have thrown them back and got free of him.

Surprisingly, the women did not take offence that I had stepped out of the undergrowth. It did not mean they would be helpful.

'The name's Falco. I'm looking for Nobilis.' No surprise at that, it seemed. 'I think I took a wrong turn. You're . . . ?'

'Plotia,' said the one with laundry. 'You want Nobilis?' She nodded to the centre shack. I had the impression it was empty. 'Gone away.'

'Beach holiday at Baiae?'

'Gone to visit his grandma.'

'Is that a joke? I hear he's a tough nut.' Plotia just stared.

I walked closer. After the incident with Fangs, I looked around, in case there were other guard-dogs. Reading my thoughts, Plotia said, 'We never have animals.' Her gaze flickered; she stated sombrely, 'Well not for long.'

I swallowed. Petronius once told me that pathological murderers tend to start their killing sprees while they are children. Find a man who takes prostitutes off the streets as a personal vocation, and he'll probably have a set of neat jars with his childhood collection of dissected rats. I had suggested all boys are curious about dead animals. Petro said most just pick them out of the gutter; we don't trap them on purpose and deconstruct them. Most of us don't eviscerate our own pets.

'What is your connection to the Claudii?' I asked the women.

'I'm married to Virtus.' It was still Plotia answering. 'Byrta belongs to Pius.' *Belongs to* was a term that would have delighted our ancestors; my Helena would disdain it. [Note to scribe: delete that 'my'. I don't want my balls pickled.]

Before I could ask, Plotia added, 'Both not here. Pius and Virtus work up in Rome.'

That was news. Petronius would be sure it was not good news.

'I'm from Rome.' I played friendly. 'What do your men do there?'

Plotia just shrugged. A Roman wife may be her husband's closest confidante in theory, but not around here. I guessed marriage was a one-sided contract among the Claudii. Wives had to take foul language, thrashing and forced sex, if I was any judge. Then they bore endless children, who were battered and buggered too. They would all learn to keep their heads down, to judge carefully from bad moods what it was safe to say or do, and never to ask questions. They were bound to have been ordered not to talk to strangers.

Many a slave knew that existence. Maybe it was how the Claudius men had learned to impose themselves on weaker souls.

'Nobilis have a wife?' I asked.

'She left.' At the mention of escape, Plotia looked jealous. Even Byrta perked up. From her perch she was listening to everything. 'He never recovered.'

'I bet there was all Hades of a row.' Plotia laughed briefly. 'Still, she got away from him?' Neither woman reacted to the way I phrased it. 'Where did she go?'

'No idea.' That meant not allowed to tell. 'Nobilis knows. Antium, I think. She set up with someone else, so Nobilis stopped that—'

'Really! How?'

'The usual way!' Plotia said scornfully. 'The girl took refuge with her father afterwards, I heard.'

'What's her father's name—and *her* name?'

Plotia and Byrta glanced at each other. This information must be on the banned list. Nonetheless Plotia told me the father was a baker called Vexus. The wife was Demetria.

'Does Nobilis now accept her going?'

'Yes—if "accept" means constantly saying he'll get the girl one day.'

I sighed. 'When did they split?'

'Three years ago.' And it still rankled with the husband? Demetria must be a brave soul to break free of that control. Or was she so badly crushed that *anything* was better than life with Nobilis?

'If that's his house, can I have a look round?'

'He won't like it,' Plotia said flatly. Strangely, she then made no objection. It might be part of the Claudian plan to appear helpful whenever they were directly confronted. I took my chance and went to the door. It was unlocked—almost a jeering invitation to search. Even at that point, entering the house Nobilis lived in sent a shiver down my spine.

I wondered if the posse from Antium had searched here. It must have done them no more good than it did me. The freedman's house was crammed with stuff with an obsessive neatness. The collection of rubbish looked as if Nobilis had lined it up in rows, just waiting to upset enquirers by failing to provide clues.

Plotia came to the door behind me. She was gazing around as if she too had never stepped inside before. 'He keeps everything. He's got stuff that goes back decades.'

That was true, but if Nobilis killed Modestus, he had not kept the statue-seller's lapis lazuli signet ring. There were no locks of hair from victims, no lovingly cared for boxes of different girls' underwear. I found no old calendars with scored marks to signify killing days. No bloodstained weapons. No ropes with cut ends that could be matched to ligatures around dead men's necks.

I had been an informer long enough to expect disappointment.

I searched until I had had enough, then I came back outside.

'Find anything?' called Plotia, now squatting alongside her sister-in-law, with the early evening sun on her face.

'No. Does Nobilis have anywhere else he hangs out? Some special annexe, where he plays boys' games alone?'

Both women merely gave me odd looks.

This place was a shack to me, but maybe it had a subsidiary hovel, some even more secret hideaway where Nobilis committed his worst deeds. If so, either he kept it from his relatives or they were playing dumb. 'Just one last thing—did either of you see the quarrel with a neighbour called Modestus?' Both Plotia and Byrta shook their heads, rather too quickly. 'You know who I mean?' I insisted. 'He disappeared after a bust-up here, then his wife came to look for him and now she's missing too.' When the women continued to blank me, I said in a sombre voice, 'Modestus is dead. Murdered—on a journey to petition the Emperor. This isn't going away, so you may as well tell me. You still deny seeing the argument?'

'Probus and Nobilis talked to the old man.' For the first time Byrta found her voice. She had a common country accent and her attitude was the wrong side of aggressive. 'It did get heated—Modestus was an idiot, and pushy with it. Our lads never did anything to him. He just went away.'

'You sure of that?' I don't know why I bothered asking. I included Plotia in the question; she was keeping quiet now. She looked away and I knew she was not going to help me. 'Nobilis and Probus were the ones Modestus argued with?'

'They never touched him,' repeated the pale, thin woman as if this was a religious chant and if she said a word wrong, some sacrifice would be invalidated.

'That right? I'll be off then.'

'We'll tell the boys you came!' Plotia mocked my wasted effort.

'Don't do that, please. If there's talking to do, I'd rather do it myself.'

Then, Plotia and I shared a brief glance. It was possible I had made a connection with at least one of these drear, isolated women—some bond that might help our investigation later.

More likely, she was just thinking I was an idiot.

21

I met my companions as I walked back through the woods.

'Next time you want to play good officer/bad officer,' Petro rebuked me mildly, 'let's agree it in advance, shall we? You know I hate always being the nice fellow. When is it my turn to put the boot in?'

I asked if his being sweet to Probus had achieved anything; he growled, 'Guess!'

'I wish I'd hit him harder, then.'

'Yes, if it helped whatever's eating you!' He knew what that was. Petronius was a loyal, affectionate family man. He knew I had grief I had not yet dealt with, and I was guilty about leaving home.

He smacked me on the shoulder, then we walked side by side. The others watched us warily, letting Petro play nurse. I outlined what the women had told me, not that it moved us forward.

The others had been carrying out sweeps, searching the woods in wide circles, looking for bodies. We went back along the path, passing the three hutments. Justinus stayed there to search the two women's homes with Auctus, one of the vigiles. The rest of us moved forward.

Looking for a good spot to camp because there was no chance we could return to Satricum that night, we were heading for what seemed to be more open country. Justinus and Auctus caught us up, having also had a fruitless search at the shacks. We kept moving along the boundary fence, distancing ourselves from where the Claudii lived. We found a place where the fence had been broken down and rebuilt; a notice had been erected on the far side, warning off trespassers in the name of Julius Modestus. Despite its fierce semi-legal language, only a short way further on we came upon another boundary breach. A group of wild-looking cattle which probably belonged to the Claudii stood on the Modestus land, eyeing us inquisitively.

No one said anything, but we kept going, rather than pitch camp too close to the big-horned beef.

We had a tent, but the ground was too wet and spongy for pegs to grip so we just hung an awning off the side of Nero's cart. As dusk drew in, I fetched out the ointment Helena had provided. This time there was no grumbling. As insects bothered us incessantly, we all dipped our fingers in the pot and slathered it on. Everyone tugged down their tunic cuffs and tightened their neck-scarves.

We lit a fire, which may have kept off some of the wildlife, though there was still plenty. We ate a nearly silent supper, not even discussing our plans for tomorrow, because we had none. Any chance of sleep was finished off by hundreds of croaking frogs. Then cattle turned up too, splashing, huffing and coughing, sounding enormous as they do in the dark. The vigiles jumped up from time to time, to shoo beasts away. Groaning, we tossed and turned all night, between bouts of miserable scratching.

At first light, people made a move stiffly. Basic ablutions were tackled. Lentullus, a shy soul, went off by himself. Soon a frightened shout alerted us: the Claudius cattle had found him in mid-pee. Although he was country-born, he was no match for these mad-eyed, jittery bullocks and heifers, who were galloping around trying to herd him against the fence. His bad leg had stopped him escaping fast enough.

'Typical Lentullus!' muttered Justinus, as we all set off to rescue him. It took a while. We had to drive the cattle to the far side of the boundary fence, then we clambered over it and left them safely out of reach. Behind us, they lowed hoarsely in frustration.

When we made it back to camp, we found a disaster. Straight away we saw that our ox was missing.

'Was he loose?'

'He was not!' Rectus was quick to clear himself of blame. 'I had him hitched to the cart.'

The cart was still there, along with some of our kit, though it was strewn around. The vigiles' two mules, who were almost uncatchable, stood under a tree looking on.

'How could strangers get Nero to go with them?'

'A bucket of feed would have him trotting off without a murmur.'

We searched around, following deep, water-filled hoofprints, but the trail lost itself in the maquis. Now we were stuck: miles from anywhere in a dangerous marsh that was inhabited by criminals of every type, knowing somebody must have been watching us—and they had stolen our ox.

22

We did keep searching as long as it was feasible. Several more days passed, but we lost heart now we were walking and carrying all our kit. We still had our mules, though once we lost Nero, Corex and Basiliscus had odd looks in their eyes as if they wished they had bolted; Corex had never been a group player anyway. We had to abandon the cart, another expensive loss for the Petronius brothers. Our task came to seem pointless. Nothing that bore any relation to a crime scene turned up. Looking for corpses in that sodden, scratchy, empty area was hopeless. The marshes were endless, horrible, ominous. Without a definite lead, we could wear ourselves out until the flies and disease finished us, yet achieve nothing. Depressed beyond bearing, we took a vote and agreed to give up. We had done our best. We had done more than anybody else had ever bothered to do.

The trip back took a long time and the first stage, heading back to Satricum, made us more sore-hearted than anything. When, still humping our packs, we passed the shack where Claudius Probus lived, he sniggered openly. He blamed the ox theft on the bandits who were supposed to have colonised the marshes. Curiously, we never saw any sign of such bandits. My guess was that the Claudii had seen off all the competition in these parts years ago. Most bandits are cowards, who avoid serious confrontation.

When we reached the good road and collapsed at the Satricum inn, the landlord expressed great surprise to see us. However, he was eager to hire us extra mounts, and very conveniently had some donkeys available; the two vigiles went with him to inspect them. Petronius sat set-faced, glaring as if he now thought the landlord was responsible for our loss of Nero.

Helena's brother Justinus went indoors to talk to the waitress, Januaria; neither Petro nor I had the heart. He returned looking thoughtful. 'She was talking about foreigners—that's anyone they don't count as local, I suppose. Some foreigners who take a road through the marshes don't come back; well, not this way.'

'That is because they have had their transport stolen!' Petro snarled.

Quintus and I exchanged glances. If the girl had made him think what she said was significant, I trusted him.

Petronius continued to resist. 'You head south, because you're going south. When you get there, that's where you want to be. So you stay there. In the south.'

'Logical,' I cracked. 'For simpletons!' I was feeling tetchy myself.

He carried on ranting. 'It follows that miserable inn-folk to the north don't see you again. They won't see *me* again either, once I get back to Rome.' Petro took a swig of wine from his beaker, spat, slammed down the cup in high disgust, then strode out, shouting to us all to move. He had had enough of the countryside. He was going home.

Petronius Longus and Petronius Rectus drove us all mad, maundering on at one another about the value of their stolen ox and abandoned cart. At least that ended when Rectus took his leave at the Via Appia. He returned to his farm in the Lepini hills. 'He was my bloody ox as well!' shouted Lucius Petronius after his departing brother.

I knew why he was so livid. The theft showed him up. He expected another ear-bashing from the cousins who owned part-shares in Nero. They were bound to suggest that an officer of the Roman vigiles ought to be able to hang on to his draught animal, especially when stuck in the middle of wetlands that were famous for criminal activities. 'My barmy brother was in charge of him—I should have known what was coming!'

I was welcomed home quietly. Helena had a sniff at me to ensure I had been using the anti-insect ointment. Ever the thoughtful husband, I had made sure I rubbed in some more just before I turned my door key. Helena herself was still subdued. Once we would have rushed straight into bed together, but with the baby's death so recent that would not happen.

I prowled around, checking the house. Things seemed well under control. Helena ran a good household and she had grown up in a senator's house, full of staff. Slaves from Pa's house were being tried out here a few at a time. I had never been able to buy good ones because I found the process so uncomfortable, but these seemed to know what was expected of them.

'Just tell me which you want to keep,' I told her, discussing slaves in order to avoid more painful subjects. Tired as I was, I raised a laugh. 'I can't believe I said that!'

'All you need to decide,' Helena answered drily, 'is whether you intend to continue your old frugal life, or should I now plan domestic extravagance and show-off socialising? We need more style. I changed from pottery beakers on the breakfast table—Gaius found some flagrant gilded goblets at the warehouse that I think will pass as morning water cups, though they won't do when we are entertaining consuls and international trade moguls.'

'Oh I leave all that to you, fruit. Don't skimp; just commission new from the most fashionable designer.'

Helena continued the joke. 'I'm so glad you said that. I've found a man who does the most *marvellous* art glass. I think it is important, Marcus, that our girls grow up knowing the finer things in life—even if they promptly break it . . .'

We tired of playing games. I flopped on a couch and Helena knelt to help pull my boots off. She was simply dressed for home in a long white tunic, with plaited hair just wound in a circle and secured with one long bone pin. My real wealth lay in the love in her eyes. I knew that.

Albia was still moping; she had stopped throwing perfume bottles at the wall, though she had taken to disappearing out of the house for long periods. Perhaps she went walking by the river, wafting along like a water sprite wronged by some heartless god. When she did come home, Helena suspected she was writing screeds of tragic poetry. 'I blame myself, Marcus; I gave her the education. Is this to be the Empire's heritage: putting barbarians at a social disadvantage—yet equipping them to complain?'

'Any further visits from Aelianus to inflame things?'

'No; he's busy. Father decided that now both Aulus and Quintus are married, it is make or break time to put them up for the Senate.' That was all I needed: electioneering. Helena grimaced too. 'I mentioned that it would be inconvenient for you, just when you are tied up with the legacy and need them to assist in your casework. But Papa is giving them one last chance to become respectable—he hopes to inveigle Minas of Karystos into a financial contribution.'

I scoffed. 'We know Minas better than that, I think!'

'Yes, he is as much use to Aulus as an in-law as he was as a professor. I suppose it has struck you,' Helena murmured warily, 'that *you* are now in line to be badgered for money, Marcus.'

'What? Everyone always supposed I wanted your father to pay *my* debts. Can the senator now be hoping to sponge off me?'

'I believe he may try to talk to you,' Helena admitted, smiling.

Thank you, Geminus. Now I was a plebeian-born, middle-class upstart who had to play banker to his aristocratic relatives. 'Will it cause a family crisis if I say get lost?'

'Not from me,' said Helena. 'Neither of my ridiculous brothers is fit to govern a beanfield, let alone the Empire.'

'Then they will sail into the Senate. Perhaps I *should* make an investment, then demand political favours from them? If a bunch of ex-slaves living on frogspawn can have friends in high circles, why not me?'

'You don't need favours from anybody, Marcus.'

I kept my head down for a few days. Life ran its usual furrow in the Aventine, though his tribune was back, so Petronius Longus had too much work at the station house. Invigorated by the sea air of Positanum, Rubella started sniping because Petro kept nipping off to the Forum Boarium, the riverside cattle market, to scrutinise any animals that came in. 'Just in case Nero turns up.'

'Nero's long gone,' I snapped, for which I received a mouthful of bad language. Fine. I told the high-handed Petronius that I had plenty to do at the Saepta Julia. So I immersed myself in my own business. We were not estranged, just having one of those tussles that keep a good friendship fresh.

Without my restraining presence, Petronius Longus chalked up a 'missing' poster in the Forum. It gave Nero's identifying features: answered to Spot, left-hander when yoked in a pair, dun coloured, four legs, tail, left-eye squint. Petro even drew a mug-shot. His depiction of Nero's perpetual line of dribble was particularly sensitive, in my opinion. I saw two granary clerks almost wetting themselves as they guffawed over the artwork, but they took it more seriously when they saw what size reward my stubborn friend was offering.

He was presented with a lot of mangy animals by rustlers who had just 'found' oxen wandering, but never his own.

The day I saw the poster, I was at the Forum to meet my banker, that morose ledger-fixer, Nothokleptes. His fingers could fiddle an abacus like no other's. He wanted to hire me a larger bankbox (for which there would be a larger fee) while I needed to explain that my sudden acquisition of large sums was not due to illegal money-lending scams or fraud on twittering old widows. Nothokleptes was quickly convinced I was legit; with a fine grasp of Roman nomenclature, he stopped referring to me as 'Falco, you shameless bankrupt' and now schmoosed, 'Marcus Didius, my dear respected client'. He claimed he had always known I would come good, though I had no recollection of this astrological forecast in the long dark days when I was begging for credit.

I still had to get used to my new position. I admit I was surprised when Nothokleptes seated me at a little bronze-legged table and sent out a lad to buy me a custard pastry. It was soggy, with not enough nutmeg topping, but I saw that my financial fortunes must have officially turned around. Thanks again, Pa!

Mellowed by egg custard, though with mild indigestion, I climbed up the Aventine to visit my mother. She was out, putting the world to rights. So I called at the house nearby where Petro and Maia now lived. She said he was sleeping. Then she backed me into a daybed on their sun terrace and forced a dish of salted almonds on me. I was beginning to see why men of wealth were also men of girth.

'Lucius has come home from Latium in a foul mood, and it can't just be losing that ridiculous ox. I blame you, Marcus!' Maia tolerated me more than my other sisters did, but she followed the trend. Petro's first wife, Arria Silvia, always thought I was a bad influence. That was even though, according to me, our worst adventures had always been his idea.

'I never did anything!' Why did a discussion with relatives always make me sound like a truculent five-year-old?

'I suppose that's what the low-lifes in the marshes all said too! Lucius keeps mum, but I can tell you got nowhere. You'll have to buck up,' Maia instructed me. She was a decent sort, when not being abrupt, hasty-tempered, condemnatory and unreasonable. That was her good side; her wild side was frightening. 'Get this case moving, will you?'

'It's his case.'

'He's your responsibility.'

'No—he's thirty-six years old and a salaried officer. Besides, he wasn't even my responsibility when we were young soldiers drinking our way across Britain while the tribes rampaged around us.'

'I can't live with him this grouchy,' Maia insisted. 'You're supposed to be the investigator, so stop loafing and get sleuthing.'

I promised I would, but sloped off home. Helena was slightly more sympathetic—if only because she felt her role was to appear always more rational than my female relatives. Putting their noses out of joint with her blameless serenity was, according to Helena, in the noble tradition of Cornelia, the mother of the Gracchi, every wise matron's heroine.

'You are not going to send me out pavement-bashing with a flea in my ear, I hope, darling?'

'Of course not.' Helena paused. 'Though I am *very* surprised, Marcus, that you have made *no* attempt to find those Claudii who work in Rome, or learn where Claudius Nobilis went off to!'

I knew when I was beaten. I crawled out of the house like a slug with a spade put halfway through him.

I had no intention of being bossed. Pa, who knew just how to live a worthwhile masculine life, had bequeathed me one thing of greater worth than its book-value: I now possessed his bolt-hole. As nonchalantly as possible, I took myself to the Saepta Julia.

Now I was so prosperous, I even had two bolt-holes. I was still paying rent on a cubbyhole Anacrites and I once hired, back when we were working on tax matters. I had affection for the place that had acquired me middle rank. I was using it now for the legacy paperwork, so it was stuffed with scrolls and piteous pleas for the inheritance tax clerks to give me time to pay. I didn't need more time, but today Nothokleptes had impressed upon me the need to delay bills so he could invest the capital in short-term sure prospects. 'The more you have, the more you can make, young Falco. You realise that, surely?' I certainly realised the more I had, the more my banker could cream off for himself. 'Only the destitute pay up prompt, for fear they won't have any money later.'

I had told Nothokleptes I would have to get used to this principle—but that I was a fast learner.

I sat in the cubbyhole, thinking, until boredom took over. Then I sauntered along the Saepta's upper gallery, enjoying the vibrant life going on at this level and below, just as Pa used to do. I could see why he loved this place. There was never a dull moment, as fat jewellers and paranoid goldsmiths swaggered around trying to bamboozle would-be customers, while pickpockets tailed the customers and guards wondered absently whether to tackle the pickpockets. There were constant cries from food-sellers who wandered the building with gigantic trays or weighed down by garlands of drink flagons. Wafts of grilled meat and suet patties vied with the reek of garlic and the stench of pomade. Every now and then some man of note—or a nobody who thought he was one—pressed through the throng with a train of arrogant slaves in livery, trailing sweaty secretaries and put-upon fan-danglers. Disdainful locals refused to be pushed around, resulting in loud altercations.

I enjoyed watching the gallery rage, then stepped over a vagrant and entered the office. My nephew Gaius, Galla's second eldest, was loafing there. He looked me over. 'You don't want to waste your time here, Uncle Marcus. Why not give me a couple of thousand a week and I'll run the place for you?'

He was at an indefinable point in his late teens, old enough to be useful, not old enough to trust. He looked like a tattooed barbarian, though with infected sores where the woad should be. He was a sweetie underneath; we sometimes used him for babysitting.

'Thanks for the kind offer, Gaius. I don't need help. We just put chipped old pots on show by the door and idiots rush in to pay huge sums for them.'

Gaius dropped into a stone throne, his favourite lounger, where he spread himself like a potentate. He was drinking Pa's flagon of Campagnan red, supposedly kept for celebrating big auction gains or for numbing the pain of losses. He waved me to a cheery cup that advised me to drink now for I would die tomorrow; as I poured a tot, Gaius warned me in serious tone, 'You want to take a lot of water with that, Uncle Marcus. It's probably too strong for you.'

'Yours is neat?'

'But I am used to it,' smiled Gaius. His brass-necked cheek came straight from my louche brother Festus, from Pa, and a long line of previous Didii. I made no attempt to remonstrate. Like Lucius Petronius, I was thirty-six and had learned when there was no point arguing.

We talked, with surprising sense from Gaius, about an auction held in my absence. 'Things are looking up again, no question. People stayed away to begin with, thinking nothing would be the same without Grandpa, but customers are trickling back.'

'They are learning you're up to it. One or two may even have heard good things about me.'

'Don't bank on that, Uncle Marcus! Yet again, we failed to shift that two-handed urn with the centaurs battling, but that's been around for over a year; the artwork's crap and people are bored with the subject. I'm going to organise fake bidders next time. See if we can force some interest.'

'Geminus didn't really want to sell that pot,' I said. 'It hung on so long, he grew fond of it.'

Young Gaius shook his head like a Greek sage. 'There's no scope for sentiment in this business!' Then, to my surprise, he asked shyly whether Helena and I were getting over the baby, and complimented me on my handling of Pa's funeral and memorial dinner.

Business over, I called in a passing peddler, bought Gaius a flatbread stuffed with chickpeas, and left him to it.

I sauntered back towards the centre of town, passing the Theatre of Balbus and the Porticus of Octavia as if I had no clear idea where I was going. I had made up my mind, however. I turned away from the river, then climbed up to the Palatine via the Clivus Victoriae. I gained entrance by telling the guards I needed to see Claudius Laeta. But I was going to see Momus.

23

'Falco! You cack-handed, two-timing, pompous backstairs bastard—seems a century since I laid eyes on your ugly bum-crack!' Momus represented the refined element of the Palatine.

He was sprawling on a bench like a big blob of sea anemone, one that had let itself go. Even his headlice were low-grade. He had a paper of nuts lying next to him, but was too lethargic to dip in and munch. 'Torpor' would have been his cognomen, had he been refined enough to want his entitlement to three names.

Thinking about imperial freedmen, as I was for the case, I asked him what family name he used. Momus gave me a wide shrug, astonished anybody asked that question. He was so informal he had never bothered to work out his nomen.

'Who was on the throne when you got your cap of liberty?'

'Some useless pervert.'

'Sounds like Nero.'

'Probably the Divine Claudius.' Momus made 'Divine' sound like an obscenity, which in the case of that old duffer Claudius it traditionally was.

I leaned on a wall, as far away from his body odour as I could get without retreating into the corridor. There was nowhere to sit. Most people who came to see Momus were slaves he was brutalising. He didn't offer them a stool for beatings and buggery. He might be as low as a palace officer could get, but he was one level up from them so he took the traditional seat of power while they cringed in whatever desperate position he chose for them and waited for their punishment.

'So were you a contemporary of an obnoxious bunch of imperial freedmen called the Claudii? Most live in the Pontine Marshes, though I'm told they have connections with Rome.'

Momus took a long time rubbing his bleary eyes, then surprisingly he said no.

I said quietly, 'I thought you were famous for knowing the entire *familia*?'

He pulled a face. He was not intending to help me. That was unusual. Normally our loathing of Anacrites and our distrust of Laeta made us allies.

'Somebody knows them,' I said. '*Somebody* is rumoured to protect them.'

'Not me, Falco.'

'No, I never saw you as the patron type!' Even just talking to Momus always made me feel I had let down my own moral standards. I may be an informer but I do have some.

Momus laughed, but no ice was broken in his reception of my joke.

'Half the towns in Latium are shit-scared of treading on their nasty toes,' I told him. 'And you claim you don't know them? Leaving me no choice, old crony, but to suppose you must be shit-scared of this *somebody* who watches over them.'

Momus did not move a muscle.

I blew out my cheeks slowly, as if impressed by the scale of the problem. That was easy. I was genuinely marvelling. Momus liked to be outspoken. His silence was not part of his routine sea-anemone lolling. If he had had tentacles, he would have stopped waving them as soon as I mentioned the Claudii. Momus was taking a lot of trouble to show no reaction, but his grime-engrained skin acquired extra sheen. I could have wiped his greasy, sweating face and then oiled a wheel-axle with the rag.

Eventually he growled, 'Don't mess with this, Falco. You're too young and sweet.'

He was being ironic, but the warning had a note of real concern. I thanked him for the advice and took myself to see Laeta.

I knew he would be there. In the first place, he enjoyed pretending his burden of work was terrible—and in the second, he really was the most important scroll-bug in the imperial bureaux. At this time in the summer, the betting was that all three of his masters, Vespasian and both his sons, were taking their ease at some family villa, perhaps out in the Sabine hills where they originated. When that happened, Claudius Laeta was left at the Palatine to run the Empire smoothly. Few people ever noticed that power was temporarily in his hands.

As an informal gesture to the fact that it was after business hours, Laeta had a singer intoning an epode. The musician was heavily em- phasising the iambic trimeters and dimeters in a long, slow, lugubrious piece that used the style aficionados call affected archaism. It was music you could never dance to, nor would it lull you to sleep, raise your spirits or encourage a fine-featured woman to sleep with you. Laeta had one finger placed against his brow to indicate subconscious delight. I wondered why men who listen to such torture always think themselves so superior.

The Dorian dirge subsided. Laeta had made an almost impercep- tible gesture, so the singer left. Going voluntarily saved him having me drag him outside and bind him by his tasselled wristbands to a fast-moving cart.

'I'm glad you dropped by, Falco.' Always a bad start.

Laeta then told me that Anacrites was back from whatever mis- sion the Emperor had let him loose to ruin. Instead of waiting for more orders, the Chief Spy had taken it upon himself to follow up the Modestus case. 'I have informed Marcus Rubella he can drop the investigation,' said Laeta, barely looking up from his deskful of documents.

'That stinks!'

'It's a done deal, Falco.'

'You think Anacrites is fit for this?' I demanded.

'Of course not.' At this point, Laeta did look up and meet my eyes. His were clear, cynical and unlikely to be swayed by protests. 'Think yourself lucky, Falco. Tell your vigiles friend too. This case may go very mouldy before it's over. If the spy thinks he wants the job, that's typical of his misjudgement—but let him go ahead and bungle it. We can all watch Anacrites get nasty black squid ink down one of those barley-coloured tunics he insists on wearing.'

Laeta always wore white. Classic. Expensive and aristocratic. By implication incorruptible—though I had always assumed he was very corrupt indeed.

I dropped my voice. 'What's going on, Laeta?'

He laid down his pen and leaned his chin on his hands. 'Nothing, Falco.'

I folded my arms. 'I can spot official lying. You can tell me the truth. I have the Emperor's confidence. I thought you and I worked from the same order sheet.'

'I am sure we do.' Claudius Laeta gave me the look some bureaucrats use. It made no denial of a cover-up and seemed to assume I knew everything he did. I felt I could see distaste for whatever game Anacrites was playing.

'I thought this was a confidential enquiry. How did Anacrites even find out about it?'

'Your crony Petronius put in a claim for a replacement ox and cart. An auditor strolled up the corridor and mentioned it to the spy.'

'Oh no! I wonder what that was worth? I do see the Treasury will quibble—but the adjudicators are perfectly capable of turning down expenses without bringing in Anacrites. It's nothing to do with him.'

Laeta for once allowed himself to be rude about another official:

'You know how he works. He spends most of his time spying on his colleagues rather than enemies of the state.'

'Shall I challenge him on this?' I asked.

'I advise against.'

'Why?'

Laeta's eyes were keen and oddly sympathetic. 'Take a steer from a friend. Anacrites is always dangerous. If he really feels he wants this work, stand back.'

'That's not my style.'

Laeta leaned back with the palms of his hands on the edge of his table. 'I know it's not, Falco. That's why I am taking the trouble, out of respect for your qualities, to say, just let this one go.'

I thanked him for his concern, though I did not understand it. Then I left his office wondering what exactly the Chief Spy could find fascinating in a bunch of belligerent marshfrogs killing a neighbour in a feud about a boundary fence.

My style was, as Laeta may have realised, to march straight up the corridor to Anacrites' office, intending to ask him.

Once again he was absent.

Two of his men were there this time, eating folded flatbreads. I had seen them before. I reckoned they were brothers, and for no logical reason I had placed them as Melitans. Anacrites had had these idiots watching my house last December. I was looking after a state prisoner temporarily and, in his own tiresome style, he tried muscling in. Just like this, really. If he thought I was being noticed by the Palace, he could never leave me alone.

The legmen had taken over his room as if this was their base, where they were allowed to eat their supper before they were sent out on their next assignment. One was actually sitting in the seat Anacrites normally used. Even spies have to eat. That included the unfortunates Anacrites employed. Any over-familiarity was his problem.

When I looked in, the pair straightened up slightly; they rearranged their foreign-looking features so they seemed helpful, though neither bothered to ask what I wanted. They made vague attempts to hide their vegetable turnovers until they saw I didn't give a damn.

'He's out?'

They nodded. One raised his bread two inches as an affirmative. I didn't ask where he had gone, so they did not need to tell me. They knew who I was. I wondered whether they guessed why I wanted to talk to Anacrites.

He was obsessively secretive, too close to make a good commander. His men probably had no idea what he was up to. That was the problem with him: half the time he didn't know what he was doing himself.

24

For some reason, when I left the Palace, the night seemed full of threats and unhappiness. Rome had its seamy side. I seemed more aware of it tonight. I noticed caterwauling and unhappy cries, both near and distant; there seemed to be a bad smell everywhere, as if while I was in the Palace some major disaster with the drains had occurred. Darkness insinuated lower areas, creating pools of menace where there ought to be streets. Monuments that stood amidst a few lights looked cold and forbidding instead of familiar.

Back at my house, however, there was peace. The children were in bed, perhaps even asleep. Albia was in her room, plotting against Aelianus. The lamplight was mellow, there was food and drink on a side table, a sleepy Nux thumped her tail at my appearance then went straight back to snoring in her happy doggy dreams.

I sat sideways on a reading-couch with a cup of wine in one fist, not even drinking yet. Helena curled up beside me. She was sweet-scented from the baths and now wearing an old, comfortable red gown, no jewellery, with her hair loose. She put a light rug over her bare feet for comfort, wriggling her toes. I looked for signs that her grief for the baby was diminishing; she allowed my scrutiny, though with pinched lips as though she would flare up if I asked the wrong question. But then she took my hand; she was judging my progress back to normality just as I assessed hers. I too concealed my feelings, as I rubbed my thumb over the silver ring on her third finger.

Once we both relaxed, I told her about being pushed to and fro at the Palace. Sharing news was our habit, always had been. I passed on what Laeta and Momus had said, while Helena at first listened. When I ran out of details and sipped my wine slowly, she spoke up.

'Anacrites has commandeered the job because he is jealous, perennially jealous of you—and of your friendship with Petronius. He thinks you have a better life than him. He is afraid you may jostle him aside and gain favours from the Emperor. He wants what you have.'

'I don't see it.' I put down the winecup; Helena reached over and sipped thoughtfully, before replacing the cup. I half smiled but kept talking. 'Sweetheart, he has status; from what I hear, he has money too. Jupiter knows how he got there, but he's top man in intelligence. Even that time he took out of action with his head wound never seemed to affect his position. He has a secure career, salaried and pensioned, very close to Vespasian and Titus—whereas I'm a luckless freelance.'

'He envies your freedom,' Helena disagreed. 'It may be why he tries to sabotage your cases. He realises your talent, hates how you can choose to accept or refuse work. Most of all, Marcus, he longs for you to be his friend. He *loved* working with you on the Census—' He drove me mad on it. 'But he's like an angry young brother, jumping up and down to get your attention.' She had two younger brothers. 'He has done this before to you and Petro. So, treat him like a tiresome brother; just ignore it.'

I went with the simile. 'I don't want the nasty little menace to have a fit and smash my toys!'

'Well, keep your toys on a high shelf, Marcus.'

It was late. We were tired, not exhausted but not yet ready to go up to bed. In a family household, this was a rare moment of quiet. We stayed hand in hand, savouring the situation, re-establishing our strong partnership after a period of upset and absence. Helena caressed my cheek with her free hand; I bent and gently kissed her wrist. We were a man and his wife, at home in private, enjoying one another's presence. Nothing really intimate was occurring—or not yet—but the last thing we wanted was an interruption. So that was when the bastard came, of course.

I mean, Anacrites.

I was dimly aware of noises downstairs—not urgent, no cause for us to involve ourselves. Then a slave I did not remember owning knocked and came in. This was what it meant to be wealthy: total strangers were living in my house, knew who I was, addressed me humbly as their master.

'Sir, will you receive a visitor?'

The visitor must have had a suspicion what my answer would be. He followed the lad and rudely pushed in after him. 'I do apologise for calling so late—I just heard about your father, Marcus. I came immediately!'

Helena murmured, 'Thank you,' to the young slave, so he would know we saw it was not his fault. He slipped away. She and I remained in position just long enough to let anyone less crass than the spy see he was intruding. He had probably come from the office; he even looked around as if hoping for a titbit tray. Failing a guest went against our idea of hospitality, but like stoics we refused to offer him refreshments.

I stood up, sighing openly. A mistake, because it allowed Anacrites to bound right up, grasping my hands in his. I wanted to snatch back my paws, apply them round his beautifully barbered neck and strangle him; but we were standing on an attractive rag rug, and I was reluctant to defile it with his corpse.

'Ah, Marcus, I am *so* sorry for your loss!' He let go of me and turned to Helena who had stayed on the couch out of his reach. 'How is this poor fellow doing?' His voice was doleful with sympathy.

Helena sighed glumly. 'He is managing. The money helps.'

Anacrites took a second to catch on. 'You two! You joke about absolutely everything.'

'Graveyard humour,' I assured him, resuming my place beside Helena. 'A grimace in the teeth of Fate, to hide our desolation. Though as my smart wife says—Geminus left me a stupefying legacy.' I bet Anacrites had made sure he knew that before he came. 'Apart from the inconvenience of probate, rummaging through his coffers does assuage the grief.'

Anacrites took a seat opposite, though we had not invited him to do so. He leaned forwards, elbows on his knees. He was still addressing me with the unbearable earnestness people ladle like sweet sauce over the bereaved. 'I am afraid I never really knew your father.'

'He kept out of the way of people like you.' This was not always true. Once, Pa had thought Anacrites was sniffing too closely around my mother like a gigolo—an idea so unbelievable we had all believed it at the time. My outraged father, taking it personally, rushed to the Palace and took a swipe at the spy. I was there and witnessed the crazy fist-swinging. Anacrites seemed to have forgotten. Perhaps the bad head wound a few years ago excused selective memory loss. It did not, however, excuse anything else he did.

'And how is your dear mother?' He had been Ma's lodger for a time. Though she was so shrewd in many things, she thought he was wonderful. He in turn spoke of her with veneration. He knew it made me sick.

'Junilla Tacita bears her loss with fortitude,' Helena interposed gravely. Anacrites looked at her, grateful to encounter a normal platitude. 'She only gloats in the afternoon; she says in the mornings she's too busy around the house to taunt his ghost.'

I smiled gently at the spy's discomfiture.

He wore an umber-coloured tunic, his idea of sophisticated camouflage. His skin looked strangely plump and smooth; he must have come from the baths. With that oiled hair and a straight bearing, he could be called personable; well, by a woman of the night, with time on her hands and bills to pay. I doubted that any decent woman ever looked at him, not that I had seen him seeking female company since Maia dumped him. I was convinced he had no friends.

He was a strange mixture of competence and ineptitude. Undoubtedly intelligent, he was an able public speaker; I had heard him spout excuses like any clerk covering up his failures. There was no need for him to endure a tiny office and low-grade agents; his was a high public position, attached to the Praetorians; he could have conjured up a decent budget if he had applied himself.

His next foray was to say to Helena, 'I hear your brother is back from Athens—and married! Wasn't that unexpected?'

This was typical. Laeta had said Anacrites only returned to Rome three days ago, yet he had already discovered private facts about my family and me. He pressed too close. If I complained it would sound paranoid, yet I knew Helena saw why I loathed him.

'Who told you that?' She sat up abruptly.

'Oh it's my job to know everything,' Anacrites boasted, giving her a significant smile.

'Surely you should only watch the Emperor's enemies?' Helena retaliated.

'Helena Justina, you were pregnant!' Anacrites exclaimed, wide-eyed, as if it had only just struck him. 'Has the happy event occurred?'

'Our baby died.' I bet the bastard knew that too.

'Oh my dears! Again, I am *so* sorry . . . Was it a boy?'

Helena bridled visibly. 'What does that matter? Any healthy child would have pleased us; any lost child is our tragedy.'

'Such a waste—'

'Don't upset yourself over our private troubles,' Helena said coldly. He had pushed her too far. 'I suppose,' she jibed, 'a man in your position does not know what it is to have family? You must always have looked intelligent. When some unknown slave girl bore you, were you taken up as soon as that was spotted, to be regimented in a soulless stylus-school?'

Anacrites relied on pretending we were all best friends; otherwise, I fancied there might have been real venom in his expression. 'As you say, they could spot potential. I was indeed favoured with government training from a young age,' he replied in a quiet voice. Helena refused to show shame. 'I knew my alphabet at three, Helena—both in Latin and Greek.'

Though she did not remark on it, Helena had already taught our

Julia both alphabets, plus how to write her name in rulered lines. Perhaps she relaxed slightly, however. For one thing, Helena always enjoyed sparring. 'And what else did they teach you?'

'Self-reliance and perseverance.'

'Is that enough for the work you do now?'

'It goes a long way.'

'Do you have a conscience, Anacrites?'

'Does Falco?' he countered.

'Oh yes,' replied Helena Justina sternly. 'He leaves home with it daily, along with his boots and his notebook. That is why,' she said, fixing him with a steady gaze, 'Marcus was so interested in working on the Julius Modestus case.'

'Modestus?' Anacrites' bafflement seemed genuine.

'Compulsory letter-writer,' I put in. 'Dealer from Antium. Found stone dead in a tomb—hands cut off and hideous rites committed—after a squabble with some marsh-waders known as the Claudii.'

I thought Anacrites twitched. 'Oh you were involved with that?' It was disingenuous; he knew it, and looked shifty. 'I pulled back the case from Laeta. He should never have been involved. In fact, I'm glad I've seen you tonight, Falco. I need a handover review. Shall we say mid-morning tomorrow at my office? Bring your vigiles friend.'

So not only was he pinching our case from Petro and me, the unmitigated bastard wanted to pick our brains to help him solve it.

'Petronius Longus works the night shift,' I said curtly. 'He needs his mornings for sleep. You can have us at the start of the evening, Anacrites, or go begging.'

That would give us two time to liaise first.

'As you wish,' responded the spy; he managed to make out I was surly and unreasonable, while he was all sweetness and toleration.

I was burning with frustration, but just then the door of the room crashed open and in flew Albia. 'I heard there was a visitor. Oh!' She must have been hoping for Aelianus.

'This is Tiberius Claudius Anacrites, the Emperor's chief of intelligence,' Helena told her, using over-formality to rile him. 'You met him at Saturnalia.'

'Oh yes.' A friend of her parents: Albia lost interest.

'Why Falco,' the spy then exclaimed. 'Your foster-daughter is growing into a fine young lady!' This was the kind of indefinable threat he had taken to throwing at me. If I ever caught him so much as saying good morning to Albia unsupervised, I would truss him with poultry string and pay to have him cooked in a baker's oven. By the slow-roast method.

'Flavia Albia has led a sheltered life and is extremely shy.' Helena always supported the girl, though sometimes gently teased her. 'But she will be a delicate ornament to womanhood any day now.'

'Well,' Anacrites answered silkily, 'you must bring Flavia Albia with you—oh how silly; I didn't mention this—we have so much catching up to do! I absolutely insist you come to my house for dinner. The formal invitation will be here the minute I can make arrangements.'

I did not bother to decline. But King Mithridates of Pontus had the right idea: the only way I would eat at the spy's house was if I had first spent three months taking antidotes against all known poisons.

'I thought I might lash out on a Trojan hog,' Anacrites confided in Albia, as if they had been close friends for years. He was a man with poor social skills trying to sound big in front of a young girl he thought would be easily impressed; she of course stared at him as if he was crazy. Then she flounced off, slamming the door behind her so hard the pantiles on our roof must be in danger.

As soon as Anacrites had gone, Albia reappeared. 'What is a Trojan hog?'

Helena was dousing lamps as we made our way to bed. 'Exhibit cookery. Only a show-off would serve it. On the principle of the Trojan horse, it carries a secret cargo. A whole pig is cooked then slashed open suddenly at table, so the contents spew out everywhere; the guests think they are being bombarded with raw entrails. The innards are usually sausages.'

Albia considered. 'Sounds brilliant. We had better go to that!'

I groaned.

25

Petronius and I walked into the Palace next evening side by side. We were silent, our tread measured, both outwardly impassive. Anacrites had played this trick on us before. It didn't work then— trust him to repeat the same manoeuvre.

As we neared his office, one of the pair I called the Melitan Brothers came out. When the man drew level, we made space for him to pass us. Afterwards we both stopped, pivoted on our boot heels and stared after him. He managed to keep looking ahead all the way to the end of the corridor, but could not help glancing back from the corner. Petro and I just stood there, watching him. He nipped away out of sight, ducking his head anxiously.

We strode into Anacrites' room without knocking. As Petronius opened the door, he said loudly, 'Standards are slacker than ever. He looks too foreign to be scuttling about like a rat, so near the Emperor—if I had a Palatine remit, I'd make him prove citizenship— or he'd find himself in a neck-collar.'

'Who's your runt?' I demanded of Anacrites. He had been lounging in his usual pose, with his boots—a rather fine pair of russet calfskins—on his desk. He swung rapidly upright, knocking over an inkwell, while his clerk sniggered.

'One of my men—' Petronius guffawed at that, while I winced, miming pity. Anacrites mopped ink, thoroughly flustered. 'Thank you, Phileros!' That was a hint for the clerk, a puffy, overweight Delian slave, to make himself scarce so the spy could talk to us confidentially.

I pretended to think it was an order to fetch refreshments. 'Mine's an almond tart, Petronius likes raisin cakes. No cinnamon.'

Petro smacked his chops. 'I'm ready for that! I'll just have mulsum with it, not warmed too much, double honey. Falco takes wine and water, served in two beakers if they run to it.'

'Hold the spice.' I steered Phileros on his way as if the rest of us needed to get on. The clerk left, and Petronius made a point of closing the door.

It was a small room, and now there were three of us filling it. Petro and I took over. He was a large character, with substantial thighs and shoulders; Anacrites began to feel cramped. If he looked directly at one of us, the other went out of eyeshot, probably making rude hand gestures. I seized the clerk's stool, shoving all his work aside, none too gently.

Then we sat still, with our hands clasped, like ten-year-old girls waiting for a story. 'You first!' ordered Petronius.

Anacrites was beaten. He abandoned any attempt to follow his own agenda. We were all supposed to be colleagues; he could not force us to play straight with him.

'I have read the scrolls—' he started. Petro and I glanced at each other, grimacing as if only a maniac ever read the case papers, let alone relied on them. 'Now I need you to sum up your findings.'

'Findings!' said Petronius to me. 'That's a sophisticated new concept.'

Anacrites was almost pleading with us to settle down.

Abruptly, we became fully professional. We had agreed in advance we would give him no excuse to say we had been uncooperative. I briskly set out that I had encountered Modestus' disappearance through his business deal with my father. I did not mention his nephew, Silanus. Why should I? He was neither a victim nor a suspect.

Petro described the discovery of the corpse and its identification from the letter Modestus was carrying. He spoke in a crisp voice, using vigiles vocabulary. He gave an account of our visit to the Claudii; how we had interviewed Probus; searched the area; found nothing.

'What were you planning next?' asked Anacrites.

'Since the next move is all yours, what do you think?' snapped Petro tetchily.

Anacrites ignored the question. 'Do you have any other leads?'

Petronius shrugged. 'No. We have to sit back and wait until another corpse turns up.'

Anacrites applied a sombre expression, which we dutifully mirrored.

'Look, you can leave this all to me now. I can handle it.' Time would show if that was right. He closed the meeting. 'I hope you two stalwarts don't feel I took your case away.' We refused to look sore.

'Oh, I have plenty to do chasing tunic-thieves at the baths,' sneered Petronius.

'Well, this isn't quite on that level . . .'

'Isn't it?'

Anacrites then brought in the ploy he'd tried on me last night: he mentioned his plans for a dinner party, inviting Petronius too. 'I had such a wonderful time when Falco and Helena entertained me at Saturnalia—' Saturnalia may be a time for patching up feuds, but believe me, I was pushed into that hideous arrangement. 'Such a glorious family atmosphere . . . Have you eaten with them at their house, Lucius Petronius?' Of course he had! He was my best friend, living with my best sister. 'I feel it's time I issued some invitations in return . . .'

Previously noncommittal, Petronius Longus straightened up. He looked the spy directly in his weird eyes, which were almost two-toned, one shifty grey, one browner—and neither to be trusted. He stood up, placed both fists on the spy's table and leaned across, full of menace. 'I live with Maia Favonia,' my pal declared heavily. 'I know what you did to her. So no thanks!'

He strode out.

'Oh dear! I was hoping to smooth over any unpleasantness, Falco!' Anacrites was ghastly when he whined.

'Not possible,' I told him with a sneer, then I followed Petro from the room.

Outside, Phileros was hanging about nervously with such an enormous tray of confectionery his stretched arms could hardly hold it. Petronius cared about the poor, since he so often had cause to arrest them. He had ascertained it was all paid for out of the spy's petty cash, not the shabby clerk's own pocket. So we swept up as many cakes as we could carry, and took them away with us.

We gave them to a tramp, of course. Even if they were not dosed with aconite, to eat anything provided by Anacrites would have choked us.

There was no chance we would allow Anacrites to have our case. Earlier in the day Petronius and I had agreed on the same system as the last time he tried muscling in. We would proceed as normal. We would simply keep out of the spy's view. Once we solved the case, we would report to Laeta.

According to Petro, he had Rubella's support. I did not press for details.

Although we had implied to Anacrites we had reached a dead end, we had plenty of ideas. Petronius had issued an all-cohorts notice to look out for the runaway slave called Syrus, the one who had worked for Modestus and Primilla then was passed on to the butcher by their nephew. Petro's men visited the other cohorts to inspect any slaves they had found roaming. There was another alert too: for the missing woman, Livia Primilla, or more likely her body.

It was too risky to have official warrants for Nobilis or any other Claudii; Anacrites was liable to hear about it. Nonetheless, efforts were being made to trace the couple who were supposed to work in

Rome, using word of mouth among the vigiles. There was also a port watch for Nobilis, arranged through the Customs service and the vigiles out-station at Ostia. Meanwhile Petronius was having his clerk go through the official records of undesirables, looking for members of the family listed in Rome. If the two called Pius and Virtus had become astrologers or joined a weird religious cult, that could turn them up.

Rubella would not permit Petronius to leave Rome again, so I was going back to Antium: I would be looking for the estranged wife of Claudius Nobilis, hoping to hear about life on the inside with the Pontine freedmen.

First, came an assignment close to home. When I returned, Helena met me at the door.

'Marcus, you have to do something and it must be now, while Petronius is at the station house. Your sister sent a message; she sounds upset—'

'What's up?'

'Maia needs to see you. She doesn't want Lucius told, because he will be too angry. Maia had an unwelcome visitor. Anacrites went to see her.'

Never mind Lucius Petronius. I was damned angry myself.

26

My sister Maia Favonia had more locks on her door than most people. She had never recovered from coming home one day a couple of years ago to find everything in her home destroyed and a child's doll nailed up where the knocker had been. Anacrites left no calling card. But he had been haunting her neighbourhood after she split from him; she knew who had given her the warning.

I had moved her out the same night. I took her away with us on a trip to Britain and by the time she came back, she and Petronius Longus were lovers; her children, a bright bunch, had democratically elected that friendly vagabond as their stepfather. Maia took a new apartment, closer to Ma's building. Petro moved in. The children preened. Everything settled down. Even so, Maia installed a tumbler lock and a set of large bolts, and she never opened the door after dark unless she knew who was outside. She had been fearless, happy and sociable. Terror left its marks. Maia would never get over what the spy had done.

Petronius and I had sworn an oath together. One day we would exact retribution.

———

They lived, as most city people did, in a modest apartment. One floor up, a communal well in the courtyard, a small set of rooms to arrange as they liked. Petro, who was handy with a hammer, had fixed the place up in shipshape style. Maia had always had her own casual glamour and, given her work for Pa at the Saepta, she furnished it with dash. Our mother's house centred on its kitchen and a table where onions were always being chopped; Helena and I liked to relax in private in a room where we read together. Any house where Maia lived had a balcony as its heart. There she kept a trough of plants that could survive breezes and offhand treatment, plus battered lounging chairs with mounds of well-squashed cushions, between which was the bronze tripod where she served a constant supply of nuts and raisin cake.

I wondered if Anacrites had been allowed into that insiders' sanctum this time. He knew how things worked. The damage to Maia's previous much-loved sun terrace, when he trashed her place, had been particularly vile.

Helena had come with me tonight. Maia greeted her with a sniff. 'Oh he's brought a woman to worm out all the secrets, has he? You think I'll be softened up by girls' chat?'

Helena gave an easy-going laugh. 'I'll sit with the children.' We had glimpsed them, doing schoolwork in subdued silence: Maia's four, who ranged from six to thirteen, plus Petronilla, Petro's girl, who lived here most of the time now because her mother had a new boyfriend. Petronilla had condemned Silvia's latest conquest as 'a lump of mouldy dough'. She was eleven and already scathing. So far, Petro was still her hero, though he expected daddy's little girl to begin disparaging him any day now.

A shadow darkened Maia's face. 'Yes,' she said urgently. 'Yes, Helena. Do that.' So the children knew Anacrites had been here, and they needed comfort.

I was shepherded to the balcony. Maia closed the folding doors behind us. We sat together, in our usual positions.

– 148 –

'Right. You had a visitation. Tell me.'

Now we were private, I could see how badly Maia was shaken. 'I don't know what he wanted. Why now, Marcus?'

'What did he *say* he wanted?'

'Explaining is not his style, brother.'

I lay back and breathed slowly. Around us were the noises of a domestic district at nightfall. Here on the Aventine, there was always a sense of being high above the city and slightly aside of the centre. Occasional sounds of traffic and trumpets came from a very great distance. Closer to, owls hooted from the gilded roof trees of very old temples. There were all the normal wafts of grilled fish and panfried garlic, the rumpus of angry women berating tipsy men, the weary wails of sick or unhappy children. But this was our hill, the hill where Maia and I grew up. It was a place of augury, foliage gods and slaves' liberation. It was where Cacus the hideous caveman once lived and where the poets' association traipsed about singing silly odes. For us the flavours were subtly distinct from every other Rome region.

'Better start at the beginning,' I told Maia in a quiet voice.

'He came this morning.'

'If I am to evaluate what this bastard is really up to,' I said quietly, 'then start *right* at the beginning.'

Maia was silent. I gazed across at her. Normally you think of your sister as she was at eighteen. Tonight, by the flicker of a pottery lamp, every year was etched on her. I was thirty-six; Maia was two years younger. She had survived a wearisome marriage, births, the death of one daughter, a cruel widowhood and ensuing financial hardship, then a couple of crazy dalliances. There were at least a couple; I was her brother, what would I know? Her worst mistake was when she let Anacrites home in on her.

'You never really told us: was it serious?'

'Not for me.' For once Maia was so unnerved she opened up. 'I met him, you know, after he was hurt and you took him to Mother's to recuperate.' Maia was the kind of daughter who was always popping into Ma's house to share a cabbage—keeping an eye on the old tyrant. 'After Famia died, Anacrites turned up one day. He treated me respectfully—that was a change after Famia using me as a boot scraper for all those years . . .'

'You liked him?'

'Why not? He was well dressed, well spoken, well set up in an official position—'

'Did he tell you about his work?'

'He told me what it was. He never discussed details . . . I was ready,' Maia admitted. 'Ready for a fling.'

I could not resist my next question. Be honest, legate, you would have begged to know too: 'Good lover?' Maia merely stared at me. I cleared my throat and played responsible. 'You made it clear all along that you wanted nothing permanent?'

'At first it could have gone anywhere.' I controlled a shudder. 'But I soon felt he was pressing too close. There was something about him,' Maia mused. 'Something just not right.'

'He's a creep. You felt it.'

'I suppose so.'

'Instinct.'

'I certainly see him as a creep now.'

'I don't understand. I *never* understood why you had anything to do with him, Maia.'

'I told you. He comes over well when he wants. The man had had a terrible head injury, so I thought any oddness was because of the damage.'

'Well, I like to be fair—only I knew Anacrites long before he had his skull bashed in by some bent Spanish oil producers. He was sinister from the start. I've always thought,' I told Maia, 'the head wound only made his character more visible. He's a snake. Untrustworthy, obnoxious, poisonous.'

Maia said nothing. I did not insist. I never wanted to push her into admitting she had been fooled.

'We had nothing in common,' she said in a depressed voice. 'As soon as I told him there was no future, I felt so relieved it was over—' So true. Women are not sentimentalists. I remembered how she had immediately begun flirting with Petronius, who happened to be available.

'Anacrites would not believe that we were finished—then he turned vindictive. You know the rest, Marcus. Don't make me go over it.'

'No, no,' I reassured her. He had hung about, morosely stalking her, until the fateful day he had her home destroyed. I could see my sister growing tense as she tried to avoid those memories. 'Just tell me, what happened today, Maia?'

'For some reason, I opened the door—I don't know why. He hadn't knocked. There he was—standing in the passage, right outside. I was completely shocked. How long had he been out there? He got inside before I caught my breath.'

'Then what?'

'He kept pretending everything was normal. It was just a social call.'

'Was he unpleasant?'

'No. Marcus, I hadn't seen him, not to talk to, since I gave him his marching orders.'

'Were you scared?'

'I was worried Lucius would come home. There would have been a horrendous row. Anyway, I pretended he was there, asleep indoors, so I shooed the spy away. You know Anacrites—I thought he probably realised I was lying.'

'So what did he say?'

'That was the funny thing.' Maia frowned. 'He tried small talk—not that he knows how to do it. His conversation is zero. That was one reason I couldn't continue with him. After Famia, I needed a man who would respond if *I* talked to *him*.'

I laughed. 'Oh, you get banter from Lucius Petronius?'

'He has his hidden side; don't all of you!' scoffed Maia. 'I was about to mention the *incident,* when Anacrites actually brought the subject up himself. Apologised. According to him it was "an administrative mistake". Then he pleaded his injury, said he couldn't remember properly. He tried to make me sorry for him by telling me how tired he had been, how he had to cover that up so he didn't lose his job, how he had lost years of his life through being bludgeoned . . . Anyway—and this is what I wanted to tell you, Marcus—Anacrites seemed mainly interested in that case he's taken off you,' said Maia. 'The warty melon kept trying to extract from me just what you and Lucius have found out.'

'And you said . . . ?'

'I had nothing to tell him. You know Lucius.'

Petronius never believed in discussing his work with his women-folk. Anacrites should have approached Helena instead—she knew everything; not that she would break my confidence. He was too scared of her to attempt it, of course.

Anacrites had upset my sister for nothing. He had angered me too—and if Petro heard about this, he would be livid.

Maia and I agreed that Petronius had better not be told.

27

With Petronius stuck in Rome, grounded by his tribune, I made another trip to the coast.

This time Helena came with me. I took her to see Pa's maritime villa. I brought Nux as well, since my household was completely ruled by the dog. Luckily tearing through the pinewoods and racing along the beach suited her just fine. Nux was prepared to allow us to keep this wonderful place.

Helena also approved, so we spent several days discussing how to arrange things to suit us, turning the house into a seaside family home rather than a businessman's retreat. While we were working, some of the slaves reported a man hanging around in the woods. He was a stranger to them, but from their description, I wondered if it was one of Anacrites' agents.

We knew a woman who lived with the priestesses at a temple in Ardea. Driving off with a deal of commotion, Helena went to visit her. I stayed at the villa; I made myself visible shifting furniture and artwork to outbuildings, then spent time loafing on a daybed on the shore while the dog brought driftwood to me. The mysterious sightings stopped. I hoped the agent had gone back to Rome to report that I was at the coast for domestic reasons.

It would be typical of Anacrites to waste time and resources. He should have been pursuing the Claudii. Instead he was obsessed with Petro and me. He knew us well; he knew we would try to pip him on the case. But that cut both ways. We understood him too.

On Helena's return we went down to Antium. We were enjoying our break from the children, and we did love to be out and about on enquiries. She was right: I must never stop doing this work—and when it was feasible I must always let her join in.

Helena was charmed by Antium, with its shabby, outdated grandeur. As always happens, there was nothing we wanted to see at the theatre, though old posters told us annoyingly that the week before Davos, our old contact who was Thalia's lover, had presented a play here. I would really have liked the chance for a chat with Davos!

Exploring more successfully than I had had time to do with Albia, Helena and I managed to find decent local baths then a cluster of fish restaurants. We lingered over a fine meal, eaten out of doors with grand sea views from the lofty precipice where Antium stood. This was always an hour when we liked to come together, to relax, review the day and reassert our partnership. With just the two of us tonight, it was like old times—that elusive condition married people should seek more often.

As we savoured the last of our wine, I took her hand and said, 'Everything will be all right.'

'The case, Marcus?'

'No, not that.'

Helena knew what I meant.

We enjoyed the evening a little longer, then I went to pay the bill and ask the restaurant-keeper where he bought his bread. His baker was not Vexus, Demetria's father; still, the man gave me suggestions where to start looking next day.

———

I went on my own, leaving Helena to take Nux around the forum.

It took me some tramping of narrow streets. Vexus worked at the edge of the city, with one small oven and not even his own grind-stone. It was a rough, depressed quarter with dusty streets where half-starved dogs lay on doorsteps like corpses. There were better shops, with a better clientele, in the smarter areas. This man, a short, thick-set ugly-faced fellow, baked heavy dark ryebread for the poor. He looked as if he had been miserable for the past thirty years. I began to understand how his daughter, growing up here without a future, might have settled for one of the Claudii. Even so, there seemed nothing basically wrong with the home she came from. Unless she had only one eye in the middle of her forehead yet failed to attract men with her novelty value, there was no reason for Claudius Nobilis to assume she was so desperate he could treat her badly.

I bought a bread roll to start the conversation; it never works. As soon as I said what I wanted, Vexus turned unhelpful. He had not overflowed with customer care to start with. I introduced myself and I might have been trying to sell him a silver-boxed ten-scroll set of Greek encyclopaedias. Used ones.

'Get lost.'

'I want to help your daughter.'

'Leave my daughter alone. She's not here and she's had enough trouble.'

'Can I see her?'

'No.'

'I don't blame you—but my enquiry won't harm her. Maybe I can get the Claudii off her back.'

'I'd like to see that!' Vexus implied I wasn't up to it.

'Will you at least tell me about Nobilis?'

'Mind your own business.'

'I'd like to—but those wastrels on the marsh have become the Emperor's business. I'm stuck with investigating. So let me guess: your girl married Nobilis when she was too young to know what she was doing—against your advice, no doubt? It went sour. He beat her.' I wondered if the father was violent too. He looked strong, but controlled. Still, men from boot-menders up to the consulship have been known to conceal their domestic brutality. 'Did they have any children?'

'No, thank Jove!'

'So Demetria decided to leave, but Nobilis would not let her go. She came home; he hated it. She found someone else, and he put a stop to that . . . Right?'

'Nothing to say.'

'Is she still with her new man?'

'No.'

'Nobilis put the scares on?'

'Half killed him.'

'In front of her?'

'That was the point, Falco!'

'So the new man caved in?'

'He got rid of her,' agreed her father bitterly.

A ghastly thought struck me. 'Don't say she went back to Nobilis?'

Vexus pressed his lips together in a thin line. 'Thankfully, I put a stop to that.'

'But she was so frightened, doing what Nobilis said became a possibility?'

'No,' said the baker, with heavy emphasis. 'She was so frightened it was *never* a possibility.'

That was all he would tell me. I left details for Demetria to contact me, if she would. No chance. I heard the tablet with my name on it thump into a trash bucket before I got back outside to the street.

I asked about Demetria around the neighbourhood. I met nothing but hostility. The atmosphere felt dangerous. I left before a riot could start.

28

I had another lead to follow: Petronius and I had been told by the waitress at Satricum that Claudius Nobilis worked for a corn dealer called Thamyris. He lived outside town. I took Nux and Helena and drove out to his place, a scattered set of barns and workshops off the coast road that went south.

Thamyris was a wide, squat, shabby typical countryman, in his sixties, wearing the usual rough tunic and a battered hat which he kept on even though when we arrived it was the lunch break. He and his men were gathered on benches, a peaceful group. They had mastered the art of making their working day revolve around the time they took off. Some were eating, some whittling. There was easy-going chat. Nux jumped from our cart and went to sit with them. She guessed correctly they would pet her and feed her titbits.

Nobody showed any curiosity about us. If we had wanted to buy grain we would have had to wait. The men stayed where they were and carried on enjoying their break; Thamyris stayed put and talked to us. Helena was allowed to sit on one of the benches, which a lad willingly swept of straw first, using the back of a fairly clean hand.

I explained what I wanted. Thamyris replied slowly and thoughtfully, as if he had answered these questions before. I asked him; he said he was always being consulted these days about Claudius Nobilis. For years the man had worked in this labour gang unremarked, but now the local authorities had a definite eye on him. It might have been awkward, had he not already taken himself off somewhere.

'Do you know where he's gone?'

'He said something about the family. Knowing what they are like, I kept my nose out of that.'

'So who else has been asking about him?'

'Men from Antium. A man from Rome.'

'I'm supposed to be the man from Rome—who was the other bastard?'

'Someone like you!' The grain dealer enjoyed the joke. I pressed him for details and came to the conclusion he had been visited by one of Anacrites' runners.

While I brooded on that, Helena changed the subject pleasantly: 'What was your impression of Nobilis when he worked for you?'

Thamyris summed up like an employer who noticed things: 'He did the work, though he didn't push himself.'

'Did he fit in? Was he one of the lads?' I asked.

'Yes and no. He never said much. If we were all sitting around like this, he would be with us. If we went out for a drink together in the evening, he would tag along. But he always tended to move off a little distance from the group.'

'Did he strike you as at all odd?' Helena then wondered.

'He had his obsessions. He liked talking about weapons. He collected spears and knives—nasty big ones. He seemed a bit too interested, if you understand me.'

I nodded. 'Trouble?'

'He never gave me any.'

'But he came with a reputation?'

'That I don't deny. People said he had been accused of thieving as a child, and I did hear that years ago a woman said he had raped her.' Thamyris seemed unconcerned. On the scale of country crime, rape tended to rank with shouting boo at chickens.

'So why do you think he left?' asked Helena. 'We heard he was "going to see his grandmother", whatever that means. What's the mystery?'

'A classic excuse.' Thamyris gave a laugh. It was the irritating kind that suggests someone knows a lot more than you do and intends to take a very long while revealing it. 'When people want time off.'

Helena asked, 'So what was up with him? Was he upset? Did he have a quarrel?'

'Better ask Costus.' Hearing his name, a corn cockle on another bench looked over. 'Nobilis!' called his boss in explanation.

'Oh him!' The younger man exclaimed dismissively; then he just went back to whittling.

I raised my eyebrows. Thamyris dropped his voice. 'Had a fling.' I showed that I still didn't get it. 'Costus.' The voice lowered even further. '*With Demetria!*'

I left Helena to draw out anything else she could from the dealer, and strolled across to Costus. He was a handsome chunk, who looked none too bright—in fact, if he had moved in on the wife of the violent Nobilis, he couldn't be. 'You're brave!'

'Stupid,' he conceded.

'I'm looking for your war wounds.' I could see no recent bruises, though his nose and one ear had a squashed look. Without a word, he pulled up the lower edge of his tunic to reveal a ferocious, fairly new knife scar running from below his hip to his belly-button. It was healed, but he must have been laid up and in some danger for a long time. I whistled through my teeth. '*Very* brave—and no wonder you seem subdued.' The Claudius women had told me it was three years since Demetria had left Nobilis. She must have already known Costus, through his working with her husband; were they lovers before, or was it only after she left that this young man had provided a consoling shoulder? 'Did Nobilis stop working here because his wife left him for you?'

Costus shook his head. 'She just left him. Then he went to pieces. He couldn't accept it.'

'You took her over afterwards?' A couple of his workmates were now watching us quietly. 'Do you know where she is now?'

– 159 –

'Nope.'

I bet he did.

Costus lied to me, and his comrades impassively watched him do it. They were all in the cover-up. But I had seen that his lunch consisted of a variety of items, which had been folded up for him in a very clean napkin. The package was not bought from a food-seller. Unless Costus was living with his doting old mother, he had other female company. He was a duffer, in my view, but a woman might find him good-looking.

I thumped him on the back in a rueful gesture. Just as I had with the baker, I wrote my name and other details on the back of an old bill from my pocket, which I placed on the wooden table. 'Better be off. We're heading back to Rome tonight. Probably stop over at Satricum to admire the scenery . . .'

Helena and I thanked everyone for their helpfulness, then we left. We took the road that went across the marshes, stopping at the inn for a night in Satricum as I had mentioned.

We hired a room, and took our time settling in. Easier said than done; the rooms here might be tolerable to men on tough missions where each needed to show the others he was hard. As a husband and wife we would need to hug together very tightly, to keep the bed-bugs out. We stuck it in the room as long as possible then went to find a meal.

I hid a smile when Helena told Januaria, 'I hear you made friends with Camillus Justinus!'

'He's a bit of all right!' agreed the waitress admiringly.

'My brother.'

Januaria was taken aback, but briefly. 'Is he married?'

'Oh yes. He has two little boys.'

The girl sniggered. 'I bet his wife curses him!'

How true.

We ate, then sat behind empty bowls regretting it. Night fell. We had almost given up when the gods smiled. Nux growled a warning in the back of her throat. Costus with the straight nose and biceps from the corn-supplies place sidled up out of nowhere. After shy negotiations, promises of confidentiality, and a small inducement in coinage, he wriggled back into the darkness, then reappeared, leading by the hand a woman we knew would be Demetria.

The baker's daughter was bolder than I expected. That probably meant her relationship with Nobilis had been tempestuous. Sometimes it works that way. Demetria had an ugly air of defiance, probably not caused by her past history. She came with it from the egg; her truculence was a symptom of social ineptitude. Had she ever gone to school, which I doubted, she would have been the awkward one on the back bench.

She was in her twenties, plain-faced with a snub nose, loose, fly-away hair and a faint sour smell as if somebody spilled milk on her several days ago. She wore a drab brown dress with one sleeve rolled and one to the cuff. It wasn't a fashion statement. She was too lazy to notice it. Her girdle was a rope that would have doubled as a bullock halter. She wore no jewellery. I guessed she had never worked, so had no money herself, and the men she chose were never generous.

It was all a waste of time, of course. Demetria admitted she still lived with Costus, pretty well in hiding. He had dragged her along tonight to see us hoping there would be money in it. She might have had enough spirit to run away from Nobilis, but on the whole Demetria's instincts were to do as she was told.

She would not talk about her marriage to Nobilis. She did not accuse him of violence against her, nor of battering her lover. Whatever pressures to keep quiet had been embedded in her by Claudius Nobilis, they were still firmly in place.

She had no idea what Nobilis got up to nowadays or where he had gone off to; she had no contact with the family—though when I said I had spoken to the other two women, she asked after Plotia and Byrta. She swore she knew nothing about what happened with Modestus and Primilla and since she hadn't lived with Nobilis then, it seemed reasonable. When I asked if she had ever had reason to suspect visitors were vanishing at the compound, she denied it.

'So why did you come to find me?' I demanded in exasperation.

That was when she came straight out and said Costus wanted her to beg for money. I could hardly complain. As Helena sniggered afterwards, offering facts for a cash reward was what I did as an informer.

I replied that when *I* made the offer, facts did exist.

There was one outcome. I asked Costus if he had been there when the man from Rome that Thamyris mentioned had turned up. According to Costus, it was a couple of days before. The description he gave of peculiar eyes, greased hair and smooth-talking sounded suspiciously familiar; it could almost be Anacrites himself.

'Did you hear what was said?'

'He took Thamyris out of earshot.'

'So you've no idea what he wanted?'

'Oh yes!' Costus seemed surprised anyone should think his employer would keep a city man's secret. 'He ordered the boss that if anyone came asking about Nobilis or the other Claudii, he was to say nothing.'

'Did he reinforce that order?'

Costus laughed bitterly. 'One or two suggestions. Just in case we forgot. Like—he'd close down the business, crucify Thamyris, sell his wife into a brothel, send us as slaves to the galleys and cut off our goolies first. Do you think he can do it?'

'Oh yes. It's the regular tactic used by the Praetorian Guards.'

29

On the journey home, Helena and I discussed the situation. Costus' story confirmed all the rumours about the Claudii having protection. Whoever was looking after their interests must be powerful, if they used the intelligence network to do their dirty work. Anacrites had not dared threaten Petro and me; even he was not that stupid. But he had no scruples about intimidating members of the public. He assumed we would never find out. For us, this signalled ulterior motives. He would know that if we once became intrigued, we would latch on to him like rat-dogs.

He had slipped up. I for one would not rest now until I uncovered his real interest—and Petronius was the same. I was all set to tear into the spy's office and threaten him with the same punishments he offered Thamyris—especially the part about castration. Maia must have the old veterinarian tools her dead husband used when he looked after the Greens' chariot horses; she would happily loan me his equine nut-crusher.

Helena urged me to play clever. 'Don't alert him, Marcus. Let's carry on as normal, pretend his agent wasn't spotted. I suggest when we get home, we see if he has invited us to dinner as he threatened. If he has, we should go along to his house, and sniff the air before you tackle him outright.'

'I would rather sniff a heifer's bum, after a week's diarrhoea.'

'Your rhetoric is so refined! . . . Listen to your wife's good advice.' Helena shook her finger warningly: 'Find out just whose fixer Anacrites is. Who wants him to protect these marsh-men's interests?'

'You are right, as ever.' It was time to address the point. 'It must all be to do with these Claudii having an imperial background,' I told Helena. 'I sensed that Laeta and Momus know what's going on. Some old influence has carried over . . . I don't believe it's the Emperor.' Vespasian had a few close cronies; his cabinet of private advisers were men like Helena's own father who had known him for years, long before he counted. He had never been regarded as someone who protected favourites.

'Nor Titus,' Helena decided. She and Titus viewed each other with admiration—more admiration than I liked. Still that just meant Titus Caesar was a fine judge of womanhood. Like his father, he was basically straight.

Helena was still ticking off candidates: 'Domitian's more questionable.' I had a feud with Domitian. He didn't scare me, but if he was in on this it was best to know. 'Of the great and powerful at the Palace,' Helena concluded, 'there would only be Claudius Laeta. He would not have invited you and Petro to investigate Modestus, if his interests lay in a cover-up.'

'Give the man credit—he knows we're too good!' I grinned at her.

'Laeta does not take stupid risks,' she corrected me coolly. Helena had a wonderful sense of humour, though little tolerance for silly beggars' backchat. 'He doesn't play with knives for a cheap thrill. He sees his role as protecting the administration, so the Empire can run smoothly.'

'So what do you think?'

'It could be some consul or ex-consul who has never crossed our path.'

'Most of them!' We kept out of general politics.

'I can ask my father. Not that he tends to know strong-arm thugs.

His friends in the Curia are benign. Men who read Plato over their lunch, philanthropists who think a commission should look into health issues among the urban poor.'

I said the Claudii were a health threat in Latium.

Helena was still considering the argument. While I ducked out if there were too many alternatives, she liked to be thorough, with no feeble 'decide that later' topics; she worked through every point. She would say I was a typical man; I thought her a highly unusual woman.

'We ought to consider, Marcus, not just who this person of influence is, but *why* he supports the freedmen. It's been a long while since mighty men in Rome aligned themselves with criminal gangs.'

'People like Clodius and his terrorists? He provided himself with brutal enforcers; everyone was scared of them and together with his very patrician name, it gave him enormous power . . . Nothing like that happens in the city now.'

'It cannot be about anything the Claudii offer to their protector,' Helena said. 'He may be ambitious, but he must be able to manage his career without their help. So why does he bother? What hold do they have over him?'

She was right and I agreed: 'What's he scared of? A bunch of second-rate ex-slaves, living out in a marsh, miles from civilisation, selling scrap and beating up their wives? I can't see how they have any influence with anyone who carries serious weight in Rome. And he must have weight. It takes a real someone to make Anacrites jump.'

'Could it be simpler?' Helena suggested. 'Could they be under the protection of Anacrites himself?'

We both laughed and agreed that was totally unlikely.

Back in Rome, it emerged that the visitor who had threatened Thamyris could not have been Anacrites. The man who went to Antium must have been an agent. Petronius confirmed that the spy had been in Rome. The vigiles had seen him.

Things had moved on. While Helena and I were away, the Seventh Cohort had been called out to the necropolis on the Via Triumphalis.

This burial ground was across the river, north of the city, unlike where Modestus was discovered. Passers-by had alerted a caretaker to what looked like a shallow grave, dug without permission close to the road. In it was a fresh, mutilated corpse.

30

Julia and Favonia had been playing quietly on the floor with their pottery animals. As soon as we walked in, they remembered they had been abandoned by us, their callous parents. They jumped up, grew red in the face and ran away screaming loudly, real tears streaming down their faces. It was a classic scam.

Helena Justina gave me a quizzical look. 'Maybe two is enough?'

'Agreed!'

Albia, too, refused to welcome our return but stalked off like an offended dog. That gave Nux the same idea, even though she had been on the trip with us.

The message from Petronius about the new murder was irresistible. I changed my tunic and boots, then washed my face. I thought about a comb-through but settled for the windswept look. Being back in Rome had fired me up enough; being neat would be too much excitement. Sometimes I needed to remember when I lived in Fountain Court and was a rough rascal.

At mid-morning I set out from home, with a knife down my boot and just enough money in my purse to cover emergencies. My mind was clear and my step spry. However, I had the faint edgy feeling of a man who needs to reimpose himself on his customary surroundings. Adultery and cart-crashes could have occurred without me knowing it. I might have missed the crucial capture of that balcony thief from the Street of the Armilustrium. Old Lupus could have gone on his long-promised cruise of the Mediterranean—for all I knew, taking that pudgy waitress from the Venus Scallop, instead of his miserable wife, the one with pigtails who was always cadging off Brutus from the fish stall. Once I reached Maia's, she would fill me in on these essentials, but first my way took me to the Fourth Cohort's station house.

Petronius had finished the night shift and gone home. Fusculus was there and gave me the story.

'Same modus as before?'

'Apparently. Body found at the necropolis—though not in a tomb this time. There's a difference from the Appia and Latina sites, where you find patrician surnames and bloody big mausoleums. The Via Triumphalis is a big burial ground with a mixed clientele, slaves to middle rank. Its burials are mixed, everything from old skeletons popping out of shallow graves to grey stone urns with nice pointy lids or half a broken amphora lying on its side to hold the deceased's ashes.'

'About our level!' I said, grinning.

'Not as fancy as that inscription your papa fixed up for himself, Falco! No *This is my memorial which may never be sold, with a front-age of a thousand feet*; no pretty Etruscan funeral altar, with dear little wings on it.'

I was not yet ready for jokes. I could satirise losing Pa, but thinking about my tiny son demanded respect. 'Fusculus—that's a large cemetery with a litter of confusing graves. Why did this corpse attract attention?'

'You know some crazy killers want to yell out, *Look at me; I've done what I wanted and you can't catch me!* Petronius reckons the dead man was placed near the road specially, so someone would notice.'

'Did you see the body?'

'That was indeed my privilege.'

'Modestus was middle-aged. Someone similar?'

'No, this one's young. Slight build—easy to overcome.'

'How was he set out?'

'Obviously ritual. Face down, arms outstretched sideways like a crucified slave. Well, when I say full length, Falco, that is excluding both his hands which, having been hacked off, were placed very neatly either side of his head. Same groundplan as Modestus. And like Modestus, when the Seventh rolled him over, they found him sawn open from his gullet to his privates.'

'Any other mutilation?'

'That was enough!'

'As vindictive as the Modestus killing?'

Fusculus gave that thought. 'Maybe not. He had been thumped, but probably during initial attempts to subdue him.'

'Then apart from the fact he lost his hopes in life, you could say he did not suffer?'

'So nicely put! His clothes were there. Shoes, neckerchief—and bright new wedding ring still on his severed hand. Mind, I don't think anyone would try selling what was left of his tunic in the flea market—not after he was slit open.'

'Ring left behind—so theft not a motive?'

'No money on him, so maybe. His donkey's missing, but anyone could have pinched that from the roadside if the killer left it.'

'And do we know who he is?'

'We do, in fact!' Fusculus left me waiting. It was the end of the night and he soon lost interest in teasing. '. . . A carter reported his courier missing. Young fellow. Just got married, so the bride started jumping as soon as he failed to report for his dinner. Her very first attempt at seafood patties—now he'll never know how terrible they were . . . He'd been sent out with a parcel—the Seventh haven't found the parcel, but it was in his donkey pannier. That caring citizen, his master, reported him gone because he thought the lad had simply scarpered with the goods.'

'So this parcel-boy was heading out of Rome, not coming into town? And not on the Pontine Marshes side?'

'No. So the Seventh *were* assuming it's the same killer, because of the method, but those on high say different.'

'Not the Claudii? That's the Anacrites verdict?' I was angry. 'Tiberius, my lad—this points us in the other direction much too obviously!'

'Funny thing,' murmured Fusculus. 'That's what Petronius Longus decided.' He pretended to look impressed that we two could so swiftly come up with the same suggestion. 'Mind you, he always likes to be a wild man over theories. If seven people say a cabbage-seller did it, the mighty Longus will arrest the baker. He'll be right too. Clever bastard.'

Going on my way, when I reached the door I whipped back with a sudden last question. This was a trick to reserve for suspects, really, but Tiberius Fusculus was one person in the vigiles who appreciated stagecraft. 'Have you discounted a copycat?'

'Ah, Falco, there's always that delight to cause confusion!'

Petro had been going to bed when I arrived, but he stayed up to gossip. We went out to the balcony. He closed the folding door. That was how he did things. Through the slats I could see Maia waggling her fingers at us and sticking out her tongue. Ma would have listened secretly. Helena would have dragged the door straight open again and brought a stool for herself.

He gave me further details. The Seventh Cohort, all halfwits in Petro's opinion, had been first on the scene. The Via Triumphalis, which runs out of the city on the north-east side, was the Seventh's beat; they had jurisdiction over the Ninth and Fourteenth districts, including any burial ground just outside the boundary. They consulted the Fourth Cohort. They knew Petronius had the Modestus case, though they had been unaware of the Anacrites complication. The Fourth's tribune wanted to be a Praetorian Guard and spies were a Praetorian subdivision, so as it had a bearing on his own position Rubella stuck by the rules. He notified Anacrites of the new linked case so fast the hot wax seal burned the spy's fingers. Anacrites had allowed the Seventh to continue with routine enquiries. Either they lacked the taint of association with Petronius and me, or he just thought they were too stupid to get in his way.

'As they are,' said Petro.

'You're tired.'

'I'm right.'

'Of course. So what do you think? Fusculus says the new official view is that the Triumphalis death indicates random killings on any road near Rome. It's supposed to tell us the Modestus death was just a traveller's unlucky accident.'

'Yes, apparently that is a luminous truth.'

'Modestus getting topped on his way into Rome has no relation to the Claudii but is pure coincidence?'

'Wrong road, wrong time.' Petro paused, as Maia came out with a dish of stuffed vine leaves, checking up that we were not enjoying ourselves too much without her.

'He needs his rest, Marcus.'

'We've nearly finished.'

'I know you; you haven't even started.'

'Buzz off and let us get on then.' Petro's tone was affectionate. My sister put up with it.

I chomped a vine leaf. Home made. Wheatgrain and pine nut filling in a slightly tart dressing. Mint. Good, but I stayed gloomy. 'Spill, sunshine.'

Petro took a snack between one thumb and finger, but merely waved it as he talked. 'Marcus, here is my personal list of anomalies. First, why did the Modestus killers cut off his hands? I still think for revenge: those hands had repeatedly written angry letters to complain about the Claudii. Someone must have heard about Cicero— murdered for railing against Mark Antony. Cicero's hands, which wrote his polemics, were removed and stuck on spikes either side of the head up on the rostrum where he had made his speeches.'

'One hand.'

'Pedant.'

'The allusion seems too literary.'

'No, it's not. Everyone knows what happened to Cicero. Even *I* know!' boasted Petro. He had been to school, but whereas my adult hobbies were drinking and reading, his were drinking and drinking some more. 'Besides, what do you think Nobilis and Probus do all day at their miserable shacks? They sit down with a learned scroll to improve their minds, don't they?'

'Show me proof! But I go with revenge against the petitioner's hands. Next anomaly?'

'I had had our doctor, Scythax, take a look at the remains before we got Modestus cremated. Scythax thought he was probably still alive when his hands were removed. Nobilis may know about the death of Cicero; he intended Modestus would appreciate his fate.'

'Meanwhile, the courier's boy never wrote poison pen letters.'

'No, he couldn't read or write.' Trust Petro to have asked the question. 'His body may have been stretched out like Modestus, but his slashed belly is different. Scythax tends to be cautious forensically, but he reckons the Modestus killer cut open the corpse after death. I mean, he probably came back and did it several days later.'

I cringed. 'What was that for?'

'Who knows why? Reinforcing his power, maybe.' Petro munched his snack now, thinking about perversion and frowning. 'Anyway, the courier was opened up the same day he died. We can be sure, because he set off in the afternoon and was found at first light next day. He was practically warm.'

'The murder sounds hurried—that's untypical of repeat killers.' I could tell from the way Petronius had paced his narrative, there must be at least one more discrepancy. 'What else?'

'Whoever killed Modestus, from the detritus left nearby, I suspect more than one man was there. And they stayed around the crime scene for several days. *After* the killing, I mean. Possibly someone came back to slash Modestus open—but I say, the bastards never went away.'

'Jupiter! This happens?'

'With perverts. Of course, people who hold other theories will argue that around the Via Appia tombs there are plenty of comers and goers, squatters and campers, so how can we tell?'

'And how can you?'

'As well as the post mortem filleting job, we found seats that had been moved out of the tomb; discarded amphorae; obvious food evidence. There was human shit and it was the right vintage.'

I winced. 'Your job is charming.'

'My job is to get it right and not let bastards bamboozle me.'

'If the Modestus killers had wanted to play with the courier's boy like that, all they had to do was take him away from the road out of sight. Instead they placed him right beside the road-edge ditch, where he was bound to be spotted immediately.'

'Funny, that!' observed Petro. 'The whole thing stinks—though a stupid spy might fall for it.'

He did need his rest and while he brooded, Petronius Longus fell asleep. I did not disturb him. I sat on there, letting him snore on the other daybed, while I continued thinking.

Maia looked out once. She brought me some warmed honey mulsum, silently curling my fingers around the beaker, then roughing up my curls. After these sisterly attentions, she left us to it.

31

It was time to look harder at Anacrites. Helena was right about how we could do that. Escorting my womenfolk to a soirée at his old-style Palatine mansion would not have been my choice, but his invitation had arrived and Rome is a city of civilised dining. Commerce and corruption of all kinds are furthered by social evenings of this type. I wanted to get close enough to him to work out why he wanted to be close to me.

At my members-only gym, Glaucus' at the back of the Temple of Castor and Pollux, I bathed and put myself in the safe hands of the sneery barber. First, I had Glaucus give me a fierce weapons practice, followed by a session with his most brutal masseur. When Glaucus asked if all this preparation meant I was off on another dangerous mission overseas, I told him where I was going that evening. His advice was to watch my footwork, watch what I was given to eat, but above all watch my back. He had met Anacrites. When the spy had applied to join the gym as a regular, Glaucus found he was so oversubscribed he could only put Anacrites on the very competitive waiting list . . . Anacrites was still there.

'Say no when he passes you the mushrooms,' Glaucus hinted. An old Roman allusion to poison. 'Better still, here's an idea. You got plenty of slaves off your old man when he died, didn't you? Take one along as your taster. Be sensible, Falco. You're paid up here until the end of the year—you don't want to waste part of your subscription.'

'I regard my slaves as family,' I protested with a righteous air.

'All the more reason to bump a few off!' replied Glaucus. Nobody would know he had a good-looking wife he doted on and an athlete son who was his pride and joy.

According to Helena it was more trying for a woman to get dressed when she wanted to look as if she had gone to no trouble than when she was trying to show vast respect to some possible patron in order to advance her husband (never applicable in my case) or to impress a man she was sizing up for passionate adultery (not applicable in Helena's, I hoped—though if that was her intention there was not much I could do about it; she was far too devious). I lay on the bed watching proceedings, naked and hoping the scent of the masseur's crocus oils would evaporate. His goo was useless for attracting women. Helena Justina had just wrinkled her nose in mild curiosity, as if I had come home with an arm missing and she was subconsciously wondering what was different about me. The hour which we could have filled with lovemaking went to trying on gowns, searching for girdles and picking through her jewel casket. When she was halfway through applying face paint, she rushed off to supervise Albia, who had decided that since her parents never took her anywhere, she would wear all the sparkle she possessed while there was an opportunity.

'We need to look as though we know it's not just borage tea and a pickled egg,' I heard Helena telling her. Two room doors had been left open, to facilitate the shrieks as the only good gown in the chest was found to have had honey spilled down it and the clasp on each chosen necklace broke under frantic fingers. 'But that we don't think enough of Anacrites to bring out our best.'

'And why is it we hate him?' Albia asked with her fastidious curiosity. She tended to act as if all things done in Rome were crazy beyond belief to anyone born in the provinces.

'No hatred. We treat him cautiously,' Helena reproved her. 'We find his jealousy of Falco a touch unhealthy.'

'Oh—as in, he tried to have Falco splayed on a rock for carrion birds in Nabataea?'

'Quite. Trying to arrange a long-distance execution was not acceptable etiquette.'

'So will the spy try short-distance Falco-killing this evening?' Albia sounded far too interested.

'No, darling. Anacrites is too shrewd to try anything with you and me there. I'd poke his eyes out, while you rushed for a lawyer.'

That was reassuring. I hauled myself upright and sorted out a tunic I was willing to wear.

'Oh Marcus! You're not going in that disaster. Wear your russet.'

'Too smart.'

I had always loathed the russet, which made me look like some praetor's pimpled equerry. Naturally, that was what my stylists made me wear.

At the Anacrites establishment, which he must have acquired with his Census earnings, the murderous watchdog had been sluiced with scented water and told to bark more quietly. That would be a bonus for the wealthy neighbours who were usually too scared to complain. The formidable gates had been oiled so they could be forced wide enough; Pa's old six-bearer litter sailed us through. We were cleared by the bestubbled porter and passed into the custody of liveried greeting slaves.

They were slick. So slick, Helena guessed Anacrites had hired professional party-planners. His house was busy with Lusitanians in matching snowy tunics. There were garlands in themed colours. A young lady facilitator in platform soles and a faux fur bustband picked out bijou little guest-gifts for us (I got dice, that would only land on three). At the spy's back door must be a train of carts bringing the accoutrements of outside caterers—bronze buckets of fancy seafood from specialist suppliers, slightly worn table linen, and their own griddles. For Anacrites, this evening clearly meant much more than a comfortable supper among friends.

I pinched Albia cheerfully. 'Assume the Trojan hog is on!'

The greeters whipped away our outer garments and shoes. A rumpus at the door announced further visitors. Since one of the voices was that of Camillus Aelianus—sounding a little weary perhaps—that boded ill. We had hardly reached the atrium and Albia already looked surly. Then I heard the hideous baritone of Minas of Karystos. He must have stiffened his resolve with cocktails before the party set out.

Helena and I shuffled past the atrium pool, towing Albia. Tiny lamps like fireflies, the kind designers think sophisticated, twittered around the pool, many already going out. While the newcomers were shovelled into their dining sandals, we found our way through the murk and came upon our host reclining on a reading-couch, like a man who was trying to calm his nerves.

He jumped up, wearing one of his slimfit tunics (great gods, the vain fool must have darts put in, to make him look trim). I was very put out that his was a brown shade rather close to mine. I'd half expected him to have a torc around his neck, but he had confined himself to matched gold cuffs on his upper arms. He exercised. He had enough muscle to show off, though his arms were oddly smooth, as if he had the hairs individually plucked.

'You invited my brother!' Helena barked at him. Anacrites had changed her from peacemaker to firebrand in one move. Even he looked startled.

'Dear Helena Justina—' Oh it was formal names tonight! 'Since Lucius Petronius and Maia Favonia unfortunately had other commitments, I invited *both* your brothers.' He made it sound as though he was doing her a favour, as if the noble Camilli were incapable of arranging a family party for themselves. What it really meant was that he only knew us. I was right: he had no friends. 'I hoped you would approve,' he whined.

Fortunately the band struck up.

He had three lyres and a light hand-drummer. They accompanied a short troupe of fairly good tumblers in almost new costumes, followed by a girl who sang brief Cretan shepherd songs after long explanations from a man in a shaggy goatskin cape. Ignoring this, we waved cheerily to Justinus and his wife Claudia, less cheerily to Aelianus, his new wife Hosidia and his tottering father-in-law. 'Cretan was the best I could get at short notice to compliment Greeks,' Anacrites whispered as he went to welcome the Camilli. As a host he seemed anxious, a new and surreal side to him.

We watched Anacrites wonder whether he could—or should—kiss Claudia and Hosidia, or if he should, or could, embrace Helena's brothers. (He had not hugged me. I'd like to see him try.) Minas, the bearded, exuberant law professor, threw himself upon Anacrites, whom he had never met, as if they had rowed the same oar in a galley for at least twenty years. Hosidia shrank against Aelianus, who nearly stepped back into the atrium pool. Claudia was too tall for the spy to kiss and she just shook hands with him briskly; the hem of her gown fell victim to the sting of the firefly lights but Hosidia considerately flapped out the sparks. Aulus and Quintus Camillus as one stayed at arm's length from Anacrites. I noticed they both wore heavy new chalk-white togas, ready for electioneering. They introduced their womenfolk, who then clustered with my two so they could all admire each other's outfits. Claudia, who had a warm heart, greeted Albia very fondly. Hosidia stood about looking supercilious. It was her natural expression, as far as I could tell.

'Would you like us to speak Greek?' Anacrites asked helpfully, in fluent administrative Greek.

'Naturally I speak Latin,' Hosidia answered—though she said it in Greek. That failed to solve anything; so we were headed for a bilingual evening—feasible, but distancing.

Two pale, flat-chested girls in long white uniforms arrived with snack trays. The snacks were small but tasty; there was no obvious sign that house-slaves had nibbled them. Young boys with their hair oiled into silly points brought the first drinks, in garish decorated cups that the caterers probably supplied. Minas, who needed no cheering up, cheered up loudly. The women guests then demanded that Anacrites give them a tour of his house. Looking worried, he let himself be swept off; he had the expression of a man who knew he had left a pile of dirty loincloths on his bedroom floor and failed to close the cupboard containing his winged phallus lamps.

This left Minas, the Camilli and me standing in a square, each holding a crayfish tail and asking one another what in Hades we were doing there.

Justinus reminded me that we knew from a previous visit Anacrites kept obscene statues in a secret room. Minas brightened, hoping for a private view. 'This should be a good night, Falco!' he boomed. I saw Aulus, who had a keen idea of Minas' liquid capacity, smile fixedly. 'I am so looking forward to it!' Minas confided to me, leaning close in a hideous aura of lunchtime wine and garlic. 'This man must have very great influence, I think? He knows important people? The Emperor, perhaps? Anacrites can do us favours?'

I nodded gravely. 'Tiberius Claudius Anacrites would be proud to know you believe that, Minas.'

32

We were called to dine.

The old dining room was indoors and a touch cosy. The hired hands had decorated its three crushed-together stone couches with coverlets in some shiny fabric the colour of pomegranate juice. They must have misjudged what kind of bachelor Anacrites was. A single rose, suspended from the centre of the ceiling, made the traditional statement that anything we said would be in confidence.

'Surely,' Albia piped up, all wide-eyed innocence, 'only an idiot would mention any secrets in a spy's house?'

'Now I remember your daughter!' cried Minas, clapping me around the shoulders so hard I nearly lost my footing (he had only just remembered *me*, I reckoned). 'This minx is too astute!'

'Oh these days intrigue is the only game in town, Minas.' Thanks to the bagginess of the russet tunic, a good wriggle helped me slide free of the Greek's grip. 'Anacrites loves people to come here and commit treason. He gets a thrill thinking they are his guests so he can't arrest them.'

Anacrites looked disorientated.

We were nine at dinner, naturally. To break convention would be too daring for our host. He must have given much thought to his placements, but when the rest of us arrived in the triclinium, Helena was shifting people around to avert awkward situations: making sure I could grill Anacrites; putting Albia and Aelianus apart; not imposing the bombastic Minas on anyone shy . . .

Minas thought he should take precedence, but this was Rome and he was foreign; he stood no chance. 'Both brothers Camilli are standing for the Senate—' Anacrites said, as he tried to guide them into his chosen places. They were talking about the races and failed to notice him.

'They'll be voted out,' snapped their sister.

'Oh thank you!' they chorused half-heartedly. She just grabbed each one and shoved him where she wanted him. For would-be empire-governors, the duo submitted like wimps. Albia was chortling at this, until she was frogmarched to the end of the inferior couch. 'Young girl's prerogative,' Helena soothed her. 'You get the easy exit to the lavatory and you can reach the food trays for seconds.'

Minas still took too much interest in which was the seat of honour. 'The one on the right-hand corner of the middle couch, I think . . . ?' Fired up by some tourist guide to Roman etiquette, he was aiming his big belly in that direction.

Helena shepherded me there. She pushed Minas to the other end. 'With the best views of the garden and statuary if we were out of doors—' Due to the deficiencies of Anacrites' house, we were facing a dowdy corridor. 'Marcus is the only person who has held a significant public post, Minas; he was Procurator of Juno's Sacred Geese.' If I was top man, and by virtue of supervising a flock of birds, that showed this dinner's low status.

Minas pouted. I grinned and to distract him I explained, 'It's a sad story, Minas. Government short-sightedness. I lost the job ignominiously, in a round of treasury cutbacks.' I always wondered if Anacrites had had something to do with it. 'Juno's Geese and the Augurs' Sacred Chickens were heartbroken to lose me. Their loyalty is touching, in fact. I go up on the Capitol regularly to see the clucks for old times' sake; I shall never lose my sense of responsibility.'

'You are fooling?' Minas was only half right.

'Forget convention. *I* think the best places are the centre of the couches—' Still struggling to seat everyone, Helena steered Anacrites between Minas and me. Aelianus had to go at the top of the left-hand couch, talking across the corner to Minas, with Hosidia behind him; Justinus was opposite Hosidia with Claudia above him, adjacent to me across the other top corner. Albia was below Justinus. He was a good lad and would talk to her; she would probably hope to upset Aelianus by being friendly with his brother. At the far end of the left-hand couch, Helena was stuck with Hosidia. Good manners would have placed Helena next to me, but she had demoted herself in order to put the spy in my range. At least I could wink down the room at her.

During the appetisers, our host led the conversation—as much as he could do, with Minas tipsily interrupting. We had seen him in action; as a symposium-crawler no one could touch him, even in Athens' exhausting party whirl.

The wine was better than good; Anacrites discussed it fluently. Perhaps he had taken himself to wine-buffery classes. At any rate, he served palatable mulsum with the appetisers, not too sweet, then a very fine Caecubian. One of the best wines in the Empire, that must have cost a packet. He also introduced us to an unfamiliar variety he had just acquired, from Pucinum; he was dying for us to ask where Pucinum was so he could show off, but nobody bothered. 'What do you think, Falco? The Empress Livia always drank Pucinum wines, ascribing her long life to their medicinal qualities.'

'Very nice—though the phrase "medicinal qualities" slightly puts me off!'

'Well, it kept her going to eighty-three, outliving her contemporaries—'

'I thought that was because she had poisoned them all . . .'

I asked for a separate water cup and drank the wine sparingly. Anacrites knew me well enough to have seen me do it before. I had a curious sense that tonight he wanted to relax for once—yet now he was torn, in case loosening up gave me some advantage.

While he continued to hold forth on vintages, I chatted to my other neighbour, Claudia Rufina. The three Camillus siblings were all lofty but Justinus had married a woman tall enough to look him in the eye; this Claudia now saw as necessary since he could be a rogue, an edgy character who needed constant watching. On a dining couch designed for our stumpy republican ancestors, she was having problems twisting herself to fit. But once she settled, Claudia gossiped with me on the current situation in the senator's house. 'Things are tense, Marcus.'

Minas had emptied the Camillus wine cellar in about five days. The amiable senator declined to restock, so Minas got huffy. Then Camillus senior hit on the idea that Aelianus and his bride should live next door; he owned the adjacent house, where his brother had once lived. It was decreed that Minas must stay with the couple. 'Julia Justa said, *So nice for him to see a lot of his daughter, before he goes back to Greece* . . . I don't think the professor intends going back, Marcus!'

'No; he is determined to be a big rissole in Rome.'

'I would have thought,' said Claudia, who was a kind-hearted girl, 'the newly-weds might be given some time to themselves—especially as they don't seem to have had much opportunity yet to get to know each other.' That was ironic. Claudia and Quintus would probably stick out their marriage (she had an excellent olive oil fortune which encouraged him mightily), but they were experts at communication failure.

'You presuppose, my dear, that either of them wants familiarity.'

'You cynic!'

'I've lived. Still, we must be hopeful . . . How are the lovebirds getting on?'

Claudia lowered her voice. '*They have separate bedrooms!*'

'How fashionable! Though not much fun.'

'They will never have children.' Claudia and Quintus had produced two small sons very quickly; she assumed everyone wanted the same.

At home we joked that Quintus could get his wife pregnant just by kicking his boots under the bed.

Babies were still a painful subject with Helena and me. To stop Claudia detailing the wonders of their newest son, I turned back to Anacrites. Forcing Aulus to endure a bout of Minas, I grabbed our host's attention. 'So! Tell us all about the big secret mission. Where did you go? How long did you stay? How many barbarians tried to garrotte you? Do tell me some at least tried. And what were you doing abroad in the first place, acting as the Emperor's messenger-boy?'

'You're just jealous,' Anacrites replied coyly.

'Cobnuts! Now, I don't mind you playfully pretending it's a state secret—just so long as you confess all.'

'It was nothing.' Everyone was now listening, so Anacrites had to answer. 'It seems that when his mistress Antonia Caenis was alive, Vespasian managed to discover for her that her ancestors came from Istria.' Minas looked puzzled yet again, so Anacrites explained that our affable old Emperor had lived much of his life with an influential freedwoman who filled a wife's place. 'Senators are forbidden to marry freedwomen. Apparently Caenis had not known her origins and I suppose it bothered her. Once Vespasian assumed power, he had access to the records. Someone finally looked up answers.'

'That's a romantic story,' Claudia said.

'It was true love.' Helena supplied the fact that Caenis had managed to visit her homeland for nostalgic reasons before she died. 'I met her; I liked her enormously. Did you know her, Anacrites?'

'I knew who she was, of course,' he said, in that careful way of his. From what I had seen, in a couple of meetings while she was alive, Antonia Caenis had more sense than to cosy up to the spy.

'I wondered if your backgrounds were similar?' Helena pressed. The spy, not deft with a spoon, concentrated on chasing a langoustine nibble around his foodbowl. I admired my sweetheart for many fine qualities, not least her ability to denude a silver comport of its most succulent seafood while seemingly engaged in chat. Helena served herself to three from the central table while he fumbled. If we had been seated together she might have passed one to me. 'So what were your duties in Istria, Anacrites?' Nobody else will have noticed, but Helena was aware of the way I was smiling down the room at her.

'Merely ceremonial. Falco would have been impatient with it . . .' I leaned on my elbow and glared at him sternly. Anacrites was just too good to show it made him uncomfortable. 'Vespasian endowed various public buildings, in honour of Caenis. An amphitheatre at Pola, for instance, needed restoration—'

'He *paid* for it?'

'He loved her, Marcus,' Helena called reprovingly. 'Go on, Anacrites.'

'I was sent to represent him at the inauguration. So, Falco, it was nothing sinister!'

I laughed off this weak attempt to make me appear paranoid. 'My dear fellow, any time you have the chance to cut civic ribbons in a two-bit foreign town, you do it. I am surprised you could be spared for such matters.'

He flushed slightly. 'Pola is a major city, *Colonia Pietas Iulia Pola Pollentia Herculanea.* I was owed leave. I was honoured to go. It suited me too,' he let slip.

'Oh?' I was on it at once.

'I have connections there.'

'Connections?' I patted his shoulder. 'Can we be learning personal secrets?'

Anacrites shifted. 'It is very beautiful along the coast.'

'Full of pirates, lurking in the rocky creeks, according to my Uncle Fulvius. He watched their movements for the fleet,' I told the spy, trying to make him think this undercover work had been for some mysterious higher agency. Fulvius was in Egypt now, or I would never have mentioned it. No rose suspended from a ceiling was protection enough; had Fulvius still been engaged as a 'military corn factor' (a ridiculous myth, because no corn factor is ever what he seems) he would not have thanked me for interesting Anacrites. 'So what was the real draw, Anacrites?'

'Oh . . . an opportunity to get my hands on some Pucinum wine!' The man was indefatigably slippery.

To his obvious relief the servers cleared the starter tables and brought in the main course. While this was organised, the tumblers tumbled off for a break and a professional singer swanned up to delight us. He must be all the rage; I recognised this caroller from Laeta's office. Immediately I wondered if he was Laeta's plant, observing Anacrites at play. The thought kept me happy until the new food-bowls were laid.

Time for business. (Anything to avoid listening to this singer.) 'So Anacrites, how are you getting on with the Modestus killing?'

'Don't ask, Falco!'

'I just did. Now listen, happy host, I am your guest of honour. While I stretch out on my elbow here in the best place, the consul's spot, my every whim is yours to fulfil—so come clean! What's the situation?'

'There has been another death.' The spy had a wide-eyed honest look that made me want to screw bits off my bread roll and stuff him like a trigon ball. 'It bears similarities to the Modestus killing . . .'

'But?'

'Either it's some sad mimic—plenty of people knew what happened to Modestus; the vigiles may have said too much in public—' Oh yes, blame them, you bastard! 'Or I think it is a ploy, Falco— falsely implying that the killer works from Rome. Of course, I am not fooled so easily. Modestus had been tailed on his journey; he was deliberately targeted. This was different.'

'Interesting!' I was shocked. Was Anacrites really so shrewd? I almost wondered if he had a nark in the vigiles' patrol house who had eavesdropped on Petronius and me.

Aware of my surprise, he applied fake humility. 'What do you say, Falco? I'd like to hear your professional evaluation.'

'Oh you seem on top of things.'

'Thanks. Did you know about the second killing? Have you discussed it with Petronius?' He really wanted to know whether we were still monitoring his case.

'Yes, we heard about it.'

'And what was his verdict?'

'We think a crazed copycat killer knifed the poor courier . . . So are you still looking for those Claudii?'

'Of course.' It was the right thing to say. He was smooth as a wet rat sliding down a drain. Still, I never expected Anacrites to be totally incompetent, let alone appear corrupt. He was too good to show what he was up to.

He turned away, readjusting a pomegranate silk cushion so he could converse again with Minas. 'We don't want to talk about a murder over dinner, Falco.'

You could tell he rarely entertained. He had no idea that far from being squeamish, guests would be eager to hear about gore.

When the main course arrived, he had overdone things. There was no need. His caterers were first class; we would have been flattered by anything they cooked. A couple of roasts, a simple platter with a fine fish, a vegetable mélange with one or two unusual ingredients, would have sufficed. But he had to over-impress. Although he had complimented Helena and me on the warm atmosphere of our Saturnalia gathering last December, Anacrites had failed to analyse it: good food, fresh ingredients not overcooked, a few carefully chosen herbs and spices, all served in a relaxed style with everybody mucking in.

Instead we had tired old Lucullan oysters—'I'm sorry, Falco; I know you were in Britain, but I could not get Rutupian!' After flamingo tongues and lobster in double sauces came the ridiculous climax. Albia squeaked and sat up on her couch in happy expectation: a major-domo clinked an amphora to call for attention, spare servers stood back expectantly, the tumblers' harpists (who must have finished their boozing break) rattled off dramatic arpeggios accompanying a drum roll. A pair of sweating waiters dragged in the Trojan hog. Though young, it was a big brute, presented on a trolley upright on its feet, wearing its hair and tusks. From the glaze on its cheeks and the delectable odours, it had slow-roasted most of the day. Fake grass, full of pastry rabbits, nestled around its trotters. A crown of gilded laurel topped it, wired on between the piggy's shining ears.

A master carver approached, perhaps the chef himself, wielding a vicious meat sabre. I wouldn't trust him on a dark night round the back of a seedy posca bar. His blade flashed in the lamplight. With one mighty sweep he cut open the boar's belly. Glistening innards tumbled out towards us, like raw guts. As Helena had said, they were sausages. While we still believed they were hot viscera, he tossed a quick-fire barrage into all our foodbowls. There were screams. Someone clapped briefly. Minas took a moment to grasp what was happening, then exploded with delight. 'Excellent, excellent!' He was so thrilled, he had to beckon a server to fill up his wine goblet. A hum of appreciative voices congratulated Anacrites, while Helena and I looked on patiently.

It was a shock—though not if you knew what was coming. The trouble with the tired old Trojan hog trick is it only works once. Was I jaded? I made an effort to look excited—well, mildly—though even Claudia forgot her natural generosity and muttered to me, 'Those Lucanian sausages look very undercooked! I don't think I'll eat them.'

The crackling was good, though full of bristles.

33

Some time while everyone was gnawing tough pork, then picking their teeth discreetly, I noticed that Albia had slipped away from the table. Her absence went unremarked by others. As the main course ended, people were behaving informally. One by one they went out for a natural break, on their return taking the opportunity to move around and talk to different guests. Justinus was now alongside his brother. Helena abandoned Hosidia and crossed the room for a chat with Claudia.

I was bored with Anacrites' well-clad back as he listened to Minas. Luckily the gloopy singer reappeared; he had picked up the Cretan shepherds' habit of explaining everything long-windedly— so often, of course, lamenting young sailors lured to their doom by sinister sea-nymphs or brides who had died on their wedding day. When he announced, 'The next song is a *very* sad one', I went to find a lavatory.

I explored in a desultory fashion, but I had been in the house before and seen all I wanted of the layout, décor and cold living arrangements. I found the kitchen, with the caterers engaged in washing bowls—most of them, anyway; I had passed a couple sidling about, probably pinching Anacrites' fancy curios.

The services were, as I expected, next to the kitchen—functional, but with the faint unscrubbed odour you expect in a male establishment. (I was well trained; in a strange house it is a man's duty to report to his wife what the facilities are like.) Emerging, I took a wrong turn somehow.

I ended up in servants' quarters, a series of undecorated small rooms that served routine purposes. There were sacks of onions, buckets and besoms. Even a spy has to endure the domestic—though I bet Anacrites put his onion-seller through an oral security test. That would explain why he had been sold mouldy, sprouting ones.

I spotted a figure ahead of me, slipping down a passageway. He did not hear me call out for directions, but he had left a door open and I heard voices. In one of the rooms, Anacrites' two legmen were sitting with a draughtsboard. I was surprised; I would expect him to keep work and home separate. Instead, the Melitans, as I called them, gave the impression this was a regular haunt. Their room had a sour smell that hinted of long-term use.

The duo were not playing, just talking. They could be arguing about whose turn it was to remove their food tray (there was a large jumble of used crockery and utensils piled ready to go back to the kitchen). They barely troubled to react to my appearance.

'Lost my way.'

Neither spoke. One waved an arm. I turned out of the room, pointed myself in the direction he indicated, and departed. After I walked off, their voices stopped abruptly, however.

They might not be Melitan, but they definitely were brothers. They had the same facial looks, the same dress code (dingy tunics; open-strapped shin boots), the same movements and accents (I had noticed they talked Latin). Most of all, the way they behaved together was the way Festus and I used to be: that blend of spats and tolerance only brothers have.

Back on familiar ground, curiosity drew me to a colonnaded peristyle, formally planted around a statue of three half-size nymphs. This was where the dining room really ought to be situated. I wondered if there was in fact a better triclinium than Anacrites had assigned to us.

I was looking for Albia. Sure enough, she was there on a low wall, looking in at the courtyard. She was just sitting, so I paused. Albia had gone out for a break from watching Aelianus being polite to his wife. It would be best if she could work through her heartache privately.

Someone else interrupted her reverie: Anacrites strolled through the colonnade opposite. Crossing a corner of the garden, he went straight over to Albia. He sat on the wall beside her, not so near as to make her nervous, though near enough to worry me.

'There you are!' he said easily, as though she had been missed, not perhaps by the company but by him. To reinforce his position as a careful host, he added, 'I am glad I saw you hiding here. Helena Justina told me all about your unhappiness.'

'Really!' He would have his work cut out with Albia. He played it well, saying nothing more until she asked in her blunt way, 'What are *you* doing away from your guests?'

Anacrites rubbed the tips of two fingers against his right temple. 'Sometimes commotion disturbs me.'

'Oh yes,' Albia, the unfeeling adolescent, answered. 'I heard you had your head smashed in.'

He managed to sound rueful. 'I don't remember much about it.'

'Does it affect your work?'

'Not often. The effects are random. Days may be good or bad. It's very frustrating.'

'So what happens?'

'I think I have partly lost my powers of concentration.' It must be three years since his head wound; he had had time to learn how to cope.

'That's awkward. You might lose your job. Do you have to conceal it from everyone?'

'Whoa!' In the teeth of Albia's relentless attack, Anacrites made it jocular: 'I'm the spy. I'm supposed to ask the heavy questions.'

'Ask one then!'

Anacrites leaned back his head against a pillar. He was savouring the peace and quiet, resting. 'Do you like my little garden?'

Oil lamps had been dotted around the rest of the house, though there were none out here, probably to avoid attracting insects. In the last light of evening, only outlines of climbers and topiary showed, though there were pleasant scents and a faint splash from some informal water feature. A boy grotesque, pouring from a vase, maybe. I did not see Anacrites as a two-doves-on-a-scallop-shell man.

'It's not bad.'

'I have it looked after by professional horticulturalists. They claim they need to visit every day to keep things trim. It costs a fortune.'

'Are you rich?'

'Of course not; I work for the government.'

'Spies don't do gardening?'

'No idea how to.'

'Falco can dig and prune.'

'Unlike your father, I never had a country background. Do you call Falco your father, by the way?'

'Of course.'

'I was not sure what kind of arrangement Falco and Helena had about you.' Anacrites was obviously hinting there was something irregular he could use against us.

'I have my citizen's certificate!' Albia slapped him down.

Anacrites jumped on it: 'Was that after appearing before an Arbitration Board?'

'Not necessary in a foreign province,' Albia sneered. 'The governor has full jurisdiction. Frontinus approved it. Didius Falco and Helena Justina adopted me.'

'So formal?' So necessary, with people like him out to get us.

'Well, there you are, Anacrites. You don't know everything about Falco!'

Though I grinned at the way she attacked him, I kept absolutely still. I was standing in shadow, by a great tangle of foliage supported on some kind of obelisk. Anacrites' eyes wandered one way and another. I reckoned he suspected I was somewhere watching and listening.

'You talk as if you think I am pursuing Falco! He and I are colleagues, Albia. We have worked together many times. In the year of the Census, we worked very hard in a perfectly good partnership; the Emperor congratulated us. I remember that as a happy experience. I feel very affectionate towards Marcus Didius.'

'Oh he loves you too!' Albia chopped the subject off. 'Tell me about Antonia Caenis and Istria. Why did she care so much about where she came from? Was she hoping to find her ancestors?'

'That I don't know. Perhaps she was. We all have a yearning to discover our background, don't we?' Anacrites' question was incongruous from him.

'I think what matters is the person we are now.'

'That sounds like Helena Justina talking.'

'She speaks good sense.'

'Oh yes; I too admire her immensely.'

'Are you jealous of Falco for having Helena?'

'Certainly not. It would be inappropriate.'

'Why are you not married?'

'Never seemed to find the time.'

'Don't you like women? Do you prefer men?'

'I like women. My work tends to mean keeping very much to myself.'

'Not many friends then? Or no friends at all? You were a slave too—like Caenis. Do you know about your own family?'

'I have some idea.'

'Really? Did you ever meet them?'

'My earliest memory is being among the palace scribes.'

'So you must have been taken away from your parents very young? Was that hard?'

'I never knew anything different. Where I found myself, we were all the same. I enjoyed my training. It seemed normal.'

'So—I always want to ask people this—don't you want to try to find your relatives? If anyone could do it, a spy should be able to.'

'I suppose you ask this question because *you* feel a driving need to find your own people?'

'Oh I shall never discover who I first belonged to. I accept that. I was orphaned in the British Rebellion. I'd like to think I am a mysterious British princess—that would be so romantic, wouldn't it? But I don't have red hair and the poor people I grew up with firmly believed I was a Roman trader's child. I suppose there were circumstances that suggested it, back when they found me. Because of the terrible events and confusion, that will be all I ever know. I am realistic. The uncertainties can never be cleared up, so some avenues in society are closed to me.'

'Is that why you are unhappy, Albia?'

'No, it's because men are deceitful pigs who use people for convenience then look after their own interests.'

'Camillus Aelianus?'

'Oh, not just him!'

'It is sad to hear a young girl speak so bitterly.'

'Now who is being romantic?'

'I suppose your anger is because Aelianus betrayed your hopes and married Hosidia . . . Hosidia what? Does she only have one name?'

'Her family know her as Meline, but "Hosidia Meline"—a Roman name then a Greek one—would sound like a freed slave. She is not one, of course. Some people despise professors, but it goes without saying, they wouldn't have got to be professors if they were poor. Minas must have a prosperous family if he went to Athens to learn law. Still "Meline" wouldn't do, not among senators. Vespasian may have got away with his mistress, but he is an unusual character. The Camilli have to look respectable.'

'I am very impressed, Albia. How did you dig all this out?'

'That's my secret. I've watched Falco. I could do his work. I could do yours.'

'I would be charmed to have you—but, unfortunately, we don't use women in the intelligence service.'

'Yes you do. I've heard of Perella, the dancer. There was a lot of talk about Perella in Britain. You gave her an assignment to eliminate a corrupt official.'

'Oh *really*?'

'Anacrites, don't bluff.'

'I know Perella, certainly. She is a superb dancer.'

'She cut a man's throat. To get rid of him and avert a public scandal. Everyone knew you sent her.'

'I heartily deny that rumour! What a slur on the integrity of our beloved Emperor and the high ethos of his staff. Don't spread this story, please, or I shall be forced to impose a gagging order . . . Anyway, you are much too sweet to want to do work like that.'

'I would not want to *do* it, but I would like to know *how*. Skills give you confidence and power.'

'I would say you have quite enough confidence, young lady. And you had better be kept away from power!'

'Spoilsport.'

'There you sit, looking neat, thoughtful and demure. That, I am sure, is how your adoptive parents are bringing you up. Falco and Helena would be shocked to hear the way you have talked to me.'

'Regretful, maybe—but not surprised.' She was only half right; I was startled by the way she took the spy on.

'Well, *I* am shocked, Albia.'

'You're easily shocked then. Why? You do filthy work. You are a spy and you co-operate with the Praetorian Guards. That means unfair arrests, torture, intimidation. Nothing I have said is so very outrageous, just honest. Life made me hard. Harder than the average Roman maiden of my new father's rank, or some pampered girl brought up in higher circles. I'm harder even than the daughters of poor craftsmen, who have to work in the family business, but who are free to chatter away their days until some dumb husband claims them. I come from the streets. I am sure you poked about and learned that about me.'

'Why ever would I investigate you, my dear?'

'It's what you do. To put pressure on Didius Falco.'

'That's a myth—and libel.'

'Better hire an informer then, to make your case in court . . . So you say you are above jealousy? Why then, Anacrites, do you do stupid things like stealing that case Falco and Petronius worked so hard on? They had their teeth into it, and are perfectly capable.'

Anacrites jumped up in a spurt of irascibility. 'Olympus! If the Modestus enquiry means so much to them, that ridiculous pair can have it back. There was nothing underhand; it just seems a suitable case for my own organisation! A normal redistribution of the work-load, once I was available to supervise.'

'So the terrible Claudii don't have some hold over you?'

'Who thinks that? Don't be ridiculous!' The spy was pacing about in the courtyard. Albia, my dogged, darling fosterling, stayed where she was. Briefly, Anacrites put both hands on either side of his fore-head, as if troubled again mentally. 'Falco asked me just now how the case was going. He was satisfied with my answer.'

'I doubt that.'

Anacrites stopped. 'Did Falco put you up to this?'

'Rubbish. He would be frothing at the mouth if he realised you were talking to me. What—out here in the dark, away from the com-pany, a young girl who has only just begun to go to adult parties and a man in a position of public authority, her host, maybe thirty years her senior?'

'Quite right!' Anacrites' voice was clipped. He held out an arm for-mally. 'I have enjoyed our talk, but I should return you to our fellow guests. Come!'

It was Albia's turn to stand up, swishing her skirts to put them back in order. She kept out of reach. 'I shall return myself, thank you. If we went back together, after so long away from the couches, my parents would be bound to think you had been making dreadful overtures.'

'Your father makes his own crazy decisions about me—though I would hate Helena Justina to suppose I harbour guilty thoughts.'

'You don't?'

'I do not.'

'You mean, because you respect Falco too much?'

'No, Albia,' replied Anacrites, returning to his insidious smooth-ness. 'Because I respect you.'

It was the perfect answer—if it was honest. Albia should be flattered, impressed and charmed. Producing that smooth reply just proved what I had always thought: Anacrites was deadly dangerous.

As he led her away, he looked back and his pale eyes swept the colonnades again. He was wavering, no longer certain whether I was hidden there. Knowing me, he just thought it must be likely.

Albia had kept him hopping. But much of what he said must have been aimed at me.

34

I let Anacrites and Albia go ahead. A tall, slim figure separated off
from near another corner of the garden. A woman called in a low
voice, 'Marcus! Is that you?'

'Helena!' We met along one of the colonnades. My hand found
hers. 'So how long were *you* lurking there? Did you hear all of that?'

'Most of it.'

'I didn't put her up to it—so did you?'

I felt Helena bridle. 'I would never put her in such danger! I came
to find her.'

'Did you really tell Anacrites about her yen for Aulus?'

'Of course not. Anacrites was lying, and I shall make sure she
knows that. For one thing, whatever occurred between her and my
brother—or whatever Albia thought at the time—she really has not
talked about it. Besides, give me credit; I have more loyalty to her.
Marcus, she's just a girl. He frightens me.'

'I was impressed by how she handled that.'

'It's not safe for her.'

'We'll have to see she never comes within his orbit.'

'Too late! He knows about her,' Helena told me morosely. 'He knows he can hurt you—us—through her. And I'm afraid she, too, will be hurt in the process.'

As we went around a really dark corner, I pulled her close to kiss her and take her mind off her fears. It failed to work on Helena, though it cheered me up.

Temporarily.

We ran into Aulus and Quintus, chortling in a corridor. They admitted they had nipped off so Quintus could show his brother the cabinet of obscene statues. 'How did you monkeys get in there?'

'We asked ourselves what you would do, Marcus—then we broke the lock.' Justinus spoke as if he had brought along a crowbar specially. 'The spy can blame his fancy caterers. They are crawling everywhere.' That fitted my fancy that Laeta was paying them to observe.

'And was the "art" collection revolting?' Helena asked. The lads assured her they were shocked. However, Justinus reckoned there were fewer pieces than when he stayed here last winter; Anacrites may have felt alarmed that other people knew about his filthy gallery so he had sold the most sinister pieces. A spy needs to avoid scandal. Besides, as I knew from Pa's business, he would have made a killing from any of the private pornography collectors.

We returned to the dining room, all in a jolly foursome, so Anacrites might think we had been together all the time. I had not yet decided whether to tell Albia about us eavesdropping. She was now staring at the tumblers' pratfalls, as if planning to run away to join them.

Claudia looked weary after being left alone to cope with Hosidia. I thought Hosidia brightened, as she watched Justinus sprawl back on his couch opposite her. Could his easy manners and good looks be attracting yet another young woman who really belonged to his stodgier brother? Claudia had once been betrothed to Aulus, but she dumped him—which her new sister-in-law had probably realised . . . But Hosidia would need some nerve to flirt with Quintus. If threatened, the once-shy Claudia Rufina fought for her rights with Hispanic bravura. In fact, being the senior bride in the Camillus family seemed to have fired up her confidence. Helena and I liked her; she was tougher than she looked.

Hey ho, I had convinced myself the Camillus family were about to enact a Greek tragedy . . .

Anacrites' evening was starting to deteriorate. Dessert was the least impressive course he provided. It consisted of browned fruit and lacklustre pastries. I reckoned Anacrites had got this far in the caterer's estimate then drew a line through any extras. He had a frugal streak. When I worked with him, it had always been me who went out for honeycakes to break the monotony.

While we toyed with grapes, Minas reappeared. He boomed that he had seen one of the chefs stealing a picture. Anacrites now seemed too deflated to deal with it. I jerked my head at the Camillus brothers. He was a host to avoid, but we were guests with manners. The lads needed no further telling. We three, tailed by the dispirited spy, marched to the kitchen to investigate.

We found the hired caterers packing up. Observed dully by Anacrites, Aulus, Quintus and I lined up the Lusitanian workers, pushed them about, searched them, insulted them, then went through their equipment. They had not been too greedy—just one or two small but good artworks that the spy might not have missed for weeks, a painted miniature pulled from a nail in a wall panel (that was what Minas had seen them taking), then a pitiful assortment of nick-nack bowls and cutlery. The two female servers were the worst offenders; they each had dainty reticules that doubled up as swag-bags.

One very suspicious item was a jewel, which Quintus found rolled up in a used napkin in the laundry hamper. 'This yours?' he asked Anacrites in some surprise. The spy shook his head initially; it was hardly his taste.

Suddenly he changed his mind. 'Oh—a girlfriend must have left it. Give it me, will you—'

'What girlfriend is this?' Aelianus joshed him.

'Oh you know . . .'

'Ooh! Anacrites has had a home masseuse!'

'Sent out for special services!' Justinus joined in.

'You dirty dog!' I said. 'I hope she's registered with the vigiles and you had her credentials checked. This could be a serious breach of security—'

Anacrites looked embarrassed. He was so close about his habits, assuming he had any, that being teased made him red-faced and uneasy. He was holding out his hand for the jewel but Quintus moved away, still inspecting it closely. Aulus stopped the spy, slapped him on the back, spun him around and clapped his cheeks as if he was a youth we had all taken to be 'made a man' by a sought-after courtesan in a luxury brothel. If that was the kind of woman he had summoned here, he would have paid through the nose for the house call.

We gave the caterers a stiff lecture. They were shameless, but we were drunk, so we kept at it with pedantic gusto. Minas loomed up and threatened to prosecute them, but it was not the kind of big law-work that would gain him notice; he wandered off again to search for more of the spy's fine wine.

Minas should have stayed: once he sent the caterers on their way, Anacrites brought out a small flagon of exquisite Faustus Falernian to thank us. We four sipped it together in the kitchen, though socially it was a stiff moment. This had never been a party that would extend to the small hours so I tossed back my tot, followed by the two Camilli. We were accompanied by mothers of young children, a girl, a newly married bride—all good excuses to disperse. Most of us felt weary too. The dinner had been hard going. Minas would have dallied, but when we returned to the triclinium, he was persuaded to tag along home with the Camilli.

We all thanked Anacrites who, frankly, looked done in. He made weak protestations that it was far too early for us to leave—then thanked us rather too fervently for coming. As he led us to our transport, which had already materialised at his entrance porch, he said he had had a wonderful evening. Compared with his normal lonely nights, it probably had been.

'I hope we have mended some fences, Falco.'

I kept my face neutral, watching Helena as she kissed Quintus

Camillus goodbye, undeniably her favourite of the brothers, as he was mine.

Aulus came up to me. Briefly he clasped hands. It was an unlikely formality, especially as I was being chilly with him over Albia. I met his eyes properly, for the first time since the news of his sudden marriage; amazingly, he winked. Something small and cold passed into my hand from his.

I curled my fingers on it. In the darkness of the lurching litter going home I opened my grip but could not tell what I had been given.

At our own house, oil lamps in our familiar hallway greeted our late return. I looked again. Upon my open hand lay the special cameo we had retrieved from among the soiled linen. The Camillus brothers must have done a swift lift-and-pass, neat as Forum pickpockets.

'Oh I like that!' exclaimed Helena.

It was oval, and looked like a pendant from a necklace; it had a granulated gold loop on top, though the chain was absent. The workmanship was fine, the design aristocratic, the cutting of two-tone agate quite remarkable. While a really expensive whore might afford such a thing, it was serious quality. That must have alerted Quintus when he handled it. He was not renowned as a connoisseur—or had not been before he married; Claudia came with her own overflowing necklace boxes, so why should he learn? Yet Quintus moved in society; he had seen plenty of custom gems, hanging from the crêpey necks and scrawny lobes of wealthy high-class women.

I understood exactly why Quintus and Aulus had palmed it. This bauble required investigation.

35

Anacrites was a sad case. Nobody else would turn up before breakfast to ask if last night's guests had enjoyed his dinner. That was his excuse anyway.

'I have mislaid that jewellery.' He had already trekked to the Capena Gate to enquire after the cameo. The two Camilli denied all knowledge, so he came to me. Anacrites still pretended this loss could make life awkward with the item's owner, though he did not want to give more details about which floozy that was supposed to be.

'What's her name, your bird of expensive plumage?'

'You don't need to know . . .'

He was in a dilemma, drawing attention to the piece, when he clearly wished we knew nothing about it.

I was determined to investigate that cameo's history. I lied, therefore, and said I did not have it. 'I'd forgotten all about it. Maybe those light-fingered caterers of yours saw somebody drop it and picked it up a second time . . .' No; he had been to ask them, he said. Jupiter! He must have been busy. 'Who were they anyway?' I asked. 'You'd have to lock up the family silver if you hired them, but that chef was wonderful.'

Briefly, Anacrites glowed under my praise. 'The organiser is called

Heracleides, sign of the Dogstar by the Caelimontan Gate. Laeta put me on to them.'

'*Laeta?*' I smiled gently. 'Taking a risk, weren't you?'

'I checked their credentials. They provide imperial banquets, Marcus.' Anacrites sounded stiff. 'Gladiators' last meals before a fight. Buffets for seedy theatre impresarios who are trying to seduce young actresses. All very much in the public eye. The proprietor has too much good name to risk losing it—Besides, the thefts were carried out by minions, mere opportunism. And I was protected. I had my own security—'

'I saw your house guests!'

'Who did you see?' Anacrites demanded.

'Your dilatory agents, playing board games in a back-corridor hole . . .' Some flicker disturbed his carefully cultivated, steady gaze. If I understood that half-hidden reaction, the Melitans were in for a nasty half hour when he next saw them. He could be vindictive. If they didn't know that already, they were about to find out. 'I meant, was a suggestion from Laeta safe for *you*, dear boy?' I gazed at him and shook my head slowly. 'Given his well-known wish to winkle you out of office?'

The spy's eyes widened.

'No, he wouldn't!' I cried. 'I'm being ridiculous. Laeta is a man of honour, he is above conspiracy. Forget I spoke.' Although Anacrites had imposed iron control on his face muscles, I could see he now realised Laeta might have wrong-footed him.

He changed tack quickly. Gazing around the salon where I had been forced to entertain him, he noted the profusion of new bronze statuettes, polished expanding brazier tripods, fancy lamps suspended from branched candelabra. 'Such lovely things, Falco! You're very prosperous, since your father died. I wonder—does it affect your future?'

'Will I give up informing?' I laughed gaily. 'No chance. You'll never be rid of me.'

Anacrites smirked. All last night's affability had dissolved with his hangover and he went on to the attack: 'I'd say your new wealth exceeds due proportion. When a man receives more from Fortune than he should, winged Nemesis will come along and right the balance.'

'Nemesis is a sweetie. She and I are old friends . . . Why don't you come out straight and say you think I don't deserve it?'

'Not for me to judge. You don't bother me, Falco. Compared with you, I'm fireproof.'

He had to have the last word. I could have allowed it because it meant so much to him—but we were in my house, so I patted back the ball. 'Your confidence sounds dangerously close to hubris! You just said it, Anacrites: presumption offends the gods.'

He left. I went off to breakfast with a lighter step.

Helena and I amused ourselves over the bread rolls discussing reasons why Anacrites could be so worked up about the jewel. After all, he had money nowadays. If some night-moth complained she had lost part of her necklace during their frolics, he could afford to buy her a new one to shut her up.

Some wrangles are meaningless and soon forgotten. Anacrites and I often exchanged insults; we meant them to bite and we meant every word, though it never stuck for long. But the clash we had that morning insidiously stayed with me. I continued to believe that cameo was significant—and I wanted to know why Anacrites had panicked.

36

The Heracleides company was run by one man who lived over a stable block. It was a large stable. Up in his elegant apartment he certainly did not tread on hay. His personalised loft had been floored with highly polished boards; a team of slaves must skate around with dusters on their feet each morning. Instead of mangers, there were sumptuous cushioned couches with dramatic flared legs like whole elephant tusks. He went in for ivory—always the snobbish side of flash. And the flared leg is much beloved by stagy folk (I was thinking like Pa.)

Heracleides ran his outfit from a line of stabled wagons that contained his staff's cooking and serving equipment. Where these staff lurked by day was not immediately obvious. Heracleides, I already knew, believed in distance supervision. He flattered clients with promises of individual attention, yet stayed away from their big night. According to him, his highly trained personnel had been with him for decades; they were safe to leave alone and his presence was unnecessary. At a venue, he would not so much as place a violet in a vase. I guessed his only interest was in counting the profits.

Younger than I expected, he was a pampered specimen—too much time at the baths, probably baths which offered stodgy saffron cakes and erotic massage. His tunic had a fringed hem; a narrow gold fillet bound his suntanned brow. You know the type: all high-stepping insincerity. Not safe to buy a rock oyster from, let alone a three-course dinner with entertainment and flowers.

Trying to impress me, he paraded his business ethic: love of fine detail, competitive rates and a long list of very famous customers. I wasn't fooled. I understood him straight away. He was a chancer.

I took a flared-leg chair, which needless to say had its back at the wrong angle for the average spine. One of the fancy legs was loose too.

I mentioned to Heracleides that sadly the staff he spoke of so highly had been involved in an incident last night. At once the operatives who had supposedly been with him for years became temporaries who must have come to him with false references, bad people whom he said he would never use again. I asked to see them. Hardly to my surprise, that was impossible. I stated calmly I would come back with the vigiles that evening and if the person I was looking for was not then present, Heracleides would be in trouble.

I spelled out the trouble: 'Got a function tonight, have you? Lucky you don't supervise in person or you'd be forced to cancel. Looks like you'll be stuck here answering five hundred questions about the status of your boy and girl helpers until the moon comes out. Any of them got form? Past arrests for pinching clients' pretty manicure boxes? Your women ever been on the vigiles' prostitute lists?' In the service industry that was inevitable. Waitresses were there to sleep with. 'And what about you, Heracleides—what's your citizen status? Did you answer your summons for the Census? Got any imported artwork you never paid port duty on? Where did all this charming ivory come from—would it be African?'

He tried to play tough. 'What do you want, Falco?'

'I want whichever of your staff picked up a fine cameo pendant at the spy's house. If they talk to me today, I can promise no comeback.'

'I wish I'd never taken that brief.'

'Think of this as structured learning. Now, show me your managerial expertise: kindly produce my witness.'

He liked the jargon. He disappeared to ask the group which of them was guilty. He wasn't long coming back. His minions must be curled up in the stable stalls downstairs.

'It's my chef. He's not available. I sent him on a meat-carving course. Sorry—you've had a wasted journey.'

'He slashed the Trojan hog with panache last night. He doesn't need extra training. You're lying. Let's make a little trip downstairs, shall we?'

We made the trip. I walked at my favourite pace, steady but purposeful. Heracleides stumbled more jerkily. That was because I was holding him up by the back of his tunic, so he had to walk on tiptoe. Draught mules watched thoughtfully as we appeared together in the stable.

'Call your chef.'

'He's not here, Falco.'

'Call him!'

'Nymphidias . . .'

'Too quiet.' I reinforced the request painfully. Heracleides yelled Nymphidias' name with much more urgency and the chef crawled out from behind a barrel. He was the man who stole the miniature painting yesterday, I knew. In view of his expertise with knives, I kept my distance.

I let go of the party-planner, shaking my fingers fastidiously. Heracleides fell headlong into some dirty straw, though of course I had not pushed him. I squared up to the chef. Not having his big carver with him, his bravado crumbled.

I extracted the facts fast. Yes, Nymphidias stole the cameo. He had found it in one of the small rooms down the corridor where I got lost earlier in the evening. In the room had been a narrow bed, a man's spare clothes, and a luggage pack. The jewel was in the pack, wrapped carefully in cloth. Everything else there had looked masculine.

I described the Melitans. The chef knew who I meant. They had both come into the kitchen at one point, asking for a meal. Nymphidias said it was a cheek—not in the party contract and they had demanded double portions too—but he prepared some food in a slack moment, which he personally took to their quarters as an excuse to look around. They were in the room where I saw them sitting, not the same as where he found the cameo.

It started to look as if all kinds of agents slept at the spy's house, on occasions. He must be running a kind of runners' dormitory.

'You see anyone else apart from the two who were hungry?'

'No.'

'Nobody who stayed in the single room, where you found the jewel?'

'No.'

I did not believe it. 'There was someone else—I saw him myself.'

'Party guests came to use the washroom. So did the musicians. That singer was hanging about like a spare part—we run into him at a lot of dos.'

'He's called Scorpus,' Heracleides put in, trying to seem helpful. 'Always takes an interest in how much money the hosts have, who their wives are sleeping with, and so on. Very persistent. It's all wrong; in our business you have to be discreet. These clients are high-status; they expect complete discretion.'

'So unprofessional,' I sympathised. 'He sings appallingly too. Whose nark is he? Who pays him?'

'You'll have to ask him.' Heracleides looked jealous, as though he thought Scorpus might receive more for information than he did.

'And who do *you* spy for?'

'No comment.'

'Oh him! I've met that shy boy "no comment" before! There are ways to make him less bashful—and they are not pleasant.'

I returned my attention to the chef. He said the spy's household staff had kept to themselves all evening, annoyed that outsiders had been hired. Apparently that was common. When Heracleides ran functions, he told his staff to make sure the house slaves did not spike drinks or spoil dishes. Anacrites dressed his slaves in green (how sickly; he would!); when they did wander about, they were easy to identify.

'So,' I enquired of Nymphidias, 'from its position and appearance, what did you think when you found this jewel?'

He sniffed. 'I thought whoever had it must have no right to it. It was hidden away too carefully. The rest of his stuff didn't look at all swank. The gem couldn't be his. So I might as well take it off him, mightn't I? Just the way,' he whined, with a new aggression in his tone, 'you've taken it off me.'

'The difference being,' I answered quietly, 'I shall hand it in to the vigiles, so they can find out who really owns it.'

Standing beside me, Heracleides laughed. 'Anacrites won't like that!'

He was right. But Anacrites would never know, until there was a good reason for Petronius and me to tell him.

Before I left, I took Heracleides out of hearing of his staff. 'One last question. Who is so keen to know what goes on in Anacrites' house?'

'I don't know what you mean, Falco.'

'Pig's pizzle. Anacrites is supposed to be the Chief Spy—but more observers sneaked in last night than deluded fathers and clever slaves in a Greek farce. What if I float the name Claudius Laeta past you?'

'Never heard of him.'

'You're tiring me out. Anacrites may be simple-minded, but I can spot infiltrators. Admit it; you do the same as Scorpus. You get paid to poke around houses, on likely nights . . . Indiscretions happen at parties. People drink too much, there is unfortunate groping, you overhear talk of an illegal betting syndicate, someone says Domitian Caesar needs a good spank, someone else knows about the Praetor's nasty habit—'

Heracleides looked wide-eyed. 'What habit?'

I had started a rumour. Well, it was probably true. 'Educated guess . . . We can make a deal. You tell me about Laeta, and I'll make sure you will hear no more about your staff's pilfering last night?'

'Can't help you, honestly. Oh leave it alone, Falco—we've got a good racket, and it's harmless. The hosts can all afford it. And we don't keep the stuff ourselves.'

'What racket's this?'

At once Heracleides regretted the slip. He soon drooped and confessed. 'We lift a few pretty things that look as if they may have sentimental value. We pass them to our principal. He goes along to the house a few days later. He tells them he has heard on his special grapevine about some property that belongs to them. He thinks he can get it all back, and will retrieve it as a special favour. Of course there is a premium to pay . . . You know.' I knew all right.

'So who is this?' It could not be Laeta. He had more class. Blackmail was his medium, not ransoming heirlooms.

'Someone I'm not prepared to mess with, Falco.' Well, the scam was almost irrelevant. I handled property-hostage hustles sometimes, but my present interest was in bigger things.

Heracleides seemed genuinely afraid. Joking initially, I finished up, 'That settles it. I shall have to assume that you work for Momus!'

Then the party-planner shuddered. 'Yes, but he scares me! For heaven's sake don't tell the filthy bastard that I told you, Falco.'

Momus, as well as Laeta?—Now this was really getting complicated.

37

I managed to screw from the party-planner directions for finding the torch singer. It took me an hour to locate his block, and identify which attic he festered in. Scorpus was fast asleep on his bed. That's the beauty of witnesses who work late nights. You can generally find them.

I sized him up before I woke him. He was chunky, though not athletic. He had a red face, a grey moustache, fairish hair receding badly. He looked like a tax lawyer. He probably played for them.

He slept in a disreputable loincloth; I threw a blanket over him. He woke up. He thought I wanted his money or his body, which he took in good part; then he saw that I was holding his lyre and he panicked. There was no need even to threaten him. It was such a good instrument it would have hurt even me if I had to smash it. He would talk. In great alarm he struggled to get up, but I pushed him back prone, using one foot. I did it gently. I didn't want this aesthetic type to collapse with anxiety.

'My name's Falco. Didius Falco. I expect you know that. And you're Scorpus, the disgusting highbrow singer of doleful dirges—'

'I play in the respected Dorian mode!'

'What I said. Minor keys and melancholia. If your listeners aren't sad when you start, by the time you stop, the poor idiots will be suicidal.'

'That's harsh.'

'Like life . . . Just lie there and co-operate. It won't hurt. Well, not as much as refusing, trust me . . . We can save time, because I know the score. Whenever there is a gathering at an expensive private house, with hired-in food and entertainment, half the specialist artistes are collecting and selling information. You certainly do it. I want to know your paymaster, and anything you saw of interest last night at the Chief Spy's house.'

He yawned insultingly. 'Is that all!'

'It's enough. Let's start with Claudius Laeta. Did he pay you to collect dirt on Anacrites—or have I got this the wrong way round: when you play for the great Laeta at the Palace is somebody else giving you kickbacks to observe him?'

'Both.'

'Ah Hades!' I twanged a lyre string vacantly, as if seeing how far I could make it stretch before it snapped. I can play a lyre. I use it for disguises. I know what happens when a string breaks and was really not keen to have whipping animal-gut flick at high speed into my eye. Scorpus could only see the threat to his precious instrument.

'Please don't do any damage!'

'Who's spying on Laeta? Momus? Anacrites?'

'Both—Everyone thinks I am working for them. Really I'm freelance.'

'Freelance, as in you'll take anybody's money? And you'll shit on anybody too?' I sneered. It made no impact. He was shameless. Well, I knew that from what he twangled for helpless listeners. 'You can do better than this, Scorpus.'

'What are you after?' He caved in. He had no interest in the fine practice of resistance. I was almost disappointed.

'I want to know what you saw.'

'Much the same as you did, I suppose,' he retorted defiantly.

'I was a guest. I couldn't look around freely, and anyway I've been in that house before. I know he has a pornographic art collection, so don't try to pass that off as news.'

'Has he?'

'He's sold a lot of it. Somebody must have warned him he's under observation.'

'I can't think who would warn that man of anything.'

'Then you have more taste than I supposed! What have you told Laeta?'

'I am bound to secrecy.'

'Let me unbind you.' I inspected the arms of his instrument, while prising apart the elegant yokes, forcing them against their cross-strut . . .

'Oh leave off, Falco! I had nothing to tell Laeta, except a list of who attended. The Greek with the big beard was dire, I have to say.'

'That Greek is a master of jurisprudence. He could sue you in three different courts for insulting him. He might even win.'

'He'd have to be sober!' The singer fought back with spirit. I had to stop this; I was starting to like him.

'I know that the caterers were stealing, for a ransom scam. You must have seen them at it, at other parties. I know who's paying them as well. Momus. You don't want to tangle with that bastard.'

'His money's good, if you're desperate.'

'So you work for Momus too?'

'Not if I can help it. Sometimes the landlord here is very demanding . . .'

I looked around. The place was bare and unappealing. Not as squalid as rooms I myself had parked in, but unsuitable for a court musician. He wouldn't want Laeta to spot fleabites. 'Whatever the rent, he's overcharging! You can afford better.'

'Who cares? I'm never here.'

'Have some self-respect, man!' I was turning into his wise old nurse. 'What do you spend your fees on?'

'Saving for a once-in-a-lifetime cruise to Greece.' That figured.

'Did it last year—not all it's cracked up to be. Still, book it and go now. You could die of self-neglect and your efforts would all be wasted. So—who were the tumblers and the band working for?'

'No one special.'

'What? We're talking about Cretan shepherds in hairy coats!'

'Cretan my rear end! The tumblers arrived last week from Bruttium and all the rest came straight over the Tiber from Nero's Circus.'

'You amaze me! And they have no money-making sidelines?'

'I didn't say that. I believe,' said Scorpus, with disgust, 'the strummers have been known to sell stories about indiscretions for the dirty scandal page in the *Daily Gazette*.'

I winced. 'That's low!'

'I agree—though I believe there is cash to be made.'

'Fortunately the Camilli—to whom I am related, by the way, so watch it—are models of tedious morality. As for Anacrites, snitching on him would be madness: you could end up holding your next musical evening with Praetorian Guards, answering an arrest warrant signed by Titus Caesar, before they drag you on a very short walk to your death.'

I plucked his lyre, reflecting that the musicians he sneered at as strummers had played seven-string lyres too—their instruments probably costing much less than this fine pearl-inlaid walnut specimen. The singer gave me a sideways scrutiny. 'So what were *you* doing there, Falco?'

'Oh all I got was indigestion and a sore head.'

Thinking this had made us friends, Scorpus tried again to get up. I shoved him back angrily. 'Oh get this over with! What do you want, Falco?'

'Who did you see? There were two agents lurking in a back room—was somebody else with them?'

He had had enough time between playing his sets for a thorough reconnoitre. He knew about the Melitans. But Scorpus claimed, convincingly it seemed, that he saw no one else; he did not know who occupied that other room, where the pilfering chef found the cameo.

I gave up and went home for lunch.

The singer had lied to me. I did not know it at the time, but when I found out afterwards, I felt no real surprise.

38

After lunch my secretary needed me to attend to business; in superior homes it might be the other way around, but not with Katutis. He told me what I had to tell him to do. I complied. Still, I was lucky to have my hour with him. Now I was known to have a secretary, other people continually borrowed him. Katutis was supposed to take down my case-notes and start collating my memoirs, but he spent whole afternoons writing out soup recipes, curses and laundry lists.

Next, Helena wanted to discuss household matters, which meant more meek compliance. My daughters then had an urgent need to show me drawings and ask for new shoes like those their friend three doors down had been given by their spoiling parents. Even the dog stood at the front door with her leash in her mouth.

Only Albia tried to avoid anything to do with me, but I took her out anyway. That would teach her to tell Anacrites she could do an informer's job.

I was taking the cameo to Petronius. By the time we reached Maia's apartment, it was so near to evening we only just caught him before he left for duty.

'Hold on. I want to show you this, off vigiles premises.'

He got the message.

With Albia watching, we inspected the jewel. It was carved from sardonyx, the redder form of onyx. 'It's like an agate, Albia—layered hard stone.'

'More education!'

'Listen and learn, girl.'

Petronius held the gemstone in his mighty paw while he tried to work out what was going on in the picture. It was a two-layered cut, in low relief. The onyx banding was white and red-brown, beautifully executed. The lower half of the design showed a gloomy bunch of captured barbarians. On an upper frieze, gathered around twirly horns of plenty, minor deities were applying triumphal crowns to the noble brows of bare-chested noble personages. An eagle, probably representing Jove, was trying to muscle in. 'Claudian imperial family,' Petronius guessed. 'They always have that clean-cut, very close-shaven look. They were all untrustworthy midgets really.'

Albia giggled.

'He's exaggerating, Albia. Lucius Petronius, being a great hulk himself, likes to make out anyone dainty is deformed. However, this is so special it may even have belonged to Augustus or someone in that family, either commissioned by them or given as a gift by a syco-phant.'

Petro's eyebrows shot up. 'It's that good?'

'Trust me; I'm an antique dealer. Without provenance it's hard to be sure, but I would say this could be the work of Dioscurides. If not his own piece, it certainly came from his workshop.'

'Dio who?'

'Augustus' favourite cameo-cutter. Well, look at the workmanship! Whoever carved this was brilliant.'

Petronius leaned towards Albia and growled, 'Have you noticed how Falco keeps sounding like a bent auctioneer these days?'

'Yes, at home we all feel we are living with a fake-wine-jug seller.'

'Rag away!' I grinned. 'Whoever owned this—I don't mean some mystery lodger at the spy's house—knew its worth. The purchaser, who may have been a woman because it has been a necklace pendant, had the money and the knowledge to buy real quality.'

'Someone in mind?' asked Petro.

'I hope we can tie it to Modestus' wife, Livia Primilla. From the nephew's vagueness when I asked about any distinguishing jewellery she wore, I don't think he would recognise it, but he said she wore good stuff.'

Petronius perked up. 'If it was her, and if she was wearing this when she disappeared, there is a chance we can identify it.'

He told us that the Fifth Cohort had picked up a runaway slave living rough near the Porta Metrovia, who was called Syrus. They were bringing him over to the Fourth that night, for quizzing about whether he was the Syrus given to the butcher by Sextus Silanus—the one who had waved Primilla off when she went to see the Claudii.

'Couldn't the Fifth have asked him for themselves?'

'They could have tried,' said Petro. 'But the slave's scared to talk and everyone knows Sergius is the best in the business.'

Sergius was the Fourth Cohort's torturer.

At this point I would have left Albia at Maia's house; sensing a brush-off, she insisted on coming to the station house with us.

Sergius was waiting for Petronius to arrive before he started. He had stashed Syrus in a small cell, like someone marinating a choice cut of meat for a few hours before grilling.

'You could just ask the man,' Albia suggested. It could have been Helena talking.

'Not half the fun,' said Sergius. 'Besides, the slave's evidence will only count if he screams it out while I'm thrashing him. The theory is, pain will make him honest.'

'Does it work in practice, Sergius?'

'Once in a while.'

'How can you tell whether what he says is true or not?'

'You can't. But then you can't tell when you're questioning a free citizen either. Most of them lie. That applies whether they have something real to hide—or are just being buggers on principle.'

I thought Albia might have been upset by the whip man's attitude, but young girls are tough. She listened quietly, filing away the details in that strange little head of hers. 'If this is the right slave, what will happen to him?'

'He will be whipped hard, for causing us trouble, then returned to whoever owns him.'

'No choice?'

'Certainly not. He is their property.'

'A non-person?'

'That's the definition.'

Albia accepted this as one more fact that showed Romans were cruel—assuming that idea was what caused her enquiry. Sometimes she was unreadable.

Albia turned her pale little face to me. 'Do you think coming from a rough, hard background, being treated badly in their slave generation, explains why those Claudii turned out as they are?'

'Maybe. But some groups, some families are feckless by nature. People carry their character defects from birth, whatever their origin. You find freedmen who are loyal, kind-hearted, hard-working and decent to live with. Then you find noblemen who are vicious, deceitful and intolerable to be around.'

Albia smiled. 'Helena would say, "I blame their mothers!"'

Petronius clapped her on the shoulder. 'There may be some truth in that.'

'So how does this theory explain Anacrites the spy?'

Petro and I both laughed. I said it: 'He is just a poor sad boy who never had a mother!'

Albia gave me a long look. She did not say, since she could see I had just remembered it, that until Helena picked her off the streets in Londinium, she herself had struggled with neither parent.

Petronius, a father of girls, recognised her mood. 'Falco is right. Most people do seem to be born with a character inbuilt. So you, Flavia Albia, are destined to be decent, sweet and true.'

'Don't patronise me!' Of course, being Lucius Petronius, he had charmed her.

We left it there. Sergius, with his long whip, was impatient to begin.

He got as far as ascertaining that the terrified fellow the Fifth had brought us was indeed the slave Livia Primilla owned. When she went to see the Claudii, she had given him instructions to wait three days then if she failed to come home, to go to tell her nephew. Syrus, who looked as if he had come from the interior deserts of Africa, was able to describe the scene: Primilla mounted on a donkey, wearing a round-brimmed travel hat. The slave was poor on garments but thought her outfit was in shades of dark red, with a long fringed stole that was also red or damson coloured. Petronius showed him the sardonyx cameo; he failed to recognise it.

One new piece of information emerged. Petronius demanded: how could her staff, despite their duty of care to their mistress, have let Primilla go off alone to see the Claudii—especially after Modestus had already gone missing? Syrus said Primilla had intended to meet up with someone: the overseer who looked after the property and who had first found the broken fences, a man called Macer. This was a development. This man had not previously figured in the disappearances. He must be one of the family slaves who had run away.

At that point, we were thwarted. Loud hammering at the mighty gates of the station house announced unwelcome visitors. The gates were kicked open. In burst a small group of large armoured men. Plumes danced in their glittering helmets. Violence curdled the air.

Three tiers of military cohorts kept law and order in the city; neither law nor order had much to do with the feud between them all. The Praetorian Guards despised the Urban Cohorts and they both hated the vigiles. But the Praetorians protected the Emperor and were commanded by Titus Caesar now; whenever those thrusting bullyboys strode from their camp and appeared in public, there could be no contest.

They burst into the exercise yard like dam water after a leak. There was no stopping them. Petronius did not try. Somehow Anacrites had learned we had the slavey; he had sent the Guards to snatch Syrus. They made it plain, it would be foolish to request a warrant.

'Take the ungrateful bastard; I don't want him. Our budget's too tight for feeding runaways.' Well, Syrus was a slave. Nobody was going to make an issue of it. 'I heard the Fifth had found him,' Petronius told the Guards' leader helpfully. 'My plan was to check the facts and send him up to the Palace with a note. You're doing me a favour. He's all yours.'

'Oh he is!' snarled the Guards' leader. 'Word of warning—don't meddle!'

'Are you speaking for Anacrites?'

'None of your business who I'm speaking for—back off, soldier!'

I could not believe the spy had been so crude—and it went against the careful pretence of comradeship he had been laying on thick at his dinner party. But that was him, since his head wound. He was highly unpredictable. Capricious mood changes damaged his judgement. The one thing a spy needs is self-preservation—and that demands self-knowledge.

Syrus was hauled from the interrogation cell by the Emperor's élite thugs while we stood around like puddings. Terror overtook him so his legs gave way; the Guards virtually carried him. His eyes rolled white and he shat himself. It had nothing to do with Sergius, who despite our teasing of Albia had barely touched him. Petronius was not preparing a witness statement; he had wanted answers, answers he could trust. Instead, as the Praetorians dragged the slave away, the poor creature knew his fate. He would be dead in a ditch within the hour. Anacrites, we were starting to suspect, either knew the answers already or he did not care.

Petronius cursed. He knew nobody would ever see that slave again. At least we still had the cameo. Petro retrieved it from a murky bucket of water where he had quickly dropped it when the Guards crashed in.

As for them giving us orders to back off, it was blatant intimidation. Nothing new for the Praetorians; not so new for the spy—but foolish. So stupid, in fact, that Petronius and I wondered if Anacrites had lost his grip.

39

Y ou two great men have lost yourselves!' Albia was a frank
wench; it was liable to get her into trouble. 'Why don't you ask
the big question: if the cameo really belonged to Primilla, and if it
was taken by a killer—*how did Anacrites get it?*'

I pointed out coldly that I had spent all morning among the dregs
of artistic society trying to find out. 'Anyone else, Petronius and I
would go along to his house, pin him to a wall with a meat skewer
and demand an explanation. But the spy can't be handled like that.
He claims it belongs to some woman he had had at the house.'

Petronius snorted. 'She must be desperate.'

'So many are, sadly,' Albia commented. 'That is how you men get
away with things.'

'Helena is teaching her a lot!' said Petro.

'Sarcasm especially. It's always possible the spy does have a girlfriend.'

Albia biffed this aside. 'The jewel was found by the hog-chef, tucked
away in luggage that we think belongs to the Melitan brothers. If they
are Melitan. Or even brothers. Who said so? Nobody. This is just a
fantasy Falco dreamed up last Saturnalia, when he had had too much

wine with his hot water. I remember the pair of them watching our house, and the only thing we could tell was that they were idiots.'

'You ought to be at school, young lady,' Petronius instructed her. 'Not hanging around a vigiles house, causing upset.'

'I'm making sensible suggestions. And, by the way, I am home-tutored by Helena.'

'Oh take her home, Falco.'

'I can't. You and I have to talk about this cameo—'

'Send her then. Albia, be off with you!' Petro lowered his voice to me. 'I could assign a man to escort her—'

'I don't need a bodyguard!' snapped Albia. 'I'll go by myself.'

She went.

Petronius Longus stared at me. 'You let her walk in the streets alone?'

'Nothing else is practical. You allow Petronilla out unchaperoned, don't you?'

'Petronilla is a child. Much safer. Your girl is marriageable age.' He meant beddable.

We left it.

'She's right,' I grumbled. 'We need to explore how the cameo came to the Melitans.'

'Surely you mean the idiotic agents of unknown origin?'

'Bastard! I'm sure they look like brothers. Listen—if there is an innocent explanation for them having it, that saves us trying to link this to the Pontine killings. Maybe Anacrites really does screw women. Asking him for more details will be a waste of effort—but we could find his unknown-origin agents and ask them questions. He won't like it, but by the time he finds out, it's done. Can't you put troops out to look for them?'

Petronius groaned. 'I'd love to. I haven't got the manpower, Falco. If Anacrites keeps them close to him at home or in his office, those are no-go areas. I can't send troops into the Palace and I am not getting a formal reprimand for watching that swine's private house—

especially not on a case I was told to drop,' Petro concluded reasonably.

'Last night, he suggested they were his bodyguards.'

'Then the whole idea is definitely off.'

'You didn't tell me it was on.'

'I'm thinking about it.'

In the end, Petro taxing his brain proved unnecessary. One of my nephews turned up at the station house, bringing a message. Katutis had written it out. His writing was so neat, I always had difficulty deciphering the letters.

'What exactly is the point of your secretary, Falco?'

'Oh he goes his own way. That keeps him happy.'

Petro got his clerk to decipher. Albia had spotted one of the hang-dog Melitans. Anacrites was watching my house again.

'The bastard! He's made this too easy for us—'

Petronius grabbed my arm. 'Now hang on, Marcus; we need to plan this properly—'

I nodded. Next minute he and I were scuffling in a doorway, laughing like ten-year-olds, as we each tried to be first through as we dashed out to run down the Aventine by the nearest steps to the Embankment. We knew that in taking on the Melitan we would be taking on Anacrites. Nothing of what happened next had been adequately considered. But with hindsight, it is fair to say Petronius and I would still have done it.

40

We separated and approached from two directions.

It was still light. The day's heat had diminished slightly, but blue sky still soared over the marbled bank, the Tiber, and the low hills opposite. The frenetic hum of city life had lost a little of its persistence as businesses slowed down and individuals thought about going to the baths. Those bath houses that had already opened would have just allowed admittance to their outer porticoes. Stokers were busy raising a smoke, ready for the formal entry to the changing rooms when the bell rang. There was plenty of banging and shouting, which carried further across the water as the last boat relays brought goods up to the Emporium from Ostia, making the weary stevedores curse as they longed to down tools and bunk off to wine shops.

Surveillance could not be easy. My house had no side or back approaches. The front looked straight out across the Tiber over the Transtiberina slums, towards the old Naumachia where Augustus had staged mock-sea-battles. Nobody here kept topiary in terra-cotta pots, suitable to hide behind, because if we did night-time drunks just rolled them over the road and pushed them in the river. Occasionally carts were parked, but as the Embankment was a main thoroughfare and a commercial artery, the street aediles had them moved to avoid congestion. All an observer could do was hang around in the road chewing a bread roll, hoping I would not appear in person and spot him. Last time the two so-called Melitans were watching us, the whole family used to wave at them as we came and went. Even the dog once ran up to wag her tail and say hello.

Albia was right. He was there. One of them, on his own. I wondered where his brother was. Maybe the two agents were taking turns—or if Anacrites was thoroughly obsessed with us, the other might be outside Petro and Maia's apartment. We would have to find out. My sister would become hysterical if she thought the spy was having her watched.

What we did next was totally unplanned. Petronius and I had been in this kind of dark situation once before, in Britain. An officer who betrayed our legion had to be dealt with. Justice was done. Maybe it gave us a taste for hard revenge. I for one had hoped we'd never find ourselves in such a situation again, but when we ended up here on the Embankment with the spy's agent, neither Petro nor I thought twice.

The man saw me coming, as I walked directly up to him. He was considering resistance when Petro tapped him on the shoulder from behind. We were already too close for him to run or fight. So we had him. We simply took him into custody.

At the time we presumed he thought Anacrites would rescue him. Perhaps he did think that. Perhaps we did. He may have expected we would merely argue about the surveillance, at worst throw a few punches, then order him to stop harassing me. That may even have been what we initially intended.

We searched him. It was no surprise to find that he was carrying: four knives of different sizes plus a short piece of rope that was only suitable for strangulation. We kept him standing in the road while we stripped him of this armoury, not bothering to be polite, though since it was a public place, we were not particularly brutal. He grunted a bit. Petro and I were feeling our way towards a decision.

Once we made him safe, we took him into my house. He had not expected that. Neither had we, to be honest; it seemed to follow on naturally from the search process. In this way we took him off the street and out of sight very rapidly—and we saved Petronius the potential awkwardness of imprisoning one of the spy's men at the station house. As soon as we stepped inside and the front door closed, everything became intensely serious.

We put him in a downstairs room. It was one of the damp ones I reserved for summer storage. In August he would not develop asthma or foot rot. The walls and door were thick. I pointed out that nobody would hear him call for help. Then we gagged him anyway. By this time, the black implications were growing. For him, there could now be no happy ending. For us, too, there was no going back.

We worked quietly. He endured it with resignation. This would not be a job for the vigiles punishment officer, Sergius and his metal-tanged whip; we would give it our personal treatment. The agent was an unimpressive specimen, but it was soon clear he would be professional. We bound his arms behind his back, tied his ankles together, then picked him up like a long parcel and roped him carefully to the top of a heavy bench, face up. We turned the bench on its end so he hung upside down, then left him to think about his situation while we went for refreshments and warned all my household that the room was out of bounds. Albia would probably have rushed straight in there, but she was out on one of her long solo walks.

Helena was apprehensive, though we tried to avoid her concern. She could tell Petro and I were beginning to feel raw. We had no regrets about our capture, but we had put ourselves in a grim deep hole. Helena drew herself up and said, 'I live here with very young children. I want to know what you are intending to do to this man.'

'Ask him questions.' Ask him questions in a particular way, a way that would produce answers—eventually.

'And if he refuses to answer?'

'We'll improvise.'

'How long should it take?'

'Perhaps a few days, love.'

'Days! You are going to hurt him, aren't you?'

'No. There's no point.'

'Am I to provide food and drink for him?'

'That won't be necessary.'

'I wish you meant he won't be here that long.'

'No. We don't mean that.'

'You cannot starve him.' We could. With this kind of man, we would have to. And that was just the start.

'Well, maybe a bowl of delectable soup, with an aromatic scent,' suggested Petronius with a smile. 'After two or three days . . .' To stand in the room and tantalise.

'What about toilet facilities?' Helena demanded angrily.

'Good thinking! A bucket and a large sponge would be wonderful, please.' We would clean up as we went. Petro and I had fathered babies; we could look after a prisoner hygienically. A regime of squalor has been known to work, but Helena was right; this was our house.

Our first conversations with him were civilised.

'Anacrites sent you—agreed? How long have you known him?'

'Couldn't say.'

'I can check the payroll. I have contacts.'

'Couple of years.'

'Who is the other fellow I've been seeing with you? A brother of yours, I'm thinking.'

'Could be.'

'Where is he?'

'Gone to see his wife.'

'Where's that?'

'Where he lives.'

'Don't be funny with us. You two look like twins.'

'And you two look like donkey-fuckers.'

'I'll overlook that, but don't push us. Do you have a name?'

'Can't tell you.'

'Are you from Melita?'

'Where?'

'Small island.' Ma had a Melitan lodger once. Thinking about it, at close quarters, this man was not olive-skinned, hairy or stumpy enough. He was hard to place—not from the East, but not from as far north as Gaul or Britain either.

'Don't insult me. I'm from Latium,' he claimed.

'You don't look like it.'

'How would you know?' A generation back, on Mother's side, I was from Latium myself. His accent was right: Latin, though countrified. This was almost the first occasion I had heard him speak. Three-quarters of Rome sounded just the same.

'What part of Latium?'

'Can't tell you.'

'Could be anywhere from Tibur to Tarracina. Lanuvium? Praeneste? Antium? Come on, what's the harm? Be specific.'

Silence.

'At least he never says, *Find out yourself!*' Petronius weighed in. 'He's being wise. That only leads to a big kicking.'

'Not our style.'

'No; we're soft little cupids.'

'So far.' I think we knew we were on the cusp of surprising ourselves.

'He doesn't like you, Falco. Perhaps he has a point. Let me talk to him. I expect he wants to deal with a professional.'

'Just don't thump him. You'll defile my house.'

'Who needs to touch him? He's going to be sensible. Aren't you, sunshine? Tell us your name now.'

'Find out yourself.'

Oh dear. Well, Petronius Longus had warned him.

We left him soon afterwards. It was dinnertime. For us.

41

We continued. One at a time, then in tandem. Long pauses. Short pauses. For the agent, existence became concentrated on events in this small room. When Petronius and I left the door open briefly, so he heard a child's cry or a rattle of pots in the distance, it must have seemed otherworldly.

'What's your name?'

'Can't tell you.'

'Won't, you mean. Why did Anacrites order you to watch my house?'

'Only he knows.'

'We may have to ask him, then. So much easier all round, if we can stop him knowing you were so easily spotted and caught . . . No, I'm wrong. He must realise by now. How soon do you think he missed you? Can't have taken long. Where is he, I wonder? What's he going to do about you? You would think Praetorian Guards would rip in here to grab you back for him. Has he given up on you? Perhaps he's away—could he have gone to the Pontine Marshes, working the Modestus case? Looking for the Claudii—have you heard about them?'

'Can't tell you.'

Petronius Longus suddenly spun the cameo in the air. 'Did you have this?'

'Never seen it before.'

'You or your brother?'

'Better ask him.'

'Now I'm depressed, Falco—imagine having to talk to two of them!'

'Suits me. One each. You could take yours to the station house, give him a real thrashing, use your implements. I could keep one here to play with.'

'Yours would talk first. You wear people out with your wonderful kindness. Villains cave in, weeping. They want the brutality they are used to. They understand that. You being their lovely benefactor just confuses people, Falco.'

'No, I think people respect humanity. After all, we could pull out his fingernails and crush his balls. Instead, what does he get? Moderate language and a pleasant manner. Look at this one—he admires restraint, don't you?—Oh don't hit him again; he's going to tell us everything without that . . . I still think he and the other one are twins. Twins can communicate through thought, you know. I bet his brother's sweating. What's your name again?'

'Can't tell you.'

'What's your brother's name?'

'Can't tell you.'

'Where did this cameo come from?'

Long silence.

42

O nce, I thought he had been weeping while we left him alone. On my return, his eyes were dull, as if in the long interval of solitude, he had been remembering old pain. But his resistance stiffened. Someone had spent years conditioning this man. We could not touch him. He would endure all, without weakening and collapsing. He would ride it out, even curbing signs of hostility, until we gave up.

We were tiring of the game. He had stopped refusing to tell us things. He stopped talking to us at all.

'I'm going to throw a bucket of cold water at him.'

'No don't do that. This is my house, Petro. I don't want water everywhere. You go and have a bite. There's some really good goat's cheese, just came from the market this morning, strong and salty. And I've put out a flask of Alban wine; believe me, you really need to try it. Leave me with our friend here.'

Petronius left the room.

'Now, here we are, cosy and private. How about you tell me who you are and what you do for Anacrites?'

No answer.

I threw a bucket of cold water at him.

43

A development.
   Helena Justina had been brooding ever since we first brought the man into the house. Now she braced herself, waited until everyone else was preoccupied, then came down to see what was happening.

We had the bench standing properly at that time. He was looking up at the ceiling, or he would have been, had he not appeared to be asleep. Petronius and I were standing back, arms folded, thinking up our next move. At that quiet moment, Helena must have been surprised by the ordinary atmosphere. She may have felt relieved by the lack of violence. Then she realised it was more sinister than it appeared.

   Petronius and I greeted her affably. Outwardly normal, we could have been two men in a workshop who had been preoccupied with a big carpentry project; she could be the woman of the house just making sure two simple lags were not drinking nettle beer brewed in a billycan or reading pornographic scrolls. Our sleeves were rolled up high. Our attitude was businesslike; though drained by days of concentrated, unsuccessful effort, we were feeling weary.

   The man on the bench seemed aware that Helena had entered the room. His eyelids flickered, though his eyes stayed closed. She stood there: more gaunt facially since she lost the baby, tall, positive though wary, dressed in drifting summer white, wafting a light silver-blue stole, as cool as refreshing sorbet chilled in a rich man's snow-cellar. He might smell her citrus perfume. He must hear the quiver of her bangles and her clear voice.

Observant and intelligent, she absorbed the scene. I watched her looking for signs of what we had been doing—while dreading what she might learn. There was nothing to see. Everything looked clean and neat. She focused on the man. She saw his exhaustion, how hunger, thirst, isolation and fear were bringing him close to hallucination, despite his ferocious will to resist. He had to fight now, to stop his mind wandering.

Helena realised how our task had dispirited Petronius and me too, how our power over the helpless man would soon defile us. Most men would have been corrupted from the moment the prisoner was taken and tied up, his helplessness freeing them from moral restraint. Even we had to struggle to avoid being most men.

'This is too brutal. I want you to stop.' The words were firm, but Helena's voice shook.

'We can't, love. It's about long-term sanction of bad neighbours' bullying. It's about murder, and official cover-ups of murder. He seems to be involved. If his activities have an innocent explanation, he only has to tell us.'

'You are being bullies too.'

'Necessarily.'

'He is close to collapse.'

'He has endured worse, we can tell.'

'Then you won't break him,' Helena said.

We ourselves were starting to dread that. We had learned that he had been ready for the ordeal. He had put himself into a state of passivity. His background must be bad. His past experience hardly showed physically; there were no old marks or scars. We could not deduce what his previous life consisted of, though we could tell he knew humiliation and deprivation. When we made threats, he knew that situation too. He was in many ways quite ordinary, a face in any crowd. He was like us, and yet unlike us.

Helena had come with a prepared speech. Petro and I stood at rest and heard her out.

'I have only agreed to what you have been doing because Anacrites is so dangerous. I am horrified by what you have done to this man. You have toyed with him, teased him, tortured him. You have obliterated his personality. This is inhumane. It goes on for days, he never knows what will happen in the end—Marcus, Lucius, can you explain to me what difference there is between your mistreatment of this man, and the way that the killers of Julius Modestus abducted and abused him?'

'We have not used knives on him,' said Petro bleakly. The urge to keep up pressure on the agent got the better of him: 'Well—not yet.' He gestured to the hideous collection we had taken from our abductee. 'Those are his. Assume he carried them to use.'

It was an instinctive response, not the real answer. I knew Helena, loved her, respected her enough to find a better reply: 'There is a difference. We have a legitimate purpose—the general good. Unlike the killers, we don't relish this. And unlike their victims, this man can easily stop what is happening. All he has to do is answer us.'

Helena still stood there rebelliously.

'He has a choice,' Petronius reinforced me.

'He looks half dead, Lucius.'

'That makes him half alive. He is better off than a corpse—by a long way.'

Helena shook her head. 'I don't approve. I don't want him to die here in my house. Besides, you are running a huge risk. Surely Anacrites could burst in to rescue him any minute?'

The man on the bench had opened his eyes; he was now watching us. Had mention of Anacrites revived him? Or did Helena's spirited speech awaken hopes he had not known he harboured?

Helena saw the alteration. She moved closer, inspecting him. His light-skinned, now heavily stubbled face had a faint scatter of liver spots or freckles. His nose was upturned; his eyes were pale, a washed-out hazel colour. He could be, as he had told us, from Italy, though he looked different from true dark-eyed Mediterraneans.

In a much lower voice, Helena spoke to him directly. 'Anacrites will not be coming for you, will he? For some reason he has abandoned you.'

The man closed his eyes again. He shook his head very slightly, in resignation.

Helena breathed in. 'Listen, then. All they really want to know is where that cameo jewel originated.'

At last he spoke. He said something to her, speaking almost inaudibly.

She moved away again and looked at us. 'He says it was found in undergrowth, out on the marshes.' Helena walked to the door. 'Now you two, I want him out of here, please.'

She refrained from saying, *That was easy, wasn't it?*

We refrained from pointing out he could be lying; he probably was.

When she had gone, Petronius asked him, in a quiet, regretful tone of voice, 'I don't suppose if we took you to the marshes, you would point out the spot where you say this cameo was found? Or tell us more about the context?'

The man on the bench smiled for once, as if he let himself enjoy our understanding; he shook his head sadly. He lay quite still. He seemed to believe that the end was coming. It looked as if he had decided there was no hope now, never had been any.

He spoke to us, the first time in two days. He croaked, 'Are you going to kill me?'

'No.'

We had our standards.

44

The next time I emerged from the room, I was shocked to find the hallway full of luggage. Sheepish slaves carried on moving chests out through the front doors, clearly aware that I had not been told what was going on. I bit my lip and did not ask them.

I found Helena. She was sitting motionless in the salon, as if waiting for me to interrogate her as roughly as we were dealing with the agent. Instead, I merely gazed at her sadly.

'I cannot stay here, Marcus. I cannot have my children in this house.' Her voice was low. Her anger was only just under control.

The usual thoughts passed through my head—that she was being unreasonable (though I knew she had tolerated what was going on longer than I could have expected) and that this was some overreaction in the grief she was still feeling after the baby's death; I had the sense not to say that.

I seated myself opposite, wearily. I held my head in my hands. 'Tell me the worst.'

'I have sent the girls away and now that I have spoken to you, I will be joining them.'

'Where? How long for?'

'What do you care?'

Flaring up like that against me was so rare, it shocked me. A terrible moment passed between us as I held back the urge to retaliate with equal anger. Perhaps fortunately, I was too tired. Then perhaps because I was so exhausted, Helena was able to see me as vulnerable and to relent slightly.

'I care,' I said. After a moment I forced out the question: 'Are you leaving me?'

Her chin went up. 'Are you still the same man?'

The truth was, I no longer knew. 'I hope so.'

Helena let me suffer, but briefly. Staring at the floor, she said, 'We will go to your father's villa on the Janiculan.'

She started to rise. I went across to her; taking her hands in mine I forced her to look at me. 'When I have finished, I will come and fetch you all.'

Helena tugged her hands free.

'Helena, I love you.'

'I loved you too, Marcus.'

Then I laughed at her gently. 'You still do, sweetheart.'

'Cobnuts!' she snapped, as she swept from the room. But the put-down she had used was a habitual one of mine, so I knew that I had not lost her.

I had to bring this to a finish.

Petronius and I had told the man we would not kill him. We could never give him back, however. Capturing one of the spy's agents was irreversible. So what happened to him next would involve more terror, cruel treatment and—soon, probably, though not soon enough for him—his death, even if it was not at our hands.

Petro and I had talked about a solution. We abandoned our efforts to extract information and made final arrangements. I had thought of a way to do this, so there would be no comeback.

I left the house, the first time I had been out for days. I went to see Momus. For an eye-watering sum, Momus fixed it up for me. I did not say who we wanted to put away so discreetly, or why; with his sharp grasp of a filthy situation, Momus knew better than to request details. When he wrote out a docket he just asked, 'Are you telling me his real name—or shall I give him a new one?'

We still did not know who he was. He was so hard, he consistently refused to tell us. 'Anonymity would be ideal.'

'I'll make him a Marcus!' Momus jeered, always one for a joke in bad taste.

I was startled how easy it was to make somebody disappear. Anacrites' man would be taken away from my house that night. The overseer who worked for the Urban Prefect was now expecting an extra body; when we delivered the Melitan, he would be infiltrated among a batch of convicts who were going for hard labour in the mines. This punishment was intended to be a death sentence, an alternative to crucifixion or mauling by the arena beasts. Protest would be pointless. Convicted criminals always claimed to be the victims of mistakes. Nobody would listen. No one in Rome would ever see him again. Chained with an iron neck-collar in a slave gang in a remote part of some overseas province, stripped and starved, he would be worked until it killed him.

We told him. I had once worked as a slave in a lead mine, so I knew all the horrors.

We gave him a last chance. And he still said nothing.

45

Soon after I returned home alone after removing the agent, Anacrites came to the house.

I had bathed and eaten. I had devoted time to making sure all trace of recent events had been removed. I was in my study, reading a scroll of affable Horace to cleanse my sullied brain. It was late. I was missing my family.

A slave announced the spy was downstairs. Would I see him? This was how things worked now; I would probably get used to it. Helena must have stiffened the staff, teaching them not to let visitors get past them. It gave a prosperous householder a few moments to prepare himself—much better than the days when any intruder walked right into my shabby apartment, saw exactly what I had been doing (and with whom), then forced me to listen to his story whether I cared or not.

I paused to wonder at the spy's timing—did he *know* we had shed our prisoner? Then I went in my house slippers to greet him.

He had no Praetorians. The other 'Melitan' was not with him either. He had brought a couple of low-grade men, though when I invited him up he left them below in the entrance hall. Taking no chances, I put slaves to watch them. I had known him when he only had available a legman with enormous feet and a dwarf; later he hired a professional informer, though he was killed on duty. A woman worked with him sometimes. This pair today were a grade up from basic, ex-soldiers I guessed, though pitiful; in a peaceful province they would have been relegated to rampart turf-cutting or in war they would have been expendable, mere spear fodder.

'I called in to wish you good fortune, Falco, on the Feast of the Rustic Vinalia,' Anacrites bluffed. I rarely honoured feast days, whether mystic or agricultural; nor did he, in my experience. I had sat with him in our Census office, yearning in vain for him to leave early to go sardine-munching at the Fishermen's Games in the Transtiberina or to pay his respects to Invincible Hercules.

'Thanks; how civil.' I refrained from bringing out a rock-crystal flagon of *rotgut nouveau*.

Anacrites favoured guarded sobriety while he was working—so different from Petronius and me, abandoning care at every opportunity and living on the edge. He made no attempt to cadge a festival drink. Significantly, as was also his tendency, he straightway lost his nerve. Despite having probably spent hours perfecting an excuse, he came right out with it: 'I have mislaid an agent.'

'Careless. What's it to me?'

'He was last seen outside your house. You won't object if I take a look around here, will you, Falco?'

'This is hardly an amicable gesture—and after we all had such a rollicking time at your hog-roast too! Still, help yourself. I dare say there is no point objecting. If you find him squatting on my property, I'll want compensation for his upkeep.'

This terse banter was interrupted by new arrivals. For an instant I thought the spy had brought the Guards after all. Someone banged the front door knocker in a military manner, though then a key scratched in the lock angrily: Albia. She had been roaming on her own again. I knew Helena had been unable to find her when the others left for the Janiculan; I was supposed to send the girl on. She looked disgruntled and, curiously, was accompanied by Lentullus.

'Thanks, jailor, you can go now!' she ordered him crossly. She stalked across the vestibule. From choice I would have ordered Lentullus to wait, so he could explain out of the spy's hearing. Albia turned back from the stairs and made furious signals for him to clear off.

Lentullus stood to attention and announced, 'Camillus Justinus asked me to return your young lady, Falco. He saw her outside our house, staring—it's a habit she's prone to recently.'

'Oh Albia!' I dreaded having to play the heavy-handed father.

'Looking is not a crime,' she snarled.

'You have been harassing a senator,' I disagreed, all too conscious of Anacrites listening in. 'If I know you, girl, you do your best to make your glare upsetting. Lentullus, please apologise to the senator. Thank Justinus for his kindly intervention, and assure them all this will not be repeated.'

'It's just that the Greek lady was getting spooked,' said Lentullus. 'The tribune said we'd better whip your girlie back home today and have a word with you about it.' He beamed at Albia, showing his admiration. 'She's a bit of a one, isn't she?'

'One and a half,' I grumbled. 'Anacrites, would you just excuse me for a moment while I sort out a reward for Lentullus—'

Anacrites waved me away, since he was then able to approach Albia. I heard the bastard offer that if she ever needed a refuge from family troubles, she knew where his house was . . . This evening had become a disaster.

Behind the spy's back I quickly passed to Lentullus the cameo jewel, pressing it against his palm the way Aulus had given it to me. Being Lentullus, he needed a really big wink to help him get the point. 'Remember the time we hid the tribune in that old apartment of mine? Can you find it again—above the Eagle Laundry in that little street? Could you possibly take a detour up there on your way back home?' I muttered where there was a hiding-place in my old doss, and Lentullus promised to conceal the jewel.

Albia had broken away from Anacrites and barged up, thinking I was talking about her. She sensed me making arrangements with Lentullus. 'I'll take Nux for a walk—if I'm allowed out?'

'You've just been out—but you are not a prisoner. Just stop stalking

Camillus Aelianus—and keep away from other men as well.' I meant the spy. Lentullus was too much of a clown to count.

I returned to Anacrites and his planned search of my house. 'Who are you looking for?' Better to ask, rather than admit I knew. 'Does your lost lamb have a name?'

'State secret,' Anacrites mumbled, pretending to make a joke of it.

'Oh, one of your precious bodyguards, would that be?' This was like trying to squeeze a dry sponge, one that had been desiccated in the sun on a harbour wall for three weeks. He nodded reluctantly, so I added, 'Aren't there two? Where's the other one? Doesn't he know what his brother's been up to?'

Anacrites shot me a suspicious glance. 'How do you know they are brothers?'

'They look like brothers—and in some passing conversation, they told me, you idiot. I don't waste my time trying to find out sordid details about your useless staff.'

Anacrites then set about peering into all our upstairs rooms, while I ambled along with him to ensure he saw nothing too private. I encouraged him to look under beds, if I knew there were chamber pots; I wished we had put snappy rat traps just inside cupboards. A toy donkey fell down a step and nearly made the spy take a tumble, but the beds were neatly made, shutters closed, lamps trimmed and filled. We had staff; order had seeped into my domestic life like a leaking drain. None of the slaves were discovered rifling papers or money chests, none were screwing one another in the guest rooms or playing with themselves alone in linen cupboards. Something about Anacrites made them all scuttle for cover even though I, their reassuring master, was escorting him, with my half-read scroll of Horace still tucked under my elbow and an expression of pained tolerance at his damned intrusion.

We glanced in every room, then went out on to the roof terrace. 'If he's up here, I'll throw him off.' By now I was curt. 'This has gone far enough. What's going on?'

'I told you—my agent has gone missing; I have to find him. He has family, for one thing; if something's happened, they will want to know.'

'Married?' I felt a strange need to know. I had shared three crucial days in that man's life. His worthwhile existence reached its end in my home. Petronius and I were his last civilised contacts. Remembering Helena's furious comparison, I wondered if psychopathic killers developed this warped sense of relationship with their victims.

'Yes, there is a wife—or so I believe.'

'Parents living?'

'No.'

'And he has a brother who looks like a twin.'

'They are not identical.'

'Oh you know something about them then, Anacrites?'

'I take care of my men. Give me credit for being professional.'

'An impeccable employer! He's probably fallen victim to a street mugger, or been knocked down by a wagon and hauled off to a healing sanctuary. Try the Temple of Aesculapius. Maybe he ran away because he couldn't stand his working environment—or couldn't stand his superior.'

'He wouldn't run away from me,' Anacrites said, with an odd expression.

We returned downstairs. On reaching the lower hall, Anacrites decided to search the ground-floor rooms. 'We don't use them,' I said. 'Too damp.'

He insisted. He looked ready for a fight with me, but I did not quibble.

When he looked in the room where we had kept our captive, Anacrites sniffed slightly. No trace of his missing man remained, though like a bloodhound, the spy seemed to harbour doubts. If I had believed in supernatural powers, I would have thought he was picking up the aura of a soul in torment. The room stood empty, apart from a well-scrubbed bench against one wall. The floor and walls looked spotless. The air was clean, pervaded only by a faint smell of beeswax where the boards had been given a buffing very recently.

'I used this as a holding cell,' I told Anacrites gently. 'For my late father's slaves—' Mentioning my bereavement made the bastard look humble. I wanted to kick him. 'While I was assessing which were for the slave market. And if, in your role as an interfering state auditor, you intend to ask—yes, I paid the four per cent tax on every one I sold.'

'I would not dream of implying otherwise, Marcus.'

Every time Anacrites called me Marcus it just reminded me how impossible it would be ever to call him 'Tiberius'.

He left eventually. I wondered if the unpredictable swine would come back for another attempt. Anacrites often did a job, then half an hour later thought of three things he had missed.

His 'search' was just a surface skim. He could be inept—yet he could also be more thorough when the mood took him. Tonight he just gave my house a casual walk-through. I even wondered if he had left his visit until now because he'd known all along where the agent was, and actually wanted to lose him from his payroll. After all, he knew I always spotted surveillance and would take against it. He had just claimed to be a concerned superior. When the Melitan went missing, it should not have taken him three days to act.

Luckily, at heart Anacrites was so obsessed with outsmarting me that once we engaged in mental tussle, he noticed little else. He seemed unaware that, while I walked him around, my heart was beating fast. When Albia left with Lentullus and called Nux for a walk, the madcap mongrel had raced downstairs eagerly. Our dog was carrying her latest toy. It was a short piece of rope; she liked to fight people for it, gripping on like fury, shaking it from side to side and growling with excitement. Nux would have offered to play the tugging game with Anacrites, had he shown the slightest interest. Instead, wagging her tail crazily, she scampered away after Albia.

As far as I could tell, the spy failed to spot that my dog's prized new toy had once been his agent's strangling rope.

46

Anacrites did not dare search Maia's apartment in person, though he sent his two ex-soldiers. They were very polite, especially when they found that only Marius (aged thirteen) and Ancus (ten) were in. They must have been warned to expect a termagant and possibly a large angry vigiles officer, so finding a scholarly boy and his very shy little brother caught them wrong-footed. My elder nephew wanted to be a rhetoric teacher; so, Marius practised legal disputation on them (the rights of a Roman householder) while they quickly peered about, found nothing, and fled.

Petronius heard about it later. He would have been furious, but by then something big had blown up. Something so big, that since no harm had been done at the apartment, he left the issue alone. He had noted it, though. He was adding it to the long list of outrages for which Anacrites would one day pay.

I was setting off to Helena at the villa when I received an intriguing invitation. I was to meet Petronius at a bar called the Leopard, one we never frequented. He suggested I bring my Camillus assistants. A cryptic note on his message warned us *Play by Isca rules.* Only I knew what that meant: it referred to a secret court-martial we once took part in. So, this was a meeting of high importance, to be kept from the authorities. Nothing that was said today at the Leopard would ever be acknowledged afterwards. No one could break faith. And for me, there was a subtle indication that somebody of status—Anacrites?—was about to be formally shafted.

Aelianus and Justinus were agog and turned up willingly at my house. We had a brief moment of tension when Albia stalked down to the hall while we were assembling. I overheard Aelianus plead with her, 'Won't you at least speak to me?'

To which Albia coldly answered, 'No!' She stormed out of the house, giving me a filthy look for my contact with Aulus. At least I knew this time she was not rushing to the Capena Gate to stalk him.

'You're an idiot!' said Quintus to his brother—who did not deny it.

When we arrived at the bar, Petronius was already there. He had a man with him. It was a large place. They were in a room at the back, which they had managed to keep to themselves. Money probably changed hands for that.

Brief introductions ensued. 'This is Silvius. He'll tell you himself what he does—insofar as he can say.'

The draughtboard and counters had been allocated to our room, a cover for us being there; we seemed like an illegal gambling consortium. While drinks were ordered, I sized up Silvius. He was lean, scornful, capable. Maybe early fifties. A semi-shaved grey head. One finger missing. Been around the houses—on good terms with the householders, maybe even better terms with their wives. I would not like him staying in *my* house. That did not mean I could not work with him—far from it.

'What are you thinking, Falco?' Petro asked, with a mild smile that meant he knew.

'Silvius is one of us.'

'Honoured,' said Silvius. He had an easy-going baritone voice that had ordered up plenty of flagons in its time. He had spent long nights in smoky bars, talking. Either he was a lyric poet, a speculative saucepan-seller—or he traded information.

The drinks came. Sides arrived simultaneously in pottery dishes. There would be no need for the waiter to trouble us again.

I saw Silvius eyeing the two young Camilli. Petro must have given him the rundown on us all. They had left their pristine togas in the clothes press and were turned out professionally: neutral tunics, serviceable belts, worn-in boots, no flash metal buckles or tags on their laces. Neither went in for jewellery, though Aulus had a rather wide new gold wedding ring; Quintus was not wearing his, but I thought he had had it on when he escorted his wife to the spy's party. You could just about take these two down an alley in the Subura without causing a rush of pickpockets, though they still had to learn how to pass along the streets completely unnoticed. At least they looked nowadays as though they might see trouble coming. As they thickened up in their middle-to-late twenties, each looked as if he might be handy when that trouble reached him. Their hair was too long and their chins too clean-shaven, but if we were soon to have action, I knew they would enjoy making themselves more scruffy.

'They will do; they are fit,' I said in an undertone. Silvius heard it without comment. Both Camilli noticed the exchange. Neither flared up. They had learned to accept how you edged towards acceptance in new professional relationships. When work was dangerous, each man had to make his own judgements about people he would be dealing with. Aulus leaned back on the bench and subjected Silvius in turn to scrutiny.

We raised a quiet toast, then set our beakers down again as Petronius prepared to speak.

'Is this about our Modestus case?' Having been to the marshes with us, Quintus was over-keen and jumped in. I laid a finger to my lips. Good-natured, Quintus shrugged an apology.

Petro began slowly. 'Marcus Rubella, my tribune, introduced Silvius to me, but officially, Rubella never met Silvius—and nor have I. *Officially* we surrendered the case into the safe hands of the honest Praetorians, together with their intellectual comrade, Anacrites the spy.

There's a poor interface with his organisation. We all let Anacrites play by himself.'

Aulus asked, keeping his voice level, 'Who are "we all"? The vigiles, the Praetorians, and whoever Silvius' people are?'

Petro gave a satirical growl. 'Here is how co-operation works, boys.' He branched into a lecture I had heard him give before: 'The Praetorian Guard provide the Emperor's security—hence the link with the intelligence outfit. Titus Caesar commands them, to keep them under control—though who will control Titus? They spend a lot of time nowadays arresting people whose faces Titus does not like. Upset Anacrites, and that could be us. The Urban Prefect is Rome's city manager. Duties include investigating major crime—note that. Then come the vigiles. Duties: sniffing out fires, apprehending street thieves, rounding up runaway slaves. When we catch minor criminals, we give them on-the-spot chastisement—otherwise we parcel them up for the Urban Prefect, who charges them formally. So another point to note, Aelianus: we have good lines of communication with the Urbans. Very good.'

I leaned on one elbow and pointed one forefinger at Silvius. Silvius nodded. He belonged to the Urban Cohorts.

The Camilli watched this interchange. Justinus asked pointedly, 'The Guards and the Urbans live in the same camp. Are they not natural allies?'

'You might think so,' admitted Silvius. 'Though not for long. Not once your keen eyes observed how the Praetorians behave like gods, looking down on the Urbans as their poor relations—while also thinking that the vigiles are puny ex-slaves, commanded by has-been officers.' Petronius spat out an olive stone. 'Pity the pathetic Urban who has bought the myth that it is easy to pass from one section to the other, merely on talent and merit,' Silvius continued in complaint. I wondered if that was what he had tried to do, and failed. 'No vigiles officer, I suspect, would even waste his time thinking it could happen.' Ah. Tell that to Marcus Rubella, whose dream was to rise on snowy wings to wear the Praetorian uniform.

'So you work in Rome,' Aulus pressed Silvius.

'Personally, no.'

We all raised our eyebrows—except for Petronius who calmly supped his drink and waited for Silvius to explain.

'The Praetorians,' said Silvius, with sly satisfaction, 'have to remain with the Emperor. The Urban Cohorts are free to roam. Our remit covers major crime—not only in the city, but anywhere within a hundred miles. Because, you see, any horrible criminal activity in that area might affect the sacred capital.'

'Now it makes sense,' said Aelianus. Even in the shaky hands of Minas of Karystos he had absorbed enough legal training to care about jurisdictions. 'For instance, the Modestus case would fall to you?'

'Yes, but Anacrites wants it.'

'So?'

'There is a magistrate at Antium—'

Justinus laughed. 'The invisible man!'

It was Silvius' turn to raise an eyebrow.

'When Modestus and Primilla disappeared, a posse from Antium was sent to investigate. Before Anacrites waded in and stopped our activity, Falco, Petronius and I tried to liaise with the magistrate but he declined to meet us.'

'You assumed Antium dropped all interest?' suggested Silvius. 'No, there is more to the man than that, boys. When he found nothing in the soggy marshes, it's true he went home and seemed to keep his head down. You may suppose he just spends his life enjoying the sea breezes at Antium, but this togate beach bum has a sense of duty— for civic rectitude, he could be one of our clean-living, right-thinking, porridge-slurping ancestors. Nor does bureaucracy scare him. Amazingly, he went on digging. He looked through records. Then one fine day, he was entertaining the Urban Prefect—our beloved commander, who, it has to be admitted, had gone out to Antium using official expenses in order to scout for a cut-price villa, to keep his bitching wife quiet. Over the men's sophisticated luncheon, words were exchanged of a diligent nature. Feel free to marvel.'

Aulus leaned in, scooping seafood from a dish. 'What have they found?' He had no truck with fancy narratives. Minas probably thought Aulus was not a natural lawyer, but his plain gruffness satisfied me.

'The magistrate has been following up reports of missing people, people who had disappeared while travelling mainly, so unlikely to have caused a local outcry. A list was prepared. Footmen were sent out into the countryside, some carrying long probes. And they *found,*' said Silvius, enjoying the chill he laid on us, 'two double sets of bodies.'

Aulus dumped a chewed prawn head in an empty saucer. 'So far.'

Silvius looked at me with only a trace of sarcasm. 'He catches on!'

'Thanks. I saved him from ruination: army and the diplomatic—he was a slow slug until I took on his training . . .' While Aulus seethed mildly, I pressed Silvius, 'You work outside Rome—so when the Antium big bug talked to the Urban commander, you were assigned to the case?'

'That's right. "Liaison officer". Keeping the locals on track—while letting them believe they have control.'

'Did you see the bodies yourself?'

He moved a little on his bench, disturbed by memories. 'Yes—one lot while still *in situ*. They were old bones. Nothing to identify. One pair much more recent than the other. Shallow graves, one trench to each body, each two of a pair lying close to each other—no more than ten feet separate—but the two pairs were half a mile apart. To find more, there will be a lot of ground to cover. The locals are still looking. And we've kept it secret.'

'People will soon know.'

'Sadly they will, Falco. So we need movement. I was sent to Rome to chivvy it up—only to learn the Modestus case has been passed over to the spy. I'm disgusted. This is no job for Anacrites. We Urbans won't cave in to him and the Praetorians. So our Prefect talked to the Vigiles Prefect. I've now been sent to communicate with you boys—very, very quietly. It's imperative the Praetorians don't know until they have to—and, until we can make arrests, nor must the Claudii.'

We all breathed in, or whistled through our teeth.

Petronius pushed aside his beaker. 'I'd like to hear more about the circumstances of these other deaths. How, when, where, who?'

'The graves are a few miles out of Antium. The oldest, just skeletons, may date back decades. The others are maybe five years old. How can anyone tell? A gravedigger from a necropolis was brought in to confer, but he couldn't say anything more specific. Because of their condition, impossible to say what had been done to them, though there could be cut marks on bones. We can't attach names—no clues to identity, though using the missing list, we may make guesses.'

'How were they laid out in the graves?' I asked.

'Arms at full stretch—like Modestus and that courier.'

'Any hands removed?' That was Petro.

'No. One corpse had an arm missing, but the grave had been disturbed, probably by animals. One had a foot off—maybe he kicked out and was given special punishment.'

'Any clothing or other items?'

'Nothing useful. Rags mostly. No money or valuables. It all looked careful, by the way. Marcus Rubella told me the courier's burial seemed rushed?'

'We're keeping an open mind on the courier,' I told Silvius. 'Even Anacrites thinks it could be a distraction, according to what he told me . . . Maybe it's him all along, trying to divert attention from the Pontine connection, to protect the Claudii.'

'Why would he want to look after those bastards?'

'Who knows? Have you met him? Do you know what he's like?'

Silvius spat contemptuously.

After a small pause Petro kept niggling. 'Did your four bodies give up any hints about the killer? Was there more than one, for instance? Did they stay on the scene afterwards, to commit further defilement?'

Silvius was pecking at snacks now, undeterred by the subject under discussion. 'The sites were too old. I wouldn't even say for sure that the deaths occurred where we found the graves. Two were in a lonely spot. It's a deep ravine, a place with a real sense of evil. We hated being there.'

'A ravine?'

'Water channel scoured out by a river at flood time. Dry in summer.'

Petro pushed back from the table, arms braced. 'So—this is the question: what makes you decide your very old corpses, discovered close to Antium, are linked to the Claudius family who live—insofar as we can call what they do living—away across the marshes.'

Silvius paused. He liked to milk a situation. We all waited.

'Petronius Longus, this is what I need your help for. There is a witness.'

'*What?*'

'Somewhere in Rome, we hope. Ten years ago, a young man fell into a street bar near Antium. He was hysterical and claimed he had been led off the road and nearly murdered by two villains. One man who seemed friendly and helpful had lured him, then suddenly jumped him and took him to an accomplice, an extremely sinister presence. He was obviously planning to commit terrible acts. The intended victim somehow escaped their clutches.'

Silvius himself shuddered, while the rest of us moved in our seats and variously reacted.

'Nobody took much notice at the time. If there was any kind of enquiry, it dwindled away fast. All the locals now think it was a couple of Claudii—Nobilis and one of his brothers. They were never interviewed, nor put in front of the victim for identification. They must reckon they got away with it. But we know the young man came from Rome—which of course wouldn't have helped him get attention in Latium. He is believed to have returned home after his ordeal. So, highly recommended Watch Captain with the interesting friends—' Silvius raised his beaker to the Camilli and me. 'You are requested to help me find him.'

47

All they knew was that the young man with the narrow escape was called Volusius. He was thought to be a teacher. Silvius had no details of his address in Rome. Petro had already tried the teachers' guild. A pompous official, possibly detecting that Lucius Petronius despised formal education, said he would ask his members but it would probably take time.

Petronius had cursed him for a piece of offal—but he managed to reserve this view until he was alone. Perhaps the guild master would come good. Wrong. It took him no time to 'consult his members'—in other words, he had not bothered. He said he had no member of that name on his current list and nobody had ever heard of Volusius. He declared the lad must have been an impostor. Petronius asked why would anyone ever lower themselves to claim fraudulently that they thrashed schoolchildren for a living? The guild master offered to demonstrate his big stick technique. Petro left, not hastily but without lingering.

The vigiles cohorts keep lists of certain undesirable professions (mine, for instance), though teachers are excluded. *Impersonating* a teacher, as the master had suggested, ought to be illegal but there were no lists for that either: probably because the pay was so low, fraud was in fact so unlikely.

Rubella still refused to allow Petronius to leave Rome. So by the time our meeting broke up, I had volunteered for another trip to Antium, to reinterview people at the bar where the escaped Volusius had turned up screaming for help ten years ago. If the bar was still there, which Petronius doubted, someone surely would remember a hysterical youth falling on the counter while screaming he had been abducted and scared witless. Even in the country, that must be more unusual than calves being run over by hay wagons.

The bar was there. It had been sold to a new owner who knew nothing about the incident. His clientele had changed. They knew nothing either.

Or so the bastards told me.

I pointed out quietly that if they left these killers on the loose, one of them could be a body in a shallow grave one day.

'Never!' a wall-eyed sheep-stealer assured me. 'All of us know better than to accept an invitation from Claudius Pius to go for a little walk down a marsh track to see his brother's spear collection.'

'Who mentioned Claudius Pius?' I asked in a level tone.

He rethought rapidly. 'You did!' he snapped. 'Didn't he?'

They all agreed that I had done so, despite it being obvious I had not. So against expectations I had discovered who lured away the victims—though this feeble conversation would not count as proof.

'Anyone seen Pius around here recently?'

Of course not.

'So tell me about "seeing the spear collection". How do you know that was the lure?'

'It's what the teacher said.'

'I thought you knew nothing about the teacher?'

'Oh no, but that's what people around here all reckon.'

'Anything else people around here know? Which brother's spears were on offer, for instance?'

'Oh Nobilis, bound to be. Probus has some, but nothing by comparison.'

'Any recent sightings of Nobilis?'

No. They said anyone who saw Claudius Nobilis would quickly look the other way.

'So what exactly are you scared of?'

They looked at me as though I was demented if I had to ask.

I was ready to give up. This bar might seem a safe haven to a young man escaping two murderers, but as a watering hole it was deadly. If this was the best place to buy a drink where I lived, I would emigrate to Chersonesis Taurica, die in exile like Ovid at the back of beyond, yet still think I had the best of it.

Preparing to leave, I glanced around the dismal place, then had one last try: 'I just can't work out what a teacher from Rome would have been doing on this road in the first place. None of them earn enough for a summer villa on the coast. I don't suppose "people around here" know why he came, do they?'

'He was coming to Antium to be interviewed for a holiday job.'

'Is that right!'

To my amazement, it turned out to be well known in those parts just which wealthy villa owner had summoned him. Incredibly, the rich man still had the same villa.

I never met the prospective employer, but it was unnecessary. He was the type who, faced with a potential hire who had come to grief, insisted that full details of the man's experience must be written down; in case Volusius tried to sue for compensation, presumably. A transcript still existed. I was shown it. They would not let me take it off the premises, but a scribe sat down and copied out the ten-year-old statement for me.

Volusius described meeting the man everyone now thought was Claudius Pius, who made friends and lured him off the road to meet his brother. Despite having no interest in weapons, the naïve young teacher found himself agreeing to accompany Pius. They went further than he expected, down extremely remote tracks, and he was already worried when they encountered the promised brother. This man was sinister. They met him in a clearing, as though he had been waiting. It made Volusius realise he had been deliberately stalked. He knew he had been brought here for evil reasons.

Volusius had made a terrible mistake. Although he felt he was about to be murdered, he managed not to show he understood his danger. Perhaps because there were two of them and they thought they could easily control him, the brothers were careless. Volusius broke away and managed to run off. Shaking with fear, he hid in a thicket for hours, overhearing a discussion about fetching a dog to track him down. As soon as he thought the men were out of earshot, he made a break for it, and ran until he reached the road and found the bar. The barkeeper at the time took him to safety at the villa where he had originally been heading.

The villa owner had clout. A search was conducted, though nobody was found. No one then made a link with the Claudii. Volusius gave a description of the two men, but it was too vague. If he had heard names, he could not remember them. He went into shock, too jittery to be of use as a witness. Some people even doubted his story. There was not a scratch on him. Nobody had seen him with the strangers. His fear might not be caused by trauma, but a pre-existing mental problem that made him imagine things. Enquiries petered out.

'And did he get the job?' I asked the slave I was talking to.

'Out of the question. He was a gibbering wreck. A man in that state could not be allowed to give lessons to respectable boys. He never even met them.'

'What happened to him?'

'He went back to Rome.'

'Was he fit to travel? After such an ordeal, didn't he panic at the prospect?'

'We kept him here a few days. He was allowed to write a letter and his mother came for him.'

'Got her address by any chance?'

'Afraid not, Falco.'

'We've lost him then . . .'

'Why do you need to find him? It's all here.'

'And it's invaluable, thank you. But we now believe the two men existed all right and there is an idea who they are. Volusius, as the only known survivor, might be able to identify them.'

'I bet he'd still panic, even after all these years.'

'Maybe. We have to hope seeing them in custody will reassure him . . . Tell me, what was the point of offering him a job here? Don't boys in a wealthy family have their own private tutor? Were they so dumb, they needed extra cramming in the summer holidays?'

'Excuse me! Quite the opposite. My master's sons had an all-round education in which they both excelled. This was to give them special lessons, because they were so gifted and mentally demanding.' It was to keep them occupied, I guessed, to stop them groping the maids and setting the house on fire. 'Volusius had a sideline—expertise in algebra.'

Now we were getting somewhere. The vigiles do not keep track of the miserable, half-starved souls who teach urchins the alphabet under street corner awnings, not unless there is a *very* large number of reports of sexual abuse; or, better still, complaints about noise. But in Rome, playing about with numbers carries dark undertones of magic. Like prostitutes, Christians and informers, therefore, mathematicians are classified by the vigiles as social undesirables. Their details are kept on lists.

48

I had one more task before I left Antium. I went to the workshop which had once belonged to the famous cameo-cutter, Dioscurides. He was long gone but an atelier still existed, where high-class craftsmen made every kind of cameo, not just from gems and from coral brought up from the Bay of Neapolis, but wondrous pieces carved from two-tone layered glass. I bought a small vase for Helena, an exquisite design in white and dark blue which I could either save for her birthday in October or hand over now to win her round if she was still being distant with me.

Remembering that I owned an auction house, I even made enquiries about bulk purchase—but the snooty salesmen sneered at that; they wanted only to deal direct with customers and take all the profits. Pa would have wangled some deal, I knew. I wasn't my father; I refused to become his ghost.

Exclusivity did help, however. When I asked about the jewel found at Anacrites' house, I was told they would have records of who made it, who bought it and when. I described it. They professed admiration for my eloquent detail. They sent me out for lunch. When I returned, a small piece of parchment was handed over, which they insisted was in confidence. The cameo had been made a long time ago for an emperor who died before it was finished; it had remained at the workshop, awaiting the right buyer, until very recently.

Sadly, the eventual purchaser was not Modestus or his wife Livia Primilla, but a man in Rome called Arrius Persicus, who must have oodles of bullion, from the price he paid. It was not written down, though proudly whispered to me. The gem left the workshop only a few weeks ago. That too ruled out Modestus and Primilla. It also left no obvious link to Anacrites. Unless Persicus had disappeared mysteriously in the past month, the agent's claim to Petro and me that the cameo was found 'in undergrowth on the marshes' became suspect.

It was possible Persicus had been done in on his way back to Rome with his expensive new bijou. Petronius would have to check if he had been reported missing.

'Is he a collector of precious objects, or do you know who he bought it for?'

'Confidential, Falco.'

'Girlfriend, you mean?'

'We rather thought so.'

'I'm sure you get a smell for it . . . Is he married?'

'Presumably. He bought a second piece that day—very much cheaper.'

How sad life could be.

I returned to Rome, passing straight through and making my way to the Janiculan. Communicating with my own sweet wife Helena Justina was now an urgent issue.

I dumped my luggage in the porch. Times had changed: I knew people would take it in for me. I could hear my little ones romping in the gardens, with Nux barking. Instinct drew me down a path away from them. I found Helena seated on a bench that had been set up close to where we held my father's funeral. A new memorial stood there, with an inscription to Pa and a sad last line naming our lost baby son. *Also Marcus Didius Justinianus, beloved of his parents: may the earth lie lightly upon him.* I had not been able to ask Helena anything about this; I had to arrange it myself. I had not even seen it since the mason set it up.

Helena's attitude suggested that she came here regularly. She was not weeping, though I thought I detected tears on her cheeks. If she was managing to mourn, that was an improvement on her previous tight, tense refusal to acknowledge what had happened.

After I met her gaze, I sat beside her in silence, then we looked at the memorial together. After a time, Helena of her own accord placed her hand on mine.

It was some weeks to Helena's birthday, but when we returned to the house I gave her the blue glass vase anyway. She was worth it. I told her that; she told me I was a hound, but she still loved me. 'I would have been just as pleased at your return without a gift.' A man in my line of work has to be cynical, but I believed her.

'Just so long as you don't see it as a bribe.' This would be our only mention of Petro and me keeping that man at our house.

'Even you can't afford the size of bribe you would have needed.'

'Oh I know. At least, unlike the wife of Arrius Persicus, you know *I* haven't bought a bigger present for some secret mistress.'

'No, darling. Spending even this much money must have been enough of a shock.'

'I'll get used to doing it. For you.'

'Well,' said Helena graciously. 'You had better go and tell Petronius Longus what you found out.'

'You're giving me a pass out of barracks!—Not tonight, though, honeycake. I'm staying in with you.'

'Don't overdo it, Falco—or I will think you have something to hide.' Helena Justina was almost her old self again.

I really felt too travel-weary to seek out Petro but sent a message to him with news of Volusius being a mathematician and Arrius Persicus buying the cameo. He would follow up these leads. I suggested we meet up for breakfast at Flora's next day. I burrowed back into domesticity—patted the children, tickled the dog, played mental tug of war with Albia about nothing much, bathed, dined, slept.

'Anyway,' Albia had demanded, 'what did you do with that scraggy bit of rope you took away from Nux? We spent hours searching for it while you were away.'

'I burned it. You don't need to know why—nor does the dog.'

'That was a waste. She loved her tugging rope.'

Nux was a scamp but I liked to think even she had standards. She might not have loved the rope if she knew what it was. Besides, with Anacrites repeatedly dropping in on us like an annoying uncle, the dog's toy had to be sacrificed.

While I was in Antium, he had even come up to the villa, Helena said. She told him I had gone to Praeneste for a client. She claimed it was a very attractive widow for whom I carried out unspeakable personal services; Anacrites had commiserated with her in apparent shock and sorrow.

'He said, *This is a new side to Falco.* So I snapped, *You are not a very good spy if you think that!* Don't relax,' Helena warned me. 'The man is not stupid. He didn't believe a word of it. Marcus, he will be wondering where you really did go.'

Next morning Helena arranged to bring the family back to our house. I had the impression she had been pretty well ready to do it even if I had not arrived to fetch them. I left the villa earlier. Even up here, I checked carefully that I was not followed. The spy was a man down now, though; perhaps he would stop haunting me.

Flora's Caupona was a decrepit drinks place in my family's part of the Aventine, run by my sister Junia. Luckily she had not yet arrived, since her mornings were occupied with the needs of her son, who was profoundly deaf. Junia had proved an inventive, devoted mother who spent hours coaxing him into basic communication. She had already had plenty of practice with her supremely dull husband, so perhaps her patience with little Marcus was not all that surprising.

In her absence the waiter Apollonius produced what the workers who formed the caupona's early passing trade had to endure as stamina food: stale bread and weak posca, the vinegary drink that is given to slaves and soldiers. Nobody who hoped for a sociable outdoor breakfast would ever come here. The tuck had one advantage, though; it was better, and safer, than what Flora's served for lunch.

Apollonius had once taught geometry at an infant school; he taught Maia and me. It would have been a neat coincidence if he had known the victim Volusius—a coincidence to find only in a Greek adventure yarn. In real life it never happens. 'Can't say I've heard of him, Falco.'

While I waited for Petro to show, I wondered glumly if the stricken young teacher half dead of fright at Antium could also have left his job and become a wine waiter. If so, in this city with hundreds of thousands of street bars, we would never find him.

I could tell by the jaunty way Petro approached that he had made progress. During the night shift, he said, the new facts I brought from Antium turned into excellent leads.

We told Apollonius to go into the back room and stay there, reading a long scroll of Socrates.

'What if customers come?'

'We'll serve them for you.'

'You can't do that!'

'My sister owns the joint.' Wrong. *I* owned the joint now; Junia just managed it for me. A terrifying thought.

'You mean you'll send my customers packing!'

'Relax. We'll call you.'

One or two latecomers did try to buy stuff. We told them we were hygiene inspectors and had to close the bar down. Then indeed we sent them packing.

49

Even after his shift, Petronius was buoyant. 'Let's start with the gem-buyer. Marcus, my boy, you've done well.'

'Persicus?'

'Persicus! He meant nothing to me, but Fusculus recognised the name.'

'Fusculus is a lad.'

'He's a sparkler. Too good, I'm afraid. Rubella will probably transfer him to another cohort for "career development".'

'How does he know about Persicus? We were not aware of him before, surely?'

'We could have been. He never showed on a statement, but while the Seventh Cohort were formally telling Rubella and me about that murdered courier, a couple of troops waited outside; talking to Fusculus, they gave up extra details. Their written reports are as skimpy as a whore's nightgown. I suspect their clerk can't even write—one of their centurions' halfwit cousins, who got the job as a favour . . .' He calmed down when I grinned. 'But their enquiry chief asked the right questions. The carter was forced to supply details of the courier's package, in case it was relevant—or the Seventh even found it.'

'Have they?'

'Don't make me weep! The carter said the parcel was a load of cushion stuffing, sent by a client to his country estate.'

'The client was Arrius Persicus?'

'Correct. This is the good bit. He's alive and well and has never mentioned losing any fabulous cameo.'

I guffawed. 'In case his wife finds out he has a girlfriend! Shouldn't cushion stuffing go the other way? Wool, feathers, straw—they all come from the country *into* Rome.'

'Exactly.' Petro tried to winkle crumbs of the stale bread we were gnawing from between his teeth. The crumbs clung on resolutely. Junia must have Apollonius spread it with cow-heel glue as some new gourmet fashion. 'The crucial parcel didn't sound significant initially— which was a clever ploy. The Seventh thought they could forget about it. So let's think: why dispatch a load of cheap stuffing via an expensive courier?'

'Obvious: something costly was concealed inside.'

'You bet.'

We sat quiet for a beat, thinking.

'Anyway—don't let's get too excited too fast. Fusculus has gone to ask the carter about it on the sly. We still have to pretend we're not intervening in Anacrites' case. If the cameo *was* in the courier's parcel, then it's a lead—but you and I need a long, hard think about the implications . . .'

'I'll start thinking too much now, unless you distract me. So, what about the teacher with the numerical sideline?'

Petronius perked up. 'Found him. Easy. The mathematicians list is one of the shortest: thank you, Jove. Volusius may have died eight years ago. At any rate, he vanished from our records—which is hard to achieve, once we have a rascal in our blotted scroll.'

I groaned. 'Dead end?'

'Not quite.' Petronius gave up on Flora's breakfast and threw what was left of his bread to a pigeon in the street. It flew off, affronted. He sniffed the acetic posca then dashed that into the gutter too. 'He lived with his mother, off the Clivus Suburanus, close to the Porticus of Livia. I'm whacked and old dames don't have enough verve to keep my eyes open. I'm going home to bed but you, being a layabout with time on your hands, may fancy a chat with her.'

I said I was always available to do work the noble Lucius found too much for him. And while he could only chat up pretty things of twenty, I was more versatile and could charm even older women.

Petronius let me get away with that, because he was bursting with one further fact. 'While I had the old documents spread around the room, my eye fell on something.' Calm by nature, he seemed excitable now: 'I found one of the Claudii!'

'Speak, oracle!'

'I'm sure it's him. Two years ago, a Claudius Virtus, newly arrived in Rome from Latium, appeared as a person of interest.'

'What had he done? Joined a dodgy religion?'

'Depends how you categorise cults, Marcus. We have him down as taking an interest in astrology.'

'Stargazing?'

'People-forecasting—wickedness. I hate that stuff. Life's dire without finding out in advance what will be dumped on you by Fate.'

'According to Anacrites, when he turned on me recently, when Fate gives you anything worth having, if you dare to enjoy your good fortune, remorseless Nemesis will fly up to snatch it away.'

'Is he sniping at your legacy?'

'You guessed. Is Virtus still living in the same place?'

'Who knows? We don't always update our records unless some name bobs up in a new offence.'

I said that in addition to Volusius' mother I would visit Virtus, but Petronius would not reveal the address. He would meet me for lunch after a few hours' rest, then we could go together. I promised to round up one of the Camilli, or both, to accompany us. Lunch could be at my house; Flora's had lost our custom.

'We should go armed. These bastards collect spears. The Urbans carry swords and knives—why don't we ask Silvius for back-up?'

Petronius Longus was a vigiles man and he would never change.

Despite the supposed joint operation with Silvius, he assumed a vague expression. 'Let's you and I just take a quiet recce first.' He was as keen on inter-cohort co-operation as a fifteen-year-old boy thinking about purity.

'Fine. We'll tiptoe up like cat burglars . . . I could knock on the door for a horoscope—but I don't want Virtus to look into my future and see when he and his stinking brother Nobilis will be arrested.'

'Don't worry.' Lucius Petronius had no faith in clairvoyance. 'He won't even be able to foresee what he's getting for lunch.'

'Right. What's your star sign, by the way? You're under the Virgin, aren't you?'

'Believe that, Marcus, if it gives pleasure to your childish mind.'

50

I sent a runner to tell Aulus and Quintus to come over for lunch. Meanwhile, I went alone to find the teacher's last known address.

It was a dismal mission. I found the apartment, in a tangle of narrow lanes on the way to the Esquiline Gate; indoors, as she generally must be, was the ancient, widowed mother. I guessed she had lost her husband young. Perhaps there had been a legacy; the rental where she lived—where she had brought up her only son Volusius—was cramped but just about tolerable. She was the proud kind, to whom poverty must be perpetually shameful. She had scrimped to get her boy an education, investing all her own hopes in his obvious potential. Although he became a teacher, because of his experience at Antium only disappointment followed. She was now half-blind, but taking in tunics to mend, to keep from starving.

Volusius was dead. His mother said he had never recovered from his fright that day at Latium. It affected him so badly he could no longer teach. He lost his job at the local school, then failed to find other work. He moped around as a loser, became mentally disturbed and committed suicide—threw himself in the river just after the second anniversary of being abducted.

'Did he talk about what had happened?'

'He could never bear to.'

'You went there to fetch him home afterwards. Was he in a bad state?'

'Terrible. He knew we had to pass the place where he had met those men. He froze at the memory. He was shaking so much when we tried to set off home, the people at the villa had to give him a sleeping draught and send us in a cart. Once I got him home, he woke up in familiar surroundings and just broke down crying. He kept saying to me he was sorry—as if what happened was somehow his fault.'

'I was hoping, if I could find him, he could describe the men who took him.'

The mother shook her head. *'Scum!'*

Such vehemence in the mouth of a civilised woman was ugly. The lasting effect on her was an extra consequence of the killings. This mother had not only lost her only son, too young, but all her own hopes. What happened to Volusius was on her mind daily. Now she lived alone, dwindling arthritically into fear and despair. There was no one left to take care of her. She was going to need looking after soon, and I could see she knew it.

When I said that now we thought we knew who the abductors were, she just waved me away. It was too late to save her son, so it was too late for her.

Angrily, I renewed my vow that this time we would find justice, for both Volusius and his mother.

51

Peace in the home. What a wonderful thought. If only I had it.

The Camilli had already arrived—anything to get away from Minas of Karystos and their wives. Nux was chasing around the house, barking loudly. Slaves were pursuing her, unaware that this only aggravated the dog's excitement. Albia would normally have waded in to sort this out, but she was shouting at Helena over me having invited Aulus. Julia and Favonia had picked up the idea of complaining and were wailing their heads off. As soon as I turned up, slaves began crying too; I could not see what that was about. Perhaps they were the ones I intended selling. I had not told them yet, but a list existed. They could have bribed Katutis to reveal it. Katutis was keeping out of sight, which clinched it.

Lunch. Very pleasant. Rather tense, but that is what lunch at home exists for.

No Albia. Helena had sent her on an errand to my mother. Ma would be taking me to task about the girl soon.

No dog. Worn out, Nux had fallen asleep in her basket.

No children. I had ordered them out of the room when Favonia threw a foodbowl on the floor and Julia giggled.

No slaves. I was not yet ready to treat a crowd of feckless strangers as extended family, with more domestic privileges than I allowed to my own relatives. I would house them, feed them, express gratitude and affection on a moderate scale—but no more. Nema, previously Pa's bodyslave, commented that he was very surprised by my attitude.

'We could have met at a bar,' Quintus suggested.

'Are you saying,' demanded his sister in a voice like an ocean breaker as it stripped barnacles off rocks, 'my house is badly run?'

'No, Helena.'

A meeting convened. Katutis appeared with a bunch of note-tablets and a hopeful expression; he was upset when I told him not to take minutes. 'Why else, Marcus Didius, would a man hold a meeting, but to have its conclusions recorded?'

'This is confidential.'

'Then good recording practice is to write "Confidential" at the head of the scroll.'

'So the next time Anacrites raids my house, he sees that and backs away bleating, *Oh I am not allowed to look at this!* In fact that's a certain way to make him grab it.'

Katutis slunk off, muttering like a malevolent priest.

The big, comforting presence of Petronius Longus soothed those of us who remained. Helena, whose meal had been interrupted by the various ructions, was still chewing flatbread. Dabbing chickpea paste ferociously on to her bread, she had the look of a woman who knew she would soon have heartburn. 'Oh don't wait for me to finish!' she scolded Petronius, in a tremolo of agitated bracelets.

Petro cracked on smartly. 'There is news. It's good—though it will pose questions. Since Fusculus proved the link to Arrius Persicus, I let him call on the carter, and thump him until he squeaked—'

'Can you not do anything without unnecessary violence?' Not a good idea to remind Helena about our treatment of the agent.

Petronius had the grace to look guilty. 'The carter now admits his spendthrift, two-timing client was indeed posting off a secret love token—and not for the first time. It was a routine arrangement. She's a lucky little pullet. This is why the carter panicked when his courier vanished—he thought the newly-wed had gone bad now he had a wife to support, so he pinched the gem. Later the carter kept quiet about that, in a misguided attempt to protect his customer.'

'Did the carter know what the hidden gift was?' Helena asked.

'A cameo on a chain. Persicus had bragged to him about it.'

'The chain is news,' I said. 'It's not been found. Who has got their sticky hands on that, I wonder? . . . Need we interview Persicus?'

'Not at this stage. If we want a deposition for the Prefect later, Fusculus can go along and scare him shitless then.'

'Back to basics then. The cameo comes from Antium, Persicus is sending it to his mistress. The gem is in some unconvincing wadding, in a parcel, in a pannier. The young bridegroom sets off on the donkey, no doubt whistling a jaunty measure and thinking about enthusiastic sex. Then what happened at the necropolis?' I ticked off possibilities: 'Better consider it: *did* the courier steal the gem?'

'No,' said Quintus. 'He wouldn't commit suicide and stuff himself in a shallow grave.'

'So was he robbed by somebody who knew what he was carrying? Did the carter himself set it up, even?'

'If so, he was foolish to report his courier missing.' Quintus again. 'And why would he kill his man?'

'As for someone else knowing,' Petronius said, 'Fusculus heard they were always very discreet when they had valuables to transport.'

'Models of good practice?'

'Fusculus said the carter swears the lad was tried and trusted. Could be relied on to avoid attracting notice.'

Aulus, who had been subdued since Albia had hysterics, recovered enough to add his thoughts: 'So, did the young man just classically happen to be in the wrong place at the wrong moment? Was his murder random—though then his attackers found our exquisite cameo in his donkey pannier and thought it was their lucky day?'

'That seems right,' I agreed. 'Being chosen by a cruising killer was an accident.'

'Someone who looked harmless, stopped him,' said Petro. '*Excuse me, what's the way to Clusium?—My pocket lodestone's broken* . . . I don't suppose this time the lurer said, *Do you want to look at my brother's lovely spear collection?*—but we'll never know.'

Helena had calmed down. She tidied bowls into piles. 'Now stop tiptoeing around the big question.' We men sat quiet, our backs a little straighter, our faces grave. 'How did someone in Anacrites' house get their hands on the cameo?'

Petronius drained his water cup. 'As far as the Seventh Cohort know, the donkey and its pannier disappeared. Suppose later, while Anacrites and his men were investigating, they found the donkey wandering?'

'Not right,' I said. 'He let the Seventh carry on with routine enquiries. Unlike you and the Fourth, he has no beef with the Seventh. Anyway if, for once, he actually found evidence, he would have boasted about it.'

Helena scoffed too: 'Even if his men had legitimately discovered the parcel, why did the cameo end up hidden in their luggage?'

'Are his agents screwing Anacrites—pinching evidence to sell?' Normally deadpan, Aulus looked cheery at the thought.

'Has been known,' Petro confirmed dourly. I knew the problem was endemic among the vigiles. House fires gave particular scope for pilfering from victims. 'But Anacrites knew about the gem, didn't he, Falco?'

'No, in fact.' I cast my mind back to the scene when the Camilli and I were pulling up the caterers for theft, with Anacrites watching us. 'When he saw the cameo, he first denied knowledge. He took a moment to realise what it must be. Am I right, lads?'

Both Camilli nodded. Aulus said, 'He looked annoyed—but he chose to protect the agents. Thinking fast, he came up with that limp story about a woman.'

'He became very jumpy,' added Quintus.

'Yes—jumpy enough for you to think the cameo was significant, and to palm it!'

'Ooh, naughty!' said Petro, grinning.

Helena frowned. 'Why would Anacrites protect his men if they are corrupt? Wouldn't he be livid that they stole evidence and jeopardised his chances of cracking the case?'

Petronius thumped a clenched fist several times on the table. The beat was measured, the meaning grim. 'You can have the wandering donkey theory—though I think it's bullocks' bollocks. Try this: during the courier's murder, one of his killers took the cameo. It was a trophy. It was secreted away to gloat over, the way killers' trophies are.'

I agreed: 'And it never left the killer. He took it home and hid the thing in his room. When Anacrites saw what the caterers had found, it took him a moment, but he knew what it meant. Why? Because he already knew he had a killer in his house. Work the rest out, lads—'

The Camilli made the connection immediately. Justinus said, 'The so-called Melitans are the two Claudii who work in Rome. They are Pius and Virtus.'

Helena sat back as it all made sense. 'Anacrites himself is protecting the Claudii—and not just since Modestus died. He has actively been their patron for much longer.'

I nodded. 'I'm slow. As soon as he let slip that his agents were twins, it should have rung bells. Too much coincidence.'

'It's good. It was another bit of very simple concealment,' said Aulus. 'Once you know, however, the subterfuge leaps out. I don't know how he thought he could get away with it for much longer.'

'Arrogance. He believes he is untouchable.' Petro claimed the big finish: 'Two of the murdering Claudii actually go out to kill *from the spy's house.* Anacrites himself has given the twins a base in Rome, providing them with a locale. He knows—but he still let them get away with it. So what is his game, Falco?'

Baffled by the spy's stupidity, I shook my head. 'He is crazy. I suppose he may be struggling to contain them. On an off-day, *he* may even stupidly have told them to provide a corpse north of the Tiber to distract attention from the Modestus killing on the other side of Rome.'

Helena had been thinking fast. 'Anacrites cannot have known originally what these men were. He must have taken them on to work for him—which we think was a couple of years ago—' That was what Pius or Virtus, whichever we had held captive, had told Petro and me, though I did not remind her of the circumstances. 'He found out later. Then he may have been attracted by a hint of danger attached to them. You know how he is; he would never admit that he made a mistake in hiring them.'

I agreed. 'When he learned the truth, he would simply convince himself he had chosen ideal staff. He would think having a colourful background made them just right for his work's "special nature".'

Justinus barked with laughter. 'So, being perverted murderers equates with "special intelligence skills", does it?'

Aelianus had once been a recruitment target; he knew the spy's sales patter: 'Anacrites maintains that spying is a little over the edge of legality. That's exciting. He sees himself as cunning and dangerous. He gloats that he can get way with using assassins "for the good of the state"—well, think about Perella.'

I thought it a good diagnosis: 'He would tell himself he could control them. But when he came back from Istria and discovered the Modestus murder had drawn attention to the Claudii, faced with them getting out of hand, he tried to take personal control.'

'Marcus, I'm afraid your involvement must have made it all worse for him,' Helena told me ruefully.

'Too right. Not only must he bury the problem before the Claudii are exposed, he has to distract me.'

Justinus blew his cheeks out. 'And there's no chance for us to expose his position, you know. He will only accuse us of interfering in some covert operation, endangering the Empire.'

'We are stuffed,' said Aelianus. He was young. He gave up easily.

I was older. I knew how the world worked. I was starting to think he had the right idea.

Petronius let out a grim laugh. 'Well, one of the twins is dealt with. Either Pius or Virtus has been removed from society—without us even realising who he was.'

I myself would not have mentioned that again. Helena glowered. The Camilli sensed awkwardness and did not ask what Petro meant.

Of course it explained why Pius or Virtus would never admit his name to us—and why Anacrites also glossed over his men's identity. It also explained why the agent—child of a cold, controlling father and a remote, neglectful mother, growing up with sadistic brothers— had managed to resist our interrogation.

And it explained the knives he carried. I tried not to look at Helena Justina as we both grasped that I had brought a perverted killer right into our house. I felt queasy remembering we had kept him here, in the same building as my wife and children.

Petronius may have picked up what Helena and I were thinking. He lowered his voice. 'So, Marcus Didius, my old tentmate, who volunteers to confront Anacrites?'

'Not us—not yet,' I answered.

Ever cautious, Petro nodded too.

52

Claudius Virtus lived in the Transtiberina. Petronius had found the address in the vigiles' lists. This was the Fourteenth District, a hike across the Tiber, an area I had always distrusted. It had a long history as a haunt of immigrants and outsiders, which gave it a reputation as a refuge for low-grade hustlers. Officially part of Rome for several generations, it retained a tang of the alien. Its dank air was imbued with murky hints of cumin and rue; alive with harsh, foreign voices, its dark, narrow lanes were populated with people in exotic cloaks who kept strange birds in cages up above on their windowsills. Carts here regularly tried to ignore the curfew. The vigiles, whose station house was just off the Via Aurelia, rarely made their presence felt, even to tackle the soft option of traffic nuisance. This area was attached to Rome, yet kept from full participation by more than the yellow-grey loop of the Tiber. The Transtib would always stay separate.

As I walked with Petro, Aulus and Quintus, I was still remembering that night at the spy's house. 'I saw someone else. Just a glimpse. I think he had been with the two agents. Could it have been Nobilis? Nobody we've questioned seems to have spotted him, though the chef did say Pius and Virtus asked for double portions with their meal—that could have been a cover for their brother. I certainly saw enough used dishes for three.'

'Description?'

'No good. He was too far away, and in a gloomy corridor. It was after dark by then, and Anacrites is mean with lamps.'

'So who do you think it was, Falco?'

'I don't know—but don't let's forget him. According to the caterer's chef, the third man was the one with the cameo.'

Virtus rented a room above a row of crumbling shops. It was in the same building as the bar we chose when we arrived, immediately above us. If he had been there, he could have jumped through a window and landed right on Quintus. But there was a fifty-fifty chance he had gone away, and would not be coming back.

The barman, who knew him, said Virtus had not lived there full-time for six months. He kept the place on, and had been coming back to check his stuff once a week. Not just lately, however.

'Sounds as though he's living in with a girlfriend? Keeping up with his rent because he thinks she's going to throw him out. Or he may want to dump her?'

'Not as far as I know. He's married, I believe.' That did not rule out Petro's girlfriend theory. 'Working in Rome to earn some cash, but he goes home.'

'Where would "home" be?'

'No idea, sorry.' We knew: the Pontine Marshes. The wife's name was Plotia. I had even met her. Petronius had searched the rustic shack where Virtus left her. Not much cash seemed to find its way back there.

'Where else might he go?'

'He mentioned a brother.'

'Pius?'

The barman shook his head. 'Means nothing, sorry.' He was very apologetic. According to Petro, as we went upstairs, the man in the apron should have been apologising for his lousy drink.

Petronius shouldered in the door. He didn't care if the occupant learned we were after him. The landlord could claim compensation; from the state of his building, he wouldn't come around to notice the damage.

It was a one-room apartment, its interior kept with the squalid housekeeping we recognised as the Claudius trademark. Flies lived here as subtenants; they soared about with the lethargic flight of insects that had gorged on unpleasant decay, close nearby. The smell in the room was familiar: an unclean, earthy odour I recalled from the spy's house, in those mean corridor rooms where the Claudii were lodged.

There was no space for four healthy adults. I volunteered to search, with Justinus. Petronius reluctantly agreed to wait downstairs in the bar with Aelianus.

'It's a simple room-search, Lucius. Let me handle it. Back off; you're worse than Anacrites!'

'I don't want you to cock it up.'

'Thanks, friend. Any time Quintus and I can shaft you in return, assume we'll be available.'

The 'stuff' Virtus came back to check was minimal. Apart from the landlord's basic furniture—sagging bed, lopsided stool, a skinny old sack on the floor for a rug—we found only a filthy foodbowl, empty wineskins, and a used loincloth which Aulus lifted up on the handle of a bald broom from the corridor then dropped in distaste.

We found no trophies from killings. However, hidden behind the inevitable loose wall panel, there were more knives. These were bigger and nastier than the ones we took off the agent.

After Quintus and I went downstairs again, Petronius insisted on going up to double-check.

'Jove, he's finicky!'

'Doesn't want to make a mistake with the Urban Cohorts watching.'

'Doesn't trust you, Falco!'

I asked more questions of the barman. This time he changed his story; he now remembered he had met the tenant's brother. His wife had appeared, curious about us. He was short and sparely built; she was shorter and enormous. She had met the brother too. The fond couple engaged in a hot marital argument; the barman maintained the brother was a scruff and a shambles, which the wife doggedly disputed. 'Kept himself nice. Good threads. Combed his hair.' They went on disputing, until it almost sounded as if they had seen two different brothers. Given the numbers of Claudii, this was possible.

'Fancied him?' asked Aulus, cracking the grimace he used for charm.

'Not likely—he had funny eyes.'

It was the wife who knew the real reason Virtus came back so regularly. 'He's one of Alis' regulars. He comes every Thursday.'

'Is Alis the local prostitute?'

'Not her! Fortune-teller. Just around the corner. She does a bit of witchcraft when people want to pay for it. Thursday is her night for seances. Virtus always went.'

As Petronius could not tear himself away from the room upstairs, I left the Camilli to wait for him. I strolled past a veg stall, a pot shop and a sponge bar, tripped around a corner by a fountain that was so dry its stone had cracked in the sun, and parked myself in a peeling doorway in order to inspect the fortune-teller's. The place I had been told Alis lived in was anonymous. These women work by word of mouth, usually hoarse whispers passed on in the environs of un-scrupulous temples. Anyone who has enough sixth sense to find a horoscope-hatcher, doesn't need her services.

After waiting a while, I went across and knocked. A frizzy baggage came to the door and admitted me. She was middle-aged and top heavy, wearing peculiar layers of clothes, over which were dried-flower wreaths with funny feathers sticking out of them. I expected a dead mouse to drop out any minute. The prevailing colour of her wardrobe was vermilion. It was amazing how many scarves and belts and under-tunics she had managed to acquire in that far-from-fashionable shade.

She moved with a shuffle and was slow getting around. Only her eyes had that sly, kindly glint you find in folk whose livelihood depends on befriending people with no personality, banking on the possibility that the vulnerable might part with their life savings and have no relatives to ask questions.

'My name's Falco.'

'What do you want, Falco?'

'You can tell it's not a love potion or a curse, then?'

'I can tell what you are, sonny! You won't fool me into drawing up a lifeline for the Emperor. I practise my ancient arts fully within the law, son. I pay my dues to the vigiles to leave me alone. And I don't do poisons. Who sent you?'

I sighed gently. 'No fooling you, grandma! I work for the government; I want information.'

'What will you pay?'

'The going rate.'

'What's that?'

I looked in my purse and showed her a few coins. She sniffed. I doubled it. She asked for treble; we settled on two and half.

She toddled into a corner to brew herself some nettle tea before we started. I gazed around, impressed that one elderly woman could have collected so many doilies and corn dollies, so many horrible old curtains, so many amulets with evil eyes or hieroglyphs or stars. The air was thick with dust, every surface was crammed with eccentric objects, the high window was veiled. I bet every superstitious old woman from a two-mile radius came here for her special Thursdays. I bet half of them left her something in their wills.

Nothing that smacked obviously of witchcraft was out on view. The desiccated claws and vials of toad's blood must be behind the musty swathes of curtain.

Eventually she settled down with her tea bowl and I learned Claudius Virtus was a regular at the seances. 'He was interested in the Dark Side. Always full of questions—I don't know where he got his theories. From his own strange brain, if you ask me.'

'Are you going to tell me what you do at your meetings?'

'We try to contact the spirits of the dead. I have the gift to call them up from the Underworld.'

'Really? And did Virtus ask about anyone in particular?'

'Usually he watched the rest. He tried to talk to his mother once.'

'Did she answer?'

'No.'

'Why would that be?'

Abruptly, Alis turned confiding: 'I got the creeps, Falco. I don't know why. I just felt I didn't want to be in the middle of that conversation.'

'You have some control then?' I asked with a smile.

The seer sipped her nettle tea, with the manners of a lady.

She told me Virtus had never missed a meeting until a few weeks ago. His mother—Casta—had died a couple of years before, he told Alis; he claimed to be close to her and said all the family adored the woman.

'My information is she was vicious,' I said. 'She had twenty children and was reputed to treat them all very coldly.'

'That's your answer,' replied Alis comfortably. 'It explains Virtus. He tells himself she was wonderful; he wants to believe it, doesn't he? In his poor mind, his ma is a darling who loved him. He misses her now, because he wants her to have been someone he should miss. If you were to say to him what you just said to me about his mother, he'd deny it furiously—and probably attack you.' I believed that.

Alis had winkled out of him that his father died before his mother, and that he had other relatives, some in Rome. 'More than one?'

'I gained that impression. He spoke of "the boys".'

'There are sisters too.'

Alis shrugged. She knew about the twin, believed he lived not far away, but had never set eyes on him. Plotia, the wife, had never been mentioned. When I commented that I was not surprised, Alis pulled a face and nodded as if she knew what I meant. Of course I despised this woman and her arcane dealings—yet in her frumpy, frowsty way, she was a good judge of character; she had to be.

'Did you think him capable of great violence?'

'Aren't all men?'

Virtus had ceased coming to the meetings, without warning. I took this as evidence that he was the agent we had sent to a hard death in the mines.

Alis put down her tea bowl. She sat motionless, as if listening. 'I don't feel we have lost him, Falco. He is still among those who wander the earth in body.'

I said I was sure she knew more about that than me, then I made my farewells as politely as a sceptic could.

This conversation had made me feel closer to Virtus now than in all the time Petronius and I had spent with him.

53

We men had a short case conference as we walked back towards the river. We would have preferred to stay at the bar, but that meant the helpful barman and his inquisitive wife would have listened. Anyway, Petro hated their drink.

We agreed it was futile for *us* to tackle Anacrites. However, the time had come to explore whether any higher authorities would take an interest. Camillus senior was on friendly terms with the Emperor; the senator might speak on the subject next time he was chatting with Vespasian. It would be tricky: so tricky, I shied off it until we gathered better evidence though I instructed Aulus and Quintus to tell their father what we believed. We had convinced ourselves, but that was not the same as proof.

Titus might be open to an approach, though his reputation varied from kind-hearted and affable to debauched and brutal. As commander of the Praetorians, he was Anacrites' commander too; that could rebound on us. If we failed to persuade him the spy was compromised, we could unleash a violent backlash from Anacrites—all for nothing. Even if Titus believed us, it could look as if *he* had misjudged his man. Nobody wanted Titus Caesar as an enemy. His dinner parties were more fun than the spy's—but he exercised the power of life or death over people who upset him.

I said I would have another word with Laeta and Momus. All the others thought that an excellent idea. They went to a bar near the Theatre of Marcellus that Petro reckoned was really well worth visiting, while they waved me off to the Palace.

I saw Laeta first, my preference. He did not turn me away. His method was to greet you with interest, listen gravely—then if your story was unwelcome politically, he let you down without a qualm. Unsurprisingly, he let me down.

'It's too thin. On what you've got, Falco, I don't see this going anywhere. Anacrites will simply say he made a mistake when he employed those men, and thank you for pointing it out to him.'

'Then he'll get me for it.'

'Of course. What do you expect with his background?'

'What does that mean?' I raised an eyebrow. 'As far as I know, his background is the same as yours. An imperial slave who made good—in his case, for unfathomable reasons.'

'He is bright,' Laeta said tersely.

'I've known pavement sweepers who could think and talk and grade dog turds to a system as they collected them—but such men don't end up in senior positions.'

'Anacrites was always known for his intellect—though he was more physical than most secretaries, which suits his calling. He had pliability; he could bend with the political breeze—which, when he and I were coming up the staff list, was a must!'

'He adapted himself to the quirks of emperors, whether mad, half-mad, drunkard or plain incompetent?'

'Still at it. Titus thinks well of him.'

'But you don't. You have a singer spying on him at home,' I threw in.

Laeta brushed it aside. 'The same man who observes me for Anacrites! Suspicion is a game we all play. Nevertheless, Marcus Didius, if you find genuine proof of corruption, I am sure I can persuade the old man to act on it.'

'Well, thanks! Tell me what you meant about the spy's background,' I persisted.

Laeta gave me a fond shake of the head—but then what he said was enlightening: 'Many of us feel he never fitted in. You compared him with me—but my grandmother was a favourite of the Empress Livia; I have respected brothers and cousins in the secretariats. Anacrites came up the ladder by himself, always a loner. It gave him an edge, honed his ambition—but he never shakes off his isolation.'

'Not isolated enough for me; he crushes up against me and my family.'

Laeta laughed softly. 'I wonder why?' He went no further, naturally. 'So, Falco, dare I ask: are you and your cronies still investigating the Pontine Marsh murders?'

I gave him a straight look. 'How can we, when our last instructions were to drop the case? Instructions, Claudius Laeta, which you gave us!'

He laughed again. I smiled with him as a courtesy. But as soon as I left, I stopped smiling.

Momus, I was certain, never had a slave grandmama who was cosy with the old Empress. He must have crawled out of an egg in a streak of hot slime somewhere. Any horrible siblings were basking in rich men's zoos or their heads were on walls as hunters' trophies.

Momus reacted eagerly to news of the spy's implication in sordid crimes, until I hankered for Laeta's measured thoughtfulness instead. Momus even promised to help—though he freely agreed it was hard to see what he could do.

'Momus, I still don't think the Claudii showed up and got jobs with the spy by accident. Are you ever going to tell me what you know about them?'

'Falco, if I knew how they control him, I'd be controlling him myself.'

'Do you admit you've put in people to watch him?'

'Of course I haven't,' he lied.

I left, reflecting ruefully that Momus had always been useless.

There was one more possibility.

Anacrites sometimes used a freelance on very special assignments, a woman. Helena and I had run into her a few times, and although I had a professional respect for her, we viewed her warily. She killed for Anacrites, killed to order. She took a pride in a beautiful performance, whether it was death or dancing. Dance was her cover. Just like her assassinations, it was clean, prepared in every detail, immaculate and took your breath away. Her talent gave her access to people Anacrites wished to remove; distracted by her brilliance, they were at her mercy. As often as not, no connection was made between her dancing and the discovery of a shocking corpse. Her name was Perella. She used a thin-bladed knife to slit her victims' throats. Knowing her method, I never let her stand behind me.

The first time I met Perella, before I knew her significance, it was at her home. Though a few years had passed, I managed to find the place again: a small apartment near the Esquiline, inexpensive but endurable. She let me in, barely surprised to see me. I was given a bowl of nuts and a beaker of barley water, urged to take the good chair and the footstool. It was like visiting a great-aunt, one who looked demure but who would reminisce about times when she juggled three lovers all at once—and who was rumoured to still do it, passing them on to the baker's wife, when she felt tired.

What made me remember Perella was my encounter with the mystic Alis. Perella, too, was of mature age and build; in fact more years of age than it was kind to mention. The skilled diva remained supple. She had power too; not so long before, I saw her kick a man in the privates so hard she wrote off all chance of him producing children.

'Didius Falco! Whenever I see you, I feel apprehensive.'

'Nice courtesy, Perella. And I take you very seriously too. Still working?'

'Retired—generally.' That figured. Her hair, never stylish, had once passed for blonde; she was letting the grey work its way out through the lopsided chignon. The skin on her neck had coarsened. But her self-containment did not alter. 'Yourself?'

'I had the chance—came into money. I decided work was in my blood.'

'What are you working on?' Perella was eating pistachios as if all that mattered was splitting their shells. She tossed off the question like casual conversation—but I never forgot she was an agent. A good one.

I let time pass before I answered. Perella put the nuts down. We gazed at one another. I said quietly, 'As usual, my role is complex. I cannot trust my principle—insofar as I have any, given that the case I was investigating for a dead man's nephew was then grabbed by Anacrites.'

Perella folded her hands on her full waistline, as if she was just about to ask me where I got my stylish wrist purse. 'My whimsical employer!'

'Still?'

'Oh yes. You mean the marsh bugs, I suppose? He sent me there, if you're interested.' I must have looked surprised. 'I can swat flies, Falco.'

'And which fly,' I asked with emphasis, 'was he wanting you to swat?'

'A vicious coward called Nobilis.' Although Perella worked for Anacrites, he never quite managed to buy her loyalty. She was more likely to connive with me, a fellow professional. 'Nobilis must have heard I was coming, so he fled abroad.'

I could not blame him. 'So that's why he vanished! How did he know you were coming for him?'

'I wonder!' scoffed Perella. She implied Anacrites let it slip.

'Do you know where he went?'

'Pucinum.' Where had I heard that name recently? 'Fled into hiding with his grandma,' Perella said, sneeringly. 'That's where they come from, those animals. I could have gone over there and dealt with him easily.'

'Did Anacrites run out of cash for your fare?'

'Much more intriguing! Anacrites was going that way himself.'

'Aha! So Pucinum is in Istria!' I whistled through my bottom teeth, to give myself thinking time. 'I've remembered—he bought wine there on the trip . . . Has Anacrites done the business? Has he finished Nobilis himself?'

Perella gave me an odd look. 'Well, just like you, I'm off the case. But, just like you, I never let go. He didn't. Nobilis is back, according to my sources. Seen in Rome. Anacrites must have reprieved him.'

'Or he just bungled it.'

'Not so,' said Perella softly. 'Claudius Nobilis came home on the same ship as the spy. The pair of them together, tight as ticks.'

'Anacrites brought him back? But not in leg irons—I haven't seen a trial announced!'

'Surprise! You'd think,' Perella told me in disgust, 'if he wanted Nobilis dead, as he told me, he could have found the chance to put a boot in the small of his back and shove the bastard overboard. Anacrites is handy enough—and I hear you know all about that!'

'What?'

'A little bird twittered "Lepcis Magna"?'

'That birdie must fly absolutely everywhere! I'll wring his neck for tweeting.' Anacrites had fought as a gladiator at Lepcis. It was illegal for any but slaves. Citizens who fought in the arena became non-persons. News of it would make Anacrites a social outcast; he would lose his job, his ranking, his reputation, everything. I smiled gently. 'You *are* well informed. It's true; he spilled blood on the sand. But that information is mine to exploit, Perella. I was there.'

'I won't step in—even though I want his job.'

'*You want his job?*'

'Why not?' Indeed! The Praetorians would never accept her, yet Perella was just as shrewd, experienced and ruthless as the current incumbent. More intelligent, in my opinion. She had the talent. Only the ancient traditions of keeping women beside the hearth interfered with her qualifications. No tombstone yet had ever said: She kept the house and worked in wool—*and slit a few throats for security reasons* . . . 'You could destroy Anacrites, Falco—and presumably he knows it. Can you ever feel safe?'

'I have protection: other witnesses. If he touches me, they'll tell. So he's the one who lives in fear. I'm saving the information for the sweetest possible moment.'

The dancer took up her barley water peacefully. She still sounded like a well-disposed aunt, giving me career advice: 'Don't wait too long, my dear.'

54

I found my team, not as tipsy as I feared, merely unreliable. I said it was good to associate with happy men. Petronius had to work, or at least take a nap at the station house. The Camilli, being persons of leisure, rolled along with me. They had reached the clingy phase, where I was their best friend. Trailing them like seaweed stuck on an oar, I went up the Aventine to Ma's house, intending to collect Albia.

She had left, for home my mother said. 'Anacrites was here—he drops in, to see I am all right,' she confided in Aelianus and Justinus hoarsely. 'He knows my own don't give me a second thought. When I am found stone dead in my chair one morning, it will be Anacrites who raises the alarm.'

I cursed this libel and sat down on a bench. The Camilli did likewise, fitting in fast, as people did at Mother's house. They were clearly thinking: what a dear little old lady. She sat there, tiny and terrible, letting them believe it. Her beady black eyes rested wisely upon them. 'I hope my good-for-nothing son hasn't taken you drinking.'

'They were drinking; I was somewhere else, working,' I protested. 'Now I shall have to take them to the baths, have them home to dine, and sober them up for their trusting wives.'

'I don't expect trust comes into it!' reckoned Ma. The senators' sons looked shifty. Belated doubts about the dear little old lady filtered through their blearied brains.

Ma then described a cringe-making scene at her house earlier between Anacrites and Albia. 'He said "I always admire Junilla Tacita; you should come to her when you are troubled, dearie".' He cannot have called Albia 'dearie'; it was the word Ma used, to avoid truly accepting this outsider as a granddaughter. Albia saw Ma's reservations; she only came up here when Helena sent her. 'We all had a nice chat, then when your Albia was ready to go, he *so* kindly offered to see her home. Beautiful manners,' Ma insisted to the Camilli.

Aulus said in a solemn, lawyer's voice, 'You can tell a man's character by the way he treats young women.' He thought he was being satirical: big mistake, Aulus.

'You are the one who broke her poor little heart, are you?' asked Ma, with her crucifying sneer. 'Well, you would know all about character!'

I judged it time to leave.

Albia was safe at home. Anacrites had left her on the doorstep, merely sending in greetings to Helena; he probably knew this would only increase her anxiety—and my wrath. Albia failed to see what the fuss was about.

She dined with us, despite Aulus being present. Nothing kept Albia from her food. So she overheard us relating our progress. Helena summed up: 'Virtus has been dealt with; let us not remember how. He said Pius had gone home to the Pontine Marshes. Perella believes Nobilis is back in Rome, though you have no leads, unless it was him Marcus saw at the spy's house. Now we know the "Melitans" are his brothers that does seem likely. You won't get in there a second time to look. Relations with Anacrites are deteriorating, and he will hardly invite us all to dinner again—'

With yelps of pain, her brothers and I pleaded to be excused if he did.

'I could go to his house!' piped up Albia. 'He is perfectly nice to *me*! He says *I* can go at any time.'

'Keep away from him,' snapped Helena. 'Have respect for yourself, Albia.'

'Don't listen when he makes out you're special!' I said crushingly, 'Saying he's never met anybody like you is a very old line, sweetheart. When a man—any man—who has a collection of obscene art invites a young girl to visit, there is only one reason. It's nothing to do with culture.'

'Is this from experience, Falco?' Albia asked, disingenuously. 'How did you meet Helena Justina?' murmured our little troublemaker.

'I worked for her father. He hired me. I met her. She hired me as well. I never invited her to my horrible hutch.' Helena turned up there of her own accord. That was how I knew enough about strong-minded girls to be afraid for Albia.

'Was it when you lived at Fountain Court? I've seen it! I went with Lentullus, hiding that cameo. Is that how you know how the art invitation works, Falco? Did you lure girls up to your garret, pretending your father was an auctioneer so you had curios to show them—then when they had climbed all those stairs and found out there was nothing, it was too late and they were too weary to argue?'

'Certainly not,' Helena interrupted calmly. 'Marcus was such an innocent in those days, I had to show him what girls were for.'

Albia broke up in giggles. It was good to see her smile.

I topped up everybody's water cup while I tried to reassert the myth of a respectable past.

We agreed it was time to go after Claudius Pius. Assuming his brother had told Petro and me the truth, then Pius was visiting his wife, that fragile soul Byrta. It meant another trip into the marshes, though at least that would let me go over to Antium and liaise with Silvius, of the Urban Cohorts. Petronius had checked with Rubella, who still refused to release him from Rome, even to work with Silvius. So Justinus, with his experience on our first trip, won the ballot to come with me.

Next day at dawn, I was all packed and about to mount a mule outside my house, when Helena ran out after me. She told me anxiously that Albia was not in her room. Our conversation the day before had had unwelcome results. The girl had left a note—at least she was that sensible—to say she was going to Anacrites' house *'to have a look around'*. If she went last evening, he had kept her overnight.

'Don't worry,' Helena reassured me, though her voice was tense. 'You get off—I'll fetch her back somehow.' I wanted to stay, but I had five slaves chomping at the bit behind me and had made arrangements with Justinus to depart at first light. 'Leave it to me, Marcus. Don't fret. Take care, my love.'

'Always. You too. Sweetheart, I love you.'

'I love you too. Come home soon.'

As I rode through Rome in the thin air of a very early morning, on my way to collect Justinus at the Capena Gate, I thought about those words. How many people have said them as a talisman, but never saw their precious love again? I wondered if Livia Primilla, the elderly wife of Julius Modestus, had spoken the words when her husband rode to challenge the Claudii. If I failed to return from this journey, Helena Justina would come after me too. I should have told her not to do it, not without an army. But that would have meant planting the suggestion that her brother and I might be in serious danger.

At the Capena Gate, Aelianus emerged to wave us off. He was mildly jealous, though as an assistant he always enjoyed being left in charge. I mentioned what had happened to Albia. 'Aulus, it's not your affair. Obviously this is awkward for you, but could you check with Helena that everything is all right? Will you tell her I had a thought as I came through the Forum: if she goes to see the spy, take my mother.'

'Will he listen to your mother?'

'Mediation! Helena will know—in a crisis with an enemy, it's a fine Roman tradition to send in an elderly woman, with a long black veil and a very stern lecture.'

Justinus suggested leaving behind Lentullus, who could bring us news later.

So Justinus and I, taking a handful of slaves as back-up, rode off once more to Latium. Thirty miles later, as near we could get discreetly, we camped overnight, not showing ourselves at any inns where landlords might give advance warning of our presence. We planned the traditional dawn raid.

At first light, with the promise of an unpleasantly hot late August day, we reached the end of the track. Here, we knew, three of the Claudius brothers lived when it suited them, in poverty and filth, with two skinny, subdued wives and innumerable wild children. We had already passed the shack where their brother Probus mouldered; we saw no sign of him, nor his ferocious dog, Fangs.

The woodlands were sultry. Fetid steam rose from depleted pools as the marshes dried out through the summer. It must have rained recently; there was a dank, unpleasant smell everywhere. Clouds of flies rose up from tangles of half-decayed undergrowth, skirling in our faces in predatory black curtains as we disturbed them. The insects were worse than we remembered, the going more difficult, the isolation drearier.

We rode up as quietly as possible. We all dismounted. With drawn swords, Justinus and I went straight to the hovel where Pius and his wife lived, while our slaves checked around the back. We banged the door, but there was no answer. The hutment which belonged to Nobilis looked as deserted as before. While we continued knocking, a man appeared in the doorway of the third hut. A woman's voice sounded behind him.

'What's that noise?' he shouted. It was the other 'Melitan'. I recognised him, and he recognised me—though he cannot have known quite how familiar he seemed. Anacrites had said the twins were not identical; maybe this one was half a digit taller, a few pounds heavier, but there was little in it.

'Claudius Pius?' If so, he was on the wrong doorstep, growling over his shoulder at the wrong woman. Mind you, it did not surprise me that one of the Claudii should be screwing his brother's wife.

He rounded aggressively. 'No. I am Virtus.'

I believed him. We had muddled them up. I should have known. Anyone who has ever seen a theatrical farce would expect the wrong one to pop out of a doorway. That's what you get with twins.

55

He could be lying. Impersonating each other to fool people is a lifelong game for twins. When I was at school, the Masti were famous for it; their loving mother helped by always dressing them in identical tunics, with their hair curled in the same ridiculous quiff. They spent their days tormenting our teacher, then later were reputed to swap girlfriends. Causing confusion would have gone on for ever, if Lucius Mastus had not been run over by a stonemason's wagon. His brother Gaius was never the same afterwards. All the joy went out of him.

Virtus had the same build, skin, freckles, light eyes and upturned nose as the man Petro and I had captured. I felt uncomfortable with it, though I did not believe the telepathy of twins could have told him what his brother went through. I suppose I had a bad conscience.

After grumbling noises from indoors, Byrta sidled into view next to him. In the act of re-draping her clothes, she hitched a scarf around her neck. Maybe it was to hide love bites, if she called their relationship love. It was some rich red colour, decent material. I supposed Virtus must have brought it for her from Rome as a present.

She vouched for him being Virtus not Pius. I said he had to come with us. He reluctantly complied. His wife did not rush to pack him a travelling bag. We searched his home before we left, but found nothing, not even weapons. If he really was Virtus, he had left his armoury in the Transtiberina apartment, so it was now secured at the Fourth Cohort's station house. The woman stayed behind with their children.

We asked about his brother Probus. Virtus said men had come and arrested him—Silvius and the Urban Cohorts, presumably. 'Why didn't they get you at the same time?'

'I heard them coming.'

We took him with us to Antium, where we joined up with Silvius. Silvius confirmed he had Probus in custody. Probus seemed to be breaking ranks and denouncing Nobilis, though it was too early to say if he would distance himself enough to give us evidence. When Silvius wanted to question Virtus, I had had enough with the other twin, so I gave him the prisoner without quibbling. Justinus and I sat in. I insisted on that.

In two days of hard questioning, Virtus said little useful. His line now was that he had never had anything to do with any of his brothers' cruel practices—and, as he knew well, we had nothing to tie him to the murders.

'None of us ever knew what Nobilis was up to.' That tired cliché. 'These things you are saying about him and Pius are terrible. Thank the gods our father will never know about it.'

'Aristocles was no moralist! Look at the disgusting rabble he and Casta produced. Strong family bonds, have you?' asked Silvius, insinuating.

'Oh I see your game! I repudiate my brother. I reject Nobilis. If he and Pius did those things, I dissociate them from our family. They shame us. They are blackening the family name.'

'*What family name?* Don't make me spew.'

Virtus just stared at Silvius. He was not a clod. None of them were. That was how those of them who committed the crimes had covered up their tracks for so many decades.

'We'll get the truth,' sneered Silvius. 'Probus is here in custody, you know that. Your Probus seems a fellow with a conscience. Probus has begun telling us a lot of helpful things—all about his perverted brothers.'

'Probus is just as bad as them,' scoffed Virtus.

When Silvius needed a break, I was given a go. 'Tell me about your connection with Anacrites, Virtus.'

'Nothing to say.'

'When did you find out about him?'

'Around two years back. We went up to Rome and asked him for work. He thought he could use us, so it was fixed up. I know when it was, because our mother had just died.'

'Casta? Was her death something to do with you going to see Anacrites?'

'Yes and no. When we lost her, we felt cast adrift.'

'Oh you poor little orphans!'

'Have a heart, Falco!' Justinus broke in, grinning. Silvius let out a short laugh too. He had bad teeth, not many left.

I had remembered something someone told us about Casta. Unexpectedly, I strode up, grabbed the prisoner by his hair, then turned his head to demonstrate he had part of an ear missing. 'Did your mother do that to you?' I yelled.

'I deserved it,' said Virtus, immediately and without blinking.

We had to stop then, because news came in about the discovery of more bodies.

Justinus and I went with Silvius to inspect the site. On the way, Silvius owned up that the Urbans had been using Claudius Probus for the past few days to help them identify places where his brother Nobilis might have buried corpses. 'We believe Probus is himself implicated in the abductions, though not as the principal.'

'How did you make him talk?'

'We had to provide immunity. The way it works, Probus suggests places that Nobilis liked—secret lairs he had, on his own or with Pius.'

'Pius was the one who lured the victims; he brought them to Nobilis?'

'Seems so. These spots are difficult to access, so Probus takes us and points out where to look.'

'He knows too much about it to be innocent.'

'He admits that. He says he was young, and coerced by his brothers. He claims he became too horrified and stopped joining in.'

I hated him being given immunity. Sometimes you have to compromise, but if Probus was directly involved in the deaths, immunity was wrong. Silvius just shrugged. 'When you see the terrain, you will understand. There is no other way we could ever find the bodies. My seniors conferred. It's worth it, to clear up the old disappearances.'

Silvius was quite right about the dreadful terrain. The first place we went was a forest, a few miles out of Antium. A thick canopy of slim-trunked scented pines, intermingled with stunted cork oaks, filled this thickly wooded area. At ground level, dense brushwood impeded movement. Nobilis must have used a narrow track. A slightly wider access had been bashed down by the Urbans. Following a guide, we struggled along it to a dell. We went in silence. When we reached the activity, the shocked hush continued, broken only by rustles and chopping spades as work went on slowly at the sordid scene.

Bodies had been excavated and placed on flattened underbrush. There were eight or nine, of different ages; their poor condition prevented an exact tally. Most were now collected in proper array, but the bones of one or two could only be hopelessly jumbled on a sack. The troops had lifted most remains from their resting places and laid them in a row—except one. One body lay apart and they had not touched it. One was new.

The men stood back. Silvius, Justinus and I went to look. While the workers waited, watching us, we surveyed the remains, pretending to be experts.

Most of the recovered bodies had been found in the ritual position, face down and with outstretched arms—the mark of the Modestus killers. There were no more severed hands. Petronius must have been right that this was the letter-writer's particular punishment for making appeals to the Emperor.

We had all seen dead men. Dead women too. We had seen flesh battered and bones treated disrespectfully. Even Justinus, the youngest here, must already know the swift sag of the stomach that comes in the presence of unnatural death. That smell. The mocking way skulls grin. The shock at the way human skeletons can hang together even when entirely stripped of meat and organs. The worse shock, when long-dead bones suddenly fall apart.

What lay here was in one sense no longer human; yet these bodies were still part of the wider tribe we belonged to. Most had died years ago. Many would never be identified. But they called on us as family. They imposed responsibilities. I cannot have been the only one who silently promised them justice.

The newest corpse was a woman.

'How long?'

'Two days, at most.'

Her killer must have been fleeing from the forest almost as the first troops approached. Perhaps the noise of them stomping down thickets had disturbed him. Perhaps he even glimpsed them through the trees.

She lay on her own, not with the others. Those who found her had felt she was different—still close enough to living to count as a person, not simply anonymous 'remains'. Indeed, it would have been possible to recognise her face—had her killer not battered her badly. She had suffered; large areas of her skin were discoloured by bruising. Someone suggested much of the beating was inflicted after death; we preferred to think so. Either her trunk was swollen because of what had happened internally during the violence, or she had been pregnant. Unlike the other bodies, which were deposited face down in scraped graves, this one had been left unburied and looking at the sky. She had not been ripped open. He had not finished with her corpse.

Around her neck still lay a gold chain that must have been the means by which Nobilis managed to get close to her again. The expensive granulation looked like the hanging loop on the Dioscurides cameo. I could see the fastening. I forced myself to bend down over the body, unhook it, and remove the chain. It had dug into the flesh, but I pulled on it as gently as I could.

'I know who this is.'

I recognised her dress. I remembered that sad rag from when she was brought to see Helena and me in the inn at Satricum. It was Demetria, daft daughter of the morose baker Vexus, obedient lover of the foolish grain seller Costus—and one-time wife of Claudius Nobilis, the pernicious freedman who so relentlessly refused to release her from his possession, that he finally came after her and slaughtered her.

56

Word of the grisly discoveries in the forest had inevitably spread. The bodies were carried out on hurdles; we left a small group of men still searching. When we came back to the road, a crowd had gathered. A few, who must have lost friends or relatives in the past, rushed forwards as the cortège emerged from the woods, and had to be held back by troops. Also there, though keeping to themselves in a tight knot, was a group of women I was told were from the Claudius family: three sisters, plus the sisters-in-law, Plotia and Byrta.

They neither spoke to us, nor we to them. They stared, blank-faced, as we removed the dead. It seemed to me they would never speak, never assist with any knowledge they had of the crimes, never even defend themselves. Others kept away from them; who could believe these women were truly innocent of the crimes their men perpetrated? How could they really have known nothing? They would be ostracised. They and their children were further casualties. A grim cycle would repeat itself. The children would grow up angry and isolated. Already none of them knew anything except neglect and violence. Which descendants of Aristocles and Casta could ever escape the stigma of this bleak family? To start a new life would be too hard; to learn new behaviour impossible.

I knew Plotia and Byrta had been friendly with Demetria, but her corpse was well covered; we kept her identity secret until we informed her family. Silvius and I did that. First, we sought out her father, Vexus. From what he told us, we were partly prepared when we visited the cottage where Demetria had lived with Costus. Costus had been taken in by his mother two days ago. Our news would not surprise him; he must count his lover already dead. Two days ago he had come home from his work to find Demetria gone. Their home had been trashed. Every pitiful stick of furniture they owned was wrecked. Vegetables and grain were scattered in the road outside. Pottery, skillets, brooms, rush lights, and a few personal possessions, were all stamped on, thwacked to pieces, shattered and smashed, the quiet means of domestic life pointlessly desecrated. And on the street door, we found a crude symbol: fixed with a long nail through its head was a doll.

A shiver ran through me. I recognised this savage witchcraft.

I knew now who came and destroyed my darling sister's treasured home on the Aventine two years ago. Anacrites must have sent some of the Claudius brothers to frighten Maia and her children; his messengers included the depraved Nobilis.

57

Despite the long summer days, it was nearly dark when we turned in at our inn that night. Silvius had still not finished; he had gone to report to the magistrate.

The finds in the wood were only the start. Painstaking work would now begin on the few scraps of material from the graves which might provide clues, with attempts to work out physical details of the human remains—height, body-weight, sex—if it were possible. Only that way might at least some of the bones be identified, to close missing-person cases and give release to distraught survivors.

From one comparatively recent body, which had boots a local cobbler recognised, we knew the troops had uncovered Macer; he was the overseer who worked for Modestus and Primilla—the man who was beaten up when he remonstrated with the Claudii about the broken boundary fence and who accompanied Primilla when she went to challenge them about her missing husband. We knew we had not found Livia Primilla. I can say now that nothing of her ever was discovered. Her nephew would only ever be able to guess what must have happened.

I was ready for bed, though my head was thrumming with today's experiences. I would not sleep. I sat up with Justinus, neither drinking nor talking. We were staying near the beach; most places at Antium fringed the coast so not only rich men's villas but even ordinary homes and business premises had good views. Stars and a slim moon rose over the motionless Tyrrhenian Sea. The beauty of the scene was both calming and subtly disturbing. My young brother-in-law and I, experienced in dark adventures together, remained silent. Our terrible experiences today removed any need to communicate.

Suddenly we heard familiar voices. One was Lentullus. The piping tones of that nincompoop split the night with cries of mundane bewilderment as he tried to find us. Justinus smiled at me ruefully in the feeble outdoor lamplight; he half rose and called out. My secretary Katutis burst on the scene with Lentullus. They joined us, excitedly. Food and drink had to be supplied. There was a minor commotion, soon reduced as the hungry travellers ate.

While Justinus organised, I demanded, 'Has Albia been found?'

'Oh she's all right!' Lentullus assured me, ripping into bread ravenously.

Katutis had burrowed under his long tunic to produce a letter from Helena. 'She wrote it herself!' He was annoyed at this breach of etiquette. I felt off-kilter because letters between Helena and me were rare. We were infrequently apart for long.

I took the sealed document aside, taking a lamp so I could read in privacy.

Helena wrote to tell me a lively story.

For a couple of days back in Rome, much activity had revolved around my foster-daughter. Helena now knew Albia had betaken herself to the spy's house, convinced she could discover for us whether he was harbouring Claudius Nobilis. It began well. At first Anacrites kept up the pretence that he and Albia had some kind of special relationship. Once she wheedled her way in, she used the age-old excuse of needing a lavatory; then she hastily explored the corridor of utility rooms where I had seen Pius and Virtus playing draughts. She found the room with a third bed. Baggage was still there. Unfortunately, so was the occupant. Albia came face to face with Nobilis. She knew it must be him from the sinister way he turned on her; Albia was terrified.

Luckily for her, Anacrites appeared. She wondered if he had actually been watching her progress. He sent Albia back to the main part of the house. Being her, she disobeyed and dawdled. She heard Anacrites quarrel with the man. He shouted that now Nobilis had been seen by Albia, he had to leave; the only safe course was to go home to Antium. Anacrites said he would deal with the girl.

Albia did not wait to see what that meant. She ordered a little slave boy to tell his master she would seek sanctuary in the House of the Vestal Virgins—the one place in Rome, she said, that not even the Chief Spy could invade. Then, although the spy's house was always heavily secured, our streetwise Albia found a way out.

Now she had to decide where to hide for safety. Coming home that night was out of the question; Anacrites would follow her. Helena did not tell me in the letter where Albia was, although she said she knew. Her mother, friend of a retired Vestal, had obtained curious inside information. The spy had turned up at the Vestals' House in the Forum, mob-handed with Praetorian Guards. The idiot tried to enter this sacred place that was barred to men. He outraged the Vestals, those revered women whose sanctum had been inviolable since the foundation of Rome six centuries ago (and just when, chortled Helena, they had settled down for the night with hot mulsum and dunking biscuits). When they caustically denied any knowledge of Albia, Anacrites refused to believe them. It was horrible to contemplate how severely the Vestals slapped him down in return. Only he would have taken on a group of vicious professional virgins who had six hundred years of training in how to reduce men to shreds. He retreated ignominiously.

All this had taken place before Helena and I realised Albia was missing. Next day—very soon after I left for Latium—Anacrites turned up at our house, alone, pretending to be concerned about her. Of course she was not there either. Helena showed him the door.

He tried my mother's house. This was another bad mistake and as a result he had now lost her previously unshakable goodwill. Ma was dozing in her chair—anyone of sense would have tiptoed out again. He woke her. He was so het up, Ma could see he intended Albia no good. Despite her devotion to this worm whose life she had saved, Ma rallied; she might have been lukewarm about having Albia in the family, but in a crisis Ma always defended her grandchildren. Furious, she ordered Anacrites to leave, threatening to upend an onion casserole over his sleek head. Even he had to see their cosy relationship had ended.

Anacrites next convinced himself Albia must have run to Helena's father, to ask the senator to intercede with the Emperor. This was the spy's worst mistake. She was not there—never had been—but my winsome father-in-law became incensed when Anacrites forced a house search on him. Camillus Verus called for his litter and immediately had himself carried off to complain to Vespasian.

Not content with jumping into this vat of steaming dung, Anacrites stormed next door to the house where Aelianus now lived with his wife and the professor. Minas of Karystos was ecstatic at the outrage. Wielding a wineflask in one hand and a bread roll in the other, he rushed from a late breakfast to pronounce loudly on the rights of a citizen to live without interference. Unbeknown to us previously, he was a populist democrat, fiery on the subject. Even with omelette in his curly beard, he was good. He bounced outside into the street, seeing his big chance to advertise his hireable expertise to all the well-heeled inhabitants of that fine patrician quarter. Before a rapidly expanding crowd, Minas had already quoted Solon, Pericles, Thrasybulus the defeater of the Thirty Tyrants, Aristotle of course, and several extremely obscure Greek jurists, when aediles turned up to investigate the street disturbance. The aediles did nothing; they were so impressed by his luminary erudition and the interesting points he was making, they brought him half a barrel to stand on.

Anacrites did not find Albia. Officially, her whereabouts remained unknown.

As I read on in weary amazement, Lentullus crept up to me with his usual confiding manner. He burped shyly. 'Falco, I know where your girlie may have gone—'

I raised a finger. 'Stop! Don't say it! Don't even think about it, Lentullus, in case Anacrites can read your brain.' In fact not even the devious spy could untangle that ball of wool, but Lentullus sat down obediently by me on the bench, full of joy that we were sharing this Big Secret.

While he carefully kept quiet, I read the rest of Helena's letter. That was personal. You don't need to know.

Afterwards, I folded up the document and tucked it inside my tunic. We all sat a while longer, listening to the whispers of the dark ocean, each contemplating death and life, love and loathing, the long years of tragedy that had brought us here, and the hope that at last we were ending it.

A faint breeze had got up and morning was not far away, when we said our goodnights and for a few short hours all sought our beds.

58

A lot of things had happened in the past few days. I told Silvius what we could now deduce about Nobilis and his movements. Anacrites had ordered him to leave Rome; Nobilis must have obeyed, much at the same time as Justinus and I left. We could easily have encountered him on the road down here.

His killing of Demetria confirmed his arrival. He must have been doing that while we were in the marshes arresting Virtus. We knew Nobilis must have carried out the attack on his ex-wife alone, because both Pius and Probus had been in custody. With troops swarming everywhere, he was probably pinned down in the Antium area. We set up a search.

If he went into the Pontine Marshes, we had no hope. The wild bogs stretched for nearly thirty miles between Antium and Tarracina, and between ten and fifteen miles across. This great rectangle of terrain was impossible to monitor. Nobilis knew the marsh intimately, had roamed there since childhood, had lived there all his adult life. He could elude us for ever.

Catching Nobilis quickly was now imperative. We had to hope that activity during the forest search had prevented him slipping away. The troop movements could have trapped him close to Antium itself, or forced him west. We searched the town—no luck. A polite house-to-house was set up among the handsome coastal villas. Of course we encountered resistance from their wealthy owners, who would rather put up with a depraved killer in their midst than let the military check their property. Each huge spread possessed innumerable outbuildings, any of which could be a hiding-place. Justinus and I spent half a day attempting to mediate with the rich and secluded; Silvius had reckoned us respectable (a senator's son and a man with his own auction house) so he assigned us the role of winning over the landed classes. For the most part, they saw it differently, though only one set the dogs on us.

We held a midday conference. Silvius had convinced himself that once Nobilis knew we had found the forest bodies, he would not just hunker down but would try to leave the area. Available roads were either north along the coast, taking the Via Severiana towards Ardea, Lavinium, and ultimately Ostia, or else the main road that skirted the northern edge of the marshes. That would take him over to the Via Appia, on the way to Rome. In Rome, could he still call on Anacrites for protection? Even if not, Nobilis could easily vanish into the city alleys as so many criminals had done. Ostia, if that was his choice, would give him access to ships bound for anywhere.

We pulled everyone off the property searches. It turned out to be the right choice. While we were still sitting around our lunch packs, co-ordinating our next moves, Lentullus edged up to Justinus and me. He asked if we wanted to know something funny about an ox cart that had just passed. The driver had seemed like any of the locals who pottered around. 'He looked all right—for a farmer, if that's what he is,' said Lentullus. Lentullus had come from a farm originally. 'And guess what—he had an ox that was just like Nero!'

'*Spot!*' Quintus and I roared at him, as we scrambled to our feet.

We all mounted up; we had a mix of mules and donkeys. Checking our weapons, we piled in pursuit. If this was just some inept ox rustler, we would look stupid, but we knew where Nero had been stolen so none of us believed that.

The countryside was gently rolling; when he turned off down a dirt track, we were close enough behind to see him leave the highway. A bullock cart can put on a fast turn of speed, a fully grown ox less so—and Nero had always been a plodder. Nonetheless, it was two miles before we caught up. It was Petro's ox all right, but by then abandoned. No mistaking that dun-coloured hunk of beef, with his mournful low and his permanent stream of dribble. He was even hitched to our own cart, the one we had had to leave in the marshes after the ox was taken. There was no time to make jokes about salvage rights, but Petronius and his po-faced brother would be delighted.

Nobilis had left the cart and taken off on foot. I made Lentullus stay with the ox. His bad leg would have hampered him, and those two simple souls could look after one another while the rest of us, the hard men, tracked our killer. We stayed on mule-back as long as possible, but soon, like him, we had to leg it. He vanished down a deep ravine and there was no choice but to follow him in.

'I know this place,' said Silvius. 'It's where we first found bodies!'

Italy is a strange country geographically, so long and narrow, with its great spine, the ever-present Apennines. They were there in the distance, low-looking grey ridges far away but visible beyond the undulating foreground plain. Even in summer, towering clouds rise over those hills. You can see them as you approach Rome. After storms and in winter, rain pours off the Apennines. Trapped water causes the Pontine Marshes. Here close to Antium, groundwater lay very close to the surface but instead of forming marshes, rivers carved phenomenal channels through the alluvium, down which they sucked the surplus to the sea. For century after century it happened, creating strange caves, deep seasonal gullies, and incredible ravines. You would not know they were there. From above, the countryside seemed featureless. The presence of these gullies made farming harder, so only a short way past Antium was a near wilderness. In this dire place, Claudius Nobilis had struck down one of the deep ravines. There was nothing else to do: trusting our souls to the gods—those of us who believed in gods—we went in after him. A few who did not believe in a deity until then may have offered a swift apology for doubting and beseeched divine protection after all.

Why does it always happen to me? In the course of my work, I had been at the bottom of some ghastly holes. This was another appalling experience. Nobilis had scrambled into a fissure in the earth that became fifty feet deep in places, though never much more than six feet across. The sides rose perpendicularly. Soon we felt quite cut off from the world; we feared we would never manage to return. No place I had ever been in contained such a sense of menace. It felt like one of the approaches to Hades.

He kept going. Hours seemed to pass as we struggled slowly after him. The ravine's formation reminded me of straight-sided rock-cut corridors I had seen in Nabataea, places so narrow a claustrophobic man would have to turn back afraid. In high summer, it was dry. One of our men, who had local knowledge, told us that when the rains came, such a ravine would contain raging water to waist height. In summer its soggy bottom fed the sturdy roots of unyielding under-growth. The going was almost impossible. Bright green frogs croaked everywhere; flies tormented us. Sweat poured off us as we strove for-wards. As we trampled on, scratched and torn by ferocious scrub plants, we became rapidly exhausted.

The place nearly defeated us. We were not the first to come here. Generations of criminals must have used this hateful crevice. They used it to hide themselves, their loot, their weaponry. They left be-hind sordid litter. Bodies must have been dumped here too. They would never be found. The undergrowth would conceal them, the floods would carry them away.

Ahead of us, the killer also struggled. He knew the ravine of old, yet found no easier way through it than we did. If paths had ever ex-isted, harsh foliage had reclaimed them. Its prickly growth was im-penetrable. The atmosphere, the heat, the smell, drained us. Being in a group, we just about kept up our spirits, and were closing the gap between us and our quarry. Nobilis was alone. He was on his own for ever now, and he knew it.

In the end he could go no further. With no way out, he turned on us. We never saw him coming but suddenly we heard him, as with a long, wild yell, he crashed out of hiding. With barely time to react, we bunched closer, bringing our swords up defensively. For an instant it did seem his intention was to break out past us. The ravine was too narrow, the tangled thicket too dense. His animal howl of defeat, despair and rage continued. We braced ourselves.

Nobilis flung himself straight at us. So this man, who had killed so many people with his own crude weapons, used us and our raised swords to kill himself.

59

Once we dragged out our blades and the corpse fell to the
ground, we stood in shock. Silvius recovered first and rolled
him over. We gathered round, to inspect the remains. We had to see,
once, the man we knew to be the killer.

He looked younger than Probus and the twins. There were like-
nesses. We could see he belonged to the Claudii. He was bigger, more
unkempt, over-heavy. Dead as he was, he lay staring at the sky in a way
that made us shiver. Camillus Justinus, a man of refinement, stooped
down quickly to pull the eyes shut with one thumb and forefinger.

Just before he did so, Quintus looked up at me. 'That barman's
wife in the Transtiberina may have seen Nobilis. She said he had
peculiar eyes.' He spoke with the same throwaway manner Helena
would use in company, tossing me something to think about, for discussion later. I said nothing, but I looked—then I drew the same
conclusions.

We left the body there. We were exhausted. Dragging it back up
the ravine would have finished us. If his siblings wanted to collect
Nobilis for burial, let them.

———

'Myself, I like to go to law,' said Silvius, back in Antium. 'A quick show trial, and a bloody execution. Deterrent to others. Suicide-by-cohort never works the same.'

Since the Urban was in a vengeful mood, he then let on that Claudius Probus was to remain in custody.

'What happened to his get-out clause?'

'Ah, Falco, I just remembered! I am not empowered to offer it. Immunity from prosecution is reserved to the Emperor—and he, I gather, never intervenes in criminal cases . . . So it's thanks for the help, Probus—but tough luck!'

The surviving twin, Virtus, was also in trouble, potentially. Despite his insistence that he kept aloof from his brothers' activities, Justinus had remembered something: 'When we picked him up at their shack in the marshes, I noticed his wife, Byrta, was wearing a good quality scarf in a dark red material. Silvius, if you can ever find any of the runaway slaves who belonged to Modestus and Primilla, you must show them that scarf. Primilla was wearing something like it when she left home.'

Piece by piece, we were linking the Claudii to their victims. We also had the unusual chain that Nobilis must have given to Demetria; I was confident that belonged with the cameo taken from the Rome courier on the Via Triumphalis. Petro would send the cameo for comparison; Silvius would take it to the Dioscurides workshop for absolute confirmation.

We asked both Probus and Virtus about their connection with Anacrites. Both blanked us. In my view, now Nobilis was dead, they were afraid they would bear the full burden as public scapegoats, but they believed the spy would extricate them. I thought they were wrong. 'No; he will distance himself now. I know him. He will sacrifice the Claudii to save his own career.'

'I thought they could put pressure on him?' said Silvius.

'We still don't know what—though Justinus and I have a theory we intend to check. I suggest you process Probus and Virtus here in Antium. Do it fast, Silvius. But if you can, please give me a couple of days, before you send word to Rome about Nobilis.'

'What's the plan, Falco? I can see you have one.'

'Let me keep it to myself. Silvius, you don't want to know.'

Silvius and the Urbans stayed in Latium to process the survivors' trial. I and mine set off for home. Lentullus was bringing Nero and the ox-cart for Petronius, which meant the usual maddening slow progress. It took us a day to reach Bovillae. Next morning, Justinus and I left Lentullus to drive in without us, while we rode on ahead up the Via Appia.

We passed through the necropolis where the corpse of Modestus had been found. After that came the Appian Gate, then a long straight run through garden suburbs until we hit the dark shade of two leaky aqueducts at the Capena Gate. I excused myself, and left Quintus to pass on greetings to his parents and his wife. We arranged that he and his brother would come to my house the next day, for a catch-up meeting.

I moved on, reached the southern end of the Circus Maximus, where I veered left. Since I had a mule to do the hard work, I pressed him up the hill. He carried me uncomplainingly to the crest of the Aventine, with its snooty ancient temples on the high crags, around which beetled the vibrant plebs of this place where I was born.

After life on the coast, I felt assailed by the busy racket. More shops and workshops were crammed together on this one hill out of seven than traded in the whole of Antium. The crowds were loud—singing, shouting, whistling and catcalling. The pace was fast. The tone was coarse. I drew in a deep breath, grinning with joy to be home again. In that breath I tasted a strange brew of garlic, sawdust, fresh fish, raw meat, marble dust, new rope, old jars and, from the dark doorways of ill-kept apartment blocks, the reek of uncollected sewage in flabbergasting quantities. My mule was jostled, insulted, barked at and cursed. Two hens flew up in our faces as we wove a passage through garland girls and water carriers, ducked out of the way as a burglar dropped down off a fire porch with his clanking swag, turned off a narrow road into one that was barely passable. At the end of *that* lay the disguised entrance of the sour alleyway called Fountain Court.

A pang of nostalgia hit me like last night's undigested Chicken Frontinian. The street was not much wider than the ravine where Nobilis killed himself. The sunny side was shady and the shady side was glum. A deplorable smell rose and wavered around like a bad genie outside the funeral parlour, while a fierce fight about a bill was spilling on to the pavement by the barber's. To call it a pavement was ridiculous. The customer who was threatening to kill Appius, the barber, was sliding on molten mud. To call it mud as it oozed in through gaps in his sandal straps was optimistic. I rode by without making eye contact, though my sympathy was with the barber. Anyone so stupid as to patronise a tonsure-teaser who had the sad comb-over Appius gave himself should expect to get fleeced. Even a *quadrans* was too much to pay.

I dismounted stiffly at the Eagle Laundry and tied up the mule among the wet flapping sheets in what passed for a colonnade. Lenia, the laundress, emerged nosily: a familiar figure, all frenzied red hair and drinker's cough, tottering on high cork heels, unsteady after her afternoon bevvy. She winked heavily. She knew why I was here. I gave her a wave that passed for debonair, and as she snorted easy insults, I set off up the worn stone stairs. My rule was, three flights then take a breather; two more then pause a second time; take the last flight at a run before you collapsed among the woodlice and worse things that littered your path.

The doorpost of my old apartment still had the painted tile that advertised my name for clients. An old nail, carefully bent about ten years ago, was still hidden in a pot on the landing; as a spare latch-lifter it still worked. I put the nail back, pushed open the door very gently in case someone jumped me; I went in, feeling an odd patter of the heart.

It looked empty. There were two rooms. In the first stood a small wooden table, partly eaten away as if it were fossilised; two stools of different heights, one missing a leg; a cooking-bench; a shelf that once held pots and bowls but was now bare of fripperies. In the second room was just a narrow bed, made up neatly.

I called out that it was me. I heard pigeons flutter on the roof.

There was a folding door from the main room to a tiny balcony. I jerked the door with a special hitch that was needed to move it. Then I stepped out through the opening into the old, incongruously glamorous view over Rome, now bathed in warm afternoon sunlight. For a moment I soaked up that familiar scene, out over the northern Aventine to the Vaticanus Hill beyond the river.

Albia was basking on the small stone bench. Coming from Britain, she adored the sun. The building was so badly maintained by its landlord Smaractus that one day the whole balcony would fall off, taking the bench and anyone who was sitting on it. For the moment it held. It had held for the six or seven years that I lived here, in view of which it was easiest to continue to have blind faith than to try and make the unbearable Smaractus carry out repairs. The kind of builders he used would only weaken it fatally.

My fosterling wore an old blue dress, tight plaits, a simple bead necklace. She sat with her fingers linked, pretending to be happy, calm, and unafraid. There was no chance she was afraid of me. I was her father, just a joke. But she must know her situation. Someone else had terrified her.

'I thought I would find you here.' She made no answer. 'You had better stay until I have a chance to straighten things out with Anacrites. Are you all right, Albia? Do you have food money?'

'Lenia gave me a loan.'

'I hope you fixed a good rate of interest!'

'Helena came. She settled up.'

'Well, I'll send you an allowance until it's safe to come home.'

'I won't be coming,' Albia informed me suddenly and earnestly. 'I have something to say, Marcus Didius. I love you all, but it cannot be my home.'

I wanted to argue but I was too tired. Anyway, I understood. I experienced deep sadness for her. 'So we failed you, sweetheart.'

'No.' Albia spoke gently. 'Let's not have a family argument, like other tiresome people.'

'Why not? Arguments are what families are for. You have a family now, you know that. You're stuck, I'm afraid. Try not to be estranged from us, the way I was from my father.'

'Do you regret that?'

I grinned abruptly, even laughed out loud. 'Never for one moment—nor did he, the old menace! . . . Have you told Helena this big idea of yours? Striking out on your own?'

'She was upset.'

'She would be!'

Albia turned to me, her face pale, her blue-grey eyes dark with panic despite her attempted bravado. 'You gave me a chance; I am grateful. I want to stay in Rome. But I am going to make myself a life, a life that is suitable and sustainable. Don't tell me I cannot try.'

Huffing gently, I squashed in on the bench beside her. Albia moved up, grumbling on principle. 'So let's hear about it?'

Uncertain of my reaction, she confided, 'I cannot have the life you hoped to give me. Adoption only half works. I stay provincial—if not a barbarian. Someone who hates us might find out where I came from. In this city, spiteful rumours could damage you and Helena.'

'Anacrites?'

'He intends to do it.' Albia spoke quietly; all self-confidence had drained out of her.

I wondered how he had so badly crushed her spirit. 'And what about you? Did he try something on?'

'No.' Albia was inscrutable. She had made up her mind not to tell me. If Anacrites had seduced or raped her, she would spare me incandescent anger; she would protect Helena, too, from the pain of knowing. But even the fact that Anacrites had lured her into danger gave me motives to pursue him.

'You sure?' Pointless question.

'He was not the same. He had changed—or at least had stopped hiding what he is really like. You were right about him: he looked lecherous. I decided straight away I must escape. Then I found Claudius Nobilis.'

'Did *he* lay hands on you?'

'No. He meant to. But Anacrites barged in and said "leave her to me".' Albia shuddered, looking older than her years. 'Repulsive man!'

'Don't you think we are all the same?' I teased, alluding to her opinion of Camillus Aelianus.

To my surprise, Albia smiled sweetly and replied, 'Not quite all of you!'

'So, Flavia Albia, you are leaving home. What are you planning?'

'To live here. Do what you did.'

'Right.'

'No argument?'

'No point. So you want to be an informer? Well, that could work.' I put my head back against the rough surface of the wall, remembering the experience. Part of me was envious, though I hid it. 'Start small. Work for women. Don't accept any job that comes along—gain a name for being picky, then folks will feel flattered if you take them on. It's a hard life, depressing and dangerous. The rewards are few, you can never relax, and even when you achieve success, your miserable cheating clients will not thank you.'

'I can do this,' Albia insisted. 'I have the proper attitude—the right bitterness. And I have sympathy for desperate people. I have been orphaned, abandoned, starved, neglected, beaten, even in the clutches of a violent pimp. There will be no surprises,' she concluded.

'I see you have convinced yourself! Nothing scares you—even when it should.' The romantic in me wanted to have faith in her. 'You are too young. You have too much to learn,' I warned, as the father in me took over.

'I have been pushed into it before I'm ready, so it's not ideal,' replied Albia coolly. She had spent several days here, thinking up answers to thwart me. Then, because Helena Justina's teaching had made an impression, she added demurely, 'But I shall have you to teach me, Father.'

My throat went raw. 'First time you ever called me that!'

'Don't get overexcited,' Flavia Albia answered matter-of-factly. 'You have to earn it, if you want it permanent.'

'That's my girl!' I exclaimed proudly.

I stood up, easing my stiff back. I needed to see Glaucus at the gym, get back in shape. Before I left the apartment, I made a few adjustments to the old potted rose trees, pinching off dead wood from spindly branches. 'Professional question, Albia: when you encountered Nobilis—did you notice his eyes?'

She jumped up eagerly. 'Yes! I wanted to tell you—'

'Save it. Come down to the house tomorrow. It will be a good exercise in moving around Rome unrecognised.'

'What for?'

'Family conference. We need to talk about Anacrites.'

60

I awoke late. I was alone, Helena's side of the bed long cooled. I could hear the house thrumming with movement and casual noises, everyone going about their business without me, as they must have done while I was absent, as they would do if I stayed dozing. I was the master, but expendable. However, a wet snuffle under the door from Nux waiting patiently outside told me the dog was aware of my homecoming last night.

I let her in, endured a quick greeting (she was a polite dog), then allowed her to jump on the bed, which was her real purpose. The whiskery fright was not allowed on beds or couches; that made no difference. Nux curled up and went to sleep. I washed my face, put a comb through my curls, dived into a favourite tunic. I was ill-shaven, hungry, stiff from travel and subdued. I had no casework I was aware of and would have to look for clients. In most respects I could have been back in the life I once led in Fountain Court. Once again, I felt mournful and bereft of my youth.

Downstairs, slaves saluted me with only mild disdain. A good breakfast and my alert assistants were waiting. My wife came in and kissed me. My children appeared in the doorway, made sure it was me, then ran off back to their games. A buffet slave refilled the bread basket with warm rolls as soon as I took a serving, poured hot water on to honey for me, cut smoked ham slices. The napkin laid upon my lap was fine linen. I drank from a smooth Samian beaker. When I came to rinse my hands again, scented water in a silver bowl was immediately offered to me.

I had forgotten I was rich. Helena saw my reaction; I noticed her amusement. 'Jupiter!'

'You'll get used to it,' she said, smiling.

My new status brought responsibilities. Clients were lined up, awaiting favours shamelessly.

I dealt briskly with Marina, wanting money of course, then ignored a message from my sister Junia about the caupona needing a refurbishment. Helena said there were queries at the auction house, not urgent; I could attend to them when I visited the Saepta. Next came another, much more serious, family problem. The usher (I now required one, it seemed) ushered in Thalia.

She was visibly pregnant, puffing slightly. It had not persuaded her to wear less revealing clothes. The two Camilli, waiting for me to be free for our planned meeting, exchanged startled glances. Arrayed in a few wafts of gauze and long strings of semiprecious beads, Thalia patted the bump that was supposed to be Pa's offspring. 'Not long now, Marcus!'

'How are you feeling?'

'Terrible! The python knows; he's off colour, poor Jason.'

'Still dancing?'

'Still dancing! Are you hoping exertion will bring on a miscarriage?'

'That would be irresponsible.'

'Gods! Money has made you so sanctimonious!—Now listen, I need to talk to you.'

'Well, make it quick. I'm about to begin a business meeting.'

'Stuff that,' replied Thalia. 'A little child's life is at stake here. We've been let down, Falco, this poor baby and me. I've had words with that scheming shark, Septimus Parvo—your devious father's utterly useless lawyer.'

'He seemed competent.' Thalia's annoyance was cheering me up now.

'You would say that. He tells me he has looked into things further and the will's rotten. It won't hold up. My poor little one has been cheated—and he is not even born yet!'

'I don't know what you mean, Thalia.'

'According to Parvo,' she enunciated with high distaste, 'if a legacy is given to a posthumous infant, the child must be born of a legal marriage.' Thalia was a tall woman of majestic stature; as she rounded on me fiercely, I felt some alarm. 'Geminus said Parvo would sort everything out for me. I know what's gone on here. This is a fiddle. You bastard, Falco—you must have put him up to it!'

Not for the first time since my father died, my first thought was to lay wheat cakes on a divinity's altar and exclaim, *Thank you, for my good fortune!*

Aulus leaned forward, his face serious. 'Parvo is quite right, if you don't mind me saying so.'

'My brother Aelianus,' Helena told Thalia helpfully. 'He has had legal training.'

'I don't trust him then!' Thalia scoffed. Aulus took it well.

'There can be no doubt, I'm afraid, Thalia.' What an excellent fellow Aulus had turned out to be. 'Didius Favonius remained married to his wife of many years, the mother of his legal children.' Helena may have discussed all this with Aulus. He was a better scholar than we expected, but only with advance warning. He must have looked up the law specifically. 'Everyone at Geminus' funeral saw Junilla Tacita taking her place as the widow. She was acknowledged as such by all those friends, family and business colleagues who knew her deceased husband. Moreover,' Aulus continued relentlessly, 'to become an heir, the child must be referred to in the will itself. I do not believe a codicil will count.'

'All that is as may be!' Thalia could be worryingly firm. 'I am here to make arrangements. Things have to be set up properly.'

I gulped nervously.

'Here is the deal, Marcus Didius. When this child is born, it has to be looked after. Don't expect me to do it. I can't take a baby on tour with the circus! My animals would be dangerously jealous, it's not hygienic, and I don't have the capacity.'

'That's very sad,' Helena interrupted. 'Children give so much pleasure and can be a comfort, Thalia.'

'He'll get in the way!' Thalia replied, as riotously honest as when she discussed her sex life. Then she dropped me in the midden. 'You will have to bring him up, Falco.'

'What?'

'I thought about it. This is what Geminus wanted. You know it is. He told you in that codicil: you were to see my baby as your own sister or your brother. You can't argue with a *fideicommissum*.' She was calm. She was composed. Before I could bluster excuses, Thalia added the death blow: 'The best thing will be, Marcus darling, if as soon as he is born, you take him off me and adopt him.'

I closed my eyes while it sank in. I had expected troubles to come with money. I knew some of them would be complex, many crushing. Cynical though I was, nothing of this magnitude had crossed my mind. There was no escape, however. Pa had landed me absolutely.

I said I had to consult Helena. 'That's right,' Thalia agreed composedly. 'Then the dear little thing can grow up with you two, and be part of your beautiful family.'

Those quick brown eyes of Helena's told me she foresaw everything, just as I did.

So I acquired a 'brother', who was almost certainly not my brother but whom I had to adopt and endure as my son. I would have shared the money with him fairly willingly, but now I had to give him a decent chance in life as well—quite another proposition. This could only go wrong. Helena and I anticipated from the start that little Marcus

Didius Alexander Postumus (as his mother would name him, poor noddle) could never be grateful. We would offer him a home, education, moral guidance and affection. Pointless. A soulless waste of effort. He would be difficult to raise and impossible to console for the arbitrary fate that had been dumped on him. He was bound to seethe with jealousy and resentment. And I would not even blame him.

Thank you again, Geminus.

61

There had been slaves pootling around us, but we dismissed them. Katutis did not even try to argue; he was learning.

We sat in the salon. Helena had moved things around while I was in Latium. We reclined on day-couches with bronze fittings. Cushions in soft shades of blue and aqua lay under our elbows. The walls, newly painted last year, were respectable tones of honey and off-white, plain panels delineated by fine tendrils and elegant candelabrum motifs, intermittently relieved with discreet miniature paintings of birds, done in faint brushstrokes. These were civilised, though unpretentious surroundings. With her own sure taste, Helena had scaled down from when my father lived here, using less grandeur than when he had the place bursting with antiques. The salon made a quiet setting for the sombre discussion we were about to hold.

Others soon joined us: first Albia, then Petronius and Maia. I had considered including Ma, but my habit of keeping secrets from her was too great. Helena rose to close the double doors for privacy. Before she resumed her seat, she stood for a moment: tall, wearing white with coloured bands and informal jewellery, just a matron at home, as ever on the edge of domestic harassment, always alert in case she was called away to scorched meat in the kitchen or bruises in the nursery . . . It would not happen today. Arrangements were in place. Here she was, the woman I loved, taking on the wider role of a Roman wife and mother: steering her family towards great decisions and the righting of intolerable wrongs.

I smiled at her faintly. She understood what I was thinking. I had made a good choice.

Helena said, 'This will be a family conference—in every sense, because we are all members of a family, and families are what we have to talk about. Nothing that is to be said in this room today may be mentioned outside it to anyone.'

'*Sub rosa*,' said Aulus.

'Isca rules,' nodded Petro.

'*Our* rules,' my ever-caustic sister Maia corrected him.

A formal family conference is the symbol of emergency in Roman society. It happens rarely, because it only happens after outside measures have been tried and have failed. A fallback when public systems have collapsed, it is used for both utterly private reasons and for arranging a challenge to political tyranny. This is the last meeting before assassinations, executions, exile or disgrace. This is where wives are summoned to account for adultery by stern old-fashioned husbands, then humiliating punishments levied with unpleasant aunts' encouragement. It is where necessary usurpation of rulers is plotted. Where suicide or honour killing is carried out, after rape or other violation.

Our family council was where seven of us, my closest and dearest, assembled to unpick the full connection between the Claudii and Anacrites. Then we would decide what to do about it.

First, Quintus reported events in Latium. I watched him, tall, still boyish in appearance though increasingly firm in manner. He had his father's straight rather spiky hair, his mother's bearing and good looks. He was more slightly built than his brother, though Aulus had lost weight since his marriage: stress, presumably.

Quintus was concise, his tone almost pleasant. He could have been assessing routine logistics for a fort commander in a frontier province, as he concluded: 'We never had a chance to interrogate Claudius Nobilis. Everything else about him has to be conjectural—except one thing: his eyes. After he died, Marcus and I noticed they were odd. Nobilis had pale eyes, eyes that were neither one colour nor another. Part grey, part brown. Extremely unusual.'

I heard Maia catch her breath as she made the link. Albia was twisting her hands in her lap.

'Neither of the twins, nor Probus, had that aberration,' Quintus continued, after a quick glance at Maia. 'Marcus and I checked the survivors. But we all know one other person whose eyes look two-coloured with some tricks of the light: Anacrites.'

Helena took up the story, taking the narrative from her brother as smoothly as the sacred torch is passed in a Panathenian relay race. 'This explains many things. Let us go back to two slaves on an imperial estate in the days of the early Empire: Aristocles and Casta. Of course they could not marry while they were in slavery, but let's assume they met, matched and even perhaps began to have children then. They were freed, some say to get rid of them because they were so difficult. They had many offspring. Some died. Some of the girls broke away, at least partly, and married. The eldest was Justus, who died not that long ago, perhaps of a bad conscience. Nobilis was among the youngest, pushed out more, perhaps; having to jostle more for attention, maybe even for clothes, space and food.'

My turn. 'One of the boys was called Felix. His brother Probus sneered: *Felix, the happy and fortunate—and a clever little sod too; well we lost him early, naturally* . . . How did they "lose" him? We know now. When he was three years old his intelligence was officially noticed and he was removed from the family. In Rome, he was arbitrarily assigned a new name. It happens to slaves. So the man we know as Tiberius Claudius Anacrites began life as Claudius Felix. He may not always have remembered where he came from—but he certainly knows now.'

At that point, it was Maia, Maia who might have been expected to be harshest, who put in a word for him. 'Imagine how it might have been for a child so young to be forcibly removed from the people he thought were his own.' Shaking her head, she went on in a low voice, 'Aristocles and Casta may have been distant, even violent, as parents, but I dare say they screamed and shouted when they had to give him up. From what we know, they were possessive; he was theirs, their property.'

'Casta may have tried to hang on to him physically,' Helena agreed. 'I know I would. Imagine the scenes—with the child hysterically weeping, torn from his mother's grasp by brutal overseers. Next, with Casta's screams ringing in his little ears, he was taken many miles away, nobody telling him why or where he was going. Perhaps he felt it was a punishment for some unknown naughtiness. Plenty of punishment went on among the Claudii—he knew that concept. Dumped at the Palace, he wakes up in a cold dormitory. Other children there were strangers. They may all have been older, may have bullied him.'

'He says his subsequent childhood seemed normal to him,' I said. 'But was it really? He learned to survive—but trauma and fear moulded him.'

Petronius had been listening with distaste. Now he stretched his long legs and frame, looking too bulky for the couch. 'I'm more intrigued by where he is today. In adulthood, do you think he was aware who his family were?'

'I doubt it,' I said.

Petro grinned. 'We could ask him.'

'You could. I wouldn't. He would only lie. In fact, as long as he can, he has to. He cannot hold a high imperial post as a known relative of murderous criminals.'

'So we're getting to the heart of this, Falco. What happened to reunite them?'

'Two years ago, or thereabouts,' Helena reminded us, 'the mother, Casta, died.'

We were all silent for a while, wondering what that had been like, for the large sprawling family that Casta had ruled with her mixture of cruelty and indifference. Aristocles had gone before her. Casta's death destroyed their equilibrium, Virtus told me.

Aulus leaned forwards. 'I bet there was a mighty big funeral. The full wailing, hypocritical orations. All sorts of sentimental grief. And presumably it was around then that somebody thought of contacting their long-lost brother Felix.'

'Anacrites went to the funeral,' stated Maia. She was looking down at her feet. Maia was sitting sideways, adjacent to Petronius. Her feet were small, pressed together tidily, wearing stylish shoes in ox-blood leather. Maia looked at them as if she was wondering where the decorative footgear came from.

'It begs the question,' mused Helena, 'how did his siblings find him?'

Again Maia unexpectedly had answers. 'He told me once. He had a letter from his mother when she realised she was dying. After all, where he was taken as a child would not have been a secret. Casta must have followed his progress, either from affection or the possessiveness we mentioned. Anacrites answered her summons but when he got there it was too late. I never knew the funeral was in Latium; he kept quiet about his people living in the Pontine Marshes. It was just after I met him he told me, as a conversation gambit.'

'Was he upset?' asked Albia.

'He seemed so.'

'He could have been acting.'

'There was no reason for that.'

'That's him, though. Defying logic.'

'His feelings need not concern us,' I said. 'The funeral was his downfall. Once they knew who he was, his brothers latched on like parasites. They saw Anacrites as their crock of gold. It looked innocent to start with. The twins asked for a job. How could he say no? He employed them; he may have welcomed them—agents he felt he could control, agents who would be loyal to him.'

Petronius shook his head. 'The twins arrive in Rome. Anacrites quickly grasps his error: he will never shake them off. They start whining about conditions on the marshes. Their background is a reproach, their presence in Rome an embarrassment. They threaten the spy's ambitions.'

'He wants out?' asked Quintus. 'But they refuse to go.'

'Anacrites' unpredictability increases due to his head wound,' Helena said. 'He becomes vulnerable at work, with his position threatened by Laeta and even by Momus. At some ghastly point he learns the kind of crimes Nobilis and the others have committed. By then he cannot escape.'

'And so we come to the Modestus murder.' I screwed my thumbs into my belt and took charge of the final argument. 'Everything went wrong with the fence dispute. Up to that point, I'd say Nobilis probably carried out all his killings in the area around Antium—the bodies Silvius has found. Nobilis and various brothers abducted people for years, usually travellers, often couples. Those cases were concealed, but he lost it with Modestus. By tailing Modestus to Rome, for once Nobilis left a trail. Nobilis—presumably with Pius or Virtus— killed Modestus on the Via Appia. They spent several days at the crime site, desecrating the body, then Nobilis went home. Primilla came looking for her husband, so he killed her too, with her overseer, Macer. That meant her nephew alerted the authorities and a posse arrived to shake down the Claudii. From then on, we can assume pressure was put upon Anacrites to protect them. That may well have been when one of them told him about the murders. It made him more insecure and dangerous. Crucially, he inherited the same manipulative traits as the rest of them—a situation which they may not have foreseen. He turned on them.'

'He may have been appalled by their crimes,' Helena said, always fair.

'He was certainly furious about how it threatened him personally! Perella was sent after Nobilis, but Nobilis got away. Anacrites tried to remove Nobilis from the scene, taking him to Istria. Whose idea that was we can never know. Perhaps they really found their grandmother. One way or another, Nobilis refused to play; he would not stay in exile. Idiotically, he sailed back with Anacrites—who then must have been as close to hysteria as he ever gets.'

'Not him!' Albia scoffed. 'He thinks himself invincible. In his eyes, everything that happens is manipulated by him. He believes he is a genius. When I was in his house he said, "Falco can't touch me; I run rings around him". He had been drinking, but he meant it.'

With a glance at Petronius, I said slowly, 'He may in fact have been more clever than we think. What Anacrites achieved may not have been entirely crude. The way he grabbed the Modestus case and warned off Petronius and me seems plain stupid. Some of his actions—house searches, annoying the Vestals—seem worse.'

'Well, they were!'

'Perhaps not, Petro.'

'Oh Titan's turds!' Suddenly, Petronius saw where I was heading. He was tired after last night's shift with the vigiles. Realisation drowned him in self-disgust and frustration. 'He cannot be this clever!'

'Lucius, my old friend, I'm afraid he is.'

'He *played* us?'

'Tickled us like dim trouts in a mountain stream.'

While Petro cursed and tried to pretend this had not happened, Helena Justina took over from me, to explain the unpleasant truth. 'Anacrites had a dilemma. The Claudii were threatening to expose his background unless he protected them. He had to make them think he was looking after them—while all the time that busy brain of his, the intelligence even Laeta compliments, was desperately finding ways to eliminate them instead. He had to deal with each in turn—and without the others noticing. He found the perfect solution. Marcus and Lucius, he used you two.'

With a deep sigh I acknowledged it. 'He took away our case—knowing we would refuse to give up. A pattern existed. We had continued on cases secretly before. We hated him. He used our own doggedness against us.'

Petro shared the confession: 'He organised either the twins or Nobilis to kill that courier, so *they* would think he was cleverly diverting attention from them in the Modestus case—'

'When I asked, he even admitted the diversion idea stank,' I said. 'He made sure we had seen through it. He *wanted* us to stick to the Claudii.'

Petronius groaned. 'Then he began picking them off—using us. We did his dirty work; he looked innocent to his brothers. He sent Pius to us deliberately. He'd dispatched Virtus to the marshes, so he could not help his twin. We helpfully took Pius—'

'We fell for it like automata.'

'So whose idea was that, Falco?'

'Be fair—both of us,' I pointed out. Petronius shrugged acknowledgement. 'The spy avoided looking for Pius until he thought we must have finished him off. Even Pius realised he was abandoned. He gave up. He saw Anacrites was never going to rescue him, because Anacrites had planned it.'

'Pius could have told us,' said Petro.

'If he explained what was happening, it was as good as confessing his involvement in the murders. Afterwards, Anacrites probably told Virtus to stay "out of the way" in the marshes, so he never realised his twin had gone missing. We know he then instructed Nobilis to run for cover—just when Quintus and I were on our way to Latium, and might have run into him.'

Petronius cursed. 'I bet he knew all along we were working with Silvius and the Urbans. Jupiter, you don't think Silvius is some crony of his?'

'No. I think Silvius is straight. Concentrate on Anacrites,' I instructed.

'He jerked our string. We did everything he wanted. It is a compliment, really,' Petronius decided, with grim mirth. 'Marcus, a villain of unbelievable duplicity entrusted us with his schemes. We should feel proud he believes in us so much!'

'I am proud of the *work*. We put four criminals out of action, after they had preyed on a community for decades. That is what we do with our lives, Lucius, and it is commendable.'

Quintus and Aulus Camillus had been listening with tense expressions. I stood up. I paced the room a few times, before telling them. 'For Petronius and me, the work is not yet finished. I wanted you two to hear all this. Now I want you to go away and leave us to it. Preserve your knowledge of these facts, as curators of the truth. I need you to know, in case the rest goes wrong.'

'The rest?' demanded Quintus quickly.

'Don't do it!' muttered Aulus. 'Going after him is far too dangerous. Leave it, Falco. My father tried, but Titus spoke up for the spy. At the Palace they believe he is good at his job. The official decision has been made: Anacrites is too valuable to remove.'

'I expected that. Hence this council.'

I looked around the room: Helena; her brothers; my sister; our adopted daughter; Petronius; me. A close, closed circle, all of us touched in some way by the spy's past actions, all threatened by his future schemes.

'Helena?'

Helena glanced at Albia, then Maia. 'What do we all think?'

'Leave him—and it will only grow worse,' prophesied Maia darkly.

'He claimed he can do anything he wants,' added Albia. 'I argued that he is accountable to the Emperor—but he told me emperors will come and go. He stays. He answers only to history.'

'Hubris!' Helena retorted, as if charging Anacrites in person. 'Self-centred aggrandisement—an insult to the gods. What will the gods do about it?' she then wondered. Her dark brown eyes inevitably sought mine.

'Send Nemesis to deal with him,' I answered.

62

There were two stages: the search and the action. I may have implied to my loved ones there would be one other element beforehand: mature consideration. But Petronius and I dispensed with that.

Our division of labour was simple. We both reconnoitred the chosen location for the deed, convinced ourselves no one would bother us there, surveyed escape routes. We identified a dump site. We knew it would work; I had used it once before. Petro was bringing swords and a crowbar for the manhole. I had to find the spy.

It was important that nobody noticed me looking. That ruled out knocking on the door at Anacrites' house, pretending to sell hot sausages; his staff knew who I was. Even worse would have been showing my face on the Palatine, asking the clerk in the office, Phileros, for details of his whereabouts, allowing the rheumy-eyed Momus to spot me, contacting that snake Laeta. They might all guess my role later; I could live with suspicion. But I must leave no trace of the process. There was no point conducting this kind of operation if it left new witnesses who could apply new pressure. We wanted clean air and a quiet life, with no further harassment.

I spent much of the day checking known haunts. That was depressing. Anacrites had pitiful taste in lunch bars. I watched Ma's house for an hour or so, but she was entertaining Aristagoras, her ninety-year-old smooch. Anacrites must be in his office, working his ordinary day. Arrive, work, plot, gloat, leave for bath and dinner.

At the eighth hour I made my way somewhere I had never been before, though I had heard of it, back in the days when Anacrites and I worked together on the Census. He had told me then it was his favourite and I had stored the information in an empty brain cell, for potential use one day. It was an expensive private bath house on the south end of the Circus, in a short sunny street near the Temple of Sol and Luna.

Nobody knew me. The cloakroom boy confirmed Anacrites was there. I said I was an off-duty investment consultant and the spy had agreed to see me about buying a dog-collar factory in Bithynia. Madness always pays off. They let me in straight away.

My quarry was at that moment not plying his strigil in a steam room; he had moved on and was secluded in a curtained room, experiencing—though certainly not enjoying—the attentions of a team of personal hygienists. I could have waited for him to emerge, but not waiting was so much more fun.

They had a security system, designed to put off the inquisitive: they simply told anyone to push off, if they insensitively noticed screaming. The bouncer was a plump dwarf in a short tight white tunic, who doubled as manicurist. She offered me a half-price cuticle tidy up, but I declined without regret.

'No time, precious. I am absolutely bursting to see my dear old friend in here—don't worry, he always lets me come and watch. We have *no* secrets!'

Well, until today he had had this one.

I whipped aside a sagging length of moth-eaten purple cloth that gave clients imagined privacy. I would not have put myself in this position without an oak door, five-tumbler barrel locks, armed guards and an attack dog.

There were a couple of couches, one occupied. I had found him, and he must be cursing me. Well, he would have been, if he had not had his teeth gritted in serious agony.

Four or five practitioners were frowning with concentration as they applied themselves to the spy's selected parts. He was splayed on his front at that moment, legs apart and feet towards me. I always realised he must depilate his arms and legs. Now I knew he boasted hideous fancy stuff under his tunic. When I burst in he was not wearing one. He was naked, apart from a light coating all over with very high quality almond oil.

The hair-removers had scythed off his torso rug and defoliated his buttock fur. Now they were subjecting him to the most painful part of their expensive duties. Anacrites had bought the whole deal. The specialists were giving him what is known in louche circles as a back, sac and crack. Or so I am told. You would never catch me having it.

He was probably dying for the agony to stop, but when I entered the room those attending to him did not pause. Their instructions were probably to keep going, just as long as the customer could stand it.

'It's Falco. No—don't move an inch!' I carolled cheerily. 'This is too good to miss! I have spent many hours imagining resourceful ways to torture you—but, Tiberius Claudius Anacrites, I never thought of hot pitch poured on your exposed genitals!'

Whoever did think of it, and persuaded him to have it done, deserved to be awarded a radiate diadem.

Anacrites let out a faint mortified cry. I assured him he could take his time, make a thorough job of it with the hot pitch peel, ensure every naughty stray hair was yanked out with the tweezers. I said I could not bear to watch, but I would wait for him outside, enjoying a glazed honeycake from one of the bath house's itinerant food tray men. 'I need to see you urgently. If you are still on the Modestus case, this is about Nobilis.'

He bounced out not long afterwards, pretending nothing had happened. Perhaps embarrassment clouded his judgement from that point.

I was holding a packet of honeycakes, which I had decided would be reassuring. I announced that Nobilis had escaped capture in Latium (this was why I had asked Silvius to delay his report). According to me, Nobilis had trekked back to Rome, where he was spotted by the bright-eyed vigiles. Petronius Longus knew where he was and was guarding the location; since it was the spy's case, I had come to fetch him. 'He's hiding up. The place looks grim, but Petronius and I are with you. There's no time to wait for back-up; he has a hundred escape routes available.'

Anacrites did ask, 'How do I know you're not lying, Falco?'

'You don't,' I replied curtly—that old double bluff, which never fails if your opponent is conceited. Taking it upon himself to believe me was a daring executive decision.

He agreed to come. He had no bodyguards with him at the baths, so it was him and me. I said Petro had told us to hurry, because he was alone on guard. So we walked rapidly through Rome, just a short distance. As we strode side by side, with Anacrites trying to forget his privates were painful (but walking with great difficulty, I was glad to see), I let myself make comparisons.

Although my own family were a ramshackle feckless bunch, to Anacrites the Didii must be a thousand times better and happier than *his*: warm, vibrant, cheerful and, under their craziness, caring about one another. I was starting to see why Helena had always thought Anacrites yearned to be me—yearned for it, yet felt so jealous he wanted to destroy what I had.

This was crucial to understanding him: the contrast between my Aventine family and his swamp-dwelling relations. His set had ended up alienated and dire, all petty criminals, some venal. Mine might look hopeless and annoying but they mostly had good hearts. Clearly it was due to Ma. Her life was a struggle but she always took a determined interest in her offspring; too much, we thought, though it produced results. Anacrites, spawned in trouble and ripped from his roots, ended up amoral and friendless. I had been given tenacious ethics and could relate to most people. He might easily have gone the way of his murdering brothers—perhaps had done. I never could. One of us was unavoidably a villain, the other perhaps a hero.

A tangle of streets close to the Forum was the place Petronius and I had chosen. It was ripe to be redeveloped by some free-spending emperor. Perhaps by the time we were very old men it would be.

We met Petronius Longus at the end of a narrow alley called Nap Lane. He was carrying equipment, well wrapped up. It struck me that this alley was an urban version of that ravine near Antium. Previously known to both of us, it was a bare wagon's width across; a laden cart could lose its cargo, bashing against the walls. Steep, boarded-up façades of abandoned buildings rose either side. They made the street, which was clogged with dried mud and littered with fly-tipped debris, almost too dark to see down. Absentee entrepreneurs owned or rented decayed warehouses here, either left empty or half filled with stolen goods. Shady runaways sometimes sheltered in these cordoned-off, rotting premises; most were too scared and preferred to starve and be mugged in the shade of bridges where someone might at least find their corpses.

Everywhere was quiet. It was dinnertime in Rome. This was a fine day in early September, between the Calends and the Nones, still in the school holidays; not a festival; before the Roman Games; not a black day in the calendar. Absolutely nothing noteworthy about the day at all, in fact.

Nobody saw three men hold a short discussion, after which they all walked into the dingy alley. They were comfortably built and capable, so they all went with confidence. A few moments later, there were sounds of a short scuffle, expertly managed. It was followed by dull metallic noises, as if someone had pulled up and dropped a large manhole cover. The Great Sewer, the Cloaca Maxima, ran beneath the rutted roadway, taking sewage and storm water to the River Tiber.

Not long afterwards, two people strolled out again from that alley. Emerging into the late evening light, they walked unhurriedly, comfortable in an easy friendship. They looked like two men casually eating pastries and perhaps talking about the races. Two men who were preparing to leave the streets after the day's business and who were setting off home to their families.